MAYWOOD PUBLIC LIBRARY

3 1312 0016738265

P9-CSH-749

Maywood Public Library
121 S. 5th Ave.
Maywood, IL 60153

such sweet thunder

such sweet thunder

Vincent O. Carter

STEERFORTH PRESS
SOUTH ROYALTON, VERMONT

Copyright © 2003 by Liselotte Haas

ALL RIGHTS RESERVED

For information about permission to reproduce
selections from this book, write to:
Steerforth Press L.C., P.O. Box 70,
South Royalton, Vermont 05068

Library of Congress Cataloging-in-Publication Data

Carter, Vincent O.
Such sweet thunder / Vincent O. Carter ;
foreword by Herbert R. Lottman.
p. cm.
ISBN 1-58642-058-5 (alk. paper)
1. World War, 1939–1945—African Americans—Fiction. 2. World War,
1939–1945—France—Fiction. 3. African American soldiers—Fiction.
4. African American men—Fiction. 5. Americans—France—Fiction.
6. Kansas City (Mo.)—Fiction. 7. Jazz musicians—Fiction.
8. Young men—Fiction. I. Title.
PS3603.A79 S83 2003
813'.6—dc21

2002154280

This novel is a work of fiction. Names, characters, places, and
incidents are either the products of the author's imagination or are
used fictitiously. Any resemblance to actual persons, living or
dead, events, or locales is entirely coincidental.

FIRST EDITION

To
Duke Ellington

FOREWORD

For those of us who are used to handling manuscripts — sometimes to examine them line by line, more often to flip through the pages — it's a privileged moment indeed when we realize that we are dealing with a text destined for that small shelf of memorable literature, certain to be printed and reprinted over the years. The telltale signs, for me, are trembling hands, eyeglasses clouding over — the psychological equivalent of a thunderclap. The book you have in hand now provided all of these emotions.

But let me begin at the beginning. The time is the late 1950s, when I was just settling in Paris, endowed perhaps with fewer talents than I'd hoped, but like so many of my fellows determined, with James Joyce, "to forge in the smithy of my soul the uncreated conscience of my race." One day a letter arrived from another American in self-imposed exile, but this American seemed to have chosen an incredibly odd refuge: that overgrown village of Bern, improbable capital of Switzerland. "Joe sent me," Vincent Carter began his letter. (Joe turned out to be Joe Kramer, an American medical student I knew in Bern.) Carter was writing and hoped to be published; Joe thought that since I was closer to the center of things, I might be of use to him. At the beginning the best help I could give him was encouragement, for I much admired the literary perfection of the first manuscript he showed me, an account of his wanderings through that parochial place, where he stood out as the only black man in town.

Admired isn't the word. . . . I was charmed. I thought of his daybook as a new *Anatomy of Melancholy*. His digressions also reminded me of that earlier continental visitor, Lawrence Sterne. Indeed *The Bern Book*, which its author considered to be a record of the voyage of the mind, so defied current conventions (we were then in the angry 1960s) that it couldn't be published, however letter-perfect it may have been, for what could one do with a black American who seemingly wasn't on the firing line?

I said all these things in an essay published in 1970; that led to the acqui-
sition of *The Bern Book* by an American publisher not afraid to seem out-
moded. After that, nothing. And yet Vincent Carter was then giving the
finishing touches to what I think will be seen as the consummate account
of an African American childhood, what the Germans call a *Bildungs-
roman,* a work that cries out for distance — say from Kansas City,
Missouri, to Bern, Switzerland — as well as patience; what Wordsworth
called recollection in tranquility. Few of our best American writers, black
or white, even when they have the subject, possess the patience.

I have to go back to Joyce, whose own successive Berns were Trieste (where
he began his *Portrait of the Artist as a Young Man,* wrote much of *Dubliners,*
and the opening of *Ulysses*), and then Zurich (where he wrote most of
Ulysses, finishing it in Paris). Later Ernest Hemingway would say that he'd
had to go to Paris to write about Michigan, and would undoubtedly leave
Paris before trying to describe it.

Perhaps Vincent would have laughed had I begun to talk about Joyce
after reading *Such Sweet Thunder.* And yet I couldn't help thinking of that
stubborn young Irishman, reinventing the sights and sounds of his childhood Dublin while living parsimoniously in a strange environment, supporting himself by giving English lessons, as Vincent Carter was doing.
Each would feel the need to rewrite, and pare, and shape. (The first version
of *Such Sweet Thunder* was considerably longer than what we are reading
now, the heavy dialect more challenging.)

Carter was not an autodidact, far from it. He was born in Kansas City,
Missouri, in 1924, to parents still teenagers. He was called up for active
duty — first in a defense plant, then in the U.S. Army, on America's entry
into the war at the end of 1941; he landed on a Normandy beachhead, took
part in the drive toward Paris. Later he won a college degree from Lincoln
University in Pennsylvania, certainly paid for by the G.I. Bill, which made
it possible for war veterans to pursue their studies. He also spent a graduate year at Wayne State in Detroit. I don't believe that he ever took a
course in creative writing, yet this book contains scenes that are overwhelming in their perfection; let's just credit it to talent. But he continued
writing, all this time, against the grain. I had other black American friends,
notably William Gardner Smith, a fellow Parisian who spent his voluntary
exile keeping a sharp eye on America; by the 1960s he had written his
novels and was expressing himself best as a journalist. In 1963, the year
Vincent Carter completed *Such Sweet Thunder,* another American abroad,
James Baldwin, published his angry essay *The Fire Next Time.*

Vincent Carter had wished to take up residence in Paris, even in

Amsterdam or Munich, before settling in placid Bern, which seemed to him the least inhospitable of choices. Yet would anybody have dared to say that Carter had gone there to shelter himself from the real world? He was brought up — and surely saw himself (in the language of his family and friends) — as a "race man." Every page of his book underscores the evils of "separate but equal." His beautiful parents, whose social advancement would be measured in pennies and nickels, were living testaments to the changes that everyone expected.

Dear Vincent, I wish that you had lived to see this book published. It took a little more time than we thought it would, but in the end you found a publisher worthy of the book of your life. The book worth your exile.

God knows, we talked about getting published a lot. We shared your rejection letters, many of them from quite honorable publishers who explained candidly that the editing of this mass of paper would be too expensive for them.

I myself waited a long time to be able to revisit your manuscript. After your death I lost contact with your Bern family. The only palpable souvenir I had was *The Bern Book*, which contained the preface in which I described the still-unpublished manuscript that was to become *Such Sweet Thunder*. Nearly thirty years went by after that preface was published before a perceptive publisher, Chip Fleischer of Steerforth Press, came upon a copy of *The Bern Book*, and asked for my help in finding the lost manuscript. Thanks to a Swiss friend, who had to turn my query over to another Swiss friend, who found a third friend in Greece who knew the answer, we were able to contact *your* friend Liselotte, and the book was as good as published.

And so I have been able to read *Such Sweet Thunder* again, and to find those pages that moved me so much when you were only a border away in Switzerland. Once again I'm immersed in the life of this precocious infant as he becomes aware of the world, protected by Viola and Rutherford, even-tempered and loving, and yet so desperately young and poor, in this most moving homage to parents I know in literature. In reading, I ask myself if the book's real meaning is to be discovered in the class visit to the city's art gallery, when you — disguised as Amerigo Jones — discover the colors of things, and suddenly everything about you is either art or life, to be felt and tasted, a cause for joy and weeping. (Your intention had been to call your book *The Primary Colors*.)

Sometimes, though, especially after such moving passages, I must put the book aside, wishing to preserve my right to step away from this reconstitution of a childhood not my own, to take possession of myself again. Then I think: You are waiting to know.

But of course you are no longer waiting, no longer living in Bern or anywhere else I can imagine, although I am sure that you will find the words to convince me that you are more present than ever.

For you prove your magic all through this wondrous story.

HERBERT R. LOTTMAN
Paris, 22 May 2002

such
sweet
thunder

On a cold winter morning shortly before dawn in the year 1944, the stars shone brightly, but were now and again obscured by drifts of heavy clouds.

The Great War, which was then ravaging the earth, seemed to be asleep. Nevertheless, the soldiers slept restlessly within the confines of a large race-track on the outer limits of the northern French city of R___. The camp occupied more than two-thirds of the entire track — long rows of barracks connected by gravel lanes that extended from the periphery to a large inner field that served as a parade ground.

Now all was obscured by darkness. The hollow chamber of the huge cementlike structure that loomed over the barracks from the far end of the field had once been the reviewing stand, but was now merely a bulky mass filling in the final segment of the track. Its wooden benches and flooring had been hacked into firewood by the freezing civilian population. This shell seemed to echo the cries of death choking the throats of the French, English, and American soldiers who had slept nervously in the same encampment during the First World War of 1914.

Now the soldiers within the barracks tossed and turned while the sentries who stood watch from the nine posts along the outskirts of the camp looked warily out into the dark.

A bell rang from a tower in the town, and a beam of light flickered in the darkness. A hoarse command separated itself from the voices echoing in the shell:

"All *right*, then! You-had-a-good-home-but-you-leftit!"

The sergeant of the guard roused the sleepy men from their bunks and they stumbled out of the guardhouse, moving sluggishly, in loose formation, their rifles slung carelessly over their shoulders, their heavy boots grating against the frozen gravel.

After plodding along the track for a short distance, they broke through the open field that, covered with frost, made them look from a distance like specters tramping noiselessly through a bank of clouds.

Half asleep, shivering with cold, they straggled along, halting at first one post and then another, grunting unintelligible signs of recognition to the companions they were relieving who, impatient for the warmth of their beds, hastened back to the guardhouse.

Finally the last guard made his way toward his post. It was five or ten yards from the reviewing stand, and somewhat isolated from the rest of the camp. This hintermost area was surrounded by a dense forest, beyond which lay the southern limits of the city.

"It's Jones, Roy!" cried the approaching soldier in a youthful sonorous voice. Roy, within the hut, hastily threw the lid on the old oil can in which he had made a fire and stepped outside. "It's cold as hell!" Jones added in as manly a tone as possible.

"You think it's cold, man?" he answered.

Confused, Amerigo Jones shivered past him.

"Say, man —"

"Yeah?"

"— you can have 'er, if you want 'er."

"What?"

"What?"

But Earle had disappeared in the dark.

A hint of rose coloring burned imperceptibly brighter in the blue-black sky. A bit disconcerted, Amerigo entered the hut and immediately tried to restart the fire thinking, as he poked into the can with the butt of his rifle, that Earle must have said something quite different from what he thought he had said. Nevertheless, the words "You can have 'er, if you want 'er" stood out in bold relief in his mind, the word *her* mysteriously separating itself from the context of the sentence, filling him with a titillating excitement.

Now what did *that* mean? he pondered, standing his rifle against the wall beside the can. The great Roy Earle! He fumbled in his pockets for a match, and as he fumbled he saw Roy dressed in neat-fitting purple trunks — taller, more robust, and generally more handsome than he — prancing arrogantly in the ring of the high school gym, animated by the enthusiasm of the crowd. He tried to pacify himself with the reflection that Roy's eyes were small and puffed and that his nose was crooked from having been broken. But then he heard the voice of his mother telling him that *he* would have to develop the beauty *within* because he would never be a movie star. The thought of home, of high school, flashed through his mind, and gradually he became immersed in the warm feeling of spring.

Of a particular spring, he felt, the imperative emphasis rising to the surface of his excitement. A feeling of intense pleasure rippled over his consciousness, and he strained his memory in an attempt to discover its cause, vaguely remembering that it had somehow been provoked by his willful abstraction of the word *her* from the rest of Roy's words.

Nor did it strike him as peculiar that a burst of autumn colors now imposed themselves upon his awareness of spring, for his thoughts were stumbling on so swiftly that the unknown face hiding within the shadow of the word *her* was swept up into a flurry of words that now flooded his mind and filled him with a sweet melancholy sadness.

The rosy glow died out of the fire. *Her.*

The fire's gone out he thought, embarrassed because he could see no connection between the word and the fire. He wondered why he thought there was. His eyes came to rest upon the little square window in the door of the hut. A faint, very faint, blue light crept in through the dirty window. It was spattered with dried drops of rain, and wedges of frost had entrenched themselves in the corners.

He struck a match. The yellow flame made his shadow dance upon the wall and break into three grotesque planes where the ceiling joined the wall and caused the rusty can of dead embers to dance and bend and merge into his shadow. The floor was spotted and stained with filth. A dried-up rubber lay crumpled among the warm ashes that spilled out of the little draft hole near the bottom of the can. While impulsively burying it with the toe of his boot, he spied a piece of soiled paper just behind the can. He stooped to pick it up. The match went out. He lit another, and bent over to inspect it more carefully, but the flame flickered out before he could decipher the name of the paper under the coating of dirt. He lit another match.

The *Voice*! Damnit! He rubbed his hand to cool the stinging pain in the tip of his thumb. Anxiously now he lit another match and saw that he held a part of the society page in his hand. His eyes fell upon the face of a young woman in the center of the sheet, stained by a muddy boot print and torn in such a way that little more than eyes, nose, and a corner of her mouth, which seemed to be smiling, were visible.

It's *her!* he whispered excitedly. And the spurt of air on which the word *her* issued from his lungs blew out the light. Nervously he struck another match, but was so excited that it was only with the greatest difficulty that he was able to read.

But wait! Just as he began to read, the sound of the wind filled his ears. It whipped through the frozen trees in the surrounding forest and dashed unseen branches to the ground. It echoed in the hollow shell towering above the hut and mingled with the whispering colors of the dawn. So

striking was the effect that Amerigo half believed that a host of devils insinuated themselves into the words, as he read:

"Miss Cosima Thornton, only daughter of Mr. and Mrs. Elijah
Thornton, of this city, was wed to Mr. . . ."

A serried line obscured the identity of the anonymous man and converted the square that had contained the photograph into a triangle. The
match went out. Seconds later he felt the cold creeping through the square
blue window. He shivered, as if he could recover from the shock of seeing
the smudged mutilated face of Cosima lunge out from the shadow of the
word *her*.

It's an omen! he thought. But then — that's crazy! But still. It must *mean*
something! She . . . we . . .

The cold crept up his spine.

I must make a fire. Guiltily he considered the society page of the *Voice*.
Actually, it's only a piece of paper, he argued. And suddenly a conscienceless hand had tossed it amid the warm ashes, while the other withdrew a
knife from his pocket and whittled a few shavings from one of the two-by-
fours in the wall of the hut. He felt a pang of remorse as he lit the paper
and watched the shavings ignite and the dormant fire sustain the flame.

Forgive me, Cosima! he exclaimed. Outside the hut the icy branches
creaked in the wind.

It's strange after all this time. I didn't recognize her at first. Now there
she is, burning in that damned can. It's not Roy's fault. Whose then?
Perhaps if there hadn't been a war? If!

He shaved more wood from the post, and the fire grew brighter.

She'll be sitting by the fire, he mused. Breakfast on a cold winter morning
such as this, with Mr. What's-his-name, over orange juice and toast! She'll
unfold the crisp clean pages of the *Voice* and read beneath the photograph of
a grave young black man with eyes that peer into the very depths of her soul:

"Amerigo Jones, only son of Mr. and Mrs. Rutherford Jones, of this city,
who was killed in the heroic act of. . . ."

While he pondered the heroic act he heard her heart pounding within the
aching void of profound regret. Stirred by a deep feeling of pity for her,
rewarded for all the suffering she had caused him, he extended his small
black hand in an attitude of forgiveness, through the cold blue sky and
across the stormy reaches of the Great Atlantic Ocean! She shed a penitent
tear upon it and caressed it piously. Thus consecrated with love, his martyred body exploded into dazzling filaments of purest light.

"I will love you always!" he whispered.

From outside the hut came the sharp crack of a broken twig. He stood breathlessly still. Something stirred in the brush, hesitated, and moved again. He carefully took up his rifle, quietly shoved the bolt home, and kicked the door open.

A woman stood there.

More rose coloring had filtered into the sky, intensifying the yellow of her hair. The firelight caught her pale oval face, but the lower part of her body was in darkness.

Without a word she stepped past the muzzle of his rifle, past the astonished look upon his face, and stood shivering in the far corner of the hut.

Just a girl! Not more than sixteen.

Confounded and somewhat embarrassed by the intensity of her gaze, he leaned his rifle against the wall. Her hair looked as though it had not been combed in a long time, and her eyes were an intense shade of blue.

She stood calmly — no longer shivering now that the fire had gradually thawed the coldness in her body — and allowed his frankly bewildered eyes to ferret out the deep violet lines that circled her own. A patch of golden down fringed her thin upper lip; the bottom lip was slightly drawn, more from a sort of animal toughness than from fear of him. She's surely not ashamed, or proud. Just here: Post No. 9, 1944, twentieth century. Her ridiculous G.I. coat almost reached her ankles and was missing all its buttons but one, which was securely fastened. What he could see of her legs terminated in a pair of combat boots.

His whole consciousness became absorbed in a vital awareness of her eyes, which seemed to have swallowed all the perceptible worlds between them.

The wind rose with an anguished moan.

He glanced guiltily at the fire. It's only a dirty scrap of paper! he argued. But now it's a part of the flame.

He looked into the girl's face, as though to deny the fact that the flame cast a mellow glow upon it.

You can have 'er, if you want 'er.

He impulsively stabbed at the hot embers with the blade of his knife. Then without knowing what he did, he withdrew a package of rations from his pocket and gave her a part of its contents. She took it and ate in silence.

She's done this many times, he thought as he poured some coffee into his cup and handed it to her, drinking himself from the canteen. When he had finished he slung his rifle over his shoulder and went out to fetch wood for the fire, thinking: Maybe she'll go away. But when he returned minutes later with a few frozen branches she stood in the corner, as before. He threw some wood on the fire and then squatted before her.

"Now," she said.

He could see her body through her thin rag of a dress that was either blue or green and fastened at the neck with a pin. Her underwear, which might have been a soldier's olive-drab shorts, could be glimpsed through a bursting seam. A pair of army socks crumpled around the tops of her boots.

"I will love you always!" he heard himself saying, and a cold fear seized him. The wind rose and in its wake a procession of grotesque figures seemed to dance obscenely in the light of her pure gaze. He reeled in the upsurge of dimly perceived events flowing within his visual range with varying degrees of clarity, flaunting every previous notion of himself.

It shouldn't have been like this! he thought in despair.

He tried to remember Cosima's face. But now he was tempted to look at the woman again, as though he half expected her to *be* Cosima. Cautiously, he raised his eyes as far as her boots. Then, with a sweeping glance, he took in her body, her face, and then he looked into her eyes.

"Now?"

Wait a minute! he cried desperately to himself, for it now appeared to him that the woman's features were actually changing before his eyes. He stirred the coals in the can. The flame grew brighter.

"Cosima?"

A branch fell to the ground with a loud crash. His mouth flew open as the woman's eyes changed from blue to brown, her hair from blond to soft brown.

Is it *possible?* . . . Yielding to the dazzling sensation splashed in hot spring colors. *What if I can't stop this?*

The woman's skin grew darker. Her nose broadened at the base and her cheekbones swelled gently under her eyes, which grew larger, the lashes longer, giving them an intense dreamy expression. Her lips became fuller in a face that was radically different from that of the girl who had lain there before.

It's no use he mused sadly, but not without a subversive feeling of pleasure, as he relaxed and allowed his mind to be subdued by his fancy. It can't *all* be just imagination. But . . . but how could this be Cosima. His eyes strugged to avoid the flesh under the flimsy bodice of her dress.

And now he perceived that her body had *even diminished in size!* There can be no doubt! he thought, passionately abandoning himself to the sight and thought of her. Her lithe body now flitted upon the horizon of his fondest recollections.

The spring of '41. The gym . . . North High. The setting sun was streaming through the three great windows.

Music at four. Chester Higgens on drums and Daisy Logan on piano.

Faces crowded around the bandstand, listening to Tommy Wright on trumpet from Jay McShann's band in town.

Dancing with Cosima! Looking guardedly over her shoulder at the side of her face, at the soft wisp of hair caught in the sunlight: on the turn, at the edge of the crowd.

To the blues. Shuffling back and forth on ball and toe of nervous feet. Once, while getting ready for the turn his arm tightening around her waist, heel turning on the pivoting point, her body pressed against his, faces forced apart, yet drawn by the magnetism of inexpressible joy!

Caught, in the swing of the turn, his thigh locked between hers, heel spinning like the axis of the world, her wide skirt billowing like a sail!

Stunned! Dazed! In the middle of the floor amid the fury of applause, stamping feet and yells of enthusiasm:

Cosima?

Lost? Lost! In the wake of the furling yellow skirt, fleeing through the sea of sunlit sound! . . .

A bell rang from a tower in the town. Voices in the shell rose to a voluminous whisper:

Cosima's not there! Cosima's not there! Cosima's not there. . . .

A dull pain throbbed in his head.

Cosima!

Cosima's not there!

"It's only a *thought!*" he cried angrily. "It comes from *me!*"

He studied the woman's face.

She's smiling. Why does she smile? How small her mouth is! And then he thought knowingly: She always did look like that when she was . . . Her nose is — is like *mine!* He closed his eyes and saw the ripple of animation that broke over her smooth black face whenever she spoke.

Mom?

He opened his eyes and beheld the woman with *his* face lying on the floor. She had balanced herself upon her elbow and had drawn her left leg toward her chest. He looked beseechingly into her eyes.

And now he felt the warmth of her flesh tenderly enveloping his naked body. His tiny fists clutched at her breasts. He closed his eyes and sucked with a hungry passion.

Boom! A deep bass voice boomed in his ears:

"Such a big boy like you, suckin' his momma's tiddy!"

He looked up and saw the woman's breast protruding between his eyes and the hairy face of a man. A killing shame smote him.

"It's not *my* fault!" cried Amerigo, enraged by the sight of himself, floundering in a state of infantine helplessness. At the same time his feeling of shame was intensified by an irresistible desire to embrace the woman, to seek refuge between her parted legs. The desire grew into a great longing, like that of an intensely felt homesickness. Meanwhile his body grew smaller and smaller in an attempt to hide from the dangerous face.

"It is not *possible!*" he cried, noticing that his voice made a small, round, barely audible sound. "No!" But his body continued to grow smaller. He entered the woman's body. He allowed his thoughts to sink down into the alluvial blackness, to the rhythms of myriad beating hearts. So loud that he was reduced to a mere amorphous awareness of himself, flowing through ancient worlds of flesh and bone strewn between the canyons of buried mountains and dry seas; a whirling rainbow brightness caught in the vortex of an irresistible force.

A bell chimed from a long way off.

He discovered himself staring fixedly into the woman's eyes. He saw the night. A boy and girl appeared. They climbed secretly to the crest of a great hill covered with wild blue grass and disappeared behind a clump of bushes that shot giant sprays into the air.

Rain and the feet of many generations had worn deep hollows into the breast of the hill, so that here and there — now hidden by a soft knoll, a bush, a knot of tangled undergrowth — lay the secret place where the thing was done: *Boom!* The seed plummeted deep into the root-breeding depths of the still cool darkness. The first of the ninth month, in the year '23, on a starry night in June when the scent of maple and pine, wild rose, and lilac filled the air. . . . He saw the day: *Boom!* — and the slow rhythmic pain resounded in the girl's abdomen. . . .

The boy's handsome face filled the woman's eyes. He ground his teeth and bit into the flesh of his bottom lip until it bled. Dad? His eyes fixed upon his father's face, Amerigo felt himself drawing nearer to the brink of time, within audible range of the inevitable question. Rutherford wrung his hands and muttered to himself:

"I didn' know nothin' like this was gonna happen! What am *I* gonna do with a *baby?* Just a trap! Her word against mine!"

"Tee! hee! hee!" A strange woman's voice, but no face appeared.

"Black thing!" Another woman's voice. It was familiar, but he couldn't place it.

"A tramp!" A man.

". . . You — a father!" The voice of an older woman, which he felt he had heard many times. "Why boy, you just a baby yourself! Besides, how do you know it's yourn?"

Boom!

A shriek escaped Viola's lips, followed by a lusty cry. Rutherford studied the features of the small black baby in Viola's arms, which now appeared in the woman's eyes. Its eyes shut tight, fat hands doubled into fists, it kicked as though it were falling through space. Amerigo thought it resembled himself.

"Don' look nothin' like *me!*" said Rutherford reproachfully.

"He's too little to tell yet," said Viola. Her eyes were clear and bright with remembered pain, her lips dry and parched. "Somethin's finished in me . . ." she whispered, ". . . over. Ain' nothin' gonna change that. Not just bein' up there on that hill with my spine pressed against that knoll. That was somethin', all right. But this is somethin' *else!* This I had to *earn!* Had to suffer, *all by myself!*" She looked up into Rutherford's face and read the fear and doubt that were there. Then she turned to Amerigo and whispered bitterly: "Adam'll have as many brothers as the ocean's got teeth!"

"But they always leave you in the end!" The hoarse tubercular voice of a woman who was no longer young, but not old. "They only want you to ween 'um. Once they git on they feet, git the craze to see a diamond cut a heart, they gone. The devils!"

The woman's face appeared. She spoke as though she were ill or drunk, cursing a man with words of endearment. "Your poppa! Your poppa had eyes that could light up like hell! 'Specially when they'd git to shufflin' with them dice an' cards roun' the gam'lin' table. Mercy! Rex . . . Rex! That was my sweet devil's name. An' he was dangerous, too! Like sin. Played any-game-a-chance that was ever played. An' when them run out, he's up an' make up his *own!* Why, he'd bet on the length of the knife that was stabbin' 'im to death if the one who was stabbin' 'im would *stop* stabbin' long enough to *call* it!

"Fordy-two when I first met 'im. Darlin' Sarah, my pa — Jethro was his name — usta call me. I was just turnin' seventeen that spring. That was the year I got married to the gam'lin' table.

"Between games I had babies. First Oriece. The Lord took him away from me when he wasn' but one an' a half. But He made it all up by givin' me Ruben! An' then Viola, the baby.

"When she wasn' no more than ten it was a long hard winter. They daddy's luck was just as hard as the winter was cold. One day he hadn' been home for three days. An' pretty soon them three days was over three weeks! After that I never saw 'im no more. . . ."

"Your gran'ma," said a new voice, a woman's. "Your gran'ma cried her eyes out, but it didn' do no good worryin' 'bout how she was gonna git through the night or if Rex's game was good or bad, if he was gonna be mad — or glad — when he finally did come home."

"One glad night was worth a thousand mad ones!" Grandma Sarah exclaimed.

"Yeah, darlin', but one day he came no more."

"No more . . ." Grandma Sarah whispered. "Come 'ere, the devil said. I hear it an' hear it always like he said it the first time."

"That's just whiskey talkin', Sarah. If you ain' careful it's gonna talk you to death. An' if that don' do it, honey, T.B. *will!* Did," the woman added sadly. "An' after that Ruben supported the family. Vi was eleven. He had his momma's face — little an' roun' — with a little sharp chin. Had a way of cockin' his head on the side when he was in earnest, just like her."

A young man's face appeared that looked a lot like his mother's face and a lot like his face.

"Of course," the woman continued, "his hair was crimpy, too, but not as good as Sarah's. Nappy! she usta say when she wanted to tease 'im. He'd smile an' then look just like his daddy. An' then Sarah'd be through for the night!"

"Viola was j-e-a-l-o-u-s!" cried Rutherford.

"Yeah, I admit it!" Viola exclaimed, "but I never held it against *him!* I loved him, *too!* It wasn't *my* fault that my father died when I was too little."

"Died?"

"Went away."

A low animated murmur rose from the shell, as several unidentified voices began to speak at once:

"That Ruben had a million-dollar smile!"

"Cute, too!"

"An' *dance!*"

"The only trouble with that good-lookin' black boy is he was born too early!"

"Your Uncle Ruben was a dancer, boy!" he heard his mother saying above the other voices, and he wondered how many times he had heard her say that, especially when he couldn't do that break-step she was always trying to teach him!

"My daddy," she would say, "had hands like a devil, Momma always said. My brother had feet like a angel, an' you — you got feet like knees!"

Her face broke up with laughter, while Uncle Ruben illustrated the break-step *again*. Then he tried it with his mother, and she exclaimed, "No — no, that ain' it!"

"Even your daddy could forget," said the woman's voice that had been speaking to Grandma Sarah, "that you look more like your momma than you do him to praise Ruben's dancin'!"

"M-a-n, he sure was somethin'!" Rutherford exclaimed. "An' I don' mean just tata ta-ta-*ta!* I mean that joker could really git up an' go! I remember that night, Jack, that night at the Black an' Tan? Never forget it as l-o-n-g as I live. Where the Black Angel usta be, 'cross from the Italian bakery on the corner of Independence an' Charlotte.

"Ruben was workin' at the hotel an'-an' had to work late that Saturday. He fell in about twelve. I mean the joint was jumpin'! Them jokers was strugglin'. Layin' 'um, Jack. Drinkin' sneaky-petes from flasks that you had to hide in your pocket, or stash under the table. Them jokers was payin' three an' a quarter a half-a-half-apint, an' six bits for the ice!

"Bus Morton was playin', an' man! I mean he was really hittin' 'um! Them jokers was *rough!* Bus was on piana, an' — what was that li'l short joker's name that played the cornet, Babe?" turning to Viola.

"Knuckles."

"Yeah, that's right. They called that cat Knuckles, Amerigo, 'cause his hands was so *b-i-g!* How he could play that cornet with hands like that, I'll never know. But that joker could blow! An' *all* them jokers was rough. An' lookin' *nice,* Amerigo, in fine togs, with they moss all layin'. Them cats had c-l-a-s-s, Jackson!

"Your momma had on the toughest dress she e-v-e-r had. Silver, with a long low neck. Fell straight from the shoulder an' hit just at the knees, with fine fringes hangin' down. An' those rhinestone shoes she keeps in the closet. Boy, when that black woman brought that dress home I coulda killed 'er! She's a-l-l-ways been like that, though, even when she was a li'l girl. Always had to have the best! It took us *both* six months, workin' day an' night — I ain' kiddin', am I Babe? — to pay for it.

"But she sure looked nice! Didn' *nobody* look no better. Your momma was a dresser!"

Rutherford's voice grew thoughtful.

"I was standin' pat in ma gray bo-back, Jack!" Grinning with pleasure: "It was really hittin' me! I don' remember *what* I paid for that suit. Wait a minute! Sexton bought it for me. Yeah. He a-l-l-ways had a big roll a bills. Big enough to choke a hoss! It was my first tailor-made suit. Formfittin', Jack! With white Florsheim shoes and a dark blue tie. Silk! With a hard knot layin' right in the heart a that collar. Tab. An' then, on top a that, I had Sexton's diamond stickpin, layin' right up under that knot. So bright it'd blind the sun!"

He paused, as he always did, to fully enjoy its brilliance.

"Me an' your momma was layin' down a Camel-Walk while you was home 'sleep!"

"You always went to sleep right away," said Viola, "an' slept the whole night through!"

"Ruben fell in about twelve," said Rutherford. "Lookin' like one of those big-time cats out of Chicago or New York or somethin' with a winnin' smile that killed 'um *all!* What you say! Some niggah yelled, an' a-l-l the people started lookin'. 'It's Ruben!' they all said. Didn' they, Babe?"

Viola grinned proudly.

"He couldn' hardly git over to our table, for smilin' an' shakin' hands! Like he was the *president* or somethin'! Rachel was a-hangin' on his arm, puttin' on airs, like a *fool!*"

"Rachel!" exclaimed Viola with contempt.

"But she looked nice, though!"

"Aw!" retorted Viola.

"Rachel was no good, Amerigo," said Rutherford, "she was a bad woman. Lazy an' triflin'. Spent Ruben's money faster'n he could make it. An' d-r-i-n-k! Drink more than a man. An' she was eeeeevul! Nobody liked 'er."

Uncle Ruben did, thought Amerigo.

"But she was a pretty woman, Amerigo, one of the prettiest women — black *or* white — I ever seen! Ain' that right, Babe?"

"Rachel!" Viola spat out the word in the same tone in which she might have said *whore.*

That's what she really means, Amerigo thought. But she can't say it because of me.

"Anyway," Rutherford continued, "he held the chair for her an' ever'thin'. Ruben was a gen'leman! An' before he could set down the jokers started yellin' Dance! Dance, Ruben! Do a Buck-an'-Wing! Break 'um down with a soft-shoe! Eagle-Rock, baby!

"An' then that joker on the drums started a soft roll on the snares. It got louder an' cracked up all golden-like when that cat hit the cymbals! An' then he rattled off a finger roll. Light as a feather! All the cats got quiet, waitin' to see what Ruben was gonna do.

"Then Ruben, your uncle — it's a pity you never knowed him, he sure liked you, didn' he, Babe? Well, your uncle Ruben stepped up on the stage in front of a-l-l them jokers! Modest, Jack! That's what I always liked about Ruben. Cool! Like-a-a-aristocrat! An' he didn' let it swell his head the way Rachel did. Well, he stepped up on the stage. An' the Baby Love — the baddest drummer that ever *was!* — started to hittin' at Ruben on the cymbals!

"Ruben glided into a soft-shoe, with a easy rhythm that was g-r-a-c-e-f-u-l! Man! Wasn' it, Babe?" looking at Viola for confirmation. "Like he was dancin' on *air!*

"An' then Baby Love let loose on the snares, watchin' Ruben's feet, the bass ridin' easy: a-boom-boom-boom-boom.

"Ruben answered the niggah, an' went 'im one better. An' then he changed the beat on 'im before he could get set. But Baby Love was on 'im, Jack! Like white on rice! That Baby Love was m-e-a-n! You heah me? The joint was so quiet you could hear a rat piss on cotton."

"Rutherford Jones!" cried Viola.

"An' then what happened, Dad?"

"Then!" exclaimed Rutherford, looking at him in surprise, as though he pitied him for not having been there. "Then? Boy, Ruben closed his eyes. Like this." Rutherford closed his eyes like Uncle Ruben, and the long silk lashes fringing the lids lay upon his dark, reddish brown skin.

The best-looking man in the whole world, Amerigo thought.

"Like this," he was saying, "an' *then* he let his arms fall to 'is sides. Relaxed, Jack! An' then he danced. *Danced!* For a solid hour! An' he never did the same step twice!

"Baby Love put his drumsticks *down* an' just *watched* Ruben! An' the rest of the jokers in the band laid their instrument 'cross their knees. Every foot was tappin' while old Ruben was dancin'. Yes, sir, like *God* was callin' the steps! An' all you could heah was: *Whoom! Whoom! Whoom! To-to-to Whoom! Whoom! Whoom!* An' in between the '*Whoom!*' Ruben was dancin' every step that ever was. An' when them run out, he started makin' up his *own!*"

Like Bill Bojangles Robinson, Amerigo thought. Must a been something like that.

"Then Rachel started playin' the fool," said Viola sadly.

"Yeah," said Rutherford in a tremulous voice, "she started messin' 'round with some niggah from the south side. A one-eyed niggah. She encouraged 'im 'cause he had a wad of bills. He started feelin' all over her, an' when she tried to get away from the niggah it was too late.

"Ruben looked up just in time to see 'im kissin' her. The joint got quiet, and the people started movin' back. Ruben leaped at the niggah — from the *stage!* G-r-a-c-e-f-u-l!

"Some woman yelled out 'Look out, Ruben, the niggah's got a knife!' But he didn' have no knife, he had a gun! A twenty-two automatic. Shot Ruben in the chest — two feet away. Then he made a dash for the door, flashin' his gun. Little John emptied his forty-five at him, but he was gone.

"The hole in Ruben's chest was too small. It closed up and he couldn' bleed. By the time old Doc Bradbury got there Ruben was dead.

"They never did catch the niggah that done it."

"They never *tried!*" Viola protested bitterly. "Why should they? Just one niggah killin' another niggah."

In the thoughtful silence that followed Amerigo was smitten by a profound regret that his cousin Rachel's green eyes and soft golden skin had made a hole in Uncle Ruben's chest that was too small, and that *"they,"* who were supposed to deal with such people, didn't care at all.

"He was born too early," said Rutherford. "If that dancin' black man had been *white!*" He paused abruptly, speechless before the enormity of his speculation. "Yeah . . . an' your momma was a good dancer, too, Amerigo. Won every Charleston contest in town. An' she could do a mean Black-bottom, an' a Eagle-Rock that was better'n most, an' she could Buck an' tap an' toe. . . ."

"All I know is what Ruben taught me," said Viola. "I usta like to dance with your daddy 'cause he could do the Camel Walk so well, with those long legs of his! An' when he got a little tight he could do a real mean Shimmy, too!"

As his mother's voice faded away, his father's expression became grave. Amerigo felt vaguely uneasy, but he was not surprised or mystified by it because he gradually remembered the source of the feeling and was finally able to isolate it. He strained to catch the whisperings of the wind.

Rutherford, his five sisters, and a brother lived down on Fourth Street behind the old Field House opposite Garrison Square where the old Garrison School used to be. Opposite the schoolhouse stood Clairmount Hill.

It stood proud as a mountain, looking down upon the grand Missouri River and the huge dingy factories strewn along its banks. And upon the railroad machine shops with their sprawling yards stained with burned oil and soot, cluttered with odd wheels and dismantled engines and piles of worn-out brake shoes and all manner of wire bales, and bells and drums and bolts and rings and elbows and joints of iron and steel eaten up with rust; shops guarded by rough-hewn men in black leather jackets, closed in by strong rusty iron fences that had stood long in the rain.

Clairmount Hill was a stormy hill in spring when lightning lashed the trunks of the tall trees, raising welts of fire as the wind buffeted their splendid boughs.

The hill caught in storm raged in the reclining woman's eyes.

Then a familiar voice rose above the wind: *They ain' no better'n you!* It sounded like his mother's voice, and then again like his grandmother's, Darlin' Sarah. He thought he knew the voice, and was agitated because the face did not appear.

"Rutherford," it continued, *"grew up in that old shack down at the foot of Clairmount Hill. Every time it rained the mud washed down its sides an' flooded the street. Ran right up to the foot of the house like a volcano blowin' up with mud! The one on the corner where the street ended, a frame house with three rooms. His momma, Veronica, his sisters: Ruby, Jessy, Nadine, Edna, an' Helen — an' him — all crowded together like Cracker Jacks in a Cracker Jack box. A course, the high an' mighty Sexton didn' live with the rest of 'um, he lived up on the avenue. The oldest — if he'd a lived long enough."*

"A man like him *don' come out of* every *belly!"* Another familiar voice, a woman's. It resembled his father's voice. The face would not appear.

"She sure loved Sexton!" said Rutherford bitterly.

"Tall, an' straight! Like his father," said the woman. *"Hair like a soft bunch of feathers! Auburn. Wouldn' be no exaggeration to say he had a b-e-a-u-t-i-f-u-l face for a man: straight nose, straight as a arrow! Distinguished lookin'. Humph! No wonder the girls loved him so! I ain' ashamed to admit it. Just like his father!*

"Do you know how your father got me? He stole *me! Took me off the plantation by night! Almost killed his hoss 'cause he wouldn' stop before he crossed* three *borders!"*

"Off a what plantation did Poppa steal you, Momma?" asked a strange spectral voice. A man's. Like somebody who was dead.

"Never you mind that!" answered the woman with deep emotion.

"You scaired to tell?"

"Yes, son, I'm scaired to tell. You, Sexton, my firstborn — you was born in Saint Louie. An' your sisters, Nadine an' Jessica — twins. An' then we came west here. Your grandpa was a wand'rin' man. Here's where the rest of you, Ruby, Helen, and Rutherford, was born. An' they wasn' no space in between. My man was a half-breed!"

Amerigo gradually perceived the new face that now appeared in the reclining woman's eyes, that of his grandma Veronica. Her skin was light, almost like a white woman's, and her hair was long, dark brown, and straight. It seemed that a shadow of a smile lingered upon her face.

"Momma didn' smile very much," said Rutherford, and the gravity of his expression was softened by resignation, "except when you got her to talkin' about Will. Then she just couldn' hold back what was inside 'er. She didn' love n-o-b-o-d-y else! Unless it was Sexton. She'd follow Will anywhere he led 'er. An' I mean without complainin'!"

"He sure was a Indian, all right!" Grandma Veronica exclaimed, "but he had hair like a white man. An' blue eyes! Even wore a handlebar *mus*tache. Like Buffalo Bill. Didn' drink, didn' smoke, didn' gam'le!"

"He had seven of us, Momma!" cried Rutherford. "I think that's enough!"

Grandma Veronica's face turned a ripe peach color. As she laughed through her closed mouth, her cheeks swelled up under her hazel eyes and a fine spray of spittle escaped her lips, while the bluish green vein that divided her forehead into two equal parts broke up the stern effect caused by her thin nose and set chin. Her yellow skin was smooth, like Cosima's, and her long silky hair was parted in the middle, with the halves swept back and wound into a soft ball.

"An' Momma never did talk about herself much," Rutherford continued distractedly. "In fact, she didn' talk 'bout *nothin'* much! More Indian than anythin' else. Crow, she *says*. But how she got to be Crow when her momma, her name was Anna, was a slave ain' never been clear. What happened before Poppa was *supposed* to a come along on his hoss is as plain to you as it is to me. But he was her weakness!"

"Made his livin' doin' odd jobs, mostly outdoors," said Grandma Veronica. "That's one man sure liked to be outdoors. Will looked ridiculous pent up in a house! Had a natural way with the sick."

"Old Will was a medicine man!" shouted Rutherford. "Hot dog!"

Amerigo tried to catch a glimpse of his grandfather, but all that came to mind was Buffalo Bill.

"No matter what you had," said Grandma Veronica, "he'd go trailin' off in the woods an' turn up a couple a hours later with a little deerskin sack he usta carry around full a roots an' herbs. He'd take off to the kitchen by hisself an' cook 'um. Make a polstice or a stew. An'-an' — no matter *what* you had, if you was normal you got well! An' *whistle!* Like a bird. Predict the weather just lookin' at the sky. Fish? Hunt? Humph!"

"Her lips," said Viola, "would always tremble in the end, and she'd start crying, like Momma. Even though she *was* blind! Funny how blind eyes can cry. An' especially *hers,* because she always *seemed* to be such a self-willed woman. I'll never forget how when we got married she . . ."

"She *did* have a strong will!" Rutherford broke in angrily. "How do you think we lived when Sexton wasn' nothin' but nine an' I was a baby — still crawlin' — with five girls in between. An'-an' Buffalo Bill walked off! Into the woods somewhere, an' never *did* come back!"

"Just couldn' stand sleepin' in a bed!" exclaimed Grandma Veronica.

Rutherford's expression grew bitter; his eyes narrowed and his voice quavered.

"*We* usta *have to* keep in bed *a-l-l day,* just to keep warm, while Momma was out workin' for the white folks. Five dollars a week for cookin' an' cleanin' an' washin' an' ironin'. I sold papers on the streets when I was five, an' had to give every penny to Momma.

"An' rough! That evil woman was *terrible!* Huh! She'd say, do it! An' if you didn' — an' I mean *right now* — *boom!* You'd be busted upside the head. An' no cryin'. Better *not* cry!"

Rutherford looked at Viola for sympathy, but her expression was hard, insistent. *Say it!* it seemed to say.

"My brother Sexton was a pimp, Amerigo. . . ."

"What's a pimp?" he asked.

"He kept women. You know . . ."

"Aw . . ."

"They said *I* wasn' good enough for your daddy," said Viola, "'cause I was black an' my hair was nappy."

"Aw Babe!"

"But *my* brother wasn' no *pimp!* They found they previous yellah-baby sister Ruby, who was too good to come to our weddin', dead in a *whore-house!* She was lousy! With T.B. to boot! 'Scuse me, Amerigo, but it's the *truth!* Ask your daddy! She had to be buried in *my* dress 'cause her *own sisters wouldn' give 'er* none!

"My brother this an' my brother that they say, but they don' never do nothin' for 'im, 'cept *beg* 'im out a every dime they can git. An' where does he have to git it from? From *me!* I work just as hard as he does. Every scrap of furniture that's in this house, every crust of bread we eat, I help to pay for it! An' him, like a fool — too weak to say no! They been diggin' our grave ever since we been together! It just *kills* 'um to see us turnin' out so good! An' when your gran'ma went blind. She had three daughters, but she had to come and live with us 'cause *they* wouldn' take 'er. We had to *shame* 'um! Ask your daddy!"

All the faces disappeared except those of Amerigo and his mother.

"I will love you always," he said.

"Will you?"

"You'll see! I'll do somethin' big! An' be famous, an' you'll be proud. I'll buy you a big house an' pay for ever'thin'!"

No sooner than he had uttered these words than the face of his father appeared next to his. He whispered plaintively in one ear while his mother whispered plaintively in the other. Strains of an unbearably sad music filled the air. He shut his eyes but he could not shut out the sound.

If they say just one more word, he thought, I'll die!

"You gotta give Momma credit for one thing, Babe."

"What's that?"

"She always did love our son. More'n she loved *me*, even!"

"That's true," said Viola, "because he always loved *her*."

The sad music died away, and with a feeling of relief, he once again saw Grandma Veronica's face. It appeared as it was most familiar to him: stern, placid, with hazel eyes.

"I'll love you always!" he whispered.

"Amerigo's a dreamer," she said, "just like my Will. I had big hopes for Sexton, but the women killed him."

"It was cancer, Momma!" said Rutherford.

"You kin call it *cancer* if you want to. Call it anythin'. He's dead. Ruby, my baby's dead. She was the prettiest of them all. I guess she never got much of a chance. A pretty girl likes pretty things.

"An' then Nadine went an' married old John Simpson!"

"Yeah, Momma, but *ever'body* — white folks, too! — called him *Mister John!*" said Rutherford admiringly. "Yes, sir! That's a *man!*"

"A one-handed, bald-headed old man!" said Grandma Veronica. "Lost it in a sawmill, they *say*, just as he was turnin' nineteen. Married my girl when he was forty-five! An' her nothin' but eighteen. Trashman!"

"Collected things," said Rutherford. "He had a ol' horse an' wagon, Amerigo, that he usta drive up and down back alleys, pickin' up newspapers an' rags, an' copper an' all kinds a lead an' aluminum pots an' pans — anythin', no kiddin'! Plumbin' fixtures, old furniture, books, bolts, screws, wire! Anythin' he could bundle up and sell at the junkyard. An' s-m-a-r-t! Read a-l-l the time!"

"Smart enough to collect my daughter!"

"Yeah," Rutherford retorted, "an' a little later he bought 'im a new horse, too. An' *now* he's got a *truck!*"

"An' *three* kids!"

"He ain' *got* but one hand, Momma!"

"Amerigo's the best of the lot of you. He's got *two* hands, an' he ain' forty-five. An' he can *see*, thank God! Dreams wide awake, even if he don' look like no Jones!"

"That always *was* a mystery to Momma," said Viola, "how somebody can have any sense an' *not* look like a *Jones!* If you ain' high-yellah, with a little Indian-red, a little stray-brown mixed in, accidental-like, you ain' nothin'! An' even when the Joneses *was* a little dusky, like Nadine, they just *had* to have good or passin'-good hair!"

"No nappy heads in my family!" said Grandma Veronica. "An' the faces are reg'ler!"

"Everybody does when the wagon comes!" said a familiar voice. Amerigo stirred attentively.

"Ain' it the truth!" Viola exclaimed.

A woman's face appeared and gradually merged into Viola's face, at which Amerigo experienced a feeling of deep, almost reverent love.

Aunt Rose? Aunt Rose! That was *her* voice talking to Grandma Sarah! That's *her,* all right! But different, younger.

Her forehead was exceedingly high. Domed and smooth. Bad hair! Smiling warmly at the part in her coarse black hair. It gave her a girlish air. Needs a pink bow-ribbon.

"She began to dye it when she was about forty," said Viola, "when the first white streaks began to show. It's a secret."

Aunt Rose is no beauty, Amerigo reflected, but she has a beautiful mouth. Sort of like Mom's. But it makes her head look smaller than it really is. Still it's small enough. Like a little Gothic tower!

He allowed his fancy to play freely upon the features of her face. Her brows hovered nervously above her eyes like the wings of a bird silhouetted against the sky, while the eyes themselves were animated by a nervous energy that seemed to register every emotion that rose to the surface of her consciousness. They were hungry, curious, saddened by what they saw — when they weren't too busy laughing. And they were laughing most of the time.

"She's fat!" snapped the resentful voice of a young woman.

"Ain't you heard, honey?" Aunt Rose retorted, *"fat meat's* greasy!

"Lordy!" she sang, *"Lordy look down, look down, that lonesome road,* before *you travel on!"*

A gust of wind broke through the forest and shattered into many fragments of sound that spoke of Aunt Rose. He listened in an attitude of discovery.

"If Aunt Rose ever lost her tongue," said Viola, "she could talk more 'n most people just with 'er eyes!"

"Yeah," said Rutherford, "she sure kin! She kin praise you with humor."
"Blame you!"

Ardella! thought Amerigo.

"I'd sure hate to be her enemy!" An unidentified voice.

"Just like Ruben," said Rutherford, "born too soon. If that black woman had a been white!"

"That sure is the truth!" said Viola. "An' she didn' git no further than the third grade neither. But if you could see her handwritin', you'd think *she* went to college, instead of Ardella!"

"*She's a fool!*" said Ardella.

"They *say*," Viola replied, "blood's thicker than water, but she's been just like a *momma* to me! I don' know *what* we'd a done without her. Especially when we was just married, without a dime to our name an' no place to go after Momma died!"

"A course, she had her weaknesses, just like ever'body else," said Rutherford. "Old Billy was *her* downfall! With that guitar of his. He could tell 'er that the moon was made of John the Conquer Root an' she'd believe it!"

"Aw, she didn' believe it," said Viola, "she just didn' care no more."

"Ain' that funny Babe, how she could love a niggah like that?"

And suddenly Amerigo was sitting in a room filled with women, facing a little stage where an old black woman stood, hovering over a silver ball. She wore a black turban and a cape that fell to the floor. One of its edges was thrown back over her shoulder, exposing its red lining and a long white dress underneath. She wore large crescent-shaped earrings, and when she raised her eyes and hands to the ceiling many rings with big pretty stones of different colors glittered on her fingers. The room grew dark and the silver ball lit up like a moon. The whites of her eyes and the silhouette of her thin fingers were visible against the light. She stood motionless. After several minutes she moved toward Aunt Rose and looked deeply in her eyes for a long while. Then she folded her arms upon her chest and said, in a still voice that was hardly above a whisper: "Sister, you coulda been a great woman if you hadn' a-married the man you married!"

"Lord knows I've made mistakes!" said Aunt Rose with a heavy sigh, as the room faded away and her face reappeared. "I done the best I could. I got a mirror an' I look at it all the time. But a mirror don' show what's inside a person, an' people just don' never seem to have the time to look. I've had to scuffle all my life for somebody *else!*: for Momma, till she died; for Poppa when he went blind; for the white folks. An' then there was Billy. He was a soldier, an' you *know* what soldiers are! Cavalry! It was the army that made a tramp out a him. Oh, I know! I know a-l-l about him. He's a weak, shiftless, good-for-nothin' who never gave me nothin' in my whole life 'cept Ardella an' a helluva lot a trouble! But he was kind an' good-natured, an' he had a good heart. An' in the dark wasn' nobody but just me an' him. Now that's how my corset fits!"

"*My pappy!*" exclaimed Uncle Billy's jocular voice, "*was a soldierin' man!"* The handsome smiling face of a bald-headed man appeared beside that of Aunt Rose. His skin was the color of burned saddle leather, and a blue stubble of perhaps two days' growth covered his face. His eyes twinkled and his teeth shone white and strong. "Wounded twice! Seventy-nine. An' I'm a soldierin' man. Got mine in the left shoulder in 'seventeen. Under fire twenty-one days! Hot damn! . . . But I want you to know somethin'." His smile deepened, dimples welling on either side of his beautiful mouth. "I had my black fun! Yes, sir! You ever see a French gal do what they call the Can-can? M-a-n they sho' kin Can-can! Good Godamighty! Usta hit the meat houses e-a-r-l-y in the mornin'! Before they had time to pee! Ha! Ha! Ci-vil-ians civilians a-l-l-ways squawkin' about war, but a real soldier — I mean a reg'ler, not one a these cake eaters — don' like nothin' else *but!"*

"Hush, Billy," said Aunt Rose.

"Hush! Woman I was a warrin' sonofa — "

"What's war, Uncle Billy?" asked the child.

"War? W-a-r!" Uncle Billy's mouth flew open. He stared into space, as though he were looking there for the answer.

"Boy, you'll find out soon enough. You think ol' Jerry knows fat meat's greasy? One a these days, boy, one a *these days.* I won' live to see it, but *you* will. One a these days you'll hear a b-i-g sound, an' that'll be *war!"*

A volley of wind crashed against the side of the hut and ricocheted against the walls of the shell. . . . Unconsciously his mind quickened to the melody of an old song that he had heard many times: "Joshua!" he muttered, "an' the walls come tumblin' down!"

"Men!" said Aunt Rose contemptuously. "I been soldierin' a-l-l m'life without a uniform an' all that rigamarole. Try bringin' up a daughter in a good-time house through the depression, *an'* Prohibition, an' see if that ain' hell! I bet General Sherman ain' never tried that!"

"But it was fun, though," said Uncle Billy. "'Course, it wasn' nothin' like the good ol' days oversea!"

"Rose was a good mixer!" said a husky male voice. *"An' a damned good cook! Bis-cuits just melt in your mouth! When a man sets down to Rose's table he kin leave his teeth at home! Not only that, she was a woman a man could talk to an' know she'd understand what he was talkin' about!"*

"Usta break 'um down e-v-e-r-y Sad'dy night!" Another male voice. A whiskey voice. *"Porters an' waiters'd hit town, pockets jinglin', just dyin' to spend it!"*

"Fried chicken an' collard greens!"

"Hush!"

"Black-eyed peas! Red beans an' rice! Pig feet — ears, snoots, tails.

Wasn' nothin' *she didn' know 'bout no* hog! *An' plenty a good corn liquor an' gin an' ice-cold beer to warsh it down. Now what I say!"*

"An' man, them broads that usta come down to Rose's place sho' was hot! Sheeeeeiiiit!"

"That li'l Georgie May, that was 'er name — yeah, Georgie May! — had a twis' that'd break a sand hog's back!"

"She sure could make you holler, all right. But Baby Sister wasn' no drag neither. That li'l bowlegged gal could git up an' go! An' I ain' got no cause to lie!"

"Big-leg woman, keep yo' dresses down! You got somethin' make a bulldog hug a houn'. Big-leg woman, eh!, keep yo' dresses down! *Ah! ha! ha! ha!"*

"Tee! hee! hee! Eh . . . uhm . . . An' you know one thing?"

"Naw, what?"

"Rose was makin' pots a money!"

"Wish I had a nickel for every dollar I spent!"

"She had a business head, all right."

"Pick the gold out a your teeth, if she ketch you nappin'!"

"If you ketch a fool," said Aunt Rose, "bump his head! You couldn' never keep a dime in your pocket no way. But let me ask you somethin': You ever been hungry when I wouldn' feed you? Did you ever ask me for a drink when I wouldn' give you one? Ever had to sleep in the cold as long as I had a roof over my head? Huh? Answer that! You whinin' niggahs make me sick! None a you no damned good! I been takin' in stray dogs ever since I can remember — an' what thanks do I git?"

"That's true," said a woman's voice. *"She took all kinds a crap from those niggahs just so's she could give Ardella a decent life."*

"A chance *I* never had!" said Aunt Rose. "Only the *Lord* knows what I been through."

"I hope," said Ardella, "I hope the Lord hasn't got a one-track mind, Momma, 'cause I'm my mother's daughter."

Her face appeared between those of Aunt Rose and Uncle Billy. "It wasn't no choice of *mine* to look like Momma. She's fat and I'm tall and skinny, but my ankles and feet are swollen just like hers. And like Momma I've never had any luck with men."

"Actually, Ardella's got a *good* heart," said Viola earnestly. "An' she's smart, too, just like Aunt Rose. But smartness don' get you *no*where if you can't get along with folks. Or yourself, for that matter!"

"Two years in *college* couldn't make no *saint* out of me!" retorted Ardella. "I grew up in Momma's good-time house, pouring out drinks! When I wasn't doing that I was keeping an eye out for the police. And helping

Momma clip the niggahs of those dirty one-dollar bills! When I went up to bed I could hear Georgie May, Baby Sister, and Queenie Johnson giggling with the porters and waiters in the rooms next to mine. And I heard *every-thing,* for years! And then we moved to the city, to a bigger house!"

He remembered the house.

"On the corner of Fifth and Beadle Street, across from the old court-house. Looked out over the trafficway . . ."

The sounds of an endless stream of cars flowing down the broad thor-oughfare, and the clang and rumble of the Fifth Street trolley filled his mind. He saw Aunt Rose's big two-story redbrick house with its rambling porch extending the length of the front. It was perched on a rather high hill that rose abruptly from the street. Looks like a grotesque nest! he reflected, recognizing the tangled undergrowth that sprang up around its foundation, his eyes sweeping down the hill that gave onto a wall of solid rock that dropped fifty feet to the street. And there was Mr. Antonini's fruit stand at the corner. The stairs! His attention was drawn now to the winding wooden stairs that he had often climbed to the upper reaches of Aunt Rose's stronghold. It squeezed its way upward between the high rock wall that supported the base of her house and the wall of the adjoining building, a nightclub, "Dante's Inferno!"

"What does *in-fer-no* mean, Aunt Rose?" Amerigo asked.

"Hell, son."

The red house flared up like a great flame before his eyes; it fired the rose and raspberry bushes and ran down the sheer wall to the street where it inflamed the streetcar tracks, which picked up the burning light and fled west down Fifth Street. With a quickening sense of recognition he now smelled the pungent aroma of massive quantities of fruit and vegetables mixed with the odor of live poultry — white and fluttering in wire cases strewn with feces and dried corn; or dangling heads-down in bunches with outspread wings — of butchered meat, fish, cheeses, spices. Sawdust and gasoline and burned oil; horse manure, human sweat, and summer heat ground into busy fragments of sound: the cling and bang of cash registers, the roar of truck motors, and the whinny of horses amid the clang of trolley cars and the swarm of flies, the barking of dogs, and the energetic cries of children and farmers. Now he saw the four square blocks of fruit and vegetable stalls surrounded by the knot of banks and the sprawling mass of hot dingy office buildings with signs on their windows in raised porcelain letters.

The old city market! Fifth and Main, you have to go north to get to Admiral Boulevard. His eye followed its broad concrete bed into the gaping mouth of the long, steel-ribbed viaduct that spanned the industrial area along the north and south shores of the great Missouri River. No-man's-land! He felt rather than saw the spectral forms of odd Italians, Mexicans, Irishmen, Negroes, occasional Indians, and those anonymous, raceless men who slept in dirt houses dug into the banks of the river.

A strange breed. They filtered in and out of the innumerable factories, warehouses, and mammoth packing plants that filled the area known as the Bottoms.

He could hear the low of stalled cattle drifting up from the stockyards, the bleat of sheep, the squealing of hogs.

"*But the smell of blood,*" a voice whispered. "*The sound of death is the loudest. So loud that you can see it!* Floating overhead like a wad of blood-soaked cotton, at sunset, when the wind shifts and the stench takes your breath away. The bottoms! A dangerous place if you don't know what you're doing."

"*They ride aroun',*" began another voice, "*in big black armor-plated see-dans! My old lady's doin' Little John's warshin'. Knows his momma an' all of 'um down there. Tourin' see-dans with bulletproof windows.*"

"Yeah," exclaimed another voice, "*an' ifya git crossed up with one of 'um they take you for a buggy ride! Just like that! An' then yo' number's up — you hear what I say? I'm tellin' you what I know! Not just what I heard, what I know! Or else you wind up in the river with a belly full a lead an' a rock aroun' your neck — or under one a them vi-dock piers with your eyes poppin' out a your head! An' ain' no use askin' who done it! Who'd be fool enough to tell even if they knowed?*"

"Yeah! That was *my* battleground!" said Aunt Rose bitterly. "An' they wasn' no bugles blowin', an' no fancy metals! The Lord works in myste-rious ways. Seems to me that sometimes the quickest way to heaven is *down!* In them days I could whisper loud enough for the right ear to hear it. But I ain' proud of it. I'm just tellin' it like it is."

"Aunt Rose was a talker, Amerigo!" Rutherford in a voice that revealed awe and pride. "I seen 'er! I seen that woman stand up on a platform at election time, in front of a crowd so big it covered the w-h-o-l-e street! Ain' that right, Babe? An' talk to 'um, Jack! An' I mean lay-it-on-the-*line!* With all them high-powered political words an' things. She kin really put it down when she wants to. An' when she got through, the votes poured in, an' the breaks came her way. She could git you a job on the city. She could git you on relief durin' the depression, on the WPA. Yeah! She could git you a pension if you was cripple or blind or anythin' like that. She helped Momma, Amerigo. Don't you never tell this to *no*body, but she could even git you out a *jail* — even if you *killed* somebody! — providin' it was a Negro an' you had some cash stashed away. What *they* care? Just as long as it wasn' no white man.

"Ha!" Rutherford laughed, "ol' Billy retired from the army and laid up there and spent it as fast as she'd let 'im!"

"An' what he didn' run through she spent on Ardella," said Viola, "on fancy clothes an' sendin' 'er to college. But that gal just wouldn' do right. What *wouldn'* I'a done if I'd a had a momma who'd a given me the opportunity to make somethin' out a myself?"

"I done all I could for that gal," said Aunt Rose, "but she don' appreciate nothin'."

"You waited too late, Momma!" said Ardella in anguish. "How do you think I felt when my nice friends would ask what my mother's profession was? When the nice young men would say, I was at your momma's *joint* last night, and click their teeth at me. They call me Black Mariah!"

"The blacker the berry the sweeter the juice."

"Momma, you got to *pick* it before you can find out! Besides, I'm not so sweet, I've been on the vine too long."

"You had it too easy," said Aunt Rose. "You got no gumption. You coulda *tried* to stick it out. If not for me, then for your*self!* You let 'um *run* you away! You're an' ungrateful child. Marryin' a niggah like Jessy just 'cause he's yellah! An ugly good-for-nothin' yellah niggah that ain' got a dime to 'is name nor a brain in his nappy head! You're a thorn in my heart. But I done had my say. I done cried enough tears over you. I'm through . . . through."

"Momma, you haven't got a heart!"

"After Ardella got married," said Rutherford, "Aunt Rose started readin' the Bible. Never knowed *no*body to read the Bible like *she* did — except maybe Mister Simpson. Man, she could recite chapter an' verse out a her head whenever she had a mind to. An' she'd always drive her point home. Sund'y mornin' when she'd drop a roll in the collection plate big enough to choke a mule, you ought to a seen them jokers buckin' they eyes!"

"But she wasn' no happy woman," said Viola sadly. "After Billy died an' Ardella got married, her heart started botherin' 'er and she thought she was gonna die. Ol' Jessy and Ardella was standin' pat — waitin'."

"You, *too!* Ah ha ha ha!" Rutherford laughed mischievously.

"Why *Rutherford!* How-on-earth could you *say* such a thing like that! After *a-l-l* she's done for me!"

"Many a mornin'," said Aunt Rose, "I'd wake up e-a-r-l-y in the mornin' an' ask myself what I done to deserve the life I've had! Lord, why do You break my heart! My own child, my own flesh and blood! You know I done it all for *her!* Times was *h-a-r-d!* If only Billy coulda helped me a little. Woulda . . ."

He saw Aunt Rose in a semidarkened room, stretched out on a blue bed, a blue light filtering through the window; lying in an attitude of listening.

She began to gasp for breath. Her heart pounded violently and she began to cough, and then to laugh at the same time, a terrifying laughter, which, interspersed with coughing, burst in volleys of explosive sound upon the still air. Then she lay still. Silent.

"Aunt Rose?" Amerigo whispered.

Her lips parted and said:

"I could talk to Darlin' Sarah when I couldn' talk to nobody else but the Lord!"

"At the bottom of every poor woman's heart," said Darlin' Sarah, *"is a man. Rex ain' never comin' back, an' my baby, Ruben, ain' neither. Why?"*

"The Lord knows, but He won' tell me! I carried Ardella in my womb nine long months; even married Billy to keep 'er. Now *he's* gone, an' *she's* gone — an' in the dark ain' nobody but *me!* But at least Ruben was a credit to you. Ruben was a golden child!"

"I wish I hadn' a been such a burden to 'im."

Grandma Sarah's voice trailed away into a silence that lasted for several minutes. Viola's face appeared beside that of Aunt Rose.

"With Darlin' Sarah gone, Viola, honey, you all by yourself. But you young an' strong, an' you got a lot a courage. An' now you even got a baby. Lord! *An'* a husband! When I look at you I can't help thinkin' about when I was your age, just startin' out! I got myself a man, too. An' I watched 'im sap up all my strength with his lust an' triflin' ways. 'Course, you an' me an' your momma ain' the only ones. It's many a black woman that's had to go the same way. What good's a man to a woman who ain' no man! When you come right down to it color don' matter. An' it ain' just bein' poor. Now it ain' no harm in your gittin' married, even if you ain' nothin' but a baby. You done good! But you started it, for better or for worse! An' you gotta stick it through, else you just ain' *nobody!* You understand me?"

"Yes'm."

"There's a lot a wonderful things ain' never gonna happen to you an' Rutherford, 'cause it's gonna take all your strength just to survive, git ol', an' buy a decent funeral. Times is changed! Like I told Ardella, you gotta have book-learnin' nowadays. Gotta git somethin' in your head 'sides foolishness if you wanna keep up with the white folks. Yeah! They gonna try to keep you back, but you gotta learn what they learn just the same! Learn it better! An' work hard, harder 'n they do, kin, or even will, just to git half as far!

"The baby's got a chance. He's the beginnin' of somethin' that ain' got no end. You just listen to what I tell you! I promised the Lord I'd make it up to Him if He'd just give me another chance!"

Amerigo's face appeared between his mother's face and the face of Aunt Rose.

"Amerigo," said Aunt Rose, "the Good Book says, love thy father an' mother that thy days may be long, 'specially your momma, 'cause she'll be with you a-l-l-ways!"

"Through thick and thin," said Viola earnestly. "I *know!* My father left me when I wasn' nothin' but a *baby!*"

"Life'll bring it home to you one day," added Aunt Rose, "when you big enough to understand."

"There's things I've had to put up with I ain' never told nobody," said Viola. "I hope the Lord strikes me dead if I'm lyin'. I took it, an' kept on goin'. Just for *you!*"

Amerigo watched his child's face torn with pity.

"When I git big," he muttered tearfully, "an' git to be a man, I'm gonna be somebody *real* big! An' you'll be proud an' . . ."

"Momma!" cried Ardella, "if you could have been to *me* what you are to *them,* it could have been so different, you and me."

"You ain' never been no real daughter to me. Kin you give me a grand-child to love? Naw! 'Cause it ain' no child's love in you. You done growed hard inside. Like a tree turned to stone. Why, Ardella? Why?"

"You're blind, Momma!"

Ardella's words were drowned by a sudden upsurge of wind that stormed Clairmount Hill and shook the branches of the trees until the leaves floated down. *Boom! Boom! Boom!* — They flew helter-skelter over the planes of his mother's eyes like faces. "Grandma, Veronica, Uncle Billy, Ardella," he called after them. "Darlin' Sarah! Aunt Ruby! Uncle Ruben! Rex! Will! . . ."

Boom! Boom! resounded the falling leaves *(Boom!),* growing into a rolling swell of sound that forced him through a series of dimly perceived rooms filled with smells that prodded his sensibility with the reclining woman's question:

"Now?"

"Ah yes! I remember!" But then he was forced to pause before the enor-mity of the word *I. I?* Making a terrific mental effort to bring the swirling morass of sounds, smells, and colors into harmony with his deeply rooted need to answer the question:

The first thing I remember?

Unconsciously he slipped back through intervals of time, back to the state in which he had been suspended within an aura permeated by brilliant points of light; from which he had finally emerged into a state of mind that was strange and yet familiar, that of a baby with a face anticipating his own, within the deep wells of the woman's eyes.

Sitting upon a floor of clean planks whose worn, polished nail heads reflected the sunlight that filled the room; light shining through a green shade behind a white curtain, the burning points of sunlight like stars. A great volume of sunlight flooded through the door, beyond which a little dirt yard gave onto an alley paved with cobblestones. Across the alley was a one-story redbrick house with a yard shut off by a sun-blistered gate.

A clock ticking. A clock ticking on a table in front of the window where a boulder of sunlight crashed under the partly lowered shade and came to rest upon the blazing white tablecloth where the clock stood, ticking, its large black hands indicating four o'clock.

Now and then it broke the slumbers of the old black woman in the denim dress, creaking in the rocking chair by the big black coal stove.

Miss Corina! Tommy's grandmother! She used to keep me when Mom and Dad were at work. When I was one? One and a half? Two? Dead!

The woman with an immaculate white cloth tied around her head now and then looked at him. The polished glass shade of the coal oil lamp reflected the coarse strands of silver hair that shone against her black skin and the luminous blue of her dress. It mirrored the contours of the room, elongating her blue-bodied figure until it stretched to the center of the floor where he sat, rooted within the vortex of the black cracks between the planks, listening to the tick of the clock, striking the membranes of his infant ears with a loud, explosive *Boom!*

Finally the noise was absorbed by the gauze-gray shady back room of a low redbrick house. Then, a wedge of sunlight severed the bare legs of a stout young woman just below the knees. Her coarse black hair was uncombed, the neck and armpits of her loose-fitting dress were stained with sweat; fine beads of perspiration glistened on her forehead, on the tip of her nose, and on the smooth black skin of her arms.

A plain table stained with water rings, from dripping glasses filled with ice water, was strewn with dirty dishes and flies that had settled upon the drying scraps of bread and grains of spilled sugar. With an expression of misery upon her not unattractive face, she struck out at the flies as she ate. Now and then she took some of the chewed food from her puffed jaws with the tips of her fingers and stuffed it into the mouth of the tiny brown baby she held in her arms.

Miss Lena! Tommy's mother. Dead. That must be Lem in her arms. Watching the boy that was himself gazing at her in silence from where he sat upon the ground in the yard near the door, he was shaded from the sun by a big black thing.

Big Tom's old Model T Ford! Hell! we used to climb all over it and sit in it. It would rock like a baby buggy when we pushed it when the brakes were on. And roar like a lion when Big Tom got in and pushed the pedals down and wiggled the skinny sticks that stuck out from under the steering wheel. Smoke shot out of its rear end as it shook and rattled down the alley: *Boom! Boom! Boom!* Hot dog!

The boy sat in the sun. The sun scorched the gray dunes of dirt that he preened with his fat fingers, as a wet sticky feeling crept between his legs. And suddenly the canals he dug were miraculously filled with dirty bubbling water emptied from a tin can by a pair of wild mud-caked faces with glistening hands and arms high above his head. Tommy and Turner! They were dancing around the canals, laughing excitedly, as cities, nations, worlds arose from the gray dust only to be squashed, quite suddenly, by the great silver bubbles that now fell from the sky, splaying the earth with a constellation of stars.

He tried to pick them up, to handle them before the muddy puddles swallowed them and they burst into cool streams flowing in rushing cascades under the wide wooden gate and into the alley, over the cobblestones and down into the sewers where they whirred with a strange music. He stared at the bubbles as they fled under the gate, through the gate, across the alley and the facade of a one-story redbrick house with a screen door, and a black dirt yard beyond.

Pondering the mystery, laughter mingled with the wet of falling rain, a blunt-nosed little boy picked him up and set him in the door of the house facing the yard. Then the rain turned to hail, bombarding the earth with explosive volleys of white sound.

Boom! Boom! Boom! cried the boy: *Boom!* as the neighboring house, barely visible now, faded out of mind.

How long after that? A month? A year? He questioned a sky of burning blue that illuminated a long silver lane bordered by stretches of blue-green grass sprinkled with yellow, white, and purple flowers. They swelled into gentle mounds of flowering bush and tree and crowded the broad, shaded porches and the spacious windows of white wooden and brick houses. Down the lane the sky finally sloped into the mouth of a smooth asphalt street on the corner of which stood an old unpainted house with a large garden with many fruit trees.

A few crumbling cement steps led to a little grassy terrace filled with flowers springing up without plan or ceremony through a heap of old tires and inner tubes, between rusty buckets of paint, a hardened bag of cement and a pile of sand, a little pile of gravel, rusted toys, a naked one-armed doll, marbles spilling out of a cigar box, a tricycle seat, a keg of nails. Rambling roses amid a pile of new bricks. Irises caught in the crook of the arm of a half-buried Victrola whose disengaged speaker nosed the grass.

"He collected things," Rutherford said, as Amerigo took in the porch.

At the far end a swing suspended by two beads of rusty chain. Motionless. But he could feel it sweeping out over the garden, unconsciously drawing up his legs in case they got caught on the forward swing! Gradually he got used to its phantom movement amid the blooming vines and potted plants. Beside the door (advancing and receding) was a tall rubber plant, a small palm tree, and a huge fern.

The swing stopped. A short young black woman with a sad but handsome face stood in the frame of the front door. Aunt Nadine! And Uncle John! A brown-skinned man with a perfect bald head and laughing, intelligent eyes that perched out from a beautifully sculptured forehead now stood beside her. His gloved left hand rested on the shoulder of a small handsome boy with black satin hair. Martin! Next to him was a smaller boy whose skin was like the man's but whose hair was coarse. Edwin is good looking like Uncle John . . . — and Hortense! A handsome girl in braids appeared, the tallest of the three, standing beside the man.

"He only had one hand, Momma!" he heard Rutherford exclaim, as his aunt and uncle and three cousins smiled a greeting to Rutherford and Viola (who carried him in her arms).

It must have been summer, shortly after one and a half — or was it two?

Viola and Rutherford were leaving, leaving him in the woman's arms. Just then a speckled rooster followed by a red hen and a brood of chicks darted from behind the house. Frightened, he reached for his mother, but she was gone!

Then the sky flushed silver-cold and the windows grew frosty, and the belly of the big iron stove in the dining room glowed cherry-red. A green tree as tall as the woman appeared in the parlor, aflame with bright colored lights, and from the tip of its topmost branch a star! It shone until the sky flashed bright with streaks of lightning followed by thunder and rain, after which the frost ran down the windowpanes and the white color ran out of the green that surrounded all the houses in swirls of muddy water that overran the shallow puddles and seeped through the cracks, until later they were dried by the sun and the earth under the grasses and trees grew firm.

Then Viola and Rutherford appeared on the porch steps, and the images of Aunt Nadine and Uncle John, surrounded by Martin, Edwin, and Hortense, the chickens, ducks, pigeons, and turkeys, and two Scotch terriers, the old and new thawed-out things, receded in the distance, until they were out of focus, and his eyes gradually grew accustomed to the dull red glare of burnished cobblestones, and his legs had grown just strong enough to lever his bottom high enough to let it fall with a *Boom!* upon the taut skin of a little red drum: *Boom!*

"Did you see that, Babe?" Rutherford exclaimed.

A room with a window, the curtains billowing against the screen on a hot afternoon. Must have been Sunday. A brass bed covered with a patched quilt stood against a wall. In another corner a rusty little coal stove with a broken leg balanced upon three half bricks. A small table was opposite the bed and a washstand in another corner with its bowl and pitcher. He sat, fat, naked upon the drum, looking up at his father who was saying:

"Did you see that, Babe?"

Viola stood in the door with a bath towel wrapped around her head, kneading the towel with her hands in order to dry her hair.

"If that little niggah kin raise his big behind high enough to set on that drum, by God he kin walk!"

"Now Rutherford!"

"Don' now Rutherford me! That boy's two and a half years old. Shoulda been walkin' *years* ago! Well, I'm sick a this mess! Boy!" The corners of Amerigo's mouth turned down. "Git-up-off-a-that-drum an' walk! You hear me?" Viola moved nervously toward him. "Stand back, woman. This little niggah's gonna walk — *now!* Amerigo, *come here!*" Big tears swam in his eyes. "You'd better not cry a drop. *Walk!*"

Slowly his lips straightened out. The tears that stood upon the rims of his eyes quivered there. His fat round hands gripped the edge of the drum and dimples appeared in his knees. He slowly raised his bottom and stood up straight on his short fat feet.

"Looka there!" Rutherford exclaimed. "I told you that boy could walk! Come here, son. Come here, Amerigo." He took another step, another, and another, and then wobbled and fell. Rutherford gathered him into his arms and pressed his face against his, while Viola looked at them with an expression of wonder.

"*Boom! Boom! Boom!*" went the drum, and volley after volley of hilarious laughter rolled up from the pit of his stomach and gurgled in his throat. Tears filled his eyes and streamed down his face, mixing with the slobbers that bubbled from the corners of his mouth and hung in shimmering droplets upon the edge of his fat dimpled chin.

"*Boom!*" the drum resounded.

"That boy'll laugh himself to death with that drum!" Viola exclaimed with a smile that was undermined by a tremor of grave concern.

Rutherford watched her pick him up from the floor, wipe his mouth, and press his head against her bosom. A dark shadow clouded his eyes.

"You a father? Why, boy, you're just a baby yourself! Besides, how do you know it's yourn?"

Grandma Veronica's voice trailed away into silence in the void of which the *Boom* resounded again, dissolving the image of the Sunday room with the billowing curtain and the brass bed with the patched quilt.

And now he sat, looking down upon his father from the tremendous height of three years from the rump of Mr. Clark, the old horse of the ragman, Mr. Andrews. The sun burned hotly overhead. Mr. Clark struck his iron shoes against the cobblestones in front of Big Tom's house until sparks flew. A squadron of beautiful blue-green horseflies swarmed over the sores in his running eyes and nose, and crawled along the iron ring attached to the foam-flecked bit, in order to reach his hairy lips. They swarmed over his rump, also sprinkled with sores, which Mr. Andrews had smeared with a yellowish green salve. They crawled under his tail and between his trembling legs. Smarting with pain, Mr. Clark jerked his head over his shoulders and snapped his yellow teeth at them and rolled his bloodshot eyes and frantically swished his tail.

Meanwhile Amerigo clung fearfully to the crags of shifting bone, struggling to keep his balance at the insistence of Mr. Andrews.

"Set up there, A-mer-reego, an' let ol' Mister Clark see how it feels to have a m-a-n on his back!" he cried, grinning a toothless grin amid the little crowd of black, brown, and beige faces, which also grinned. Viola looked at him with an expression of joy and wonder, subsumed by a nervous flow of love streaming from eyes that were the twins of his own.

"Do you think he'll be all right, Rutherford?"

"You let 'um put 'im up there. Now let 'im set on his hoss!" Rutherford shook his head in feigned annoyance, shading his eyes from the sun, which stood directly behind his son's head.

Suddenly a fly darted up Mr. Clark's nostril. He snorted violently and dipped his head forward in a wild way, falling to one knee as he did so, and then flung his head up into the air, raring as high as his trappings would allow. Amerigo let out a soulful scream and bounded heavily to earth. Terrified, he felt the heavy mass of bony flesh churning under his small body.

But before the tears could swell from his eyes and the muscles of his face fully express the fear and rage that contracted them, a voice rang out, sharp and clear, over all the upturned heads and outstretched arms and hands with fingers extended in emergency gesticulations, cutting the hot humid air like a knife:

"That boy's got a head like a preacher! Open your mouth, boy, and give us the word!"

Old Jake slowly advanced from the rear of the crowd, his clear blue-gray eyes fixed upon him. Mr. Clark stood still, as though in a trance, hypnotized by the intensity of Old Jake's gaze. The flies suddenly droned away and settled on the manure heap that lay cooling in the elliptical shade cast by Mr. Clark's belly.

The old man was smiling, but it was not the kind of a smile that one dared to take lightly. His skin looked tough and a blue-white stubble covered his sharp protruding chin, and he had a pointed nose with widely distended nostrils. He wore an old battered hat stained with sweat and a faded blue denim shirt under a worn dirt-brown overcoat. His huge right hand grasped the sagging neck of the sack, while the other held a staff whittled from the branch of an ash tree. A serpent entwined itself around it. It looked as though it had grown in his hand.

The little crowd looked at Old Jake and then at him, waiting attentively, as though they were expecting something apocalyptic to happen.

"Speak, boy! Tell us what you see!"

Ah yes! I remember, Amerigo whispered. But then he was forced to pause before the enormity of the word *I* — I? I? Making a terrific effort to bring the pulsating, swirling morass of sounds, smells, and colors into harmony with some vague, deeply rooted determination within himself to *be*.

The first thing I remember, he thought, unconsciously slipping back through vast intervals of time, to a state in which he was suspended within an aura permeated by brilliant patches of light, from which *he* finally emerged, in an attitude that was strange and yet familiar to him.

Just then a black crow screamed from the branch of a persimmon tree and swooped down in front of Mr. Clark's eyes. Mr. Clark lunged forward, and he tumbled off his back and would have been trampled to death had not Old Jake been quicker than Rutherford, who had moved just an instant too late to catch him in his arms and hand him to his mother.

"The Lord's sure got His arms around *you!*" she cried, at which Rutherford looked into the darkened sky.

"*Boom!*" A shimmering, opaque pellet of rain hissed downward and splashed upon the hot cobblestones: *Boom! Boom!* Another, and another, leaden, crowding the earth and sky with coolness, scratching cat's paws in the dust, upon the roofs of houses and porches and in the streets, running, gushing in rivulets down gutter pipes into sewers, causing the crowd to scurry away, emitting shrieks of surprise, giving utterance to their bewilderment as to the mysterious ways of God. All except for Old Jake; he stood the storm unflinchingly.

"*Boom!*" resounded the thunder, preceded by flash of fire, illuminating the spot where the old man stood.

"Ever since I kin remember, or anybody else," said Rutherford, "you could see that old man walkin' up an' down the alleys, or sometimes w-a-y down by the river! Once we saw him on top of Clairmount Hill — you remember, Babe? — all by hisself, at *night!* Talkin' to hisself. They say he's crazy. I don' know. But whatever that old man is, he's got a look that'll strike the fear of God in the average joker, you heah me!"

And the aftertones of Old Jake's "prophecy" spread far and wide, dissolved in the falling rain and washed down the banks of the great river whose replenishing waters heralded the blossom of cherry, apple, and peach tree! And busy-bee, fly-droning summer days that waned with a sun pregnant with five o'clock.

Five years deep within the gauze-gray of still another room Viola was searching for something under the cover of the kitchen table.

"What could I have done with it?" she asked herself aloud, looking next in her purse and then under the flowered paper covering the pantry shelves. Rutherford entered the kitchen, tired and hot and serious.

"Supper ready?" throwing his cap on the laundry hamper behind the door and rolling up his sleeves in order to wash his hands at the kitchen sink.

"Rutherford, did you take some money from the table?"

"Naw, how much is missin'?"

"A dime. I need it to buy bread to go with the meat."

"Did you look good?"

"I looked everywhere."

"Aw, Amerigo probably took it, he's gittin' to that age. I remember the time I stole a whole quarter from Momma an' bought a quarter's worth a candy — wineballs an' jellybeans! That ol' woman give me a beatin I ain' got over yet!" His lips tightened. "Ah that strap!" He dried his hands. "I'll have to teach that little niggah a lesson! Us workin' like damned dogs to feed 'im, an' 'im stealin' the bread out a our mouth to buy candy!

"Boy!" Amerigo dropped the neighbor's cat and ran in from the back porch. "Did you take that dime off the table?"

"No, sir."

"Yes, you did. Didn' you? You took it — an' bought wineballs an' jellybeans at Goldberg's. Stick out your tongue." He stuck out his tongue. "You took it! Admit it!"

"I didn' take it, Dad."

"Don't you lie to me, damnit!"

"I didn' take it!" he shouted, trembling with indignation.

"W-h-a-t did you say?"

"I said I didn' take it! *W-h-y* do you keep *sayin'* I did it when *I* say I *didn'!"*

"Who in the *hell* do *you* think you are — to-to be accused. *Ever'body's* accused!"

"I'm Amerigo Jones!"

"Git me that strap! We gonna see who you are, mister!"

He went to the kitchen and got the razor strap from the nail in the toilet door and handed it to his father.

Rutherford struck several heavy blows upon his bare arms and legs.

He doubled up his fists and drew his lips in stubborn defiance.

"You doublin' up your fists at *me?"* Rutherford struck again. He did not move, and did not cry.

"Usually," Rutherford had said later, "when I'd punish him, he'd cry an' jump around tryin' not to git hit. I didn' actually hit 'im much, no way. Just make the strap make a loud noise against the wall, or the back of the chair. He'd think he was gittin' killed. But this time he didn' move. Just stood there, stubborn-like. I'd never seen 'im like that before!"

Viola looked on with tears in her eyes. Rutherford raised his strap again.

"If you hit him again I'll *leave* you!" she screamed.

"Maybe he didn' take it, but I'm still the man in this house — an'-an'- he's gotta respect me or I'll see 'im in his grave! An' don't you threaten me, neither!"

He struck again.

A welt rose upon the child's arm.

Viola rushed forward to protect him.

"Stand back! I *mean* it!"

He struck again.

She broke past Rutherford and threw her arms around him.

"Beat *me!"*

"D-i-d you take the money?"

"No, sir!"

Rutherford dropped to one knee before the child and his mother. The strap fell from his hand.

"I believe you. I'll always believe you, as long as I live. If anybody — anybody! — ever says you did something you said you didn' do, I'll believe *you.* Excuse me."

He extended his hand. The child threw his arms around his father's neck and wept. Viola wept, too.

Through their sobs he heard the refrain of the duet that Aunt Rose and Viola often sang:

". . . Love thy father and mother that thy days may be long. Especially your momma, 'cause. . . ."

It struck his ears with a new dissonance that modified the melody that subsumed the vibrant tremor of life that flowed through him. It grew with a roaring swell that exploded with a loud *Boom!* which now articulated a deep and persistent impulse that hardened the blue in the sky over Post No. 9 with a warlike yellow. Poised upon tingling calves, back flattened against the wall of the hut, he peered into the eyes of the reclining woman and saw the world he lived in as a child spring alive. The murmuring wind within the shell was saying:

"*In the city of your birth men said that times would not get better.*"

"*They gonna git a lot worse!*"

"*A helluva lot worse!*"

"*Work's already as scarce as hen's teeth!*"

"*A woman usta cost two dollars. Now you kin git all you want for a piece a bread!*"

"*It's the Republicans that's ruinin' ever'thin'!*"

"*Well, Abe Lincoln was a Republican, an' I'm a Republican, an' I'm gonna stay a Republican!*"

"*Humph! Republicans freed you, but they sure ain' feedin' you. Fool!*"

"*What did they do, Dad?*"

"*They made the depression, son.*"

"*What's the depression?*"

"*The depression!*"

Amerigo, his mother, and his father sat at the supper table on a hot summer evening as an amber ray of sunlight shone upon the threshold of the kitchen door. Rutherford had just scooped up a big spoonful of navy beans from his plate and was raising it to his mouth.

"What's the de*pression.*" His mouth flew open with astonishment, he dropped the spoon, and bean juice spattered against the front of his shirt. Viola was grinning.

"De*pression!*" Rutherford said, looking incredibly at Viola.

"Depression is: is beans an' fatback instead a T-bone steak an' red gravy! It's workin' seven days a week an' gittin' half your pay — or nothin' — on payday an' bein' glad to git that 'cause almost ever'body you know ain' even got no job an' have to be on relief!"

"But beans an' fatback's *good!*"

Rutherford regarded him with a look of stupefaction. A hot wave of fear shot through him and he felt the mass of bony flesh churning beneath him as Mr. Clark clawed the hot cobblestones. A truck rattled down the alley, echoing his words, growing fainter as it reached the mouth of the alley where it paused before spreading the news to Independence Avenue.

"Mom, kin I go down on the front porch?"

"Yeah, I guess so."

He went down to the front porch and sat on the top step and gazed into the alley, watching the blue smoke from wood fires curling up from the chimneys. The smell of coal oil; corn bread and pork fat sizzling in frying pans; and fried cabbage and salt pork penetrated the air.

"Good evenin'. Mrs. Derby, Mister Derby." Viola descended the steps all dressed up. Mr. and Mrs. Derby were just coming out onto the porch, and Aunt Lily had just struck her head out the door.

"'Evenin', Mrs. Jones!" Mrs. Derby answered. Mr. Derby nodded.

"Hi, Aunt Lily!" Viola smiled. Aunt Lily smiled back.

"Hi, honey! My, you sure look nice!"

"Thank you, ma'am!"

As she passed him, she gently laid her hand on his head and whispered: "Now you go up to bed soon, you hear? Don' want your daddy to have to tell you. Bye, hon . . ." and kissed him on the cheek.

"She's goin' to the show." He followed her to risk movements up the alley while the neighbor's comments titillated his ears.

"Sure is a f-i-n-e lookin' woman! Strut, girl!" cried Mrs. Derby.

"She sure dresses nice, all right!" said Aunt Lily. "Oughtta make you proud, son. If you don' remember nothin' else, remember to love your momma. Nobody in the w-o-r-l-d's gonna love you like *she* will. I know all about that!"

"She sure ain' tellin' no lie!" said Mrs. Derby.

"Yes'm," he replied respectfully, a deep feeling of tenderness for his mother rising to his throat. And then he thought of his father and felt profoundly embarrassed. After that the feelings were overwhelmed by the memory of the sheer happiness he had felt when she had touched him. He had smelled her fresh sweet body and watched her walk up the alley through the early blue light of evening perforated by points, squares, rectangles, triangles, and arcs of soft, cheese-colored light from coal oil lamps; the hard naked brightness of electric bulbs burned through veined window shades and poured out from the edges of lowered shades and window ledges into the falling darkness.

From somewhere down the alley came the soulful sound of the blues picked out on a steel guitar. From the top of the alley came the low constant whiz of the dangerous stream of traffic along the great Admiral Boulevard. At the bottom of the alley was a parallel plane of glittering light from Goldberg's windows, and the red, blue, and white neon light from the signs in the windows on the taverns on both corners at the mouth of the alley — The Blue Moon and The Saw-Dust Trail — were like laughing mouths filled with shiny teeth!

Now three rowdy dogs scrambled madly from a neighboring yard in hot pursuit of a dog-eared cat that ran for his life and won it while Sammy, Policeman Jackson's mongrel hound, lay regally upon the lower step of his master's porch — feared, respected, the acknowledged ruler of all the dogs and cats in the alley — withdrawn from the anxieties of the chase.

The streetlights came on and were greeted by a buzzing throng of flies, moths, gnats, and june bugs that huddled up under the white galvanized shades for warmth. One lamppost stood opposite the porch. Its glare gave the cobblestones a dusky earthen color and caused the tiny fragments of broken glass strewn among them to shine like stars, which caused him to look up and be surprised by a host of cool blue points of light twinkling in the heavens.

Star light, star bright.

However, a secret wish forced him to contemplate the circle of light thrown by the shade of the street lamp, to peer beyond it, where the cobblestones shone shadow-black. Suddenly he was surprised by his recollection of the daytime, of the fact that the cobblestones ran to the top *and* to the bottom of the alley, that they led everywhere he knew how to go, even though he could not see that far from where he sat now.

"My name is Amerigo Jones an' I live at six-eighteen Cosy Lane an' my father's name is Rutherford E. Jones an' my mother's name is Viola E. Jones an' my telephone number is Harrison three-three-eight-seven," he muttered softly, but with determination. Trembling slightly, he peered into the darkness, looking a bit anxiously toward the entrance and exit from the alley, the conduits through which the Republicans bearing the dreaded depression might attack at any moment!

"That's *right!*" he heard Rutherford saying, "if you ever git lost . . ."

Boom! The imminent possibility of getting lost loomed ominously in his mind. Blazing sunlight crashed through a window just beneath a green shade that was cracked and veined like a leaf, letting in points of light that shone like stars. An old black woman dozed in a rocking chair, while a baby sat in the middle of a scrubbed floor and stared at the big silver clock.

He looked down the alley and found the house, its windows now filled with darkness. He heard the squeaking of the rocking chair, stilled now by the rumor of death, the clock ticking four o'clock. Shortly before seven o'clock, four years later, the alley sprang alive and made him feel as long and as wide as the space between the great Admiral Boulevard and Independence Avenue: filled with many rooms, crowded with faces of many colors whose expressions were enlivened by the multicolored voices that were an indispensable part of him. It was as though he were a complex congealing of air held in this peculiar shape by these parallel rows of dingy redbrick houses, covered by this particular sky, scented by a profusion of pungent odors — of vagrant dogs and cats, steaming urine of man and animals that stained walls, poles, and porch banisters; of rainwater and sewage water filtering through the crevices between cobblestones strewn with ashes, rusty cans, occasional piles of damp horse manure, blood, rotting carcasses of rats and cats run down by speeding vehicles, dripping oil from leaky carburetors, melting ice and falling coal, splinters of chopped wood, watermelon rinds, and rinds of cantaloupe and honeydew, dew, rain, hail, soot, spewed tobacco juice, sawdust, sand, onion skins, cabbage leaves, rusty nails, screws, hot melting running tar, spit-out wads of chewing gum and gin-soaked balls of asafetida. Rising and falling with the seasons like waves of sea.

"That's right," Rutherford was saying, "if you *ever* git lost, Amerigo, just walk up to a policeman — even if he *is* white — an' tell 'im that, an' he'll show you how to git home."

"*Boom!*" A carburetor exploded on a neighboring street.

"*Did you ever see them French gals do a dance called the Can-can? M-a-n — they sure kin Can-can!*"

He tried to peer through the mystery that was war.

Just then Sammy cocked his right ear and growled at a rustling noise issuing from a heap of rusty cans in the empty house next door. The siren of a police car whined down the avenue. Heads popped out of windows up and down the alley. The sound passed. Heads popped in again. Seconds later a car crept into the alley without lights and stopped noiselessly in front of the empty house. Two white men got out and rushed to the back of the car and opened the trunk. Sammy growled menacingly.

"Hush Sammy!" whispered one of the men. Sammy hushed, while they hastily carried two twenty-gallon whiskey jugs into the dark shoot between the two houses. A minute later the men returned and quietly got into the car. As it rolled into the alley, the man who was driving leaned out the window and tossed up a quarter that missed the step where he sat by an inch. The coin tinkled down the steps and onto the cobblestones, where it rolled for a short distance and fell.

"Let it go!" said Aunt Lily quietly. "An' if anybody ask you if you seen this or that, you ain' seen *nothin'*! An' don' take *nobody's* money for *nothin'*!"

"She's tellin' you right, son," said Mrs. Derby.

"You wanna go with me, daddy?" said a teasing alto voice down the alley, and he shivered in the descending darkness, suddenly frightened by the enormity of himself, with so many rooms filled with faces, voices, and smells, throwing shadows beyond the aura of light where the French girls did the Can-can and the Republicans were armed with the depression!

And now he lay in bed in the front room in the dark, looking out at the cool blue stars that shone just above the shade of the lamppost just beneath his window, trying to stretch out his body to the farthest limits of himself, up to the brilliant points of light in the sky. He was suddenly astounded by a great secret feeling that he had had earlier in the evening, a feeling he had never spoken of to anyone, nor even articulated to himself — in his whole life: I've been up there, up there with the stars, before! A deep excitement stirred within him, as he tossed nervously, unable to sleep, straining to remember every nook and cranny he had ever squeezed his small frame into, trying hard now to glean from the host of talkative words that strayed through his mind some reference to the occasion of that visit.

But sleep dragged him down into the glaring circle of light that radiated from the lamppost, and his mind was besieged by a profusion of shadowy movement and sound teeming within the boundaries of a world partly perceived by his eyes and partly conceived by his imagination. The words and sounds slowly crystallized into a feeling that was *his* city, the city of K___, the area known as the north side. Under the darkened skies of his shut eyelids he emerged with his city from the south shore of the Missouri River. "The longest river in the world," Rutherford said. From the river he expanded southward, engulfed Clairmount Hill, and swept down again, westward, until he came to the summit of a great bushy hill where Aunt Rose's big red house stood — and away! Along the streetcar tracks that whisked him to the old city market, which he circled twice. Then he raced on shadowy wings up Main Street, south to Independence Avenue, so swiftly that he had to run its full length several times before he managed to slither into his alley and float through the globules of circled light, and toward the known but seldom-seen frontiers of the great Admiral Boulevard. North, for half a block east, and then north again, up Campbell Street to Ninth Street and down Ninth Street to Harrison Street, where a great burst of song rose upon the air and filled the myriad ears of his being.

He flowed toward the sound, followed it through the great oak doors and into the huge vaulted auditorium. It was divided into three sections, a great middle section marked off by tall pillars with wings on either side. Its long wooden benches were covered with wine-red cushions.

He moved down the center aisle into the great assembly of men, women, and children of all ages and took a seat among them, his face numbering one among the many that were black, various shades of brown, almost white. Each of the faces had two eyes that contained more colors than the rainbow, and each face had a nose that was flat, or thick; long, thin, pointed, hooked, or skinny. Noses! Each face, according to the light in his eyes, had a mouth with lips that were shaped as variously as the noses, and as the ears, and that their heads were covered with hair like his, like the wool of sheep. Like grass, like horse's hair — Mr. Clark's! Like Crow-feathers, like Grandpa Will's, like corn silk on the cob, like tar with finger waves the way Mom does it!

And all the heads from whose throats the song issued were turned toward the pulpit. It was covered with a red carpet, and five large imposing equally distanced chairs with high backs and seats upholstered with red velvet spanned its width. Their sturdy arms were decorated with carved figures of lion's heads in roaring attitudes, lambs in attitudes of piety, and flowers surrounded with foliage.

In the chairs sat four serious, conservatively but richly dressed men, in immaculate white shirts, perfectly tailored summer suits, with jeweled fingers and diamond stickpins. Each wore a pair of long, infinitely long, black sparkling shoes.

Then suddenly the reverend emerged from behind the podium and stood over the huge gold-edged Bible illuminated by a little silver lamp that rested upon its slanted top. His gaze rested upon the Bible for an instant. Then he took a sip of water from the silver decanter upon the little table next to the podium.

In a faultlessly tailored frock coat and gambol-striped trousers, he squared his shoulders and looked at his flock with an air of grave concern. His black silk tie (the pearl stickpin lying modestly within the vortex of the white cord embellishing the collar of his vest) gave him an official air, while the rounded lapels that fell away from his coat gave his vest the appearance of the great door of a shrine upon whose altar lay the bloodred heart that had been bathed in the blood of Christ.

Gradually his face took on an expression of fiery exaltation, his eyes loomed large behind rimless glasses, which, reflecting the light of the great candelabrum hanging from the dome by a golden chord, glowed like suns.

He raised his palms toward the heavens. All eyes looked upward. An expectant silence filled the room.

Amerigo beheld the dome with its great oak beams and small round windows of colored glass, similar to the long narrow panes of the tall windows that graced the walls upon which were depicted in amber, ocher, maroon, and grass-green scenes from the life of Christ.

His gaze descended and was surprised by a host of faces in a great half circle along the balcony. He followed the chain of faces around until it gave onto the three choirs filling the choir stands immediately behind and a little above the pulpit.

There were men, women, and children in three great bodies, four rows deep, in robes of blue and black with stoles of gold, orange, and silver.

Every eye was lifted toward the heavens, as though the reverend were supporting it with his upraised palms.

And now there came the full terrifying blast of the great golden organ. The building and everyone in it trembled as it echoed the words that issued from the reverend's mouth:

"My heart is bathed in the blood of Christ!"

"A-men!"

"Yes, yes!"

"Good to be heah!"

"Open your mouth an' tell us what you see!"

He twisted and turned in his seat. Beads of sweat rose up on his forehead. The dome, the candelabrum, and the dazzling array of faces whirled before his eyes. Fear seized him. The reverend began to sing.

"A — maz — ing Gr — race!"

"A-men!"

"How sweet the sound!"

"Oh Lord!"

"that saved — a wretch — like me!"

"Yeah!"

"I once — was lost, but now —"

"Now?"

"na-ow, oh now,"

"Tell what you see!"

"I'm found! Was blind, but now — I see!"

"Ooooooh!" the shrill soprano voice of a small black woman wearing a silver stole that almost matched her hair. "Ooooooh!" hands clutching her chest, eyes closed, the pearling, soaring note filling the great dome and invested the earth-shaking vibrato of the organ with a body of feminine sound: "— a — ma — zi — ing grace!"

"How sweet the sound!" answered the reverend, in a deep baritone that seemed to swell up from the alluvial depths of the sea and engulf him in the powerful desire to surrender, to breathe deeply and sink to the bottom of the profound blackness that was its primeval source.

"that saved a wretch — like me"

Together the soaring soprano and the earth-rooted baritone:

"I once was — lo — ost, but na-ow"

"Now?"

"I'm fou-ound, wa — as blind, but na-ow I see!"

"My heart!" cried the reverend, "— is bathed — in the blood — of Jesus! I say, my heart — is bathed — in the *blood!* Help me, Lord! of Jesus! An'-an' I'm askin' you to open up your heart to *Him!* For who among you *here,* sittin' in God's house *taday,* has never sinned! — Listen while *I* open up *my* heart to you! — I say who among you here, taday, hasn' got some secret locked up tight in your heart that makes you look the other way when you see your neighbor comin' down the street; that turns sleepless nights into weary days, that stands between *you* an' God! Jesus knows!"

How does He *know?* He squeezed himself down into his seat in an effort to grow smaller and drown within the sudden flurry of movement, for now the congregation was rising to its feet, flushing a great bevy of bright colors into the beams of light streaming through the windows, accompanied by a rustle, a cracking and a popping of two thousand heads bowing in prayer. Quiet hissing intonations of reverence fluttered in the air like the soft wings of birds.

Amerigo stole quietly down the aisle and stepped out through the great doors, just as a new burst of song filled the great room. It pursued him as he fled in terror out into the street.

"Twelfth and Vine!" said a voice, and he turned east along the shining tracks.

"The main drag!" said still another voice.

"We usta break 'um down till the times got better!"

But now a streetcar filled with yellow light overtook him. Its trolley hummed along the electric cable overhead and drew sparks of fire at intersecting streets. In every window was a black, brown, or yellow face, singing, accompanied by a great clapping of hands, with great exhaltation:

"Let us have a little talk with Jesus! Tell 'Im all about our troubles!"

Tell 'Im *what,* he cried desperately, cringing beneath the obtruding breast that lowered overhead like a dark inverted cloud.

Another streetcar whizzed by, in the opposite direction, the throng singing the song backward, rhythms reversed! And no sooner than it had roared out of sight than two streetcars heading east and west blasted his sensibility at the same time, the converse and reverse strains of the song clacking within the vacuums of swiftly shuttling squares of light reflecting in one horizontal plane the sweaty sheens of distorted faces that were attenuated into a spectrum of burning movement.

Wearily he made his way down the dangerous street. The song gradually submerged into the larger, general sound shot through with the flickering light of cars speeding in all directions, firing the fringes of a cool grassy island laced in a bright border of blooming flowers that lay voluptuously in the midst of a broad boulevard.

"The Paseo's a pretty place in summer!" said Rutherford, "an' 'em niggahs keep it lookin' nice, too! . . ."

He stood before two small cannons facing the street with their nozzles aimed at the high stone wall with broad stone staircases on each end that led to the upper reaches of the park.

"Commemoratin' the *first* world war!" Rutherford remarked sarcastically, as a streetcar nudged its way through the traffic that swarmed around the staircases. He was swept into the thickening crowd of black folks where the song throbbed beneath the brutal clash of a cymbal, against the sobbing of an alto saxophone, quickening to the pulse of a bass fiddle, or the pertinent click of hickory sticks upon taut snares, or an Englished cue banking an eight-ball in a corner pocket for a quarter.

"Let us have a little talk with Je-sus!" sang the blind man on the corner, to the accompaniment of his guitar. He stared dumbly into the man's face, struck by the fact that he looked just like — *Dad!*

"Wanna go with me, daddy?" said a young honey-colored woman in a tight dress.

Mom?

"I got the dime, baby, if you got the time!" a man replied, smiling like Rutherford.

Dad! Mom! The man's and the woman's faces blended into the shifting mass of faces that all looked like Rutherford and Viola. He followed them down the street and around a corner where the street grew darker and the crowd got thinner, where the din faded as though he were hearing it from a distance.

Nearing Eighteenth Street the sound of milling black folks grew louder. Soon he was among them. They all looked like Rutherford and Viola. Streetcars filled with them rumbled through the field of flickering light. They clapped their hands to the beat of the song with great jubilation.

By the time he reached Woodland Avenue he heard the song only in sporadic bursts, through a suddenly opened door, issuing from the darkened interior of a taxi turning down Nineteenth Street.

He continued up the hill, crossed the overpass under which sped the east- and westbound trains that stopped at the great Union Station to discharge and take on passengers before continuing the two-thousand-mile trek over mountains, plains, and deserts to the sprawling West Coast of the United States of America.

He moved cautiously beyond the summit of the hill. A feeling of uneasiness stole upon him, as the song, barely audible now, diffused itself among the shadows of strange streets with cultivated trees whose branches swayed noiselessly in the night air. Cozy houses rested quietly in faultless lawns surrounded by shrubs and blooming flowers frequented by coiffured dogs with collars and registered pedigrees. Only occasionally now did he see the flickering lights of a passing auto, the sound of which caused him to quicken his pace.

Fainter still the song. A white woman entering a house. "Mom?" Two black women passed under a lamppost and disappeared beyond its circled light, beyond the pale of song, walking carefully, with restrained step, speaking in hushed indignant voices of the floors they had scrubbed, the clothes they had ironed, and the children they had loved who were not their own.

Silence.

As he slowly drew himself up into a tight little ball, he felt his body contracting through the maze of crowded streets and avenues filled with the faces of Viola and Rutherford, weaving in and out of traffic, moving under globules of lamplight, accompanied by the song and the frenzied clapping of hands. Returning home.

Suddenly he had opened his eyes and was staring at the light filtering through the window. Listening to the clock ticking in the middle room. What time is it? Peering into the darkened room where his parents' bed loomed up in a big bulky shadow.

He closed his eyes once again. The springs of the big bed whined. She isn't home yet! He was startled by the pop and flash of a match head grating the thumbnail of Rutherford's right hand. He followed the trace of its yellow flare to the tip of his cigarette. Rutherford's face shone like a yellow mask in the darkness and disappeared, while the crimson glow at the end of the cigarette grew brighter, and then fainter, in a nervous pulsing rhythm, as he drew the clouds of hot smoke into his lungs and spewed them out into the dark.

The bed lamp flashed on. "Twelve-thirty!" Rutherford muttered angrily.

Where could she *be?* Amerigo wondered.

"Show's out at the latest," said Rutherford, "twenty minutes with the streetcar, an' three-quarters of an hour on foot. But that gal ain' gonna do no whole lot a walkin' — not at *this* hour."

Father and son tossed nervously, measuring the questionable distances from the periphery to the center of the circled light.

The clock ticked one o'clock, one-one, one-two, one-three,

The crimson tip of Rutherford's cigarette grew brighter and then fainter: *"You a father! Besides — how do you know it's yourn?"*

The cigarette flared like a danger signal, "like the stoplight at the top of the alley."

One-four, five, six

"Love thy father and mother that thy days may be long,"

"Especially your mother," Aunt Rose insisted, *" 'cause your mother'll be with you a-l-l-ways!"*

"Through thick an' thin!" said Viola.

A car zoomed down the alley, slowed up at the foot, and turned into the avenue.

One-seven-one-eight . . .

"Want somethin' to go with that pint a whiskey, daddy?"

"Hell naw!"

A burst of secret laughter between a man and a woman.

Rutherford ground the top of his cigarette in the ashtray on the table beside the bed and squirmed under the covers.

Silence for three minutes.

He pulled the chain on the bed light, leaped out of bed, and tiptoed barefoot through the front room to the front window and looked out. The son stared at the father's back silhouetted against the window. The alley was quiet, except for the bugs that buzzed around the hot globe of the streetlight. A man staggered into its bright circle, and urinated against the shed opposite the house, and then staggered into the shadows.

Rutherford went into the kitchen and turned on the faucet and let the water run until it got cold. Then he filled the battered old aluminum cup that Uncle Sexton had brought back from the war and drank until it was empty. Then he went to the toilet. After that he returned to the middle room and sat on the edge of the bed, lit another cigarette, got in bed, and turned off the light.

Night light filtered through the window.

One-thirteen. One-thirty-seven-and-a-half. Thirty-eight.

Rutherford sighed deeply and arranged his pillow. He turned on his side and stared out over the roof of the empty house next door. Whiskey fumes rose from the still on the first floor. A door opened and threw a long oblique beam of light across the roof and the twang of a guitar stirred the night air.

"Black gal!" sang a man with a voice as high as a woman's: sad, plaintive. "Black gal! Woman what makes yo' head so hard?"

The door closed. Darkness and silence for two, three, four minutes.

A car turned discreetly into the alley, rolled down past the house, and stopped. The door opened and shut, followed by the click of iron-plated heels on the cobblestones, and then the soft thud of toes tiptoeing up the stair. A momentary silence broken by nervous fingers fumbling for a key, and then the jingle of several keys before one stabbed the lock. The front door swung quietly open, and then a cool rush of night air.

Viola undressed hurriedly, quietly. Rutherford lay dangerously still. The clock ticked unbearably loud.

"*Boy!*" cried Uncle Billy, "*you'll look up one a these days an' it'll be war! . . .*"

Rutherford stirred as though her movements had awakened him. He turned on the lamp and the room flushed rose. Viola, caught in her underskirt, was hastily slipping off her stockings. The naked glow of the bulb shone directly upon his angry face. It drew deep hard shadows under his eyes.

"Do you know what time it is?" He picked up the clock and looked at it. "Well?" He rose threateningly upon one elbow.

Why don' she *say somethin'?* he implored.

"*Yes.* I-know-what-time-it-is."

"This crap's gotta stop! This is the second time this week. You're a married woman! Out gallyvantin' till-till almost two o'clock in the mornin'. What you take me for, a damned fool? Sick an' tired a this shit! Workin' like a damned dog — an' for what?"

"What you startin' all that rigamarole for?" Viola retorted. "I went to the show. An' then I met Susie an' Mabel on Eighteenth Street. She was with Bill. An' they asked me to have a drink with 'um at Elk's Rest an' I went with 'um. We got to talkin', an' it got late. That's all!"

"'Em lies gonna trip you up one a these days an' I'm gonna break your damned neck!"

"If I was big," the child muttered to himself, "if I was big I'd *kill 'im* — talkin' to *her* like that. To *my momma!*"

Tears rolled down his face. He stirred angrily in his bed in protest.

"Go to sleep, boy!" Rutherford commanded.

Viola got into bed, and the lights went out.

"Anyway, she's home," he whispered to himself. "She's home!"

Viola and Rutherford tossed angrily for a while and finally pushed themselves to the opposite sides of the bed. In the silence there was only the sound of their troubled breathing, of wild hurting thoughts flitting through the dark like hungry mosquitoes.

Where was she? Don' she love us? He tried to sleep. Will he *really* break her neck? What will happen to me? What will happen if he goes away? *Go away!* Is Dad goin' away?

"Open up your heart to Jesus!" said the reverend. The great choir began to sing. The great throngs milling under the globules of lamplight took up the song.

Mom? Dad? The faces and the light and the song grew fainter, as his eyelids grew heavy, until he became aware of only the quiet darkness interrupted by the fiery twinkle of starlight falling between his eyelids. And then they fell shut.

A heavier, fluid, more transient darkness descended upon him. He sank to the depths of a great forest that was blacker than night. He was going somewhere, but he had lost his way. He couldn't find the path. He was afraid. Something, someone was after him. He had to get away, to hide. He ran, stumbled as he ran, faster and faster! A long black hand with claws tried to catch him by the neck, to *break* it! Faster and faster he ran. He grew tired. He grew weary. He was afraid to stop, couldn't stop because the hand was getting closer and closer. *Boom!* He stumbled over something big and hard. He fell down, down, down, down, through an endless sky full of dazzling stars! He screamed a loud piercing scream, but his voice made no sound.

Suddenly he was sitting upright in bed, his body covered with sweat. He was no longer falling. He looked anxiously into the middle room to see if his mother and father were still there. He listened to their quiet breathing. Then he fell back upon his pillow and sank into a deep oblivious sleep.

The sparrows were twittering in the eaves of the empty house next door. He lay awake at the foot of the bed, naked, having torn off his pajamas during the night. The bedcovers lay crumpled on the floor. The streetlight was still burning.

It's night.

But then he noticed a faint blue color that crept into the sky. He sat up in bed with an air of incredulity. The streetlight went out.

He surveyed from memory the faded flowers on the papered walls, the plump outline of the sofa that opened out into the bed on which he slept.

He discovered the grape-blue leaves designed upon its velvet surface. It stood against the north wall. A big overstuffed chair stood in the northwest corner, its color and design matching that of the sofa. He remembered the evening when Rutherford had come home and found it there — a whole brand-new living room suite!

"Don' you know there's a depression, woman?" he had said. "The whole damned country's starvin' an' *you* buyin' *furniture* — on credit!"

"This place looks like a pigpen!" Viola had protested. "Maybe we gotta be poor, but we *ain'* gotta give up livin'! Besides, I'm gonna be in debt, too. I work just the same as you do. I'll make enough on the side sewin' an' doin' hair to make a big part of the payments!"

During the days that followed Rutherford had grumbled. But after that he was proud! Even invited T. C. and Mr. Zoo and Mr. Elmer and Miss Vera over to see it. They had a party and danced.

A fresh burst of twittering from the birds distracted him and caused him to look suddenly at the bird-of-paradise that strutted proudly through a garden of exotic flowers on the shade of the tall floor lamp. It had silk fringes on the border that swayed when there was a breeze, or when someone moved the lamp. The fringes stirred now, ever so gently. He looked questioningly at the magazine rack between the lamp and the chair, but it remained merely a dumb shadowy form engulfed in a faint, almost misty aura of blue, cluttered with detective-story magazines, last week's copy of the *Voice* and yesterday's copies of the *Times* and the *Star*. Their pages appeared uncommonly white, fusing into the blueness pouring into the room. It created a ghostly impression.

He was looking at the east wall, at the door that opened on to the middle room where his mother and father lay sleeping. He relived a sudden painful curiosity undermined by fear, which caused him to shift his glance to the left of the door and examine the straight-backed upholstered chair that stood against the wall. He tried to separate the blue-black mass resting upon its arms into three grape-blue cushions that converted the folded bed into a sofa. And then he was surprised by the discovery of a long thin thread of light that hung vertically suspended in the air less than a foot from the chair. It gradually revealed itself to be the stem of the floor lamp with the pink pleated shade that Viola had made. It was a dusky blue-gray color now.

It was getting lighter. His eyes fixed upon the chromium ashtray near the sofa. Now there was even a dull metallic sheen of light upon its black enamel base. He tried to see himself in the mirror that hung next to the window: a soft ghostlike image rendered animate by two large eyes set wide apart, with neither hair, ears, nor a nose. He looked away, down, at the top of the humidor that was partly reflected in the lower right-hand corner of the mirror. A lace doily covered its square top, upon which rested a cut-glass vase containing artificial roses whose blossoms almost touched the mirror, causing them to appear double. His eyes traveled up the edge of the mirror, and suddenly he caught the reflection of the little gas stove in the upper right-hand corner, standing in the opposite corner of the room behind him; it was partially hidden by the overstuffed chair, which had been turned toward the door because it was summer. The lacquered floor in front of the stove reflected the criscross patterns of light from the fire-brick columns dancing upon the shallow crests of the blue flames at the base of the burners. It was like a miniature stage.

Will Dad go away? He studied the fine and suddenly perceptible layer of soot that stained the wall behind the gas stove. He looked questioningly at the dark skies of the large velvet landscape that hung on the south wall of the room. Will he? Unconsciously he entered into the scene: a silver velvet moon shining upon an old velvet mill, a velvet moonlit stream turning the velvet waterwheel shaded by a row of soft green velvet poplars, while silver-feathered birds winged the blue-black velvet sky beyond the rolling banks of the silver clouds.

What'll happen to me! he asked the gaily festooned plaster of paris staring at him from the opposite wall. The bird did not say a word. When Viola had bought it at the five-and-ten-cent store it was white. She got paint in little tubes like toothpaste and painted it. Dad watched until he got sleepy and went to bed and then we finished it together. Last winter . . . we ate a whole bowl of popcorn!

The Spanish lady came after that. He shifted his gaze a little to the right of the parrot. She wore a wide silver hooped skirt and a white satin bolero blouse, a little black vest, and a big red wide-brimmed hat, like a cowboy's . . . Buffalo Bill, Grandpa Will. She stood proudly upon a silver balcony leaning against a silver balustrade amid bushes of poinsettias, palms, and ferns. She looked out into the black night studded with silver stars, gazing at them while eating a big red apple with a little green leaf attached to the stem. He remembered with deep emotion how his mother had stayed up half the night filling in the outlines of the thinly sketched forms, which she finally framed in glass.

Somewhat relieved of his anxiety by the things he could only partially see, but which he knew were there, even though the light *was* out, he got out of bed, pulled on his pants, and tiptoed through the middle room where his mother and father lay sleeping in the big bed that occupied more than half the space. Viola lay on her side on the edge of the bed facing the window; Rutherford lay on his side facing the interior of the room. He paused for a moment in the little space between the bed and the vanity dresser. Its drawers were filled with cosmetics and miscellaneous odds and ends, and in the bottom drawer on the right-hand side beneath Rutherford's underwear and socks and handkerchiefs was a little twenty-two-caliber revolver like the one that killed Uncle Ruben. The top of the dresser was crowded with an assortment of perfume bottles of various shapes, sizes, and colors, with and without sprayers, with tassels and tops of silver and brass and stems of crystal.

He glanced at the mirror that composed the upper half of the dresser, extending from its top to a distance the height of a short man's head. He saw Viola seated upon the low wicker stool in front of the mirror (matching the wicker-bottomed rocking chair in the corner opposite the dresser, between which was a narrow closet crammed mostly with her clothes) surrounded by comb and brush and a large hand mirror, patiently performing the miracle that never failed to dazzle the eyes of father and son.

What with the large four-poster bed and the vanity dresser there was hardly enough room for the chest of drawers, squeezed into the corner between the bed and the wall. It was filled with slips and panties (snuggies), purses, ribbons, scraps and cuttings of dress patterns, and knitted caps and belts and bunches of artificial flowers — paper violets, roses, and cherry blossoms Viola had made. And on the floor protruding from under the edge of the chest of drawers was a line of shoes, Rutherford's, Viola's, and his: house and street.

The ashtray on the end table was filled with cold dirty-gray ashes strewn with crumpled cigarette butts with black grotesquely splayed ends. Meanwhile a beautiful Indian maiden smiled sweetly upon the scene from the calendar on the wall above the table. Her black hair was decorated with beads, her long graceful legs supported a proud straight body that stood under the sweeping boughs of a willow tree beside a birch-bark canoe that nosed a quiet little cove nibbled into the shore by the smooth waters of a blue-green lake, which in turn sprawled out over the numbered days of September written in large Gothic letters.

A shiver ran up his spine when he looked at Jesus sitting at the Last Supper table in the picture that hung over his parents' heads. He cast a knowing glance at his companions, as if to say:

Who among you *here in God's house* — *today!* — *ain' got some secret locked up in his heart!*

He fled to the kitchen, a moderately sized room with a linoleum floor with a flowered pattern of various shades of apple-green, and a breakfast set with apple-green flowers that Viola had painted. And a gas range. A R-O-P-E-R — Roper! Rope, dope, swope, park.

He opened the screen door and stepped out onto the back porch. The sky was brighter and the air was cool, sweet, and fresh with the scent of wet

e looked down into the backyard. Wild grass, weeds, the tall stalky
wers in the lot behind the empty house next door, and the vegetables
Mrs. Crippa's garden glistened with dew. The squarish concrete yard
between his house and Mrs. Crippa's house opposite was wet in the cracks,
as though it might have been rained on during the night. No flies buzzed
around the big trash box standing with its back against the wooden fence
on the south side of the yard jammed against the upper half of the outer
wall of the narrow shed on the porch below.

He studied his yard with a curious fascination and with a vague feeling
of dread. The yard itself formed a little plateau that began on the second-
floor level of the back of the house, which was built into the hill that
swelled up from the alley. A wooden staircase led up from the ground floor
— necessarily a dark damp musty place because the sheer dirt wall that
supported the yard afforded neither sunlight nor fresh air — up through
the porch below and from there up to the third floor where he now stood.

There was a drain as round and as deep as the half of a scooped-out watermelon in the middle of the narrow concrete shelf below where the neighbors
poured dirty dishwater and water from the big tin tubs they took baths in
every Saturday night. The cloudy stream souring in the crevice leading to the
drain was as yet unvisited by flies, nor did they swarm merrily around the
garbage can where the smell of rotting food rose with the sun.

Now the sky was fragrant with the smell of blue air washed with dew; of
growing vegetables, the pungent scent of two tall elm trees over three stories high in Mr. Fox's and Miss Ada's backyard; of white and red wine,
which rose from huge vats in Mr. Crippa's cellar; and of corn whiskey from
the still below.

He looked through the shoot into the alley. It was still asleep except for
the crickets chirping in the grass and the incessant twittering of the sparrows. One suddenly swooped down upon the banister near his hand and
then darted through one of the paneless windows of the empty house.

The voice of the choir sang softly in his ears and gradually filled the
morning with song:

*I sing — be-cause I'm hap-py! — I sing — be-cause — I'm free — ee!
He's got His eyes aw — on t-h-e spar-row, an' I know He — ee wa — ah
— ches me!*

A robin stepped from behind a sunflower stalk with a worm in its beak
— and took his breath away!

"I hope it never changes!" he murmured with a rush of deep emotion.

I — I kno — o — ow He — ee — ee — wa-ches — me! whispered the
choir, and he was stricken by a feeling of uneasiness.

How does He *know?*

He sat down opposite the kitchen door on an orange crate and tried to cope with the fragments of his dream, which now rushed helter-skelter through his mind. He closed his eyes and shut out the stars, and fell down, and was afraid, and ran and ran in order to escape the hand that was trying to break his neck. And then he awoke. He opened his eyes. Objects in the increasingly bright morning light came more sharply into focus and he heaved a sigh of relief for having escaped the fatal hand.

But then he remembered the sound of bedsprings, his father tossing in his bed, waiting for his mother to come home. Then suddenly the flash of the match and the tip of the cigarette glowing in the darkness, and his father's masklike face silhouetted against the sky full of stars.

"Up long, son?" said a voice.

He looked through the kitchen screen at the shadowy apparition of his father looking down upon him as though he were reading his thoughts:

"Up long, son?"

"No, sir," his eyes vacantly staring at the worn boards of the porch floor.

Rutherford turned into the kitchen and Amerigo watched him brush his teeth and wash his face in the sink and throw the dirty water into the toilet, next to the door, that they shared with the neighbors. Then he went into the front part of the house.

Minutes later Rutherford reappeared in the kitchen dressed, with the *Times* rolled and bent like a boomerang. He unbent the paper, unrolled and glanced at it with a heavy sigh, laying the paper on the table while he began to prepare his breakfast.

Amerigo thought: Black coffee two cups, two strips of bacon, two pieces of toast — with plum preserves!

He read the paper as he ate. And when he had finished eating he fixed his lunch . . . beans left over from supper. . . . He poured them into a little grayish white enamel bucket that he would warm at twelve on the little gas stove in the basement at the hotel where he had worked ever since the child was born . . . hoppin' bells!

Amerigo watched him put on his cap and his suede jacket. *Mom bought him these for Christmas. . . .*

"So long," said Rutherford, "an' don' forget to stay in the yard an' play."

"Yessir."

Rutherford disappeared into the interior of the house. He waited until he had heard the click of the Yale lock on the front door and then he ran through the house and down onto the front porch. He sat on the top step and watched his father walk up the alley with long rhythmic strides, falling back on his slender legs as he climbed the hill.

That's my father! he thought aloud, looking around for someone to tell, but as there was no one, he watched the tall young man fade out of sight in silence.

No sooner than he had turned into the great Admiral Boulevard than an old Model T Ford came zooming down the alley, its radiator boiling like a train. Bra Mo coming from the icehouse! The truck was loaded with frosty cakes of ice covered with gunnysacks and a big tarpaulin to keep the ice from melting. Brother Moore put on the brakes and climbed down from the driver's seat and went around to the back of the truck and pulled the chain through the tailgate with a loud rattle, causing the gate to bang against the truck's iron bed. Then he started removing the sacks and the tarpaulin from the ice.

He slipped down from the porch and ran up the hill to Brother Moore's truck to watch.

"Mawnin', 'Mer'go!" looking down at his bare feet. "Boy! Yo' momma's gonna *kill* you, traipsin' through this alley wid no shoes on!"

"Yessir," smiling broadly because Brother Moore smiled broadly, his small black face breaking up into an expression of tenderness.

"Mawnin' folks!" He heard his friendly voice drifting down through his memory from a year's distance. Brother Moore had just moved into the alley, into the house next to the empty house where Aunt Nancy and Erwin, her feebleminded nephew, lived.

"Mawnin' folks! Me an' ma wife jus' moved up from Nawth Car'lina. Durham. Gonna settle down up heah. Ice an' coal an' kin'lin' wood. Sho would like to serve you folks!"

He suddenly burst into a smile, for now he saw Mrs. Derby's image. She and her husband lived on the second floor, north. A short, strongly built black woman with kinky hair and a pleasant, pockmarked face. Her left eye was blue and her right was brown and her husband was a hunter like an Indian, quiet. Mrs. Derby talked all the time, and dipped snuff! You could see it bulging under her tongue under her bottom lip. Ugh! Whenever she wanted ice she used to come out onto the porch and yell: "Bra Mo! Aw, Bra Mo!" and all the kids and grown-ups would laugh. It wasn't until he joined St. John's that the child found out that *Bra Mo* was a diminutive of Brother Moore!

Now Brother Moore grabbed the tongs from his shoulder and clawed one of the cakes on the end and pulled it away from the others with practiced ease. He slid it onto his shoulder and shifted his weight until the balance was right and carried it down to the far end of the basement to the icebox and eased it off his shoulder.

"Whew!" turning to the child who had followed him, "I sho' hope you don' nevah hafta work like this!" He returned to the truck and brought in another cake, and another, and soon the truck was half empty.

Meanwhile the sun was advancing rapidly down the alley. It sprawled lazily upon the rooftops. Soon now the raw freshness of the morning would have to give way to the hot sultry air of the summer's day.

"Betta run 'long, son, yo' momma's gonna be worried when she wake up an' you ain' theah."

"Yessir. S'long, Bra Mo."

"S'long, 'Mer'go!"

He ran swiftly back to the porch. He tiptoed halfway up the hall stairs and listened to see if his mother was awake. Satisfied that she was still asleep, he quietly descended the stairs again and feasted his eyes on his alley, knowing that the alarm clock would ring any minute now and she would wake up — she always slept until the last minute — and spring suddenly out of bed and descend upon him like a fresh sparkling little whirlwind! She would whir down the alley — run! — all the way to the laundry more than eight blocks away and arrive just before the whistle blew. Then she would begin her long hard day on the mangle in the steamy basement of Jefferson's laundry until twelve o'clock when the whistle blew. And then she would run the eight blocks home in her white apron with a white hand towel wrapped around her neck to keep the sweat from irritating the rash that came because of the intense heat. Just to fix his lunch, and eat with him, with a smile on her face and her mouth set for a laugh! When she laughed her eyes and her pearly teeth would sparkle, and he would forgive her for making him suffer the humiliation of not being able to protect her when his father shouted at her and swore because she came home late. He understood a little why Rutherford might not go away, as he always feared he might, if not today then tomorrow, because Viola flowed like a bright stream of light through their lives, like the sun advancing down the alley.

He thought of noon already. How long it would be until then! Until then he would have to be alone in the backyard.

"But she ain' woke yet!" he declared happily, deciding that he would remain on the porch as long as possible. The blue sky was now streaked with blazoning rays of golden light. Almost like it was evening. Only now the blue was harder, pregnant with a light composed of many bright hues. It feels funny, he thought, whirling within the dizzying swirl of brightness.

Magically the subtle shades of blue lifted like veils, revealing a world washed in clean morning air, transforming the dirty-gray earthen colors of the worm-eaten porches that leaned against, clung to, the dull redbrick facades of the houses. Taut green blades of grass pushed up between the cobblestones and rusty cans and piles of ashes and clinkers in the foundation of the empty house. Strong rays of yellow light converted little knots of trees into church windows and made the cobblestones look orange.

They'd never been as red as that! Except, perhaps, at sunset. In late September, or October when the moon rose early. As red as a pomegranate!

The lights within the houses had long since flickered on here and there and had already begun to grow pale in the face of the advancing sun. Smoke from chimneys spiraled into the sky. Doors opened and raw-eyed men and women left their houses and headed up and down the alley for work. Suddenly the alley was caught in the crossfire of traffic from the boulevard and the avenue. The alarm clock rang upstairs.

He crept quietly up the steps and stole into his mother's bed and snuggled in her arms and pressed his face against her breast and squeezed her tight.

"Be still, Amerigo," she whined sleepily.

He struggled to keep still but his heart pounded with love, and his thoughts flitted around the speculation as to what would happen to him if his father didn't come back. The Republicans would get us, or the depression! Jerry'd come and we'd have a war one day when I looked up and — *Boom!* He kicked at the covers.

"If you don' keep still!" said Viola.

A ray of sunlight crept in the window. Suddenly feeling the full intensity of his heat upon her face, Viola leaped out of the bed with a shriek and ran into the kitchen. The splash of cold water, the sound of teeth being brushed. Seconds later she shot into the middle room, dressed, and dashed clackedy-clack down the front steps, the child at her heels, and down the alley.

"Jus' like a fiah en*jine!* God damned!" shouted Mr. Daniels, a tall thin yellow man with a long nose. He smiled, baring tobacco-stained teeth, swinging his pegleg in one direction and his crutch in the other, mimicking her as she yelled back over her shoulder:

"You be good, an' don't you set a foot out a that yard! 'Cause if you *do,* I'll know it, an' your daddy'll know it, too! An' you know what *that* means!"

"Yes'm!"

"Yo' maw's tellin' you right, 'Mer'go!" cried Mr. Daniels. "A-l-l-ways do what your maw says. If I'd a done what my maw said I'd be walkin' on two legs taday 'stead a three! Ah-ha! ha!"

"Told me you had four legs last night, you old devil!" declared a woman's voice from the screened interior of the house next door.

Miss Maggie.

"Hush yo' filthy mouth, hussy!" cried Mr. Daniels.

"Sixty-six, eighty-nine, an' twenty-four on the big book," said Miss Maggie, "an' seven, six, nine on the little 'un. I had a dream. An' if you bring me some money, you kin show me all the legs you got!"

Mr. Daniels plucked a long yellow pencil from behind his right ear and whipped out a thin narrow book from his vest pocket and quickly wrote the numbers down. Then he detached the carbon copy and stuck it under the screen.

"Lord knows I could use a little luck!" said Miss Maggie as her sickly yellow hand took the proffered ticket. Mr. Daniels nodded, and hobbled up the alley, his shoulders appearing grotesquely powerful under the crescent-shaped shoulder rest of his long yellow crutch.

"Hi! You li-li-lit-little schhharp-mouthed thing!"

"Hi Unc!" Amerigo smiled broadly at the little brown-skinned, bald-headed, sharp-mouthed man who stepped out of the apartment on the south side with quick nervous movements. He wrinkled his nose mischievously and thumped him gently on the head with his thumb and forefinger as he passed him on the stair.

"Dead," said a voice.

"That little niggah usta be a big shot!" Rutherford's voice declared. "I mean a big-time gam'ler. Had a different suit for every day of the week an' carried a wad that'd choke a elephant! An'-an', Amerigo, he had a Rolls-Royce. Red! I remember hearin' Sexton talkin' 'bout Mister Dewey! An' then, all of a sudden his luck run out. Lost a-l-l his money. Then he started hustlin' an' sellin' policy. Usta be married to a high-powered broad — a lady. She must a been a looker. I think she died, or left 'im. Somethin' like that."

"I wonder how he ever met Aunt Lily?" Viola asked.

"Yeah. I wonder what ever made 'im do a thing like that?"

"Maybe he loves 'er!"

"Yeah, but a cripple woman!"

"Can't a cripple woman have feelin's just the same as anybody else?"

"How'd she git cripple?" Amerigo asked.

"A horse kicked 'er when she was a little girl," said Viola in a tremulous voice, "no bigger'n you, an' 'er hip went stiff, an' she ain' never been able to walk straight since."

"What's them black spots on 'er face?"

"Them's warts," Rutherford replied. "If a frog splashes slimy water on you, you git 'um."

"Well I can say this for 'er," said Viola, "I ain' never heard 'er say nothin' nasty or mean about *nobody,* an' nobody else ain' neither! I don' think she could tell a lie if she tried!"

"Hot damn!" Rutherford exclaimed, "a-l-l them stray dogs an'cats! I ain' kiddin', a-l-l the stray dogs an' cats, an' birds *love* 'er!"

"She's got a son," said Viola, "a tall black good-lookin' number."

"Yeah! He just up an' left home when he was sixteen I heard, an' never did come back. An' didn' even *write* unless he wanted somethin'. An' no matter how broke she is, she always finds a few pennies somewhere to send him! Old Unc's got a good thing. Don' have to work much, if he don' want to. Just lay in there, Jack, an' let 'er take care of 'im."

Rutherford's voice died away, and conflicting passions besieged Amerigo's mind: deep feelings of anger, love, and revulsion, so that now when he heard Aunt Lily's greeting he did not quite know what to do.

"Hi, honey! How's my baby?"

He looked into her smiling face, a longish horselike face, with a slightly crooked nose and a large mouth filled with big perfect yellow teeth. Her lower jaw protruded to the extent that she couldn't completely close her mouth. Her long hair was thick, coarse, and very black, while her eyes were large and spaced rather far apart, the irises flecked with rust-colored spots and the pupils brown. Though she smiled her expression was sad.

He tried not to mind that she was crippled, or that her teeth were yellow. He threw his arms around her waist. She bent down for him to kiss her, but when he saw the tiny warts on her face he just couldn't, in spite of the expression of calm understanding that now crept into her face in the wake of violent nuances of subtle pain that animated her eyes. She pressed his head to her breast, and then tried to gently disengage him.

He tightened his grip on her waist.

"I gotta go, son! You know I can't keep white folks waitin'."

He released her, and watched her twisted movements down the steps. He tried not to look at her, and distracted himself with the thought: She works at the Golden Laundry, remembering that he had passed by it one day with Viola and that she had pointed to the big steaming building and said: "There's where Aunt Lily works. She's one a the oldest girls there."

"Did you stay in the yard today?" said Rutherford, and on his way up the front stairs he tried to grapple with the mystery of the strange power that his father had over him: to be able to draw the secret from his eyes, no matter what it was — *even before it happened!*

How does he *know?* he thought, pausing for breath on the top stair.

At that moment a man ran heavily up the steps and almost knocked him down in his hurry to enter the opposite apartment. He wore a white sweat-stained cap, a pair of smudgy gray trousers, and rusty black run-over shoes that showed his naked grimy heels. His unshaven face was dirty and there was sleep in his eyes. His cheeks were drawn; large beads of sweat rolled

down his face. His teeth chattered as he continued to beat on the door as
if to break it down. During the anxious little pauses in which he listened
for signs of life within the apartment, he continually rubbed his arms.

"*Boom! Boom! Boom!*" He banged again, and finally the door opened.
The man mumbled something through the crack that he couldn't quite
hear. Then the door opened wider and he rushed in, knocking over a chair
as he did so. The door banged, but it didn't shut because it had been
banged too hard. Miss Sadie was standing by the little table next to the bed
where Mr. Nickles lay sleeping on his side, with his back to them. Miss
Sadie, a medium-sized yellow woman with sleepy eyes and a pockmarked
but not unattractive face, stood as though she were in a daze, her silk negligee falling apart, revealing her naked body. He started at the patch of reddish brown hair between her legs, until his attention was distracted by the
sudden violent movement of the trembling man who had grabbed her by
the shoulders and was shaking her roughly. Mr. Nickles, without turning
over, ran his hand under the pillow and withdraw a big blue gun and said:
"Make the niggah show his money!"

The man fumbled nervously in his pockets and withdrew some dirty
crumpled bills and threw them on the bed. Mr. Nickles turned over and
counted it. "All right," he said, and turned back over and went to sleep.

Miss Sadie took a little bottle from the table drawer and stuck a needle
attached to a syringe in it and drew a clear liquid into the syringe. Then she
stuck it into the man's outstretched arm. Seconds later he sighed profoundly, an ecstatic smile took possession of his face, and he stepped into
the corridor as though in a dream.

Miss Sadie noticed him as she was about to shut the door: "Hi, honey,"
self-consciously pulling her negligee together. "Want some candy? Wait a
minute." Half walking, half stumbling into the middle room of the apartment she returned seconds later with a peppermint stick. "Here, baby!"

"No'm, thank you, my momma told me not to take nothin' from
nobody."

"Aw, it's just a little piece!" Her negligee fell open again, as she lifted him
into her arms and rocked him back and forth, as though she would lull him
to sleep. Her bosom was hot and she smelled like sweat and perfume,
talcum powder, cigarettes, burned Vaseline, and sleep. She kissed him on
the cheek and pressed his head against hers. Her lips were moist. Mr.
Nickles stirred in bed and she immediately put him down, making a sign
for him to be quiet, and pushed the peppermint stick into his pocket. Then
she gently eased him out the door.

She's pretty, he thought. Not as pretty as Mom, though. A deep sad
feeling welled within him and made him want to cry. He stared at his front

door until the sadness gave way to a blind passion that filled him with nervous excitement, and before he quite knew that he had done so, he had violently pushed the door open and banged it shut. . . .

He moved desultorily toward the table model radio and turned the knob. It cracked and hissed and popped. "Slap it!" said Rutherford. He slapped its rounded shoulder with the palm of his hand and sweet oily voice spewed out into the air:

"And now, ladies, the sitting-up exercises for slim figures and happy futures!"

He straightened the covers on his bed, folded it up into a couch, and put the three big cushions in place.

"One! Two! Three! That's right! *Again!* A-one!"

He moved the coffee table with the glass top in front of the sofa, folded the papers neatly, and placed them in the magazine rack.

"Ummm! Doesn't that feel g-o-o-d. Lift up those legs! High now! One! Two! Three! That's all, that's all, ladies, un-til tomorrow morning at the same time when McClimmerick's Salted Crackers presents. . . ."

"In this matchbox of a house," he heard Viola saying, "if you don' hang up ever'thin' just as soon as you get through with it, it looks like a pigpen!"

His eyes flashed with the sudden brightness of remembering: peanuts, and chewing gum maybe, and maybe some peanut brittle! He began searching all the suspicious corners for something good to eat.

Soft piano music flowed from the speaker, sad, majestic, quite unlike the music Viola and Rutherford and all the people he knew always listened to, but beautiful just the same. It made him think about the alley in the evening just before nightfall, about Miss Sadie, about Aunt Lily whose son had left her. He hummed the melody.

"What's the name a that?" he had once asked Viola.

"That's classical music."

"Aw."

"Ivy Flakes presents: Mary Marvin! The story of a beautiful woman who tries to find happiness after thirty-five!"

"That sure is old!" He was full of sympathy for poor Miss Marvin.

"And now for our sensational announcement! We of Pocter and Kantrell are proud to present the newest and most extraordinary addition to our distinguished family of luxury soaps: Ivy Flakes Debutante! The newest. . . ."

He resumed his search for goodies, looking in the purses in the chest of

drawers for chewing gum. Instead of gum he found half a roll of Life
Savers, and stuffed the whole half roll in his mouth.

Soft piano music. He paused and let it sweep his thoughts way out,
beyond the circled light, beyond the southernmost limits of the polished
floors and boiling clothes and fondled babies who did not belong to the
black hands that caressed them.

And then *she* spoke, in a dulcet voice. The prettiest voice in the w-h-o-l-e
world next to Mom's! And then old Mary sighed a heavy sigh, over a letter,
a love letter, in a garden reeking with the scent of roses, the announcer said.
He said that a bird sat in a nearby tree and sang his heart out — Tweet!
tweet! — mad with intoxication at the mere sight of her, suffering from
unbearable pangs of jealousy, while she wondered why Geoffrey, the young,
handsome, marriageable millionaire and heir to the Winthrop fortune, hesitated to ask her for that which she had already given to him a hundred
times over — her hand, her heart, her soul!

Geoffry ought to have his ass kicked! Shit! Amerigo stalked into the middle
room. Mad, he made up the big bed, puzzling long and hard over the wine-
red stain on Viola's side of the bed. He tried to break 'er neck! The sheet
trembled in his hands. When he had finished making up the bed, he hung the
clothes up in the clothes closet and dusted the powder off the vanity dresser
and emptied the ashtray, carefully laying the cigarettes aside against the day
when his father might not have fifteen cents for a new package.

An organ flourish. He looked up with surprise, disappointed that he had
not heard what had happened to Mary Marvin:

"Palm Oil presents! The story of the little suburban community of Five
Points and Doctor Sweetridge, the parish priest, in his daily struggle to
come to grips with the problems in a modern suburban community." Then
Amerigo and Dr. Sweetridge said:

"There is a destiny that makes us brothers,

"For none goes his way alone:

"An' all that we send into the lives of others

"Comes back into our own."

Organ flourish:

"And now, ladies, have you been wondering . . ."

He entered the kitchen and started to prepare his breakfast.

"When last seen, Kitty was talking to the notorious gangster known as
the Hawk, trying to discover a clue that would lead her to Terry, who has
been missing ever since he received the mysterious phone call from the
unknown woman from the red house. . . ."

He ate his cornflakes and condensed milk diluted with water, and sugar, and
bread and butter sprinkled with sugar and cinnamon, and plum preserves.

"*Boom! Boom! Boom!* Terry!"

He carried his cornflakes out onto the porch and sat down on the orange crate within the bright wedge of sunlight that fell across the outer corner of the porch. He surveyed his alley, the shoot and empty house next door, the backyards of the adjoining houses up and down the alley and those of Campbell Street.

Suddenly there was a burst of excitement streaming through the windows and the door of the Crippa kitchen. He was fascinated by the torrent of strange passionate words. "Momma! momma!" cried Tina, interrupting her mother. She was thirteen. Pretty brown hair. Sure mad about somethin'. Her teary speech was now partially drowned out by the sound of music.

"Midmorning Interlude!" the announcer was saying.

Meanwhile Tina spoke vigorously against the music. Then Carl, the youngest brother, joined in. He has a balloon-tire bicycle! His broken falsetto tones of rage tumbled into the midmorning sunshine, mingling now with:

"Gershwin's *Rhapsody in Blue,* played by Paul Whiteman and his orchestra!"

Then suddenly the loud bang of a fist crashing upon the top of a table. Glasses and dishes rattled, spoons tinkled in cups. "Goddama! Basta! Baaaa — sta!" Silence, filled by the low wailing tones of a mournful clarinet. Mr. Crippa appeared at the back door with a huge white towel in his hands, with which he dried his smooth massive face. A big, iron-gray mustache filled the space between his well-shaped nose and upper lip, which was almost completely hidden. Now he curled the tapered ends with his thumb and forefinger and rubbed with his giant hand the broad sweeping avenue of scalp that had once been adorned with rich, curly, chestnut-brown hair.

He talks so loud! Amerigo thought, looking at him out of the corner of his eye. Must take a g-r-e-a-t *big* pot of beans and fatback to fill *him* up from his feet to his head! A million dollars' worth! He gazed with fascination upon the thicket of iron-gray hair that forced its way through the collar of his snow-white shirt.

Meanwhile Mr. Crippa looked with satisfaction out over his chest upon the yard and the house that he had rented to Rutherford and Viola, Aunt Lily and Unc, Miss Sadie and Mr. Nickles, Mr. and Mrs. Derby, to the bootleggers and Miss Anna and Monroe Benton on the first floor. He spied Amerigo looking at him with wide eyes.

"HALLO TONY!"

The earth seemed to tremble. He felt himself being lifted out of his mother's arms by two huge hairy hands that grasped him under the armpits, while he stared excitedly into a pair of eyes in a big pink mustached head that became two attenuated lines of feathers fanning a pair of ballooning red cheeks that swelled up under the eyes causing the lips to expand in a broad fleshy smile. This apparition grew suddenly smaller, as he felt himself soaring through the air, his feet flying back — and up over his head — until his frightened eyes stared directly down upon the waxen scalp of Mr. Crippa's head, his volcanic voice booming all the while:

"WHOA UP! WEETHA SUCHA BEEGA HED ANNA SUCHA BEEGA EYEES YOU SHOULDA BEA, WE GONNA CALLA YOU TONY. EH! YOU LEEDLE DAGO EENYWAY EH? A-MEREEGO VESPUCCI — EH! YOU DEESCOVER AH-MER-RI-KA — AYE, TONY!"

"He usta be a general!" said Rutherford's voice. "At least, that's what Shorty says."

"What Shorty?" asked Viola.

"Shorty! Aw, you know that li'l niggah, Babe!"

"I can't place 'im."

"A little buck-eyed niggah with his pants hangin' down under his belly that usta flunky for Bernard when he had that gam'lin' joint down on Fourth Street. Usta be sweet on Pretty Girl. . . ."

"Him? I thought he was Lucy's ol' man!"

"Maybe he was, I don' know. But anyway, that's him."

"How does he know?"

"He's flunkyin' for the dagos, runnin' hootch for 'um. He heard 'um talkin'. He says that the ol' man was a general in the war. An' after that he made a pile a dough off a black-market sugar to set 'im up in the States."

Mr. Crippa turned into the kitchen and Mrs. Crippa opened the screen door and stepped out onto the porch dressed in black. A quieter, calmer flow of conversation followed her. Mr. Crippa who reappeared in the door looked down upon her and replied now and then to her animated gesticulations with a low sympathetic growl. Her eyes twinkled and the finely wrinkled skin around her eyes and mouth expanded and contracted as she spoke. Gradually the talk and the faces faded out of mind, except that now Mrs. Crippa was approaching him.

"Eh Tony! Here! You wanna banana, eh? I geeva youa banana!" pressing a dark brown almost black banana into his hand.

"Throwitaway!" he heard his mother's voice whispering angrily. "Take it down an' put it in the garbage can, an' if she says anythin' to you, you tell 'er I told you to do it!" "*Last week,*" she had said to Rutherford, "*she come givin' 'im a box of cornflakes that the mice had messed in!*"

Mrs. Crippa entered the house and all was quiet, except for the unfamiliar music from the radio; it sounded like march music.

I wonder what they were talking about? he asked himself. Nobody got killed, so I guess they weren't really mad. Maybe they talk like that because they eat a lot of tomatoes and drink wine all the time instead of water! He turned over in his mind the image of Mr. and Mrs. Crippa going every evening and sometimes during the day down to the basement with a large glass pitcher to get wine from one of the four huge vats. He remembered the tall stacks of red and white grapes that came every year. She always gives me big handfuls, and last year we stole a w-h-o-l-e lot, and ran around in the shoot and ate them, and squeezed them until the insides squirted out. He thrilled to the memory of the delicious sensation, and to the fear that had smitten him when he had faced Viola with his face and trousers all stained from the grapes:

"Boy! Where-in-the-w-o-r-l-d have you been?"

"Nowhere."

"Did Mrs. Crippa give you those grapes?"

"Yes'm! You kin go an' ask 'er!"

Now he smiled a faintly guilt-ridden smile of triumph as his mother's voice faded out of hearing. His eyes swept down upon the yard next to Mrs. Crippa's where the vegetable garden was. Rose Marie, her daughter, lived there. Just got married to a fireman! A Irishman! Patrick Kelly! Pat, with a r-e-a-l pretty vegetable garden and a pretty new house that cost f-o-u-r-t-h-o-u-s-a-n' d-o-l-l-a-r-s!

"Must be true," he heard Rutherford say, "Shorty can't be lyin' about *that!* This is the depression. Who else can afford to buy a house like that in times like these?"

"The Farmer's Bulletin!" said the announcer. "What are your problems, farmers? The weather? Predictions of . . ."

His glance took in the backyards that staggered in tiers down to the vacant lot just behind the row of buildings facing the avenue from which he now heard the rumble of a trolley and the large vague hum of traffic interspersed with the concerted sound of many voices. He was surprised to hear the birds still twittering in the trees. Resting his elbow upon the banister he watched the sun shining through the branches of the elm trees into the lot of the empty house. Then he thought: It's about time for them to be going through the shoot to go to school.

"That's the way you'll be goin', too, pretty soon!" said Viola. "Then you won' have to stay in the backyard all day by yourself no more while we're at work. That's the same way we went: through the avenue to Troost, an' down Troost till you git to Belvedere Holla, an' then through the holla to Fores', an' then straight down Fores' till you come to the Field House."

"Like when you go swimin'!" said Rutherford. And the hot sunny way opened up before his mind. He followed the burning path through the lot, past neat rows of foreign-looking redbrick and stone houses facing clean paved streets, cleaner than the alley, past the bars and cafés of "dago town" with benches outside filled with old men smoking little black cigars, wearing bushy mustaches like Mr. Crippa, and caps, and who like Mr. Crippa always talked excitedly, waving their hands in the air and speaking volleys of words he couldn't understand. He saw the men sitting under maple and cottonwood trees, and others hovering excitedly around little wooden balls that they rolled along the hard-packed earth. Just like kids playing marbles! He saw along the way the neat little gardens like Rose Marie's and Mrs. Crippa's in the front yard of the houses with shallow flights of concrete steps that were covered — almost every one — with a white or green trellis decked with grapevines.

In the early autumn the grapes would swell on the vines and fill the air with a pleasant musky scent, they'd fall and squash upon the cement steps and in between the rows of fat round vegetables growing in the gardens.

The smell of grapes and autumn mixed with the smell of pureeing tomatoes spread out upon a large white breadboard in the sun. A world of fresh cold, crisp, ripe fruit passed before his mind and its aromas lingered in his nostrils. And then suddenly, miraculously, they became mixed up with all the impressions he had derived from his experience of the word *dago*.

"What's a d-a-g-o, Dad?" he heard himself asking.

"An I-*ta*lian, you mean?"

"If they I-*ta*lians, why do they call 'um dagos?"

"For the same reason we're Negroes and they call us niggahs!"

"How come?"

"'Cause we're different."

Two bumblebees shot into the bright beam of sunlight that blazed the path to Garrison School.

"Yes, sir!" said Rutherford, "after Labor Day you'll be going to the kinnygarden! Ha! ha! Aw, m-a-n!"

"Under Miss Vi-o-la Chapman!" Viola added.

He followed the bee's darting movements as their words registered upon his memory, and he began to imagine that it was they who spoke:

"Time sure flies, don' it?"

"Yeah!" said Rutherford, "just think, me an' your momma both went to Miss Chapman, an' now you'll be goin' to 'er, too! An' ol' lady Moore! Ha, haa! That is a *mean* woman! Oooooooo-whee! What's two times four she'd ask you, an' you'd *better* know the answer! When you didn' knowit, after she done explained it to you, she'd hit you 'cross the knuckles with that ruler. It had a rubber edge on it an' h-u-r-t! An' don' cry! Better not cry! Ain' I tellin ' im, Babe?"

"She was rough, all right."

"Looked just like a white woman with long straight, coal-black hair. Kept it wound 'round the top of 'er head in a big coil like a thick black snake! Fastened with a big pretty comb made out a ivory . . ."

"Looked like a wig, Amerigo."

"That wasn' no wig, Babe!"

"Sure looked like one."

"Anyhow, when you left that ol' woman, an' you wasn' dead, you knowed somethin', Jackson, let me tell you. Didn' you, Babe?"

The little bee that looked like Viola nodded in the affirmative.

"She was just like Momma," said Rutherford. "Hard but fair. An' let me tell you somethin' else . . ."

He could visualize his father's face clearly now, and deep currents of emotion rose up from the depths of his awareness, rose and fell with the intonations of his voice. Rutherford's sincerity moved him.

The bees suddenly darted into the shade, and the events of last night rushed through his mind in a strange way. He trembled to a pleasant defiant sensation that caused him to articulate the following thought so clearly that it almost seemed as though he had spoken out loud:

Her no more than him!

He looked fearfully, guiltily, this way and that, as though he suspected that his mother and father might have heard his thoughts.

"An' let me tell you somethin' else," he was saying, "that Negro woman had c-l-a-s-s! I mean *dig*nified, like a queen!"

He tried to imagine going to school. A fragmentary image of Miss Chapman passed before his mind and he tried to imagine what she looked like. What someone looked like whom one had never seen but to whom one would have to go when one went to the kindergarten. A passionate feeling of love and devotion swelled in his breast as he exhumed the word: *Viola!*

Maybe she's my momma, too! Her no more than him. And then he thought of Miss Moore. What's a queen like? Something big, I bet. Like Grandma. He saw her riding through the night on Grandpa Will's horse. Queen of hearts, diamonds, spades. The smooth face of Grandpa Rex came to mind, his fingers shuffling the queens on the playing cards that Rutherford kept in the drawer of the vanity dresser.

"How come," he heard his voice interrupting his father's speech. "How come Bra Mo and Miss Moore got the same name, an'-an' she's white, an' he's black?"

"Names ain' got no colors," said Rutherford. "Your gran'ma don' look like no hundred percent Negro neither!"

"But if you got one-sixteenth Negro blood in your veins, you're a Negro just the same!" said Viola.

"How much is that?"

"Enough!" she said bitterly. "Now hush up your questions. You make my brains tired!"

"Let him ask!" Rutherford exclaimed, "askin' don' do no harm. If you don' know, an' you don' never ask, how you ever gonna find out?"

"Miss Moore sure was crazy about your daddy!" said Viola. "He was a funny-lookin' thing! You ought to a seen 'im, Amerigo!"

"Me funny?" Rutherford exclaimed. "The one *you* shoulda seen was your *momma*! Boy, your momma was a reg'ler little soldier! Walked straight as a stick! Shoulders all throwed back, hair shinin' an' fulla things, you know: ribbons an' pins an' stuff like that. An' a-l-lways late! I mean *every day!* E-v-e-r-y mornin' that gal'd come to school five, ten, sometimes a hour late! I ain' kiddin'! She even came at re-cess! Ah-ha! ha!"

"Aw, Rutherford!" buzzed the little Viola-bee.

"I ain' exaggeratin', Amerigo, that gal came to school at *n-o-o-n* even! You'd hear that nine o'clock whistle blow, an' ever'body'd take they seat all quiet an' nice-like, waitin' for school to start, an' then you'd hear a rush a wind like a storm blowin' up!"

"*R-u-t-h-e-r-f-o-r-d J-o-n-e-s-!* How you expect to git to heaven lyin' like that!" cried Viola.

"Amerigo, I hope the Lord strikes me down dead, right heah where I'm sittin', if I'm lyin'. You know, you'd hear a . . . hear a . . . thunderin' sound, like a herd a stampedin' hosses! Haw! Haw! Tearin' down Fifth Street. The whole buildin'd start to *shakin'!* That was your momma burnin' a path to school. An' don' you git in 'er way! Better not git in 'er way! Git trampled to *death!* An' then, Amerigo, she'd git right up to the door an' stop an' git all quiet an' then come *tiptoeing in*, Jack! Just like nothin' had happened!

"An' ol' lady Moore'd be sittin' there, Jack, cool as a cucumber, ready for her. Ol' Vi'd e-a-s-e the door open an' come sneakin' in, an' Miss Moore'd say: 'V-i-o-l-a!' 'Yes'm?' she'd say, 'er eyes all wide an' innocent-like, like she thought she was on time or somethin'.

"'What happened *this* time?' An' the ol' lady'd level those eyes on 'er.

"Viola'd look at the ceilin', set her mouth, an' start lyin' up a breeze! That gal could really *go* you hear me? She'd start to lyin' an' the little niggahs'd git to laughin', ol' T. C. louder'n all the rest! That joker was as big as he is now, Amerigo! He'd let out a horse-laugh. Miss Moore'd say, 'Thomas!' she called that niggah Thomas, 'you may go out in the hall and finish laughing. When you're through, you may remain after class.'"

"But wait! talkin' about horses!"

"Aaaaaaaaw," cried Viola, don' you start *that* lie again! You done told it at least a thousand times, and e-v-e-r-y time it's different!"

"Aw, but wait Amerigo, T. C. played hooky from school *more'n your momma!* She was just late all the time, but T. C. played hooky *ever' day!* An' Pr'fessor Bowles, J. J. Bowles, the principal —"

"A wonderful man, Amerigo," said Viola.

"She's tellin' the truth!"

"A *race* man!"

"I mean a real educator! Well Principal Bowles almost had to dynamite that niggah out a elementary school! Ha! ha! Ah-ha! ha! ha!"

"Amerigo!" said Viola, her voice trembling with laughter, "he was in the *seventh grade,* fixin' to *graduate,* an' didn' even know his ABCs!"

"Pr'fessor Bowles shamed him before the whole class!" Rutherford said. "Look at Rutherford an' Eddie an' Viola, here, they're at the head of the class. Your momma an' me was the best! I was the president, Jack! An' ol' Vi was the class secretary!"

"Ol' T. sure was dumb! Tee! hee!" Amerigo giggled.

"Naw he wasn', Amerigo!" Rutherford replied. "Naw he wasn', that niggah was *smart!* He knew all about fishin' an' huntin', an' hosses. An' he knew e-v-e-r'-b-o-d-y's first, middle, an'last name, an' they brothers' and sisters' names, an' when was they birthday an' when they was sick an' what they *had* — an' not only this year, but *last* year — an' the year before that, too! He knew what you liked an' what you didn' like, an' he would give it to you, too, if he could. If you could catch him in one place long enough. T. C. had a heart a gold! A-l-l the gals was *crazy* about that niggah! *Nice* girls, too! An'-an' a-l-l the teachers, an' even Pr'fessor Bowles. He never did nobody no harm, except maybe hisself, but then he had so much fun doin' whatever he did that it didn' make you feel bad, even if it was against his-self. Naw-naw, that joker wasn' dumb, Amerigo, that cat was lazy!"

"I don' even think he was lazy," said Viola tenderly. A feeling of shame rose to Amerigo's throat.

"Naw. That's right, Babe," said Rutherford thoughtfully. "He was just bigger than the rest of us, tall an' powerfully built for his age. He just flunked out all the time 'cause he never came to school, 'cause he was ashamed to have to sit with all us little kids. So he'd just goof off."

"An' even then," said Viola, "he couldn' stay away from the playground.

At recess he'd come ridin' up on that big old white horse. Whose horse *was* that, Rutherford?"

"Ol' man Benson's, I think. Anyway, Amerigo, that horse was so ol' that he didn' have no teeth."

"Aw, Rutherford!" exclaimed Viola.

"Well, he didn' have many!"

"That's true."

"That old nag's beard was so long he almost tripped over it every time he'd start to run!"

. . . Huge drops of rain splashed upon Amerigo's face as the crowd dispersed and old Mr. Clark galloped wildly down the alley dragging the wagon bearing Mr. Andrews in its wake. . . .

"T. C.," his father was saying, "T. C.'d come ridin' up on that old horse like Tom Mix a-grinnin' and a-showin' off, lettin' ever'body ride. The bell rung for 'um to go back in but didn' nobody hear it 'cause those little jokers was havin' so much fun. When all of a sudden, before anybody knowed what was happenin', there was Mister Bowles, standin' in the midst of them little niggahs. E-v-e-r-y-body got as quiet as a mouse. T. C. tried to make that old horse stand still, but he got all nervous and started to rarin' up!

"'Thomas Corning Belcher!' Mr. Bowles cried out, an' all the little niggahs started howlin'. 'Corning,' they hollered. 'Man! Where'd you git a name like *that?*' Old T. C. looked down all shamed and ever'thin'.

"'If you ever bring that beast, *Beast!* Ha! Ha! — beast on school property again, I'll have you expelled from school. Now take that thing away and be in my office in the next thirty minutes. As for the rest of you, you have three minutes to be in your seats. Once more, the whole school will remain after the last bell for one hour!' An' I mean he laid it down in *good English,* Jack, just like I said it. M-a-n — you ought to a seen those jokers scramble!

"Yessir," Rutherford continued dreamily, "ol' T. C. was a lot a fun, Amerigo. An' nobody better *not* bother me an' Viola! He'd run them li'l niggahs wild! An' they was some tough jokers, too, Amerigo, m-e-a-n li'l niggahs, with knives, an' they'd use 'um, too!

"Me an' a whole gang a niggahs usta go snake huntin' ever' Sad'dy on Clairmount Hill an' all up in them woods 'roun' Cliff Drive an' down by the railroad tracks. An' don' let us come 'cross no cats! M-a-n, we was *rough* on cats! We'd throw 'um up in the air by the tail an' chunk rocks at 'um!"

"Rutherford, you oughtta be ashamed of yourself, teachin' that boy things like that!" said Viola. "Amerigo, don' listen. That's mean!"

"I usta just look at a cat an' git m-a-d! They kin look at you so mean an' evil-like. Besides, we was just havin' fun, Babe. Anyhow, we never killed no cat more'n once or twice!"

"What foolishness you talkin' now, Rutherford?"

"Well, they got nine lives, ain' they? Ha! ha! ha! Anyhow, anyhow, no sooner'n ol' T. C. got out a elementary school, he up an' run off with a carnival. Some cat named Tex talked 'im into *boxin'*! One day the carnival came town an' there was ol' T. C. prancin' in the ring! An' that cat looked keen, too, Amerigo: tall an' heavy built, broad shoulders an' all. Hey-hey! the jokers all cried. Look at ol' T. C. We got our tickets an' ever'thin'. Battlin' T. C. B.! he called hisself. Ha! ha! You ought to a seen 'im, Amerigo. 'Battlin' T. C. B. takes on all challengers!' that niggah Tex yelled out. An' then a skinny wiry little joker, quiet, looked like he couldn' whip a fly. What was that joker's name, Babe?"

"I think it was Baby Li'l John, or somethin' like that."

"Yeah, that's it. Baby Li'l John! Well, Baby Li'l John stepped in the ring an' all the cats started agitatin': Throw that worm back! No fight! No fight! T. C.'ll *kill* that joker! An'all the time Baby Li'l John was quiet. Didn' say nothin'. Didn' even *look* at the niggahs! Then the bell rang an' m-a-n! He liked to *killed* T. C. We had to goose ol' T. back in the ring a couple a times! Hot damn! An' that wrapped that boxin' jive up.

"After that he got a job at the station, swingin' one a them big seven-foot mops! Naw, that ain' right. First he was cleanin' out the trains, the coaches, an' after that he started janitorin'. An' Amerigo, he knew e-v-e-r'-b-o-d-y in the whole Union Station! Every porter, brakeman, all the conductors. He coulda had a *good* job, an' not just no janitor, 'cause the station master was crazy 'bout 'im! But he just-couldn'-do-right-to-save-his-name! No sooner'n he'd get paid Sad'dy he'd start drinkin' with those low-lifers on Twelfth Street an' that'd wrap it up! Four hours after he'd get paid he'd be broke. He'd turn up missin' from work for days! An' they'd always take 'im back. But they couldn' give 'im no job with no responsibility. It's a cryin' shame! Why, why, with that niggah's personality he coulda been president! I ain' kiddin'! Amerigo, you ain' seen 'im dressed up. But you git 'im dressed up in a *blue serge suit* with a *white shirt* an' a *tie,* ain' *nobody,* white *or* black, handsomer than that black man! Looks like a Philadelphia lawyer! An' then he went an' married old Fenny. Old enough to be his momma. That ol' woman was so ugly an' ol' that he was ashamed to let people see 'im on the street with 'er!"

Rutherford's voice droned on and the welter of familiar names and voices of half-remembered, invisible men and women, some dead, flitted in and out of the broadening rays of sunlight and flickered like mirrored reflections upon the windows of the autos whizzing in horizontal planes at the head and the foot of the alley. Singular images now and then darted within the range of a tangible perception: thus the tall handsome figure of Uncle T. C. stood out clearly and filled the brilliant air between the lot behind the empty house and the burning sky that rose beyond the crest of the rise at the top of the alley. His face was smiling and his perfect white teeth flashed a greeting!:

"Hiya, 'Mer'go! Looka there, Rutherford, look how that boy's growed! He's gonna be bigger'n me pretty soon! An' strong as Jack Johnson! Let old T. feel yo' muscle!" He flexed the muscle of his skinny little arm into a proud little knot and heard T. C. exclaim admiringly:

"Wow! Feel that li'l joker's arm!" T. C. lifted him into his own powerful arms and pressed his face against his shaven face that nevertheless felt like the bark of a tree!

Then the images and voices gradually faded. He slowly discovered that school loomed large in his mind: the place where something was going to happen to him that had happened to his mother and father and T. C. Something big and long and strange that he could do nothing about. A stubborn resentment crept into his confused feelings and stirred him with an uneasiness that made him wish that twelve o'clock would come, and then five o'clock, night, and then sleep — very many times, and very quickly, until, at last, it would be time to go to school, and do all the things he had to do, and get it over with, so that he could get back up there (he scanned the sky for sign of a star) where it's really real — *really* real!

But twelve o'clock did not come quickly. Seven-thirty came. And eight o'clock and five minutes after that: minute by minute, second by second, as though only things were moving and time were standing still, like the people on the radio, interspersed between the movements of cleaning up, from the front room to the kitchen.

He was just about to enter the house when he caught sight of Old Jake walking slowly up the alley.

"That ol' man's crazy!" said a voice.

"He ain' crazy!" said Rutherford, "He's deep. That man sees things that just any joker can't see!"

What's crazy? he wondered aloud, just as Old Jake turned into the shoot on the far side of the empty house and suddenly appeared in the lot. He peered into one of its paneless windows as though he were looking for something. He poked his staff into the rubble heap that rose from the caved-in floor.

And then he looked up into the child's eyes. He tried to look away but he could not. Old Jake walked to the gate and stopped.

"Mornin', Mister Jake," he said nervously.

"Mornin', 'Mer'go." He let his sack slide carefully from his back and leaned his staff against the gate. Then he fumbled in the sack and finally brought out a bright object, which he held up in the air so that he could see it.

"What you got, Mister Jake?" He ran down into the yard.

"With them big eyes a yourn you oughtta be tellin' *me!*"

"Looks like a star made out a glass!"

"By Gawd, that's what it is! Found it down by the dump. I saved it for you!"

"Thanks, Mister Jake." He took the star and held it up in the air as the old man had done so that the sunlight shone through it, reflecting brilliant points of red, green, yellow, and blue light from its beveled edges, just like the rainbow!

He turned to thank Old Jake again, but he was gone! He didn't see him anywhere. Seized by a sense of mystery, he gazed warily at the empty house, as though it had swallowed Old Jake up. He had the sudden desire to look there himself, to look in ordinary places and find extraordinary things, like Old Jake. *He ain' crazy, he's deep!* That's why he could find a star when nobody else could. It's made out of glass. He put it in his pocket and kept his hand upon it. I wonder if it can shine in the pocket, like real stars shine in the sky. He returned to the porch, moving carefully so as not to break the star.

Again he started to enter the house, when he caught sight of a little knot of children cutting through the shoot: three big ones and three little ones. Tommy Johnson, Turner an' Carl Grey — big. Willie Joe an' Blanche an' Cornelie — little. In patched pants and dresses, odd jackets and sweaters and can-scarred, rock-scarred, marble-scuffed shoes, with pigtails with and without ribbons, with big red Indian Chief tablets and pen-and-pencil boxes and lunches wrapped in brown paper sacks and newspaper. They kicked at cans and rocks and laughed and yelled, looked this way and that as they passed under the elm trees where they came to a halt, looked up on the porch, and discovered him.

"Look at that li'l niggah up there with that peanut head! Hee! hee! hee! Wow! What a *head!* An them *eyes!* With eyes like *them,* that niggah oughtta see the *whole world* with one look!"

"Turner."

"*Dead,*" whispered a voice.

"Aw come on, man. Let the boy alone. Hi, 'Mer'go."

"Hi Tommy." Miss Corina's front room . . . The brightly scrubbed floor and the clock ticking four o'clock . . . His grandma, she's dead. And Miss Leona, his momma, dead, too.

The girls giggled and straggled behind the boys at the permitted distance. He followed their laughter through the shoot until the sound was gone, had mingled with the distant hum of traffic and with the farm news reporter's final prediction of shifting southerly clouds and probable rain.

Just then Bra Mo came out of his cellar and put up the tailgate of his empty truck and climbed into the driver's seat and released the hand brake and the truck creaked a short distance until the motor caught and then rattled down the alley in convulsive jerks, Bra Mo bobbling up and down on the springs of the driver's seat like a cork on a choppy sea.

"Toodle-lum! Aw, Toodle-lum!" croaked the hoarse voice of an old woman.

Mrs. Shields. By straining over the banister she could just see her as she stuck her head out the window, a big yellow white-headed woman with a large wart on her cheek and big dark injured eyes underlined with deep purple rings.

"Her mouth looks like it's always about to say somethin' nasty," he heard Viola say, seeing now his mother and father sitting with Aunt Lily on the front porch one evening when Mrs. Shields came out on her front porch and sat facing them.

"She *is!*" said Rutherford with a mischievous laugh.

"Now children," said Aunt Lily in a discreet tone, "Margret Shields usta be young an' pretty an' as sweet a child as you'd ever wanna see. An' then her momma died, an' she had to take care of a mess a brothers an' sisters. An' then she *had* to git married, an' had a mess a kids of 'er own. An' you *see* how they turned out. An' what with hard times an' all, she suffered a lot. Poor child's got the blues an' can't git rid of 'um. The blues makes some people able to laugh a little, an' other folks they just git bitter an' spiteful. But she don' mean no harm."

"Sh-sh-shee's jus', jus' mmm-mad 'c-c-ccause she's a-a-a-niggah!" stammered Unc Dewey. "Th-th-th-that darkie's mad, mad at the whole world. Sh-sh-shee'd lllike to gggive it a kkick in — the ass!"

"They just ruinin' poor Toodle-lum!" Rutherford said. "Toodle-lum! What a name to torture a child with!"

"Yes, hon," said Aunt Lily sweetly, "but you're forgettin' somethin'. He's all she's got! You lucky. The Lord's been good to you an' Viola. Amerigo's a good boy, an' one day, just like Old Jake said, he's gonna be a blessin' to you. He is already. I ain' heard from that young 'un a mine in *ten years!* If you was like her an' you had a grandson you'd hope that at least he could turn out to be somethin'. Only thing is that she don' know that you kin love somebody too much!"

"Toodle-lum! Aw, Toodle-lum!"

"Yes'm, Big Gran'ma, Big Gran'ma." A thin frightened little voice, followed by a burst of laughter from a bunch of little kids whose voices he knew as well as his own: Annie, William and Lem, Victor and Helen-Francis and Sammy and Frank.

"You come in that yard where I kin see you or I'm gonna tan your hide!" shrieked Mrs. Shields.

"Oh, ho! ho! ho!"

"Hee! hee! hee!"

"Yoo — hoo!"

"C-o-m-e Toodie-woodie," cried the children.

"Little devils!" cried Mrs. Shields. "If'n you was mine, I'd kick the holy shit out a the whole damned lot of you!"

"Sho' glad I ain' her'n!" giggled a muffled voice.

"What you say, li'l niggah?"

"Nothin'."

"Toodle-lum, if you don' stay 'way from them little dirty nappy-headed niggahs I'll *kill* you!"

Charles! That's his real name. Charles Baxter.

The delicate little boy went up on his front porch and sat on the top step and looked at his companions in the alley with an apologetic expression. Meanwhile the children ran barefoot back and forth in front of the porch, dancing and prancing and poking fun at him. They stuck out their tongues, stuck their fingers in their behinds, and pulled off monkeyshines until they made him laugh through the tears that rolled down his face.

He's pretty. He thought of Toodle-lum's brown eyes with the extraordinarily long lashes, like Mr. Crippa's. Thin nose, big mouth. When he laughed or smiled his lips — like Mom's an' Aunt Rose's, with the ridge coming to a point just beneath the base of the nose — suddenly expanded the full length of his small face and made his peach-colored cheeks swell into rosy mounds under his eyes so that one could hardly see them. His big curly head was balanced upon a long skinny neck just like a baby bird!

Skinnier than a telegraph wire! Pigeon-toed. Can't fight, can't go out of the yard. Shoots marbles good, though.

A wave of pity for Toodle-lum swept over him. He's crazy! Watching him laugh and cry at the same time, wondering how it was possible — with just a flicker of his lashes or a flash of fire that he coaxed into his eyes. Just like a girl!

And now he felt shame mixed with jealousy at the memory of how Toodle-lum always shied away when Amerigo hit him because he was mad because he had won his marbles. Amerigo cried until he gave them back, and then wanted to do something wonderful for him like giving him his wineballs, or lending him the jackknife that he got for Christmas to play mumble-peg with or something like that.

His mother's name was Hazel and she was Mrs. Shields's youngest daughter. And then there was Margret who was twenty-eight but pretended to be twenty-four. And then Jimmy, the oldest next to Maggie. Old lady Shields couldn't bully her, she worked for her living. Lived down on the first floor next to Mr. Dan. Jimmy was a porter in a hotel out south, and George didn't do anything but drink, until the old lady started to giving him hell, then he would get a job for a few days until she quieted down.

Miss Margret's pretty! He saw her thick black hair and dark daring eyes and followed the line of her lips from memory. They were always smiling at the men who passed by. He wished he were a man.

He remembered sitting on the back steps of her house one Saturday morning when she was bending over a tub full of dirty clothes. A thin trickle of sweat rolled down her neck and between her breasts, which were exposed by the sagging lapels of the bathrobe she'd clumsily fastened with a safety pin. She looked up just in time to catch him looking down her bosom.

"What! What-you-lookin' at you little *black rascal!*" she exclaimed. "Why *you* — he's — ha! Are you lookin' down my bosom, boy? *Already!* Why, you filthy li'l bastard! Git out a my sight! An' go tell that *ugly biggidy* momma a yourn that if I ever catch you — or hear tell a you — lookin' at what ain' none a your black business *agin* I'm gonna slap the piss out a you! Now git!"

He looked like his mother. She was sick all the time and her eyes were always red. She cried a lot and laughed a lot. But not the way T. C. laughed, or like Mom and Dad's, or Bra Mo's or anybody's.

"Them's hustlin' women, Amerigo," Rutherford was saying. "You stay away from that house. You let Toodle-lum come over *here* if you just gotta play with 'im."

"Yeah," said Viola testily, "or maybe your daddy could go over an' play in his yard if he can't come over here. That Margret don' do nothin' but swish 'round on that porch half naked an' make eyes at 'im, no way!"

"Aw Babe, what I want with a tramp like that?"

"The other evening," Viola interrupted with narrow eyelids, "she was over there just a singin' to beat the band — 'I kin git more men than a passenger train kin haul!' — in that loud twang a hers when Hazel, 'er own sister, yelled upstairs: 'You can't git none of 'um to marry you!' an' laughed — you know the way she does? Heeee — all high like she was wheezin'. The folks up an' down the alley sure had a laugh on her!"

The Shieldses' house loomed up in an ominous shadow in the falling darkness, its bulky mass perforated by the soft yellow light of coal oil lamps that filled the windows. Silent figures of white and black men slipped in through the back from the Charlotte Street side. The blues spewed out in the sticky air, shadows danced upon the walls, a carelessly closed door idled open: Margret sitting on a white man's lap, holding out a glass into which Mrs. Shields poured whiskey, while the white man ran his hand up under her dress between her legs. "You quit that now!" she giggled, just before Mrs. Shields prudently shut the door.

The image faded away and blended into the expansive feeling of a Saturday morning when Viola let him go out and play in the alley because it was a holiday and she didn't have to work. He slipped over to play marbles with Toodle-lum. Toodle-lum won, and then they sat on Mr. Everett's windowsill. Mr. Everett, a bald-headed old man with the face of a devil, heard them arguing about the marbles, which Toodle-lum had won, and poured a can of ice water through the screen onto the sill and wet their bottoms. Then they went up on Toodle-lum's back porch to sit in the sun and dry themselves. Presently they heard a sound like that of someone struggling in the bedroom. A bar of shade falling across the screen of the bedroom door enabled them to look in. Miss Hazel was lying on the bed and a man was lying on top of her. She was scratching him and whining and he was kissing her and squeezing her titties. The noises they made sounded funny. The man started to tear at her dress.

At this point Mrs. Shields came out of the kitchen downstairs and called: "Toodle-lum! Aw-Toodle-lum!"

"Yes'm! Yes'm!" answered Toodle-lum. Amerigo hit him hard in the ribs but it was too late. Miss Hazel, hearing voices just outside the door, jumped up from the bed, ran to the door and looked out. Her dress, which buttoned down the front, was open. The children stared at her naked body. Her hair was all in her face and her red eyes flashed angrily.

"Git away from here you li'l black muthah-*fuggah!*"

Meanwhile Mrs. Shields came grunting up the steps as fast as she could, slowly enough, she being a fat old woman, to allow them to rush past her, but not before she could swat them twice with the broom.

"Little sons a bitches!" she exclaimed. Amerigo ran home as fast as he could. From his front porch he heard the old woman screaming. "Toodle-lum, you *git* in this house! I'm gonna warm your little behind!"

"Yes'm, yes'm." His frightened voice hung — stuck — in the air, and Amerigo felt a heavy depressive loneliness steal upon him.

The sun was burning its way through eleven o'clock, diffusing its hard blatant light through the alley, raising blisters upon the ancient porch banisters and drying the cracks in the cement yard.

The cool, dank bouquet of vatted wine rose from Mrs. Crippa's cellar and mixed with the smell of parmesan cheese hanging in mold-encrusted loaves from the ceiling while blue-green flies buzzed happily around the half-shut garbage can in the yard at the foot of the porch steps. The putrid odor of rotting food permeated the air.

He descended the steps and lifted the lid of the can and gazed at its contents with an expression signifying both curiosity and revulsion. Swarming in the midst of a bile-green mass of decaying food — which in turn rested within the center of a dull, brick-red substance that appeared to have once been chili-beans — was a heap of tallow-white maggots! The smell was revolting, but he was fascinated by the colors, for now he discovered the volatile yellow hues of several lemon rinds strewn among the green, and that the outer edge of the mass of chili-beans were of a lighter shade of reddish brown, having dried more quickly in the sun. He narrowed his eyelids and discovered that the colors blended in a remarkable way, the whiteness of the maggots causing the lemon rinds to appear of a more saturated yellow, almost white, and at the same time adding a richness to the deep brown, almost black, watermelon seeds!

Then something moving on Aunt Lily's porch attracted his attention. He turned his head and peered between the banister railings into the shadows of the porch. At that instant the sharp putrid odor from the garbage can stung his nostrils with the intensity of some volatile poison. Ugh! he cried aloud, and clamped the top down over the can and hammered it more firmly with the heel of his bare foot.

The odor safely sealed in the can, he returned his attention to the porch. A small kitten emerged from the hidden corner formed by the concrete wall and the shed. It was about six months old. It advanced with some difficulty up the three concrete steps into the yard. It approached Amerigo and paused a few feet from where he stood. He picked it up and stroked its soft blue-gray fur. He looked down into its yellow eyes and they regarded him with a savage tenderness. He felt its delicate spine tremble in his hands, reverberate with a gentle purring murmur.

"Me," said Rutherford's voice, "an' a gang a niggahs usta go snake huntin' ever' Sad'dy on Clairmount Hill an' all up in them woods 'roun' Cliff Drive an' down by the railroad tracks. An' don' let us come 'cross no cats! M-a-n, we was rough on a cat. We'd throw 'um up in the air by the tail! An' chunk rocks at 'um."

He saw his father's mischievous smile as he spoke, he heard his mother's reproach and his father's reply: "They got nine lives, ain' they?"

He trembled with a deep sense of mystery, fear, and curiosity. He stroked the cat gently. Again. It purred and fanned its tail with a gentle show of satisfaction. Gradually, unaware that he did so, he gripped the kitten tightly in his hands and moved breathlessly up the steps. He stood over the banister and rested his elbows upon the rail, but he did not feel the heat of the sun upon it, nor did he hear the distant hum of traffic that rose from the boulevard and from the avenue. He did not see that the elm trees in Miss Ada's yard swayed gently and that their branches cast cool transparent shadows against the back wall of the empty house. The kitten wriggled in the free air beyond the railing. His arms, then his hands grew gradually numb. He looked at the soft fur of the kitten's head until it blurred out of focus. And suddenly his hands were empty. His eyes followed it down . . .

"Boom!" he whispered softly, almost in an attitude of prayer.

On her feet! he cried excitedly, stealing frenziedly down the steps as if in a dream. When he reached the yard he seized the trembling kitten, clutched it to his breast, and again ascended the steps, and let it fall.

Boom!

Not hard enough.

This time he ran down the steps and grabbed the kitten by the nape of the neck, and when he had gained the porch he took her by the tail and flung her high in the air. She screamed, arched her back and stretched her four legs wide apart — as she sailed through the air and down with a wild static freedom Boom!

She stood trembling, dazed, where she landed.

Why doesn't she run away? Beads of sweat gathered on his forehead. He breathed in short hectic gasps and his heart pounded in his ears. Go away, cat! But she didn't go away. She trembled where she stood. All right then, I'll show you!

He snatched her up and scrambled to the porch and blindly flung her over.

Boom!

Boom!

How many lives did Dad say? Four to go! Four!

Boom!

Boom!

Boom!

Weary in his soul, sick with shame and mortally afraid he approached the kitten again. Each step he took with dread, but he couldn't stop.

"Stop!" cried a voice, and he looked about him and tried to ferret out the witnessing eyes of the hot sultry morning. He studied all the windows and all the doors of all the houses carefully. Not a soul in sight. He listened. No sound save the sound of his heart pulsing in his throat against the background of the sound that came from far away, from the top of the alley, from the avenue, a large cruel indifferent sound that was suddenly drowned out by the voice that shouted in his ears:

Why don't you die, cat?

At that instant a cloud drenched the yard in shade. A cool breeze blew over his face, chilling the sweat upon his brow.

"Run away! Shoo!"

She stood trembling at the foot of the steps. He stooped down to pick her up and she looked at him. He took up his heavy burden and flung it down once more. He followed her descent out of the corner of his eye.

Boom!

He stood before her, his whole body aching with fear. Just as he reached down to pick her up another cloud passed over the sun. Her eyes flashed demonically in the light. He sprang away from her, jamming his knee against the stone at the foot of the steps. A sharp pain shot through his knee and the bruise started to bleed. He grabbed her by the tail and, burning with a sort of terror, carried her up to the porch. He swung her forward, then backward, in order to get enough momentum to swing her as far as he could. But on the backward swing a sharp pain seared the back of his hand. His knuckle was torn and blood flowed from the skin around the bone.

He put the kitten down and looked at her. She trembled at his feet. He bent down and stroked her fur. Then he went into the kitchen and filled a bowl with cornflakes and milk and spread a spoonful of plum preserves upon it. He took it out to the porch and placed it before her. But she did not eat. She trembled where she stood.

Presently a trickle of blood oozed out of the corner of her mouth. She began to cough violently. He ran to the farthest corner of the porch and looked at her. Gradually she ceased coughing. She half fell, half lay down before the bowl of cornflakes. Her eyes shone with a dull glare. They were looking at *him!* The blood continued to flow from her mouth, but she did not move again.

The twelve o'clock whistle blew.

He dashed into the front room and got an old copy of the *Voice* and wrapped the cat up in it. Then he slipped quickly down the steps and into the lot of the empty house and threw it into the hole filled with trash where the floor had caved in. Then he ran back up onto the porch and into the kitchen and found the scrub rag in a pail by the sink. He filled the pail with water and got the broom and carried them out onto the porch as quickly as he could.

Bra Mo's truck rattled down the alley. Big Tom zoomed up the alley in a red truck and stopped in front of his house. And now he heard voices in the alley, people were coming home to lunch!

He hastily splashed the water on the bloodstains and swished the broom over the spot where the cat had laid its head, drying it thoroughly with the rag. When he had finished he took the rag, pail, and broom back in the kitchen and put them away. Then he went into the toilet and vomited. After that he washed his face with cold water and waited for his mother to come.

"Did you stay in the yard like I told you, babe?" Viola asked, filling his plate with warmed-over beans from last night.

"Yes'm."

She fished out a piece of fat meat and put it on his plate. Then she chopped up part of a Spanish onion and strewed it over the beans and poured out a glass of cold buttermilk from the bottle she'd brought with her.

"Ain't you hungry?" noticing that he wasn't eating. She took a pan of corn bread out of the oven, sliced a wedge, and put it on his plate.

"No'm."

"What's the matter with you? You look a little ashy in the face." She noticed his hand and his knee. "What happened to your hand an' your knee?"

Jesus knows! replied a voice.

I killed the cat nine — *ten* times! . . . he thought, but no sound escaped his mouth. His heart pounded and the sick feeling rose once more to his throat.

"What happened to your hand an' your knee? . . ." Viola was asking.

"I hurt it."

"Where?" examining the wound more closely.

"On the step in the yard."

"You got a nasty gash there." She led him into the middle room and sat him down on the vanity stool. She rummaged in the middle drawer for bandages. Then she washed and dressed the cuts on knee and hand. "There, is that better?"

"Yes'm."

She took him in her arms.

"No wonder you look so peaked. Come on, now, baby, an' eat your lunch. You'll feel a lot better with some hot food in your stomach."

The one o'clock whistle blew. Viola had dashed out of the house a little before twelve-thirty promising to bring him something nice if he would be a good boy and not go out of the yard.

He sat on the orange crate waiting for five o'clock. He looked at the spot where the cat had died. It had dried and was cleaner than the rest of the porch. "Like there never was a cat!" His heart gladdened to the idea.

Jesus knows! said a voice. It sounded as though it had come from the hole into which he had thrown her. He glanced nervously at the empty house.

Who among you here in God's house today ain' got some secret locked up in his heart!

This time the voice came from behind him. He turned around and saw Mrs. Crippa's lips moving as she stepped onto her porch. He held his breath in fear that she would come over and accuse him. Instead she descended to the cellar carrying a glass water pitcher. A few minutes later she returned with the pitcher filled with wine. Looks like blood!

One o'clock slipped into two o'clock. He went down into the yard and leaned over the fence. He stared at the empty house for a long time. He peered into the hole where the cat lay. Then after a while he went down to the shed on Aunt Lily's porch and took out an old hammer, some old rusty nails and a saw, and some scraps of lumber Rutherford had brought home. I'll make a jig.

"A three-wheeled wagon shaped like a triangle," he heard Rutherford say. "With a long axle supportin' the back wheels an' a short one — an iron rod — in front."

He worked lifelessly at his task in the far corner of the yard near the gate separating it from the shoot that led to Campbell Street. It was shady there because of the great oblique shadow thrown by Miss Ada's house.

Suddenly a lean hungry-looking tiger cat jumped up on the fence and walked along its edge. Its shadow fell upon the yard. He froze with terror. The cat! He turned to see if it really was really *her.* The strange cat jumped onto the shed and sniffed and then jumped down onto Aunt Lily's porch and stood for a moment within the shadows where he had discovered *her.* Suddenly its head appeared over the edge of the concrete wall. It was ascending the steps. It was in the yard. It sat on the stone step at the foot of the staircase where he had hurt his knee. It sniffed at the dried blood. He lowered his eyes and stared at the cracks in the yard. He felt the cat *looking at him!* He lifted his eyes and the cat stared at him for several seconds. The sun shone fully upon its face, upon its eyes.

"Git away, cat!" He raised his hammer threateningly. A chilling breeze wafted his body. The shade seemed darker, though the sun shone brightly.

"*Scat!*" again raising the hammer. The cat retreated, but paused on the middle step halfway up the stair, and continued to stare at him.

"Go away, *cat!*" The cat ran up to the porch. It sniffed at the clean spot. Then it sat on and stared at him, as before.

How does he *know?* He threw the hammer at the cat, but missed and tore a hole in the bottom of the screen. The cat leaped in three bounds from the porch onto the shed and into the lot of the empty house and disappeared into the hole into which he had thrown *her!*

"What your momma a-gonna say abouta that, Tony, ey?"

Mrs. Crippa stood on her porch looking at him.

She *knows!* She'll *tell!* "About what?" he exclaimed desperately.

"That hole in the door!" waving her forefinger at him, her face wrinkling into a smile. "Ah Tony, you a bad boy, but I gonna geeva you somatheeng just the same!"

He went over to her porch and she handed him two over-ripe peaches.

"Thank you, ma'am."

She went back into the kitchen and he threw the peaches over the fence. Just then a swarm of flies swooped down upon the lid of the garbage can.

Two o'clock slipped into three o'clock. But not before many leaves had fallen from the elm trees, and Bra Mo had made several trips to the neighboring houses burdened with heavy cakes of ice, not before many sparrows had scavenged crumbs from the porch banisters and windowsills and pigeons had made love on the hot roofs. From the alley came the smell of burning tar, which meant that Mr. Harrison was repairing the roof of Aunt Nancy's house. Shorty had made several sorties up from the ground floor and had finally disappeared within the shadows of the neighboring back porch. Unc Dewey had come to the back door and looked out and then returned to the middle room where he lay across the bed and cooled himself with a palm-leaf fan. Now Miss Sadie appeared on the back porch in her slip.

"Kin you go to the store for me, honey?"

"No'm, Mom told me not to go out a the yard."

"I'll give you a nickel, baby."

"I can't."

"That's right, honey, you do what your momma tell you. Bless your li'l heart!" She stepped back into the house. Then Mrs. Derby came out on her porch.

"My, my! What a good little boy you is, 'Mer'go! Just a-playin' all by yourself, just like a li'l man, so quiet an' peaceful. Your momma gonna be proud a you one a these days. Heah, baby, I got a piece a choc'lit cake I been savin' for you." She started into her kitchen.

"I can't!"

"What? You can't eat no choc'lit cake? Your momma won' eat you if'n you take a little piece. Just a teeny-weeny li'l piece!"

He took the cake.

Policeman Jackson's dog, Sammy, a mongrel hound with a long body, short legs, and a half-chewed-off right ear, trotted casually through the shoot from the Campbell Street side, paused at the gate, and stuck his head through the space at the bottom. Then he cut through the yard of the empty house, hoisted his right leg, and emitted a stream of urine against the door frame and then sniffed into the hole. He growled menacingly, baring his teeth, snorted, and backed away. After he had disappeared around the side of the house he heard familiar voices:

"Aw man, how do *you* know!"

"You don' know *neither!*"

"Don' *none* a you niggahs know?"

The voices grew louder, accompanied now by the sound of scuffling feet and a stick scraping against the bricks of Mrs. Crippa's house.

"Man, I done s-e-e-n it!" exclaimed the first voice, as four boys and a girl finally issued from the shoot.

"Turner Grey an' Carl, his brother, an' Tommy, Sammy Hilton — an' Etta, his sister!"

Carl's dead, said a voice.

"What you say, 'Mer'go?" Carl said with a friendly smile.

He's blacker than I am, he thought, looking at his coarse black shiny hair. Better than Turner's — he glanced quickly at Turner's hair — and mine. It shines like r-e-a-l black feathers. He followed with his eyes the glistening arches of hair above Carl's eyes and the silken brushes of hair that issued from the lids. There was a line of soft fuzz over his upper lip. He wanted touch it, the smooth skin of his face.

"What you say, 'Mer'go," he was saying, as though his tongue were made out of butter.

"What you say, m-a-n?" said Turner with an amused sneer.

Turner must have been about seven because Carl was only in the kindergarten while Turner was in the second grade. A long skinny rawboned boy with tobacco-brown skin and kinky hair. He smiled at Amerigo with a sly knowing expression that made him fidget uneasily. Now Amerigo's eyes darted among the faces of the others. Measuring their reactions, as though he were peering through a web of schemes and plans behind their eyes while concealing his own.

"Hi," he said, greeting Sammy Hilton obliquely because he was the oldest and the meanest. Eight, with a thick crop of hair that he slicked down already. He glanced at the girl. She's mean, too. Six.

"Them's tough little jokers, Amerigo," he heard Rutherford saying. "You stay away from 'um, you heah? You git to fightin' with one of 'um — an' you have to fight 'um both! They momma was like that, too. An' still is! Tougher'n a bunch a rattlesnakes! Li'l black skinny gal!"

"You'd never think it to look at 'er now," said Viola, "she's fat an' squat as a mushroom!"

"An' fight!" said Rutherford, "Why, you'd have to kill 'er to stop 'er! The whole family — the whole kit an' kaboodle — black, ugly, an' mean!"

"Hi, 'Mer'go," said Tommy.

"Hi," looking at his hands to prevent their five pairs of eyes from discovering his thoughts.

"You cats comin' or ain't you?" Sammy scowled impatiently. His brow wrinkled in three vertical lines between his eyebrows. He shrugged his little square shoulders, as though to reinforce his plea.

"Where?" he asked.

"What you care, niggah?" cried Sammy, sticking his thumb in the shoulder strap of his dirty overalls. "We don' want no little eggheaded niggah like you followin' us around!"

"Tee! hee!" giggled Etta showing her big white rabbit's teeth, with her nappy hair standing all over her head.

She looks like something between a cat and a bird, he thought, observing her small face: sharp eyes, sharp nose, wide thin-lipped mouth — like Toodle-lum's — and a sharp tongue.

"Aw, let 'im come!" said Carl soulfully.

"Yeah, let the li'l niggah come," Turner encouraged. "Your momma won' care if you come out a the yard just a little while, will she, buddy?" He smiled a devilish smile, eyes twinkling.

"Where?"

"Tell 'im, smarty!" said Tommy.

"Yeah! Yeah, I'll tell 'im!" Sammy replied. All eyes were immediately fixed upon his face. His little round eyes grew so bright that all of the meanness seemed to have burned out of them. Slowly, majestically, he raised his skinny little arms and lifted his head beyond the tops of the tall trees, as though he beheld a great vision in the sky.

My heart is bathed in the blood of Christ! declared the reverend.

"Yeah, I'll tell 'im!" Sammy was saying: "I know a place! A r-e-a-l pretty place! Where you kin git a-l-l you want to eat! Anything you want! All you have to do is ask for it!"

"But beans an' fatback's good!"

"Aw, you crazy!" Tommy said.

"Crazy *nothin'!* I'm *tellin'* you, you kin have — have — fried chicken, if you want it!"

"What you mean, if you want it?" Etta exclaimed. "Huh?"

"An'-an':" Sammy stammered, "ice *cream!* An' *cake,* man!"

"Hot dog!" Carl said, licking his lips.

"Yeah!" Sammy continued, "an' chili, an' ice-cold watermelon! An' dill pickles an' wineballs —"

"Let's go!" he declared.

"Yeah! Let's go!" Etta cried.

"Shucks!" Tommy declared, "you niggahs is *crazy!*"

"Don' go then!" Sammy yelled angrily. "Come on, gang!"

"Where is it?" he asked, moving anxiously, timidly through the gate, surveying the forbidden world outside with fear and wonder.

"I'll show you, *man!*" said Sammy.

They walked through the lot behind the empty house. The sun burned hotly on the grass. Grasshoppers crawled along the fuzzy stems of the tall sunflowers and settled on the leaves. Flies buzzed in and out of the cool cellar, which had a musky rotting smell from garbage thrown into the caved-in lower floor. His eyes sought out the hole where he had thrown the cat. He saw the edge of the paper. It had a bright pink bloodstain on it. Flies swarmed around the paper.

They trooped down the alley, and he looked left and right in wonderment, regarding it with the reckless and yet wary abandon of a prisoner just escaped from prison. His eyes ravished the houses and faces of the lower half of the alley, which he had only seen until now under quite peculiar circumstances: when he went to the store or to the movies or for a walk with Viola and Rutherford, or when he went to pay Aunt Rose a Sunday visit. From the standpoint of adults he had seen it, from the vortex of the lower end of a triangle, or looking down from the unstable height determined by the length of a pair of masculine or feminine legs. Fleetingly he had seen it, from the front porch in the evening after supper, once from the floorboards of a little one-story house to the ticking of a silver clock blazing in the sun.

Down the alley he moved, toward the avenue end, a cobblestoned corridor bordered by squatting half-pint houses with little two chair porches and four or five or seven steps leading to the alley.

They passed Old Jake's house, a condemned one-story house with windows of cardboard. And Old Lady's house, a two-story house with a huge sprawling roofless porch that ran the building's full length.

Th-th-th that o-o-ol' wu-wu woman's at least at least a hundred an' tw-tw-twenty! he heard Unc Dewey declare.

"Aw Unc!" Viola had exclaimed, "you oughtta be *ashamed* of yourself for tellin' 'um like that!"

"Th-th-th-think I-I'm lyin' huh? Huh? Well, le-le-let me tell you one thing, bbbbaby, when mmm*my* momma was ssstilla a a li li little girl, th-th-th-that ol' woman was was st-*still* a ol' woman! She had gr-gr-gray hair an'-an'-an gran'-gran'-children!"

"She is pretty old, Babe!" said Rutherford. "They say she was a slave, even, an' I heard Mr. Simpson say he knew her when *he* was a boy! An' he ain' no spring chicken! I don' think she knows how old she is herself. But she kin tell about things can't nobody else remember. Git to drinkin' that catnip an' she'll tell you 'bout the time she saw Lincoln!"

"I sure wish I had a nickel for every lie you told, boy! I'd be settin' pretty for the rest of my life!"

"No stuff, Babe! That old woman kin drink more'n *me!* Yes, sir! She just sets there in that old rockin' chair — for centuries, Jack! — just a rockin' an' swattin' flies. An' every now an' then you see 'er duck down under that old apron an' come up with a jug an' take a li'l nip! Wipe 'er mouth with the back of 'er hand. Ahhha — hey! Hey! As far back as I kin remember eeeeever'body called 'er Old Lady!"

"Well," said Viola, "I ain' gonna tell no lie. I don' know how ol' that ol' woman is, but she's the oldest human bein' I've ever seen!"

He was directly in front of the house now. He looked up at the old woman with awe. Her thin white hair was braided in little braids. Patches of scalp shone through the thin matting of hair and the skin on her face was saddle-leather brown and smooth, tightly drawn into the hollows of her cheek-bones, which stood out strong and severe and puckered around her mouth.

Looks like a baby. He grinned, but then checked himself when her gaze fell fully upon his face. One large brown eye and one clouded snot-green eye froze him with terror.

She knows! Staring her image out of focus, her face took on a sinister air. He saw her ancient figure shrouded in a faded blue dress as though underwater. The waves washed her back and forth in her rocking chair. It creaked against the floorboards of the porch, which seemed to sway as though it might collapse under her weight at any moment. He stared into the cool reaches of the porch beneath her and waited for her to fall.

Under the porch on the ground floor were two apartments. Mrs. Farnum lived in one and Mrs. Clark lived in the other. Miss Milly Clark was a big yellow woman with a sad plain face and a wide pink bruised-looking mouth. She wrote numbers and had three daughters. Annie was the smallest, four maybe. Cornelia, six, and Blanche, the oldest, about ten or eleven: eyes didn't match, feet didn't match, a big kindhearted, loudmouthed buxom girl. And Willie Joe. Willie Joe, the only boy. Four, or three. Little! Fudge-colored, snotty-nosed, barefoot, and dirty. He had big, sad, wet eyes.

They ran out onto the cement porch and looked up over the concrete wall that gave onto the floor of the alley, four pairs of eyes, and said in unison:

"Hi, 'Mer'go, Sammy, Etta, Carl, an' Turner, an' Tommy!"

"Girls!" cried the boys in disgust.

"Girls!" shrieked Etta louder than all the rest.

"Et-ta's a tom-boy!"

"Et-ta's a tom-boy!"

"Et-ta's a tom-boy!"

Whereupon Etta and the boys started throwing rocks at them. Willie Joe managed to escape while his sisters' attention was being absorbed by the barrage, and followed the boys down the alley.

"Willie Joe!" cried Blanche, "you come back here, boy! I'm gonna *tell!* I'm gonna tell Momma on you, just as soon as she comes home! You just wait an' see if I don'!"

A stray rock cracked against the window of the house next door. A tall lean iron-gray-haired woman appeared in the door with a small white naked baby in her arms. His hair was a mass of fibrous golden waves and his eyes were blue. Little Delbert! And Mrs. Farnum's his grandmother.

"I seen you throw that rock, Sammy!" she was yelling in trembling voice that was too weak to give vent to her anger, as though she had been sick and was still weak. "You li'l demon!" shaking her forefinger at him.

"Look at ol' Delbert!" exclaimed the child, excited by the strange-looking baby.

"Shame on you, Tony!" cried Mrs. Farnum, "I'm sure surprised at *you!* Your momma an' daddy tryin' to bring you up decent, an' you runnin' the streets with them bad li'l hoodlums!"

His gaze fell nervously upon the cobblestones. He was suddenly shaken by a sense of fatality that smote him in the pit of his stomach. It made him dizzy and caused his heart to beat violently and his lips to quiver.

"I'm gonna tell your momma on you!" Mrs. Farnum was saying, "this evenin' when she comes home! Just you wait and see!"

He grinned foolishly in a reflex of fear that was very near panic.

"What?" cried Mrs. Farnum, "You laughin' at me, young man? Well you just wait till your momma come home!"

With that she banged the screen door shut and hooked it: *Boom!* He felt the sting of his father's razor strap on his arms and legs: *Did you take the money?*

"You comin' or ain't you!" Carl yelled, and he realized that the others were already at the foot of the alley. He hesitated for a minute and then started after them. He stumbled on a brick, which threw him off his balance and made him tear his pants on a nail sticking out of the telephone post that stood a few feet from Mrs. Farnum's house. He felt a throbbing pain in his knee. He had reopened the bruise. A fine trickle of blood ran through the bandage. He wanted to cry.

"Come on, man," said Carl, helping him up by the arm. When he tried to walk he discovered that he had stubbed his toe. The brick had torn a thin sheaf of skin from his big toe just under the nail. Even the air that rushed against it when he hobbled along was painful.

The gang entered the avenue. The pavement was hot and burned his feet so badly that he could only make progress by seeking out the shaded spots. Men in overalls stood in front of The Blue Moon and dummies with clothes on stood in front of a store that had three big golden balls hanging over the door. *That's the pawnshop* he heard Rutherford say, as he limped past Jew Mary's dry-goods store where there were a lot of clothes and shoes in the window. *There's where Katie works. Old Lady's 'er gran'ma.*

The other side of the street was lined with stores: Wineberg's ice cream parlor, Magedy's grocery store, Goldman's grocery store, the Green Leaf restaurant. John Henry was sitting outside Magedy's beside his bicycle. He delivered the groceries.

"Hi, John Henry!" he shouted.

John Henry, a strong, black, bright-eyed boy of fourteen with a big handsome smile, looked condescendingly in his direction. He grinned mischievously, bearing his large white perfect teeth: "Aaaaaw, I'm gonna *tell* your momma you out a the yard!"

He laughed a little frantic laugh and ran on, with Carl's help, after the others. The moist raw flesh on his toe was drying fast. There was already a thin coating of dirt on it. Although it throbbed every time he took a step, he was getting used to the pain. His feet were gradually toughening to the pavement and a sort of hysterical exhilaration drowned out the pain from his knee.

They came to a large storefront. The bottom of its big plate-glass window was painted black and the upper half was painted tan. They peered through the cracks scratched in the surface of the glass with a penknife.

"What's this?" he asked, able to see only a few empty tables and the long legs of a woman whose dress was raised well above her knees sitting near a piano.

"What's *this!*" cried Turner. "You don' know nothin', man! This is a fine broad!"

"Aw, I don' mean that, I mean this place!"

"The Black an' Tan — a nightclub," said Tommy patiently.

An' Ruben fell in about twelve! said Rutherford. He saw his uncle Ruben:

With his eyes closed like this, his arms at his sides, dancin' every step that was ever known! An' then, when all the known steps run out . . .

"Come on, you cats!" Sammy urged.

The rumble of chair legs and table legs and the excited shuffle of feet from the path of danger.

"Look out, Ruben, he's got a knife!"

Boom! *went the gun, blowing a hole in Uncle Ruben's chest, which, by the time Doc Bradbury came, had closed, sealed up the life of Uncle Ruben, while the man who wielded the gun that shot him got away because the people who should find the people who did things like that didn't care.*

They came to the corner of Independence and Charlotte and stopped before the polished window of Pete's candy store to admire the black and red wax pistols with their barrels loaded with syrup, and licorice and peppermint sticks, and rock candy, orange grains of candy corn, teeming in tall cylindrical jars with crystal tops.

They pressed their palms and the tips of their noses against the pane and sighed with unstinted longing, ejaculating unrestrainable exclamations, such as:

"Unnnnnnnh-unh! That sho' looks good!"

"Bet you I could eat eeeeever'thin' in that window!"

"Bet you couldn'!"

"I bet you *I* kin!"

"Huh! I kin git all that what's in there — an' more where we goin'!" Sammy declared.

"Solid, man!" said Turner.

Now they noticed that the window of the Italian bakery opposite the candy store was mirrored in the candy store window. It was filled with chromium trays on glass and marble shelves laden with cupcakes and creampuffs and cinnamon buns and jelly rolls sprinkled with powdered sugar. In one corner by itself stood a huge tray piled with golden-brown doughnuts.

"Looka there!" Amerigo cried, and they all stared at, were transfixed by the double image that was suddenly broken by the swerving movement of a black touring sedan traveling south up Cherry Street toward the corner where they stood. A curly-headed white man in a blazing white shirt with the sleeves rolled up to the elbows hopped onto the running board. There was a shot:

"Boom!" And another: *"Boom!"*

Louder than a cherry firecracker! he thought, watching the man in the white shirt fall off the running board and hit the hot asphalt pavement with a hard slapping sound and roll over one, two, three times before his head crashed against the curbstone a few inches from the fireplug with a dull thud that sounded like the hammer that squashed a big piece of ice wrapped in a gunnysack when Viola made ice cream.

They stared at the man. His shirt was stained with dirt and a shiny sticky red color seeped through the dirty white. Blood! He was getting sick in his stomach, watching it gush in heavy spurts from the gaping hole in the man's neck, while his eyes walled in his head and the irises formed a dull blue ellipsis floating in two bulging spheres of white.

In a matter of seconds the children were surrounded by a mottled crowd of black and white people who looked curiously at the dying man and whispered queries in anxious voices. A gray-headed old white lady who looked like Mrs. Crippa brought a pan of water and tried to wash the bleeding wound. But the blood only flowed faster, gushing in rhythmic spurts, bright red now like strawberry soda-pop. It ran into the street, cutting a path through a thick layer of dust that gathered at the corner and ran down the drain in front of the fireplug.

"A neeger done eet!" said the old woman, still bent over the man. Amerigo looked about curiously, as if to identify the "neeger" who could have done such a terrible thing. All the eyes were looking down at him. He felt a faint tug on his arm, and turned around in time to see Carl, Turner, Tommy, and the others seeping through the crowd.

A siren whined down the avenue. Seconds later a big white car with big red headlights swerved into Cherry Street. Two white men dressed in white got out, ran around to the back of the car, and pulled out a stretcher. The crowd gathered around the men. Amerigo, having reached the edge of the crowd, turned on his heels and ran as fast as he could. But he could not run very fast because he hit his knee again when he brushed past the window of the candy store. With every step the pain shot through his whole body, while the coolness of the air against his stubbed toe caused it to throb with a private, separate pain that was very intense. And the pavement still burned his feet. He looked down the avenue after the others, but there was not a soul in sight. He began to cry. Unable to run anymore, he slowed down to a walk. He hobbled along, blinded by the pain and the fear, no longer seeing or caring where he went.

Suddenly he heard the siren whining threateningly behind him. They *know!* They're after *me!* He forced himself to run. His bleeding toe left a thin trail of blood upon the dusty sidewalk. Just as he was crossing the alley where the meat market was, a voice whispered to him:

"In here!"

It was Carl. He darted into the alley. The ambulance screamed past, followed by a police car. They ran to the other end of the alley and cut through a yard, climbed a fence, and turned once more into the avenue six streets away.

"Here's them cats!" Etta yelled. They approached the little gang who stood waiting on the corner in front of a large building whose little windows were covered with wire grating looking up onto the street from the basement below. The boys peeped down into a large room full of women. They were of all ages. Some were black, and some were yellow. They wore white aprons with white rags or handkerchiefs around their heads. Strong jets of steam spouted from a big machine that filled the room with a rumbling noise, while the acrid odor of strong soap and wet clothes agitated by an unbearable heat hung heavily in the air. The women shouted loudly and laughed as they went about their work. Some removed the steamy clothes from the machines, while others silently, resignedly ironed the collars of shirts, and still others untied the bundles of dirty clothes, which they sorted and counted.

One woman attracted his attention. He could hardly see her because of the steam. She stood over in the far corner of the room, all to herself. She wore a white apron like the rest and a white towel around her head. Fine beads of sweat stood out on her forehead. Her lips moved, as though she were talking to herself as she worked. His gaze, however, was fixed upon the white hand towel around her neck.

That's because of the heat bumps, he explained to himself unconsciously, noticing also that she handled the bundles carefully: to keep her nails from breaking off.

Suddenly the woman looked up through the steamy air and wiped the sweat from her forehead. She looked at the window, directly into his eyes, fixed him with her gaze. He held his breath. She started to move toward the window, a distance of some fifty feet, but then seemed to change her mind, and returned to her station. She grabbed a fresh bundle of dirty clothes and started counting again.

Meanwhile he knelt before the window, frozen to the spot, his heart throbbing as though it would burst the hollow of his chest.

"Come on, 'Mer'go," said Carl quietly, touching his shoulder, and he hobbled after his companions.

They turned into a broad street. There was a steady stream of cars whose bodies and chromium parts glistened in the sun. They ran down toward Fifth Street. He kept up as well as he could.

Nearing Fifth Street he saw a big red house on a hill, nestling in a thicket of flowering bushes. A man sat on the porch sunning himself. Uncle Billy!

He looked for signs of Aunt Rose. Stealthily he crossed over to the north side of the street, hovering close to the stone wall in order to avoid being seen. He passed by the nightclub with the neon sign that read: DANTE'S INFERNO.

"That means hell!" he said out loud.

"Aaaaw, you said a *bad* word!" said Willie Joe.

"What means hell?" asked Carl. Etta sniggered mockingly.

"In-fer-no!" he replied, pointing to the sign.

"How do *you* know!" asked Sammy, "when you can't even read?"

"Aaaaaw, yes I kin!" he declared, glancing back up through the bushes, quickening his pace now, almost running ahead of the others His toe was again caked with dirt, and the blood on the bandage around his knee had dried into a crust that stuck fast.

They stopped at the corner of Fifth and Main and gazed at the old city market and then turned up Main Street until they reached Sixth Street.

"This way!" cried Tommy, and they turned down Sixth Street and proceeded for a block and a half east.

"You see! I told you!" cried Sammy, pointing to a dingy old four-story building on the north side of the street. The upper floors appeared to be filled with offices. Signs were printed on some of the windows with white paint, while on others they were printed with raised white porcelain letters. The ground floor of the building was a big storefront separated by a large screened double door. Big words were printed on these windows, too, but with white stuff that rubbed off when you touched it, like the words on the window of Magedy's store.

Through the window he could make out two long counters, behind which were five Negro men dressed in white jackets and tall stiff white hats and handkerchiefs or towels around their necks like Viola and the other women at the laundry. The handkerchiefs and towels were wet with sweat and beads of sweat rolled down their faces and glistened on the backs of their hands as they dipped into the huge steamy pots with long dippers. He had to imagine the plates because he could not see very well from between the hips and legs of the crowd of men who gathered around the window.

"You'll have to go to the rear of the line and wait your turn, son," said a voice. He looked up into the kind blue eyes of a tall thin white man dressed in neat blue summer pants, spotlessly white shoes, and an equally white polo shirt. The fine golden hair on his arm shimmered in the sunlight as he pointed to the end of the line. Carl and the others who were peeping in the window on the opposite side were also directed by the handsome man to go to the end of the line, but by the time they got there he was already ahead of them.

The line curved from the door in a wide arc that trailed down Sixth Street. It moved slowly through the screen door on the right, while another stream passed out through the door on the left, causing him to imagine that they were both a part of the same line.

A skinny one in and a fat one out! he thought with a smile, momentarily forgetting his toe until he jammed it against the heel of the man in front of him. The pain that throbbed through his body reminded him that he was sorry he had come. An awareness of his uneasiness of the previous night swept over him and he was sorry about what had happened to his mother and father. He thought about the morning and he was sorry about the cat, about the man with the bullet hole in his neck, and about the nigger who did it. The quiet peaceful yard that he had forsaken seemed more remote than ever. He tried to remember all the streets he had come through, but he got lost in the alley where the meat market was.

What time is it? he wondered with a sudden feeling of desperation. I have to get back in time!

"I'm gonna tell your momma on you, you just wait an' see if I don'!" cried Mrs. Farnum.

I don't care, he thought defiantly, feeling quite beside himself. He gazed at his bizarre companions in the line: silent, unshaven men with sunken faces and dumb eyes that stared at the ground. Some, however, looked with candid impatience toward the door, while others shyly tried to avoid the eyes of their companions and to hide themselves from the view of passersby, maneuvering themselves behind others.

The sun slanted over their right shoulders, deepening the red tones in their faces, while their shadows cut a black chain of slowly moving figures into the amber light that fell upon the dirty concrete wall.

Looks like a fence, he thought.

Jesus knows! A tiger cat walked across the fence of heads.

He tried to press forward, to make the others hurry.

"Take it easy, sonny," said a short thin white man who stood in front of him. His eyes were brown and watery and there were flecks of dried blood around his mouth, as though he had gotten the worst of a not-too-serious fight. "I reckon there'll be enough fer you."

He glanced down the fence of shadowy forms and then up the line of living faces. He noticed that their expressions were different when they left the room behind the plate-glass windows. Some of them smiled, others smirked and walked jerkily, gingerly away with a show of arrogance. He tried to think of the ice cream and cake and wineballs and fried chicken that he was going to get.

The line moved slowly forward. Now there were as many men behind

him as there were in front of him, a long line of hip pockets and baggy
knees attached to an odd assortment of run-over shoes and dirty socks —
when there were socks — the holes of which exposed grimy heels, tired feet
with corns and bunions. Amid cigarette butts, scraps of paper, and freshly
spat spit, the air was saturated with the odor of the sultry heat of the late
afternoon mixed with the sweat of unbathed bodies, burned shoe leather,
and tobacco. The more volatile odors of wine, whiskey, and beer spewed
into the air through the numerous mouths and noses and through the pores
of sweltering flesh.

"Over there!" said the man with the kind eyes who had directed him to
the end of the line almost an hour ago. His white shirt was not fired by a
tinge of red.

It's getting late!

"Over there," he was saying, arm extended, forefinger pointing to the
shaded interior of the room. He followed the finger into the full glare of the
sun, which now split the double door into a triangle; one half was light, the
other half dark. He was moving into the room, astonished by the slowness
— and at the same time by the swiftness — of time. The screen door banged
behind him, and he went toward the empty stool indicated by another white
man. He squeezed in between two men who ate eagerly and stared at the big
white bowl on the cleanly scrubbed counter. He looked on either side of him
and saw that the counter was lined with bowls like his and that beside each
bowl was a big spoon and a big white cup very much like the cup from which
Rutherford drank his morning coffee. Here and there was a huge plate piled
high with slices of bread and at every third or fourth place stood a salt-and-
pepper shaker. Turner sat three places farther down on his right and Carl sat
next to the end. Then the men started to ladle food into the bowls.

One of the cooks was a tall black man with a long skinny nose and fleshy
lips. He recognized him because the skin of his bottom lip was very purple.

"Mister Jenks!" he cried. Mr. Jenks who had been looking down — from
the pot to the bowls — had until then taken no cognizance of the faces of
the men before him, but now he suddenly looked up:

"What the hell!" he exclaimed, dropping the ladle in the pot. Confounded
by the sight of the child, and overwhelmed with a powerful emotion not
unmixed with embarrassment and pity, he nodded sadly at him, and passed
on to the next plate, mumbling: "Well I'll be damned!"

He looked into his bowl; it contained a thick milky liquid with flecks of
a dull orange color. Carrots. Thinking of the lemon rinds within the mass
of bile-green in the garbage can just before he had clamped the top down,
he unconsciously scooped up a spoonful. Ugh! He spat it back into the
bowl. He felt sick. A man tugged at his arm:

"Give it to me if you don' want it, kid!"

He looked into the face of a tall white man who stood behind him. The rims of his eyes were raw and his lips twitched. He stared at the soup, and his Adam's apple shuttled up and down the skinny column of his neck several times. He timidly nodded consent and slid down from the stool and sneaked quietly outside and waited for the others to take him home.

The sun was lower in the sky. His toe quietly throbbed now that he stood on his feet, but he noticed it less than before because of the deepening red of the sun. He watched the door anxiously. After several minutes Turner came out followed by Etta, then Sammy and Tommy, and lastly Carl and Willie Joe.

They started down Sixth Street. They walked quietly, guiltily, not looking at each other. They gathered at the corner to wait for the light to change. The heavy stream of evening traffic ground dangerously by.

"If any a you niggahs tell on *me*, I'm gonna beat your *head!*" cried Sammy suddenly, looking suspiciously at him. Etta thumped him on the head and said, "He means *you*, niggah!" The light flashed green and they ran across the street.

The sun shone redder on the strange long street, flooding his face with fiery amber light, flicking in blinding flashes from the windshields of speeding autos. The constant stream of cars whizzing up and down the boulevard made him feel that he was moving at a snail's pace.

It's too late! he thought, seeing his mother and father already sitting at the supper table waiting for him to come. *Where you been?* he heard Rutherford asking, and a heavy sense of dread added to the misery in his feet with each step he took. . . .

After a long while he recognized the island covered with bushes that separated the boulevard into two great thoroughfares. His heart gladdened, though anchored by the weight of a great fear.

Minutes later he was hobbling through the shoot. He paused wearily at the gate and glanced absentmindedly at his house. The lot of the empty house was completely cast in shade and the hole in the caved-in floor was silent, except for the buzz of flies.

He unhooked the gate and entered the yard. The shade of the houses and of the trees had cooled the concrete floor. He shot a glance upon the back porch. I forgot to lock the back door! Did I forget it? They're *home!* He listened breathlessly. All was still.

Now he noticed the scraps of lumber, the nails, the saw, scattered about the yard. He quickly gathered them together, put them into the shed, and locked it. A stench rose from the sewer in front of Aunt Lily's porch and flies swarmed around the thin stream of cloudy water that stood around its rim.

He stole quietly onto the porch. He spied the clean spot where the cat had died.

She isn't home *yet!* Not yet! — looking at the sunlight falling across the screen to check the time. Not five o'clock *yet!* Unwilling to believe that the oblique ray of sunlight had not yet reached the hearthstone of the kitchen door.

Past the troublesome spot, he grasped the knob of the screen door and discovered — because he grazed his toe on the hammer — the *hole* in the screen! It was torn in the shape of an L and much larger than he had realized.

Maybe I can fix it. A slight wave of fearful resourcefulness caused him to pick up the hammer and hide it behind the orange crate. But then, as though the act of hiding the hammer had exhausted all that remained of his will to resist, he reflected that it was too late, and entered the kitchen.

The dirty dishes were on the table from lunch. He lethargically gathered them together and placed them on the drainboard, rinsing the wet dishcloth that lay in the sink where Viola had hastily thrown it. He wiped the corn bread crumbs and the few drops of dried bean juice from the table and then took the broom and swept the fallen crumbs on the floor under the sink between the bottles of beer that Rutherford and Viola made every year.

Gradually a familiar cracking, popping sound came to his ears. He stood still and listened for a second, and perceived that it came from the front of the house. He hobbled into the front room. The pilot light on the radio was burning. He touched the radio; it was hot. Just as he turned it off the sound of the key in the lock of the front door. His heart pounded wildly.

Already! He was surprised that he had not heard her foot on the stair. Viola entered the room. She wore a clean white apron. She looked exactly as she had looked at noon, except that now a bright fire danced in her eyes.

Why don' she *say* somethin'?

She looked him fully in the face. Fear, guilt, and confusion harried his expression and turned down the corners of his mouth and filled the huge orbits of his eyes with tears.

Her eyes swept up and down his dirty little body. "You're as filthy as a *pig!*" Tears rolled down his face, washing two paths through the dirt on either side of his face. *"Come here!"*

He hobbled toward her, but stopped just beyond the range of her arms.

"I ain' gonna hit you! You don' have to be scaired a *me! Look at me!*" He looked into her eyes. "Miss Farnum said she saw you in the alley — bare-footed! — with Sammy Hilton. She said you threw a rock at her window, an' when she chastised you, you *laughed* at 'er, an' ran down on the avenue. Where'd you *go?* Can't you *talk! I'll* tell you where you went.

You want me to tell you where you went? You was smack dab in the middle of them I-talians when that man got shot!"

How does she *know?*

He looked incredibly at his mother.

Her lips trembled and now she began to cry.

"You didn' know it was dangerous, did you! You just wanted to see a man *gittin' shot to death!* An' then, an' then you wanted to have a look at the laundry where I work. Just-just curiosity, that's all!"

She squeezed the brown paper sack she held in her arms to her breast. The paper turned dark brown where her arms pressed against it.

"That was all, wasn' it?"

The bag burst. A thin trickle of tomato juice dotted with bright yellow seeds oozed down the front of her apron.

"An' Amerigo? Whatever possessed you to go to the *soup line?* Well, this is one day you gonna remember for the rest of your life!" She trembled all over now. The sack slipped from her arms. Fresh tears rolled down her cheeks. "Git in the kitchen!"

He hobbled into the kitchen, Viola following him. Blindly she took the strap from the toilet door and began to lash out at him, not seeing where she struck. Tears rained from her eyes. "You, you coulda been *killed!*" Whap! — "In the avenue! With all them cars, all the way *downtown!* Lookin' like a tramp!" Whap! "What'll people *think!*" Stinging blows landed upon his arms, upon his legs. He jumped up and down with pain, hobbling about the kitchen as well as he could to avoid the blows. She noticed his bruised foot. It bled freely, a thin trail of blood glistening on the floor.

"Ah! Your *foot!* Baby!" Whap! A stinging blow upon his rear, unable to stay the impulse that was already in motion before she noticed the blood. "You gotta promise me you won' go away like that again! Me workin' all day in that steamin' basement to buy you clothes, *shoes,* an' *you* — like a *fool* — goin' *bare*-footed!" She started at the bleeding foot.

"Bra Mo, Aw-Bra Mo!" Mrs. Derby called from downstairs.

Viola dropped the strap to the floor, filled the teakettle, and set it on the stove. "Sit down, here, boy!" He sat on the edge of the chair. When the water was hot she poured some into the pan, added cold water until the temperature was right, and washed his feet. "You never done a thing like this in your *whole* life!" wiping the tears from her eyes with the back of her hand. When she had washed and dried his feet she painted the stubbed toe with iodine and bandaged it. This done she washed out the wash pan, poured in some fresh water, and washed his face and hands, scrubbing his neck and ears until he thought the skin would come off. When she was satisfied that he was clean she fished in her pockets and withdrew the "something nice" — a little bag of wineballs — she had promised him that morning and made him sit out on the back porch.

He sat on the orange crate — very quietly, penitently. He watched his mother wearily bathing her face in cold water. After that she disappeared into the front room and returned seconds later with the sack she had dropped and started supper.

It's all over, he thought to himself. It's all right again. He rubbed the welts on his arms. The hole in the screen door caught his attention. She hadn't seen it yet. He looked up at the trees, he looked at the sky. A dirty stray dog meandered through the shoot and crossed the lot of the empty house and sniffed in the hole as Sammy had done and snorted and ran through the shoot into the alley. He caught sight of Bra Mo coming through the shoot with a cake of ice on his shoulder.

Who's that funny-looking man? He surprised himself with this thought, hearing now the high-pitched, snuff-soaked voice of Mrs. Derby nudging its way through her bloodred throat past two fine rows of even white teeth: "Bra Mo! Aw-Bra Mo!"

That's when she dropped the strap.

He plodded through the shoot and cut across the lot and paused at the gate long enough to shift his left hand to the handle of the tongs, which drew his left arm across his chest and caused his knuckles to stand out in bony ridges across the back of his small black hand, the fingertips of which were extraordinarily large and round, with nails of a light pink color. Like dolls with no clothes on. His old dirty cap hugged his head and sweat ran down his small oval face. There was a bulge like Mrs. Derby's under his bottom lip, and his face looked like it was cut out of wet black stone.

Bra Mo grunted under the weight of the melting ice as he fastened the gate. Then he shifted his tongs to his right hand and crossed the yard dressed in sweat-wet blue overalls and heavy shoes. He shuffled down the steps past Aunt Lily's door, shoulders bent, legs bent, eyes straining forward. Amerigo's gaze followed him under the staircase into Mrs. Derby's kitchen.

"Whew!" he exclaimed, opening the screen door.

He said that this morning! "Whew! Sho' hope you don' never have to work like this!"

"Sho' is hot, all right!" said Mrs. Derby.

"You sho' said *that* right!" said Bra Mo.

With a strange frightening detachment he heard the cake of ice grate against the metal rim inside the top part of the icebox with the metal lining painted white, flecks of silver showing through where the paint was peeling off. He smelled the wet soggy butter and cold water in the big bottle with the rusty grooves where you screw the top on, and little plates of leftover food: a grease-stained off-white paper containing a piece of fat bacon, a can of Carnation milk, a couple of eggs, a small can of lard, and half a cantaloupe.

"Looks like this heat ain' never gonna let up!" Bra Mo was saying.

"Sho' don'," said Mrs. Derby, "but it don' do no good complainin', the Lord's gonna have *His* way *anyhow!*"

He could mentally see Bra Mo taking out his dirty little blue book with its curled edges and its little stump of a yellow pencil with the blunt point, licking his black club of a forefinger with his sharp little red tongue and fingering until he came to a page with sprawling numbers, and as his heavy finger slowly ascended the column his brows arched, causing his smooth forehead to wrinkle. Then, wetting the point of his pencil with his tongue:

"Eh, that makes —"

"Put it on the book, Bra Mo," said Mrs. Derby with a slightly embarrassed sweetness, "Mr. Derby'll pay you Sad'dy. What does yo' reck'nin' come to?"

"That makes, eh, eh, a dollar an'-an' sixty — a dollar-sixty!" with a triumphant smile.

"All right then," said Mrs. Derby.

The screen door whined again and Bra Mo came out of the kitchen and ascended the steps to the yard with a lighter step. His long arms hung at his sides. He withdrew from his pocket a big blue print handkerchief and as he wiped his face, it took on a dull velvet tone that was very beautiful, Amerigo thought. Pleasantly surprised, he inspected his friend's face more closely. He had a rather large nose with a high bridge that made him have to look up and out — over — at the world when his shoulders were not burdened with heavy cakes of ice or baskets of coal.

He looked up at Amerigo and grinned. His thin shapely lips drew away from his deep pink gums, revealing two rows of small fine white teeth, like corn on the cob.

"Whew!" His grin deepened. "Sho' been hot taday, ain' it, 'Mer'go? Boy, I could heah you sweatin' clean out in the alley. Hee! hee!"

He dropped his eyes with embarrassment.

As soon as he had disappeared behind the empty house Mr. Derby appeared on his back porch. He swung a big wet gunnysack carefully from his back onto the porch floor, revealing a dark spot on his blue jumper where the sack had rested. As he shuffled into the house, his black rubber boots made a swishing sound on the worn hearthstone of the kitchen door.

He came out a few seconds later with three fishing nets and several bamboo fishing poles from four and a half to five feet long. He stood them in the far corner of the porch and hung the nets on a nail to dry.

One day I'll be big enough to go crawdadding, he thought. The words sounded so strange that he imagined that he could see them, that he could rub his finger through them, and that the white stuff would come off on his hands. Just then he heard Mr. Derby say:

"When you git high enough to stand waist-deep in three feet a muddy water I'll take you. But you have to mind me boy, an' do like I tell you. Then you kin go. 'T won' be as long as you think — a couple a Fourth a Julys an' Christmases or so — an' you'll be crawdaddin' afore you know it!"

The words resounded as though he were hearing them from somewhere down the alley. Then suddenly thinking and talking stopped. He became all eyes because Mr. Derby was taking down the No. 3 tub that hung against the wall beside the kitchen window. Now he withdrew from his pocket a huge jackknife with a handle like the bark of a tree and cut the string around the neck of the sack. Then he grabbed the sack by the open, sagging end with one hand, grabbed hold of the bottom with the other, and tilted it so that the crawdads tumbled into the tub.

He watched the small grayish green crawdads scrambling futilely in the tub, their long feelers wavering, their sharp claws viciously biting the heads, legs, and tails of their neighbors. They all scrambled to reach the top of the pile, to gain the uppermost rim of the tub — to be free. The tub was so full that some of the big ones, which were almost six inches long and as round as Bra Mo's thumb, almost escaped. But as soon as an apparently unnoticed one was about to get away, one of the others, which until then had also escaped notice, sometimes a little one not half as big, would catch him in his pincers by the tail or hind leg and pull him down again.

"People's like that, boy," said Mr. Derby without looking up: "Just like a mess of crawdads." He nodded agreement to the back of his old brown hat knowing that the man whose attention was bent upon his work had seen him nod. *How* does he know? Amerigo looked at the sky, at the trees, at a cloud floating just above Mrs. Crippa's roof; they all nodded, too.

Jesus knows! Mr. Derby was spreading his sacks out on the floor of the yard near the garbage can to dry. Then he stepped into the kitchen and returned immediately with a big can of salt. He poured it over the squirming crawdads:

It's the Republicans that's ruinin' ever'thin'.

"That's to make 'um puke," said Mr. Derby.

He says that every time! — watching the crawdads scramble more confusedly than ever, their black beady eyes glistening on the outsides of their heads like miniature stars. It looked like they had been snowed on.

Mrs. Derby came out of the kitchen carrying a No. 2 tub, a little smaller than the No. 3. She placed it beside the other one and without a word went back into the kitchen. Then there was the sound of a rush of water beating against the bottom of a tin bucket from within the kitchen, and of water splashing against water, and of the pipe moaning just before she turned off the tap. Then came another bucket and the same medley of sounds, after which she immediately appeared on the porch with two buckets full of water, which she poured into the No. 2 tub. She patiently repeated this process four times, until the tub was full. Then she returned to the kitchen and did not return for a while.

She's making the fire. Mr. Derby bit off a plug of his Brown Mule chewing tobacco, which he had withdrawn from his left jumper pocket. The plug made a bulge in his jaw. He put the rest of the plug back into his pocket and set to work, pulling out the entrails of the crawdads.

"You have to git hold a that middle tail fin an' yank it out clean, 'Mereego," he said, "the entr'l is connected to that. Like the bowels in humans."

Mrs. Derby stepped back out onto the porch, carrying the seat of an old wooden chair that had a broken back.

"You kin come down an' help, if you wanna, 'Mer'go," she said, looking up with a warm smile, unconsciously cleaning the cracks between her teeth with the chewed end of a match, which she wielded with her free hand. She put the chair down and continued looking up at him, shading her blue eye with the palm of her stool hand, placing the matchstick hand on her generous hip.

He looked through the screen door in order to read the answer on his mother's face, but she was already out on the porch leaning over the banister before he could utter the question, much less decipher the answer. Standing upon the clean spot upon which the cat had died she was saying: "This mister don' deserve no kind treatment today, Mrs. Derby, not after the boner *he's* pulled." He heard the words but he didn't really understand them because he was busy framing his question: "Mom, Mrs. Derby says kin I come down an' help clean the crawdads?" But before he could hear his own thoughts articulated into words the screen door had swung open and Viola had stepped out onto the porch and was leaning over the banister, her feet planted on the spot. *Boom!*

"This mister don' deserve no. . . ." But that was a long time ago, he suddenly realized now, noticing that the sun was deeper, redder, and that a cool breeze rippled through the shade that drenched the porch! *A searing pain shot through his hand and bared the bone of his knuckle. He put the kitten down.*

"Good evenin', Mister Derby," she was saying. "Why looka there! You sure caught a heap a good 'uns taday! You gonna have some for us?"

"A course!" said Mrs. Derby, "I'll bring you up some myself — just as soon as they git done." Mr. Derby nodded assent, still bent upon his work.

"What my boy do, Mrs. Jones?" asked Mrs. Derby.

"This smart young man," He listened with interest, as though she were talking about somebody else, noticing that a deep amber ray of sunlight cut Mrs. Derby's face into two parts, reflecting fiery points of light within the pupil of her blue eye on the sunny side and casting her brown eye in shade, while her short, neatly combed, kinky hair blazed in fine filaments of rainbow-colored light:

Boom!

"This smart young man went traipsin' off into the alley — bare-footed! After me workin' like I don' know what to buy 'im shoes an' things, an' him with that bad little Sammy Hilton an' his bunch. He let 'um talk 'im into goin' *all the way downtown!* To *the soup line!* I *know* he didn' think that up hisself, but he's gotta learn to do what me an' his daddy tell 'im, else it's gonna be too bad, Jim! Imagine how I felt when I come home an' find out that he's been in the *soup line?* People think we ain' feedin' 'im!"

"*Naw!*" cried Mrs. Derby, "my boy ain' been in no *soup line!* Why, I don' believe it! 'Mer'go ain' just no ord'nary boy. Just look at that head! An' them big bright eyes a his'n. Honest to goodness! Sometimes that child kin look plumb through you. He never coulda done a thing like that all by hisself. Why, when I saw 'im this mornin' he was playin' as pretty as you please."

"Yes'm, I know, he's a good boy. I ain' braggin' just 'cause he's mine, but ain' a child in this alley as well mannered or as well spoke of as he is, but he's gotta learn not to let the other boys lead 'im astray!"

"You sho' said that right! You gotta make 'um walk the chalk line 'cause Lord knows it's hard enough to bring 'um up an' have to go out an' work for the white folks every day. The way folks is fightin' an' a-killin' each other nowadays, ain' no tellin' what'll happen next. Did you hear 'bout what happened down on the avenue today?"

"Ask *him*," pointing at Amerigo. "*He saw it!*" lowering her voice discreetly, covering her mouth with the palm of her hand.

"*Naw!*"

Mr. Derby looked up from his work. His eyes were also blue but of a darker shade than Mrs. Derby's. The whites were rusty while hers were clear. He looked curiously at the little square patch of mustache under his pointed nose. It wiggled up and down as he munched his tobacco. He threw back his head and spat out a long brown stream of tobacco juice that landed on the sewer grate.

"Yeah," his mother was saying, "him an' that little bunch a ragamuffins was right in the middle of the whole thing! My heart, I'm tellin' you, almost jumped out a my mouth when I heard about it."

"How did you find out?"

"Mr. Gol'berg told me. John Henry told him. . . ."

"Boy, you hadn' oughtta be scairin' your momma like that!" said Mrs. Derby. "I *heard* all that commotion up there but I didn' know what in the world he was gittin' a spankin' about. What's his daddy gonna say?"

Boom!

"I guess he's had enough whippin' for one day, but he's sure gonna git a good lacin' down, all right!"

Just then Mrs. Crippa came out on the back porch and descended the steps with her wine pitcher. They all watched her with a suspicious silence.

"Good evening!" she said with a grunt, as she heavily ascended the cellar steps and started the short climb to her porch. She set the pitcher on the windowsill and went once more to the cellar, this time returning with a long red water hose.

"Good evenin'," said Viola with a faint smile.

"Evenin'," said Mrs. Derby.

Mr. Derby worked silently without looking up. He skillfully pulled the middle fins from the tails of the crawdads, threw the long grayish entrail tracts into a can and the freshly cleaned crawdads into the No. 2 tub.

"Well," said Viola, throwing a significant glance at Mrs. Crippa, "I guess I'd better git back in the kitchen an' git that man's grub on the table. It just don' do for 'im to come home from work — all hot an' tired *an'* evil — an' supper ain' ready!"

"If you think your man's bad 'bout that, this'n heah's *worse!* Sometimes I think men ain' nothin' but stomachs, an' you know what I mean!"

Viola went back into the kitchen and the Derbys continued their task together, while Mrs. Crippa hooked up the water hose, turned on the water, and screwed the nozzle until the water came out in a fine spray. It sparkled in the sunlight that caught the edge of the garden, arched high in the early-blue evening air, and descended upon the thriving rows of green things that sprang up from the rich black earth.

I'm going to have a garden when I grow up and water it every day. With tomatoes and radishes and onions and . . . His thoughts trailed off into the little river of muddy water between the rows of vegetables, down over the concrete wall in front of Mr. Derby's porch, and into the drain, disturbing the quiet of a little swarm of blue flies.

The pleasant smell of fish frying, sizzling in the frying pan, came from the kitchen. Mr. Derby, having finished the crawdads, poured off the dirty salt water and threw the entrails in the garbage can. Then he swished them around in clean water, poured that off and added fresh, until they shone clear. They no longer scrambled over each other, clawing and scratching. They lay clean and still and dead.

Meanwhile Mrs. Derby had gone into the kitchen to attend to her boiling pots and to prepare the seasoning. Mrs. Crippa had finished watering the garden and was propping the hose between the prongs of a tall forked stick, leaving the water to flow by itself. She dried her hands on her apron and wiped the wisps of silvery hair from her face, taking the pitcher of wine from the sill on her way into the kitchen. Several minutes later she appeared on the porch with a torn paper sack containing cucumber peelings. Lifting the lid of the garbage can, she smiled up at him and said:

"Ah, To-ny-eh! You beena a badda badda boy? You beata yo' momma? Tisch! tisch! tisch!" sucking the spittle between her teeth and smiling until her nose wrinkled and the cat's paws around her eyes deepened into fragments of humor throughout the lower part of her face like cracks in a piece of shattered glass.

Boom!

He looked at the kitchen door. Rutherford stood behind the screen, looking at him. Sunlight broke across the toe of his right shoe and painted it red. He shifted his weight and the foot disappeared while his outline remained barely visible behind the screen.

He heard Bra Mo's truck in the alley.

"What you say, boy?" said Rutherford.

Up long? he heard him asking, his head silhouetted against the stars while bright crimson rings of light enshrouded in smoke bathed his face:

"What you say, boy?"

The door swung open and the torn screen flapped quietly, dangerously, as Rutherford stepped out onto the porch, propping the door open with his left foot while he reached into the kitchen and lifted two large suitcases onto the porch.

He's goin' away!

His face turned ashy and his lips quivered.

"What's the matter with you, boy?" Rutherford asked, setting the suitcases against the wall.

"Nothin'."

"Oh, it's *somethin'*, all right!" cried Viola from within the kitchen. "Ask 'im what happened to his foot! Ask 'im where he's been taday!" She stepped to the door, her face between his and the light.

"Move over there, son, an' let your daddy set down."

He moved over onto the few inches of hearthstone that protruded between the screen door and fixed his gaze upon the boards of the porch. A fly perched upon the crust of blood that filtered through the gauze wrapped around his toe.

"What happened to your foot? Where you been taday? Your momma told me to ask you."

"In the alley."

"But how did you git in the alley when you was in the yard?"

He shrugged his shoulders.

"What happened to your foot?"

"Stubbed it on a rock."

"Where?"

"In the alley."

"Ain't you got no shoes? What happened to your shoes?"

He shrugged his shoulders.

"What you say? I can't hear you."

"Nothin'."

"Your momma told me to ask you where you been!"

"It ain' funny, Rutherford!" said Viola angrily.

"I know it ain'!" fixing her with a meaningful glance. She diverted her attention to Amerigo.

"Where you been, son?" he asked mockingly.

"Down on the avenue."

"An' then where?" Viola asked.

"In the soup line."

"In the *soup line!*" Rutherford smiled broadly.

"*Men!*" cried Viola in disgust, sharply turning into the kitchen.

"What give you that idea?"

"Sammy said you kin git ice cream an' cake an' things for nothin'!"

"For nothin'! An' you believed 'im? Unh! You *is* a fool! Go in the house an' git me that paper, boy!"

He went into the house.

"You let your son go in a soup line, Babe?" said Rutherford.

He returned with the paper.

"Thank you, son."

Viola appeared in the door with a tomato and a paring knife in her hands.

"*Ten* people told me they saw 'im. What're they gonna *think? Our* son in a *soup line* with a bunch a tramps, an' us slavin' all day long to keep 'im decent. Well, *I* care, even if you *don'!*" She slammed the door. The pane rattled.

"Unh-*unh!* She sho' is mad, ain' she? Boy, you done the wrong thing — makin' *that* woman mad. I bet she sho' brought the tears to your eyes!"

He looked down uncomfortably at the porch. The kitchen door opened.

"You kin come in an' git your supper. An' wash your hands an' face —
both a you! Comin' down to the laundry with all them little brats — an'
him dirtier than all the rest!"

"Was you at the laundry, *too!* M-a-n! Now I *know* she got you! Lettin'
those niggahs — an' white folks, too! — see you when you wasn' all shined
up." Looking down at him though the towel. "Say, you got a bandage on
your knee, did she break any of your bones, do you think?"

"He coulda been *killed,* Rutherford! A dago got shot in the head an' he
was *there when it happened. He stayed there to watch him bleed to death!*"

Rutherford finished drying his hands and face, and gave the towel to
Amerigo. The smile had left his face. He sat down at the table with a
serious air, his back to the door. Viola sat on his right in front of the sink
and he sat opposite his father.

"Say the blessin', Amerigo," he said gravely.

"Lord, we thank Thee for the blessin's we are about to receive." When
he had finished Rutherford looked up and said:

"Well, son, I guess your momma's punished you enough for one bad
thing. She's tellin' you right." Viola put a helping of buffalo fish fried in
cornmeal and some fried potatoes on his plate. She filled his glass with iced
tea. "Why do you think we try to keep you out a the alley? 'Cause we like
for you to have to stay cooped up by yourself ever' day? It's dangerous in
the alley! You kin git killed by a car. It coulda been you that got hit by that
bullet 'stead a that I-talian, or by a stray bullet! Just from lookin'.
Curiosity! We live in a tough neighborhood. We got some a *ever'thin'!*
Hustlin' women, dope peddlers, bootleggers all around us. If we tell you to
keep away from those things, we know what we talkin' about. It's hard for
a child to grow up in this slum an' not git hurt, maimed for life by dope or
whiskey or low-life habits. My sister an' brother came to a bad end 'cause
a things like that. Now, listen to me: If this ever happens *agin,* if ever I even
hear *tell* a you gallivantin' all over the street like that *agin,* you gonna hear
from *me!* You heah!"

Tears welled in his eyes.

"Yessir," thinking: *Her no more than him.*

Rutherford helped his plate to the fish and potatoes. Viola passed the
corn bread. He said: "It's gittin' so's a man's half scaired to walk on the
street." He poured himself a glass of tea and took a swig while Viola ate
silently. "But when *I* was little it was even worse!"

Through the screen behind his father's head he could see the large globe
of light shining through Mrs. Crippa's curtained window. "It was so bad
that the cops had to walk four abreast." All the doors on either side of Mrs.

Crippa's house were open, filled with soft light that seemed to have grown brighter since he first noticed it. "The cops had to walk four abreast! All except Mister Carter! There *was a* policeman, Amerigo! A colored man, a big black handsome niggah. An' *smart!* He usta walk the avenue by h-i-s-s-e-l-f! Aaah! An'-an' he didn' need no gun. He could throw that stick an' git you a block away. I mean break your leg! Yessir! When that man, an' I mean *man,* when *he* walked the block, the niggahs, the paddies, an' ever'-body else got just as quiet as mice at Sund'y school!

"'G'd evenin', Mister Carter!' all the broads'd say. 'Evenin',' he'd say. 'Evenin', Jack!' A bad man. An' he wasn' killed neither, or took for no ride. Mister Carter died *in bed.* He had one a the biggest funerals that's ever been on the north side!"

The sharp pungent aroma of boiling crawdads filtered into the kitchen as Rutherford's voice died away. They were hot and red with red and black peppers, Irish potatoes, and sweet white onions. The smell of craw-dads mixed with the smell of buffalo fish and fried potatoes, and sausages and Boston baked beans from next door. And now a shuffle of feet in the little toilet separating the two kitchens followed by a heavy masculine grunt and the splash of water in the toilet basin and then the sound of newspaper being torn from a sheet and crumpled in an unseen hand and finally the drag and flush of the flush-box. They looked embarrassedly at the table.

"Here kitty!" cried Aunt Lily from downstairs.

He froze with terror.

"Aunt Lily an' her cats!" said Viola. "She's got the cats an' the mice eatin' out a the *same* plate!"

"Here kittykittykittykitty!"

"Looks like that 'un ain' hungry," said Rutherford distractedly, his eyes aglow with the memories of times past. "Yeah, things was tougher than they are now. Money flowed like water! Sexton was a big shot. Comin' home to Momma with a big wad a dough. That's when he bought me that bad box-back suit. My first suit!"

He laid the piece of corn bread he'd been eating on the side of the plate.

"Ain't you hungry?" asked Viola.

"No'm."

"Well, eat anyway. After all you been up to taday, you need some food in your stomach."

He forced the fish and potatoes down and sipped his tea.

"Kittykittykittykitty!"

"You'll be goin' to school soon, the same as me an' your mamma usta, an' you gonna have to learn to look out for yourself," Rutherford was saying: "An' there's one thing I don' never want you to forgit — mind your own business! If you happen to be where there's a fight — shootin', cuttin', any kind a trouble — you go 'round it. An' don' go gittin' into no fights with them little tough niggahs. Ah'm twenty years old, an' —"

"Twenty-one," said Viola cautiously. They exchanged significant glances, and then Viola dropped her eyes.

"Yeah, yeah, that's right — your momma an' me was, was sixteen when you was born. Anyway — what was I sayin'? Aw, yeah, I'm twenty-one years old an' I never carried a knife or nothin' in my life, not even a penknife. If a man's got a knife or a gun an' trouble does start, he'll use it nine times out a ten. But if he's clean, he's gonna do his best to stay out a trouble. If you can't talk your way out a trouble — run! It ain' no disgrace to run. But if you can't run, then fight! But *fight!* To *win!* An' don' do no lot a playin' 'round with them little jokers. A joker starts to playin' with you, see, 'Let's box,' he says, or 'Put up yo' dukes!' Well, you hit 'im right away — *hard!* An' then you say, 'Aw did I hurt you? 'Scuse me!' An' from then on that cat's gonna let you alone! An' if you git to fightin' with a joker, fight fair. An' if he says he's got enough, let 'im up, but don' turn your back on 'im — don' turn your back on *nobody!* An', Amerigo, don' never force no man in a corner; the biggest coward in the world'll kill you if you git 'im hemmed in with no way out! But if you git beat up, git up an' brush yourself off an' keep on goin'. Okay, you tell yourself, I got beat that time. Can't nobody win 'um *all.* They's always somebody — you heah me? They's all-ways somebody *stronger* an' *quicker'n you.* Just as much in one hand as it is in the other, so you don' have to be ashamed. Give me a little more a that fish there, Babe. You must a put your finger in it, it taste so good!" She helped his plate to more fish. "An' comin' an' goin' to school, anybody ask you. 'Did you see So-an'-so doin' such-an'-such?' or 'Did you hear So-an'-so say this-an'-that to So-an'-so?' you don' know *nothin'!* Meddlin' git you killed quicker'n lyin'. Don' *nobody* like a meddler!"

"An' don' go doin' no whole lot a signifyin'!" added Viola. "You have to git along with people. They got a lot a tough girls down at that laundry, an' I keep my distance. I don' kid with *none of 'um*! They git to lyin' an' jokin', playin' the dozens, an' the first thing you know there's trouble."

"What's the dozens?"

Viola flushed with embarrassment. "It's, it's — "

"It's a nasty game," said Rutherford, "a way of supposed to be jokin', talkin' 'bout each other's mommas. Aw, it don' mean nothin' for real, an' sometimes it kin be funny. But then one wisecracker loses an' ever'body laughs at 'im, an' he can't take it. He takes it to heart. An' before you know it they're swingin' on each other! I see your momma's wearin' a new wig!

says one joker. Yeah, she borrowed your ol' lady's G-string! the other joker answers. An' then it starts. Is that so! says the first joker. An' then — "

"That's enough, Rutherford, he'll learn that filth soon enough."

"That's the way it *is!*" Rutherford protested.

A soft knock on the screen door.

"Yeah?" he said, turning around in his chair.

"Ain' nobody but me," said Mrs. Derby, smiling broadly, thrusting a large steaming plate through the door, piled high with bright coral crawdads, with little round potatoes and onions that had been cooked in the juice. Here and there appeared small black peppers and red-hots and bay leaves and pods of garlic, the savory odors of which spiraled upward in coils of steam.

"Unh — unh!" Rutherford exclaimed. "Looka that, Babe!"

"You really laid it on us this time, Mrs. Derby. How much are they?"

"Aw — take 'um for nothin'!" she said in a low cautious tone, making sure that Mr. Derby could not hear.

"Aw, thanks a lot!" said Viola in a tickled whisper.

"Yeah, that's sure nice a you," Rutherford added.

"Just send 'Mer'go with the plate when you git through," waving her hand in such a way as to indicate what she really meant: when *he's* gone, meaning, her husband.

"Aw-yeah, I see," said Viola, taking the plate. Mrs. Derby shuffled quietly down the back steps.

No sooner had she gone than there was a knock on the toilet door. Rutherford looked at Viola and then got up and unfastened the hook and opened the door. Miss Sadie stood in the toilet with a box under her arm. She held the bosom of her dress as she spoke, hardly above a whisper:

"Kin I come in, Mrs. Jones?" peeping past Rutherford at Viola.

"Why, a course, Miss Sadie, come on in."

Rutherford's eyes swept up and down her tight-fitting dress. It was thin and there was nothing under it. Amerigo stared at her vacantly, remembering the smell of her body when she had held him in her arms that morning. Now he stared at her high-heeled house shoes trimmed in white fur.

"I was downtown today. I know Tony's goin' to school next week, an' I saw this li'l suit, an' I bought it. I thought if you wouldn' mind. I bought it for him."

She nervously opened the fancy box.

"From the *Palace!*" Viola exclaimed.

"Unh!" Rutherford grunted.

"Ain' that cute, Mrs. Jones?" Miss Sadie exclaimed.

"Velvet britches!" Rutherford exclaimed. "If that boy goes to school wearin' velvet pants, they sure are pretty an' all that, I ain' sayin' they ain', but he's gonna have to fight e-v-e-r-y li'l niggah in school!"

"But he'll look so sweet!" argued Miss Sadie. "An' look, there's a top to match, pure silk, with a little collar!"

He beheld the suit with awe. He touched the pale green mother-of-pearl buttons along the waist to which the top part was attached and rubbed his fingers over the dark green velvet pants. He spied a pair of pea-green anklets in the corner of the box.

"Look!" He held them up.

"Them's to go with the en-semble," Miss Sadie explained with a grateful smile. She had forgotten the collar of her dress, and now the deep lapels from which the two top buttons were missing dropped away from her bosom. Viola rose suddenly to her feet, stepped between Miss Sadie and Rutherford, grabbing the suit from her hands as she did so, holding it in front of her exposed body:

"My, my, Miss Sadie. I don' know what to say! That's about the cutest little suit I've ever seen, ain' it, Rutherford?"

"Unh."

"You'll have Amerigo goin' to school lookin' like a rich white boy!"

"Then he kin have it?" asked Miss Sadie.

"I guess so, if it's all right with his father. What you got to say, *Father!*"

"Who, me? It's, it's all right with me if it's all right with his momma."

"Well, it's all right with me."

"Then it's all right with me," Rutherford replied. "We're much obliged to you, Miss Sadie."

"Do you like it, baby?" asked Viola with a broad smile.

"Yes'm!"

Miss Sadie ran around to the side of the table where he sat and took him in her arms and pressed him to her bosom and kissed him on the cheeks. Viola's eyes darkened. She took him out of Miss Sadie's arms saying,

"Not that he deserved it. He runs off from home an' acts like a hoodlum, an' Mrs. Derby gives 'im crawdads an' you go an' buy 'im a pretty new suit. If things go on like this, this boy'll end up *never* knowin' the difference between right an' wrong!"

"Tony's just a boy, that's all! Why I'd give anything on earth if'n I had a little boy like him!"

"Well, why don't you just up an' have one?" Rutherford asked.

"Rutherford Jones!" Viola exclaimed censoriously.

Miss Sadie sadly dropped her head. She discovered that her dress was open. She hid her bosom self-consciously.

"What did I say?" Rutherford exclaimed.

"Nothin'!" said Viola, turning tenderly to Miss Sadie. "We, we thank you very much for this nice suit an' these pretty socks, too! I'll-I-dress 'im all up in his new suit an' his black shoes! They oughtta go just fine. An' I'll bring him over to show you when he's all ready an' ever'thin'."

Miss Sadie stood silently, wavering now from side to side, as though she had not heard. Her lips moved silently. Like somebody praying, he thought. Her hands still fumbled clumsily at her bosom. For an instant it appeared as though she could not stay on her feet. Rutherford reached out to prevent her from falling, but Viola cut him with a sharp glance, and moved toward her herself.

"There, there, Miss Sadie, are you all right?"

"I was just wonderin' if, if 'Mer'go could, could go with me to the circus next week. I done bought the tickets. Only, I ain' got no little boy to take. Red, my *husband*, he's just a little boy, but he don' like to go nowhere, 'cept to bed with all the whores in town! Oh! 'scuse me, honey!" tenderly touching his head. She looked anxiously at Viola. "I'm awfully sorry, honey, talkin' like that in front a the baby. I'd treat 'im nice, hones' I would," smiling dreamily, "just like he was my own li'l boy."

"What's the circus?" he asked.

"Hush," said Viola. "Well, I don' know yet, Miss Sadie. We'll have to see. Anyway, there's still plenty a time yet."

"You be a good boy, baby," said Miss Sadie, "an' do like your momma tell you, an' you kin come with me an' see the clowns an' lions an' tigers an' elephants an' all kinds a strange an' excitin' things! Ain' that right, Mrs. Jones?"

"We'll see."

"Unh-unh! The circus!" cried Rutherford. "You know, I forgot a-l-l about the circus."

"I gotta git back now," said Miss Sadie, touching her pursed lips with the tip of her forefinger. "'Fore he gits back. If he ever found out," she whispered now, "he'd *kill* me!"

"It'll be all right, Miss Sadie," Viola whispered uneasily, pushing her gently through the toilet door. She fastened the latch, and looked at Rutherford with a slightly worried expression. He was talking to his son, his eyes were aglow:

"We usta go out an' feed the elephants, Amerigo. Boy that was somethin'! We'd work like dogs, just to git in free!"

Viola folded the suit nicely, quietly, and laid it in the box, lulled by the sound of the circus.

"Ruben took me once," she murmured softly. "If he hadn' died, been killed on account a that no-count Rachel, I'd a been to the circus every year."

"I remember that blue dress your momma got once," said Rutherford, "an' those paten'-leather shoes that Aunt Rose bought 'er on sale at Jew Mary's."

Gradually the hands that had been tying the cord around the box — looping it carefully over the corners and drawing the ends toward the center — began untying it. Presently the box was open again, and the rose tissue paper in which the suit was wrapped laid neatly aside. She took the suit in her hands and caressed the soft velvet gently. She laid the green silk upon her smooth black arm.

"Sure is pretty, ain' it?" said Rutherford.

She's prettier than everybody in the whole world! thought Amerigo.

"He'll look fine in it," she said: "Just like me."

"He's the spittin' image of you, all right!" she heard Darlin' Sarah say.

"Ha! ha! I kin just see 'im on the way to school, an' somebody askin': Whose little boy is that?"

"An' I'll say, My name is Amerigo Jones an' my momma's name is Viola Jones an' my father's name is Rutherford Jones an' I live at six-nineteen Cosy Lane, third floor, south — Garr'son three-three-eight — five!" He grinned with pleasure.

"He's very bright," said Rutherford, getting in on the game, too. "Ol' Jake said he's a great man, an' there ain' much that that old man don' know. He's gonna spin the world on its head one a these days when he gits big enough to be a man, an' learn how to *not* go traipsin' off in the alley without his shoes, so his daddy won' have to beat his brains out, or put 'im in the sideshow with the freaks!"

"What's a freak?"

"People that ain' normal. Like people with three heads instead a two, or people with eyes in they stomachs, or little boys that go around lookin' at dead people gittin' shot!"

"Ruther-f-o-r-d!" cried Viola, "you stop fillin' that boy's head with that nonsense! Don' listen to 'im, Amerigo, he don' know what he's talkin' about."

"What did I *say*, Babe?"

"You know good an' well what I mean. You ain' no fool, even if you *do* act like one!"

"Aw-aw — you done made me mad, woman! Git me that paper, boy!"

He fetched the paper. Rutherford began to read while Viola put the craw-dads away and scraped the dishes and stacked them on the drainboard. Meanwhile he took the tablecloth out on the porch and shook it out over the banister. The crumbs fell into the shoot where the sweet pungent odor of alcohol rose and mingled with the smell of the crawdads, and this mix-ture reminded him of Miss Sadie's bosom, and of the maggots in the garbage can, whose stench now mingled with that of the cloudy water around the sewer in front of Aunt Lily's porch. Mysterious, this mixture of odors now that evening was falling between the trees and the houses, now that five o'clock had come and gone in a twinge of throbbing pain that shot through his big toe.

As he drew the outstretched tablecloth over his head in order to fold it, he heard a step on the stair. He peeped from under the cloth and saw Miss Ada. Where did she come from? He was astonished that he had not seen her descend the steps of her apartment, pass by Mr. and Mrs. Woolf's door, unhook the gate, and cross the backyard. *Irish* he heard Rutherford say, thinking of Mr. and Mrs. Woolf's gray hair and blue eyes. Like Mr. McMahon, the Irish policeman next door, remembering that he, too, had blue eyes and gray hair, and that his sister had blue eyes and gray hair also. Their blue eyes and gray hair confronted him with the fact that Miss Ada wasn't Irish because her hair was black and long, noticing that though it was thick like Viola's it hung down her long neck. Her face was of a smooth beige color, like Miss Sadie's, only Miss Sadie's had little holes in it and Miss Ada's didn't. And her eyes were brown. He surveyed her long thin face with its slightly turned-up nose and wide eyes set far apart.

He stared at her swollen belly — Where did she come from? — surprised that he had not seen her when she had passed through the squarish shadow of yellow light that now stretched out over the little concrete wall in front of Aunt Lily's door.

"Hi, boy!" she was saying.

"She's gonna have a baby." He remembered the way Viola had looked at him when he had asked, "Where do babies come from?"

"Hi, boy." He lowered his eyes and did not speak.

"Yoo-hoo! Anybody home?" She tapped on the screen and entered before anyone had time to answer.

"Hi, Sister Bill!" said Rutherford.

"Hi, Ada!" said Viola with a smile.

"Sit down, you all, an' take a load off a your feet!" Rutherford said with a grin.

"All right, smarty," replied Miss Ada with feigned embarrassment, her smile revealing a row of even white teeth separated in the middle by a gap an eighth of an inch wide. She slid heavily into the chair and grunted, "How you doin', girl?"

"I'm doin' all right. How *you* doin'?"

"Gittin' heavier ever' day! Tryin' to work for the white folks in *my* condition ain' no fun. An' then to have to come home to a evil niggah that don' do nothin' but argue all the time to boot!"

"Maybe you don' keep 'im busy enough, Sister Bill!" said Rutherford coyly.

"How do you think my belly got like this, man? You crazy! My problems is how to slow 'im down! But once they got you like me, ain' nothin' you kin do 'cept try to git along with 'um."

"I know just what you mean," said Viola sympathetically.

"Yeah, but you're lucky! You got a man to marry you, but a woman jus' livin' with a man ain' got no comeback!"

"You seem to be doin' all right."

"You don' know half the truth, honey. I'm so sick an' tired a this mess, sometimes I think I jus' can't stand it no more."

He looked into the kitchen from the porch, his nose and palms pressed against the screen. He watched the tears well in Miss Ada's eyes. He wondered what the screen tasted like, and licked it. It felt cool and rough and gritty. He let his tongue lie flat against it. The tears rolled down Miss Ada's cheeks.

"I promised Momma before she died that I'd try to do right, to live decent. Lord knows I've tried. But these no-good men, all they know is one thing."

"Well, Ada," said Viola consolingly, "ever'body — I don' care where you look — ever'body's got his burden to bear."

"Oh, but wait!" Miss Ada exclaimed in the midst of her tears. Now her slender brows arched cunningly over her beautiful eyes. "I almost forgot to tell you what I come to tell, if you don' know already —"

"Yeah, I know," said Viola grimly.

"Ain' no tellin' just what these young 'uns'll think a next!" Sucking the air through the gap in her teeth. "When Jenks come home an' told me that *Viola's* boy, Amerigo! was in the *soup line!* Why, why, I said to myself, Jenks must a made a mistake, Amerigo wouldn' do nothin' like that, not with Viola an' Rutherford workin' every day tryin' hard to feed 'im an' clothe 'im an' make a man out of 'im. I *know!* G-i-r-l, Jenks said he almost dropped the spoon!"

"The rest of 'um talked 'im into it," said Viola shortly, "after all, he's only five years old, goin' on six, how in the world would a idea like that come into his head all by hisself? As good as we treat 'im at home!"

"He's a man, ain' he! They don' need *nobody* to give 'um no ideas 'bout how to git into mischief, honey! Next thing you know you'll look around an' he'll have some poor innocent girl in trouble! When mine do come, I'm sure gonna make 'um toe the line. After all I been through with these no-count men, no daughter a mine's ever gonna have to go through what I been through. I'd kill 'um first!"

"Aw, Ada," said Rutherford.

"You kin *smile*, Rutherford Jones! A-l-l you men kin smile, while we women have the babies!"

"I didn' say nothin', woman, what you beefin' at me for?"

He came in the kitchen and stood at his mother's elbow.

"'Bout time for you to go to bed, ain' it, mister?"

"Aw Mom!"

"What time is it, Rutherford?"

"He's got a little while yet."

"What else I wanted to tell you was how much I liked the way you straightened an' marcelled my hair. Honey, you do my hair better'n all them gals in the beauty parlors an' you just picked it up!"

"Learnin' don' mean nothin' if you ain' got it in you. I kin see it once an' come home an' do it just as good — if not better!"

"What they gonna do 'bout club meetin'?"

"I talked to Susie on the telephone, an' it's gonna be on Wednesday from now on. I was gonna call you an' tell you if you hadn' come over."

"Kin I have a crawdad?" he whispered in his mother's ear.

"Now, what did I tell you 'bout whisperin' in front a people!"

"'Scuse me."

"Got a name yet?" asked Miss Ada.

"I thought The American Beauty Art Club," said Viola.

"That sounds nice, but you better call Vera an' Mabel an' git together on it *before* the meetin'. 'Cause you know how contrary them gals kin be! That biggidy Miss Waters can't let *nothin'* pass without a argument!"

"Yeah, that's what I thought, too," said Viola, giving Rutherford a quick sly look.

"You oughtta be the president, anyway."

"I been the president once!"

"That don' cut no ice, you oughtta run agin. We got a democracy, ain' we? We kin vote on it!"

"Craw-pappy! R-e-d — hot!" A singing cry resounded from the top of the alley.

Mr. Derby! thought Amerigo. In his big white cook's hat and his white jacket with the white buttons and his apron — all white; with a tray with big, big crawdads on a little wagon. Coming down the alley. Hot dog!

"You always presidentin' anyway," continued Miss Ada, "might as well do it legal. Some people just cut out to be president, an' honey, you one of 'um."

"*Craw-pappy! R-e-d — h-o-t!*" Mr. Derby was coming closer. He tugged impatiently at Viola's arm. Rutherford looked up from his paper.

"Well, I'll have to leave you an' the president to look after the country, while I go down on the front porch with the crawdads an' a bottle a home-brew an' have a look at the alley with my son. Come on, boy!"

"Yessir!"

"Aw naw you don'!" cried Viola in the same mocking tone in which Rutherford had made his speech. "You don' go nowhere with them crawdads without *me!* Come on, Sister Bill."

"Naw, girl, I gotta git back over there an' fix that man's supper."

"What?" exclaimed Rutherford, rising to his feet. "You mean you ain' fixed the man's supper *yet!* It's a wonder he ain' *killed* you!"

"My belly's already full! If he can't wait till I git over there, he kin cook it hisself. He's a cook!"

"Hot damn! Tell 'im, Sister Bill!" cried Rutherford.

"*A-d-a-h.*" A loud voice from across the yard. All eyes turned toward the kitchen door. A tall thin black man in a white short shirt stood on the porch framed in the kitchen door, which was flooded with light.

"*A-D-A-H!*" Mr. Jenks called again. Amerigo saw his purple bottom lip as he ladled out the soup.

"Aw — I'm comin'," said Miss Ada, rolling her eyes.

"Well, *come on, then!*"

"I thought you was gonna tell 'im to cook it hisself!" said Rutherford. "Git out a my house, girl, before that niggah comes over here an' kills you an' gits my floor all bloody an' I have to call the law!"

"Guess I *had* better go," said Miss Ada, laughing nervously. "Well, take it easy," moving toward the door.

"You take it easy yourself," said Viola, rising from her chair and following her to the door while Rutherford pulled back the curtain in front of the sink and took a bottle of beer.

"Unh! No *wonder* there's so many flies an' bugs around here! Looka here, Babe."

"HI, JENKS! I'M SENDIN' 'ER TO YOU RIGHT NOW!"

"HI, VI! IT SHO' IS A GOOD THING YOU SENDIN' 'ER 'CAUSE IT WOULDN' DO FOR ME TO HAVE TO COME OVER THERE AN' GIT 'ER — HUNGRY AS I AM!"

"Babe!" cried Rutherford from within.

"CRAW PAPPY! R-E-D H-O-T!"

Amerigo slipped quietly into the toilet and sat on the stool. Very still.

"What?" asked Viola, turning around.

"Looka here!" pointing to the dust and dirt that had been brushed among the bottles. "That boy kin think a more ways to git in trouble taday than . . ."

"Now what the —" cried Viola suddenly, looking down at her stocking. There was a small tear in it. She looked at the bottom of the screen and saw a thread from her stocking caught in the wire fringe of the torn screen.

"What's the matter?" asked Rutherford.

"I tore my stocking." She bent down and examined the screen. "Why, there's a hole in it! Amerigo!"

"BOOM! BOOM! BOOM!" resounded suddenly from the alley.

"What's that!" cried a voice from the yard.

"Shootin' — what you think?" said another voice.

"Where's Amerigo!" cried Viola.

"Aw — 'em ain' no shots," said Rutherford, "that's just a carburetor explodin'!"

"GIT CHO RED-HOT CRAWDADS — CRRAW PAPPY — R-E-D-HOT!"

"Over here, Mister Derby!" cried a voice.

"I'll have a mess of 'um, too!" yelled another voice. Miss Jenny, he thought, still sitting on the stool, waiting for the excitement to die down. In the dark he heard the clang of a slightly out-of-tune piano accompanied by a guitar.

"Listen to that joker cut down on that bass!" said Rutherford, opening the bottle of beer. A rich creamy foam oozed out and he quickly stuck it in his mouth. In the dark the child could see it all.

"BIG-LEG WO-MAN — " A raucous baritone voice rose between the beat of the bass and the wang of the guitar. Amerigo deceptively pulled the chain. "KEEP YO' DRESSES DOWN!"

"CRAW PAPPEY!"

"Mister Derby! Aw — Mister Derby!"

"R-E-D — HOT!"

"YOU GOT SOMETHIN' MAKE A BULLDOG — OOOO-WHEE!"

He came quietly out of the toilet and latched the door.

"Wash your hands," said Viola.

"HUG A HOUN' — BIG-LEG WOMAN! KEEP YO' DRESSSES DOWN!"

A door slammed and the music ceased.

"Bring a chair an' I'll bring the pillow," said Viola, taking the dish of crawdads off the oven.

"How come I always gotta bring the chair?" Rutherford complained. "Boy, bring a chair for your momma!"

"Yessir."

He quickly took a chair and ran on ahead of his mother and father, down the front steps and onto the front porch.

"Lu-lu-lu-look who who who's here!" cried Unc Dewey. Amerigo put the chair down next to Unc's and smiled. Then he had to laugh, because Unc's glasses looked so funny, resting on the tip of his nose. Unc put his paper down and looked at him. "You you you le-le-laughin' at *me?* — you-you-you li-li-little sharp-mmmmouthed thing! You oughtta-ta-ta be cccry-cryin', the wa-wa-way I heard heard you bbbeat-beatin' your pppoor momma ta-ta-taday!"

"What?" cried Mrs. Derby, who suddenly appeared behind her screen. He looked up at her soft dark smiling form in a freshly starched print dress. "— 'Mer'go, did you whip your momma, boy?"

Viola and Rutherford stepped onto the porch:

"Evenin', Mrs. Derby! Hi, Unc!" said Viola.

"Hi, Mrs. Derby, Unc!" said Rutherford, turning to the old gambler, "any big doin's taday?"

"Nnnuthin'-nuthin' mmuch — a fffew, a few ttttwo-bit catches."

"I ain' never caught nothin' in my whole life!" Rutherford exclaimed, sitting in the chair that Amerigo had brought.

"Toodle-lum! Aw — Toodle-lum!" cried Mrs. Shields from the back of her house.

"When you ever played policy?" asked Viola, settling down upon the top step after having placed the cushion to her liking.

"Ain' no sense in it!" said Rutherford.

"Nnnothin' ven-ventured, nnnothin' gained," said Unc.

"My momma played policy every day of her life, an' I don' never remember her winnin' *nothin'!* Not much, anyway. An' even if you do win a little somethin' it don' add up to nothin' like what you lose in a year, let's say. Naw, people play policy like religion — or somethin' like that."

"Policy ain' got nothin' to do with no religion, Rutherford!" Viola exclaimed. "Now don' start talkin' like that!"

"Hazel? Aw Hazel? You seen Toodle-lum?"

"Naw, Momma, I ain' seen 'im!" cried Miss Pearl from the front room upstairs. "He's around here somewhere!"

"I didn' say it had nothin' to do with no religion!" said Rutherford. "But what you call it — to give all your money away, like them muckle-headed women up there at Saint John's — for a whole year! For they whole life! An' ain' winnin' nothin'! They *think* they gonna win! They *hope* to win! Like havin' faith or somethin'?"

"Well, if-if-ifyou ain' gggot nnno-nnothin', an'-an'-aaaan you cccan't *git* nnnothin', an'-an'-anyou ain' you-you-you ain' never ggonna gonna ha-have nothin', you-you gotta ha-have ffffaith in in ssomethin'! Be-be-*besides,* pppeople, people win eever' day!"

"Then why is it that them-them —" pointing downstairs where the whiskey still was and lowering his voice cautiously, "— why is it that they gittin' rich, an' you *ain'*?"

"What, what you bbbeefin'-beefin' 'bout, li'l ni-ni-niggah, when when you dddon' even play?" cried Unc excitedly.

"There!" cried Viola. "You got 'im, Unc!"

"I was just sayin'," said Rutherford with a boyish grin. "Man got a right to speak his mind, ain' 'e?"

Meanwhile Viola had spread out her little blue-and-white-checkered cloth on the top step beside the cushion and placed the dish of crawdads on it. Amerigo slid through the banister rail onto the step and sat at her feet. She offered the crawdads around while Rutherford and Unc bantered pleasantly back and forth, badgering each other on first one topic and then another. Presently the little company was eating, and glasses flushed darkly under a seething lather of foam.

He looked at the crawdads with their black beady eyes and long thin feelers with pleasant wonder. He remembered the squirming mass of bluish greenish gray creatures clamoring in the No. 3 tub, and squirming in their own vomit after Mr. Derby had poured the salt on them. *Like snow.* And now with a sense of pleasant revulsion he broke off one of the sharp barb-edged pincers and sucked the juice from its hollow shell. He crunched the shell between his teeth and chewed until the good taste was gone and spat it out.

People's like that, he heard Mr. Derby say, as he severed the tail from the body and dug out the soft juicy meat with his stubby fingers and stuffed it into his mouth, taking just a sip of the dark malty beer that Viola allowed him.

I hope it never changes! he thought, as the animated conversation on the porch waxed and waned in a pleasant drone that receded into the background of his awareness. He looked from the height of his contentment into his alley. From the many doors and windows, from the host of familiar faces on the porches rose a gentle swell of talk and laughter interspersed with music — from a radio, a Victrola, from someone singing or playing a guitar or playing a harmonica; accented by the sound of babies crying, a glass shattering against a floor, of automobiles whizzing up and down the boulevard, up and down the avenue.

It filled his eyes and ears with the sweetest sound he had ever heard. He sat listening, his eyes wide open, head erect, gazing at the sky, as though he were listening *years into the future* to the sound of his thought, which now toned like a bell from a high tower.

"Yyyou-you'll bbbe-be gggoin' to-to school Mon-Mond'y, won'-won't you, bbboy?" said a voice. He suddenly realized with a sense of thrilling anticipation and dread that a sharp, teasing, yet friendly voice had detached itself from the great body of sound that reverberated throughout the alley. He looked first toward the boulevard and then toward the avenue, as though the sound had come from there. A tall black man was crossing in front of Magedy's store. He had on a white shirt with the sleeves rolled up. The upper part of his body seemed to be detached from his arms and legs, which were barely visible:

"Yyyou-you'll bbe be gggoin' to-to school Mon-Mond'y, won'-won't you, bboy??"

"Don't you hear Unc talkin' to you, Amerigo?" said Viola.

He looked up into his mother's eyes. She fixed him with a warm questioning gaze. He saw the soft swell of her breast obtruding between his upturned eye and the voice. He looked down, unable to speak.

"Daydreamin'?" asked Viola tenderly, laying her hand upon his head, causing him to burn with a sweet nauseous confusion.

Just then a baggy little man with a huge steel guitar slung over his shoulder came through the shoot on Aunt Nancy's side, followed by a little white mongrel dog.

"Look at that cat, Babe!" cried Rutherford. The man leaned against one of the paneless windows of the empty house. "That joker looks like he was *born* in that suit!"

"I *know* 'im!" cried Mrs. Derby. "I forgit his name. Always with that there dog an' that music box. Sleeps with 'um, I reckon!" She grinned.

A ripple of amused excitement swept through the alley.

"Now, what's his name?" said Mrs. Derby, scratching her forehead in an effort to remember. "Come to think of it, I ain' never heard nobody call 'is name. Geetar man's all I kin remember right now. He sho' kin play that thing!"

The man arranged his guitar in front of him, his dog settling himself at his feet. He lifted his hat high in the air and said:

"Is ever'body ready?"

Silence followed by sporadic laughter.

"It's f-r-e-e! An' *no* preachin'! Haw haw haw! Know what I mean! All rightie, if ever'body's ready, I mean *ready!* I'll ask my fingers how *they* feel. Fingers? How you feel? Mister Thumb; you ready?"

He pressed his fingers on the strings in a peculiar way and struck a loud chord:

"Fingers is ready! Thumb?"

He struck another chord, and another, filling the air with a wiry disso-
nant sound that was both sweet and sad, burning with a fire Amerigo could
not see, but feel. I've heard that music before! he thought with an uneasy
feeling. Aunt Rose's voice whispered in his ear: *Love thy father an' mother
that thy days may be long. . . 'specially your mother, 'cause. . . .* Her voice
faded away, gave way to the pulsing rhythms that issued from the guitar, as
Mr. Geetar man's fingers struck the strings. Now he was tapping his foot.
Boom! Boom! Boom!

Amerigo was mildly aware of a throbbing pain. It burned a little. *Boom!
Boom! Boom!* He looked down and saw that he was gently knocking his
injured toe against the step. *Boom! Boom! Boom!* The toe began to throb
more severely. But the music sounded so good. He couldn't stop. He looked
at his father. There was a smile on his face, and he, too, was tapping his
foot, and his head swayed from side to side. Viola, Mrs. Derby and Unc
Dewey, and all the people on all the porches within range of the compelling
sound were tapping their feet.

"Oh, baby, p — l-e-a-s-e don' go!" sang Mr. Geetar man.

"Yeah!" shouted Miss Anna Benton from downstairs.

"Wo-man, please don' go — oh!"

What if he goes away? Amerigo thought suddenly, seeing the two large
suitcases on the back porch.

"Just turn the lights down low just before you go, but honey pl-e-e-a-s-e
don' go!"

Mr. Geetar man's fingers insinuated a thrilling din of metallic sound from
the strings of his guitar. It caused the blood to run to the child's head.

Them French gals sho' kin Can-can!

Men! — the devils!

She's dead.

"Before I'd be your dog! Before I'd be your do-o-g-u-e! Before I'd be your
dog, I'd bring you way down here, an' make you walk a lo-o-g-u-e!"

"Unh — unh!" cried Rutherford. "Listen to that cat go! Man play like
that ought'n have to sleep in no gutter! He's good enough — good as any
a them jokers on the radio!"

Mr. Geetar man was waving his hat and bowing to the people on the
porches and leaning out the windows. Some threw down pennies, and
sometimes a nickel or a dime. He gathered and pocketed the money with
the aid of a small band of children who gathered around him. When all the
money was gathered he bowed gracefully and put his hat on his head and
ambled up the alley, smiling and laughing, as he ran his fingers over the
strings of his guitar.

He proceeded slowly up past Bra Mo's house. Bra Mo was sitting on a stool in front of his cellar. As Mr. Geetar man walked near him, he smilingly placed a coin in the hole of his guitar box, at which Mr. Geetar man stopped, faced him, and began to play. Aunt Nancy, dressed in a proudly starched apron and bonnet, rocked to and fro in her rocking chair on the porch above.

As she continued to rock back and forth, he remembered her as he had seen her many times at church, dressed in a long black dress, her iron-gray hair swept back and wound into a ball and pinned together with two big hairpins, her dark eyes set focused upon the reverend; rocking to and fro when the singing started and everybody was shouting and jumping up and down; rocking to and fro, solid-like, heavy. She seemed to hold the alley in place as the man played and everybody was tapping their feet.

Now he turned to the other side of the alley and faced the house where Tom Johnson lived. He was sitting on the steps with his new wife, Gertrude, a big, dark-brown-skinned woman with a smooth puffy face, a small thin nose, and coarse hair. At his feet sat his new stepdaughter, Dorothy, a tall skinny girl of thirteen with a smooth yellow face like Tom's. Little Tom and his brothers William and Lemuel sat on the porch with their legs dangling over the sides, giggling because they were tickled about something that Amerigo couldn't see — until he heard the mongrel dog howl and roll over on his back and howl again, while his master played and sang.

Leonard, the baby of the Johnson family, giggled from the window upstairs, which he shared with Miss Myrt, big Tom's mother, a large yellow gourd-shaped woman with dark eyes, a full head of almost black hair, and a small mouth full of fine teeth. Watching the dog, she laughed and threw up her hands.

"Look at Miss Myrt!" cried Viola. "She *lives* in that window! I don' care when it is, winter, summer, mornin', noon, or night, she's always there!"

"Gggguess that's that's why she's so so fffat!" Unc declared. "Dddon' nnnever do do nnnothin bbbut set."

"I bet she's scaired to come down out a that window," said Rutherford, "for fear a *rollin'* down the alley till she hits a nail an' bust!"

Aooooooow! The dog howled, and Mr. Geetar man continued to wang out his tune. Then he nudged the dog gently with his toe and changed the tune, playing faster and louder.

"How'm I doin'a — hey! hey! — twee twee twee twa twa!"

Miss Myrt started popping her fingers.

"Momma, you oughtta be ashamed a yourself, showin' off!" cried big Tom Johnson, grinning up at his mother, revealing three gold teeth.

"Fine-lookin' man!" said Mrs. Derby. "Got pretty wavy hair, too. An' *strong!* Make two a most mens, an' three of a whole lot a others!"

"What do you mean, boy!" exclaimed Miss Myrt in a thin high-pitched voice. "I might be old, but I ain' dead! Leastways, not yet. Why I could play to that li'l ol' dinky tune, even if'n he played it twice as fast, an' not miss a step. I know I'm fat, but fat meat's greasy. I'm tellin' you!"

"Aw Myrt, you know you ain' doin' nothin' but callin' hogs!" cried Mr. Harrison, the roofer, from his porch overhead. Short roly-poly Mr. Harrison threw his round fudge-brown head back and let out a belly laugh, his round jaws swelling, as his lips expanded, into two huge lumps on either side of his face.

"Hee! hee!" laughed Miss Nettie from the third-floor window, while Tommy was hitting her young nephew, Ralph, who had just tumbled down the foot of the steps and onto the porch, shaking with laughter.

"Laugh agin, niggah," cried Tommy, attracting everyone's attention, "I just dare you!" Meanwhile Miss Myrt yelled out to the guitar man who had long since stopped playing and become a spectator.

"Play that thing a yourn, Geetar man!" The challenge in her tone aroused Sammy, Policeman Jackson's dog, whom Amerigo hadn't seen because he had been lying under the porch of the house next to the Johnsons' house. Now he stuck his head out and looked curiously at Miss Myrt.

Meanwhile Miss Myrt, dressed in a yellow cotton housedress and Sam Brown shoes with elastic bands in the instep, ran swiftly down the steps and skipped on the toes of her tiny feet into the center of the alley.

"Aw-aw!" and "Will you look at that!" arose from the astonished crowd, who rushed up to the porch banisters and filtered into the alley.

"So grace-ful!" cried Viola, rising to her feet. "Why, her li'l head, an' tiny hands — they must be li'ller'n mine! Her legs are big but her ankles are as trim as a deer's. She come down those steps like a — a — an' she's almost *sixty* if she's a *day!*"

"Aaaaaat at least!" cried Unc. "Why, why I-I-I-I kin-kin remember —"

A roar rose from the alley.

"Looka that, Babe!" cried Rutherford. *"Unh!"*

"The *Charleston!*" cried Viola.

Miss Myrt bounced smoothly, effortlessly, gracefully to the rhythms of the Charleston, an exhilarated smile illuminating her face and firing her eyes, her tapering arms outstretched, her tiny fingers snapping like popping currents of fire wrung from her arms.

"An' on 'er *toes,* too!" cried Rutherford. The guitar man settled down to playing in earnest now, resting his guitar in the bend of his hip, with the weight of his right foot poised upon his toe, shoulders bent, fingers flying free, stringing the trills that flowed through Miss Myrt's body. The tempo increased. The onlookers began to clap their hands and shout words of encouragement to the old lady. The clapping, the solid beat, grew louder, so loud that it almost drowned out the music.

"Whew!" cried Miss Myrt.

"Don' stop now, honey!" cried Miss Nettie, baring her rotting teeth with a smile. "I knowed you could do it all the time!"

"Show these young cake eaters what it's all about!" shouted Mr. Harrison, throwing down a quarter that resounded upon the cobblestone with a tinkle.

The sweat rolled down Miss Myrt's face, and gradually the coolness of the September evening chilled her body. She slowed down to a halt. The guitar man threw up his hat. "Give the lady a hand!" he shouted, and the alley rang with thunderous applause, which, seconds later, dispersed like windblown rain in all directions, amid joyous commentary upon her extraordinary performance.

Miss Nettie gave Mr. Geetar man a bottle of homebrew, while Tom Johnson, beaming with joy, took a ribbing from his momma.

"My momma, your gran'ma, boy, could dance a jig when she was seventy-four!"

"I believe her, too!" said Rutherford, as Miss Myrt's voice faded into the background of general sound that washed against the stones and bricks of the houses and rushed into the myriad side channels of the alley, splashing against the porches and over the hearthstones into the houses, rising like the insistent waves of a great tide. "The ol'-timers! Them was *real* men — *an'* women, too, Jack!"

The sun was sinking. Sadly, his thoughts dwelling upon "the ol'-timers," he watched the guitar man sling his guitar across his back, whistle for his dog — who ran friskily behind him — and make his way up the alley past the house where old man Whitney lived. He's got a daughter no bigger than me — real old! — who is in the circus. Her name's Princess Wee Wee.

What's a freak? The guitar man was passing by Earl Lee's house. He has no momma, lives with his Uncle George, makes rice puddin' every Sunday. The guitar man was almost at the top of the alley, almost past the row of stucco houses that faced the boulevard where he now paused for an instant, and then fused into the traffic where the dull glow of automobile headlights flashing in a deep rose sky slowly dissolving into an aura of blue.

Soon the light will come on, he thought with a pang of sadness, thinking of bed and night and sleep and tomorrow, and tomorrow, until tomorrow when he would have to go to school.

The seven o'clock whistle blew! Viola shot a glance at him and he looked at her with a worried expression. She smiled tenderly at him.

Now? sure that she would send him to bed.

But then there was the whining sound of a screen door opening and the shuffle of chairs against the door downstairs. Gratefully he watched her attention being diverted by the two young white men who came out of the apartment downstairs on the south side. Pete, the short one with the slick black hair parted in the middle and the skinny nose, looked kind of like a possum. The other man was taller and better looking. He was wearing a Panama hat and a white shirt with a tie. Mr. Pete's collar was open at the throat.

"You stay away from down there, Amerigo, you hear?" he heard Viola saying.

"I'll keep a eye on 'im," Mrs. Derby promised, "A bootleg joint ain' no place for a baby!"

"I ain' no baby neither," he protested.

"Well, if you'd like to grow up to be a man," Rutherford had declared vehemently, "you better stay away from that still like your momma told you, 'cause if I ever catch you down there, even *lookin'* in that door, I'm gonna do my best to *brain* you!"

"What's a still?"

"It's a kind a contraption for makin' whiskey. You take mash an' corn an' . . ."

"You gonna teach 'im how to make it?" Viola exclaimed. "Go on out an' play, boy."

He went out on the porch and sat on the top step and peered down into the room from the banister railing. All he could see was a big table filled with whiskey bottles and a cardboard box full of new corks. Some of the bottles had funnels in them. Mr. Shorty and Mr. Pete poured something that looked like water into the bottles. Only the "water" didn't smell like water. It had a strong, sort of sweet burning smell. He watched them fill the bottles one at a time, and when they were all full they poured some brown stuff in them until the strong water turned brown, and then they pushed the stoppers in.

After that they put the bottles in a big wooden box and nailed a top on it. Then, just as Mr. Shorty and lifted the box in order to put it in the corner behind the door, he looked up and saw him watching them. He said something to Mr. Pete and then Mr. Pete said something to Mr. Shorty in funny words that he couldn't understand but sounded like the funny words that Mr. and Mrs. Crippa sometimes said, and Mr. Shorty had banged the door.

"Amerigo, set up here by me," Viola was saying. He moved to the top step and sat by his mother. Meanwhile Mr. Pete looked up at Viola and smiled, at which she pulled her dress down over her knees, drew her legs well up under her body, and looked with a stony expression toward the top of the alley.

"Hi, Tony!" said Mr. Pete. He didn't answer. Viola drew him closer to her. Then the screen door of the upper apartment of the Shieldses' house opened and banged and Hazel and Margret Shields stepped out onto the porch and sat down.

Mr. Pete and his companion looked up on the porch and grinned. The two young women grinned back. Viola and Rutherford exchanged significant glances with Mrs. Derby and Unc Dewey. No one spoke. The child glanced up and down the alley; it was quiet, too.

The sun had disappeared. There was only a faint rose stain where it had been a few minutes ago. And now he suddenly was aware of a pulsing high-pitched chirping sound that, though familiar to him, he was not aware of having heard ten minutes earlier.

Crickets! He held his breath. The air was full of cricket-sound! Nervously, excitedly, he peered into the darkened windows of the empty house where the wild grasses pushed up through the ground floor and stuck out of the mound of ashes and cans in the cellar. The sound was loudest there. They're in there! He looked at the sky, he looked at the trees, at the street lamp, and then he looked up toward the top of the alley.

Two figures appeared upon the very dim horizon, a man and a woman. They made their way slowly down the alley. The woman carried a basket on her left arm and linked her right arm in the left arm of the man. Every few yards she would halt and take something from her basket and toss it with a wide sweeping theatrical gesture to the left and to the right, bowing gracefully, touching her lips with the tips of her fingers and blowing kisses to the people on the porches.

Here and there someone sniggered, but not loudly, while most of the people looked on with a sort of respectful awe.

"Look!" he cried, as the woman stopped to greet the Johnsons, the Harrisons, Miss Nettie, Bra Mo, and Aunt Nancy, smiling gently upon the knot of giggling children sitting on the porch.

"Shut up!" cried Tom Johnson.

"We see," said Viola thoughtfully, in a tone that checked the smile upon his face.

The streetlights came on, cutting globules of light into the cobblestones.

"Aunt Tish and Gloomy Gus!" Rutherford exclaimed.

As his father spoke he noticed that Mr. Pete, who had leaned his chair against the banister at the foot of the front steps, whispered something into his companion's ear and laughed out loud. His companion did not laugh.

"But that ain' his real name," Rutherford was saying. "His real name is

— do you remember what Pr'fessor Bowles said it was that time, Babe?"

"Naw, I don'," said Viola, "Worthington? That ain' it, but it was somethin' like that. I think, anyway."

"They ain' quite right in the head, Amerigo," said Rutherford softly. "I been seein' 'um ever since I kin remember. But they're nice people, though. They don' bother *nobody* unless you bother them. Don' *never* fool with that old man! Naw sir!"

Gloomy Gus and Aunt Tish stepped into the lamplight. Just above the lamppost, diffusing a cool aura of perfectly round red, sharply impaled against the intense blue sky, stood the moon.

"An' he's always dressed proper, too!" Rutherford continued, "in that old hat, with a coat *an'* a tie an' a vest to boot! You see that coat he's wearin'?"

The child could see him quite plainly now. He looked at his baggy coat. It seemed to weigh him down.

"That's his arsenel, Jack! Rocks! Big 'uns, Amerigo! Half bricks! He goes 'round like that to protect hisself. Jokers always jokin' at 'im an' pullin' monkeyshines!"

He was looking at Aunt Tish. How did it feel not to be right in the head? Crazy? Her eyes shone darkly, brilliantly through a black lace veil that fell mysteriously over the wide brim of her tattered old black hat. At the base of the crown a large pale withered rose. . . .

"I seen him throw a rock at a niggah once," Rutherford continued, "from almost half a block away an' lay his head wide open! An' the jokers on the street wouldn' let 'im bother 'im neither, 'cause he was right!"

Aunt Tish held her head high, proudly. Like somebody important. Amerigo thought hard of someone important with whom to compare her. Old Jake, but he's a man. Maybe Aunt Rose? She wasn't old enough. He thought of Miss Moore, of Grandma Veronica. He thought of a queen. Her head high, poised upon a long slender neck that swept down to join her sloping shoulders, her nose thin and slightly arched with thin elongated nostrils, with thin lips, and a narrow chin coming to a point like a cat!

"They usta live down in Belvedere Holla," Viola was saying, "in a ol' tin shack patched up with cardboard. We usta pass by there every mornin' on the way to school, me an' your daddy, an' T. C., an' Ada, an' Dee Dee, an' Zoo — an' a whole bunch of us. Rutherford an' T. C. an' the rest of them little ragamuffins usta throw rocks at the house an' run!"

"Aw Babe!"

"Well, we did! An' hide behind the trees an' peep out to see what they'd do. An' we all laughed to beat the band when they couldn' catch us. We was just kids. We didn' mean no real harm, I guess."

And then somebody told Mr. Bowles, Amerigo thought involuntarily, his eyes fixed on the old woman.

"Somebody told Principal Bowles," Viola was saying, and he was not surprised that he had known what she was going to say. "They had a assembly in the main auditorium that mornin'."

"How's it go?" said Rutherford softly, as though he were speaking to himself: "I want to tell you a story — that's how he started! An' man, he really told it, too, I'm tellin' you! He had all 'um little niggahs cryin' an' red-eyed!"

"Once there was a beautiful young girl," Viola was saying, "she was petite an' quiet, an' very intelligent an' refined. But that didn' mean she was stuck up. She could be a lot a fun. Most of all she liked to dance."

"'Cause she was so smart she went to college," Rutherford continued. "There she fell in love with a bright han'some young man. He fell in love with her, too. He was the smartest one in his class, the valedictorian, an' ever'body said he was gonna be a great man. An' so when they finished college they got married, an' got a job teachin' in the same school teachin' school up north. They was from the South. He was a good-lookin' man with fair skin an' good hair — just like a white man. An' ever'body loved 'um an' respected 'um 'cause they wasn' stuck up just 'cause they was smart an' had a education. An' they was happy, too.

"Then they had a baby, a boy, an' a year after that they had a little baby girl, an' they was proud enough to bust.

"One night, when the boy was five an' the girl was four, they put 'um to bed an' kissed 'um good night — just like I do you — an' waited till they was asleep. Then they went to a piana recital they was havin' at Garrison School. It lasted till eleven o'clock.

"On the way home, just as they got near the house, they saw a big cloud a smoke floatin' up into the sky. They got scaired 'cause they knew that the children was at home all by theirself, an' they started runnin' as fast as they could. When they got near the house they saw the fire wagon standin' in front of the house. Big flames was leapin' from the buildin' into the sky. All the firemen was standin' still, lookin' up at the two top windows on the east side of the house. The mother an' father looked up there, too. They saw the little boy, his name was — I never will forgit it as long as I live — Mike for Michael, an' the girl's name was Rosamond. They were trapped in the fire, an' the fire was so hot that ever'body was scaired to git any closer. The firemen had to hold 'um back. They expected the walls to crumble down any minute. An' they had to watch their children burn up in that fire — alive!

"They wasn' never no more the same after that," said Rutherford. "They got old. They forgot things all the time — to eat, to sleep. People usta see 'um runnin' an' hollerin' through the streets at night. That was long ago, the old man said, kinda quiet-like, but that beautiful woman and handsome man are still alive and together. They live alone, in a old shack in Belevedere Holla. They live as good as they kin. They don' do no harm to nobody. They talk to theyself a lot, an' people think that 'cause they do that they crazy. The man has a sad an' sometimes troubled look on his face, an' he has to wear old worn-out clothes, that's why the people nicknamed 'im Gloomy Gus. The woman's called Aunt Tish 'cause she usta take scraps of colored tissue paper an' make all kinds a flowers and ribbons an' stick 'um in her hair.

"Children often throw rocks at 'um, but I suppose God'll forgive 'um both, the young an' the old people, 'cause they just don' understand. Just like I'm sure that God'll forgive Aunt Tish an' Gloomy Gus for bein' the devoted parents of Mike an' Rosamond."

All the while Rutherford had been speaking, Aunt Tish had been staring up at the streetlight.

"'Course, that ain' exactly the way he told it," said Rutherford, "but that's the idea. He spoke a English that wouldn' quit! Distinguished an' c-l-e-a-r! An' simple enough for kids to understand what he was talkin' about. Takes a real educated man to do that!"

The old lady was still looking at the light.

She's looking past it, Amerigo thought. She's looking at the moon, at the sky — through the sky! He followed her gaze and suddenly beheld with joyful surprise a thin yellow star.

A sparrow flitted off the roof of the empty house and settled on the telegraph wire. Distracted by its flight, Aunt Tish followed its sweeping movement, smiling all the while, and then, noticing the people on the porch, she extended her arms in a greeting. Her gaze rested upon his face for more than a minute.

Her face was dirty, like it was made from mud. Fine wrinkles radiated from the corners of her black shining eyes and from the corners of her mouth and veined her neck.

"Good evening, friends!" she said with a gentle flurry of movement, displaying her long tattered dress, which dragged the ground. It was of a faded rose color and was caked with dirt and soiled with dark brown stains. Now and then she gathered her skirts in order to take a mincing step, revealing coquettishly another skirt of a faded green color of some shiny material trimmed with dirty white ruffles, and another still, bright red with a torn hem, and still another, this time a bright yellow one. She was shod in tightly laced shoes that extended several inches above her ankles. They were badly scuffed and torn at the seams.

"Good evening, friends!" she was saying sweetly, bowing deeply from the waist, blowing kisses from the tips of her long grimy fingers. She took a withered rose from her basket and tossed it up to Hazel Shields, who tossed it back into the alley with a mocking laugh. Aunt Tish watched it fall. It landed near Mr. Pete's foot. His companion stooped to pick it up, but before he could do so, Mr. Pete kicked it into the middle of the alley.

"Oh! Poor dear!" cried Aunt Tish, wringing her hands distractedly, "you've lost your mother! You've fallen from your nest, precious, precious, precious. Lost? Lost! Are you lost? Lost! Lost!"

Her words echoed up and down the alley. The whizzing cars at either end of the alley seemed to take up the cry: *Lost! Lost! Lost!*

"Crazy as a bedbug!" said Miss Margret, and went into the house and slammed the door.

Mr. Pete tossed a small stone at Gloomy Gus, but he was watching Aunt Tish so intently that he did not notice. Mr. Pete picked up another stone.

"Aw-aw!" said Rutherford. "Babe, you sit up here on the porch." Viola moved without a word, pulling Amerigo with her.

"Come! Come my sweet!" said Aunt Tish tenderly to the flower, which she now cuddled in the palms of her hands. "Here you are, sir," turning to Gloomy Gus, who took it carefully. Then a look of fear came into her face. "No! No!" taking the rose from him. She smiled coquettishly: "I shall wear it in my hair!" sticking the flower between the wisps of dark brown hair that escaped from the edges of her hat. "Wheeee!" she threw her arms wildly above her head, causing her basket to slide off her arm and fall to the ground, scattering the withered flowers. There were carnations, roses, irises, and bruised apples, peaches, and oranges. They rolled over the cobblestones. "Come back, my children!" she cried, running after them. "Sweet dears!" gathering them tenderly and placing them carefully in the basket, which she now held in one hand while she gestured with the other, crying.

"Pretty things for a pretty penny! Sweet ladies! Gallant gentlemen! Apples of my eyes, sweet honeyed hearts!"

Meanwhile Gloomy Gus stood a little to the rear and to the right of Aunt Tish, near the banister where Mr. Pete and his companion were sitting. He watched Aunt Tish intently, with love and admiration, as she offered her wares to the people on the porches. Now and then he would shake his head distractedly and shove his hands deeply into his pockets, looking warily about him, as though anticipating trouble.

"Sweet honeyed hearts!" Aunt Tish was saying. When suddenly Mr. Pete tossed a stone into the crown of Gloomy Gus's hat. Feeling the stone, he jumped back in fright and looked wildly about him in order to discover what had happened. Mr. Pete began to laugh. The alley was deathly still. Mr. Pete looked up on the porch where Miss Hazel was sitting and picked up another stone. She looked down at her feet and smiled no more.

"Let's see you do that step agin, Gloomy!" Mr. Pete yelled, smiling at Miss Hazel. His companion whispered something to him. Mr. Pete shook his head. "C'mon, Gloomy, do it agin!" He threw the stone at his feet. He jumped back as before. Then he held up the palm of his right hand, as a sign for Mr. Pete to leave him alone, wildly shaking his head all the while, muttering unintelligible words to himself. He closed his eyes and began to tremble.

"Aw-aw!" Rutherford muttered under his breath.

"Give the nice man an apple, dear," said Aunt Tish. He gazed at her for an instant with a dazed expression, trying to make her realize what was happening, but at the same time struggling to fulfill her request. While still in the throes of his dilemma, Mr. Pete slipped up behind him and pulled the tail of his coat.

A murmur swept through the alley.

"Oh Lawdy!" cried Mrs. Derby.

"Rutherford, let's go upstairs!" whispered Viola. Rutherford did not move.

Suddenly, before Mr. Pete knew it, Gloomy Gus had wheeled around, dipping into his right coat pocket and coming out with a big sandstone. He cocked his right leg in the air like a baseball player and threw it with all his might at Mr. Pete, who was just gaining his chair. He looked up with an innocent grin just in time to see the stone coming. His friend jumped aside and the stone crashed against the leg of Mr. Pete's chair and sent him sprawling into the alley.

A sudden burst of hilarious laughter filled the air. His companion laughingly helped him up off the ground. Mr. Pete looked down and saw that his shirt was dirty and torn at the sleeve. His face became very red and his eyes looked as though they would bulge out of his head. He looked angrily at Miss Hazel, who was laughing at him. Miss Margret came out on the porch and sat down beside Miss Hazel and laughed at him, too.

Mr. Pete, in a rage, rushed blindly toward Gloomy Gus, who stood with his back to him, staring dumbly at all the laughing people. Tears stood in his eyes. Aunt Tish greeted this outburst of laughter as though it were an ovation. She threw more and more kisses at them and proffered her rotting fruit.

"You old son of a bitch!" Mr. Pete yelled, and slapped Gloomy Gus, who because his back was still turned did not know who had hit him. His hat flew in the air and landed on the ground a few feet away.

"Pick up that God damned hat!" said a voice. It was Big Tom Johnson, standing on top of Mr. Pete. His eyes flashed angrily and the veins stood

out on his neck. Mr. Pete looked up at Big Tom with surprise. His face grew white. He looked down at Gloomy Gus's hat, then he looked again at Tom, and from Tom to his companion. He returned his gaze without saying a word. Suddenly Mr. Pete cried out "Git the nigger!" to his friend, and swung wildly at Tom. Tom stepped quickly aside, and crashed his huge right fist against the side of Mr. Pete's head and, before could fall, jolted him with a staggering left to the midsection. Mr. Pete crumbled heavily to the ground where he lay, doubled in two, holding his belly. Then Tom faced his companion, but he did not move.

"He-he-he-heee's scaired as-a as-a as-ajjjack-rabbit!" cried Unc.

"Naw he ain'," Rutherford replied, "he's just got good sense, that's all."

Tom turned and walked up the alley toward his house.

"Don' go to bed tonight, nigger!" cried Mr. Pete, staggering to his feet. Tom turned slowly, deliberately, and said:

"I ain' intendin' to go to sleep tonight. I'm gonna be settin' right up there — on my porch. Now you take me for a ride!"

When he reached his porch Miss Myrt ran down the steps and said something to him that no one else could hear. He brushed her recklessly aside and stalked into the house. Gertrude, his wife, rushed in after him. After a few minutes Tom appeared on the porch with two shotguns and a pistol. He was wearing a jumper. He withdrew a box of shells from his pocket and sat down on the steps and started loading his guns.

"Tommy! William! Lemuel! Git to bed — all a you. You, too, Dorothy!" The children all went into the house.

By now Gloomy Gus and Aunt Tish were at the bottom of the alley. Only her voice could be heard. "Pretty things for a pretty penny! Sweet ladies! Gallant gentleman!" All the people stole quietly into their houses.

"Let's git upstairs," said Rutherford.

"I aaain' ain' gggoin' no wh-wh-wheres!" Unc stammered. "Th-th-th-this is my my porch an'-an'-an' I'm gonna gonna set on it or bbbe damned!"

"Shoot yourself!" said Rutherford with a grin. "G'night, Mrs. Derby."

"G'night, Mister Rutherford, Mrs. Jones, Tony," said Mrs. Derby. "Hope Mister Derby don' have no trouble gittin' home. That man would be gone when somethin' like this happens."

"Go to bed, Amerigo," said Rutherford curtly as soon as they were in the house. "You, too," turning to Viola.

"What you gonna do?" she asked, breathing rapidly.

"Mind your own business." He went into the middle room, opened the bottom drawer of the vanity dresser, and withdrew a small twenty-two revolver. He broke it down and spun the chambers around.

"My brother was shot to *death* with that gun!" cried Viola, "an' for nothin'!"

"What's that gotta do with me?"

"What kin you do with that, that, *bean shooter! Against machine guns,* Rutherford?"

"Go to bed!" He shut the door so that the child couldn't hear, and he took this opportunity to go to the window and peep down into the alley. All was quiet. The alley was darker now and the street lamp shone brightly. He tried to catch a glimpse of Tom Johnson sitting on his porch, but the glare of the light was too bright.

Suddenly, mysteriously, he heard the crickets singing again. He wondered if they had been singing all the while and he hadn't heard them. And while he wondered, he suddenly realized that he heard them no more:

"Tom," said Miss Myrt from the window upstairs.

Silence.

"Tom?"

"What?"

"I'm your momma. *Listen* to me."

"Git back out a that window, damnit!"

"You don' tell *me* what to do, boy! I raised you! An' I'm gonna sit in this window just as long as you set on those steps!"

"Well, you'll just git your damned fool head blowed off if you do 'cause I ain' goin' *no*where."

Silence.

Boom!

The crickets began to sing. He got in bed and closed his eyes and listened. He felt something crawling over his chest. He slapped at it with the palm of his hand. Sweat!

Boom! Boom! Boom! His heart pounded quietly. He opened his eyes and looked out the window. He gazed above the shade of the ringed lamplight.

"Tom?"

Boom! Boom! Boom! Boom! One-two-three-four stars . . . five-sixseveneight . . . the sky's full of stars!

Half asleep.

A car sped down the alley. A storm! Glass shattering, empty cans flying noisily over the cobblestones. A whining shriek from the avenue!

He opened his eyes. The storm was silent. He looked at the sky. The stars were still there!

Sparrow-twitter! He sat up in bed with a start. He pulled on his pants and tipped into the middle room. Viola lay sleeping — alone.

"He's *gone*! MOM! He's gone!"

Viola jumped up in bed.

"What time is it?"

He held up the clock before her face. She lay back in the bed and turned to the wall. "Go to bed, boy!"

"He's GONE!"

"Who's gone? What are you — " She felt the empty space beside her. "RUTHERFORD!" She bolted upright. "THE GUN!" She sprang out of bed and raced into the kitchen with Amerigo on her heels. She stopped in front of the screen door, placed her hands on her hips, and grinned: "There's your father!"

Rutherford was sitting on the orange crate, asleep. The twenty-two revolver lay near his foot. Viola stepped out onto the porch and looked over toward Tom Johnson's house. "Look! Ain' that a sight!" pointing to Tom who sat sleeping on his steps and Miss Myrt sleeping in the window above. "If ol' Pete was comin'he coulda blowed 'um to kingdom come — an' they wouldn' a even knowed it!"

"Rutherford. Rutherford . . ." She tugged gently at his arm.

He started. "What! — What's happenin'?" He yawned.

"Ain' nothin' happenin' 'ceptin' you catchin' your death a cold out there on that cold porch! Come on in the house, boy!" He looked over at Tom Johnson. "If they was comin', they'd a been here before now!"

He stood up, stretched himself, and rubbed his arms. Then he smiled a silly smile.

"An' bring that that pop gun with you!" said Viola over her shoulder.

He stood at the backyard gate fumbling in the shallow pocket of his green velvet breeches, waiting for his mother to come. Presently she appeared on the porch all dressed up in a Sunday dress, her hair freshly straightened and curled, the tiny mole on her chin darkened with the wetted tip of a lead pencil, perfumed, diamond rings glistening.

Sharp as a tack! he thought.

"You have to pee, Amerigo?" she asked, noticing that he was fumbling in his pocket.

"No'm."

"What you got in your pocket?" She quickly descended the back steps and approached the gate, taking one last look in the little hand mirror she withdrew from her purse. He pulled out his glass star.

"Where'd you git that?"

"Mister Jake."

She opened the gate and stood waiting for him to step into the shoot.

"That's nice, but be careful you don' cut yourself, those points look mighty sharp."

"My, my! Don' Tony look sweet!" cried Miss Sadie from the porch.

"Oh! Eh, hello, Miss Sadie. I woulda called you, Miss Sadie, but it sounded so quiet over there. I, I thought maybe you wasn' up yet!"

"Aw, that's all right. I just came out to say good-bye to my baby. Couldn' let my boy go to school without seein' 'im off!

"Here, honey!" to the child, "I got somethin' for you."

"You kin go git it," said Viola.

He ran up on the porch and Miss Sadie handed him a big round silver coin.

"Thanks," he said. Miss Sadie kissed him before he could turn away, and his face got all wet. She's crying, he said to himself. Women! Tearing himself from her embrace and running down to his mother. She looked at the coin, which he held up for her inspection.

"Oh! That's too much, Miss Sadie. A whole dollar, for a baby!"

"I ain' no baby!"

"He'll just lose it. Here. I'll keep it for you," Viola took the silver dollar and put it into her purse, giving him a nickel in return. Then she said to Miss Sadie, who was drying her eyes on the hem of her housecoat: "That's *awfully* sweet of you, Miss Sadie. Much obliged."

"That — that ain' nothin', Miss Jones."

"Well," Viola began, taking his hand.

"Hi, Tony!" Miss Derby, smiling from behind her screen door. "I see you on your way sho' 'nuff!"

"Yes'm."

"Mornin', Mrs. Derby," said Viola.

"Mornin', Mrs. Jones. My, you two sho' look nice! My boy's gonna be a *fine*-lookin' man when he grows up. I kin just see 'im now! You do what they tell you, an' learn all you kin, 'Mer'go, you heah me? Never had the opportunity you gittin' to git some schoolin' an' amount to somethin'. Got my schoolin' in the cotton fields down —"

"Hi, 'Mer'go!"

"Hi, 'Mer'go!"

"Hi, 'Mer'go!"

"Hi, 'Mer'go!"

"Tee hee hee!"

"Mornin', Mrs. Jones!" exclaimed a knot of children who were just crossing the yard behind Miss Ada's apartment.

"Hi," he said shyly to Tommy, Turner, Carl, Sammy, and Etta.

"Hello there!" said Viola, smiling at them, waving at the same time to

Miss Sadie and Mrs. Derby who were waving back. Viola and the children started through the shoot. Mrs. Crippa came out on the back porch to shake out the tablecloth.

"Eh! You taka Tony to school? . . . That eez gud. Ina the olda country I no go to school, buta my Karl, Frank, Johnathan, they havey money to go to school, but they no wanna, only Tina. She's a go to college — an' for what? To gita married an' hava baby? What for? *I* have a baby — two, three, four babies an' *no* go to college! Tony do the right thing. He go to school an' grow up to be a biga fina man. Keep out a trouble. No run after the girls an' buy beeg cars an' never come home to their momma!" She waved them away with a disparaging sweep of her free hand, and waved good-bye to Viola and the child at the same time, mumbling words in Italian to herself as she stepped back into the kitchen. Meanwhile Viola and the child made their way through the shoot, followed by the chattering bunch of children.

"Phew-whee! What's that stinkin'?" cried Sammy.

"Smells like a turd!" exclaimed William.

"You gonna git a knot on your head if I hear you say that word agin in front a Mrs. Jones!" said Tommy. "Now say 'scuse me, niggah, 'fore I git you now!"

"'Scuse me," said William, his big eyes clouded with shame.

"It does smell bad!" said Viola, "I wonder where it could be comin' from?"

"I smelled it comin' through the lot!" said Sammy mysteriously. "I bet it's somethin' in the empty house!"

"A rotten ghost!" said Carl.

"Aw ghosts don' stink, niggah!" said Sammy.

"Well, it's *somethin'* stinkin' 'round here!" Carl retorted.

"Whew! This is better!" said Viola as they came out on the Campbell Street side. They crossed the little grassy yard in front of Miss Ada's house and descended to the sidewalk. Miss McMahon was on her porch, talking to her brother, Officer McMahon. He was in uniform, with a silver star with numbers on it on his chest and a gun belt with real bullets in it and a gun. He smiled and waved at them. The sunlight shining on the lenses of his glasses obscured his eyes.

"Blue," Amerigo thought, waving back. "Hi, Miss McMahon! Hi, Mr. McMahon!"

"You an' your momma lookin' mighty slicked up there. Where you off to, all dolled up like that so early in the mornin'?"

"To the kinnygarden!"

"'Mornin', Mrs. Jones," she said, while Officer McMahon nodded a greeting and smiled. "Why it seems only yesterday," she continued, "that you weren' no bigger'n that!" snapping her fingers.

"No'm," he said, as they turned down Campbell Street.

"You gonna come over an' clean out the shoot Sad'dy?"

"Kin I, Mom?"

"I reckon so," said Viola.

"Yes'm!"

"All right, then, I'll be waitin' for you!"

"Yes'm."

They passed Mrs. Crippa's house. It was fronted by a little flower garden with a trellis that covered the steps leading to the broad shaded front porch.

This is a pretty street, he thought, allowing his gaze to take in its quiet cleanness, enhanced by flowers and trees. Opposite Mrs. Crippa's house was an apartment building where white people lived: *I-talians*. Next to that was an empty lot that gave onto a hill covered with grass and weeds and wild-flowers and bushes. His back to the hill, he took mental note of the fact that next to the hill, on the corner, was a big unpainted wooden house where col-ored people lived, opposite which was another vacant lot with an even higher hill covered with weeds fronted by a big billboard facing the boule-vard. A string of tumbling houses slanted back down the hill where Mr. Mose, an old iceman, lived with his daughter Freda who was black and ugly and mean. Next to Mr. Mose lived the Chauncys, a skinny yellow man with a fat yellow wife, both over fifty, with their son, Bud, of whom all the little kids were afraid because he was mean, too. "That niggah'll kill you!" he had heard Sammy exclaim. He squeezed his mother's hand a little tighter, diverting his attention to the man who lived next door. Old man Barnes. Suddenly he saw a tall black gray-headed man with bluish brown eyes and yellow teeth. He used to work on the railroad but he was retired now.

Irish! he thought suddenly, for no accountable reason. *Yesterday* . . . Miss McMahon was saying, *You were no bigger'n that!* The sound of her fingers snapping exploded in his ears.

And then there was the violent clinging of a trolley bell, followed by the loud irritating blast of a honking horn. A big truck backed out of the spaghetti factory on the corner of Independence and Campbell, blocking the streetcar tracks. The streetcar looked like a strange toy. He tried to coordinate the image of it with the sound of it heard from afar, from the back porch, in the dark, just before he fell asleep. He listened to the strange and not unpleasant sound of its motor, a quivering rhythmical sound that made him want to tap his foot and hum a tune to match it. Just as they reached the foot of the hill the truck emitted a loud belch and jerked down the avenue, and then the streetcar conductor clanged the bell a few times more, turned the stirring knob in a circular orbit and the streetcar, half filled with black, beige, brown, yellow, and one white man, rattled clumsily down the avenue, past the spaghetti factory.

"Come on, here, boy!" said Viola.

"Yes'm."

Past Goldberg's ice cream parlor, Magedy's grocery store, past the mouth of the alley, imagining it as he usually saw it from the front porch, a low streak of sunburned orange by day and a flash of pumpkin-orange perforated with squares of candle-flame yellow by night.

Viola tightened her grip on his hand as they crossed Campbell Street and proceeded up the avenue, east.

"Tomorrow you'll be goin' to school with Tommy an' you'll have to learn to cross the streets by yourself. All you have to do is stop at the corners, look both ways, and wait till you don' see no cars coming! An' then cross. But don' run! You don' have to run. If you have to run to make it, don' try. That's the way you git killed. But you don' have to crawl, neither. Just take your time an' cross as quick as you kin, without breakin' your neck you hear?"

"Yes'm."

"I'll show 'im, Mrs. Jones," said Tommy, keeping pace with them. Viola smiled at him tenderly.

Miss Leona's dead he thought, seeing Tommy's mother, sitting in the kitchen door, the sun cutting her bare legs just below the knees — just before . . . *Miss Gert's his momma now.* Viola took out her purse and took out a dime and gave it to Tommy.

"Here. You kin buy some candy at the drugstore. An' give the rest of the kids some."

"Yes, *ma'am!*" Tommy said with a broad smile, which caused him to think:

Him no more than her!

Meanwhile cars and trucks ground their greasy, smoky, paper-littered way up and down the avenue, through the lane of big brick buildings with wooden porches, interrupted here and there by storefronts filled with fruit and groceries, or signs (in big colored letters that you *couldn't* rub off with your fingers) indicating places to eat or drink, with people sitting inside. All the appropriate smells within the dominant smell of humid autumnal heat were cooled by evaporating dew, which was beginning to mingle with the dust of the streets, the topsoil of hundreds of miles of prairies. The smell of sweat and bottled liquor, fish grease, barbecue and beer, was agitated by the penetrating odor of sour wine and meat markets; of spices and fresh and cured meat; of cheeses, sour cream in wooden buckets, and big dill pickles reposing in huge glass jars of briny water spiced with little black peppers and red peppers and bay leaves; of hard candies in jars and in boxes; bread and cakes, canned goods, dry and leather goods exposed in dank gray shops; of shoes and glue and little old men with dirty hands and mouths full of nails; of pollinating trees — cottonwood, maple, walnut, oak, fruit trees, tomato vines, grapevines.

Smells attacked his sensibility firing the objects to which they adhered with myriad colors, while the sounds jolted him with the force of lightning heralding thunder before rain!

Suddenly he pressed his face against his mother's hip in a wave of passion that made him want to cry. But Viola did not notice. "There's where your Aunt Edna usta live," she was saying, pointing to a shabby frame house near the corner of the cobblestone alley they were now crossing. He looked warily at the house. "An' there's where they found your Aunt Ruby — lousy with T.B." He looked obediently in the direction indicated, but just then a passing streetcar and a transfer truck, cutting in behind it, plus the now upsurging thought of Aunt Edna's alley, which "Ain' as pretty as our'n," along with the image of Aunt Ruby when she was eighteen, so pretty and smiling, distracted his attention.

"Do you see?"

"Yes'm."

They passed in front of a place with pictures stuck on boards propped up by sticks standing out on the sidewalk and pasted on the windows and doors. On either side of the entrance was a big double door and between them a window with two holes in it, a round one in the middle and a longer narrow one at the bottom.

That's the show! He remembered that was where Viola had gone, but not to this one, to the other one on Eighteenth Street, to see Ru-dolf Valentino in *The Sheik*, four nights ago, after the day he had killed the cat and threw it in the empty house where Old Jake had poked with his stick *before* he had given him the star that morning. He touched the star within the darkness of his pocket: *The cat!* hearing Carl's voice when they passed through the shoot: Somethin's stinkin' 'round here! "Kitty-kittykitty," called Aunt Lily, and the cat crawled along the row of shadowed heads in the soup line, as the redness of the sky had threatened him with five o'clock — So soon! — and night and day three times, until he looked at the pictures stuck on the boards and on the windows and thought: That's the show and a feeling of wonder came over him.

"Gloria Swanson was *my* favorite!" he heard Viola say. "She was the best of 'um all! An' *beautiful* . . . those eyes! I usta cry an' cry." He thought of his aunt Ruby who was beautiful. He wanted to cry. A lump rose in his throat, but the tears were stayed by the sound of his father's voice:

"Yeah, what was the name of that picture she was in where she was so sad, Babe? Had *all* the niggahs cryin'!"

"*The Lady of the Camelias,*" said Viola, "or was that Greta Garbo?"

"Now, talkin' about a actress, she was great! The greates'!"

"She sure was."

"I liked 'er best with John Bowles." Viola sighed pleasantly.

"He was a great lover, Amerigo," Rutherford explained.

"Yeah, but don' forget Douglas Fairbanks!" Viola cried.

"He was a lover, too," Rutherford admitted, "but he was more of a actor, Babe. He put down some deep stuff. I never will forgit 'im in *The Count of Monte Cristo,* by Alexander Dumas!"

The smartest man in the whole world! he had thought, looking at his father with admiration.

"An', aw Rutherford, ha!" Viola cried. "An' the *Perils a Pauline*! Boy that's sure one woman *al*ways gittin' into somethin'."

"Yeah, Amerigo, she was a famous lady daredevil! She was always hangin' out a airplanes — or gittin' hung up in runaway trains!"

"But wait!" cried Viola, "Lon Chaney was *my* man!"

"Mine, too! *The Phantom of the Op'ra!*"

"*The Unholy Three!*"

"*The Seven Sinners!*"

"*The Cathedral of Notre Dame!*"

"He," said Rutherford, "was a joker who could twist his body into all kinds a twisted shapes, Amerigo. I mean, like a real humpback or a cripple or anythin'. *The Phantom of the Op'ra* — that was the one! Picture this, Amerigo: He was settin' there, playin' the organ, Jack, dressed in a — in a mean cape. Sharp, Jack. With his back to audience. He had on a black mask — always wore it so nobody couldn' see who he was. An'-an'-an' then his girl, she come slippin' up on 'im all in love with 'im an' ever'thin'. She was gonna find out who he was. An' he was still playin', all lonely-like, somethin' deep — classical, Jack! 'Cause, you see, he was in love with her, too. So she slipped up on 'im in 'er pretty dress an' all an' he didn' hear 'er 'cause he was playin' so hard he was so in love an' all. An'-an'-an' she was gittin' closer an' closer, pantin', an'er bosom was a heavin' up an' down, an' he was playin' an' playin' like a madman! An when she got close enough she jerked it off!

"Amerigo, boy, I'm tellin' you, when that cat turned a-round, he like to run e-v-e-r'-b-o-d-y out a the show! He turned around in a flash! pointin' a l-o-n-g crooked finger in 'er face, an' his face was all tore up, wrinkled an' scarred, like a monster — like a devil, Amerigo.

"'eeeEEE — YOU!' he hollered at 'er, grittin' his teeth! An' his eyes was all sunk in an' ever'thin' an'-an' then — he went crazy! An' all hell broke loose!"

All the while Rutherford had been speaking, the face of Old Jake had been constantly before his eyes, the words *crazy* and *deep,* fixing the images of the phantom and the old man firmly in his mind. He saw Aunt Ruby slipping up on Old Jake, and his heart welled with pity when the monster pointed his finger at her, and *killed* her.

Suddenly the Campbell Street hill flashed through his mind, as his eyes caught sight of the man in the big white hat, astride the big white horse rearing on its hind legs, its front feet clawing the shiny air. A posse of famous names stampeded his ears: William Mess Hart! Hoot Gibson! TOM MIX! Ken Maynard! Buck JONES! Tim Tyler!

"Look where you're goin', boy!" cried Viola, stepping off the curb at Harrison Street. They were passing a huge building with two big dirty plate-glass windows separated by a door. It was open. A big dingy room with a long wooden counter on the left side covered with dust and curious dirty boxes filled with corks and bottletops and rubber stoppers. The rest of the counter was filled with dusty green and brown bottles of all sizes and shapes.

"Let's go in there!"

"Are you crazy?"

He feasted his eyes on the barrels and jugs, on the heap of round wooden plugs on the floor. A man was hammering a plug in a hole in the belly of a big barrel.

Like a navel. He took a whiff of the gummy smell in the air, mixed with a sour, putrid smell that was like vomit, or like the smell of the garbage can when he had taken the lid off to fasten it down better with his heel.

"It's just an old barrel shop!" She pulled him on, just as the nausea was creeping dangerously to his throat. "Looka there," she added, pointing toward the corner, "they've disappeared. They must be halfway through the holla by now!"

"I ain'!" said Tommy who had been following close behind them all the while. Viola smiled at him. Amerigo pulled his mother moodily on toward the corner.

"Here's Troost Hill!" Viola declared excitedly. "It's been a long time since I been down here. Your daddy an' me, an' T. C., an' a whole bunch a us usta slide down this hill in the winter. You see how steep it is? We usta start at the boulevard an' cross the avenue, here! An' coast on down past the holla, an' — you might think I'm lyin' — a-l-l the way down to Garrison Square!"

"Boy, your daddy an' me could really *do* that thing!" he heard T. C. saying. "Him an' your momma an' me we sure usta cut 'um! We'd build a fire at the top, see, an' one at the bottom. Some a them jokers would even take off from Tenth Street an' cut across the traffic at the Boulevard. Troost Hill was enough for me, Jackson — an' your daddy, too! Ask 'im how he got that scar on his ankle. Ha! ha! ha! That little darkie like to got us both killed. M-a-n he took off from the boulevard, see? An' me, like a fool, right behind 'im — at night! Zoom! Like a bat out a hell! Down Troost Hill. An' c-o-l-d! Aw man! that north wind made you wish you was down home. Well, old Rutherford hit the avenue, see, sort a narrow-like, close to the curb. The wind was blowin' in that little joker's face so hard he didn' see the streetcar comin' till it was damned near on top of 'im. M-a-n you shoulda seen that little joker hustle, scootin' that old raggedy sled a his around an' draggin' his feet. The streetcar conductor was a clangin' and a clangin'! I thought he was gonna kick that bell to death!

"'Fall off an' roll!' I hollered. 'Fall off an' roll!' But that little monkey was so scaired he wouldn' let go. He flattened out like a pancake an' ran — Amerigo if I'm lyin' I'm dyin' — u-n-d-e-r the streetcar like a express train! The streetcar conductor slammed on the brakes an' sparks flew ever' whichaway! The wheels was slippin' on the ice between the tracks. Whew! I hope I never see nothin' like that no more as long as I live! Am I lyin', Rutherford?"

"I sure was hittin' 'um, all right," he answered.

"The conductor pulled 'is cap down over 'is eyes. He gave that cat up for dead! I shot around the streetcar an' just did miss the fireplug by the skin a my teeth. M-a-n — I was really goin'. I was headin' down the hill, see, an' when I looked up I couldn' see Rutherford *nowhere!* Lord! They done killed that joker, sure, I thought. An' when I got to the bottom of the hill, there was your daddy, Amerigo, tremblin' like a leaf! C-r-y-i-n'! 'Cause he lost his shoe! Ah — ha! ha! An' then — you know what?"

"What?" watching the morning sunlight slant down the hill, throwing elongated shadows from the trees just above the flower shop on the opposite corner.

"What?" he was asking in his mimic, as he, Viola, and Tommy turned down the hill.

"He had a gash in his ankle that long!" doubling his fist, extending his forefinger and intercepting the axis of his wrist in order to indicate a length of about six inches.

"Every time you tell that lie," Viola exclaimed, "that cut gits bigger!"

"They took *nine* stitches in it! Well, anyway, we tied that li'l cat's ankle up, it was deep, too, an' got warmed up an' then — we *did it agin!* When he got home his ol' lady like to beat 'im to death for losin' that shoe! Ah — ha! ha!"

T. C.'s laughter filled the air, crowding out all the other sounds. Amerigo looked down the long sweeping hill that extended all the way down to Garrison Square. He took longer steps, imagining that he was walking in the invisible prints made by his father and mother and their sisters and brothers. This is my street! The long blanket of asphalt interspersed with patches of cobblestone, blazed in the hard reddish yellow light, broken by the swaying patterns of tall cottonwood and soft squatting maple trees whose faint blue shadows fell slantwise, from east to west.

They came to a little clump of gray farmhouses with porches, fronted by a black dirt yard with a narrow concrete path running up to the steps.

"There's where your cousin Rachel's been livin' since Ruben's been dead," said Viola. He looked at the house, hoping she might appear.

"She's got a little girl no bigger'n you. I don' know where the daddy is. Rachel don' neither. Let's cross to the other side a the street."

They crossed the street and entered a broad cinder-strewn path bordered by a long line of empty houses in ruins. The bricks of the houses were scarred and burned and their foundations had long since been filled in with ashes, cans, and garbage from the neighboring houses. Tall weeds and sunflowers grew out of the ash and cinder piles. Moderate-sized trees with darkly grained barks and intense green leaves stood in deserted yards. *Persimmon trees,* said a voice, surprising him with information Viola hadn't given him yet.

"This is Belvedere Holla!" she said. "Look! persimmon trees! It seems like *only yesterday* that I usta run up an' down here, when there was a whole lot a people . . . an' laughin'. Full a houses." Pointing about fifty feet from the mouth of the entrance: "That ol' shack over there's where Gloomy Gus an' Aunt Tish usta live the last I remember. Usta be a little garden in front with flowers in it, climbin' all over the place."

"It's pretty! I'd sure like to have a little house like that!"

"Tee hee!" Tommy laughed. He looked around at him in surprise.

"I sure hope you don' never have to!" said Viola. "Don't you like your own house?"

"Yes'm."

Down Forest Street through the strange Italian Quarter. It looked cooler and quieter than when he had last seen it. Finally they came to a street with two sets of streetcar tracks. *Fifth Street* said the all knowing voices. Amerigo's eyes swept across the tracks, along the unpaved street that continued Troost Street, coming to an abrupt end at the approach of a steep rise from which he could see a line of one-story frame houses on the rim of a distant hill that flowed down into a valley and a dirt street lined with shabby wooden houses. This street stopped at the base of a great hill.

"There's Clairmount Hill!" said Viola in a faraway voice. He stared at it long and hard. There were blue-green grasses and bushes and trees growing on top of it.

"That's the biggest hill in the whole world!" he said, his eyes sweeping down its mud-red sides. "Same color as the bricks in the alley."

"That old house down there at the foot of the hill, it was nicer then. It's just a shack now, it's where your gran'ma lived with all your aunts and uncles."

Images of Grandma Veronica and Rutherford and Aunt Ruby, Edna, Ruth, Aunt Nadine and Uncle Sexton, rushed before his eyes.

"An' that's the Field House over there." There were tears in her eyes.

"The school's just behind it." She turned her head in the opposite direction in order to dry her eyes with the tip of her finger. He stopped dead still. He began to tremble violently. "What's the matter, baby, you sick?"

"He's tremblin'," said Tommy.

"What's — what's wrong, Amerigo?" taking his face in her hands. He threw his arms around her waist and wept.

"He's just a little nervous — the first day a school an' all. You go on ahead, Tommy."

"Yes'm, Miss Viola."

"Now, now, honey, it's gonna be all right. Why, bright as you are, why — now's your time to shine! Your daddy an' me had to quit — we quit school. But you gonna go to college an' be a smart man. You got it in you an' we gonna stick by you an' see you through. I *know* you ain' gonna let us down — an' all the folks in the alley. They think the world an' all a you! An' —"

"Mom . . ." He looked up at her. Her head was in the sun, a huge shadow in the middle of its blinding light. Her eyes appeared a yellowish green. "Mom . . ."

"They think the world an' all a you!" she was saying, "an' we wanna be proud a you, too."

"I killed the kitty," he whispered, but she, having terminated her thought, exclaimed excitedly:

"We'd better hurry up, babe! What you say?" Walking faster, he running now beside her.

"I killed the kitty!"

"Yeah, that's nice, you don' wanna be late on your first day. But wait a minute," coming to a halt. "Here, you better dry your eyes. Don' want 'um to know you been cryin'. What'd the big boys think, you cryin' like a baby on your first day! That's better!" blowing his nose.

A cool sharp breeze shot through the hot sun and chilled him to the bone.

It severed the colored leaves from the branches of the trees. Ten paces later a huge asphalt yard full of running, screaming, laughing children came into view! They looked like the leaves in Toodle-lum's yard when the leaves of the big cottonwood tree fell. The wind blew them about with a clattering, rustling sound.

Amerigo stood in the midst of them. They all *looked* at him. They *laughed* at him. They *talked* about him.

"They *know!* How do they *know?*"

A bell, like the bell of a Big Ben clock rang. The teeming throng of noisy children clamored into the building. He and Viola followed, tramped with the others up the wooden stairs, through the huge wooden corridors with the pictures of one-two-three black men and three-five white men, one with long white hair like a woman's, a long thin nose, small stern blue eyes, and a thin tight-lipped mouth.

Irish. Staring at the writing under it, distinguishing a *G* and an *E* and an *O* before Viola yanked him down one of the branching corridors with other pictures of other white men with mustaches like Grandpa Will and thick beards and heads of long bushy hair.

"Here 'tis!" Viola exclaimed excitedly. "It sure ain' changed much since the old days!"

"Good morning!" A soft black woman stood in the door.

He looked up at HER!

Boom! A door slammed somewhere down the hall and the sound echoed throughout the huge cavernous corridors.

"Good mornin' — ing, Miss Chapman! You don't remember me, I-I guess, my name is — "

"Viola? I knew I had seen that face before. Why, how *are* you, honey? Oh, I feel so old, so terribly old! How long long is it? T-e-n years! Ten years ago. And now little Viola is a woman, and married! You were very fortunate. Yes, who . . . who'd you marry?"

"Rutherford,"

"Don't tell me it was that little skinny Jones boy! With all those brothers and sisters?"

"We been, we've been married five years now — I mean six," glancing uneasily first at Miss Chapman and then at the child who had never taken his eyes off Miss Chapman's face, "as-as you kin-can see. . . ."

He looked curiously at his mother and remarked that she seemed nervous, and that she spoke more slowly than usual, and that she primped her mouth unnaturally. She looked down at him with a proud smile. She looked very young. Like a girl like he was a boy, and Miss Chapman seemed old like a woman, and they — he, his mother and father who was once a skinny little boy — were all children, all together, and Miss Chapman was a woman, but not as old as Old Lady or Aunt Nancy or Miss Myrt or even Mrs. Derby or Aunt Lily. She was undoubtably older than Miss Sadie and Miss Ada, though not so old as Mrs. Crippa or Miss McMahon, and certainly not Irish because her hair was black and her eyes looked real black, even though they were really only dark brown, and only looked black because her face was so black, but smooth and fine, with a little reddish brown mixed in it, darker than Viola, but with a different mouth, large like Aunt Tish's, as though she said only good and pretty things with it, and not crazy.

And she's clean. He was still looking her boldly in the face. Aunt Tish isn't dirty, she's dirty like a cat's dirty, or the alley, or the dirt on the hill — and that isn't really dirty, but Miss Chapman's clean! She looks like she just grew up in some air that made her eyes shine bright and her teeth sparkle like Aunt Tish's if she was young and blacker — darker — and a little fatter and not so much like a bird . . . or an old rose on a big black hat. Sorta like Aunt Rose!

"So this big healthy youngster is your son!" she was saying. He was overwhelmed by a feeling of comfort, a feeling that he would be safe, that she could protect him from the manifold dangers of the earth and sky that had plagued him these past three days.

"I gotta, I must go now, honey!" Viola was saying. He looked into the face of the little girl who was his mother with a feeling of profound embarrassment, and then he looked apologetically at the older woman, as though he hoped that she would understand something deep and mellow in him, which he himself could not understand, but feel.

"You be a good boy an'-*d* do what the teacher tells you — an'-and if anything goes wrong — you just go to her. You gonna kiss your momma good-bye?"

"Aw, Mom . . ." reluctantly proffering his cheek, after which Viola said good-bye to Miss Chapman, and turned and walked down the hall. She turned at the head of the stairs and waved her handkerchief at him, blowing her nose as she descended the steps. When she was out of sight, Miss Chapman touched his shoulder gently, and he threw his arms around her waist and buried his face in the pit of her stomach.

"Go to your seat," she said.

Boom!

An instant later he was seated in a room filled with windows. The sun shone in bright golden bars upon little lacquered yellow-pine tables and chairs occupied by little boys and girls just like him. Miss Chapman, now here, now there, like a big soft magician, yielding warmth, yielding comfort, conjured up deep bright enchanting secrets of children and things: of clean white pulpy paper and Crayola, of water paints, and lines and circles and squares filled with bird and apple and color, worm and rat, house and boy and girl and rabbit, duck, pear, and peach — elephant! — maple leaf and walnut, of a wet gummy stuff called clay that you could squeeze and pull better than mud this way and that, and pat and roll into little balls, and sticks to look like dogs and cars and houses and stars and horses and things.

Meanwhile, after a long time, the bell rang for the first time, and Viola appeared at the door, and she and Miss Chapman talked softly together so he couldn't hear, and then they said good-bye, and he said good-bye with his head because he couldn't *say* good-bye, couldn't look at her, couldn't look at Viola, either, just hold her hand like a baby and let her lead him away through all the kids as thick as leaves making a whole lot of noise, back up the long hill to the avenue, past cousin Rachel's house.

Just as they reached the little concrete path leading up to the steps he saw a youngish woman with sallow skin and red eyes, in a worn street dress with a tight bodice that revealed a perfect figure, standing on the porch.

"Hul-lo Vi — ola," she said, taking them both in with a sad defiant glance. He stared at the thick scar on the side of her handsome face. Her legs were bare and the dress was torn on the shoulder so that the faded pink strap and upper part of her brassiere were visible.

"Hello, Rachel. Amerigo, say hello to your cousin Rachel."

"Hul-lo."

"He looks just like you, Vi. An' then agin — he sort a looks like his un —"

"C'mon, Amerigo."

He looked back over his shoulder, tried to catch the word that died upon her pretty lips. He was thinking that she reminded him a little of Miss Sadie. They passed the place where his father, who was once a skinny little boy, almost got killed — but didn't — sliding down Troost Hill toward where he was now.

"Look where you goin'!" Viola shouted, pulling on his arm. The streetcar clanged past him. It was crowded now, with more white people in it. It confused him because it was going up the avenue instead of down, as when he had first seen it this morning. It crept alongside of him, placing him and Viola between it and the barrel shop, which was there *already!* — instead of only later, *after* the show and the stars of the Silver Screen, which only came now that they were crossing Harrison Street, and the streetcar was now at the foot of Campbell Street, in front of the spaghetti factory, which he knew was there, even though he could not see it yet. Now he was looking down a strangely familiar alley where Aunt Edna used to live. A black-and-white-spotted dog with short ears and no tail was lying in the shade of one of the low squatting frame houses. It isn't Sammy, he thought proudly, remarking that Aunt Edna's alley had no empty houses. It was her alley, his father's sister's alley, a skinny little girl's with all those sisters and brothers — Rutherford's.

When they reached Campbell Street he was surprised to find himself at the bottom, going up, instead of at the top, going down. With a funny feeling he placed his feet duck-footed on the wine-red herringbone bricks and looked upward toward the boulevard. He could just make out the tops of the cars, swishing east and west. The sun, reddish, different than it was this morning, was in his face, but not directly in his face, in the corners of his eyes; it grazed his hair. Now he could make out the facade of Mrs. Crippa's house, and then Miss Ada's, and then Miss McMahon's next to it, and all the houses up to the boulevard.

Saturday I'll get a quarter for cleaning out the shoot! he thought, but Saturday was a long way off.

And then he saw Mrs. Crippa's garden above the high wall that came all the way to Viola's shoulders with flowers sticking out. The concrete steps leading to the porch were wet, with dried-out patches, like in the backyard when it was dew-wet early in the morning before the sun was hot enough.

They climbed the steps to Miss Ada's yard and followed the path around to the side of the house. Miss Sarah's door was open. She lived on the first floor, north, while Mr. and Mrs. Fox, who were white and gray with blue eyes — Irish — lived on the first floor, south.

"Evenin', Miss Sarah!" he cried.

No answer.

"Prob'ly in the kitchen," said Viola.

He glanced over at Miss McMahon's porch just before they stepped into the shoot. It was dark and cool like a cellar. When they got halfway through they smelled something stinking. It came as a pleasant surprise to him at first, as though some good meat were frying. Ham and eggs. A gentle pang of hunger smote him in the pit of his stomach.

"What could that *be?*" Viola exclaimed. "Smells like something dead!"

His stomach wretched with nausea, and the bitter, sweetish taste of this morning rose to his throat.

Viola opened the gate and entered the yard, while he shot a horrific glance at the hole where the cat lay rotting.

"Better go up an' change your clothes before you git 'um all dirty, Amerigo," said Viola.

"Yes'm," distractedly entering the yard. It was bathed in afternoon sunlight. There was no one to be seen, although all the doors behind the screens were open. Nothing stirred!

Shortly after five o'clock, Rutherford asked: "How'd it go, boy?" Sitting on the orange crate on the back porch in an old pair of pants and tennis shoes, he looked up at his father through the screen, the word *boy* blending with the image of a skinny little boy with all those brothers and sisters sliding down Troost Hill, all the way to Garrison Square. He smiled with embarrassment.

"Come on an' git your supper," said Viola.

"Yooooo-hooo!" Aunt Lily cooed softly, peering up on the porch from under the palm of her right hand. "How'd our young 'un do on 'is first day in school?"

"Fine, Aunt Lily!" cried Viola through the screen. "How're you?"

"Aw, girl, you know how it is with your Aunt Lily."

"Hi, Aunt Lily," Amerigo said shyly. Rutherford waved. Then she went back into her kitchen and he and Rutherford entered theirs.

Sitting at the table the smell of crawdads and all the suppers throughout the alley crept into his bizarre impression of all that had happened during the day. Viola placed a bowl of fried cabbage on the table, which was soon accompanied by a platter of salt pork strips fried in cornmeal, a pitcher of buttermilk, and a plate of corn bread. He picked disinterestedly at his food, while Viola told about the day.

He listened to her voice with interest, as she recounted all the events, but in quite another sequence than he had experienced them, placing the accent on sights and sounds that had passed him by unnoticed, or which he had seen in another way. It wasn't like that at all! he wanted to exclaim, but Viola spoke so quickly, and he was very tired. Besides, supper was over already, and Rutherford was reading his paper with deep concentration, while he helped his mother with the dishes. When the dishes were over he would have to go to bed early in order to be up in time to go to school.

The night was quiet. The alley was quiet. In bed, in the dark, looking at the stars through the window, he thought of the previous night. Suddenly he was swept in the wake of an upsurging wave of fear, as though he were going to school tomorrow for the first time! He raced through the previous day until it was night and Tom Johnson sat on his steps and Rutherford and Viola talked softly behind the middle room door and the fear exploded: *Boom! Boom! Boom!* in his chest. He listened for the crickets. No crickets.

Now, gradually, he came to recognize Miss Chapman's face. Only it looked like Viola's face, and somehow like Aunt Rose's face at the same time, and a little like Aunt Tish's face, only cleaner, in a different way. He was lying in her arms. Suddenly her left breast protruded between his eye and a man's dark face. A deep pang of shame smote him and he hid his face in her bosom. . . .

Then he heard the birds. He stood on the back porch. The air was fresh and cool and bright and alive with the smell of dew and falling elm leaves and the aroma of coffee that Rutherford had made and soap and toothpaste and the stench that rose from the empty house.

After a little while Tommy was waiting with William at the gate. Amerigo looked into his face in order to see if he knew, then he looked at the sky, and at the trees. . . .

"Now, you be good an' go with Tommy like I told you, you hear?" Viola had said just before she had gone off in a flash to work. He felt the dime and the nickel she'd given him tied in the corner of the handkerchief in his pocket with the star. "Keep your hand on it so you don' lose it."

"Come on, 'Mer'go," said Tommy, and he went down and joined them and they proceeded through the shoot, leaped down Miss Ada's steps in a bound, and cut across Campbell. They went through the shoot beside the white people's apartment and slid through a hole in the backyard fence and came out near a row of redbrick apartments with long gray porches. Other children were coming out of their houses: Sammy, Leroy, Margie, Robert, and others he didn't know, and they all went down Harrison to the avenue.

"Lookit that little hatch-legged niggah in them fancy breeches!" Leroy shouted. "Ah! ha! ha! ha!"

"What you say, there, you little sissy?" Robert jeered. He and Leroy were big.

"Come on, 'Mer'go," said Tommy in a conciliatory tone. Sensing danger, they walked faster. Other kids joined them along the way, and finally the noisy crowd arrived at school just as the bell was ringing.

After a while the bell rang for recess. The gray asphalt immediately flashed with movement and color. Rubber and leather balls bounced, and the metal rings clanged against the poles while others flew freely through the air.

"Whee!" cried the girls in the swings, the wind billowing out their dresses. A clump of boys peeped up between their legs and sniggered, while others wrestled and fought or huddled along the little wall near the edge of the playground.

"Your momma!" cried one of the big boys, and another big boy hit him in the nose and big drops of blood dropped onto his white shirt and the ground. A crowd gathered.

"*Hit* that niggah, George!" cried one skinny little boy.

"M-a-n, I wouldn' let *no*-body talk about *my* momma like that!" shouted another with laughing eyes.

Meanwhile he was pushed by the jostling children to the front of the crowd. George and the other boy were wrestling on the ground. "Kill that niggah, man!" and "Fight! Fight! Fight!" and "If you don' beat that cat, I'm gonna beat you!" rang from all sides, as the children screamed with delight.

When all of a sudden a little man appeared among them who was no bigger than Gloomy Gus. His hair was good like Gloomy Gus's, but silvery white, and he wore a simple well-tailored black suit, a white shirt, a vest, and a blue tie. He noticed that his hands were small and fine, and that his face was of a golden color, like a white man, almost, but he was colored. He moved slowly through the crowd. As the children noticed him, they became silent, so that by the time he was halfway through, the rear half stood in awe-filled silence, while the front half still shouted and screamed words of encouragement to the fighting boys. "Hit 'im!" "Git 'im," "Hit," "Git." Silence. The two boys fought, alone. Finally, they both looked up sheepishly at the man.

"*He* started it!" cried the smaller boy, the one whom they called George, a copper-colored boy with green eyes and reddish brown curly hair. Mr. Bowles commanded silence with the raised palm of his right hand and cut his words in two, just as the larger boy, tall for his age, black, with sad hungry eyes, panting for breach, declared: "I'm gonna git you for that!" in a cold, uncompromising tone.

"I'm glad to see that you two have so much energy," said Mr. Bowles with a warmth and a calmness that mellowed but did not detract from the seriousness of his tone.

Like the reverend, he thought.

"The playground needs sweeping, and I'm sure Mr. Johnson would appreciate some help with the blackboards. And *I* would appreciate it very much if you gentlemen would come in and see me after school. Perhaps by then I shall have thought of a few other useful things for you to do with those big muscles of yours." A few sniggers burst from the crowd. "When," with a look that demanded silence all around, "when you've finished your chores, and you're not *too* tired, and you are still angry enough to fight, why, then, you may fight as long as you like — with boxing gloves! We'll have a match. And I shall be there with bells on, pulling for the best man!"

The bell rang.

"Back to class!" he said with a humorous twinkle in his eyes, raising his arms like Aunt Tish when she talked to the flowers and the birds. The children ran into the building, bustling with excitement.

He stood transfixed by the beauty of the man after the crowd had dispersed.

A fine man! said a voice.

A race man! cried Viola.

A real educator! said Rutherford.

Her no more than him. The image of Miss Chapman surprised him by its sudden appearance. He was bewildered by a kind of magic through which the faces of Viola and Rutherford — who were little kids like him — were fused with the faces of Mr. Bowles and Miss Chapman!

"You're Amerigo Jones, aren't you?" the great man was saying.

"Yessir."

"I believe the bell has rung. That means that you have to go inside with the others."

He walked dreamily toward the building at the great man's side.

"When you go home this evening, say hello to your mother and father for me. We're old friends."

"Yessir." He stumbled up the steps, while Mr. Bowles turned and scanned the playground to see if all the children were in.

The bell rang again; for the noon recess. It rang again, and all grew gradually quiet. Again it rang, and and he stood at the front entrance, waiting for Tommy who finally came.

Then the hazardous journey home by a route crowded with fences and alleys strewn with cans and rocks to kick, with hills strewn with wildflowers and thorns and briers and cockleburs and sunflowers with stalks crawling with grasshoppers. A little boy in the kindergarten named Harry Bell got hit in the eye with a rock and two girls in the third grade had a fight over the gym teacher and there was an exchange of rocks between gangs of Italian and Negro children.

"Come on!" Tommy cried suddenly, and he ran with the Negroes.

If you git into trouble, he heard Rutherford say, *run, but if you can't run, fight! But fight to win!*

"Hurry up!" cried Tommy, ducking to avoid a barrage of gravel, and he had to dispense with his questions as to the reason of his flight in order to keep up. By the time he got home the question had exhausted itself. He came to the gate, paused briefly, absentmindedly, to stare dumbly at the empty house, irritated by his growing awareness of the strong nauseating odor that came from the hole in the foundation.

The sky flushed rose, and then blue, and was shattered into particles of light; the air was pregnant with savory sound and movement that satisfied his stomach, but merely filled his mind with a hungry anticipation of what tomorrow would bring, and tomorrow, until Saturday, and then Sunday.

. . . Now I lay me down to sleep, I pray the Lord my soul to keep. If I should die before I wake, I pray the Lord my soul to take. . . . God bless Mom an' Dad . . . Dad an' Mom. . . . Her no more'n him . . . an' Aunt Rose an'. . . .

Saturday leaped into his mind in a special way: *"We usta go snake huntin' ever' Sad'dy on Clairmount Hill an' in the woods down 'roun' Cliff Drive an' down by the railroad tracks. . . ."*

And then Sunday and Sunday school. The church loomed up out of the darkness.

I'll get a quarter! And suddenly the sound of his mother's voice made him tingle with excitement.

Yeah — I guess you kin go to the show with Tommy — if it's all right with your daddy. . . .

It's all right with me, if it's all right with you.

Okay by me.

I wish Sunday was tomorrow!

He scanned the sky for a falling star.

"Hi, Vi!" cried Miss Ada the following evening after supper.

"Hi, Sister Bill, I'm ready!" Viola answered with a smile, stepping to the door to meet her. They said good-bye and rushed off to club meeting in a whirl of powdered, perfumed enthusiasm. And before he could finish his dream of Miss Chapman and Mr. Bowles she was home.

Thursday passed unnoticed.

Friday he learned a song:

Good mornin' to you, good mornin' to you, good mornin', dear teacher, good mornin' to you!

"That's fine!" said Viola.

"That boy's gonna be a Irish tenor — like his uncle Montroe!" Rutherford exclaimed with a mischievous smile.

"Who's Uncle Montroe?"

"Don't you remember him? He had the best Irish tenor on the avenue!"

He thought of a blue-eyed man with gray hair in a policeman's uniform, or a fireman's. . . .

"He usta take you 'round with 'im all the time when you wasn' no more'n two years old!" said Viola.

"Closer to *three!*" Rutherford exclaimed, "that little niggah wasn' walkin' till he was almost old as me!"

"Miss Chapman says you ain' supposed to say *nigger*, 'cause that's what igner'nt people says," Amerigo said. Anger and surprise rushed into Rutherford's face, followed by an expression of profound embarrassment. Viola struggled to suppress a smile and dropped her eyes to the floor.

"Yeah, well — anyway . . ." Rutherford stammered, "remember, Babe? He was eh, crossin' crossin' the boulevard with the pr'fessor here. He wasn' nothin' but a baby then, an' didn' go 'round teachin' his father — an' the traffic was heavy, I mean heavy! You know how it is at five o'clock! An' that little-eh-*joker* was doin' the *mess-around!*"

"Ohooo!" Viola yelled, "an' *gruntin':* unh-unh-unh-unh — messin' around to beat the band! The cars stopped on the boulevard an' all the white folks was a-lookin' and a-laughin'! I just *knew* you was gonna be a dancer like Ruben!"

"He's gonna be a pr'fessor — or a preacher!" said Rutherford wryly, "tellin' his *daddy* what to say! But Miss Chapman's right, Amerigo, we shouldn' use that word. If anybody calls you that, just ignore 'um. That's funny, if a white man'd call you that, you'd wanna kill 'im, but we call each other that all the time. I hear the Italians callin' each other *wop* all the time, but if *you* said it, they'd want to take you for a ride! The Jews do it, too. I guess it ain' what you say, as much as how you say it — what you *mean* by it. It's about time for you to hit the hay, ain' it, Rev?"

"Yessir."

"Around the breakfast table!" exclaimed the announcer through the loudspeaker of the radio in the front room, as he rushed about his tasks early Saturday morning. A man named Jack and a woman named Jane sat around the breakfast table and talked about where to buy radios and stoves and how good petticoats and hatpins and blouses and gloves from the big stores downtown were. Then they went off.

"Let's pretend!" cried the announcer, and fairy music played, and then a man talked a little, and then there was a fairy story with little kids in it just like him. It was about a beautiful prince who was turned into a bird, a swan, who fell in love with a beautiful maiden with rosy lips like berries like in the fairy books Amerigo got for Christmas, with long blond hair, and how she saved him by cutting it off.

He thought of Miss Chapman when the beautiful maiden spoke. He saw her, all pink and golden and dark-eyed and no bigger than him! And he was the Swan Prince!

"Wauk! Wauk!" he cried plaintively, his heart beating violently for the love of the lovely maiden who treated him with such kindness. "Save me from the life of eternal swandom!" he pleaded, and she understood because he spoke the language of love, which everybody could understand.

The wicked witch demanded a sacrifice:

"Your hair!" screeched Mrs. Shields hideously.

Miss Chapman, sobbing because of the pain of her love, cut off her golden hair with a golden pair of scissors.

"I'm a prince again!" cried the prince, standing beautifully, radiantly adorned, in garments of purest gold upon the banks of the lake. "And you can be my princess!" he declared to the weeping Miss Chapman. "To King Bowles, my father who'll let us in!"

"Oh happy day!" cried the good King Bowles. "Let the weddin' bells ring out!"

The wedding bells rang through the loudspeaker and they began to live happily ever after just as he was contentedly working his way into the kitchen.

Then *Midmorning Serenade!* came on, featuring Louis Armstrong and his orchestra. He can blow higher than anybody in the whole *world* on the trumpet — Dad *said* so! The announcer was saying the second half of the program would be shared by Fats Waller.

As he washed the dishes he tapped his feet to the rhythm, and broke a cup. Satch played that thing! Heedless of the cup, he sang with the music: "Aw, the bucket's got a hole in it!" He threw his head back, straining the muscles in his throat, and sang as loud as he could. It felt good. It sounded good. He stopped washing dishes and began to dance. High-class-like, like Uncle Ruben doing the break-step that Viola had taught him, that Uncle Ruben could do better than everybody in the whole world!

And then Fats Waller came on, laughing and playing and singing, playing all over that piano! — the way Rutherford said: He's got *class*, Amerigo. He kin read music, Jack! That cat's got a edu*cation*! Unh-unh! It might *sound* easy, what he's doin', to a whole lot a people who don' know no better, but Tom, Dick, an' Harry'd break their fingers off tryin' to play what that man kin play! Or blow a fuse!

Twelve o'clock.

Lunch was over and Viola was gone.

Miss McMahon's shoot was clean, the quarter pocketed.

Five o'clock. Supper: hot dog sandwiches, salad, and beer for them and strawberry soda-pop for him. It was early when Rutherford left to get his hair cut. Low feather-edge. Amerigo watched his mother cut up the Sunday chicken. As he stepped out the door, he was greeted by Miss Allie Mae who was just coming in.

"Unh! I'm early!" she exclaimed breathlessly. "Hello, Rutherford. Hi, Vi! Hello, baby! I hear you went to school!"

"Yes'm," he muttered, blushing, while Rutherford stood inside the door to let her pass.

"G-i-r-l!" turning to Viola, "my hair's a *mess!* It needs just about *ever'thin'!*" She sat heavily in the nearest chair and smiled a pretty little smile. He looked at her with admiration. She looks like a little girl! Surprise and secret satisfaction excited him strangely: No bigger than me — just a little anyway — but her hands and feet are as little as mine. He gazed with pleasure upon her shapely legs and seated himself in the chair opposite her so that he could watch his mother wash and straighten her hair.

"So long, gals!" said Rutherford.

"So long, Rutherford," said Miss Allie Mae with a sigh.

"Take it easy," said Viola.

"After my haircut, I think I'll go over an' see what old T. C.'s doin'. Maybe we'll take in a show or somethin'."

"Okay," said Viola.

"You lookin' mighty sharp, there, Mister Jones," said Miss Allie Mae with a coy smile. Rutherford winked and was gone.

Miss Allie Mae laid her bag on the kitchen table and watched Viola finish the chicken she had started. When she had cleaned it and cut it up, she put the pieces into a bowl and filled it with water and set the bowl on the drainboard.

"Just take it easy, there, Allie, I'll be through in a minute."

"Don' worry about me, honey, go on an' do what you gotta do."

Viola wiped the drainboard clean, rolling the entrails, head, and feet in a piece of paper. "Here, put that in the garbage can," she said to Amerigo. He obeyed. When he returned to the kitchen Miss Allie Mae was taking off her shoes.

"G-i-r-l, my feet's killin' me!" she exclaimed in a sleepy voice. "Them folks had me goin' *all* day! Had to do a double room at the last minute. They don' n-e-v-e-r think it's time to quit!"

"You tellin' me!" said Viola sympathetically. "Here, wait a minute, you kin slip your feet in those big old house shoes a Rutherford's. Amerigo, go in an' git your daddy's house shoes for Allie."

He fetched the house shoes.

"Oh! ha! haaaa!" throwing her head back prettily. "I kin just about *swim* in these!" Two dimples had suddenly appeared on either side of her mouth, and he observed that her teeth were even and white.

His mother's dark efficient hands with their long slender fingers and neatly trimmed nails — like bird claws, but prettier, red — pinned a towel around Miss Allie Mae's neck.

"You sure wasn' lyin'! It sure does need washin'."

"Hush, girl! I know it's a mess. I wonder if you could marcelle it like you did yours and Ada's last time. It looked so *nice!*"

"All right, but I'll have to start the curls a little farther back, 'cause your head's shaped different than mine."

"You know what you doin', girl, just fix it."

He studied Miss Allie Mae's head. It was small and shaped a little like an egg, but then he reconsidered in favor of a cantaloupe, honeydew, he studied her light creamy complexion, her slightly pug nose, her soft brown sleepy eyes and dark reddish brown hair that was almost good. He smiled with satisfaction.

"What you smilin' at!" Viola was taking the bobbypins out of her hair and laying them on the table.

"Nothin'."

"How you doin' in school?"

Viola began combing her hair. It was rather fine, and extended down to the base of her neck.

"All right."

"I bet you know more'n the teacher!"

He grinned, Viola smiled, pushing her head a little forward so that she could comb the back.

"No'm."

Her hair stood up in a soft brush. Viola took the kettle from the stove and emptied it into the dishpan, testing it with her finger, as the cold water ran from the tap. Then she turned off the cold water and put the kettle back on the stove.

"Scoot up a little, Allie Mae." She scooted her chair up to the sink and Viola dipped the soap until it was wet and streaked with grayish suds. Then she kneaded Allie Mae's scalp until her hair was meshed in a tangled mass of foam speckled with minute flecks of blue, red, yellow, and green light.

It was like Mrs. Derby's when the sun falls on it, only white like snow. He thought of Christmas and rabbits, seeing Mr. Derby tramping home in his high leather boots and big sheep-lined coat, with his shotgun crooked on his arm, carrying a bag full of rabbits with brown fur and white tails; cottontails!

Meanwhile Viola was rubbing Miss Allie Mae's scalp good, and scratching it with her fingernails, while Miss Allie Mae exclaimed "Oh!" and "Unh! — that sure feels good, Vi!" She took a clean rag and began rinsing the suds out of her hair. When most of the suds were gone she wrung it with her hands as she would a wet cloth and poured the dirty water into the sink.

"Wait a minute — " she said, reaching for the kettle, while Miss Allie Mae wiped the water out of her eyes, and when the water was right she rinsed her hair again, and again, but this time she poured some vinegar into the water, and then she rinsed it for the last time, and poured the water out of the dishpan for the last time, scrubbed it clean, dried it and hung it on the nail beside the sink. Then she took a fresh bath towel and tied it around Miss Allie Mae's head and rubbed it so hard that the whole head shook from left to right real fast, then slower. After that she wrapped the towel tight and fastened it with a safety pin.

"There now, it oughtta be dry soon."

"Sure was dirty, wasn' it!"

"Not too bad — for three weeks."

"I thought it was two."

"Well, you was supposed to pay me for the last time on the first, an' taday's the fifteenth, so it must a been three weeks!"

"Aw, that's right, girl, you know I forgot all 'bout that. Kin I pay you for the last one this time an' this 'un next time? Honest to goodness! I just don' know w-h-e-r-e the money goes! Howard was *supposed* to give me some money last week, but, girl, that lyin' man ain' showed up *yet!* These men, honey!"

"I know, Ada's singin' the blues, too."

"An' Dor'thy come home yesterday, cryin' for a new dress! An' here I am, killin' myself just tryin' to feed 'er!"

"You dress that child just like a little doll, Allie Mae. You ain' no rich woman. You'll just end up spoilin' 'er."

"I know, but Lord knows she's all I got, Vi. Her daddy went away and left her when she wasn' nothin' but a baby, an' I just try somehow to do the best I kin. On top a that, I have to take care a Momma, she's always achin', an' Lukas's always fightin' an' givin' every penny he makes to that woman. 'Course, I ain' sayin' he ain' a good man an' all — Momma's a hard woman to live with — but all that ain' helpin' *me* none. Say! Did you hear the latest?"

"Naw, girl, what?" Viola had been rummaging in one of the cupboard drawers for her straightening combs, but now she stopped and looked at Miss Allie Mae intently.

"You ain' heard?"

"Naw, I tell you!"

She struck a match and lit the gas. A ring of blue flame shot up from the burner with a windy sound, while flickering points of yellow light fringed the tips of the little powder-blue flames. She turned the gas down until the yellow went away and then laid the iron combs on the little round grate.

All this she did mechanically, while looking at the base of Miss Allie Mae's toweled head.

"Big Tom and Gert had a *wingding* last night!"

"Agin?"

"He came home half tight, an' caught 'er tight, too, an' the house was all dirty an' ever'thin', an' on top a that the supper wasn' ready, an' the kids was all cryin', an' g-i-r-l he almost had a *fit!* They had *words,* honey, an' then 'er lip slipped, an' he hit 'er an' I'm tellin' you, I *swear!* I thought the whole house was fallin' down!"

"Ain' that a shame!"

"He knocked her *through the screen!* Through the *screen,* girl — an' *off the porch!* Broke her leg!"

"Tisch tisch tisch," exclaimed Viola, sucking the spittle through her teeth.

"Ain't you seen 'er walkin' 'round all stiff-legged an' ever'thin'? Leg ain' *never* gonna be well no more!"

"He always did believe in beatin' his women. Wonder what it was all about. Gave Leona a hard time, too. She was just like Gert. He likes 'um big an' black."

"These men don' need no excuse, honey. Howard was the same way. Lord knows I done ever'thin' I could to try an' git along with that man, but he just wouldn' do right! Drinkin' an' gamblin', an' then what'd he do? Went off with a tramp! An' she treats 'im like a dog. Serves 'im right!"

"Is it broke, do you think?"

"Just as bad, all swollen up an' ever'thin'."

"That *would* be the end, honey, Rutherford hittin' me! An' me slavin' every day — just the same as him! Honey, we done had that out, once an' *for all!* You know what I went through with the b-a-b-y an' all."

B-a-b-y spells baby, he thought cunningly.

". . . all by myself . . ."

"Don't you say nothin', girl! But you lucky, Rutherford *works!* An' brings his money home, an' *tries* to do the right thing. I ain' got no man to help *me!*"

Viola's eyes darkened, her fingers dumbly unfastening the towel. She stuck the safety pin in the bodice of her dress and fastened it.

"If it hadn' a been for Miss Rose, I don' know what I'd a done — with Momma dyin' an' all. Woman's a fool to let a man have his way an' not git nothin' out of it."

"You sure spoke the truth that time!"

Viola combed her hair out again and parted it in the middle. Her scalp shone clean and yellow. She dipped her finger in the Vaseline jar and rubbed the soft transparent mass along the scalp. Then she made another part crosswise and greased the scalp as before, repeating this process until her hair was completely divided into little parted squares.

She took a hot comb from the fire and rubbed it in an old cloth and lightly combed the first little square. The comb made a frying sound going through, accompanied by a faint puff of blue-gray smoke that rose from her hair. When the first square was finished she started on the second, and the third, until the whole head was done. Then she combed it out again, parted it, and repeated the process with the longer comb, until her hair was straight and shining.

Brighter than a white woman's, he thought, noticing the fine sheens of sweat upon their foreheads and Viola's glistening fingers as she deftly plyed her task. Her hair all straight, she parted it a third time.

"How about a little beer?"

"Girl, you took the word right out a my mouth!"

"Amerigo, look in the icebox and bring a quart a beer."

"Yes'm."

He brought the beer.

"An' there's some peanuts in my pocketbook."

He brought the pocketbook to her and she took the sack of peanuts out and placed them on the table. Then she took a bowl and two glasses from the cupboard, poured the peanuts into the bowl and some beer into one of the glasses, slanting it so that the foam would not rise over the brim. She handed it to Miss Allie Mae.

"Ummm!" she exclaimed, sipping from the glass.

"I got some rasins somewhere. . . ." said Viola, looking in the bottom part of the cupboard where she found half a sack of rasins, which she emptied into the bowl of peanuts and mixed them with a spoon. "You kin take some, if you wanna," she said to him. He spread his small hand wide and grabbed all he could and ate greedily. Viola sipped her beer and went back to work.

She gathered the fine strands of hair in each little square and laid them between the open blades of the curling iron, rolling the hair around it until the iron almost touched the scalp. Then she wriggled the iron out sideways, setting the curl with the forefinger of her left hand. Then she started on the next few strands and did the same, sipping her beer quietly as she worked.

Miss Allie Mae closed her eyes and began to nod.

"Hold your head up, here, girl! Don' go noddin' on me."

Miss Allie Mae jerked her head straight and smiled with astonishment. Her eyes were glazed. "You *know* I wouldn' do a thing like that! Goin' to Sund'y school tamorra, Amerigo?" in a sleepy voice.

"Yes'm."

"I got to iron Dor'thy's dress!"

"Mom, kin I go out an' play?"

"I guess so, but don' go out a the alley. An' don't you set foot on Toodle-lum's porch, you hear?"

"No'm."

He ran through the house, out the front door, and down the hall steps. A woman in a white dress was going into Miss Sadie's apartment. He caught sight of the coal oil lamp on the little square table with the needles and cotton just before Mr. Nickles in his sport shirt, pants, and house shoes slammed the door. He stepped onto the front porch.

Aunt Lily's door was open. He peeped in.

"Hi, hon!" she murmured softly and smiled. She was ironing a slip. It was spread out over the board, which was stretched across the backs of two chairs.

"Him" sticking his nose against the screen. "Hi, Unc."

Uncle Dewey looked up from his paper and grinned mischieveously at him. He sat in the rocking chair near the door in his pants and house shoes. The upper part of his BVDs were showing. He wore a dark brown vest over it, and the pockets were filed with thin books, the leaves of which were fastened together with metal clamps and red rubber bands, and three sharp yellow pencils with aluminum clips to hold them in. He stared at Unc's bald head and marveled at the way it picked up the light from the coal oil lamp, which threw a ring of corrugated light upon the ceiling and glistened in splinters of silver upon the rims of his glasses that rested, as usual, upon the tip of his sharp little nose. The cleft in his chin deepened with his smile.

"They tell me tha-tha-tha-that you hhhha-had-had the-the *nerve* to ggggo-go to sc-sc-school!"

"Yessir!"

"Aw, Unc!" Aunt Lily exclaimed with a smile, taking the hot iron from the top of the stove and rubbing it on a piece of Bond Bread wrapping paper at the head of the board.

"IIIII bbbe-be-bet you ca-ca-can't say your ABCs, li-li-li-little nnnniggah!"

Aunt Lily winked at him. He winked back.

"WhatyougonnagivemeifIdo?"

"I'll ggggive give you aaaa dddamned damned goo good beatin' iiif if you don'!"

"How much?"

"Aaaanickel!"

He looked at Aunt Lily to see if it were really true, and she nodded her head.

"ABCDEFGHIJKLMNOPQRSTUVWXYZ — gimme!" holding out his hand.

"You a smart li-li-li-little ddddevil ain't you?" He stuck his thumb and forefinger into his vest pocket and pulled out a tarnished nickel and slid it under the screen door. "There, nnnnow, gi-gi-gi-git out a here here — bbbe-before you *steal* steal a-a-all a my money!"

"Tee hee!" sniggers from the alley.

"Aw man, give the boy back his marbles!"

Tommy, he thought.

"Aw, I was just playin' with the little niggah!"

Turner.

"Looka there!" He looked down over the banister at Carl. Then he noticed Tommy, William, Lem, Geraldine (Turkey-legs), Toodle-lum, Willie Joe, and Helen Francis — all sitting on the edge of Miss Anna and Monroe Bentley's porch. They were looking down the alley.

The avenue was bright with the lights from the store windows. The neon lights from The Blue Moon and The Saw-Dust Trail were on. Men, women, and children, cars and wagons drawn by horses moved in and out of the light. A streetcar growled by. Fragmentary bits of song poured into the alley. Mrs. Derby softly hummed the melody of "Jus' a Closer Walk with Thee" from within her apartment. Figures moved behind the orange paper curtains in the upstairs apartment of the Shieldses' house. Suddenly Miss Hazel stood in the door in her underskirt and he heard another melody cracking on the gramophone:

"In the evenin'. In the evenin'. . ."

She looked expectantly up the alley, then she regarded him for an instant with a wry smile.

"Momma, when the sun goes down. Ain' it lonesome, ain' it lonesome, when your lover's not around. . . ."

She shut the door. There was another burst of laughter from the Bentley porch. The children were still looking down the alley. Turner was pointing and grinning. He looked to see what they were laughing about and finally discovered the stumbling figure of a man, weaving his way up the alley. He was sure that it was Mr. Mun because of the way he walked. He wore a lumber jacket, overalls, and a cap. He's got a mustache, Amerigo thought, and a big purple wart on his nose as big as a pea with little gray hairs grew out of its center.

"I done had my fun — yeah Lawd! If I don' never have no fun no more!" he cried, and then he began to sing in a squeaky broken voice: "Oh — I *wish* I had wings — of an an-gel! . . . Over these — prison walls — I would fly. . . . Anna! — Aw — Anna! — Yoooo hee!"

Mr. Everett came out on his porch. He watched Mr. Mun stumble past him. Mr. Mun waved feebly and Mr. Everett smiled.

"Did you hit the numbers taday, Mun?"

Mr. Mun started to reply, but was distracted by the giggling children. He grinned and danced comically before them, sticking his thumbs in his ears and sticking out his tongue and fanning his fingers.

"Hot dog!" cried Carl, doubling over with laughter.

"Look at that cat!" shouted William who was only four.

"Every Sad'dy he's like that . . . like that," said Toodle-lum timidly, smiling like a shy girl.

"How do you know, you little half-white monkey?" shouted Turner.

"Aw — you know that boy ain' white!" said Tommy.

"Naw, he's Mexican — ain't you, Toodle-lum?" Turner ran the palm of his hand down Toodle-lum's face.

"I ain' no half-white . . . half-white . . . neither . . . neither! . . ." brushing Turner's hand away with his own birdlike hand.

"You ain' black! You ain' no coon. You ain' no mellah-brown like me. You *must* be sum'um!"

"I'm a ding-dong daddy from Duma!" cried Mr. Mun, snapping his fingers. "Aw — you oughtta see me do my stuff!"

The children made faces at him.

"Anna's gonna ding your dong when you git home!" cried Mrs. Grey. "Turner's momma."

"Don't you go signifyin' about me, old woman!" snapped Mr. Mun, "'cause — yes, yes! 'Cause e-v-e-r-y tub, you heah me? . . . Eeee e-v-e-r-y tub, got to set, on its *own* black bottom! Now, heffer, *signify* about that!"

Mrs. Grey slammed her screen door and disappeared within the house. Meanwhile Mr. Mun stumbled onto his porch, fumbled at the screen door of his apartment, and finally entered. The child ran down to the foot of the front steps and peeped in with the others. The room was dark.

"Anna!" he shouted within.

"*Boom!*" The sound of falling furniture suddenly issued into the alley.

"Aw-aw!" cried Turner.

"God-*damn!*" cried Mr. Mun, "tryin' to *kill* a man in this hellhole! What the —"

"*Boom!*" another bone-crushing sound. The children all ran to the edge of the porch. Doors opened and people came out to see what was going on.

"I'll *kill* you — you no-good-drunken-sonofabitch!" Miss Anna screamed. WHAM! "Eeeeve-ry Sad'dy night hit's the same God damned thing! You — you —" She burst into sobs, "— straggle in here *drunk!* an' *broke!*" WHAM!

"Look out, woman!" cried Mr. Mun. "Oh-oh! God damn you!"

"Serves the no-good niggah right!" exclaimed Mrs. Grey, who had returned to her doorway.

"If-if-if I git — my — git my hands on your black ass . . ." stuttered Mr. Mun, "I'll — "

WHAM! "You triflin' bastard!" Miss Anna replied.

Mr. Mun suddenly burst onto the porch, limping and holding his arm.

"That's right!" he yelled over his shoulder at the advancing Miss Anna, who held a barrel stave above her head, swatting at him as though he were a fly. "That's right — go crazy! Kill me! KILL ME *please*. 'Cause if you *don't,* your black misbegotten day is comin'!"

She threw the stave at him. He ducked in an attempt to avoid the blow and fell backward off the concrete porch and crashed against the cobblestones in the alley. He landed on his injured arm. He lay motionless.

Miss Anna tiptoed to the edge of the porch and looked at him, a small thin dark-brown-skinned woman with a small crescent-shaped scar under her right eye. Her eyes were red from crying. She trembled in her underskirt, rubbing her bare feet against the wooden post that supported the porch in a sort of nervous agitation.

"Mun . . ."

Mr. Everett, Mrs. Grey, Mr. Dan, Mrs. Shields, Miss Hazel, and others gathered around Mr. Mun. His eyes were closed. He rolled on his side and groaned with pain.

Miss Anna knelt down and took him in her arms.

"Mun? Mun, baby. Oh Lawd — somebody please call a doctor!"

Minutes later an ambulance whined down the alley and two black men in white uniforms lifted Mr. Mun on a stretcher and put him into the ambulance. Miss Anna climbed in beside him and sat holding his hand, while the men climbed into the cab and drove away.

"Poor child," said Aunt Lily, "she even forgot to put on 'er clothes!"

"Toodle-lum! Aw — Toodle-lum!"

"Yes'm . . . yes'm." He went over and sat on his porch. The crowd dispersed, laughing and whispering.

The nine o'clock whistle blew.

Just as he reached the top step Miss Myrt called Tommy, William, and Lemuel to take their baths.

"What in the world was all that commotion about?" asked Viola as he entered the kitchen.

"Nothin'. Just Miss Anna an' Mr. Mun."

"They at it agin!"

Miss Allie Mae was nodding. Her head was radiant with a mass of shining curls!

"It's about that time, ain' it?"

"Yes'm."

"You gotta go to church in the mornin'."

Miss Allie Mae's head was almost lying on her chest. Viola looked at him and then at her and smiled. She made a sign for him to be quiet, then she tickled her in the ribs with the tip of her finger.

"Who! What! Yes — yes —" she exclaimed, bolting upright. Then she grinned, the grin weakened into a smile, and the smile slowly faded, and she began to nod again, her head settling back upon her chest, as before.

"You go in an' get ready," said Viola. "I'll come in before you git to sleep. An' wash your face an' hands, you're as dirty as a gypsy!"

They can tell your fortune, he thought, and then wondered what *fortune* meant, as he washed his face. He was about to ask when Viola prodded Miss Allie Mae again.

"Oh! My goodness! What time is it? Did I go to *sleep?*"

"Did you go to *sleep!*" Viola laughed. Amerigo, his face full of suds, laughed, too, while she looked from one to the other and grinned girlishly.

She's pretty.

"Sleepin' down to tha bricks! — Huh?" she said.

"Amerigo, say good night to Miss Allie Mae."

"G'night."

"Good night, Amerigo, sleep tight," sleepily stretching out her arms, while he resisted the impulse to throw his arms around her waist and lay his head against her breast, moving shyly into the front room where he removed the pillows from the sofa and made his bed and got in it.

Light filtered in from the kitchen. His mother and Miss Allie Mae were talking and laughing. Gradually their voices droned passively in his ears. He turned on his side and faced the window. Because the shade was drawn he couldn't see above the border of reflected light from the lamppost. He tossed restlessly amid a fleeting parade of images and sounds that had been the day called Saturday.

"Did you say your prayers?"

He bolted upright. Viola was bending over him. Miss Allie Mae stood beside her, dressed and ready to leave, her hair all shining. She was smiling.

"Did you say your prayers?"

"No'm."

"Well, say 'um."

"Be seein' you, Vi," said Miss Allie Mae.

"All right, girl. I'll call you tamorra an' we'll see what we gonna do about club meetin'. Ada knows all about ever'thin' an' all."

"Okay. Bye, baby."

He glared vacantly at her.

"He's sleepy," said Viola.

He climbed out of bed after she had gone and knelt down to pray.

"Now I lay me down to sleep. . . . God bless Mom an' Dad an' Miss Chapman an' Pr'fessor Bowles . . . an' . . . an' . . ."

"What about Aunt Rose?" Viola whispered.

"An' Aunt Rose."

He got back in bed. She kissed him good night and turned out the light.

The birds woke him, as usual.

It isn't like yesterday, he thought, tingling with a fresh excitement that gripped him immediately. He felt the warm Sunday sun upon his face. It's different because Sunday is different.

He looked into the middle room. Viola and Rutherford lay side by side. They slept lightly and peacefully, as though the slightest sound would wake them. Suddenly he heard the clock ticking. It sounded different, too. Nobody paid any attention to it. Viola and Rutherford lay there beside it as though its ticking did not make any difference.

It's Sunday! he thought.

He lay quietly and tried not to make any noise. It wasn't time to get up and get ready to go to Sunday school yet. He listened to the birds singing and the clock ticking, noticing that the sun was still too soft, with too much blue in it.

A bell rang from a church tower. The church down below the spaghetti factory. It has a high pointed roof like an ice cream cone. Catholics . . . where the I-talians go.

As he lay looking out the window he thought about Jesus who was good to little children who did what their mothers and fathers told them in order to send them to heaven. A good place where there is a whole lot a singing like at St. John's and the streets are made out of gold bricks!

The alley flashed golden before his eyes! Everybody was singing. Some in the windows and some in the streets! The alarm clock rang.

"Unh!" cried Rutherford from the middle room. He looked in and saw his father sitting up in bed with an anxious expression upon his face.

"What's the matter?" Viola asked sleepily. Rutherford stared at the clock.

"I forgot it was Sund'y! Hey-hey!" he chuckled quietly, lay back down, and turned over on his side.

Once more stillness settled over the middle room.

After a while he stole naked down the steps to the front porch and got the paper. He glanced up and down the alley. It was blue and amber and sort of golden — and quiet, except for the birds. He tiptoed back upstairs and got in bed and neatly separated the funny papers from the rest and gazed at the pictures. He scanned "Popeye" and "Tillie the Toiler" — she was so pretty — and "Tarzan of the Apes." Tarzan was standing upon the bough of a huge tree with a strong vine in his hand, gazing down upon a lion that was sneaking upon a man in a hard round hat and short pants, with a gun. His eyes raced to the end of the strip, to where Tarzan jumped down on the lion's back. That was the end. He browsed over "Maggie and Jiggs." They looked funny, but he did not understand what it was all about because he could not read that much yet. Mickey Mouse is funnier! All you have to do is look at the pictures. He studied "Little Orphan Annie" and "Little Annie Roonie" and "The Two Black Crows" and all the colored pictures on both sides of every page until there were no more, and then he looked at the best ones again.

When he was almost finished Rutherford got up, got dressed in his Sunday clothes, and went to work, and Amerigo slipped into bed beside Viola and snuggled up close to her.

"Now you be still," she said threateningly. "Taday's Sund'y an' I want to git a little rest!"

He lay very still for a minute. Then he tossed and turned and kicked and sighed until she sat up in bed and looked at the clock and said:

"All right, all right! You kin git up. Put the water on an' call me when it's hot. An' put some clothes on! You'll catch your death a cold, runnin' through the house like that!"

He slipped happily out of the bed and ran into the kitchen and put the water on. Then he went out onto the back porch. Mrs. Crippa's light was on. He could see her standing in front of the kitchen table sipping something from a cup — Coffee, I bet — noticing that she was dressed in a long black dress with a shawl over her shoulders. Then the light went out and her kitchen suddenly looked dark and gray inside and he could not see her anymore.

He heard the water boiling in the kitchen. He peeped through the screen and saw that it bubbled out of the spout and from under the lid and onto the blue flames and made them turn yellow. He rushed in and turned off the gas, and then went into the middle room and woke his mother. Her eyes were pink and there were faint welts on the fine dark skin of her face and arms from the wrinkles in the sheet and the pillowcase.

Minutes later he was standing in the No. 3 tub, laughing and giggling, while Viola rubbed him all over with a big washrag. "If you don't keep still! Fidgetin' like a jumpin'-Jack!"

"It tickles!"

Then presently Already! it was over, he was dressed in his gray Sunday suit and his black Sunday shoes. She tied a nickel in the corner of a handkerchief and stuffed it into his pocket.

"Do you have to carry that star *every*where?"

"Yes'm."

"Why don't you leave that thing here? What you gonna do with a star in church?"

He made a face.

"All right, but at least put it in the other pocket."

He put it in the other pocket. They went down on to the front porch together. Tommy, William, and Lemuel were coming down the alley.

"He's ready!" said Viola. "You bring 'im straight home when church's over!"

"Yes'm," Tommy said, "I will!"

"You be good, you hear?"

"Yes'm."

He ran to join the others, strutting a little in his Sunday way, glancing down with satisfaction at his Sunday suit, his greased legs, and his sparkling black shoes.

They made their way up the alley. They passed Aunt Nancy who was standing on her porch all dressed up in her Sunday clothes, too: a long black dress with a white collar. Her hair was done up nice.

She's on the mother-board, he thought, tipping his cap the way Viola and Rutherford had taught him.

"Well now, ain' that sweet!" she smiled broadly.

"G'mornin', Aunt Nancy," said Tommy.

"G'mornin'," said William.

"'Mornin'," said Lemuel.

"Bless your little hearts!" said Aunt Nancy, following them with her glance all the way to the top of the alley.

Mr. Whitney was standing in the door of his house, a tall thin honey-colored man with straight silver hair like a white man's and a white wisp of beard under his chin. He thought of Professor Bowles who looked like a white man, too.

"'Mornin', Mr. Whitney," he said, and the others joined in. The old man smiled vacantly, dreamily, raising his fine long feeble hand as a greeting.

Earl Lee stood on his porch, next to Mr. Whitney's. His skin was dark brown, his lips were fleshy, and his face wore a suffering expression, which he now and then converted into a sneer.

"Ain't you goin' to Sund'y school?" William asked.

"I don't have to! That's for kids!"

"Aw yeah!" Lemuel cried, the smallest and youngest of them all.

"Aw yeah!" Earl Lee retorted, imitating his voice.

"You ain' no more'n 'leven, niggah!" Turner cried.

"He's just ignarunt!" said Amerigo.

"Yeah," said Tommy, looking at him with surprise, adding, "He don' know better."

They eyed each other jealously until they were out of sight.

They turned at the boulevard. The traffic lights flickered delicious flavors of green, yellow, and red: All-day suckers. They crossed between "flavors," hand in hand, south up Campbell Street. At Eighth Street they passed a row of half run-down houses where many children were playing. He tipped his hat to all the women and greeted all the men.

"Now that's what I call a gen'lmun!" said a big dark lady who was standing on the corner talking to a skinny yellow lady.

"Who's little boy is that?" asked the yellow lady.

"That's Vi-ols's boy. They live down in the alley."

"Look at that sissyfied niggah!" said a boy. Big. He had seen him at school but he did not know his name.

They crossed Eighth Street where Negroes lived on both sides of the street, continued south, and were suddenly in a white neighborhood. Farther up on Campbell Street he caught sight of Aunt Lily's laundry.

Sunday school was held in a large gray room with narrow floorboards separated by thin black cracks. They made him think of Sister Clara James. He could hear her admonishing him to follow the straight and narrow. His eyes had fallen upon the floor and followed the cracks to the wall, and through the wall, and he had resolved to be better.

He stared at the first of three round, stained-glass windows just behind her head, while she officially opened the Sunday school and started to make the general announcements. The light flooding through the opaque window decorated with wine-red flowers with beer-bottle-green leaves obscured her round dedicated face and threw her high-crowned wide-brimmed hat with its long turkey feather into full relief.

He set about imagining her face as he had seen it in the light — caramel-colored, with three chins and big dark brown intelligent eyes.

He did not understand everything she said, but he sensed that she spoke with the tired but determined voice of one who longed for a rest from the heavy responsibilities of her position as superintendent of the Sunday school, but who could not rest simply because there was no one else with sufficient zeal and devotion to carry on the Lord's work.

When she had finished she wearily rang the bell and the children shifted into little groups, and the teachers passed out the books and began to teach their classes.

He listened to Brother Jones with rapt attention. He held the book at arm's length and squinted in order to read the text. His beautiful bald head picked up the light from the windows, and he immediately thought of Mr. Everett and Unc Dewey.

Brother Jones read the story of Jesus who was the son of God, and how when he was a little boy he answered all the questions of the wise men. "An' then, children, He asked *them* questions — wiser questions — that they couldn't answer!" He concluded with the observation that those who would go to heaven must have the innocence and faith of children.

"What's in-a-cents?" Brother Jones gave a warm smile of approval.

"That's right, son, ask questions." He paused thoughtfully: "Inacence is the ignorance of sin. Sin is what you do — even think! — that's aginst the Lord's teachin's! When we are not obedient, don't do what our mother and father tell us, or our teachers, or grown folks who's tryin' to help us for our own good, we grow up to be bad! Bad men an' women who do bad things! O-bedience to the *word!* An'-an' *love* is the way of the Lord. Love'll move mountains! Love thy neighbor as thyself! That's what Jesus said. An' if you love 'im, you'll give 'im food when he's hungry, an' somethin' to wear when he needs clothes for his back an' shoes for his feet. Share the good things in life with others. Nothin's no good to you, no how, unless you share it with somebody else!"

"What's *share* mean?"

"To give to others some a what you got."

The first bell rang and the collection was taken. He put his nickel in. Brother Jones passed out little cards with pictures of Jesus talking to the wise men, with writing at the bottom. A circle of light shone over Jesus' head. Like in the picture over the bed.

The second bell rang and the scattered groups shifted into a solid mass occupying the center section of the hall and spilling over into the sections on either side.

Sister Jennings, the secretary, read the minutes, and Sister Mayfield, the treasurer, read the financial report and reported the attendance, and then reports of the various committee chairmen were made, Sister Williams for the Christmas Program Committee, Sister Kelly for the Young People's Choir, Sister Watkins for the Baptist Young People's Union, Brother Harkins for the Wednesday-night Bible Class, and Brother Bridges for the Delegation to the True Vine Baptist Church where the pastor was going to speak on the following Sunday.

After that Sister James said that they had a visitor who had something to say, a Mr. T. Wellington Harps, from the Local Branch of the National Association for the Advancement of Colored People. Mr. T. Wellington Harps rose to his feet and addressed the Sunday school assembly with a smooth easy eloquence. Like Mr. Bowles, but different. He looks like Dad — good looking, too! — but he isn't as good looking as Dad! He tried to decide if Mr. Harps was as tall as Rutherford, and came to the conclusion that he was almost as tall. Gradually he noticed that Mr. Harps's hair was not slicked down like Rutherford's, but that it looked good just the same.

"We are not yet free citizens of America," Mr. T. Wellington Harps was saying. "There is still much, much work to be done. We need decent jobs, houses, and we need bright courageous young men and women to fight for them."

He straightened up in his seat, hearing his mother's eternal injunction: "Hold up your head, an' push your shoulders back. Be a man!"

"Men with knowledge and patience to lead us. I don't have to remind you that there was another lynching last month, for I am sure that you have read it in the *Voice*! Nor do we have to read the *Voice* or any other newspaper in order to know that we live every day with racial hatred."

"A-men!" sighed Sister James.

"Ignorance! intolerance! gangsterism! disease! filth! We are no less innocent of these crimes against humanity than our white oppressors — don't forget that!"

"Heah! heah!" cried Brother Jones.

"Heah! heah!" he whispered under his breath, looking around self-consciously in order to see if anyone had heard.

"And it's not going to change overnight! The Lord might help us, but you and I know that the Lord helps those who help themselves!"

"Hee! hee! Lay it on 'um, brother," cried Sister Watkins, smiling, the light of truth dancing in her eyes, causing the mountain of chocolate-colored flesh that engulfed her to quiver like a pudding.

"For every lynching that we investigate we need a battery of trained personnel to prepare the way. We need lawyers. Lawyers have to go to college — from four to seven years! They have to be paid. We need secretaries to write letters and compile necessary information. We need offices to house them in. We need the professional cooperation of numberless private citizens in all fields of knowledge. It takes money to fight in Washington for better and fairer laws! It takes your nickels and dimes, your pennies. And if we can't have that, we need your goodwill in order to face the tremendous task that lies ahead of us. *You* — and *you* are the N.A.A.C.P. — you are Americans, just as surely as George Washington was."

George Washington! he thought, suddenly gladdened by the feeling that he had heard that name before, that he had *seen* it under the pictures in the hall! The stern-looking man with the long white hair like a woman's.

"Heah! heah!"

"A-men!"

"Praise Je-sus!"

"Now," Mr. T. Wellington Harps continued, "when the Annual Membership Drive begins next week I urge you to give. Make a pledge and give till it hurts. I know times are bad!"

"You kin say *that* agin!" cried Brother Wayne.

"But give *anyway!* Be hungry! Didn't Jesus teach us by His own example upon this earth that *it is better to be hungry and free than to be a full-bellied slave!*"

The congregation rose to its feet and clapped its hands. Sister Watkins threw back her head, opened her mouth, and a beautiful sound filled the room:

"I, I shall not I shall not be moved! I, I shall not, I shall not be moved. Just like a tree! That's planted by tha wa-ah-ter, I shall not be moved! Jesus is my savior!"

"I SHALL NOT BE MOVED!" the congregation answered, and suddenly the deep rich baritone of the reverend burst upon the air.

He thrilled to the vibrations of all the feet booming out the rhythm on the long narrow planks running through and beyond the wall behind the table where Sister James sat with a contemplative smile upon her face. He returned his gaze to Sister Watkins — She sings so pretty! — hardly able to keep his eyes off her quivering bosom. The reverend's voice soared above the voices of the whole congregation, and a pang of shame singed his heart. He jerked his eyes away and looked at the floor, at *"the straight an' narra way,"* at *"Jesus' way"* and prayed to be better.

But then at the same time, when he looked at the turkey feather in Sister James's hat, at the smiling faces and tapping feet and at the quivering bosom of Sister Watkins, he was possessed by a powerful, almost unrestrainable desire to laugh!

The reverend stood behind the table beside Sister James. He raised the pale pink palm of his right hand, and the singing stopped, as though his hand had turned the knob on the radio in the front room.

"Ain' that a f-i-n-e young man?"

"A-MEN!"

"Yeah! Let's e-v-e-r-y-b-o-d-y say A-men agin!"

"A-MEN!"

"Talk to 'im, Jesus!"

"Aunt Nancy . . ."

"A fine young man,' the reverend was saying, almost to himself. "Smart!
Went to college. Eh, that's what *I* like! An' when he got his learnin' he
didn't turn away from the Lord, neither! Or from his people! Naw! He-he
re-in-forced his h-e-a-r-t with his *head!*"

"A-MEN!"

"I-I-I feel kinda *old* comin' behind this, this fine young man. I-I started
out so long ago! Things was different then. You, you old-timers, you know
what I mean!"

"Help 'im Lawd!"

"You remember how it was, the little country school at the end of a l-o-n-g
country road. An' then that longest road, the never-endin' road — up and out
of sin!"

"Jesus knows!"

"Jesus knows?"

"In *my* day, in my day a black man wanted to be a preacher — if the
Lord called him — or a schoolteacher, maybe a lawyer or a doctor — an'
that was hard enough!"

"Yes! yes!"

"I'm tellin' you, it was h-a-r-d! But taday, *taday* a black man wants to be
— *insists* on bein' the hardest thing of *all,* an American citizen! Ain' that
what he said?"

"Sure did, Lord!" exclaimed Sister Robinson.

"Talk to 'im, Jesus!"

"Just goes to show you how Jesus works in the hearts of men. Do you
follow me? I want you to think with me for a minute. We — us! — who
are standin' upon this little piece of God-given earth *taday!* Who have
walked through the valley of despair, have grown hoarse, tryin' to separate the goats from the sheep, tryin' to git to the top a the hill where the
air is clean an' bright with the radiance of God's holy face! As we git close
to the top, it's almost, almost too much to bear! We stumble along on cal-
lused feet! Our bones ache! An'-an' then one day comes along a young
man an' he says, 'Come on, old man, let me help you up!' Aaaaaa-Lawd!
An'you reach out an' take his hand! Ah Jesus! It's, it's the clearheaded,
clear-throated voice of Mr. Harps's generation that's speakin' God's
words taday! An' an' . . ." He looked out into the room, as though he
were trying to pick the words out of the air. Then gradually his gaze settled upon the faces of the children. His eyes shone brilliantly and he
smiled.

"An' when *I* look upon the faces of these fine young boys an' girls, Mr.
Harps seems like an old man! *As old as me!* 'Cause L-A-W-D! If-if the
world kin change so *quick!* In the twenty–thirty years between Mr. Harps

an' me Jesus! What must the world be like that God is showing to these big bright eyes lookin' at me now."

"A-MEN!"

Mr. T. Wellington Harps smiled at the reverend with admiration, and the congregation, noticing it, exclaimed with proud a-mens.

"He's the best preacher in the whole world!"

The reverend scanned the faces of the children.

"What languages do you speak?" To the rest of the congregation: "Do you follow me? Do you understand what the Lord's tellin' me to tell you? They got words *that ain' never been said yet!* They already *been* places, are gonna go places, that you an' me an' even Mr. Harps, heah, ain' never gonna know! I say, the Lord works in mysterious ways! I-I — you know —"

"Help'im, Lawd! . . ."

"Hee! hee! . . .

"You know — sometimes I'd like to make the Sund'y school fill up the whole church, the balcony an' all — with bright eyes like these — an' make the church the Sunday school — to-to teach the old to see with the eyes a the young — so that Je-sus! — help me, Lord! — could have a — a birthday party e-v-e-r-y Sund'y! . . ."

"Praise the Lord! . . ."

"Yeah!"

"Talk to 'im, Jesus!"

"Ha! ha! —" The reverend laughed, nervously, ecstatically, "aaaaaa — men! — mornin' service just gonna have to be late taday! . . ."

"Preach till the Lord tell you to stop!" cried Aunt Nancy.

"Aw — He's my everything. . . ." the reverend sang, and the congregation started to join in, but were immediately prevented from doing so by the sudden admonition from the rear of the room:

"Let 'im sing!"

They quieted down, while the reverend, oblivious to all save the inspiration that lit up his eyes, continued:

"He's my ev-va-ry thing . . . Jee-suss! — is my everything. Heee's the *Lily* of the val-lay! He's the bright an' Mornin' Star! — Je — suss is my everything! . . ."

Unconsciously now, they all began to sing, all the voices blending into One Great Voice, rising and falling, chorus after chorus. . . .

I hope it never changes, he thought, gazing upon the reverend's ecstatic face. The childish serenity in it reminded him of Rutherford, a skinny little boy with all those brothers and sisters. He felt grown up. He felt old. He felt happy because he felt grown up and old. *My name is Amerigo Jones and my mother's name is . . .* He grew sad because he only *felt* grown up and old, but wasn't, could not talk like it and act like it, because he was only a little boy. Tears of rage and self-pity choaked in his throat and bewildered his mind with a sense of injustice, of humiliation in being a child, only five years old!

So little when she's so big. He wondered how old Miss Chapman was, regretting that by the time he got big enough she would be too old. Everybody in the w-h-o-l-e world will have gray hair like Old Lady! Anyway, different! He was lost in the swell of the Great Voice until finally the song came to an end, although he heard it just the same, even if he couldn't actually hear anything but the reverend saying:

"Mr. Harps, I think that I kin speak for all a us at St. John's an' say that we'll do our utmost when the N.A.A.C.P. drive starts next week!"

"A-MEN!"

He sat wearily through the first half of morning service. The seats got hard and the glare from the candelabra made him sleepy. His stomach growled. It was getting hotter by the minute. Finally he, Tommy, William, and Lemuel nudged each other and sneaked out.

"Dad home yet?" He ran into the kitchen where his mother stood in front of the stove, mashing the potatoes.

"We'll eat just as soon as he comes." She frowned as she scooped a spoonful of margarine into the potatoes. "Butter's so expensive! Almost had to fight over the chicken. Gittin' so I don' know *what* to cook with the money we got comin' in. Wash your hands and set the table."

He washed his hands and set the table. Just as he finished he heard his father running up the steps. Seconds later he burst into the kitchen and picked his mother up by the waist and whirled her around and around.

"Rutherford Jones! Are you blowin' your top?" she exclaimed with feigned displeasure. He kissed her, and Amerigo looked away with a sudden feeling of embarrassment. Unable to control himself, he ran up to them and forced himself in between them and grabbed his mother around the waist and hugged her.

"If you two want your grub on the table you better let me go so I kin cook it!"

"Hi, boy!" Rutherford exclaimed, releasing Viola. He grinned and buried his face in his mother's stomach.

"All right — what is it?" Viola demanded, freeing herself from his embrace. "Did you git paid for a change? It's almost a week now since he promised you."

"The elevator broke down!" said Rutherford.

"What's that got to do with the price a tomatoes?"

Rutherford sat down at the table, his face glowing with excitement. Like when he tells about Uncle Ruben, Amerigo thought, taking a seat at the opposite end of the table, waiting, while Viola leaned against the drainboard, looking at Amerigo with an air of expectation.

"You know, Babe, the way old man Mac is when somethin's happened? Miss Studholt come runnin' in the office 'bout to have a baby 'cause the elevator broke down, throwin' 'er hands all 'round 'cause we got all those convention folks — an'-an' no elevator! Ha! M-a-n, she sure was excited! Bill told me all about it afterward. They couldn' git no electrician 'cause it was Sund'y, an' even if they did git one it'd cost 'um double time — you know how those unions are."

"Yeah," said Viola.

"An even then it'd take 'um at least a hour before they got there.

"'God damned!' The old man cried, an' bit down on that cigar, Jack. Ahhhha! When he bites down on that rope look out! He looked up at her from under those bushy eyebrows — I kin just see 'im now — like a gen'ral, gittin' ready to send a division into battle!

"'Git Rutherford Jones!' he said an' walked *out*. Left Miss Studhope an' a-l-l those people standin' there with they bags an' ever'thin'!

"'But Rutherford ain' no electrician!' she tried to tell 'im. The housekeeper told me that. An' Bill was lookin' a-l-l over the hotel, tryin' to find me. I was in three-seventeen, ol' lady Wilks's apartment, changin' the screen in 'er window.

"'Git Rutherford Jones!' he said, an' that was all, Jack! Old Bill come runnin' up to me an' said, Man the old man's about to bust a gut! The elevator's gone an' the whole joint's about to go up in smoke!

"'What kinda jive you puttin' down, man?' I asked 'im. 'I ain' no electrician.'

"'That's what old lady Studhoss told 'im, but you know the old man. Git Rutherford Jones, he told 'er, an' then she told me, an' now I'm tellin' you what the man said. You go down an'tell 'im you ain' no electrician! It's all in your lap, daddy. You know these Jews ain' gonna pay no double time to no electrician when they kin git a boot to do it for nothin'! Hee! hee!'

"He was just a laughin'!" Rutherford continued. "An' when I gits down to the lobby it was all crowded with people an' the old man was out on the porch, lookin' across the street with his back turned on 'um. His hat was down over 'is eyes, an' he was chewin' on that stogie, deep in thought, Jack!

"'Mister Mac,' I says, 'you sent for me?' He turned 'round. 'Ah, Rutherford!' An' then all business-like: 'Rutherford, the elevator's on the blink. God damned! I just had those fellas in to look at it a couple a weeks ago — you remember — and now look what's happened. You think you kin git us out a this mess?' He looked up at me with those eyes all the time, you see.

"'I don' know, Mister Mac,' I said, lookin' back at 'im, Jack. 'You know, Rutherford,' he said, 'I got enemies all around me. That old bitch in there' — talkin' 'bout Miss Studholt! Ha! ha! — 'that woman's grabbin' ever' dime she kin lay hold a. The bank's on my neck — I don't have to tell you that, you make the payments yourself.' An' then he broke off an'give me one a those confidence looks: 'You ain' been paid yet, have you, Rutherford?' he says. 'Naw, sir,' I said. 'Well,' he said, 'we'll have to try an' take care a you. Now I want you to take a pair a pliers an' go down there an' see what you kin do for me. You're the only man I kin trust around here.'

"Take a pair a pliers!" Rutherford exclaimed. "Did you git that, Babe? That's his word, take a pair a pliers! Sometimes I think that old man takes a pair a pliers with 'im when he goes to bed with old Studhoss!

"'I'll see what I kin do,' I said. An' then I went! I went down there an' looked at that big generator an' got s-c-a-i-r-e-d! You know, Babe, I kin fix lights an'-an' refrigerators an' stopped-up sinks, or somethin' like that, but a big high-powered generator? Well, I looked at that thing, and then I sent old Bill up to turn off the current. He was just a peepin' at me to see what I was gonna do 'cause a shock from that thing'd be enough to wrap it up for a hundred years! Well ol' Bill went up an' turned the current off, an' I started to takin' things loose. I took the first things first an'-an' laid 'um aside, all neat-like, noticin' where they went. Concentratin', Jack! An'-an'-an' then, when I got it all apart, I cleaned what was dirty, put in a new part for a old one, took out a whole lot a burned-out wire an' put a new wire in an' insulated it good. An' then — all of a sudden — I seen how it all went together! I understood the whole works! Babe, from then on it was easy! Just like fallin' off a log! I seen how I had made a mistake. There was one part that should a gone over thataway an' then come down in between two little things that was so small I couldn' hardly see which way they was hooked in. Well, I changed all that. An' when I done cleaned ever'thin' — I fixed ever'thin' I could find, could see, I started to puttin' it all back tagether agin. I polished it up an'-an' made it shine like it was new! An' then I said to Bill: 'Turn on the juice!' An' he turned 'er on. An' she started up! An' I climbed up out a the pit an' went up to the lobby, all greasy an' ever'thin'. The guests was all standin' around. An' then the old man walked up: 'Did you fix 'er, Rutherford?' he says. 'I'm about to have a look now,' I said, all cool an' business-like. An' then I pushed the button! An' it started to run! S-m-o-o-t-h! You couldn' hear nothin' but a clean even hum: the current cuttin' through them wires!

"The old man looked at me, an' then he looked at them, an' then he said, an' I mean out loud! 'That's Rutherford Jones, a man you can depend on. Fine work Jones!' An' then he bit down on that stogie an' that was all, Jack!"

Viola frowned. "But he didn't pay you, did he? We can't eat praise! If you was a white man you'd have a hotel of your own! Instead a slavin' for somebody else — an' for nothin'! When things get better agin you oughtta quit and find yourself a good job."

"Aw Babe, he's gonna straighten me." Rutherford's eyes grew vacant. "It sure would be nice to have a little hotel, though. I could even run that one better'n they runnin' it now. But I'd have to change the setup. I'd break up all those big old rooms and make kitchenettes out of 'um, and have about two floors of transients. An' right there in town, too! It's comin', Babe. You wait an' see. It's gotta come! People can't afford those big old rooms and apartments no more an' have to eat in restaurants. An' there's that b-i-g ballroom downstairs, goin' to waste. All that room — just sittin' there an' ain' bein' used."

"Your bright ideas ain' gonna do you no good, Rutherford Jones. Ten years from now, you'll still be in that old hotel. Old dependable Rutherford! Doin' any and ever'thin' they say, workin' Sund'ys, workin' nights — for twelve lousy dollars a week! It's a crime! An' you fool enough to do it!"

"The old man'd stake me, I think."

"You *think!*"

"I bet he would, if I asked him."

"Why don't you *do it*, then?"

"It ain' the right time. Things is too tough — with the depression an' all. I'll wait and ask 'im right, Jack! I wouldn' even need a hotel, a six-family flat wouldn' be so bad — with a nice big lawn. I'd keep it shinin' and the grass cut, and plenty a pretty flowers all 'round, and only rent to folks with class, Jack! Out south, around Twenty-Fourth, Twenty-Sixth Street where it's quiet an' peaceful."

Viola, having finished the potatoes, put the chicken in the skillet of hot grease.

"Wash your hands, you two, so we kin eat in a little while."

He sat through a quiet thoughtful meal. Rutherford spoke further of the six-family flat and of all the things he would like to have. "And maybe a shotgun to go huntin', an' a little car, a Ford, an' ol' Amerigo could go to college an' mix with the bigshots out south an' git 'im one a them high-yellah gals to marry."

"An' each one with his own room to put his own things in," added Viola.

"An' old Vi kin buy a new dress every day! Boy, your momma sure would love that. Amerigo, that gal loves clothes! I ain' kiddin'! Always did — even when she was just a little girl. Came to school all spick-an'-span, 'er hair all straightened nice, full a ribbons, an' c-l-e-a-n! She'd take a bath twice a day! I ain' kiddin'! An' a-l-w-a-y-s- lookin' in store windows. You know I don' make much, but that gal's got a closet full a clothes. I'm scaired to look in the closet half the time. She'll work like a dog — do hair an' sew — save every penny for a year just so she kin buy somethin' nice. An' you see all the nice things we got? Yeah, we're poor, an' we ain' actually got much, but we wouldn' have that much if it wasn' for her. She'll take chances. Ain' scaired a nothin'! But I won't! I always think: Maybe we can't pay, or what if we get sick or somethin'? But your momma don' never git sick. Even when she does, gits a cold or somethin', or has female troubles, she don' go to bed. She damned near gave me pneumonia last year just breathin' down my back! Ha! Ha! Haw! haw!"

"Rutherford Jones!"

"That's *right,* Amerigo. Look at 'er the way she's built. Straight, Jack! She's always been like that. Nigg-jokers usta call 'er The Little Soldier! Who was that li'l niggah that started all the niggahs to callin' you that, Babe?"

"Aw, I forgit."

"She breathes, Amerigo! Takes one breath to my three. I ain' kiddin'. That's why she's so strong! You know what she kin do? We kin go out an' dance down to the bricks! An' I mean d-a-n-c-e, an' her drinkin' right along with me. An' after a while I git tired an' sleepy, but she don' n-e-v-e-r git tired! 'Er eyes don' even git red! They just shine a little. Even when she eats 'er stomach don't git fat like mine or most people's — it gits h-a-r-d. Feel 'er stomach, if you think I'm lyin'. An' then after ballin' an' partyin' till two or three o'clock in the mornin' she kin git up at the crack a seven an' go to work, an' really work, I mean! An' never miss a lick! An' she ain' all mean an' evil when she comes home, neither. An' if it's somethin' goin' on the next night, she kin do it a-l-l o-v-e-r agin! B-o-y, your momma kin go!

"You know what? With *her* ability an' imagination an' all, she could have a shop, dressin' hair. She's as good as any of 'um — *better!* An' ain' never had a lesson!"

"I just watch 'um," said Viola enthusiastically, "to see how they do it, an' after a few minutes I got it down pat. I always could do that!"

"She could have a shop. Hairdressin'. No kiddin', an' run it down to the bricks! An' you," turning to Amerigo, "could really git educated! With Latin an' Greek maybe. Hey! hey! Be a high-powered lawyer or a doctor. You'd make a good 'un — the way you kin make excuses to git around your momma!"

Viola looked at Rutherford with a dreamy smile.

Amerigo looked out the kitchen door. The sun shone warmly, lazily. The alley was quiet the way it always was on Sunday. Viola laid her hand on his arm.

"You kin go when you git ready. But don' stay all day. I don' wannto have to come down there an' git you."

"Yes'm."

"Where's he goin'?" asked Rutherford from the threshold of the middle room door.

"You know you said he could go to the show taday."

"Hot dog! That's right! Well, run along, sonny, an' enjoy yourself."

"Yessir." He rose from the table and started for the door.

"Wait a minute!" cried Viola. "You ain' goin' to the show without washin' your face, are you?"

"No'm."

She dampened the washcloth and rubbed his face with it. "Go an' git the comb." He went and got the comb, and she combed his hair and brushed it back with her hand, and wet the tip of her forefinger and smoothed his eyebrows back. And then, looking him over from head to foot: "An' when you git to the avenue don' forgit what I told you an' cross at the corner. Look both ways first. An' don' run! Stay on *that* side a the street. An' don' stop to talk to nobody, just keep goin' where you goin'. An' don't lose your money! Got your handkerchief?"

"Yes'm."

"Boy!" cried Rutherford from the front room: "Git on out a here! That woman'll have you here all day!"

He headed through the shoot with his stomach full of Sunday dinner and his head full of Sunday thoughts: running along the black parallel cracks of the Sunday school floor up to the wall where Sister James sat and beyond, where he could not see, into that big place called "the future." He thought of the day when he would be "a big growed-up man." And they'll be proud of me, Mom and Dad and Miss Chapman and Mr. Bowles and the reverend and Mr. T. Wellington Harps. . . .

Open your mouth, boy, an' tell us what you see! said a voice. He was startled by the knot of faces on the corner of Independence and Campbell Street. He walked across, oblivious to the din of easy-flowing traffic, to the people, colors, and smells, deeply absorbed by the world within him.

A splinter of light flickered in his eyes: the sun reflecting upon the shiny surface of the picture of the man in the big white hat on the big white horse whose hooves clawed the air. He smelled the rich aroma of popcorn, heard it popping.

Like stars! He noticed now the woman in the ticket office, discovering with delight that the hole in the middle was for her to talk through while the hole at the bottom was for her to stick her hands through when she gave him the pink ticket with writing on it, which she had torn from a big roll of pink tickets shortly after he had said: "One please," and she had smiled at him, revealing a set of whitish teeth that were partly smudged with the thick red coloring on her lips.

Ticket in hand he went past the popcorn machine where the man shoveled it into tall paper sacks through which grease spots showed for a nickel and pasteboard boxes for a dime. He was just about to open the door when the man called him back and asked him for his ticket. He gave him the ticket and opened the door himself and stepped into a big black room.

The sound of a motor running, of crunching popcorn, fried chicken, Murray's and Tuxedo hair grease, shoe polish, perfume and talcum powder, freshly ironed linen mixed with the smell of sweat and peppermint chewing gum. The whir of big electric fans. Then he felt hot. Finally he saw the thin ray of bright light streaming from a hole in the back wall. It got thicker as it flowed toward the big white wall at which everyone was looking.

Slowly his eyes became accustomed to the dark, and he noticed first the glow of the lights shining from under the edges of the seats on the aisles, and then the soft glow of white clothing, a cap, a pair of shoes sticking out of the aisle. He saw an empty seat and took it. He looked at the wall. There was a picture on it: a dark gray sky. He smiled with satisfaction, imagining himself at home in bed, looking out the window at the stars, feeling that old secret familiarity with them, just before a welter of fragmentary thoughts and pictures crowded into his mind and his eyes closed upon them and fastened them in and he grew tired and sleepy and they grew quieter and receded out of mind.

But don' stay all day he heard his mother saying. He jumped quickly to his feet and hurried out of the dark room.

"What you doin' home so early?" cried Viola who was sitting at the kitchen table straightening her hair. She held the hot straightening comb in midair, awaiting his explanation. "You couldn't a seen the show already!"

"Yes, ma'am!"

"Rutherford, come in here and look at your son. He's been to the show an' back — already!"

"What?" A rustle of papers. "What did you see, son?" He stepped into the kitchen.

"Some stars."

"Stars! You hear that, Babe? Your son is a stargazer!"

"Mom said not to say long!"

"That's all right, baby," said Viola, "you go back and tell 'um what happened. They'll let you back in. Didn't you see no people or nothin' on the screen?"

"Just some stars."

The man at the popcorn machine let him in again. He looked intently at the wall with the pictures on it: A great big man with a great big head and great big thick black eyebrows was chasing a little skinny man with big sad eyes and a little black mustache under his nose whose pants were too big and whose shoes were way too long. He shuffled funny-like when he walked and made everybody laugh. They laughed even harder when he ran. Amerigo laughed, too. He laughed so hard that tears ran down his cheeks. The big man was trying to catch the little man but he couldn't catch him because he was too quick, but he almost caught him all the time. Finally the little man ran upstairs in the room of a house and pushed a coal stove out of the window on the big man's head and the big man fell down like he was dead. All the people in the show laughed hard when the big man fell and the policeman came and got him in the end and took him to jail. Amerigo laughed, too. And then a real pretty lady came and the little man with the big sad eyes saw her and she took him by the arm and all the people went to church, even the big man with the big head and the thick eyebrows and his wife and that was the end. He told the story to his mother on the way home:

"Then that pitcher went away an' another one came on — with shootin' an' real talkin' an' horses an' a big house burned down. An' the man in the white hat — old Buck Jones, man! — he couldn' catch 'um 'cause they was shootin' at 'im — in the head! He was b-l-e-e-d-i-n' on his horse, a pretty horse, r-e-a-l white with a l-o-n-g tail! An' then he fell off an' all them cows like to run over 'im, but they didn't git 'im 'cause he rolled over behin' a big rock an' they couldn' even do nothin' to 'im! An' after that a pretty lady found 'im an' wrapped his head up, an' then he got on his horse an' run after the ones that was shootin' at 'im till they all fell off a they horses — dead! An' then the cows come back, an' then the lady kissed 'im. An' then the lights come on an' there was old Tommy an' William an' Carl an' all of 'um down front. An' then I went down where they was. An' then the lights went off agin, an' the li'l funny man an' the big man who was chasin' 'im come back agin. An' then the man with the big white horse . . . an' then you come. . . ."

"You gonna stay here all night? Fast asleep! You better *come* on here, boy!" he had drowsily heard her exclaim. And then she grabbed him by the hand and led him out of the show.

Outside the naked lightbulbs were very bright and all the lights along the avenue were on and many people walked up and down the street with their Sunday clothes on. They climbed Campbell Hill in the dark because the streetlight was out. They paused at the gate. The empty house, a big black bulky mass with points of light from the alley filtering through its windows, cast eerie shadows upon the walls. He clutched her hand.

"It's just that old empty house," she said impatiently. "You see it every day. Whew! Still stinkin'."

He entered the front room and turned on the light and got in bed.

"Ain't you gonna put out the light?"

"Yes'm, I forgot." He put out the light and got in bed and drew the covers around his neck. He fixed his eyes upon the window, upon the stars. They blended with the stars in the show and he heard the lowing of cattle mingling with the faithful voice of Sister James, encouraging him to walk the straight and narrow, while the reverend demanded of him the unspoken word whose insistent reverberations filled the wide roomy space called the future. A cat meowed in the street; a cool breeze chilled him. He pulled the covers over his head and promised God that he would be better. He fell off to sleep.

The little skinny man chased the big bad man. The big bad man picked up the empty house and threw it at the skinny man's head and he fell down like he was dead. Amerigo laughed hard, threw his head back and laughed so hard that the tears rolled down his cheeks and glistered like crystal marbles — millions of them! They rolled under the gate and ran fast down the cobblestoned alley leaving him sitting in the yard before the kitchen door of a house facing the woman who sat at the table feeding a little baby. He looked at the naked breast between the eye and the voice. It ticked four o'clock. And he laughed and laughed until the marbles bubbled up in his throat and strangled him. He woke up. Miss Chapman was bending over him.

"You just laughin' to beat the band!" said Viola. "What in the world you dreamin' about?" She rubbed his face and settled him back in bed and kissed him. Stricken with shame, he drew away and closed his eyes and fell into a deep sleep.

While washing his face the following morning he noticed a pretty ring on the drainboard. That's Dad's. He picked it up and looked at it. It was black with a shiny piece of glass in the middle. The thin part that slipped over his finger had writing on it. It was too big. He took it off and put it back on the drainboard. The glass in the middle of the black part shone like a star:

What's share *mean?*

It means givin' others some a what you got.

He put the ring in his pocket.

At school during recess when all the other children were out playing he slipped back into the classroom. He stood at the door and watched Miss Chapman for a minute. She sat at her desk, writing on some cards. She wore a blue dress. He walked slowly to her desk and stood at her elbow. He pressed his cheek against it.

"Why, Amerigo! Why aren't you out playing with the other children?" She stopped writing and looked at him with a tender but reserved expression. He blushed furiously and looked at the floor. It had boards in it like those in the floor of the Sunday school room. They ran beyond the wall, all the way down here to the kindergarten. His heart pounded. "Run along and play," said Miss Chapman, "you haven't got long. The bell will be ringing in ten minutes." He withdrew the ring from his pocket. He placed it on the desk, turned, and started to run away.

"What a beautiful ring!" She took it up and looked at it. "Is it for me?"

He looked at the floor.

"Thank you very much. It's sweet of you, but I don't think I can accept it," looking at the inscription in the band. "Why, it's from your mother to your father!" His face grew hot, his forehead cool, while his body felt hot all over. "Here" she said, wrapping the ring in a sheet of paper, "you take this back home and give it to your father. Do you hear?" He took the ring with downcast eyes and stalked out of the room.

He saw Mr. Bowles on the playground, standing by the front wall, surveying the children. His expression was calm, serene, kind. His hair was white. But he wasn't Irish because he didn't have blue eyes and his skin was of a light golden color, like Mr. Gus:

A fine man!

A race man!

A educated man!

His heart overflowed with love for the great man. When the last bell rang he dashed into the room with the big black letters written on the glass door that you couldn't see through. It said: O-F-F-I-C-E-O-F-T-H-E-P-R-I-N-C-I-P-A-L; he spelled it out. Mr. Bowles sat at his desk with his head bent over a book with fine writing in it. He looked up and smiled as he timidly approached him.

"Well, do I have a visitor?"

He stood speechless before the desk.

"What can I do for you, Amerigo?"

He took a step closer and thrust a crumpled piece of paper into Mr. Bowles's hand. Mr. Bowles unfolded the paper and discovered the silver ring with the small diamond set in an onyx ground.

"You kin have it."

Mr. Bowles examined the ring and read the inscription.

"Where did you get this?"

"I found it on the drainboard."

"You are very kind to want to give me this ring," said Mr. Bowles, "but I'm afraid it's not yours to give away; it belongs to your father. Amerigo, would you go around and ask Miss Chapman if she would come here a minute, please, and you come with her."

He appeared minutes later with Miss Chapman.

"I told him to return the ring to his father, Mr. Bowles," she said upon entering the office. He thought he perceived the trace of a smile upon her face.

"I see," said Mr. Bowles. "Well, for the time being, I will keep this. You may return to your class, Amerigo." He left the office, but Miss Chapman stayed behind a few minutes to talk to Mr. Bowles.

That evening at supper he was very quiet. He listened passively while his mother told his father about his staying late at the movie. Rutherford laughed. "That ain' nothin', Amerigo. Your momma usta take her *lunch* to the show!"

"Aw, Rutherford. You know you lyin' like a dog!"

"I swear on a stack a Bibles! If I'm lyin' I hope lightnin' strikes me dead!"

"Lightnin's gonna take you up on one a them lies one a these days!"

They laughed. He laughed, nervously.

The telephone rang. Rutherford went into the middle room to answer it.

"I see," said Rutherford in a serious tone. Amerigo looked into his plate. Viola stopped eating. "It'll be all right, Pr'fessor Bowles. I'll *talk* to 'im. . . ." Viola looked at him uneasily. Rutherford entered the kitchen. Anger flashed in his eyes.

"What was it?" asked Viola.

"Pr'fessor Bowles," he answered coldly. He took his place at the table and stared at Amerigo for several seconds without speaking.

"What's the *matter?*" cried Viola impatiently.

"Git out a my sight!" Rutherford said to him.

"Rutherford, what *is* it?" He sneaked away from the table and went out on the back porch and sat on the orange crate and looked in at his parents through the screen.

"Kin you beat that?" Rutherford exclaimed almost to himself. "After all we try to do for that li'l niggah!"

"What did he *do?*" Viola's voice was strained with worry now.

"You know how I sometimes take off my ring when I wash up, scaired I might lose it?"

"Yeah?"

"Well I missed it this mornin', but I wasn't worried 'cause you always know when you done really lost somethin'. Well, your son got it into his head to give it to the teacher! She looked in it an' saw the inscription, I guess, an' — But wait a minute! That ain' all! She gave it back to 'im an' told 'im to bring it home! But naw! He had to haul off an' give it to Pr'fessor Bowles!"

"Aw-naw!"

"*Yeah!*"

Amerigo stared into the alley. The scene blurred before his eyes.

"*Yeah!*" Rutherford was saying: "Us workin' to feed 'im, an'-an' tryin' to give 'im a nice home an' all — an' 'im *stealin'* from us!"

"He didn' know what he was doin', Rutherford, he's just a baby!" Viola pleaded.

"Didn' know, *hell!* After they *told* that muckle-head to bring the damned thing home! Boy!"

He stepped into the kitchen and stood a good distance from his father.

"COME HERE!"

He stepped a little closer, anxiously watching Rutherford's hands.

"You don't have to be scaired *now,*" said Rutherford, "Aw naw! I'm gonna wait an' git you We'nesd'y night, when your momma goes to club meetin', when it ain' nobody here but just you an' me. You lis'nin'?"

"Yessir."

"You bring that ring home *tamarra,* an put it *back* on the *drainboard* where you found it. An' *as long as you live don't you never take nothin' out a this house agin that don' belong to you.* You hear?"

"Yessir."

"WHAT?"

"YES, SIR."

"Now git the hell to bed!"

Viola placed her hand on his cheek and kissed him as he went by.

"What! Me correctin' 'im for stealin' an'-an' you kissin' 'im!" cried Rutherford in a rage. "You want 'im to grow up to be a thief! I hate a thief worse'n the devil. The Lord hates sin!"

"He stole all right, Rutherford, an' I guess he oughtta git a whippin', but it ain' really stealin' the way you mean. It'd be different if it was candy or money or somethin' like that. I *know* he didn' mean to be stealin'!"

"Don' you think I know that, woman? But he's got to learn to respect other people's property, that he just can't pick up somethin' 'cause he takes a likin' to it. He take first one thing, an' then it'll be another, an' the next thing you know, you'll be lookin' at 'im through iron bars! Momma damned near lynched me for a lot less'n he's gonna git a beatin' for! He's gonna grow up *straight* an' honest if I have to *kill* 'im to do it. An' I *would* if I had to! I'd rather see 'im *dead* in his grave!"

He lay in bed listening to the kids playing in the alley. He tossed uneasily and looked at the deep amber shadows that fell across the bed. It wasn't even night yet! A burst of laughter came from beneath his window. They're laughing at me.

The streetlight came on. The sky gradually grew darker, of a deeper blue color. Suddenly it was like velvet, like the velvet sky in the picture on the wall. A star! He pulled the sheet over his head and tried to sleep. A lump rose to his throat, tears ran down his face. I'll go away. I'll die! An'-an' they'll be sorry, too. The empty house loomed before his eyes in the dark. Old Jake looked in the window. He poked at the pile of rubbish with his staff. Amerigo looked up from the bloodstained newspaper into Old Jake's face! He *was* dead. Old Jake picked him up and took him up on the back porch. Rutherford and Viola were sitting there. Rutherford on the orange crate and Viola on the chair. Miss Chapman and Mr. Bowles stood in the kitchen door, looking out and down at him through the screen. Old Jake placed him in Viola's arms. She was naked and his face lay wet against her breast. She wept over him. Rutherford drew near and wept, too. Miss Chapman and Mr. Bowles wept from behind the screen door. Then Old Jake took him away from Viola and put him into a sack, and he fell a long dark way, through a sky full of stars!

He woke up covered with sweat. He heard voices in the kitchen. Viola was laughing about something.

They don't care. He lay back down. He felt cold. He tossed and turned and finally doubled his body into a ball and went to sleep.

Givin' others some a what you got . . . some a what you got . . . some a what you got . . . Softer and softer: *Some a what you got.*

He stepped out onto the porch, his arms laden with Post Toasties and milk, bread and butter, wineballs and chewing gum. He laid them before the kitten, who half sat, half lay on the porch with a dull glaze in her eyes: *Here, kitty! Here, kitty.*

H-e-r-e kittykittykitty!

Kittykittykittykittykittykittykitty . . . kit . . . ty . . . k . . .

★

Tuesday morning was raw and smoky. The sky was filled with a blue haze. Like fog, but thinner. Like looking at the world from behind a blue curtain. The leaves were a whole lot of different colors — some on the trees, some on the ground, and some falling.

Night came coolly and heavily, like velvet. He said his prayers but he did not hear what he said. And when he closed his eyes the pictures came. He closed them tighter, pushed them down so deep that he could not see them or hear them. He sank heavily down behind the blue wall.

Wednesday morning he woke up too early. The sun shone too brightly in his eyes. He tried to go back to sleep, but could not, and then he finally went back, but slept too long. Rutherford had to call him twice. Twice he had to answer. He ate his breakfast, too full to eat. He dillydallied on his way to school, avoided the other children.

At school he could not look at *her,* he could not look at *him. Him no more than her.* He arranged the colored leaves behind the cardboard basket that he was making.

The bell rang.

Already! Racing along the great Admiral Boulevard, trying to beat five o'clock home, with the amber sun in his eyes!

Again the bell rang. All was quiet. He looked out the window at a sparrow in a tree. He sighed enviously.

He scraped the dried clay from the palms of his hands.

"Time to wash up!" cried Miss Chapman. He looked up at the sound of her voice. He looked into her eyes. They were smiling tenderly. He let his eyes fall to the floor, and when the bell rang for the last time he did not look at her. Nor did he run, kicking cans, or laughing and talking with the others who ran on ahead. He drifted through Independence Avenue like a single solitary cloud. His eyes and ears passively perceived the colors, shapes, and sounds. They passed through his consciousness like smoke through the sky, like blue fog.

The sun shone bright and hard, almost like summer, and yet he felt as though he were walking through a winter afternoon. He shivered and felt cold.

The backyard was quiet. The bad smell from the empty house had vanished. Maybe he's gone! He climbed heavily up the back steps: *Boom! Boom! Boom!* Ten times. He paused at the clean spot, half lay, half fell on the porch, bled at the mouth, and died.

The sun sank lower in the sky.

Bra Mo came through the shoot with a cake of ice on his shoulder. He came through the yard, ascended the porch steps, and rapped softly upon the screen door.

"Hi, Mer'go! Your momma told me to bring some ice this mornin'. Lawdy! I durn near forgot!" He smiled pleasantly and entered the kitchen, opened the icebox, took the water bottle out. and slid the cake in. "There!" he exclaimed with a grunt.

He looked up at him from behind the blue wall.

"You mighty quiet taday!"

He looked at the floor. The cracks between the boards made an imprint upon the linoleum, cutting brown parallel stripes through the fading flowered design.

"Well, sir!" Bra Mo exclaimed, "I guess *I*'d better be *goin'*. Hits too chilly here for *me!* Hee! hee! Winter's here already!"

He watched him go down the steps, through the yard, past the empty house, and finally through the shoot. Then he went back into the kitchen and entered the toilet and waited for five o'clock.

Shortly before five Viola came home and began supper. Her eyes were quiet and serious. He watched her from the chair. Soon sharp savory odors arose from the stove.

"Set the table," said Viola. "Your daddy'll be home in a minute."

He checked the sunlight falling across the threshold of the kitchen door. The cool stone flushed amber. He moved dreamily around the table, laying down the plates, the knives, forks, and spoons, the glasses and the bowl for the fried corn that Viola had on the stove. It gave off a sweetish smell that made him slightly nauseous. When he had finished setting the table he stood at her elbow.

"That's a very expensive *ring*, a *di*'mond! I gave that ring to your daddy the first year after we got married. For Christmas. I don' think you meant to steal it. I *know* you didn'. But what kin I do? Your daddy's right in his way. You just gotta learn that you can't take things that don' belong to you." Her voice trembled. "An'-an' after Miss Chapman told you to bring it back! Whatever possessed you to do a thing like that?"

He looked down at the floor.

"Huh?"

She took his chin in the palm of her hand and gently raised his head. He looked up into her eyes. They blended into Miss Chapman's eyes! His lips trembled and tears ran down his face. He buried his face in her stomach. . . .

They heard heavy foot steps on the front stair.

"Shh!" — touching her lips with her forefinger and motioning for him to go out onto the back porch.

"Hi baby!" cried Mrs. Derby from her porch downstairs. "Ain' seen much a you since you been in school. You been a good boy an' doin' what your teacher tell you?"

"Yes'm," looking down at her from the orange crate. He could hear his father and mother talking in the kitchen, but he could not hear what they said.

Mrs. Crippa appeared at her kitchen door, looked out over the yard and disappeared behind the screen. After that Mr. Derby came out onto the porch and started tending to his crawdads. Amerigo looked on indifferently, straining to hear what was being said in the kitchen.

"To-ny! Toooo-ny!" He looked through the branches of the elm trees in Miss Ada's yard and saw Miss McMahon standing on her back porch with something in her hand. "Ask your mother if you kin come over here for a minute, I've got something for you!"

"Yes'm!"

He opened the screen door and looked at Viola. Viola looked at Rutherford.

"Go on," he said, "but git back over here in a hurry!"

A few minutes later he returned with a huge all-day sucker wrapped in cellophane. It had eyes, a nose, and a mouth made out of candied sugar.

"Aw, how n-i-c-e!" exclaimed Viola. "She sure l-o-v-e-s you! But you can't eat it now, put it away till after-after," avoiding Rutherford's eyes, "until after supper."

"Yes'm."

"What am *I* supposed to be — the bastard around here?"

From the front room where he had gone to put the candy away, he heard his father's angry voice: "Ain' no use in you carryin' on like this. I done said what I mean to do — an' that's *that!*"

They ate silently, without looking at each other.

"HI, VI!" Miss Ada called from her back porch.

"HI, SISTER BILL!" Viola answered, stepping to the threshold of the kitchen door, "I'LL BE READY AT SEVEN-THIRTY! WE GOT A LOT A BUSINESS TO DISCUSS TANIGHT!"

"YOU TELLIN' ME! OKAY. I'LL BE SEEIN' YOU!"

Rutherford rose from the table and went into the front room and settled down to his paper. Viola began to dress while Amerigo washed the dishes. When he had finished he went out onto the back porch and sat on the orange crate in the beam of light shining through the screen door. After a short while Viola appeared in the door dressed for club meeting. Miss Ada called from her porch:

"YOU READY?"

"YEAH, I'M READY!" looking solemnly at him. "S'long, babe." She kissed him, and then descended the steps, crossed the yard, and unlatched the gate. She paused to look back at him and saw Rutherford's tall shadow blotting out the light that streamed through the kitchen door.

"Hi, baby!" said Miss Ada.

"Hi," he replied hoarsely.

"Hi, Rutherford!"

"What do you say, Sister Bill?" In a strained voice.

The two women disappeared through the shoot.

"Come in here!" Rutherford commanded. He went into the kitchen. "Sit down there on that chair." He sat down. "You know what's gonna happen, don't you?"

"Yessir."

"Why you gittin' a whippin'?"

"'Cause a the ring."

"That's right. 'Cause I don' know no better way to make you feel the wrong thing you done. I want you to rem'ber this for the rest of your life. So that you won' never do that agin."

He stared at the floor.

"Take off your clothes."

He took off his clothes.

"Now, go git me that strap."

He brought the strap to his father, and then ran to the far corner of the kitchen, near the toilet door, covering his body with his arms and hands. Rutherford took a step toward him. He began to whimper. Rutherford raised the strap over his head, and he let out a soulful yell. Rutherford's hand faltered. Then his lips tightened with determination, and he raised the strap again. He yelled again. Louder than before.

"Whap!" the strap resounded against the toilet door. He jumped up and down, ran to and fro, shouting and begging his father not to beat him. Rutherford raised the strap again.

"eeeeeEEEEOOOOOW!" he cried.

Just as Rutherford was about to bring the strap down a second time, a voice stayed his hand:

"Stop!"

Miss McMahon stood in the door. Her eyes flashed with anger. Her cheeks were flushed with patches of crimson color, while the rest of her face was waxen and bloodless. Her gray hair was awry and her lips were purple. She breathed with difficulty.

"If-if," she gasped, "if you h-i-t that-that boy a-g-a-i-n, I'll CALL THE POLICE!"

"What?" cried Rutherford, "I ain' even TOUCHED 'IM YET! Why-why-why-whatdoyoumean — comin' in *my* house tellin' *me* what to do with *my* son?"

He stood in the corner trembling, his face wet with tears. Miss McMahon looked at him as if to see what Rutherford said was true. He could not speak. *He ain' hit me!* . . . he heard himself saying, but his lips could not utter the words, they trembled so. He only shook his head nervously from side to side.

"*Git out a my house!*" Rutherford commanded.

Miss McMahon dropped her head heavily and turned toward the door, which she opened and closed carefully behind her. She moved slowly down the steps. No sooner than she had closed the yard gate than Rutherford turned toward him. He raised the strap and let it fall upon his legs. A hot stinging pain coursed through his body. The strap fell upon his arms, and the hot pain seared his trembling flesh. He cried and screamed, darted from one side of the room to the other, ducked behind chairs and under the kitchen table. But always Rutherford's strap found him. With each blow he flinched and clenched his teeth, red and silver sparks flew within the darkness of his shut eyelids, giving animation to the pain that was not altogether unpleasant.

"NOBODY tells ME how to bring up no child a MINE!" Rutherford shouted in front of the screen door, while the child whimpered, sweat running into the welts on his arms and legs. He stood braced, ready for the next blow, the pain already half anticipated, his mouth set for the outcry.

"I guess you won't forget this evenin' in a hurry," Rutherford said. A look of compassion came into his eyes.

"Come here."

He went to his father. Rutherford gathered him into his arms and carried him into the front room. He made his bed and put him into it. He watched over his prayers and drew the covers over him when he had finished.

"Does it hurt?"

"Yessir."

"You got a real 'un this time! But m-a-n — *you* ain' seen nothin', Amerigo. Ha! ha! I usta damned near git a whippin' like that *every day!* I was b-a-d! A-l-l-ways into somethin'! Damn you, Momma usta say, I'll make a man out a you or kill you! An' she meant it, too, Amerigo. That woman was *rough!* But all in all I don't regret it. I growed up straight. Ain' never been in no kinda trouble with the law. An'-an'-an' me an' your momma got you an'-an', uh, an' we had to come out a school an' all that, but it turned out good. They all said it wouldn' — my sisters an' them, your aunts. Your momma told you, I know, but you was a bright boy an' we still together. An'-an' I'm gonna keep you good an' bright — or see you in your grave!"

He saw from the corner of his eye the heavens filled with stars. *He's the best man in the whole world!* some wild raucous feeling cried out within him. He felt deliriously happy.

Now his father was telling him stories of his childhood: of fights he had

had and won, of T. C. and all the gang, he gave him advice about catching snakes, how to determine a poisonous one from a harmless one, especially a rattler, how to make a jig, how to make a slingshot.

He laughed and wished that he had been there then. When Viola came home from club meeting — much earlier than usual — she found them laughing.

"Unh! You two laughin' an' playin' like nothin' had happened."

To him: "You playin' with 'im after he beat you nearly half to death? You are a fool!"

She undressed without uttering a word to either one of them, and went off in a huff to bed. Rutherford undressed and got into bed. Viola lay still, on her side of the bed, with her back to him.

"Babe,"

Silence.

"Babe?"

Silence.

"Aw, Viola, it's all right. . . ."

Silence.

He dozed off to sleep, fell into a deep dark silence reverberant with the suppliant sound of his father's voice:

"Babe?"

The following evening when she came home from work he stood in the door waiting to greet her, but she brushed past him.

"Aw Mom! It's all right!"

She looked at him as though he were a stranger:

"You know one thing? If you wasn't mine I'd swear you was a witch!"

"If it ain' ready, let's git it ready!" Rutherford exclaimed as he entered the kitchen. "I'm hungry as *four* wolves! Hi, there, Viola! Son, git your daddy the paper, there!"

He fetched the paper, while Rutherford washed up and took his place at the table. He washed his hands, while Viola put the supper on the table.

"Let's eat," she said, and Rutherford put his paper aside.

"That damned paper makes a man sick at the stomach!"

"How you mean?" Viola asked.

"Well, it's bad enough to have to *live* with the depression. But then you got to come home an' *read* about it! A-l-l the Republicans kin do is in-*ves-tigate*! Investigatin' ain' gittin' nobody no jobs! Looka that!" He took up the paper and spread out the pictorial section so that she could see it.

"Hogs bein' plowed under! Oranges burnin'! An' people starvin' to death! Why ain' the Republicans investigatin' *that!* Pourin' coal oil on good food! An'-an' them damned crooked politicians down at City Hall! A man's scaired to walk down the street after dark lest he gits knocked in the head, or shot up or somethin'!"

"Yeah, it's sure bad, all right," said Viola with a heavy sigh. "They talkin' 'bout cuttin' down at the laundry. 'Course, they a-l-l-ways talkin' about that! Cut off four last month. One was a driver been there twenty-three years! Ever'time you go into the office to git those few pennies they payin' you, you wonder if it's gonna be the last. How did you come out with the old man?"

"Said he'd straighten me Sad'dy. Give me five on account. Here." He withdrew a crumpled bill from his pocket and left it on the table near Viola's plate.

"That's a cryin' *shame!* You workin' like a *slave* an' have to beg for your money!"

"It's like that everywhere, Babe. Old Bill an' them ain' even gittin' *that*. *They* have to live on tips an' what they kin make off a them hustlin' broads, or handlin' booze. An' things gittin' so tight they scaired to take a chance with *that* even!

"But," he continued thoughtfully, "but things can't go on like this much longer. The national debt's higher'n it's ever been in the country's history, an' the relief roll's gittin' longer every day. Things keep up like this an' there'll be another war. I read a editorial the other day that said it's tough all over the world, Babe."

What can I do about the depression and to stop the war? Amerigo wondered silently. Suddenly he remembered the soldiers he had seen parading down Main Street last Decoration Day. The flag had gone behind the men with the drums and everybody had taken off their hats. Everyone except the women. They didn't have to because they were women. He lightly tapped his foot to the rhythm of the music. Rutherford was saying:

"Jack Deal says it's the fault of the Jews. He sure hates a Jew!"

"Why?" retorted Viola, "'cause they're smart an' stick tagether? If *we'd* stick together the way *they* do, we'd be a whole lot better off. That's why we can't git no place now — always fightin' 'mong ourselves!"

"Old Jake's a mess!" Rutherford exclaimed. "He reads all the papers just so he kin find somethin' aginst a Jew. An' he's death on Mexicans, too. 'Now I'll tell you, Ruthafahd,' he says, 'I'll tell you, R-u-t-h-a-f-a-h-d, they ain' no damned good, by God!' He come up to me, shufflin' on them bad feet a his. You know how he walks, Babe. B-i-g head, bald in front, an' b-i-g cold blue eyes. Like a fish! I ain' kiddin'!"

"What's a Jew?"

"I . . . uh . . . well —" Rutherford stammered, "uh, Jews are people like Mr. Fineberg an' Mary with the dry-goods store. Like the people in the Bible. They came from Israel a long time ago. An' people don' like 'um 'cause they keep to theyselves, I guess. An' s-m-a-r-t! M-a-n — they got you figured out before you git there! But let me tell you somethin', they ain' gangsters an' pimps! An' they don' play no dirty politics, an' they nice to Negroes. I was just a boy when I started workin' at the hotel, an' the old man always treated me like I was his son. No kiddin', Jack! I remember when I usta have to go out to his house to help old lady Mac in the garden sometimes. An' they'd be eatin' an' she'd fix a plate for *me*. At the table, Jack! An'-an'- I'd eat right along with 'um. 'You got enough, Rutherford?' she'd say, an' I'd say, Yes'm!"

"Kin I go down to Aunt Lily's?" he asked.

"All right," said Viola, "but you be back by nine o'clock."

"Yes'm."

"Hi, hon!" said Aunt Lily when he stuck his head in the door.

"Hi, Aunt Lily, where's Unc?"

"Aw he's gone to the late drawin' I *guess!* No tellin' where that man is half the time!" She shook her head with a sad thoughtful smile. "How you gittin' on in school?"

"All right."

"Forgotcha ABCs?"

"No'm!"

"Bet you have!"

"ABCDEFGHIJ . . . KLMN . . . OPQ . . . RSTUVWXYZ! — There!"

"That's fine, baby!

"But I bet you forgot how to write your name, though. Sanie Claus ain' gonna know who to bring the toys to if you can't even write a letter!"

"No'm, I ain' forgot! Gimme a piece a paper!"

"Looka there on the sewin' machine an' take a piece a your unc's paper an' one a them pencils."

He took a pencil and paper and settled himself on the floor. He printed out his name, while she looked down over his shoulder.

"That's just fine," she said. "Here I'll tell you what." She reached for an old copy of the *Voice*. "Put your paper on the top and copy out the letters that show through." He started copying the letters. Meanwhile she put her coffeepot on the stove and settled down in the rocking chair, her glasses resting on the tip of her nose, the way Unc wore his. She picked up a dress from the table and started to mend it.

He worked intently, oblivious to everything except the black letters that shone through. He spelled the letters out as he wrote:

"D. . . . E A T . . . H! . . . C O M EEEE — S TO FAT HER OF FIVE.
F-I-V-E spells five! BOY OF SIX-TEENDIES IN H O S P I T A L F R O
M P O I C E B R U T A L I T Y N A A C P D R I V E G E T S U N D
E R W A Y.

"Look!" He held up the lettered sheet of paper with pride.

"Unh-huh, that's good . . ." she said in a distracted tone, intent on her sewing. "One a these days you'll be readin' an' writin' as good as me!"

He began to trace the picture in the center of the page. There was a tree in the middle of the picture. A black man was hanging from one of its branches. His eyes were popping out.

"Don' he look funny!" he cried, holding up the paper. Aunt Lily looked at it, and then she looked at him, and then her eyes darkened.

"Naw, honey, he don' look a bit funny to me. What if it was *your* daddy?"

He studied the picture carefully. He looked curiously at the white people standing around the hanging man. He felt Aunt Lily's eyes on him. It *does* look funny! he thought, and at the same time he was stung by a feeling of shame.

The nine o'clock whistle blew.

"Mom said I have to come up at nine."

"You better git goin' then," she smiled sadly. She started to kiss him, but he stooped to pick up the piece of paper on which he had drawn the man on the tree, and ran out the door without looking back. He scampered the dark corridor steps, paused a second before Miss Sadie's door and, hearing no sound on the other side, burst into the house, holding the sheet of paper in the air.

"Look what *I* done!" showing the drawing to Viola.

"You traced it, didn't you?"

"I put it on top a the *Voice* an' wrote over the letters that come through."

"That ain' nothin' to brag out. Anybody kin copy the letters, but it takes some doin' to write it freehand."

"Look!" He pointed to the scanty tracing of the hanged man. "*I* did it!" He smiled with deep satisfaction. "Don't he look funny! Ho! ho! ho!"

"Ain' that the picture of the man that got lynched?"

"He was in the paper that Aunt Lily gimme, an'-an' his eyes was all poppin' out all funny-like!"

"Go to bed!"

"Aw Mom,"

She looked like she meant it. He stalked into the kitchen into the toilet.

"If you ain' in bed" she called after him, "in five minutes, I'm gonna tell your daddy to tell you!"

Rutherford looked up from his detective magazine, and Amerigo quickened his step. He spelled out the word of the magazine as he sat on the stool: S-H-A-D-O-W — that spells shadow!

In bed, in the dark, he thought about the man in the tree. There was blood on his shirt and all the white people standing around him had burning sticks in their hands. He saw the man's bulging eyes. They shone like bright points of light in the dark. He was dead! he thought suddenly. What's lynching? Why had his mother made him go to bed so suddenly? I didn't do nothin'! Ain' that funny! Aunt Lily's eyes grew dark. Shame shocked him awake, but he tightened his eyes upon the deep mysterious satisfaction he had gotten out of looking at the man: *Look what* I *done! Look what* I *done! LOOK WHAT* I *DONE!*

"Boom! Boom! Boom!"

"What was that!" Viola cried in a quiet frightened voice. Amerigo peered into the darkness of the middle room.

"What?" said Rutherford drowsily.

"Thought I heard some shots."

"WHATWASTHAT!" demanded a woman's voice from the alley.

Sounds like Mrs. Grey's, he thought.

"SOMEBODY SHOOTIN' DOWN THE ALLEY!" cried Miss Anna Benton. "Aw, LAWD! Mun ain' home yet!"

"What time is it?" Miss Sadie asked someone in the corridor. A second later: "Come away from that window!" And then Mr. Nickles grumbled something that he could not understand. Meanwhile he heard the doors shutting up and down the alley.

"Did you lock the back door?" Viola whispered.

"I think so," Rutherford lay in bed for two minutes, then he got up and went to the kitchen and checked the back door.

"It's locked," he said, getting back into bed. "Unh! It's q-u-i-e-t as a graveyard out there. An' d-a-r-k! I think that streetlight's burned out, or knocked out." Amerigo looked out the front window. The stars were shining here and there.

Clouds, he thought. He squirmed quietly, cautiously in his bed. Settled, he listened to his mother and father breathing. He measured his own breath against the length of theirs. Viola's breath was long and deep, Rutherford's was shorter, and his was the shortest.

She takes one breath to my three! he heard Rutherford saying. And then he felt a sharp stinging pain in the pit of his stomach. He doubled himself into a knot, pressed his hands between his legs, and waited for daylight to come.

"You come straight home from school — an' *stay* home!" said Viola before she left for work the following morning. "Don't go cuttin' through no alleys an' yards or nothin', go the venue way." Rutherford had already told him.

On his way to school he saw little knots of people along the streets, talking excitedly.

"Riddled with bullets!" Mr. Ted was saying to Miss Emmy.

"Yeah? Wheah?" asked Miss Emmy, tall short-haired, dressed in over-alls, looking just like a man, he thought, as he paused to listen.

"Back a The Saw-Dust Trail."

"Who was it?"

"Texicana. Him an' ol' Rhodes was gam'lin'."

He walked on through the shoot where they said the dead man had been found. He looked everywhere for signs of blood. He was disappointed and wondered what he looked like.

That night at supper Rutherford read the article about it in the *Star:*

"'Wilbur Rhodes, thirty-one, Negro, five feet seven inches tall and weighin' one hundred an' eighty-six pounds, was shot to death last night in a alley between Independence Avenue an' Admiral Boulevard, Charlotte and Campbell Streets, at approximately two-twenty A.M. by John Waters, forty-seven, Negro, with a forty-five-caliber revolver as the result of a quarrel. Waters is six feet three inches tall, has a dark brown complexion and an oval knife scar on his chin. He is also known by the name of Texicana. When last seen —"

The following Friday evening after supper, Rutherford unfolded the pages of the *Voice* and read:

"GAMBLER Slain in Death Valley! Ain' that a damned shame!" He looked over the paper at Viola.

"Let me see," she said.

"Here, look."

"That's awful!"

"Why," said Rutherford, "why in the hell do they have to exaggerate like that? A man reads this paper an' gits *fightin' mad*! Waitaminute!" He turned to the sports page. "I knowed it, looka here. Hot damn!: SATCHEL PAIGE! The world's greatest pitcher to appear with the K.C. Kings after a successful exhibition tour of the South American Circuit!"

"Satch is the greatest!" Viola exclaimed, "They just don't give him credit 'cause he ain' a white man!"

"Yeah, he's good, great —" Rutherford exclaimed, "but to let the *Voice* tell it you'd think that noboda else in the world kin play baseball but Satchel Paige. Just look! All you kin see: the greatest singer, the greatest dancer, an' all that stuff. Make a man think the other hundred an' ninety million people in this country ain' nothin'. An' don't let somethin' bad happen — like that lynchin' down south last week. They make it so bad that you want to kill every paddy you see. A lynchin's bad enough, but why put a picture of a bloody man with his eyes poppin' out a his head on the front page? Don' do nothin' but fill a man up with hate. An' what kin you *do!* You *gotta* go to work the next day. I say the only way to settle this race jive is to work with intelligence through the laws of this country! A man's gotta try to understand these people, be friendly an' git along with 'um or go nuts!"

Viola nodded in silent agreement, and looked at her husband with an expression of sincere admiration. Having finished eating, Rutherford fished in the ashtray for a cigarette butt, lit it, and puffed thoughtfully. Viola took another helping of okra, while Amerigo picked distractedly at his plate.

There was a knock at the front door. Rutherford went to answer it. They could hear him talking to a stranger:

"Does Mister Jones live here?"

"Sounds like Mister Harps!" he exclaimed.

"Why, yes," said Rutherford, "Ah, I'm Jones."

"Who?" asked Viola.

"It's — " but Viola hushed him.

"Aw- you want my son!" said Rutherford, "Amerigo, here's somebody — a gentleman — to see — to see you."

He went into the front room, followed Viola.

"This is my wife," said Rutherford.

"How do you do," said the man politely.

"An'-and here's Amerigo, my son."

"You are Amerigo Jones?" said the man, smiling with surprise.

"Won't you set-sit down, Mr. — I didn't — " Rutherford pointed to the sofa.

"Oh, I'm sorry, Mister Jones, I should have — Robert Jordan, editor of the *Voice*. You see, I was asked to visit you by one of our readers, and eh-eh-I decided eh-to take her advice. Ehhem. But let me explain, last week a man was killed here in this al-street, and we-we- eh-we reported it. A little too strongly for Miss Nancy Cunningham, I'm afraid. Ah-ha! ha! Yes . . ."

"Who's that?" asked Viola.

"I never heard a that name, myself!" said Rutherford.

"Me, neither," added Amerigo.

"Why, she's a neighbor of yours!" exclaimed Mr. Jordan. "A very good neighbor, I can't help thinking. She lives up the street there, at-uh-I just came from there. An old lady, dark-complexioned, with — "

"Aunt Nancy! — " exclaimed Amerigo.

"Cunnin'ham!" exclaimed Viola. "Ain' that strange: All these years an' I never even *heard* of 'er last name before!"

Amerigo smiled, finding it funny to have somebody calling Aunt Nancy "Miss Nancy Cunningham"!

"A man delivered this letter to our office this afternoon," Mr. Jordan continued: "May I read it to you?"

Rutherford nodded assent, glanced at Viola curiously, and then fixed his attention on Mr. Jordan, who withdrew a letter from a large leather wallet that he took from his inside coat pocket:

"Ehhem . . ." extending the letter to the proper distance, and began:

"To the man who owns the *Voice*. Eh, I think I should read it the way she wrote it. Mrs. Cunningham is a simple woman with, eh, not much education, but that doesn't mean that she doesn't express herself clearly — or forcefully! Eh . . ." He smiled to Viola and Rutherford and they smiled congenially back at him. "Eh, 'To the man who owns the *Voice*: I'm just a ol' lady, an' I ain' got no education, but I'm a God-fearin', God-lovin' woman, an' I been a member of Saint John's Baptist Church these thirty-five years, an' I been livin' in this here alley longer'n that. Now all that time, I seed 'um come an' I seed 'um go, an' I know one thing: As sure as there's a God in Heaven there's good folks in this world an' there's bad. But that's only to half-blind sinner's eyes like mines, to the Good Godamighty!!! They is all good! Now we got good peoples down here an' we got bad. An' we poor, sure enough! But we ain' no badder'n nobody else. We got good law-abidin' people who don' cuss an' drink an' gam'le, an' they send they kids to church *every* Sund'y, an' gits old — older'n me even — an' go to they Maker in peace. God bless they soul! An' I don' think it's right for you to go 'round sayin' in the papers for everybody to read that we's all murderers and cutthroats when it ain' so!!! Speak not evil aginst others that evil be not spoken aginst you!!! The Good Book says that! Now in our alley is a good family with a son. He got eyes an' ears in his head. An' he's smart as a whip! Got the best manners of any little boy I ever did see — black or white! An' his momma an' poppa keep 'im clean an' lookin' nice all the time. Them, too. An' they got a telephone an' a radio just like decent folks. You go visit 'um, an' see if you done right, sayin' what you said. I know the Lord'll bless you, if you do. His name is A-mereego Jones — I know I ain' spellin' it right, but that don' matter none, just as long as you understand who I mean — an' he live at six-eighteen Cosy Lane on the third floor on the south side. Now that's all I gotta say, an' may the Lord encourage you to tell things better like they is. Miss Nancy Cunningham, Mother of Saint John's Baptist Church.'"

An irrepressible smile spread over the child's face, and he felt the way he had felt when Old Jake gave him the star. He saw Old Jake holding it up to the sunlight, as Mr. Jordan sucked his teeth thoughtfully and said:

"It isn't easy to run a Negro newspaper in this town or anywhere, for that matter, Mr. and Mrs. Jones — Amerigo. I was little more than your age

when I started selling the *Voice* on the corners." Mr. Jordan suddenly
checked himself and continued in a more businesslike tone. "We have to
compete with the *Post* and the *Star*. Because we issue our sheet weekly our
coverage is usually secondhand. Even then we must deal with happenings
of merely local interest to our people. We have to report the news and try
to educate our people at the same time. And we have to *sell* the paper!" He
paused significantly, his eyes fixed upon Rutherford.

"Yeah" said Rutherford uneasily, "it-it sure must be hard all right."

"Yes," continued Mr. Jordan, "and I'm sorry to say that we sometimes get
so involved with selling the paper that we overstep the limits of propriety."

"How's that?" asked Rutherford.

"We, eh, go too far."

"Aw . . ."

"Of course, we'll print an apology in the next issue, eh . . ." Mr. Jordan
sucked his teeth again and rose to his feet. "Now," smiling cordially and
reaching for Viola's hand, "I think I have taken up enough of your time."
Rutherford and Viola stood up. "I am very happy to have met you, Mister
and Mrs. Jones, and you, too, eh-eh, Amerigo — that's right, isn't it? Yes,
Amerigo," taking his hand and flashing a restless indulgent smile upon
him. Then he withdrew a gold watch from his vest pocket, glanced at it,
and quickly put it back. "Well, Amerigo," letting go of his hand, "how old
are you?"

"I'm five years old."

"Where do you go to school?"

"I'm in the kinnygarden at the Garr'son School in Miss Chapman's class
an' Mister Bowles is the principal."

"Well . . . well — do you, eh, like to go to school?"

"Yessir."

"You're right, son, an' education is a great possession, and very necessary to our people. I'll bet you want to be a teacher when you grow up."

"Nosir."

"No? What, then?"

"The president of Amer'ka!"

Rutherford, Viola, and Mr. Jordan exchanged embarrassed glances. Then
Mr. Jordan's face took on a dreamy, slightly sad expression, the same
expression as when he had spoken of how he had sold newspapers when
he was a boy. He placed his hand thoughtfully upon Amerigo's shoulder
and said:

"Why not? Yes! Why not! A man's no bigger than his dreams. . . ."

He shook their hands again and departed, descending the steps heavily,
slowly. Like Bra Mo with a heavy chunk of ice on his shoulder.

"Unh!" cried Rutherford, no sooner than the sound of his footsteps had faded away. "Kin you beat that, Babe? A *bigshot* comin' all the way down to the North End just to apologize to Amerigo!"

Viola nodded thoughtfully, gazing at her son as though he were a stranger. Rutherford, sensing her meaning, said: "Yeah, I know. Ain' it the truth! He'll be a man before you kin look around! Time sure does fly. An' did you notice how nice he was dressed? Conservative! An' how he put down them ten-dollar words in a simple way that you kin understand. Class, Jack! Boy!" to Amerigo, "You is *somebody!* Heah me!" His face broadened into a smile.

"Are!" said Amerigo.

"Yes, Mister President, but you wait till you finish with your college an' all an' git one a them Phi Beta Kappas or a Magna Cum Laudy before you start correctin' your poppa! An' even *then* I'd advise you to *whisper* so low that I can't even hear you!" He grinned, Viola grinned, Amerigo grinned. Then after a pleasant thoughtful silence of several seconds, he said mischieveously, "Well, Mister President, I think it's 'bout time for you to hit the hay, don' you?"

He reluctantly nodded assent.

"An' don' forget to wash your hands and face an' brush your teeth!" Viola added with a grin. He grinned back with a feeling of pride mixed with embarrassment and swaggered president-like into the kitchen. Meanwhile Viola and Rutherford went into the middle room and prepared for bed.

He said his prayers: "An' God bless Aunt Nancy an' Mr. Jordan an' the president of the Unided States of Amer'ka even if he is a Republikin."

"Do you think he really meant it? What he said?" Viola asked from within the darkness of the middle room. Amerigo listened eagerly.

"He prob'ly means it — in a way," said Rutherford thoughtfully, "I mean deep down inside. But you know, Babe, it's kinda like business, you have to be nice to the customers. He's smooth, though, like a actor. Usta talkin' to people. Ol' man Mac's like that. You know, sometimes one a the guests comes all frothin' at the mouth about somethin' an' then the ol' man turns on the charm! Has 'um eatin' out a his hand. Gits 'um to talkin' about theyself. An' before you know it, they out a the office, feelin' good, an' don' know what happened to 'um. Ha! ha! An' then, an' then five minutes after they done gone it comes to 'um."

"They wake up!" exclaimed Viola.

"Yeah! What? They say, all mad agin. An' then they go to cussin' Jews *an'* Christians — an' the whole human race! Ha! Ha! The ol' man could talk a hustlin' woman out a her money! Just the same, it does make you feel better when you speak out an' the *Voice* answers back."

On the following Friday the apology appeared in the *Voice* with an account of Mr. Jordan's visit. Rutherford cut it out and stuck it in the family album, and everybody who visited the house had to read it and listen to his account of it.

The story rippled throughout the alley:

"What a *fine* young man!" he heard from the neighbors all around, as he went to and from school.

It rippled up and down the avenue:

"I hear you gonna be president, Tony!" said Mr. Fineberg.

It slid dangerously along the streetcar tracks and between the wheels of the screeching streetcar:

"Yeah, honey, that li'l darkie's got more'n space between *his* ears!"

It slid all the way down Troost Hill to Garrison Square, and walked, skipped, hopped past the Field House and onto the school grounds where it gurgled in the laughing throats of the children.

"Did you tell that man you gonna be the presaden', niggah? Hee! Heeeeee! Haw! Haw! Hee-haw!" Others took up the cry: "Heeeeee-haw! Heeee-haw!" their laughing faces matching the colors of autumn, as the story swirled among the falling leaves that were whipped into a fury by the north wind, which gradually grew sharper, in spite of the sun, which, though it shone brightly, grew progressively weaker, causing the tip of his nose to flush plumb red and his knuckles and fingers to tingle in his pockets.

"Cut the black and orange sheets of paper into strips as wide as the first joint of the index finger," said Miss Chapman, indicating the first joint of the index finger with the pink-nailed thumb of her right hand.

Index finger. He repeated the word to himself, and suddenly recognized the word *joint*.

Till the law comes! he heard Rutherford saying, just before he bent over the Victrola to put Fats Waller on.

He cut the orange and black sheets of paper into strips and made rings of the orange strips by sticking the ends together with paste and then looped the black strips through the orange rings and pasted the ends in order to make a chain.

"Like this," said Miss Chapman, holding up a sample. And the chains of black and orange rings grew longer in his sticky hands and coiled like a snake and swelled into heaps of orange and black rings that they later had to straighten out and hang with the aid of ladders brought by Mr. Johnson, the janitor, a tall black man with shiny hair, laughing eyes, and sparkling gold teeth, in sweeping arcs against the walls of the kindergarten room until it looked pretty.

Like Christmas! Only Christmas is different: red and green and white and silver — with snow that isn't really snow but soap, and Santa Claus! Red and green rings. He pondered the difference, as the red and green and silver and Santa Claus faded into the past, which was not really the past, but the future, somewhere between the present, which was Halloween.

That evening after school he stood at the foot of the front steps with the little group of children:

"I ain' gonna let no black cats cross my path tanight!" Carl declared.

"Me neither, me neither," said Toodle-lum, grinning excitedly, his store-bought paper pumpkin in his hand.

"Got the chalk?" Tommy asked.

"Yeah, man!" said Turner with a cunning grin, "An' soap, lots of it. Laundry soap that you can't rub off!"

"Look what I made you!" cried Viola as he entered the house. She lifted a little orange-and-black harlequin costume out of the trunk.

"Look at that!" said Rutherford.

He examined the costume and pulled at the orange and black balls attached to the collar.

"Here, try this on." Placing the cone-shaped hat on his head. One half was orange and the other half was black and there were two little balls attached to the peak, one orange and one black. "Well . . . it's a little small," eyeing it critically, "but I think it'll do if you push it down tight. You got a head as big as your daddy's!" Rutherford looked up from his paper and smiled. "Here's the mask to go with it." He put it on.

"It hurts."

"That little joker's eyes is so b-i-g!" Rutherford laughed maliciously.

"Go an' git me the scissors," said Viola.

He went and got the scissors. She cut the eyes a little larger.

"There — that's better, ain' it?"

"Yes'm."

There was a knock at the door.

"Come on in!" cried Rutherford.

As the door opened they heard a long low soulful whistle:

"Zoo!" Viola exclaimed. "Well Har-rold Fergison! Wheeeere in the w-o-r-l-d have you been!" smiling at the black curly-headed man who slipped quietly into the room like a beautiful shadow.

"The old Miestro!" he rasped. "Heh heh heh," laughing from the side of his mouth, from the other side issued a big black cigar. He bit down on it and smiled.

"What you say, m-a-n!" said Rutherford warmly.

Amerigo merely grinned at him.

"Glim this Jaspah!" he said to Rutherford, indicating the child with an extended right hand with manicured nails. Like a woman's. His neck sank deeper between his rounded shoulders as he gave him his hand as he would a man. "Pray hip me, what have we here? You look like you all rigged up for a spook fest! Heh heh heh. Eh . . . yeah-ahem." He grinned as he examined the costume, fingering the balls on the collar.

"We gittin' fixed up for Hallaween!" said Viola. "Tanight's the night!"

"I see!" said Mr. Zoo. "My boy's gonna be like Jack the Bear — everywhere! Heh heh heh." The vein in his neck swelled under his tight collar. The knot in his tie appeared to be so hard that he could hardly breathe. Meanwhile Viola, observing his shining hair swelling up in deep waves from his smooth black forehead, said:

"You really got your moss layin' down to the bricks, there, Zoo!"

"Heh heh heh . . . thought I'd give the broads a thrill! They like a straight wig! Eh-heh heh heh!" His huge Adam's apple slid up and down when he swallowed the juice from his cigar.

"That monkey's got a *pound* a Murray's on 'is head!" cried Rutherford. "Haw-haw! Niggah, you oughtta be hoss-whipped for ruinin' your hair like that. You got *good* hair. Was that you was whistlin' when you come in?"

"Aw, I don' know. I'm just like the whale in jail: All I kin do is blow! Eh-heh heh heh."

"That cat kin w-h-i-s-t-l-e, Amerigo," Rutherford exclaimed. "Always could. Better'n most cats kin blow a horn!"

Mr. Zoo grinned appreciatively, bearing a mouthful of perfect large yellow teeth, which because of his black skin looked almost white. Like Aunt Lily's. And his eyes were big and rusty looking, with very long lashes, longer than a woman's. They made him look mean or like he was dreaming awake, or sleeping sitting up! Grandpa Will came to mind when he discovered Mr. Zoo's prominent nose with its high "Indian" bridge. And now he even discerned a deep rich red flesh tone surging up out of the blackness of his skin.

"Old Dee-Dee usta blow a mean harp, too," Rutherford was saying. "I remember sometimes we'd be comin' home from school, or from a dance or somethin', an' those two jokers'd git to b-l-o-w-i-n'! An' that Zoo! I swear, I ain' *never* heard n-o-body whistle like that cat! Blowed his way through school. Old Zoo never would study! Haw-haw!"

"Aaaaaw," Mr. Zoo grinned.

"Pull up a chair," Rutherford said, "an' set a while. We'll open up a keg a nails!"

"Eh-heh heh heh. Don' mind if I do!"

Rutherford reached under the sink and got several bottles of homebrew. Viola set the glasses on the table and, while Rutherford poured out the beer, she placed a can of Spanish peanuts before him. There was a long silence while they took the first swig of beer. After setting their glasses down they still sat quietly for a moment, ruminating over the past they had shared in order to find something suitable to say.

"Mom, kin I go now?"

"I guess so. Who's goin' with you?"

"Tommy an' Turner an' them."

"Well, have a good time. But don' git into no mischief! Is your hat on good? Let me see." She examined him carefully, turning him this way and that.

"Aw let that boy alone, woman!" said Rutherford impatiently. "Go on, Amerigo, an' have a good time! She'll make a sissy out a you! Don't git into no mischief? Woman, what's Halloween *for*? Ha!" He slapped his palm against his knee. "Zoo, do you remember when you an' ol' Elmer an' Dee-Dee an' T. C. an' ol' Clarence an' me put ol' man Wiggins's Ford up-on-top-a-that-toilet? No kiddin', Babe! Didn' we, Zoo?"

"Heh heh heh."

"Rutherford," Viola exclaimed, "don't you start that lie!"

"Babe if I'm-if I'm lyin', listen! I'll take a oath! Them niggahs was engi-*neers*, Jack!" He turned to Amerigo: "We was engineers, Amerigo." He stood upon the threshold of the kitchen door, held by the entreaty in his father's voice. "We took two boards an' some chain an' a ol' piece a rope. An' half of 'um pushed an' the other half pulled. If that rope had a broke a-l-l 'em li'l niggahs'd been dead! I'm tellin' you! Anyhow, when we finally got it up there, we all hid around the side of the house. An' *scaired!* Ol' Clarence kept hollerin': Aw-aw-we in trouble now! An' that cat started cryin'! Haw haw haw!"

"Naw!" cried Viola.

"Yeah!"

"Eh-heh heh heh."

He grinned and tightened his grip on his mother's arm.

"An' then ol' T. C., he had to be all brave an' ever'thin', he e-a-s-e-d up to the door an' rung the bell. An' then bust out runnin'! Old man Wiggins come to the door with a *shotgun!*"

"He must a heard 'um" cried Viola.

"Yeah! An' T. C. fell! Fell, Babe. An' Mister Wiggins leveled that double-barreled shotgun down on 'im, Jack. Took *aim!* An' yelled out: HALT! An'-ha ha! *an'* T-T. C. like to-like to dug a *tunnel* in the man's yard, gittin' away! M-a-n, that joker ran so fast that the bullet just laid on 'is back!"

"Couldn' go in!" shouted Viola with a burst of laughter, tears rolling down her cheeks. "Rutherford, Rutherford, you the l-y-i-n-'es' man that ever walked. You oughtta *crawl* to church on your hands an' knees an' ask the Lord to forgive you for tellin' a lie like that!"

"Ho ho!" Rutherford laughed.

"Tee hee hee!" laughed Amerigo.

"He-heh heh," Mr. Zoo clamped down on his soggy cigar, brushing the fallen ashes from his knee.

"Them li'l niggahs was b-a-d!" said Rutherford, as the laughter died down.

"If you couldn' blow you had to go!" Mr. Zoo grinned. A long low rush of air issued from between his purple lips.

"Blow one, Zoo!" said Viola.

"Aaaaw."

"Come on, Zoo, let's git way back!" Rutherford encouraged.

"Aw come on, Mister Zoo," said Amerigo.

"What!" Rutherford exclaimed, "you still here? I thought you was havin' a fit to git out a here!"

"I wanna hear!"

Mr. Zoo settled himself in his chair and grinned embarrassedly. "I don' know what to blow."

"You'd better be gittin' while the gittin's good," said Viola to Amerigo. "It's gonna be nine before you even git started!"

Rutherford, still smiling over his story, poured himself some more beer, while Viola helped herself to the peanuts.

"Kin I have some?" Amerigo asked.

"Yeah, take some," said Viola.

He grabbed a fistful and stuffed them into his pocket through the slit in his costume. Then he took another, and another. His hand darted out a fourth time, just as Mr. Zoo was pursing his lips to blow:

"Don't be no pig!" said Rutherford. "Leave some for somebody else!"

Mr. Zoo grinned and strummed his polished fingers nervously upon his knee. A few wrinkles broke the surface of his smooth forehead. "Eh, heh heh heh. What shall I whistle? You want me to —"

"An' don' forget to stop by an' see Aunt Lily an' Mrs. Derby an' let 'um see how you look. An' thank Aunt Lily for the sewin' she done on it. You hear?"

"Yes'm."

"You gonna blow one for us, Zoo?" Rutherford asked.

"Aaaaaw," Mr. Zoo grinned cupidly. He cleared his throat. Then he reached for his glass of beer. "Better have a little swig of this righteous brew before I consult my muse! Heh heh heh." He sipped his beer. Then he lit a match. It went out. He lit another one. He took a puff on his cigar. He put the burned-out match on the table.

"Go git a ashtray, Amerigo," said Viola.

He set an ashtray before Mr. Zoo. Mr. Zoo deposited his match, but broke the crusted end in doing so and had to brush the crumbs off the table and put them into the ashtray. Then he withdrew a handkerchief from his back pocket and wiped his hands, replaced it, and suddenly he had drawn his lips together and his jaws were filled with air. A sad sound had pierced the autumn evening.

Like the whole world wasn't nothin' but a vacuum, Rutherford had said after Mr. Zoo had gone. Like it was all by itself in a place — a place where nobody has ever been before.

Amerigo watched Mr. Zoo with awe. A dizzy, whirring sensation filled his mind. I've heard that song before! And then he was suddenly bewildered by a flash of cool splendid color that illuminated the dark chambers of memory, breaking up into particles of color as it whirred. And all the colors were the same, but different. I've been here before. Where? A pain filled his chest. That isn't pain, that's just a good feeling! So good that he could hardly stand it.

Mr. Zoo closed his eyes. His silky lashes trembled upon his cheeks, while his hands folded upon his lap. His right foot gently tapped out the beat. It ran along the parallel grooves between the planks that grew broader as they got farther away, beyond the window opposite which the old black woman sat, dozing in her rocking chair, beyond the wall with the stained-glass windows where you could not see where they went. It's the same beat! Mr. Zoo tapped it out as he blew.

And suddenly the sound had stopped. The air had gone out of Mr. Zoo's jaws and his lips were still. One could hear the drip-drop of water coming from the spigot. He saw himself putting the dirty dishes on the drainboard one sunny morning when he wasn't yet in kindergarten. He heard the clank of the garbage can in the yard below, and saw the pair of wild yellow eyes staring up at him from the depths of a blue shadow that fell upon Aunt Lily's porch.

"That sure was pretty, Zoo!" Viola said at last.

"Unh-unh! You oughtta be rich! Ain' that right, Babe?"

"He sure kin whistle all right!"

"If-if-*he* that man there," pointing at Mr. Zoo with his forefinger and tapping his knee: "If you was *white* you'd be s-t-r-a-i-g-h-t, Jack! Git you one a them high-powered managers. Why you-you- I ain' kiddin'! You could whistle your way 'round the w-o-r-l-d! To-to France! An' all them places in Europe. Ever heard of Ira Aldridge?"

"Heh heh heh, eh-heh heh heh," Mr. Zoo shook his head.

"Well," said Rutherford, "he was a actor. I mean a *actor*! None a that laughin' an' gigglin' Uncle Tom stuff. I mean a *ac*-tor! Like-like he acted Shakespeare an' Hamlet — all them high-powered old cats! Famous niggah all over the world except in his own country!"

"When did he live?" Viola asked skeptically. "I ain' never heard a no spook doin' all a that. Prejudice is in France an' them places, too, ain' it?"

"Not in Europe it ain'!" Rutherford protested. "Naw sir! I'm tellin' you, Babe, while my momma an' your momma was pickin' cotton in Alabama or Georgia — wherever it was down there — Ira Aldridge was havin' supper with kings! They didn't print it in the schoolbooks, but I read it just the same. An' he never was no slave, neither! There's lots and lots a g-r-e-a-t Negroes that we don' never hear nothin' about, 'cause *they* write the history. All we read about is George Washington an' all them jokers, but it ain' nothin' never happened in this country — good or bad — that they wasn't a Negro had somethin' to do with it! Well, anyway old Zoo here could be on big time if he got a break like that!"

"Aaaaaw," protested Mr. Zoo. He sipped his beer. Then he lit the stump of his cigar, and had a fit of coughing that brought water to his eyes. Amerigo laughed.

"Boy, *git* out a here!" said Rutherford.

"I'm gone!" he exclaimed with an excited grin, his eyes and ears filled with the sounds and colors of France, of Shakespeare *an' all them old cats, Europe, the Can-can — those French gals sure kin.*

"Boom!" he shouted, slapping his hands against Aunt Lily's screen. She drew the curtain aside with a grin, but then, upon seeing him, gave a little shriek. He stared back at her masklike face through the slightly frosted window. When she opened the door and peeped out he ran down the steps, suddenly frightened by the sad sound that escaped her lips.

At the bottom of the stair a little bunch of masked faces, grinning, laughing, and grimacing, frozen within the vibrant globule of sound that suddenly broke up, shattered into a hard raucous hail of sad sound: Tramp! Tramp! Tramping down the alley — through a France of sound that swelled and clanged as the huge pumpkin filled with black, brown, yellow, and white faces rumbled along the tracks in the middle of Independence Avenue, candlelit, eerie rays of light escaping from between its teeth.

Yellow streaks of soap appeared miraculously upon store windows, followed by a rush of fleeting excitement, as tiny feet splashed against the cold concrete pavement. The sharp north wind bit through the harlequin's skin and deepened the tone of wine-red rouge on Carl's cheeks, causing Toodle-lum to tremble and cry because the procession had left him behind upon the invisible border of the no-man's-land marked by the indomitable range of Mrs. Shields's voice:

"Toodle-lum! Aaaaaw Toodle-lum!"

"Yes'm! Yes'm."

The nine o'clock whistle blew low and pathetically, its long eyelashes, longer than a woman's, pressed against its cheeks, and little blue flames issuing from the jets of the gas stove flushed warm against his face, made his ears, fingertips, and toes tingle in the light of the bird-of-paradise lamp. Viola, Rutherford, and Mr. Zoo sat snugly around the fire talking quietly about the things that had happened when they were little.

"It's about your bedtime, ain' it?" said Viola. "Did you have fun?"

"Yes'm."

"Come on to the back, Zoo," said Rutherford, "Viola's cooked a pot a chili. It's for tamarra, but we might as well sample 'er."

"Aw-heh heh heh, I don't wanna —"

"That don' matter none," said Viola. "Amerigo, go wash your hands an' face — an' don't forget to brush your teeth."

In bed, the lights out, the soft glow of the gas flames filled the room. He lay his head upon the "stage," like at the show, only in the show there was the silver screen. No blue stars, black and white. He smiled in the dark, the smile deepened into a grin, he felt it, and then, before he knew it he was laughing Hee hee hee heeeee! — from within the belly of the big yellow pumpkin as it rumbled down the avenue.

"Amerigo!"

Viola stood over him. "Dreamin' agin! Just laughin' to beat the band!" She wiped the slobbers from his chin, and he settled back into a cooler, more vibrant, yet stiller sound, where he had once been before. . . .

All the masked faces fell from the branches of the trees. They lay in heaps at the bottom of the trees. The darkened hollows of their eyes stared up at the bright silver stars, which, glistening, fell down from the sky, covering the faces — ever so faintly, lightly, at first, and then heavily, thickly, until the glistening white forms that had been the faces merged into one another, and the falling whiteness thickened until the hollow eyes could no longer penetrate it. The snow fell and swelled into deep mounds around the trunks of the trees.

Clouds came. Viola and Rutherford spoke quietly, secretly, seriously, in the bedroom in the dark, while he pretended to be asleep.

"I don' know what we gonna do for Thanksgivin' dinner," said Viola.

"Well," said Rutherford, "if there ain' no money, there just ain' no money, Babe. Don't look like ol' man Mac's gonna git up off a nothin'. Been to see 'im twice already. Keeps puttin' me off. You think we could borra somethin' from Miss Rose?"

"I'll call 'er tamarra," said Viola. "Maybe Amerigo could go by after school."

In the silence that preceded sleep he thought about Thanksgiving: That's when the Pilgrims came. He saw men in big black stovepipe hats and long black capes and tall black boots, trudging through fields of snow with double-barreled shotguns over their shoulders, carrying turkeys with speckled feathers, followed by strong stern women wearing black bonnets tied tight around their chins and long black capes and black shoes with big square buckles on them, carrying corn and pumpkins and rabbits that the Indians had given them to big long tables with a lot of people, also dressed in black, gathered around them.

"And they were cold and hungry when they set foot upon the shores of the New World, but they were not discouraged," Miss Chapman had read from the big book with the pictures.

"What's dis-ker-iged?" he heard himself asking, suddenly surprised now by the image of Aunt Nancy in a long black cape, standing upon the shores of the New World!

"They didn't give up," replied Miss Chapman. "They were thankful unto the Lord for the blessings they had received, because they had lived through hard times. . . . So they prepared a great feast. And they prayed unto the Lord. And they shared what they had with each other and with their friends, the Indians, and the Indians shared what they had with the Pilgrims."

"Pur'tuns," he whispered.

Givin' others some a what you got.

STOP! Miss McMahon stood in the kitchen door, gasping for breath.

"I'll call 'er tammara," said Viola. "Maybe Amerigo kin go by after school."

"Now you take this," said Aunt Rose on the following evenin, "an' put it in your pocket." She tied the knot with something hard in it in the corner of a handkerchief and stuffed it in his pocket.

"What's in your pocket, boy?"

"A star." He took it out and held it up.

"Well, here. Put it in your other'n. An' you go straight home an' don' stop for nothin' or nobody. You heah?"

"Yes'm."

"You hungry?"

"No'm."

"You sure?"

"Yes'm."

"Come in the kitchen. We'll see somethin'."

She moved heavily toward the kitchen on her swollen legs. He sniffed the pleasant trail of perfume that followed in her wake, while exploring the flowered pattern of her blue print dress. The bonnet was of the same material, but trimmed with little white ruffles, like some kind of flower . . . or like cake. Instantly he remembered the big three and four-layer chocolate cakes she sometimes baked when he came. Maybe she had a cake in the kitchen! But the speculation was immediately crowded out of his mind by the memory of other savory aromas: jars filled with pickled pig feet, chitterlings steaming in a pot or on a plate with pickle relish, baked opossum, *fried* chicken smothered in brown gravy and hot — piping-hot biscuits with butter oozing out the middle! A host of things that were good to eat came to his mind, so that by the time they had passed through the front corridor and entered the parlor, he was too hungry to notice the old penciled portraits of Aunt Rose's mother and father that hung over the piano in the dark oval frames. He merely took quick unconscious glances at them now, and at the Victrola. RCAVICTOR! Fixing his eye on the spotted dog that looked into the big round thing that the sound came out of.

He thought of asking if he could play some records, but he suppressed the question in lieu of what he hoped awaited him in the kitchen.

She immediately went over to the stove and lifted the lid from a pot that gave off a delicious and vaguely familiar aroma.

"You set down at that table, young man," she said with a cunning smile. "Didn' your momma tell me that you don't like no turnips?"

"No'm."

"How come?"

"It taste bitter."

"Is that so?" She stirred the pot, and then went to the cupboard and opened one of the little frosty glass doors and took out a plate and set it on the table before him and then took out the eating things from the table drawer. While she was thus occupied, he peeped into the bottom of the cupboard. It was filled with little cans and boxes with funny weeds and grasses and papers and leaves and all kinds of things to eat that made everything she ate taste so good.

But she doesn't cook better than Mom! he thought. Still he had had a funny feeling when he had thought it, just the same.

Aunt Rose was again stirring the pot.

"There," she sighed at last, "I guess that's right now. I ain' seen you in a long time, what the darkies been up to up your way? Seen where you gonna run for president!" She laughed in her reserved dignified way, her eyes flashing brilliantly: "Lawd, I almost died when I read in the *Voice* about you bein' president! That'll give 'um somethin' to think about! What'd that niggah from the *Voice* say when you said that?"

Miss Chapman says you ain' supposed to say "niggah" he thought.

"He said, Why not?"

"Bet he sure was flabbergasted — so much sense from a little boy. An' from the north wind, too!" She pushed the pot to the back of the stove, dipped into it with a spoon, tasted its contents, and said: "Gimme your plate," in a casual tone. He gave her his plate. "But it don' matter where you live or what your color is: Brains is brains! an' gumption is gumption! There's them that's got both, an' some with one or the other — an' all the rest that ain' got neither one!" She put the filled plate on the table. "Try that." Her smile convinced him that she had some prank up her sleeve. He took a mouthful of the funny-looking sauce. Her eyes sparkled when he took a second mouthful, and a third, and a fourth. She smiled quietly, admiringly while he ate. Soon the plate was clean.

"Want some more?"

"Yes, *ma'am!*"

She filled his plate again and set it before him.

"I thought you didn't like no turnips!" She arched the birdlike brow over her left eye.

"I *don't.*"

"Aw yeah? You just ate a plateful!"

"Them ain' no turnips, Aunt Rose! I *know* — 'cause turnips taste different. They bitter an' in li'l round pieces!"

"Creamed 'uns ain'!" She smiled at him like a poker player with a royal flush. "Your momma just don' know how to fix 'um!"

"She kin beat you! She's the best cook in the whole world!"

"Who you think taught your momma to cook?"

"She just knowed it!"

"Don't nobody *just know* nothin', Mister Smart Elic. I taught your momma how to cook. When you git home you kin ask 'er."

"I bet she kin beat you makin' choc'lit cake!"

"When you comin' agin?"

"When you gonna make one?"

"You might be president at that, you li'l fox!" She looked out the window. The sun was sinking. Cars streamed up and down the trafficway below. "It's gittin' late now, Amerigo," she said a little anxiously, "you better be runnin' along before the traffic gits too heavy."

"Yes'm."

"Got that han'kerchief I give you?"

"Yes'm," feeling his pocket.

"Here, waitaminute, we better not take no chances." She went to the sewing machine in the next room and opened one of the little drawers and fished around until she found a safety pin. "There, that's better," she said to herself, pinning the handkerchief to the lining of his pocket.

She opened the front door.

"Now, Amerigo, you go straight home an' don' stop on the way. An' you stay on this side of the street, an' if any of them dagos in front of Dante's Inferno say somethin' to you, you just keep on goin'. An' cross the street at the corner, you heah?"

"Yes'm."

"All right, you gonna kiss your ol' auntie?"

He kissed her on her smooth cheek and inhaled deeply of the delicious perfume that exhumed from her soft bosom. He laid his head upon it and hugged her tight.

"That's enough — li'l devil! Lawd! Sure won't be long!"

"For what?"

"You'll know soon enough. Now scat!"

She slapped him gently on his bottom, and he set out earnestly on his long trek home.

"Ain't you hungry?" Viola asked when he did not ask for a second helping of chine-bones and black-eyed peas.

"No'm."

"Did Aunt Rose feed you?"

"Yes'm."

"What'd you have?"

"Turnips."

"*Turnips!*"

"Haw! haw! haw!" Rutherford laughed over the evening paper.

"I thought you don't like turnips!" Viola exclaimed. "*I* have to *make* you eat 'um!"

"Aunt Rose is the best cook in the w-h-o-l-e w-o-r-l-d!" He bucked his eyes in exaggerated innocence.

"Aw yeah!" Viola exclaimed.

"She does put down some a the best 'possum I ever ate!" Rutherford broke in teasingly.

"Who asked you?" Viola retorted.

"I bet she kin beat you makin' raisin pie!" said Amerigo.

"Unh!" said Rutherford, "boy, you took the words right out a my mouth. Your grandma made a raisin pie like it was 'er birthmark! An' g-o-o-d!"

"When you want it?" Viola asked, looking from one to the other. "Just when!"

The child laughed with glee.

"What's so funny, you little witch!"

"Nothin'."

"Well Sund'y's Thanksgivin'," said Rutherford, winking at him, "we'll see if your momma's learned to cook by then!"

"R-u-t-h-e-r-f-o-r-d Jones — we're through!"

"Aw, you know I was just kiddin', Babe!"

"Me, too, Mom, but those turnups shooooore was good!"

Thanksgiving day morning the reverend preached a special sermon, got happy, and made everybody else happy. Rutherford worked a little later than usual, and he stayed in the kitchen at Viola's elbow nervously watching her prepare the dinner.

"What's that?" pointing to some dried leaves on the table in a little sack.

"Now don't you start botherin' me, boy! Can't yousee I'm busy? I'll never get through on time. What's what?"

"Those?"

"Bay leaves."

"Aw." He wanted to ask her what they were for, he wanted to ask her about all the things she was using, but the serious mien with which she had said "Bay leaves" caused him to think better of it. So he touched the filling of one of the sweet potato pies that were cooling on the windowsill. Viola cut him with a killing glance. He stood on one foot and then the other, made a blubbering sound by forcing the air between his closed lips. Then he went to the window and wrote his initials upon the sweating windowpane. Suddenly he heard Viola saying "Rutherford! The grub's on the table. Your hands washed?" following which they sat down to table all dressed up in their Sunday clothes, the big golden-brown goose steaming on the platter in the center of the table with the pile of maple leaves he had gathered in the lot behind the empty house. "You kin decorate the table," Viola had said, and he had gone out and gotten them: big yellow ones and brown ones spotted with red and yellow color, and yellow ones spotted with red and brown color, with purplish black edges and purplish green stems. He had arranged them in an orderly heap in the middle of the table, and had placed a big leaf beside each plate to put the knives, forks, and spoons on, and smaller ones for the cups and saucers and glasses and salt-and-pepper shakers.

"Look!" he had exclaimed when it was all finished.

"Oooooo-whee!" Viola had said: "Bea-u-ti-ful! Now git some chairs an' wash your hands an' we can call your daddy!"

His fingers slid over the surface of the sweaty windowpane, his attention absorbed by the letters written there, he heard, as if in a dream, his mother say: *"Rutherford! the grub's on the table. Your hands washed?"*

And Rutherford solemnly bowed his head in order to say the blessing, in a long black cape, the tips of his fingers enclosing a serious thankfulness: Dear Lord, we thank Thee for the blessings we are about to receive. . . . and when he had finished Viola, in black cape and equally as solemn, serious, thankful, said her New World Prayer, and then he, the Friendly Indian, and when he had finished he raised his tomahawk, made the sign of peace, and bit into it.

A rich sensation rose up from the mists of November in a rush of succulent color and sound — like a pretty bird — and flew off into the cold blue-white reaches of the wild and dangerous New World.

"Mom, you the best cook in the w-h-o-l-e w-o-r-l-d!" he exclaimed, just as the warm-winged bird dipped into the blue shades of the frosty wilderness. The funny feeling came over him.

You mean, beside Aunt Rose, said Miss Chapman.

He looked guiltily into his plate.

The movie — plus the comedy and a second feature — lasted from three-thirty until seven-thirty; it was ten to eight when he got home.

"Hi, babe!" said Viola in her underskirt and stocking feet. Her hair was freshly curled and shining and her eyes were excited.

"Hi," noticing that the house was still full of Thanksgiving dinner smells. A whole raisin pie and half of a sweet potato pie stood upon the oven shelf, and the remains of the goose stood in the big boiler beside the pies.

In the middle room discarded clothes were strewn on chairs and on the bed. Powder boxes and perfume bottles stood out of their usual order on the vanity dresser, while two of the side drawers stood open with their contents hanging over the sides.

Rutherford was standing over the Victrola in the front room with a record in his hand.

"Hi, son."

"Hi."

He beheld his father with pleasure, admiring his handsome blue Sunday suit and tan shoes, his white shirt with its tab collar and the stand-up knot in his tie. He could still see the imprint of his skullcap in the skin of his forehead.

"Whereya goin'?"

"You forgot the dance, boy! Lawrence Keys is playin' with Baby Lovett at Elks Rest! Me an' your momma's gonna be there with bells on, Jack!"

"Gonna be gone long?"

"Till the law comes!"

He headed desperately for the kitchen. Viola was rushing toward the middle room. He turned again and followed her. The record began to play. *Yes yes!* cried the singer.

Fats Waller he thought as the raucous pearling tones agitated his fear.

"Whereya goin'?" he asked his mother.

"Huh?" She was blackening her eyelids with a little brush that she dipped into some black stuff in a little red box, which she had wet with spit.

"Didn' your daddy tell you just now? We're goin' to the Thanksgivin' dance."

"How far is it?"

"Eighteenth an' Vine."

He returned to the front room where his daddy was cleaning his nails with a penknife. His fingers were long. He looked at his own; they were short and stubby. *You'd have pretty nails like your daddy if you didn't bite 'um all the time,* he heard Viola saying, and he put his hands in his pockets. He admired Rutherford's broad shoulders, the smooth skin on his freshly shaven face, his straight Indian nose. He speculated as to how long it would take for him to have a neatly trimmed mustache like his, regretting the absence of a soft blueberry mole on the left side of his upper lip.

Fats Waller had stopped playing. The needle was running in the empty groove of the record.

"Play Bessie!" said Viola from the middle room. "What time did Sister Bill an' 'em say they was comin'?"

"They oughtta be here pretty soon, Babe." Rutherford slipped Fats Waller into the cover, laid it aside and put the Bessie Smith record on the Victrola, wound it, released the brake, and set the needle in the spinning track:

"If you don't, I know who will," she sang. "If you don't, I know who will!"

He went over and stood beside the machine. He watched the reddish brown label spinning around and around:

"You may think that I'm just bluffin', but I'm one gal"

"ain' sapposed to want for nothin'," he murmured under his breath, and suddenly an uncanny feeling passed through his body. He spun around and looked at his father, who stood with his foot resting on a chair, brushing his shoes for the last time. He stared at Viola in the middle room, freshening the mole on her chin with the wetted tip of a pencil. It's all happened before! I *know* it!

A cool sheen of sweat stood out upon his forehead; the strong sweetish smell of liquor filled his nostrils. A man, tall, dark, with a little scar on his chin withdrew a flask from his inside pocket and poured some whiskey into the top that made a cup when you screwed it off and handed the flask to Rutherford, who poured some of the whiskey into a glass. They said something to each other in hushed voices, glancing cunningly into the kitchen where the women were — three or four besides Viola — just as they brought the cup and the glass together with a barely perceptible click:

"Man, you better treat me right!" Bessie was singing, "or else it will be, good-bye, John!"

The two men laughed, throwing back their heads. Then somebody knocked at the door, Rutherford opened it, and two people entered the room, a light, almost white-looking man with curly hair like an Italian and a brown-skinned woman with a short dress that slid way up over her knees when she sat down on the sofa:

"Love me till I git my fill!" Bessie continued.

"Tellit like is!" cried the brown-skinned woman, snapping her long brown red-nailed fingers meaningfully.

He observed himself staring at her pretty red lips that matched the color of her fingernails, at her ripe bosom, and at her shining hair that looked as though Viola had done it. She beckoned with her finger, dipped her head slightly forward, while the men drew their smiling faces close to hers. Her wet lips whispered something he couldn't hear, at which heads flew back in all directions, like a multicolored flower bursting into bloom at the clap of a peal of laughter.

Viola came running in from the kitchen to find out what had made them all laugh so, greeting the brown-skinned woman with an exuberant, "Why hello there, *girl!*" Then the woman whispered it to her, while the men paused with bated breath until she had heard, and when they all saw by the broad smile that stole upon her face that she had heard, they all burst into laughter, teeth and eyes flashing, hair shining, tie knots fitting snuggly in the vortexes of immaculately starched collars framed within the lapels of blue serge suits, while the women — Miss Allie Mae, Miss Ada, Miss Patsy, and Miss Vera — rushed in from the kitchen and laughed, too.

After which they dashed here and there getting dressed, sipping from their highball glasses as they dashed, eyes shining brighter, hair bursting into clusters of brilliant curls, amid the pleasant smell of soap, powder, perfume, fried hair, fried popcorn, salted peanuts, whiskey, gin, and ginger ale — agitated and stirred by excited fragments of conversation:

"I heard you got let off at the laundry, honey," said Miss Vera to Viola, running her fingers along the seam of her stocking to see if it were straight. Catching his eye gazing at her thigh, she gave him a wink. He blushed and looked at the floor.

"Yeah, girl," Viola answered.

"Ain' that a shame!" said Miss Ada, "After all 'em years you been there!" She stood in front of the vanity dresser, straightening her lip with red color issuing from a bullet-shaped dispenser. "But at least you got a *man* to help *you*. I ain' got no papers on Jenks!"

"Shucks!" Viola exclaimed, turning her back to Miss Ada. "Here, girl, kin you fasten me up?" She glanced quickly into the front room to see if the men were listening, and then, lowering her voice, talking out of the side of her mouth, she said: "Huh! If we had to live on those pennies Rutherford's bringin' in, we'd starve to death!"

"What you gonna *do,* girl?" asked Miss Allie Mae.

"The Lord only knows!" said Viola. "But what does the Good Book say? Where there's a will there's a way? You know, the Lord helps those that help themselves, honey!"

"Ain' that the *truth!*" said Miss Patsy. She sat on the little chair beside the vanity dresser watching the others as they got ready. A sly grin appeared on her face. She looked up at the ceiling, her grin deepening into a suggestive smile. Then she puckered her lips sensuously and said: "The Lord made man, an' he made women, an' I'm as *glad* as I kin be! Say!" in a hushed tone, "did you see old you-know-who at Piney's the other night?"

"Yeah, honey," said Viola, "but I didn't have much time to talk."

"Could you tell 'im what I told you?"

"I just gave 'im the note."

"He's a hot poppa — just full a fun — an' a-l-l-ways ready to break open a keg a nails!"

"Ssssh!" hissed Miss Ada, "not so loud!" glancing into the front room.

"Aw, girl, that don't matter," said Miss Vera, "they so busy schemin' theyself they ain' got no time to hear what we talkin' 'bout! I could die tamarra, an' my old man wouldn't miss me, honey. If it's somethin' he likes better'n juggin' between some woman's legs, I swear I don' know what it is. Girl, a good man's h-a-r-d to find! Bessie wasn' tellin' no lie! But you sure lucky, Vi, to have a steady workin' man like Rutherford. An' good lookin' to boot!"

"Yeah," said Viola, "but I had to git 'im straight! I had to leave home once. Gone two weeks. He kept a-writin' an' a-callin' an' a-hangin' 'round till I come back. 'Course, I can't tell you what it was all about, 'cause one a the first things you gotta learn is to keep your business to your*self!*"

"A-men!" said Miss Allie Mae.

"What happened in them two weeks is between the good Lord an' me, an' I wouldn't be ashamed to face my Maker with the details, but what *no* man don' know won't hurt 'im!"

"Oh, Lord! Did I bring the tickets?" cried Miss Allie Mae, rumaging the vanity dresser and then the bed.

"Did you look in your purse?" Viola asked.

"Aw, yeah, girl, I'm so *excited!* We better be goin', the shindig'll be over before we even git there. You remember last year, we come pullin' up to the dance an' all the folks was comin' home! Eeeee!"

"An' we had to go down on Twelfth Street, to the Sunset, to have some fun!" said Miss Ada.

"Yeah, e-v-e-r-y-b-o-d-y was out *that* night!"

"Come on in here, Allie!" cried Rutherford, suddenly entering the middle room.

"What you up to!" She grinned broadly. He grabbed her by the arm.

"Let's see if you kin still cut a rug!"

"Ohoooo! You *know* I can't dance, Rutherford!" allowing him to pull her into the front room. Viola smiled a tolerant superior smile, while the crowd gathered around, Amerigo squeezing himself to the front. He watched his father take Miss Allie Mae by the waist and pull her close to him so that their bodies pressed against each other — trunk straight, head erect — from hip to hip, to the beat of the music, then do it again, and then fall into a two-step, then a double, rushing the tempo because the music was slow. Suddenly dropping back in his right hip, he shifted his weight and swept forward, gliding into a spin, pivoting on the ball of his right foot. S-m-o-o-t-h! he exclaimed in silent admiration, as they fell away from each other, fell back, shuffled backward until they were several feet apart. Then Rutherford raised his arms, the elbows slightly crooked, fell back in his right hip, bent his left knee, and glided forward — evenly — with a graceful shuffle. That's the Camel Walk.

"Wait a minute!" Rutherford cried suddenly, "where's my old lady? Come on, Babe! Let's show these jokers how to cut a rug!"

Viola sprang into the front room. "Make room, here," she said. Rutherford stood waiting. "Shall I shimmy?"

"Aw do it!" cried Mr. Jenks.

"You hear me talkin', honey!" cried Miss Ada with a sly grin. "Do it like your momma showed you!"

"Look out, there, Sister Bill, don't gimme none a that *momma* jive!"

Peals of laughter. He smiled, then laughed, and wondered what they were laughing about. Just then Miss Vera said: "Wait a minute! Bessie Smith ain' no shimmyin' music. Here!" She put another record, wound the crank, and set the needle in the groove. A low raucous rumbling pulsing burst of chords, undulating up and down a hill of rhythmic feeling, issued upon the air.

Everybody started tapping their feet, full of smiles. The drummer took a mean cut on the snares, and Amerigo tapped his feet and clapped his hands, too.

And Ruben fell in about twelve, he heard Rutherford say, and rediscovered the fine web of fear that now worked its way into the happy, nervous excitement that flowed through his mind and body.

"Aw, it's tight like that!" cried Mr. Jenks, patting Miss Ada softly on the behind.

"Yeah!" they all cried in concert.

"I mean it's tight like that!"

Viola and Rutherford were doing a break-step, but now they fell away, fell back, stood pat, ready. He looked at his friends, his face illuminated by a radiant smile, and asked: "Shall I shimmy?"

"Yeah!"

"Well all right, then!"

He began to tremble, so subtly that one could hardly detect it at first, and then more noticably, in ripples of watery movement. He shimmied faster and faster, and s-m-o-o-t-h!

"God damned! Lookit that niggah go!" cried Mr. Jenks.

"He's a killer-diller, ain' he!" exclaimed the man with the flask and the scar.

He's got a knife! cried a voice.

"He's a killer-diller, ain' he!"

"Come on, Babe!" said Rutherford to Viola who was still standing pat.

"Yeah, cut that cat!" cried the man with the Italian hair. Miss Vera wound the crank and started the record spinning again.

Viola fell back, away, stood still, legs spread apart, arms outstretched, fingers popping to the rhythm of "Tight Like That." She began to tremble, to shake all over. Like she was made out of jelly! he thought, and was suddenly overcome by a feeling of profound embarrassment that made him look away. But when the hand-clapping became louder and the shouts of encouragement more excited he had to look, to behold with intense private pleasure the faint sheen of sweat upon her dark velvety skin. She was smiling and her teeth shone like pearls. Rhinestone earrings glittered in her earlobes.

"JESUS!" cried Miss Allie Mae: "VI-O-LA! LOOK WHAT TIME IT IS!"

"Let's git out a here!" cried one of the men.

"Unh! The dance is over at one-thirty!" said Rutherford.

"What time *is* it?" asked Viola.

"Twelve-fifteen!" said the man with the scar.

The music stopped. The taxi honked from the street below, while coat sleeves flitted in arcs through the air and scarves whisked before his eyes, his nose smarting from the intoxicating scent of perfume.

"Got the tickets?" Viola asked.

"Yeah — I think," said Rutherford, "let me see," searching his pockets. "Yeah, I got 'um."

"Where's the juice?" cried the scar-faced man.

"Hereitis," said the brown-skinned woman.

"Bye, Tony," said Mr. Jenks.

"S'long, ol'-timer," said Mr. Scar.

"S'long," he replied sadly.

A blast of cold air rushed in the door.

"Come on, man," said Rutherford, "the taxi's waitin', if we don't git out a here 'em gals never will come!"

The men moved out onto the porch, talking, laughing, blowing smoke from cigarettes. The women next, flitting between his upturned eyes and the floor lamp.

"Bye, baby!" said Miss Allie Mae.

"Bye, hon," said Viola, kissing him. "You be good, an' go straight to bed. Tell you all about it when we git home."

"Bye-bye," said Miss Patsy, Miss Vera.

"Bye," he said, but they had already rushed out the door. The taxi honked three times more.

"Unh!" cried Rutherford, suddenly appearing in the door.

"What's the matter?" asked Viola from the top step.

"Forgot *my* booze!"

"Slowpoke!"

"Come on, Vi!" yelled Miss Ada from the street below.

"I'm on my way!" she yelled back. "Bye, hon!" turning to him once more. Rutherford rushed past him.

"You take it easy, now, you hear?"

"Yessir."

They ran down the steps. He heard a burst of laughter just before the taxi pulled off. He shut the door and locked it. He turned and faced the empty house. It was filled with the glare of all the lights, with the aftertones of laughter, with the traces of hilarious movement and the smell of flesh and sweat and of things to eat and drink. All the ashtrays were full of ashes and cigarette butts. A faint cloud of smoke hung over the room. Empty and half-filled glasses stood on the coffee table, the end table, the Victrola, the floor. The furniture stood about in unfamiliar attitudes. He moved and hung up the things that were necessary to move and hang up in order to make his bed. Skipping his prayers, he climbed in. . . .

He left the lamp burning, and tossed and turned impatiently in its light, waiting for them to come back. He tried to imagine how far away Eighteenth and Vine was, and how long it took to get there. Way out south! Music filled his ears, the sound of a huge crowd of people, men and women dancing. The Black and Tan came to mind.

"They went away an' left me. They don't even care." *Boom!* he felt his chest for the hole that was too small to bleed. He was dying. They came home from the dance and found him dead. They cried and cried but they could not bring him back. *Hum'ty-Dum'ty set on a wall. . . .*

He thought of Miss Chapman — She'll be sorry, too! His lips trembled pathetically. A lump rose to his throat. Tears.

He closed his eyes against the glare of the bulb, and he was suddenly in a red-orange room. It was hot. He tried to still be dead, to imagine them suffering, to make them suffer still, and to forgive them, but death slipped from his grasp, melted and diffused throughout the hot red-orange light that filled the room behind his closed eyelids — and then it got lost in the dark.

Boom!

The front door was standing open. Viola rushed into the room out of breath, half falling over the threshold, looking anxiously behind her, holding the train of her dress in one hand and her rhinestone shoes in the other.

"Git in that house!" Rutherford shouted from the darkness of the porch. "I'm gonna show you tanight!" He appeared in the door with an angry grimace on his face. Viola was in the middle room. She turned on the lamp.

"Now don' start nothin' till I —" but he was upon her:

"WHAP!" his palm resounded against her shoulder, as she ducked to avoid the blow.

"LETME OUT A MY DRESS FIRST!" she cried.

"God damned whore! Think I'm a DAMNED FOOL or somethin' —"

And he, trembling with fear and rage, jumped out of bed and rushed toward his father with his doubled fists raised over his head.

"Don't you hit *my* momma!"

Rutherford and Viola, suddenly distracted by his appearance, looked at each other, grinned nervously, and gestured futilely with their hands, as though they did not know what to do with them. Viola was in a defensive crouch with her dress half off, while Rutherford stood in an attitude of waiting.

"Don't you hit *my* momma!" he was yelling as he charged.

Rutherford took a deep breath, placed his hands on his hips, and said:

"Li'l niggah, if-you-don't-git-back-in-that-bed I'll *kill* you!"

He froze with terror. He trembled violently. Whimpering sounds issued from his lips, but he could not cry. He gave his mother and father a despairing look. His arms fell limply to his sides.

Meanwhile Viola quickly took off her dress. Rutherford watched her dumbly, and then looked vacantly at his son, upon the small naked figure that limply slinked back to bed.

When I git big enough, I'll *kill'im!* he thought to himself, feeling Viola's pitying eyes upon him. An' to hell with *her,* too!

"Turn out that light," said Rutherford, "an' not another peep out a you."

Viola was already in bed. Rutherford turned on her.

"Who was that niggah, anyway? That you had to dance with four times! Makin' a ass out a me in front a *ever*'body! I'm sick a this crap! You hear me? *Sick of it!*" His voice trembled. Viola was silent. He threw off his clothes, got into bed, lit a cigarette, and turned out the light.

In the dark he prayed that it was all over. He watched the tip of Rutherford's cigarette blaze furiously and grow dim in a cloud of ensuing smoke, and flare out in the darkness again, and again. Meanwhile he lay awake and waited, listened, waited, listened. After a while the red globule of light disappeared, and the bedsprings whined softly as Rutherford shifted into a sleeping position. Viola breathed deep and long.

He turned quietly on his side and faced the window. He looked out at the stars, singled one out, and *longed to be there.* . . .

"What you dreamin' about, boy?" Viola was saying. He stood by the Victrola. Rutherford had finished brushing his shoes. He found it strange that his mother held the Vaseline jar in her hand. "You daydreamin'?"

"Amerigo!" said Rutherford firmly. He started with fear. "You hear your momma talkin' to you?"

"You feel all right?" Viola asked.

He could not speak.

"You look kind a peaked to me."

"Nothin'," he answered finally. And then he began to whistle self-consciously through his teeth.

There was a knock at the door. Rutherford opened it: Tall faces and excited voices of men and women rushed in behind a blast of cold night air. They mingled with the music, moved about and became a part of the music, mixed and became a part of the heat issuing from the cool blue flames streaming steadily from the jets of the gas stove, which resembled a little stage with a curtain of flame for a backdrop, dancing to and fro in the heat to the rhythm of the music.

And then there was another burst of cold air. He grinned helplessly and said good-bye to the departing host that was off to the Thanksgiving dance at Elk's Rest, and answered "Yessir" to his father's instructions to go straight to bed, and then the noisy silence of the omitted prayer, and the hot red-orange room crowded with dancing figures, and finally the quenching tears that stained the redness black.

BOOM!

The key slid quietly in the lock.

He lay very still, afraid to open his eyes.

"Hi, baby!" Viola stood over him with a smile. He looked beyond his mother's smiling face and saw that his father also smiled.

"What you say, Sonny?" he said in a racy voice.

And suddenly the early hours of the morning after Thanksgiving were filled with cold goose and beer and stories about the people who attended the dance, what they wore, who said this and that, and why, and what happened after that, and how funny exciting it all was, and then the lights went out and everyone went to bed.

He shivered from the cold. He had kicked off the top sheet and half of the blanket while he slept. He now discovered that his feet were cold. He pulled them under the covers. Then he heard his father in the kitchen, frying eggs and making coffee.

"It *is* a Sanie Claus!" he said to himself. He lay back down but kept his eyes fixed upon the little gas stove. There was no fire in it. He looked at the sealed-up chimney hole again. Then he tossed and turned and waited for Rutherford to call him. He listened to his mother sleeping, breathing long even breaths. He thought he heard Rutherford's call. He raised himself upon his elbow and listened. The faint sound of paper crinkling came from the kitchen. "He's fixing his lunch, or reading the papers." He lay back down and looked out the window. It was filled with a cold hoary light.

And suddenly he saw a silver street lined with maple trees bordering snow-covered lawns that swept upward toward the steps and porches of beautiful stone and wooden houses. His eye wandered down the silver street until it came to a low rambling house on the corner. The steps and the terrace were filled with snow. The swing on the porch was filled with snow. Chickens, ducks, and turkeys cackled, gobbled, and pecked at the golden grains of corn that lay buried in the snow. Through the front window of the house and into the parlor he wandered: a green tree glistening with colored lights, with a bright silver star on top. The round fat belly on the coal stove glowed cherry-red from the middle room. A warm reassuring feeling came over him. . . .

"All right! Let's hit 'um!" Rutherford was saying from the middle room. He focused his eyes upon the figure that stood between himself and the early-morning light filtering through the middle room window and saw that his father had his hat and coat on and his lunch under his arm. "You awake?"

"Yessir."

Rutherford moved toward the front door.

"Dad?"

Rutherford turned and looked at him.

"Old Tommy said it ain' no Sanie Claus!" he wanted to say, but before the words could separate themselves from his thought, Rutherford was saying:

"So long, son," and had closed the frozen front door behind him.

He climbed into bed with his mother. "Mom?" She stirred drowsily. "Mom?"

"Aw, Amerigo, don' start all that wringin' an' twistin' at this time a the mornin'!" She turned on her side. He lay quietly until she made him get up and go to school.

He stalked moodily through the stiff metal-gray morning, kicking at the frozen clumps of tracked mud, frozen cans and bottles stuck to the earth, paying no heed to the few trembling leaves that still clung to the trees.

A general assembly was called at nine o'clock. All the children rushed to the big auditorium. They laughed and giggled and threw spitballs at each other and thumped each other on the head. They were told to be quiet. Then a strange man got up to talk. Just then Carl pinched him.

"Ouch!"

"Mister Bowles," the man was saying, "passed away."

He rubbed his arm and tried to catch the stranger's words.

"He departed this world at four A.M. . . ."

Boom!

His heart pounded in his ears:

Mr. Bowles! Tommy said it wasn't so. . . . Mr. Bowles! The face, the hollow eyes stared up at the stars through deep layers of snow piled at the foot of a leafless tree:

A nigger did it!

Ain' no blood.

They don't care.

"School will close at twelve o'clock today — " the strange man was saying.

"Hot dog!" Turner cried amid irrepressible shouts of glee that rose up from the assembly.

"Ssh! . . . sssh!" Miss Chapman whispered.

"Shame on you!" Miss Moore whispered.

He was ashamed for Turner and for himself. Someone behind him giggled.

"Ssssh!" he whispered to the offender, and sat very still.

"A moment of silence . . ." the stranger was saying, "for a tireless and devoted leader of his people."

The silence swelled and filled the drums of his ears with the question, but Professor Bowles did not answer.

"Ain' that a shame!" said Viola when he told her what had happened.

"Well, we a-l-l got to go *some*day," said Rutherford that evening over his paper. "He was a fine man, though."

"Pr'fessor Bowles!" said Aunt Rose the following afternoon, as though she were hearing his name for the first time.

"You knowed 'im didn't you?" he asked.

"Aw yes, I knowed 'im, all right, but I never thought of 'im dyin' like everybody else — just like the hustlers an' pimps an' junkies. Just like I'm gonna have to die someday. But then Jesus died, didn' He?"

"Yes'm."

Mr. Bowles's name quivered in the vibrant hollow of the sad round tone, it floated like a bright silver ball through the air. It got hung in a tree, got caught in its branches and burst!

Boom!

"Unh!" Rutherford exclaimed that Friday evening, smoothing out the pages of the *Voice*. "I see where they gonna tear down the old schoolhouse! Next year the school's gonna be on Pacific Street where the paddies usta go."

Next year, Amerigo repeated the words to himself. *Next year.* When's that? Wasn't yesterday, and it wasn't tomorrow; the sad voluminous tone that was *next year* filled his mind, engulfed the present, which seemed to stretch out in all the snowy windblown directions. And then the words *torn down* imposed themselves upon his consciousness. He saw the "kinny-garden" filled with golden sunlight, burning the surfaces of the lacquered desks, and the soft shadowy form of Miss Chapman behind the big desk at the front of the room, her dark hollow eyes peering up, peering out from the deep layers of falling snow piled in a mound at the foot of a naked tree:

Him no more than her.

"Si-i-lun' night, Ho-o-ly night, A-l-l is calm, a-l-l is bright," they sang with solemn voices during the weeks that followed. Miss Chapman played the accompaniment on the little upright piano that Mr. Johnson had pushed in from the hall.

Meanwhile the cold north wind blew with a mellow sharpness that caused his nose and fingers to tingle like silver bells, and it sang a weird haunting refrain within the hollow chambers of the empty house. And now the moon filled the sky with a sweet, somber joyousness.

He moved his head into the silver square of light that flowed in through the front room window. He gazed steadily at it as it slid behind a massive bank of bearded clouds. Like Santa Claus! The moon came out from the clouds and shone fully in his face. Its brightness made his eyes ache, but he did not move, did not close his eyes. Presently the moon's outline blurred, and hot stinging drops of fire rolled down either side of his face and tingled with a watery coolness upon the rims of his ears.

And then the moonlight burned the light out of his eyes, and his mask-like face lay buried under the deep mound of moonlight. His hollow eyes peered into the cool blue dark depths of "Next year." A star darted into the hollows of his eyes! It curved in an arc of fire that burned its way through the drowsy depths of "Next year."

"Go tell it on the moun-tun!" they sang in the days that followed. "Over the hills an' far-a-way! Go tell it on the mountun, that Je-sus Chris' is born!"

"When I was a mourner," sang Miss Chapman in a deep tremulous voice. "I mourned both night and day. I asked the Lord to help me, and He showed me the way!"

"Go tell it on the moun-tun," he sang, swinging his head from side to side with the rest of the class, tapping his feet like the grown-ups at St. John's, "Over the hills an' ev-ry where-ere, that Je — sus Chris' is born."

"Look!" cried Miss Chapman suddenly, an expression of wonder animating her face, her soft black, pink-nailed forefinger darting over their heads toward the back of the room. The children turned in a body and stared at the walls and at the pictures that hung on the walls.

"What?" asked Chester.

"I don' see nothin'!" Harry Bell exclaimed.

"It's *snowin'!*" cried Amerigo, suddenly perceiving the huge white flakes that fell from the sky. He rushed to the window. The excited feet of his classmates stampeded to the window.

"Aw, shucks!" cried Chester, "I thought it was *somethin'!*"

"To the cloakroom, children!" said Miss Chapman. "Put on your hats and coats! Button up well!" Minutes later they were tramping noisily onto the playground. They stretched out their arms to the snow. They stuck out their tongues and let the burning flakes melt upon them. The flakes fell slowly, majestically. Like the reverend coming down from the pulpit, he thought, watching them touch the earth lightly, and disappear, like drops of rain: quietly.

That evening when they trampled home the sky was gray and wet, and the snow was gone. But it was there just the same! he protested. I *know* it was! He could see it piled into mounds beneath the trees whose leaves had fallen, it covered the leaves, it covered the faces with the hollow eyes, where Mr. Bowles was, and Jesus, too!

"It's supposed to snow tonight," said Rutherford, sitting in the front room facing the gas stove with the evening *Star* across his knees, the bird-of-paradise lamp shining overhead. Viola, who was sitting on the sofa, looked up from her knitting and shot a worried glance at him, and then said cheerfully, too cheerfully:

"Hope it'll be a white Chris'mas!"

Amerigo smiled secretly from his place on the floor in front of the fire, opposite his father. He took a sip of the sassafras tea that Viola had allowed him to bring in from the kitchen.

"It's gonna be a long, tough winter. . . ." said Rutherford gravely. The child took up his Indian Chief tablet and began to draw out his letter to Santa Claus:

"Deer Sanie Klaws . . ."

"What you want Santa to bring you?" asked Viola testily.

"A pony! an' a wagon an' a bicycle-an'-an' —"

"You could sure use a pair a pants," she broke in, speaking more to herself than to him. At that Rutherford looked up from his paper and glanced at the neat patches in his pants, unconsciously rubbing his bottom lip against the edge of his upper teeth.

"Ain' that a nice picture of Mister Bowles?" Rutherford handed the paper to Viola. Amerigo looked at it through the crook of her arm: a white-headed old man glowering from an off-white foreground bordered in black. His eyes were faded and his suit looked too black.

He's dead, thought Amerigo.

And he was suddenly staring at the sealed-up chimney hole in the soot-smudged wall behind the stove. Like a stage. He looked at the flames, which animated but did not articulate the question.

"It's supposed to snow tanight. . . ." he heard his father saying, and he gripped his pencil firmly, wet the tip with his tongue, and once more applied himself to his letter:

"Deer Sanie Klaws, pa-leese breng me a pone a wite one an a . . ."

"Let's see them shoes," said Viola. He stuck out his foot. "Gone already!"
She sighed.

"Let's see," said Rutherford peevishly, laying his paper aside. He examined the scuffed toes of the child's shoes. "How in the *hell* do you wear out
the *tops* a your shoes! Will you look at that, Babe? I ain' *never* seen *nobody*
wear out the tops of their shoes like that! If it was the bottoms, you could
fix 'um, but with the *tops* gone, all you kin do is throw 'um away!"
Rutherford's irritation was increasing. Amerigo could tell by the look in his
eyes, and by the slow, deliberately calm voice with which he now spoke.
With a deep feeling of shame and surprise he stared at the worn toes of his
shoes. He grew cautious and quiet. "An' look at the knees of that joker's
pants, will you?" Rutherford continued: "Do you *crawl* to school?"

Amerigo smiled sheepishly.

"I ain' kiddin'! You think it's funny to have to work every day to feed
you an'-an' buy you clothes?" Rutherford trembled with anger. Viola's eyes
darkened.

"You know how kids are, Rutherford," she began appeasingly.

"How kids are — be damned!"

"When you was a boy, you —"

"When I was a boy — an' no bigger'n him — I worked! Yes, sir! Sold
papers, an' had to give every damned penny I got to Momma — an' didn'
git no new shoes, neither! I had to wear Sexton's old hand-me-down shoes
with-with paper stuck in the toes to make 'um big enough! An' him —"
pointing to Amerigo, "he hasta have ever'thin' just right! You breakin' your
back washin' an' ironin'! A clean shirt every day!"

"Go to bed, Amerigo," said Viola nervously.

He rose to his feet and headed for the kitchen.

"Two weeks before Chris'mas," said Rutherford, "an' here we ain' got a
cryin' dime."

"He kin hear you. . . ." Viola whispered softly as he turned on the light
in the kitchen.

"I asked the old man for some money taday an' you know what he said?
I'll straighten you, Rutherford. An' then he darted out the door! You know
what that means! I can't hardly feed 'im let alone buy 'im a wagon. But he
wants a horse! He must think he'a rich white boy or something!"

"Aw, we'll find a way somehow," Viola was saying as he entered the
front room and started making his bed. Meanwhile they got up and went
into the middle room and also prepared for bed.

The house was dark. He breathed quietly.

"The Lord's been good to us," Viola whispered. "We stayed tagether all
this time an' ain' none of 'um got no more'n us. We got a lot a friends, an'

can't nobody say nothin' bad about us. We ain' been sick. An' we don't fight *all* the time like every Tom, Dick, an' Harry up an' down the alley. I know ever'body's got troubles *some*times, but we don't have to — I mean *have* to argue an' stuff every day — an' . . . it'll be all right. It's just gotta be all right!"

"Yeah, I know, Babe," said Rutherford with a thoughtful sigh. "But a man gits to thinkin' sometimes. He works — hard — all his life! An' the best he kin do is to live on credit. Can't git nowheres 'cause he's always payin' for yesterday's livin' taday! An' when tamarra comes, it's the same cold turkey all over agin. I know how kids is. Amerigo's a good boy! But it makes me see red when he can't have somethin' decent when it ain' my fault — an' it ain' yourn, neither."

Silence.

"Rutherford?"

"Whut?"

"Maybe I could, we could borra the money — "

"Where? From who? We ain' got no collateral. We'd have to be payin' till doomsday! Half the furniture in the house is damned near wore out already — an' it still ain' paid for!"

The moon rose and filled the child's eyes.

"Can't ask Aunt Rose *agin!*" Viola whispered. "She's been too good to us already."

"I'll try the old man agin tamorra," said Rutherford: "But what if we don' have no big Chris'mas, we kin still eat somethin'! Chris'mas ain' nothin' but just a day, no way! Spend all that money, an' then it's over! I remember many a day when Chris'mas wasn' nothin' but just another day."

A star fell! And then another! And then they rained down like rain, only lighter, softer, shinier than rain. They fell upon his face, fell through his hollow eyes. He looked up through the mound of burning whiteness — from the foot of a leafless tree — at the sealed-up chimney hole.

"Kin you beat that, Babe!" Rutherford exclaimed the following morning.

He opened his eyes. Rutherford stood in front of the window.

"What?" asked Viola drowsily, raising herself up on her elbow.

"Look how it's snowed!"

Viola looked out the window: "My, my! Ain' it pretty!"

Amerigo slid out of bed and went to the window and looked out. Fresh white snow lay upon the roofs of the houses. Like the foam on a glass of beer . . . homebrew! It stood in round boulders upon the windowsill. Whiter . . . like a handful a soap suds!

"*A — merigo Jones!*" he heard Viola exclaiming. "*Did you use a w-h-o-l-e box a washin' powders — just to take a bath?*"

"*It wasn't all the way full!*"

"*Dumbbell! Don't you know you ain' supposed to take a bath with no laundry soap in the first place, an' in the second place, you used way too much! Why this water's like* gravy *it's so thick!*"

"*Yes'm.*"

"*You got enough soapy water here to bathe a whole family a elephants! Must think soap grows on trees . . . enough to do a whole week's washin'.*" The sound of her voice grew fainter: "*Better not let your daddy see you.*" Her words fell down softly through the air like snow: "*Tight as things are.*" They were covered up by the snow: "*Gotta save all we kin!*" they whispered up through the snow, "*with Chris'mas comin' an' ever'thin'.*"

Rutherford was buttoning up his coat. He turned up his collar, put on his gloves, took his little lunch pail, and made for the front door. When he opened it a cold blast of air shot up from the corridor.

"It's really blowin' — you hear me?"

"I hope it holds out till Chris'mas," said Viola, settling back in bed.

"Hot damn!" Rutherford shivered. "I'm gonna have to shovel snow taday!" He closed the door firmly behind him and tramped down the stairs. Amerigo waited until the sound of his footsteps died down and tiptoed quietly down the corridor stair, shivering under Rutherford's old Indian bathrobe. He stepped out onto the front porch.

He first caught sight of Rutherford's tracks in the crisp glittering snow that had been blown onto the porch. He followed the tracks down the steps and up the alley, through the glow of lamplight. He could just make out Rutherford's tiny form as he turned into the boulevard. It was dark except for the faint hoary blueness that crept into the sky and made its way unobtrusively down the alley, broken by intermittent flashes of light from the early trucks speeding by.

It could be late in the evening, he thought, still searching for signs of his father at the top of the alley. Or late at night. He stared hard at the boulevard. It was almost like it wasn't there. And then he was surprised that the snow did not appear to be falling on the boulevard, that the sight of the snow and the perception of its falling disappeared just beyond the arc of lamplight.

"*It kin snow on one side of the street — an' don' snow on the other,*" said Tommy from beneath the snow. "*I read it in 'Believe It or Not!'*"

"*Aw-naw it can't.*"

"*It ain' no Sanie Claus, Amerigo!*"

"*Aw — yeah it is!*"

"Aw-yeah it kin!"
"Aw-naw it can't!"
"I read it in the papers!"
"I don't care."

His eyes drifted slowly down from the top of the alley. He gradually perceived that the hoary blueness gave way to a thick creamy texture fired by burning points of red, blue, and yellow color that grew more intense just a little beyond the edge of Aunt Nancy's porch, which barely caught the furthermost rays of the street lamp's light.

Gazing at the light, he was surprised that the snow was still falling. It's been falling all the time! He watched as the flakes drifted, fell down by starts and fits, were driven down in oblique cascades from west to east that suddenly fell off as the wind dropped and floated down with the carefree violence of spring rain. And an instant later — self-consciously they stole into the hollows of Rutherford's tracks until they almost disappeared — *Like they were never there* — smothering the sound of Tommy's voice, while other voices rose to the surface of his consciousness, saying:

Mr. Bowles passed away at four A.M.
Ssssh!
Ssssh!

Gray feathers, he thought, feeling a little ashamed of his joyous feeling, as the flakes tickled his face. Gray leaves. He saw them falling from the hugh cottonwood tree in Aunt Nadine's yard. A tree full of stars! The shadowy patterns falling within the bright sharp rings that sliced the burning whiteness into a big circle with corrugated edges. Like a pie. His lips trembled from the cold. His bare feet grew numb. A thin stream of snot trickled down from his nose. He licked it away with the tip of his tongue.

Just then Mr. Tom came out of his house in a big leather jacket and heavy boots, with his cap pulled down over his ears and his hands stuffed in his pockets. Amerigo followed his huge tracks down the alley, and at the same time he looked for Rutherford's tracks up the alley. As they were gone, he followed Mr. Tom's tracks down the alley, until the light ran out and darkness flowed into the mouth of the avenue where it exploded into balls of light that whizzed by, sparkling like gold teeth.

The snowflakes fell quietly, steadily, relentlessly. But now the wind rose suddenly and drove the snow to the east. It rained into the black windows of the empty house. It caught him squarely in the face and rushed between the lapels of his bathrobe and down his neck, melted and trickled down his chest until he was forced to check its descent by gathering the robe together in his hands.

"A-merigo Jones!" Viola cried when he entered the house several seconds later. She sat on the edge of the bed, her bare feet searching for her house slippers. "Are you c-r-a-z-y?" He peered through her thin nightgown. "Standin' out on that cold porch — naked! With nothin' on but that old bathrobe. An' in your bare feet!"

"No'm."

"You better *git* some shoes on your feet before I *kill* you!" She stood up, her supple body quivering beneath the transparent gown. "The next thing you know, you'll be sneezin' an' catchin' cold, or pneumonia or somethin'!" She moved swiftly toward the kitchen, her voice trailing behind her: "You ain' got a bit a sense!"

"Yes'm."

The way to school was streaked and cluttered with footprints and tracks from cars and trucks. Two dirty grooves about five inches deep and four inches wide and three feet apart cut a trail through the avenue as far as he could see. Near the spaghetti factory and in front of the movie theater, a pair of huge dappled-gray horses with gray manes and tails left steamy droppings and their hooves pawed the slippery pavement as they pulled the huge Glendale soda-water wagon across the Avenue at Harrison Street. The soft snow on the outer edges of the sidewalks was cluttered with dirty shovelings from the paths in front of the stores and restaurants and meat markets. The paths were strewn with ashes, rock salt, and sawdust.

He turned down Troost Hill. A pile of coal sprawled on the sidewalk in front of cousin Rachel's house. He turned into the hollow where the snow, though swiftly melting, was more or less clean and undisturbed.

Presently he had made his way through the hollow and, lost in the toil of plodding through the soft squashing snow, he suddenly found himself in the midst of a dangerous host of colors and sounds that greeted his ears with a familiar strangeness:

"Look out, niggah!" cried Leroy, a seventh grader.

"Look out, niggah!" Leroy was saying, "any a you niggahs hit me's hittin' your mammy!"

A big snowball squashed against the back of his head.

"Aw-haw haw!" Amerigo laughed, pointing at Leroy. The other children who had seen it laughed, too.

"I'm gonna git you, niggah, just as sure as your mammy got a rubber dick! You just wait'll school's out." Leroy glowered at little Frank Walker, who had thrown the snowball at Amerigo, but missed and hit Leroy by mistake. Amerigo was still laughing when Leroy turned on him: "What you laughin' at, you little *frog-eyed* niggah?" He immediately checked his laugh, but it was too late. Leroy was saying: "I'm gonna put a knot on your head, just for laughin'! Now laugh that off frog-eyes! Frog-eyes! Frog-eyes!" A crowd gathered. They laughed and clapped their hands, while Leroy chanted: "Frog-eyes! Frog-eyes!"

"F-R-O-G E-Y-E-S!" the crowd answered back.

Tears swelled in his eyes. Etta ran up behind him, grabbed his cap, and threw it up into the air: "Whoopie!"

He ran after his cap. Chester kicked it just as he was about to pick it up.

"Goin' down to the bottom!" Leroy sang: "To the *froggy* bottom! Where the folks don't hurry, an' never worry! Goin' down to the bottom an' live my eeeeasy way!" He stepped up to Amerigo and thumped him on the head.

"Aw, leave the boy alone!" said a voice. He looked up gratefully and saw that it was Tommy who had spoken.

"What *you* buttin' in for, niggah!" said Leroy threateningly. He walked up Tommy and looked dangerously down at him. Tommy's bottom lip quivered nervously, and then — *Boom!* — before Leroy knew what had happened, Tommy had let go with a swinging right to his jaw. Leroy's cap flew into the air. He was on his behind and his heels were in the air.

"Niggah, you don't call me no niggah!" Tommy cried. Fine beads of sweat stood out on his nose.

"Git that niggah, Leroy!" Etta cried, kicking Tommy on the leg from behind. Tommy turned to attend to Etta, and Leroy sprang to his feet.

"Wiiiiiilyum!" cried Geraldine, "'em niggahs is gangin' up on your brother!' William came running over from the swings where he had been swinging with Birdie Lou. He dashed into the crowd with his mouth poked out and his firsts doubled up. Tommy and Leroy were scuffling on the ground, and Etta was on Tommy's back, hitting him on the back of his head with the glass stone of a dime store ring that she wore on the middle finger of her right hand.

"Git 'er, Wi'yum!" Geraldine shouted.

William dragged Etta off Tommy's back, and she lit into him, swinging her arms and fists like a wild cat. Meanwhile Tommy kicked Leroy in the stomach:

"Ooooow!" he groaned and doubled over.

William had Etta by the hair. When she heard Leroy scream she started screaming, too. Sammy, her brother, who was just coming on to the playground, heard her scream and came running.

"Aw-aw!" Turner yelled, "I'm gonna see this!"

William turned and faced Sammy.

"Let me have that niggah, man," Tommy said.

Meanwhile Amerigo stood on the edge of the crowd and watched. While Leroy was still groaning Tommy leaped at Sammy's neck and dragged him down. Etta stooped over to pick up a stick to hit Tommy with, and William kicked her in the behind. Sammy pulled his knife out of his pocket. Tommy grabbed his wrist just as the bell rang.

All the children ran into the building.

"See you after school, niggah!" Sammy said gruffly, gasping for breath, as Tommy let him up.

"You ain' gonna see me before I see you, niggah!" Tommy replied more gruffly.

Amerigo went quietly to his seat and sat down. He looked out the window at the gray sky. He looked at the gnarled branches of the trees in the yard across the street. The sky grew darker. The streets grew wet and the wooden porches of the neighboring houses became slate-gray.

"Joy to the world!" they sang, "the Lord is come! Let earth receive her king! Let ev-ry heart. . . ." He sang distractedly, with a troubled voice.

Finally the last bell rang.

"You stick to me, 'Mer'go," said Tommy gravely when they gathered in front of the schoolhouse. William and Geraldine and Carl and Turner came up and they all stood in a huddle.

"Ready, men?" said Turner. "Look. If 'em cats start somethin', we'll git 'um!" He opened his fist and proudly exhibited a smoothly polished sandstone about the size of a duck egg.

Tommy's gang took the east side of the street, Sammy's took the west.

Meanwhile the wind rose up from the north and cut their faces and hands. They turned into the hollow. Sammy's gang lagged behind. There was a strong gust of wind, followed by a shower of rocks and cans that fell among Tommy's gang.

"Anybody hurt, men?" Tommy inquired. "Naw . . ." they answered and discharged their own rocks, cans, and bottles at the enemy. The wind blew very sharply.

Tommy's gang turned into the alley.

He climbed the front steps . . . I don't care — There is a Santa Claus! he thought. He entered the front room and lit the stove. The flames invested the little stage with a rosy light that filled the somber four o'clock shadows lingering ominously in the room.

They had just finished supper. Viola was clearing the table. Rutherford was in the toilet, smoking a cigarette.

"Mom, kin I go down to Aunt Lily's?"

"You better put your coat on."

"I'm just goin' to Aunt Lily's!"

"Put your coat on!"

"Yes'm."

He entered the middle room. Rutherford came behind him and resumed his task of washing the woodwork. He watched for a minute. It'll be Christmas soon, he thought. Viola had told him that Christmas would come in two weeks. He looked at the sweating windows. It was dark outside, blue-black. The sweat ran down the panes like strips of tinfoil that hang from Christmas trees. Icicles. He saw thin daggers of frozen ice falling sharply from the roofs of houses in the morning, when the sun shone on them and made them glisten like the pretty glass in Rutherford's ring. A diamond! He made a tinkling sound with his mouth to imitate the sound that occurred when he ran his finger along a row of icicles hanging from an accessible railing, and dashed happily down the stairs.

He lay on Aunt Lily's floor with a heap of newspapers, while Aunt Lily sipped her strong black coffee from a big white cup. He turned a page and stared into the face of a huge smiling Santa Claus. He had an enormous sack from which he emptied toys. They spilled onto the bottom of the page and piled up so high that they looked as high as Clairmount Hill: trains and dolls and flashlights and knives and shoes and boots, and all sorts of things, but no *real* horses — little wooden horses with wooden wheels on their feet to push or pull them until they ran — not even a little one. Next to a real horse he liked a wagon. It was red and had white rubber tires.

Western Flyer! he heard Tommy say when he had asked him the name of a wagon: *"That's what the name of 'um is 'cause they got 'um at the store where Tom works. I seen 'um!"*

Western Flyer, he repeated, unconsciously disturbed by the air of certainty of Tommy's tone. *"I'm gonna write a letter to Sanie Claus an' tell 'im to bring me one!"*

"Aw, man, it ain' so," Tommy's voice had tried to say, but he had turned away and ran down the alley after Toodle-lum who had followed Carl and Turner into the empty house to get firewood.

W E S T E R N F L Y E R. He copied the letters carefully. Then he held up the paper:

"Look!"

"Unh-huh! That's fine, babe, but you gonna have to work mighty hard to git it finished an' lookin' nice before Chris'mas. Why — it'll be Chris'mas before you know it!"

Two weeks. An unexpected fear filled his mind, and he grew impatient with writing. He turned the pages of the *Star*. He studied all the advertisements. They were filled with elegant white ladies dressed in expensive fur coats, funny hats, and long funny shoes. There were pictures of big shiny rings and wristwatches, and clusters of holly with little red berries. He traced them out on the clean part of the paper. He traced the pointed leaves of the poinsettias and the richly decorated Christmas trees. Viola had told him that he could buy the Christmas tree and make snow from soap flakes to put the presents on.

"Unh!" Rutherford exclaimed when he came home the following evening. "Babe, you oughtta see the Plaza! I had to go out an' help old lady Mac with some decorations for the house. It's all decorated for Chris'mas — already! An' man I'm tellin' you, Babe, it's somethin'!"

He took off his coat and washed up and sat down at the table.

"I bet it's pretty, all right!" said Viola. Amerigo remained quiet, for his father had that dreamy look in his eyes.

"It looks like a-a-a fairyland or somethin'. The streetlights got big silver stars on 'um, Babe, an' Chris'mas tree branches — braided, Jack! — hangin' from one post to the next. That's along the sides, over the side walks, but they swing up, Babe, to the big stars in the middle of the street. An' p-u-r-d-a-y! I ain' never seen nothin' like that. An' all the stores decorated *down!* Lookin' like palaces or somethin'. An' groc'ry stores an' candy stores — the stuff looks too pretty to eat! An' all around where the old man lives is nothin' but fine houses, Jack, with pretty lawns, an' nice walks lined with bushes an' evergreen trees. Some of 'um's got little crystal chandeliers for porch lights, an' when you ring the doorbell bells ring. Chimes, Jack! Makin' pretty music!" Rutherford smiled with wonder at the remembered scene. "Quiet, an' c-l-e-a-n! Can't even see not even a scrap a paper nowhere! Just think, Babe, just think — if a man could live in a house like that he'd be sittin' on top a the *world!* Don't even have to be no big one like the old man's, could be just a little one, with say, just four rooms. Why he'd be s-t-r-a-i-g-h-t hear me?" His smile broadened into a grin, as he stared out the sweaty kitchen window.

Saturday evening shone bright and clear. Shortly after supper the snow began to fall in big dry flakes that lay, like leaves, where they fell.

"Rutherford," said Viola in a worried voice, "I don' know if we oughtta let this boy go all the way out there on a streetcar by hisself."

"What kin happen, Babe? He *knows* where he *lives* — an' what his telephone number is. All he's got to *do* is git on, an' git off at the end a the line, an' walk around a little bit, an' git back on the streetcar an' come on home! Go on, boy, that woman'll keep you a baby till you git to be as old as Me-thuse-la!"

"He *could* git *lost!* Or have a accident, or anything. It happens *every day.*"

"When I was his age I didn't have no accident! *I* could go all over town by myself!"

"Who else's goin', Amerigo?" asked Viola.

"*All of 'um!* Tommy an' Eddie an' 'em!"

"Well, you go an' ask if you kin go with 'um. An then you come back here and wash yourself. An' put on a clean shirt. You kin dirty up *more* shirts! An' put on your Sund'y shoes an' . . .'"

He sat in the back of the streetcar all by himself. Tommy and Carl looked out the big rear window, while Eddie and Turner sat up front by the conductor. A current of hot air flowed up through the seat and warmed his bottom, while his feet tingled from the cold air that rushed in when the doors flew open at the stops. The streetcar's motor throbbed rhythmically. He tapped his foot and swayed from side to side, as the streetcar swayed, causing the leather straps hanging from the roof to swing back and forth like pendulums. He perused all the posters and spelled out all the letters, and then he looked out the window.

He saw the reflected image of a white lady who sat on the opposite side of the car. Her face looked like a pink shadow and her hair glistened with snow. He pressed his nose against the pane and watched the dark streets glide by. Then he turned and looked at her. She smiled. Her lips were very red.

He tapped his foot and sang a tune to the rhythm of the motor: *I'm a dingdong daddy from Duma, you oughtta see me do my stuff!* He looked at her out of the corner of his eye. He thought he saw a smile on her face as the streetcar rumbled down through the Negro neighborhood, and down past houses and apartments where white people lived, past dingy stores, restaurants, and hamburger stands, up past a big stone building with a high iron fence around it:

That's the public library, he heard Rutherford saying. *There's a lot a books in there. You kin git 'um free. All you have to do is sign a card. You kin git 'um, too, when you git old enough to read good. . . .*

"*How many books they got?*"

"*A lot.*"

"*I bet they got a million of 'um!*"

"*Well, I don' know about that, but there's prob'ly more'n you an' me's gonna read in a lifetime put together!*"

"*I'm gonna read 'um all!*" seeing the big image of Santa Claus in the *Star,* wondering if just one of those millions of books would contain a voice loud enough to silence Tommy's voice, which now rose above the rhythmic rumble of the streetcar.

"*Aw, man, it ain' no Sanie Claus!*"

They were just crossing an intersection when he caught sight of a huge
Santa Claus standing in the bed of a white truck with big signs on the sides
with writing on them. Santa Claus threw back his head and billows of
laughter rolled from his mouth, while his arms waved mechanically in the air.

"I TOLD YOU! I TOLD YOU!"

Tommy grinned sarcastically, but his protest was drowned out by Santa's
laughter.

"I TOLD YOU!" looking at the smiling faces of the men and women on
the streetcar for confirmation. They all smiled back at him. Even the conductor looked back for an instant, smiled and remained silent. Santa
Claus's laughter continued to resound above the din of the traffic. But suddenly the laughter stopped, and the cracking of a phonograph needle spinning in an empty groove could be heard in spite of the rumbling of the
streetcar's wheels. Then the laughter started again, but now the truck
turned off into a long broad street. He waved good-bye from behind his
breath-misty window.

After a while he saw a broad field of flickering lights in the distance. As
the streetcar grew closer he could make out a row of huge signboards on
either side of the field of lights, east and west, and on the far side of the field,
south, all lit up, while straight ahead lay a broad sweeping hill that looked
like a huge mound of snow swelling up from the street. At the top of the hill
there was a group of squarish stone buildings that shone coldly white, monumental, against the blackness of the sky. From the court, fronted by a huge
stone wall, stood a white stone column, at the top of which burned an enormous flame. It looks like a g-r-e-a-t big candle! he thought excitedly, his eye
sweeping down to the foot of the great wall that shone like a sheet of frosty
ice. He took in the splendor of the row of fountains at the wall's base. Their
powerful sprays, caught in the beams of the concealed floodlights, appeared
like towering white feathers wavering in the snow-filled sky!

"Looka there!" he shouted.

"Ain't you never seen Memor'al Hill, niggah?" Turner said.

Tommy hit him hard in the ribs with his fist.

"What's the matter with you, man!" Turner exclaimed.

"That's for sayin' *niggah* in front a white folks!" he whispered.

Turner bowed his head sheepishly, while Amerigo looked at Tommy with
an expression of admiration.

"Union Station!" cried the conductor. He gazed down upon the great
network of train tracks glistening with snow and spangled with constellations of red, yellow, green, and white signal lights. The tracks nearest the
station were sheltered by long narrow sheds that gave onto the magnificent
main building, which was of stone with a high vaulted ceiling.

The streetcar came to a halt. Men and women carrying bags stepped down from the car and headed for one of the great entrances and the long line of yellow taxis parked in front.

That's where T. C. works, he thought, and the bell clanged three times, and the streetcar moved away from the station. The streets grew quieter, the houses larger, surrounded by large spacious gardens and tall bushes.

Presently the streetcar stopped.

"End of the line," said the conductor, and they stirred themselves and stepped down. They were greeted by cold gusts of air that rushed up their coattails and disturbed the warmth left over from the streetcar.

Tommy and Turner took the lead until they came to a little square where they stopped and gazed at the beautiful prospect before them. To the south, on a hill beyond the lovely boulevard, stood four large apartment buildings in a row. Above the roof of the middle building he spelled out the letters B-I-A-R-R-I-T-Z in red neon light that stood out against the blue-black snow-filled sky. His eyes swept downward to the boulevard where the bushes and small evergreen trees stood covered with snow, and finally came to rest at the spot where they stood, before the square bordered by a dazzling array of beautiful stores of all kinds, the lights in their windows all shining at once!

The stores look like — like — palaces or somethin', he heard Rutherford say, and he smiled with satisfaction because it was true. The scene caused him to think of the fairy tales to that he listened to on the radio every Saturday.

He followed his companions silently, dumbly taking in all the finery in the store windows. It looks a lot better than the pictures in the *Star,* he thought, pressing his nose against the windows of the candy stores, and of the food stores, where everything looked so good, so unbelievably good — too good to eat! — as Rutherford had said.

The snow fell silently and swelled into mounds around the evergreen trees that stood in the center of the square. They glistened with tiny blue lights.

"It is a Sanie Claus," whispered the voices, seeping up through the snow from the trunks of the trees. Anxiously he looked at Tommy, who was standing in front of a little store that looked like a chapel. Its facade was covered with porcelain shingles, and two bronze urns stood on either side of the alcove through which one entered the store. A tiny bell in its miniature tower rang the hour:

"It is a Sanie Claus!" it said: *". . . it is . . . it is . . ."*

They moved on now, gazing at other wonders of the Plaza with reverence and with awe.

They were walking east. The beautiful square was far behind. They were now surrounded by large roomy houses with long generous porches.

"That's the one I want!" Amerigo cried suddenly, pointing to a bungalow with a deeply slanting roof and coffee-brown shingles.

"I'll take that one!" Turner said, pointing to a big stone house behind a tall iron gate.

"You couldn't even pay the rent money!" said Tommy.

"Aw — I kin say what I like if I wanna, man!"

"It sure is pretty!" said Eddie. "Must have twenty rooms!"

A million of them! he thought, seeing a big fireplace in every room — big enough to slide down easily!

Now they were walking west. They came to a broad shallow staircase with an expansive walk on either side of a long grassy island now covered with snow. The paths extended almost a block to another staircase that gave onto a grand stone porch supported by six great marble columns. On either side of this main stair were two moderately sized lawns enclosed by stone balustrades, beyond which were various kinds of trees and bushes whose branches now bent earthward under the weight of the ever-falling snow.

A mellow amber light glowed from a huge bronze urn hanging from the ceiling. It tinted the snow and illuminated the porch and threw the building's facade into a peaceful and yet stately relief.

They walked quietly onto the porch and peered at the great bronze doors. Suddenly the sound of crunching snow broke the churchlike silence as they walked. A flashlight flickered from the garden neighboring the lawn to the east.

"Look! A ghost!" Eddie cried.

"Aw-aw!" said Carl.

"Ssssh!" Tommy whispered, poking him in the ribs and beckoning him and the others to follow him. They stole off the porch and ran down the path as fast as they could. When they reached the street and could finally breathe again Amerigo declared:

"M-a-n — that house sure was haunted!"

"Aw, man, that's a museum!" said Tommy.

"Hee hee! You don' know nothin', man!" Turner jeered. "That's where they keep pictures a dead people an' bones an' things from the Greeks an' stuff like that."

"Yeah!" said Tommy, "an' a place where you keep pictures is a a-r-t museum, dumbbell!"

He took another look at the stately building.

"I take it back," he mumbled to himself. "*That's* the house I want!"

"What?" Eddie asked.

"Nothin'," he said, thinking, that's the prettiest house in the whole world! Moving away with the others, he stared back at the great porch.

The peace and serenity of its columns and of its facade filled him with strangely familiar emotions that were both curious and comforting. For an instant a subtle fear accompanied by the dizzing sensation of whirling through cool bright regions of space came over him. A long low growl rose up from the pit of his stomach. Gradually the fear subsided, leaving only a feeling of wonder egged on by his curiosity to know exactly what was in the building. But then his stomach growled again, and his curiosity gave way to a sensation of hunger, and then he became aware of the pains that shot through his feet as he trampled along the cold wet pavement, through cozy lanes and winding alleys lined with beautiful houses nestling behind snow-covered gardens. Only now he no longer looked at the houses, only at the soft warm light behind the curtained windows. He longed for his bed and sleep.

They had lost their way. Turner wanted to go "thataway!" pointing to a little winding lane to the left, and Tommy wanted to go "thataway —" pointing to a little winding lane on the right.

"Come on, 'Mer'go," said Tommy, and they trudged on alone. Turner, Carl, and Eddie went the other way. Finally he and Tommy came to the square. All was silent, except for the silently falling snow. The bell in the tower of the store that looked like a chapel toned eleven.

They stood huddled together in the shelter and waited for the streetcar. An automobile stopped at the corner, and three pale, dry, curious faces stared out at them from behind snow-splashed windows, and then moved away, out of sight.

Gradually now the snow turned to freezing rain. The snow that lay on the ground was transformed into a dirty gray slush flowing in shimmering streams through the gutters and down the drains.

The sky was black, and the trees stood naked and wet under the lamp-light. Glimmering droplets of water undulated along the undersides of their branches and fell slowly, heavily, rhythmically: *Boom! Boom! Boom!* against the gray gauzelike curtain of driving rain. He followed their descent to the foot of the trees where they exposed the fallen faces now glistening with rain. It dropped through their vacant eyes and gaping mouths from which raucous gurgling sounds issued and swelled until they burst into peals of laughter. He saw the huge Santa Claus standing in the bed of the truck. He looked up at a tree just beside the shelter and saw a star shining through its branches. It was attached to the lamppost. Through the crack in its rain-soaked lower point he saw the sharp hard light of an electric bulb. Then the laughter ceased. All was silent, except for the ominous sound of the phonograph needle, spinning along the empty track of the phonograph record.

Clang! clang! clang! The streetcar rumbled up in front of their shelter and turned around to the far side and waited for the time to depart. He took his seat beside Tommy. They huddled together in the middle of the car and gladdened to the hot currents of air that steamed up through their wet clothes.

The conductor stamped on the bell and the streetcar moved away from the shelter. He watched their swaying images, shot through by pellets of rain sliding down the windowpane, as the car picked up speed.

"Look!" cried Tommy, looking out the window on the opposite side.

"Where?"

"Don't you see 'em cats?"

"Aw yeah!" Turner, Carl, and Eddie stood in the middle of the track about fifty yards from the shelter, waving their arms.

"Tell 'im to stop!"

"Aw, it's too late now," said Tommy. "I told 'um it was thataway 'steada thataway!" The streetcar swerved around a little bend and Turner, Carl, and Eddie were out of sight.

"Boy! Do you know what time it is?" Rutherford cried when he entered the house. He sat on the edge of the bed, snuffing out a cigarette, while Viola slept peacefully within the rosy aura of the bed lamp.

"No, sir."

"It's damned near *twelve o'clock!* Didn't you have sense enough to come in out a the rain? There's somethin' to eat in the kitchen, but git them wet clothes off first."

Viola stirred restlessly, rolled away from the light, and faced the wall. Rutherford helped him take his clothes off, warmed his pajamas before the fire, and helped him put them on. They went into the kitchen. There was a ham sandwich on top of the oven and a glass of milk and a piece of chocolate cake on the table.

"How did you like it? Did you see all the pretty trees an' stores an' things?"

"Yessir."

"Anybody say anything to you!"

"Nosir."

He crammed the last of the sandwich into his mouth and started in on the cake, taking greedy swigs of milk between bites. His eyes were so heavy that he could hardly keep them open.

When he had finished they went to the front of the house. Rutherford got in bed and put out the light.

"Good night," he said.

"G'night."

"Don't forget to turn off the stove, you hear?"

No answer.

"Amerigo?"

"Yessir."

He stared at the light issuing from the stove. It cast a mysterious glow over the room. The little laced fire-brick columns through which the flames jutted were taller than they had ever been before. They grew taller and taller. He followed them up to the ceiling to where the urn filled with amber light hung down. Down . . . down . . . his gaze drifted with the huge flakes of snow, falling through the soft aura of amber light. He heard his shoes crunching the soft snow that fringed the edge of the great porch. Then there was a flicker of light:

"Amerigo? You 'sleep?"

"No, sir."

"Turn out the light an' go to sleep, then."

He turned out the light, and then the stove. The color faded from the columns. The room grew dark. He climbed sluggishly into bed. As he settled himself under the covers he heaved a deep sigh. Then he turned and expectantly faced the window, but it was only filled with cold gray night light. He listened to the rain beating on the roof and on the pavement. His eyelids closed under the weight of the beating rain. Just before he fell off to sleep he heard the sound of the phonograph needle, spinning along the empty groove of the record. . . .

"No luck," said Rutherford bitterly, as he entered the kitchen the following evening. Viola was dipping the big spoon into the pot of chine-bones and beans.

The telephone rang.

"I'll git it," said Rutherford: "Hello? Hello? Unh!" He hung up and returned to the kitchen. "I wonder who that is? That's the third time this week that damned phone's rung an' they hung up!"

"Wash your hands, Amerigo," said Viola in a controlled but casual voice, placing the bowl of chine-bones and beans, the plate of steaming corn bread, the pitcher of buttermilk, and a saucer of chopped raw onions on the table. After he and Rutherford had washed their hands they sat down to the table. Viola quietly scooped up some of the onions into her plate and then covered them with beans, taking the chine-bones in her fingers. She deftly pulled them apart, ferreted out the meat with her tongue, and sucked the juice from the bones. He copied her movements, while Rutherford thoughtfully sipped his buttermilk.

"I got sixty-two cents!" he said suddenly, breaking the nervous silence. "An' I got some milk bottles comin' from Miss McMahon, an' Mrs. Fox promised me a dime Sad'dy for goin' to the store for 'er, an' Miss Sadie's gonna give me a *dollar!*"

"That's fine," said Viola, "You gonna have a whole lot a money."

The telephone rang. Rutherford's body stiffened. Viola continued eating without looking up.

"You answer it this time. Maybe whoever it is'll talk to *you.*"

Viola got up without a word and went to the phone.

"Aw, hi, girl! Sad'dy? Let me see . . . what time? I think that'll be okay. Aw, so so. Naw! That's too bad. Did she call a doctor? Honey — ever'body seems to be down in the mouth this Chris'mas! Thank the Lord we at least got our health! Now who you tellin'? Ain' that the truth! I better knock on wood, though. Well, all right, girl, see you Sad'dy. Bye.

"It was Allie Mae," said Viola with deliberate coldness, as she sat down to the table and continued eating without another word.

"How'm I gonna do *my* shoppin'?" he asked, "I don't want nobody to see what they gittin'!"

"Call Aunt Rose an' ask her if you kin go with her when she goes Sad'dy, why don't you?" said Viola.

"You wrote your letter to Santa yet?" asked Aunt Rose. A rich aroma seemed to rise with each little burst of steam that escaped from the pot cooking on the stove.

"Yes, ma'am!" Warming up to the smell, he noticed at the same time that the frost had etched beautiful patterns upon the window. He thought they looked like leaves; thinner than toilet paper. Autumn leaves came to mind. He tried to remember autumn, the first leaf that fell, the last, and then he saw them all, lying in a heap around the trees.

Next year they gonna tear the schoolhouse down, he heard Rutherford saying.

Last year? The leaves swirled up in bevies of color, yelling loudly, wildly, all at once.

"What'd you ask 'im to bring you?" Aunt Rose asked.

Mr. Bowles passed away at four A.M., said the stranger.

"Sssh!"

"Chris'mas'll be here before you know it."

"A little horse an' —"

"A what?"

"A horse, a *real* one, an' a wagon, an' a bicycle. But Mom says I need a pair a pants and a pair a boots — an'-an'-an' Dad got real mad 'cause they was all wore out an' he had to sell papers when he wasn' no more'n — no older'n — me an' he didn' have no new ones — to buy no new ones 'cause Mister Mac didn't pay 'im yet after he's asked 'im three times already. An'-an' then the telephone rung an' didn't nobody answer it an' Dad got real mad! An'-an' Mom said she didn't know what she was gonna do, but we was gonna do somethin'. An' then Dad said that Chris'mas ain' nothin' but just another day, no way . . . an' — "

"B-o-y! You kin talk longer'n a eight-day clock! What kind a wagon you want Santa Claus to bring you?"

"A red 'un. A Western Flyer! With white rubber tires. They got a lot of 'um where Mr. Tom works 'cause Tommy said so. Tommy said it ain' no Sanie Claus."

"How does he know?"

"He said 'cause we ain' got no chimney!"

"Aw — I don't think a little thing like that'd bother *him* none, do you?"

"No'm, but . . ."

"You hungry?"

"No'm."

"You mean you couldn' eat a li'l teenie-weenie piece a sweet patada pie?"

She set the pie before him and poured out a glass of milk.

"If you don't want it, just let it set there. I'll be back in a minute." With that she raised herself slowly from her chair and shuffled heavily into the other room with a painful groan.

Meanwhile he ate the pie, drank the milk, and studied the patterns of frost on the windows. He was about to conclude that they looked like the tangled branches of trees when she came back into the kitchen with a secret twinkle in her eyes, like when she had asked him if he couldn't eat a "teenie-weenie" piece of sweet potato pie. Baby talk.

"You through?"

"Yes'm."

"Come on in here with me, then."

They entered the front room. She stopped in front of the trunk next to the piano and lifted the lid. It was filled with a lot of clothes and little boxes and things.

"See that bakin' powder can?" she said.

He discovered a large can with writing on it. It had a slit in the top, like the top of the box you put your money into on the streetcar.

"I went to the Plaza!" he shouted excitedly, "all by myself! I got on an' put the nickel in an' got a transfer an' rode all the way to the end of the line —

an' got off an' walked around an' looked at e-v-e-r-y-t-h-i-n-g! Reeeel pretty trees, an'-an' b-i-g big big buildin' with a lot of pictures inside! An' we saw a ghost — An' we run an' run! Gittin' out a there! Man oh man! An' when I got back home it was twelve o'clock! Old Tommy said it ain' no ghosts."

"Can't say there is an' can't say there ain'," she said, faintly smiling. "An' I don' know nobody you kin rightly ask. Them that says it is is prob'ly crazy, an' them that says it ain' is prob'ly lyin'. Never seen a dead man yet that'd come back an' tell you what happened. But let me tell you a little secret: They's a lot a folks walkin' 'round who oughtta done been in the graveyard a long time ago!" Her eyes danced and her nostrils expanded slightly, and then the faint trace of a sad smile appeared upon her face.

He picked up another photograph, in a wooden frame, about the size of a postcard. It had lain near the back of the tray, facedown. A tall thin man with a laughing face. His legs were crossed and his right arm was casually thrown around the waist of a guitar. His long strong fingers were stretched out over the keys.

"That's a ghost," she said softly.

"Who's that?"

"Don't you know who that is, boy? That's your Uncle Billy."

"But he ain' dead!"

"Naw, he ain' dead."

She carefully placed the photograph in its old position, facedown.

"Don't you wanna see what's in the can?"

Her voice trembled and her bosom shook a little. He took the can up from the corner of the tray and twisted the top off. It was full of nickels.

"Look!"

"I been savin' 'um for you the whole year. Every time I found a nickel in the corner of my handkerchief that wasn' doin' nothin', I put it in."

"Kin I have 'um a-l-l?"

"If you kin count 'um."

"He picked out one: One —"

"Ain't you forgot somethin'?"

"What?"

"Don't you know?"

He grinned ashamedly, and then threw his arms around her neck: "Thank you, ma'am." He kissed her on the cheek.

"You better git out a here, boy! It's gittin' late. You kin count 'um at home — an' call up an' tell me how many it is."

They had finished supper when he arrived. He burst excitedly into the kitchen: "Look what I got! An' it's a-l-l mine! Aunt Rose *said* so! But I have to count 'um an' call 'er up an' tell 'er how many it is!"

"What on earth are you talkin' about?" said Viola. "Did she give you somethin' to eat?"

He held up the baking powder can, screwed off the top, and poured the nickels out on the table.

"Unh!" Rutherford exclaimed, dropping his paper, "Don't forgit your pappy, boy!"

"Ain' that sweet!" said Viola.

"She's been savin' 'um all year — just for *me!*"

"She's so thoughtful!" said Viola. "Why — I remember she usta have a bakin' powder can for me, too. You remember, Rutherford? Momma'd let 'er take me town on Sad'dy, an' she'd point to the trunk an' say: Don't you wanna know what's in the can?"

"That's what she said to me, too!"

"How much you got?" Rutherford asked.

"One . . . two . . . three . . ."

Viola unconsciously tapped the can against the table as he counted, while Rutherford counted behind him. Presently, she felt something rattling in the can and looked inside, and then she stole a quick glance at them.

"Fourteen," Rutherford was saying.

"Fourteen," he repeated, looking at Rutherford with a broad smile. "Sixteen, seven-teen, eighteen."

Viola tucked the can under her apron and stole quietly into the front room. With trembling hands she shook out the folded piece of paper, unfolded it, and withdrew a stiff neatly folded bill. She clamped her hand over her mouth to keep from crying out. Then she withdrew her handkerchief from her apron pocket and blew her nose in the middle of it and wiped her eyes with a corner. She tipped to the middle room, eased the bureau drawer open, opened her handbag, and put the bill in her coin purse. Then she closed the bag carefully and quietly closed the drawer.

"Unh!" Rutherford exclaimed as she entered the kitchen, "this cat's got six dollars and thirty cents, Babe! Kin you beat that? Five years old with six dollars all to hisself! Boy, you sure is lucky, you hear me?" He smiled mischieveously: "You gonna loan your daddy enough for a haircut an' a package a cigarettes?"

"Here!" pushing the pile of coins toward his father.

"Naw, that's all right, I was just kiddin'."

Viola's eyes got wet again. She reached for her handkerchief.

"I'll loan you some, too!" he said very seriously. "How much you want? Here!" pushing the money toward her.

"You keep your money, babe," said Viola, "you gonna need it to buy all the Chris'mas presents you wanna buy. You finished your list, yet?"

"Yes'm!"

"Let's see."

Rutherford took up his paper and resumed reading while he fetched the list from his drawer in the vanity dresser.

"Eh, you an' Dad," mumbling "Dad an' you" under his breath. "An' Aunt Rose, Aunt Lily, Miss Sadie, Miss Allie Mae, Tommy, Toodle-lum, Uncle Billy, Mrs. Derby, Chris'mas tree, Ardella, T. C., Miss Chapman, Mr. Derby, Turner an' Carl an' Eddie, an' I ain' gonna give Sammy nothin' . . . an' Wi'yum an' Lem an' — "

"Ain't you gonna give Unc nothin'?" Viola asked.

"An' Unc!"

"What about your Aunt Nadine an' 'em, Amerigo?" said Rutherford, smiling over the edge of his paper.

"I guess so," he said worredly. "Aunt Nadine, Uncle Charlie, an',"

"Aw, I was jus' kiddin', Amerigo," Rutherford broke in. "You can't give all those people nothin' with no six dollars! Besides, you don't wanna spend *all* your money. Keep some — to have some fun with, yourself. All 'em jokers ain' givin' you nothin'."

"It ain' the gift, it's the spirit that counts 'cause the Lord is good to people that's good to other people that gives 'um some a what they got!"

"He's got you, Rutherford!" Viola laughed.

"Well — it's your money. But I'd be damned if I'd give it *all* away like that!"

"Yes, he would," said Viola.

"Who — *me?* Woman, you crazy? Never!"

"Yes, he would, Amerigo, your daddy's just talkin'."

Just after supper the rain froze into driving sleet. Sounds like sand, he thought. He went to the window and watched the tiny crystalline pellets bounce against the ground and scatter in all directions, as if they were alive. And then he heard the sound of the toilet flushing, followed by the swish of a woman's underwear. *Always flush the toilet when you about to do somethin'* he heard Rutherford say, as the door on Miss Sadie's side whined quietly to and the bolt slid gently home. *Then the people in the kitchen can't hear you.*

Seven dollars an' thirty cents! he thought suddenly, and at the same time reflected that Miss Sadie always flushed, but Mr. Nickles never did.

"I got *seven* dollars an' thirty cents!" he said, turning to Viola who was clearing away the dishes. "Miss Sadie's gonna give me a dollar!"

"Yeah, but you ain' got it yet, don' count your chickens before they hatch!"

He imaginatively removed the promised dollar from the six dollars and thirty cents and pushed it into the corner of his mind where Miss McMahon's milk bottles and Mrs. Fox's dime were. Then he turned to the window again and tried to decide whether or not he ought to buy Santa a present.

Meanwhile the sleet on the ground and on the roofs began to glisten within the wide circle of light thrown by the street lamp. The alley gradually came to look as though it were covered by a thin layer of polished glass. Long thin icicles hung from the lamp's undulated rim. The electric wires glittered brightly, while fine points of shimmering light shone upon the grated surface of the sewer's iron lid. The steps and the banister railings became dangerously slippery. And now, here and there, slanting streaks of yellowish light glided across the alley's icy surface and burst into powdery explosions and dust settled over thin stretches of cobblestone in front of the houses. Ashes, he thought.

At his back Rutherford dozed in the comfortable chair, while Viola sat on the sofa opposite the Spanish lady who still placidly ate her red apple upon the silver veranda, and impatiently knit a ball of wine-red wool into an afghan for Aunt Rose.

Presently she glanced at the star-spangled sky above the veranda, cast a thoughtful glance at Rutherford, who happened to look up from his dozing with a startled air, and smiled warmly, almost apologetically at him.

"It's about your bedtime, ain' it, babe?"

He let the curtain fall between him and the falling sleet and got ready for bed. Rutherford stirred sleepily, and when Amerigo wasn't looking, Viola beckoned Rutherford into the kitchen. When the front room light went out and he was settled in bed, he heard them speaking in hushed, excited voices.

"Hey-hey!" Rutherford shouted.

"Ssssssh!" Viola whispered.

And the dark front room was suddenly filled with bright silvery secret hissing whispers that shot like sparks of moonlight through the red room where it congealed into hard beads of brilliant diamond sound that gradually rained into the deep soft blackness of the black room.

"Ummm," Miss Chapman hummed the pitch note.

"Ummm," the class repeated.

Her hands swooped upward and fell:

"Si-i-lunt night, Ho-o-ly night, All is calm, all is bright!"

"*Ssssh,*" whispered Miss Chapman, pressing down the obtrusive sound with the opened palm of her outstretched hands.

"Round young Vur-ur-gin, Mo-theran'Chil', Hoooo-ly En-funt, so tenderan' mild. Sleeeeeep — in Hea-vun-ly pe-eee-ce! Slee-ee-ep in Hea-vun-ly peeeeace."

"Now once again — softly!" she whispered sweetly. "Ssssh!" cutting her thin silver whisper in two with her sharp vertically poised forefinger.

"Si-i-lunt night,"

Big moons of light hung from the ceiling, diffusing a soft glow throughout the room, while the deep amber light of December, with much blue, much silver in it, filtered through the window, silhouetting the wreaths that hung before the panes, each with a big red bow-ribbon at the top, and within each wreath a little white candle whose flames licked the hoarfrost from the windows and made it glisten like rain.

"Sleeee-eee-ep in Heaaaa-vun-ly peeeee-eace!"

"Shall we turn off the lights?" asked Miss Chapman.

"Yeah!" they cried in chorus.

"Zenobia, you may turn off the lights!"

Zenobia, the chosen one, proudly marched up to the light switch: "*Click!*"

Candlelight flared up! Each child looked into the mysterious face of his neighbor with a "Oh!" and a "Ah!"

"O, little town of Bethlehem — " Miss Chapman began to sing. The children joined in, and the candle flames twittered, as if for joy. They flickered through the eyes of the faces buried beneath the thin layer of ice beneath the silver trees. And now the hoar-blue houses beyond the window took on the air of dark faces wrapped in cellophane; their windows were eyes flooded with soft yellow light:

"An' in Thy deeeeep an' en'less sleep . . . the si-i — lunt staaaaars go by."

"Merry Christmas and a Happy New Year!" cried Miss Chapman.

"MERRY CHRIS'MAS!" rang around the room, mingling with the excited crinkle of red and green tissue paper filled with red and green candies wrapped in cellophane!

Rrrrrrrr-ing! rang the bell. And all the doors of all the rooms burst open, and the smiling laughing hilarious ring of MERRY CHRIS'MAS AN' A HAPPY NEW YEAR! poured into the halls and echoed throughout every corner of the building. All under the stern glance of the thin-lipped white man with the writing underneath his picture that said: *George Washington*!

★

"Don't slam it!" cried Viola good-naturedly, as he burst up the stairs.

"Boom!" slammed the door.

The cheerful atmosphere of the house flashed warm and rosy against his face. He laid his cap and coat on the chair and looked around with satisfaction. Fresh clean curtains stood out from the windows, and the Christmas wreaths shone through the curtains. The bright red and orange flowers in the front room rug caught his eye. He sniffed for the faint odor of ammonia water, remembering the foam it made when Rutherford had scrubbed it the way he did at the hotel. And now he saw the bed in the middle room. Actually, he had seen it the first thing, but had purposely saved it till last. It was covered with a pink silk spread, and a beautiful doll in a dress of ruffled silk sat between the two pillows. And in the middle lay the tantalizing pile of Christmas packages!

"Don't touch a thing!" Viola cried from the kitchen, and so he had to be contented with merely looking at them. At the same time he wondered:

"How did she *know?*"

The packages were wrapped in beautiful Christmas paper with cords and ribbons of gold and silver. Two were wrapped in plain brown paper and tied with stout cord string.

"Them's for Gran'ma an' Aunt Florence an' Uncle Pope in California."

"Unh" cried Rutherford as he entered the kitchen a little while later. The wind had whipped the color into his face and his eyes flashed with pleasurable excitement. "The house looks pur-d-a-y!"

"Does look nice, don't it?" Viola replied. They flashed secret signals to one another when their eyes met, and the sound of frying pork chops and yellow corn rose up and animated their glances with laughter. Amerigo laughed, too, with a secret silver joy that no longer took notice of the sealed-up chimney hole in the wall behind the stove.

And then supper was over. Talk died down. A fresh windy calmness settled over the houses and over the streets. The sound of the streetcar clanging down the alley rose on the wind, accompanied by occasional shouts and intermittent bursts of music up and down the alley. Doors flashed open and banged shut. And then silence. And the wind. And then the wind died down. And then all was quiet. . . .

"Lookie! lookie! lookie!" he cried the following afternoon, waving a dollar bill in the air, as Viola entered the door burdened with two large brown paper sacks filled with groceries. "I *told* you! I *told* you!"

"Did you thank 'er?" she asked breathlessly.

"Yes'm!"

"Close the door. My hands are freezin'! An' don' slam it!"

"*Boom!*"

"What you say?"

"Nothin'." She set one of the heavy sacks on the drainboard and laid the other on the table. "Look!" she said, emptying its contents: big red apples streaked with red and orange color, with "knuckles" on top of a big pile. Viola put them in the big cut-glass punch bowl. On top of the apples she arranged a tier of flaming oranges with "S-U-N-K-I-S-T" written on their skins in purple letters. And then came the layer of tangerines:

"Close your eyes an' open your mouth!" she said. He shut his eyes tight and opened his mouth wide:

Frog eyes! Frog eyes! he heard Leroy and Etta yelling, and then his cap flew through the air. He opened his eyes.

"Aw, you cheatin'!" cried Viola, holding on to the stem of a huge bunch of grapes that were only halfway out of the sack. "Just for that you don' git none! Here." She gave him the sack. "Some fell off you kin have *them.*" Staring at the enormous bunch of grapes, he let the sack fall, and grapes ran all over the floor.

"Muckle-head!" Viola laughed at him. "Serves you right!"

"Them's the biggest grapes in the w-h-o-l-e w-o-r-l-d!"

"Them's the biggest grapes in the w-h-o-l-e w-o-r-l-d!" she cried, mimicking him. "You forgot to say: A million of 'um!"

"Do I always say that?"

She laughed harder, threw her head back.

From California! he thought, as the laughter died down, hearing Rutherford exclaim:

"*Cucumbers as big as watermelons — almost!*"

"*Aw — Rutherford!*" Viola had protested.

"*No kiddin', Babe! I seen 'um in a magazine!*"

She arranged the grapes on top of the apples and oranges. He thought of Mrs. Crippa's grapes in boxes piled higher than Rutherford's head every year in the backyard. That's where wine comes from. Troost Hill swooped down across the avenue, across the streetcar tracks, under the slanting shade of spreading trees in front of neat little gardens with trellises filled with vines burdened with grapes, all the way to Garrison Square to the school where he would have to go until he was a man and became president.

Next year! Just then a pungent flicker of yellow color flashed before his eyes.

"I don' know what I'm gonna do with these bananas!" Viola was saying.

Next year!

"Aw — it ain' no . . ."

And suddenly there was the clacking sound of nuts rattling in a sack, followed by a *"ping"* as they crashed against the glass bowl, which was not as deep as the punch bowl: black and English walnuts!

"We usta go down in the country," he heard Viola saying, "to Aunt Rose's cousin Car'line's, an' gather 'um in gunnysacks, an' take 'um home an' keep 'um in the dark till they got ripe. An' black! My hands'd be all stained for days!"

Hazelnuts tumbled out of another little sack.

Toodle-lum nuts! he giggled. Then pecans fell, and almonds. Finally there were no more nuts. Viola took the bowl into the front room and put it on the table next to the comfortable chair, under the approving eye of the bird-of-paradise. Amerigo followed her back into the kitchen where she put the bananas into a straw basket with the dates and figs, and then she started taking things from the other sack, which she placed on the drainboard.

The rich flurry of succulent color made him dizzy as he oscillated between the front room and the kitchen. That evening when he had bought the tree all the lights were on the tree he had bought and chosen all by himself, and the bright fuzzy cords of gold and silver hung from it, with a star at the very top, and a mound of snowflake snow at the foot to put the presents on, he sat on the floor in the front room of *his* house with *his* mother and father and thought: I hope it never changes!

The streetcar pulled up to the Plaza with the little square with the evergreen trees filled with tiny blue lights surrounded by all the beautiful shops, and he thought:

I got the prettiest tree in the w-h-o-l-e w-o-r-l-d!

"Chris'mas'll be here before you know it," said Aunt Lily.

"Chris'mas is now, ain' it?" he asked his mother.

"How can it be now when Santa Claus ain' even come yet?"

"'Mer'go, boy, you aint got no chimney!" cried Bra Mo.

He allowed his eyes to wander up the wall behind the gas stove. It was clean! The flowered pattern stood out bright and clear. He could see the round, well-defined imprint of the covered chimney hole better than ever before. His glance fell to the floor upon which the crisscross pattern of light from the grating of the stove was reflected.

Where'll I hang my stockin'? he wondered with a weary yawn. His eyelids closed slowly. He breathed heavily. The rich savory aroma of all the wondrous colors that were Christmas filled his lungs. He felt himself rising into the air, coming to rest upon something cool and clean. Then a cool blue-blackness covered him. He shivered and half opened his eyes.

"G'night, baby," Viola was saying.

"Night, son," said Rutherford.

The light flashed out. The middle room door closed quietly. He lay wide awake in the dark. Gradually he perceived a thin crack of rosy light, as wide as a coarse hair, cutting the door into two unequal parts. And now a faint, very faint silver light, filtering through the window, through the hole in the middle of the wreath. His eyes closed heavily upon it. A noise! The click of the bed lamp behind the closed door:

Zenobia, you may . . .

Christmas Eve morning was cold and frosty and everything that breathed made steam. The air tingled with the sound of bells, even the bell on John Henry's bicycle. They filtered through the music, organ music, and the music of choirs singing because it was Jesus' birthday a long time ago when people rode camels.

They got humps, said a voice.

Some got two.

They keep water in 'um an' they don' have to eat every day like we do.

And he continued to think of Jesus who was born in an old barn with the mules and the chickens and the cows and things, and of Joseph who was His father, like Rutherford, and of Mary who was His mother, like Viola. They're playing and singing about that because tomorrow it will be Christmas after Santa Claus comes, and then everybody will get a lot of presents and Dad will have to work half a day, and then we'll eat the dinner with a reeeeeal big turkey like the Puritans and everything. At Sunday school they'll have a big tree with baskets for the poor people and a present for everybody in the church on it. And then I'll come home. And then Dad'll come home with a lot a money that the people at the hotel give him. . . . And then we'll eat, after T. C. and Miss Mabel come. And I'll get the drumstick!

In the afternoon the turkey came in a big package, its long dead neck dangling down, its forked feet hanging limply, toenails dirty.

The afternoon was quiet, but he couldn't go out and play because Viola said it was too cold, in spite of the fact that the sun shone brightly and hard, until the air, when he tried to look straight up from the porch, looked as though it were burning.

Toward evening Viola let him take the dime store star off the tree and put the one Old Jake had given him on the top branch.

It was dark when Rutherford came home, and they all ate, real quiet-like. After supper everybody put presents under the tree with a little card with a Santa Claus or a bunch of holly leaves with red berries on it and the name of the one it was for.

Then they watched the tree. Like it was the show. But it was prettier that the show. They played church music and classical music on the radio, and the *real* music when Louis Armstrong came on!

It got late. He laid his longest stockings — he had tried to borrow a pair of Viola's, but she had said that it wasn't the right thing to do — on the floor in front of the stove. He did not look at the chimney hole. Aunt Rose said it wouldn't make no difference to Santa Claus.

"You kin wait till he comes," Viola had said, "sit up close to the fire so you kin hear 'im when he comes through the hole — see the rain deer an' the sled when they land on the roof."

He sat by the stove and waited, and listened. He stared fixedly into the fire. Thoughts sprang pell-mell into his mind, melted like wax and ran down upon his heavy eyelids and forced his head to bend toward his chest. His chin crashed against his knee, and a sharp pain shot through his bottom lip. The leg nearest the fire began to burn. He rubbed it and scooted farther away from the stove. He stretched out his legs and braced himself against the wall and gritted his teeth. His eyes fell shut and his head again slumped over. A noise! His eyes sprang open. He looked up at the hole in the wall, at the Christmas tree in the front window. Viola was knitting quietly in the middle room. Rutherford was making his bed. He moved his lips weakly in protest, but they emitted no sound.

A wave of fear shot through him in the dark. He bolted upright in bed, threw off the covers, and stumbled over something hard — it made a rattling sound — stubbing his toe, as he scrambled out of bed. He could just discern a thin splinter of hoary blue light filtering through the window along the edge of the thing he had stumbled over. His heart pounded wildly. Maybe he came while I was asleep! Tears filled his eyes, as he clicked on the bird-of-paradise lamp. Tears coursed down his face: "LOOK! I TOLD YOU! I TOLD YOU!" He dashed into the middle room and climbed into the bed between Viola and Rutherford. "LOOK! LOOK!" he cried ecstatically until they stirred, yawned, and stretched themselves. An instant later they all stood admiring the bright crimson sheen on the Western Flyer.

"He came! He came!"

Meanwhile the Christmas tree burst into flame, and they fell upon their knees and ravaged the contents of the bright pretty packages. Merry Chris'mas! rang throughout the cold blue room. Rutherford tried on his new bathrobe and slippers, while Amerigo strapped his new roller skates to his bare feet and began scooting over the floor until he slipped and fell, drowning his pain in laughter. Viola tried on her new shoes, admired her new dress, and asked if Rutherford liked his tie and was satisfied with the cut of the collar of his shirt.

The stove flushed hot, and soon after that the warmth of the room melted the hoar-blue light that advanced steadily through the window. And coffee bubbled in the coffeepot!

"Come on an' git it!" Viola cried, and they sat down to Rutherford's favorite breakfast: waffles and eggs and pig sausages and coffee.

A hard egg-yellow tone filtered into the sky, animating the sound of the bells in the tower of the tall church on Campbell Street. Rutherford had gone to work a little later than usual, all dressed up like on Sunday. Now Amerigo said good-bye to his mother and stamped proudly down the icy steps, adroitly avoiding a rusty can as he made his way up to Tommy's house.

"Hot dog!" Tommy exclaimed, "look at ol' 'Mer'go!"

"Thought-you-said-it-wasn't-no-Sanie-Claus! He brought *me* a Western Flyer. I kin *show* you! An' these boots an' corduroy pants an' a sheep-lined coat an' goggles an' a cap!" He flipped open the knife case on the outer side of the right boot and flourished a small hunting knife.

Tommy grinned and showed his sweater, his new shoes and stockings. William came out onto the porch with a cork gun. Eddie came running up with a BB gun. Helen Francis had a doll and a new dress.

Minutes later they all spilled down the steps into the alley and made their slippery way toward Sunday school, collars up, steam spouting from their nostrils and mouths, arms flying, swaggering all the way.

Sunday school glittered warmly, impatiently, for a full hour and a half, followed by church service. When the choir sang a song with a lot of hallelujahs in it, and the reverend talked a lot about Jesus. Nobody got happy because they were all dressed up in their new clothes. Then the doors swung open and they poured out of the church with their presents from the big tree standing in the lobby, a host of smiles and merry voices, which suddenly turned all speckled and flakey, as a great flurry of snow filled the air!

"Hot dog!" Tommy shouted, "now maybe we kin go sleddin'!"

"I don't care," he said, regretting that he had forgotten to ask Santa Claus for a sled.

They entered the mouth of the alley. Old Jake was coming out of the shoot between his house and the empty house. He trudged heavily toward them, wearing his old brown overcoat with the collar turned up around his face. A worn scarf tied around his head covered his ears and chin. One hand was stuffed in his pocket and with the other he carried his sack. His feet were swaddled in gunnysacks.

He looks like he's awful cold, Amerigo thought, wondering what had become of his staff.

Just as he came within speaking range he fell into a fit of coughing. The cough came from deep down in his chest and caused his whole body to shake. His eyes shone dimly within their hollow sockets.

"Merry Chris'mas, Mister Jake!" he said with forced gaiety. And suddenly there was a tight feeling in his chest. An unexpected feeling of rage overwhelmed him. A procession of fragmentary images — hot, color-spangled, cool — whirling within a globular burst of sad voluminous sound filled his mind. *Heh heh heh.* He heard Mr. Zoo's raspy laughter.

"Merry Chris'mas, Ole Jaky!" shouted William. They giggled; he, did too, self-consciously, against his will. But the giggle froze in his throat, for the old man looked at him the very instant his mouth flew open. A cold vacant stare. And then he turned and continued up the alley.

When Amerigo reached the stair of his front porch he hit his knee against the bottom step. A cold blast of air splashed against his face. He was oppressed by a profound feeling of shame.

I forgot to buy Santa Claus a present! But Tommy said it ain' no . . .

"Merry Chris'mas, 'Mer'go!" Mrs. Derby was saying, as she closed the door behind her and started down the slippery steps. "My! Don't you look pretty! Santa Claus sure was nice to you, wasn' 'e!"

"Yes'm."

He dashed up the steps. A man stood before Miss Sadie's door. He trembled and looked at Amerigo with downcast eyes:

Who among you here! exclaimed a familiar voice, and Amerigo rushed into the house.

Viola was busy in the kitchen, like she had been at Thanksgiving, but now she was much busier. The pies were all baked, the chocolate icing was on the cake, the turkey lay stuffed on a big platter.

She asked him about church, but was much too occupied to listen when he told her: how big the tree was, how many baskets were delivered to the poor, how Brother Jones talked about Jesus when he was born and the Star of Bethlehem that stood over the barn and told the wise men where to look. There were three of them. One was a Negro: Bal-ta-zar! How after that Sunday school was over. And suddenly he discovered, as he narrated the strange colorful events, that he was repeating himself, that he had said all of that before, at some other time, that he had seen it all and felt it all — before! And the voice within him that had previously spoken rose to the surface of his consciousness and blended with the voice that now spoke to his mother. He looked through the kitchen window at the sky, he looked at the trees.

"When's Dad comin'?" he asked testily, thinking: "He oughtta come soon." A secret thrill frightened him a little when Viola answered:

"He oughtta be here now!"

And then he felt a blast of cold air that shot through the house like a prophecy: *"Boom!"* The front door banged, and Viola, shaking her head without even looking up, cried: "You just as bad as Amerigo. Why close a door when you kin *slam* it!"

"Boom! Boom! Boom!" — his father's approaching steps.

Hi Babe! Amerigo whispered to himself.

"Hi, Babe!" said Rutherford with a smile. "I'm a little late. Fetch your daddy's house shoes, there, son."

He went and got his new house shoes from under the tree. When he returned to the kitchen Rutherford was showing Viola the presents he had received from the guests at the hotel. "An' m-a-d!" he was saying: "Come givin' me a cheap two-bit tie after all the work I done for her — an' the *whole year,* Babe!"

"What you expect from those poor paddies at that fifth-rate hotel," said Viola, sliding the turkey into the oven.

"Unnnnnh-unh!" Rutherford exclaimed, "look at that bird!"

Amerigo looked at the turkey, remembering its dead dangling head and long limp horny feet. He saw the man trembling in front of Miss Sadie's door just after he had hurt his knee on the bottom step, just after . . . A sour sweetish sensation rose from the pit of his stomach and reminded him of the bile-green smell that had stung his nostrils and caused him to jerk his head toward the shadows of Aunt Lily's porch, just before he had slammed the lid down on the garbage can.

He went to the window and stared absentmindedly into the yard. Large dusty flakes of snow fell by starts and fits. They fell into the yard. They fell upon the narrow cement shelf in front of Aunt Lily's porch — he knew it, though he could not see the shelf from where he stood. Upon the three cement steps they fell. Like heavy cat's feet they ascended the porch steps: *Boom! Boom! Boom!* A gentle wind swept them onto the edge of the porch, onto the banister railing, and off again! Down down down: *Boom! Boom! Boom!* six times, seven times. Down, down. Nine times: *Boom!* They crept back up again, and half stumbled, half fell upon the porch and died. *That's a ghost,* said Aunt Rose as the snowflakes fell to the bottom of the tall elm trees in Miss Ada's yard, upon the roof of her house, in, on, through the windows of the empty house, through the caved-in floor and down through a pair of bleached hollow eyes.

His face grew hot and his heart pounded.

"Sister Bill's baby's due next month," Viola was saying.

Old Jake appeared from the mouth of the shoot and poked his staff through the window of the empty house:

"How!" he cried, turning desperately upon his mother and father, "kin Sanie Claus come if it ain' no chimney!"

"If you don't take the cake!" Viola exclaimed. "You hung up your stockin', didn't you? An'-an' you *saw* the wagon an' things! Why did you ask that — all of a sudden?"

Tears stood in his eyes. His lips trembled. A bright sheen of sweat stood out on his forehead.

"What's the matter, son?" Viola asked, taking him in her arms. His tears flowed freely. "Don't you feel good? Huh? What is it?" She cupped his chin in the palms of her hands and lifted his face toward hers.

"He's just tired, Babe," said Rutherford, "Eatin' all that candy an' trash. It's a wonder he ain' sick. He ain' really slept right in two days. Go in the front room, Amerigo, by the fire. Lay down a while. Make you feel better."

"Yeah, babe, maybe your daddy's right. Come on. Rutherford, you keep a eye on that turkey. Come on, babe."

He lay on the sofa with his head on the wine-red cushion that Viola had made. She tucked Rutherford's old Indian bathrobe around him, and felt his forehead.

"At least you don't have a fever." She turned off the bird-of-paradise lamp. The Christmas tree lights glowed in mellow subdued tones through the frost-gray light that entered through the window. It made the silver tinsel on the trees glisten, and softened the faint rose coloring that issued from the gas stove.

"There, babe," she said softly, "you try to rest a little, an' in a little while dinner'll be ready, an' you kin have the drumstick!" She tiptoed quietly out of the room.

He lay on his back with his head propped up toward the window. A bell rang from a tower in the town. His eyelids closed slowly, dreamily, indifferently, and he sank, floated effortlessly throughout the vast reaches of the gray room. Vague sounds from the kitchen filtered into the grayness. Gradually the sour-sweet taste rose to his throat. He took a deep breath, swallowed, and checked its ascent. His head began to whirl, slowly at first, then more quickly, then more slowly, as his body grew warm, then cool. In his irritation he kicked the bathrobe loose. Suddenly he opened his eyes and looked around to see if anyone had seen him with his eyes closed.

"I won't close my eyes! I won't!"

The mocking cries of children rose up in a blue-gray haze, but then suddenly disappeared at the sound of Viola's voice: *He oughtta be here by now!* His breath quickened with surprise. He swallowed the sour-sweet spittle that flowed into his mouth, and then fell into a fit of convulsive coughing, which caused the spittle to explode through his nostrils and wet the back of his hand. He wiped his nose with his hand and wiped his hand on the hem of the bathrobe:

Somethin's stinkin' around here! cried Lemuel: and the deep gray coolness gave onto Campbell Street . . . to Garrison Square . . . to the school where next year. . . . Next year swirled in eddies of gray leaves that finally came to rest at the bottom of the naked trees. . . .

T. C.'ll come an' Miss Mabel an' I'll git the drumstick: Boom! — 'cause Jerry don' know. . . .

Boom! A door banged to. *Boom!*

Those French gals sure kin . . .

That's a ghost . . .

Is it New Year's yet? . . . His voice sounded gray and distant. As if he were dead.

"*How kin it be New Year's,*" Viola replied, "*when the schoolhouse ain' even tore down yet.*" He beheld her face at the foot of a tree. Like a shadow of a shadow.

The sour-sweet sickness rose once again to his throat. The crowd gathered around him. He looked up into the circle of faces. Their tears fell in large clear drops upon his face. They fell upon the balls of his eyes.

I'm dead! . . . The hole's too little!

Rachel's fault!

Naw — I done it! he shouted to all the gray faces. "*AH DONE IT!*" He smiled triumphantly at them. He laughed. He waved his arms mechanically and threw back his bearded head, just as the streetcar crossed the intersection. And then he stopped laughing, and there was only the sound of the needle scratching the empty track of the phonograph record.

Boom! A door banged. A draft of cold air blew across his damp forehead. The faces shifted in the gray silence.

"Hi, boy!"

A black beautiful face with white flashing teeth smiled down at him. A pair of huge tapering hands reached down and picked him up:

"Hi, boy! Look what your Uncle T. C. brought you!"

He surveyed the man's face, and then the faces of Viola and Rutherford, and Miss Mabel, a soft brown woman with a large mouth and large brown eyes. They were watching him.

"Here, T. C.," said Miss Mabel, "the baby's still sleepy. Give 'im to me. There . . ." taking him into her arms. She smelled sweet . . . like chewing gum and talcum powder and soap and perfume and icing on a cake. She laid his head against her bosom. T. C. took up the package he had brought and handed it to Amerigo. He looked at it dumbly.

"Ain't you gonna look?" T. C. asked.

He buried his nose in Miss Mabel's bosom:

"Boom! Boom! Boom!" said T. C. aiming a toy rifle at him. He suddenly jerked his nose from Miss Mabel's bosom with a feeling of shame.

"Shoots corks!" T. C. exclaimed.

"Looka there!" Rutherford cried.

Jerry's got one that shoots twenty-five miles! said Uncle Billy.

"What you gonna say?" Viola asked.

Jerry's got one that shoots twenty-five miles, he thought, but said: "Thanks, T."

A steamy bubbling sound came from the kitchen.

"The milk for the potatas!" Viola shrieked, dashing into the kitchen, just as the bird-of-paradise lamp flashed on and fired the gray tone that had settled upon the rose room. The lights on the Christmas tree burned particolored holes in it. Rutherford turned up the fire. Miss Mabel placed him gently upon the sofa, and sat beside him and stroked his face with her smooth hand.

And then he gradually sensed that the warm savory colors from the kitchen were flowing through the whole house, that they were sweeping him buoyantly into the kitchen in the wake of an animated current of jovial conversation.

The golden-brown turkey lay steaming on a platter in the middle of the table with its legs tied together with a piece of thread.

And presently the best Christmas dinner in the w-h-o-l-e world lay precariously balanced upon the crest of a sour-sweet sensation that rose up from the pit of his stomach. Once or twice, when the laughter had been the loudest, it had threatened him with disgrace.

"If I eat another crumb — I'll bust!" Rutherford declared. General agreement reverberated in satisfied grunts, sighs, and smiles, sprawling around the table until the show came.

It was double-featured with two comedies interspersed with popcorn, peanuts, and Boston baked beans, followed by a cold raucous twilight home where festive preparations for the dangerous dance to the accompaniment of the spinning phonograph record were under way.

He lay alone in the red room, amid the debris of Christmas. And the darkness came, only to be bombarded by volleys of thunder at first, and then rained upon by flashes of fire, causing his sleeping eyes to perceive the room

in a sudden explosion of bright flashes, like the flapping pictures at the end
of the reel at the show when the silver screen explodes black and white and
red and big black and white and red numbers pop and crack in and out of
sight: six! five! four! three! two! one! And then a picture comes and stands
still, while people move around in it, as though they were real. . . .

From the front porch, jets of steam spouted into the black air. A barely visible man whose name was Rutherford Jones pointed the muzzle of a
twenty-two revolver at the sky in an attitude of breathless anticipation:
    Ruben fell in about twelve, he thought, pushing his way to the front of
the little crowd of tall tense bodies.
    The factory whistles blew:
    Boom! Boom! Boom! Boom! Boom! Boom! went the twenty-two, pre-
ceded by six flashes of yellow fire that burned six holes of light into the sky.
    No blood. . . . Hole's too little. . . .
    Boom! Boom! Boom! Boom! resounded the exploding shells from near
and distant quarters of the city. Bells tolled from all the towers of all the
churches in the town:
    "Happy New Year! Happy New Year!" shouted the knot of people on
the porch.
    "Is it next year yet?" he asked anxiously.
    "Naw, it's *this* year!" Viola exclaimed with a laugh, raising her glass to
her lips, and then setting it down with a crash upon the Victrola, as she
rushed into the front room and fell upon Rutherford's neck. He stood as
one struck dumb amid the noisy crowd. His shoulders bent under the
weight of his heavy brown overcoat and his eyes stared out from the depths
of their deep bony sockets. He coughed a deep-throated cough. The muscles of his stomach wretched convulsively and the sour-sweet bile-green
nausea spewed out of his mouth upon the bright orange and red flowers of
the front room rug.

"They gonna tear the schoolhouse down this year!" said Tommy.
    Next *year!* —
    This *year!*
    I don't care.

★

The January wind whipped through the paneless windows of the empty house:

This *year!*

Next *year!*

He tossed and turned in his bed:

Next year.

This year!

He faced the window and gazed worriedly at a twinkling star.

"'Mer'go! Aw, 'Mer'go!" Mrs. Derby peered up through the front corridor.

"Ma'am?" He looked down at her from the top of the stairs.

"It's Sad'dy evenin', ain' it?"

"Yes'm!"

"Well, where's my kindlin' then?"

"Aw shucks, I forgot!" He yelled into the house. "Mom, kin I go an' git Mrs. Derby's kindlin'?"

"Yeah, but you come right back, your daddy'll be home in a few minutes an' then we kin eat."

"Yes'm."

He put on his sheep-lined coat and buttoned it up tight and then put on his sheep-lined cap and pulled the goggles down over his eyes and fastened the chin straps under his chin good. And then he pulled on his new rabbit fur-lined gloves.

He had to tug hard at the kitchen door because it was stuck along the bottom where the wind had frozen the sweat that had rolled down over the panels onto the threshold. He closed the door firmly behind him and stepped onto the porch. It made a cracking sound under his weight, like the frozen branches of the elms creaking in the wind. He grabbed the Western Flyer by the tongue and pulled it to the top of the stair and half dragged, half carried it down the steps, its rear end banging noisily against each step as he descended. When he reached the bottom he pulled the wagon up to the gate.

"Hallo, Tony!" roared the huge overcoated figure of Mr. Crippa coming up out of the cellar with a pitcher of wine.

"Hi, Mr. Crippa!"

He muttered a volley of indistinguishable sounds that seemed to fall heavily upon the frozen ground as he lifted his powerful bulk up the steps. His screen door banged to just as the kitchen door opened, at which instant an angular bar of light skidded out over the porch into the yard, accompanied by an upsurge of strange husky words. The door closed, muffling the voices, while the bar of light slipped noiselessly back through the door and froze in the large yellow squares behind the kitchen window. After that he heard only the sound of the wind.

— But as soon as he had shut the gate he heard a siren from a long way off. He pulled his wagon into Miss Ada's yard and started through the shoot.

The siren grew louder.

Coming this way.

Miss Sarah's door flew open, and the light cut a sweeping path over the frozen yard, coming to rest against the corner of the empty house. Aunt Nancy's door opened, and blazed another trail of light through the yard, catching the entrance to the shoot between Miss Ada's house and Miss McMahon's house. More doors opened, firing a luminous pattern of criss-cross trails accompanied by cautious yet excited exclamations as the siren screamed into the mouth of the alley, shooting two brilliant cat-eyes of light into Amerigo's face just as he was emerging from the shoot.

A crowd drew around the ambulance in a shadowy mass, breaking the beams that streamed from the headlights as it stopped in front of the empty house. Bright silvery jets of steam issued from excited mouths, animated by fragmentary hands, fingers, feet; eyes burning with fear and curiosity; flashes of gold or silver in a ring or an opened mouth. Two black, white-uniformed men jumped out of the cab and pulled out a stretcher.

"In here!" said Mr. Dan, balancing himself upon his crutch, pointing to the interior of the empty house with his free hand, which looked very large and gray in the beams of the headlights. "Little Tom Johnson, here, found 'im."

The men disappeared into the shadowy twilight-gray interior of the house. Seconds later they emerged, straining under the weight of their heavy burden.

He caught sight of the feet first. They were wrapped in gunnysacks. The legs were stiff and straight. He stuck his head between Mr. Everett's and Miss Anna's hips and managed to catch sight of the face of the dead man just before they slid the stretcher into the ambulance. A scarf was tied around his head. His mouth was ajar and his eyes stared up at the sky.

The driver slammed the cab door, and then joined his companion who was already in the driver's seat. He gunned the motor and the ambulance shot up the alley, leaving the whining scream of the siren in its wake. The crowd dispersed in silence. He ascended the front stair.

"That's all right, baby," said Mrs. Derby when he reached the porch, "I got enough kindlin' to last till tammara a bit."

"It's a shame he had to die like that!" Aunt Lily was saying. He looked questioningly at her. "All alone, without a friend in the world."

"That's-that's sssome-somethin' every-bbbody gggot-gotta do by th-they-self, Li-lily!" Unc said from within the house. She shut the door. Mrs. Derby shut her door.

The angular bars of light that had glided obliquely through the doors and onto the porches, down the steps leading to the alley, and over the cobble-stones suddenly vanished one by one, exploding into bursts of sound — Boom! Boom-Boom! — emitted by banging doors. The alley was again quiet, except for the sound of the wind.

"Come on an' git your supper." He looked up into the face of his father, felt the pressure of his strong hand upon his shoulder, and they moved silently up through the dark corridor together.

They sat down to the evening meal of sauerkraut, boiled potatoes, and wieners. He mumbled his blessing: "Dear Lord, bless this food we're about to eat," thinking: Now I lay me down to sleep, I pray the Lord my soul to keep. . . .

"Miss Sadie said he looked like he was 'sleep," Viola was saying.

"His eyes was open!" Amerigo said, but she seemed not to hear him.

"Imagine, somebody freezin' to *death! — all night!* — in that old house. Right *next door!*"

"Prob'ly starved to death,'"said Rutherford.

He tried to imagine Old Jake in the empty house. He peered down through the caved-in floor into the cellar. *"His eyes was open,"* seeing Old Jake's face in the roots of a leafless tree.

"This year!" whispered Old Jake in a stream of attenuated sound that pierced the black room.

"Next year . . ." he protested weakly.

"Mrs. Derrrrby!" he called from the top of the corridor stair.

"Yeah, honey?" she looked up at him.

"It's Mond'y evenin'!"

"All right, 'Mer'go! I sure could use it!"

He pulled the Western Flyer into the empty house and set to work hacking up the loose floorboards with Aunt Lily's old ax. He cut enough wood to fill three bushel baskets, two for Mrs. Derby and one for Miss Ada whose baby was due soon, and once more after the first load had been delivered . . .

Next year! he thought stubbornly, staring down at the tiny wormlike baby full of black shiny hair, blindly tugging at Miss Ada's breast.

"Turn your head!" she said.

Ashamed, he turned his head, but remembered the shape, the color, and the softness of the exposed left breast, and the fire in the accusing eye, which caused him to sink deeper and deeper into the cold dark bosom of January whose frozen sky was frost-gray, as the wind licked the icicles that hung from the eaves of the houses and gutter spouts and from the shade of the streetlight. Heavy ice clung to the electric wires that spanned the poles between the boulevard and the avenue and caused them to sag dangerously, and hiss and pop and crack, while the branches of the trees crashed to the ground. Ashes froze upon the hard crust of ice that covered the cobblestones, and steamy breaths froze in droplets of ice upon the mustaches of men, and upon the gunnysacks, old coats, and blankets swaddling the freezing noses and boiling radiators of shivering trucks and cars. . . .

Tuesday morning was bitter cold. The wind rose above the twitter of the scrawny sparrows that blunted their beaks against the hard ground. His face ached and his nose, ears, and toes itched on the way to school. He pressed his pocketed palms against his thighs and bent his head to the wind. Just as he came to Garrison Square an amber streak of sunshine broke through the clouds and suffused the air with its light. The trees creaked gently in the wind and seemed to extend their armlike branches toward the sunlight. A deep mysterious joy swept over him, accompanied by a confused, complex, but familiar feeling of ridiculousness, which caused the cold muscles of his face to work themselves into a smile.

"This year!" he yelled aloud. A blast of cold air rushing down his throat made him cough until the snot ran down his nose. He wiped it away with the back of his hand, and looked around to see if anyone had seen or heard.

"Where are your gloves, Amerigo?" Miss Chapman asked, rubbing his hands between hers shortly after he arrived at school. "Go to the cloakroom and hang up your coat and hat." He hurried along with the other children to the cloakroom. Meanwhile she opened the window and chipped a wash pan full of crusted snow from the sill. "Here," she said as he approached her, "wash your hands in this snow."

"In snow?" he exclaimed. But she looked at him with such a wise and steady gaze that he could not resist her command. He took the snow into his trembling hands and rubbed them together until he felt the blood throbbing through his fingers, they tingled as though they were on fire. He rubbed snow on his nose and ears until they also burned.

"Snow's hot!" he exclaimed with a bright smile of discovery. He looked up at Miss Chapman, but then lowered his gaze. He looked at his wet hands, and then overwhelmed himself with a new and unexpected outburst:

"*Water's fire!*"

Again he looked involuntarily into her eyes, and this time she looked back at him. A wave of heat flushed through his body. He sniggered timidly. She smiled. And suddenly he felt old, older than Viola and Rutherford and all his brothers and sisters, older than Miss Chapman who was older than them, but not as old as Aunt Rose or Old Lady. The twang of a guitar burned the air that rushed into his ears, and his silent laughter was tempered by a blue sadness that was as strong as the blue wall and as thin as the gray light that had filled the front room on Christmas Day — as wide and as deep and as high as the sky. That's a star! he exclaimed to himself, seeing in her eyes the wide-open eyes of Old Jake staring up through the crowd of steamy faces caught in the cat-eye beams of light, mouth ajar, the muscles of his face fixed in an attitude of laughter, but no sound. . . .

BOOM! Boom-BOOM!

"Hot damn! That's close!" Rutherford cried, jumping up from the supper table that evening. It was about six-thirty.

"STOP 'IM somebody!" cried a woman's voice.

"Miss Ada!" he cried.

"Sister Bill! Oh Lord!" Viola cried, rising to her feet just in time to grab Amerigo before he could rush to the door where Rutherford stood peering through the tense broken silence of the late-January evening. "You sit in that chair an' *stay* there!" she commanded.

"Unh! It's Jenks!" said Rutherford. He opened the door and stepped out onto the porch.

"Rutherford!" Viola cried.

Amerigo rushed up to the door. Mr. Jenks stood on the porch in his undershirt, waving a gun in the air.

"That niggah must be crazy or somethin'!" Rutherford whispered over his shoulder.

"Jenks," said Miss Ada in a whining tone, "you can't keep people from takin' that wood!" She struggled weakly to take the gun from his hand.

"GIT BACK IN THE HOUSE, WOMAN — BEFORE I KILL YOU!" Mr. Jenks yelled. He jerked the gun out of her reach and fired another shot into the breast of the tall elm tree whose branches swept onto the edge of the porch: "*Boom!*"

The lamp-yellow doors of all the houses facing the yards were filled with animate silhouettes of people who now spilled out onto the porches, emitting steam from their mouths and nostrils.

"What's the matter, man!" said Rutherford.

"Rutherford," said Viola nervously, "you stay out a this. It ain' none a *your* business!"

"R-u-t-h-e-r-f-o-r-d?" Miss Ada cried weakly: "Rutherford — " stretching her arms out over the banister, as though she would take him by the hand. "He's tryin' to-to- stop them people from takin' that wood. *It ain' none a his!*"

Whap! Mr. Jenks's black arm arced through the air. Miss Ada screamed and grabbed her face with both hands as she fell against the screen.

"*It ain'! It ain'!*" she sobbed.

"Git back in the house like I told you!" Mr. Jenks commanded. He stepped to the edge of the porch and stared down into the frozen lot back of the empty house. "YOU! DOWN THERE IN THE YARD!"

"I don't see nothin'," whispered Amerigo, trembling in the cold. "Nothin' but that old cart." An old wooden cart with two big rusty iron wheels stood in the door of the cellar loaded with scraps of wood.

"Them cats done cut out!" Rutherford said with a chuckle.

"Unh!" Viola exclaimed, "kin you beat that?" stepping out onto the porch, "he must be losin' his black mind — tryin' to keep people from takin' wood that ain' even none a his!"

"That old house is about to fall down anyhow!" shouted Mrs. Derby laughingly from downstairs.

"They don't *belong* 'round here!" shouted Mr. Jenks. "Anyway — you keep out a this!"

"Huh," Mrs. Derby retorted, "*my* old man's got four guns! An' he knows how to shoot 'um, too! Tee hee!"

He looked over the banister just in time to see her dart behind the screen. The naked lightbulb in the kitchen flung her vulnerable shadow back out doors, across the drain in the cement shelf, a few feet to the left of Aunt Lily's porch.

Like she was dead, Amerigo thought, gradually hearing the laughter that bubbled from the doorways and porches and flooded the yards while Mr. Jenks stood defiantly upon his porch, gun in hand, staring at the empty house. The steamy laughter washed up around his feet, it engulfed his knees, it lashed dangerously at his chin.

"They *gone*, Jenks!" Miss Ada shouted from within the kitchen. And then the thin sound of a new baby crying. It mingled with the laughter and the sound of the frozen screen doors slamming.

"Her name's Dora," he whispered to himself.

"They gone, Jenks!" Miss Ada was saying, "what you *still standin'* there for?"

"Ain' nobody gonna come around takin' MY wood!" shouted Mr. Jenks.

"Hee hee hee hee! Ha ha ha ha! Wow!" exclaimed the laughing voices.

Mr. Jenks dashed into the house and slammed his kitchen door: WHAM! and the sound of shattered glass mingled with the sound of the baby's crying and with the sound of the laughter, which now rushed in the gaping hole in his kitchen window.

This year! he thought all through the windy silence of January, as the fires in the stoves burned steadily and Bra Mo grunted through the shoots and up and down steps carrying heavy sacks of coal. The wind howled through the cavernous walls of the empty house whose floors had been gutted, its broad beams and window sashes wrenched from their frames, its ribs torn out of its sides, exposing a skeleton of ravaged brick and plaster filled with ashes and rubbish and a set of fine bleached bones that the dogs no longer sniffed at.

He felt the advance of the migrant year through his bones as the mornings grew mellower and the thick crust of ice that covered the cobblestones in the alley glistened beneath the wet ashes embedded in its frozen surface. A tingling excitement, a fearful sense of dread, of expectancy and remembered pain, rose to the surface of his mind. He watched the icicles dripdrop from the shade of the streetlight, the thick coating of ice on the electric wires drip and fall in bursts of light that crashed against the floor of brittle ice below, shattering a trail of ice fragments up and down the far side of the alley, sending tiny rivulets of shimmering water shooting under the ice, which wove a fine web of silver through the dissolving ashes.

With quickening breath and an increasing sense of anxiety he watched the glistening water fill shoe, boot, and tire track. Unconsciously he slapped his hand against his breast in order to crush the flakes of snow that rained through the open lapels of Rutherford's old Indian bathrobe.

Meanwhile the crystalline water continued to drop from eave and gutter spout, to slide down banister rails and undulate along step edges. It made the branches of the tall elm trees in Miss Ada's yard glisten. The jeweled droplets swelled, and fell, softly, to the roots of the trees, while the branches stretched out, swung out in wide arcs up toward the warm beam of light that shone through the mist like a great cat-eye, burning hotly, that was suddenly drenched in the wet freezing shade of a burning silver cloud.

He looked expectantly at the trees, and again at the sky.

From the darkness of the front room he gazed through the window at a twinkling star. It grew larger and larger. . . . He stretched his body out to its full length, as though he would touch it with the tip of his toe.

"It won't be long now!" cried Rutherford, stepping gingerly into the kitchen. He glanced at the five o'clock sun advancing through the window and slanting across the hearthstone in an amber bar.

"What won't be long?" Viola asked, looking up, as she dropped some bay leaves into the hash, stirred it with the big spoon, and then put the lid on the pot.

"Sun's shinin' like California!" Rutherford exclaimed.

She turned down the fire.

"If we don't find some money somewhere, it ain' gonna make a bit a difference. Mabel said she heard they need a girl at the Biarritz."

"Unh! That's a high-class joint. In the Plaza!"

He beheld the Plaza filled with falling snow: rose through a hanging urn.

"Hi, sonny!"

"Hi."

He set the plates carefully on the table, embarrassed because his father was watching him.

"Unh!" Rutherford exclaimed. "Will you look how this little joker's growed, Babe!"

"Like a weed!" said Viola with a broad smile, measuring him with a sweeping balance. "Won't be long now. Just a little while before he'll be in the first grade! An' then high school! An' then college, an' hot dog!"

He tried to measure the time as he placed the knives and spoons on the table, watching the bar of sunlight stretch itself out until it touched the leg of the kitchen table.

"Unh!" Rutherford exclaimed.

"What?" Viola asked, inspecting the table with a critical glance.

"I was just thinkin'. Ain' that funny? As long as I kin remember there's been a Garrison School!" He gazed dreamily out the window.

"Yeah," Viola said, drying her hands on her apron.

"Aw — you'll find it all right, Amerigo," he heard her saying. "All you have to do is keep on goin' like you been goin' till you git to Troost an' then, instead a turnin' down the hill, you just keep straight on!"

"Yeah," Rutherford broke in. "Straight-on-up past Forest, past Tracy, till you git to Pacific an' then you turn. North. You have to pass by the junkyard where your uncle Charlie works. An' then comes the church, an' then a bunch a frame houses, an' then you there."

He followed the burning trail marked out by the bar of sunlight. It had reached the table leg farthest from the door. Past Troost where Dad and T. C. slid down under the streetcar on a sled until they got to Garrison Square.

Viola ladled the hash into a deep white bowl and placed it on the table. She opened the oven door and withdrew a pan of biscuits, which she tumbled out onto a plate. He gazed wonderingly at the spirals of steam that issued form the biscuits.

"Boy! I kin beat your momma makin' biscuits e-v-e-r-y day in the week!" he heard Aunt Rose saying.

Aaaaaaw naw, you can't! he protested in thought.

He grinned as Viola set the plate on the table.

"What you grinnin' about? Have to eat 'um with margarine. Butter's so high you have to be a bird to reach it!"

"We lucky to be gittin' that!" said Rutherford testily. "They let off three maids taday."

Amerigo blew gently upon the hot spoonful of hash, put it into his mouth, and hastily washed it down with a swig of sassafras tea. Then he put a piece of margarine between his biscuit, clamped the halves together, and bit into it. He chewed the pleasant hot airy mass, gulped it down, and was overwhelmed with a familiar sensation that caused him to exclaim:

"Bean's is good!"

"What's that got to do with the price of pork chops?" Viola asked.

"Aw, I mean, margarine's good!" confused by the sudden emergence of summer song from all the secret places of his alley. It flooded his mind with an unbearable sweet nostalgia.

"Unh!" Rutherford exclaimed. "Babe, your son is either a fool — or nuts!"

I hope it never changes!

"I'll leave it with you, babe," Viola was saying. She rose from the table and went into the front room where Rutherford was sitting by the fire in the comfortable chair with the *Star,* the *Voice,* and the *Shadow,* listening to the radio. She took her place on the sofa and began tying tassels on the invitations to the whist party that the American Beauty Art Club was having at Miss Susie's next Saturday night.

He strained to catch the fragments of excitement that flowed from the radio as he washed the dishes:

"Sal-ha-patica — for the smile of health!" cried the lusty-voiced

announcer. "I — pana for the smile of beauty! I-pana! Sal-ha-patica presents: F-r-e-d A L L E N! EeeeeEEEEEyaay!" roared the voices, which gradually faded away until only an animate drone interrupted by occasional
outbursts from the audience filtered into the kitchen. Meanwhile his
thoughts gradually gathered around the unheard strains of a guitar, the
rolling bass of a piano and a drum. He burst into song:

"I-I-I-'m a dingdong daddy from Duma, you oughtta see me do my stuff!"
And he was suddenly surprised by the thought:
Her lips sure were red!

The redness whirled around in the sky until it tinged the deep purplish
brown branches of the trees, and the reddish green buds burst into new
green leaves. He did not have to wear his woolen sweater under his sheep-
lined coat anymore as he strolled heedlessly over the "diamonds" now
sunk deep into the earth, over which a great wind blew that Rutherford
had said "Came in like a lion!" adding: "That March wind's trouble, you
hear me?"

The doors and windows rattled noisily, and he knew that the treetops
were swaying in the wind, as if they were glad about something. With an
inexplicable feeling of satisfaction he watched stout weeds and tall grasses
pushing up from the foundation of the empty house.

"Boy?" Rutherford was saying, "Ever see your poppa fly a kite?"
"No sir!" He grinned.
Rutherford gazed at the flowered pattern in the front room rug. "We usta
go w-a-y up on top a Clairmount Hill! I had a kite — Am I lyin', Babe?"
"Don't ask me to be no witness —"
"This big!" he stretched his arms out to their full length. "And string —
I had a ball a string that was as big as T. C.'s head. Aw-haw haw!"
"Rutherford!" Viola cried: "Rutherford Jones!"
"No *kiddin'*! Honest! You think I'm lyin'? If I'm lyin' — I'll take a
bloody oath on my *momma!* It was *that* big, Amerigo — sure enough!"
Rutherford designed a huge ball with his hands.
Amerigo grinned incredulously.
"Had a tail thirteen feet long! Out a old rags an' things. Sexton drew a
big Jolly Boy on it! Well, anyway, I finally got it up — an' m-a-n! It ate up
all that string! I had to borra some more! Amerigo — that kite flew up so
high you couldn' hardly see it!"
"Amerigo," said Viola, "don't you never tell nobody that lie your
daddy's tellin'!"

"An' the wind was a blooooowin'!" he continued. "I have to take you up on Clairmount Hill sometime an'-an' teach you somethin' about flyin' a kite! Where me an' your momma usta play — before you was born. Heh-heh." He looked at Viola with an expression that was void of awareness but suddenly changed to one of wonderment, as his laughter died away while she quietly let her eyes drop to the floor. Amerigo also looked at the floor, and saw, beneath the flowered pattern of the rug, the parallel lines between the floorboards, stretching from the confines of 618 Cosy Lane to the summit of Clairmount Hill.

"An' the wind was a blooooowin'!" Rutherford was saying. "It blowed so hard that the string broke! Heavy string! For fishin'! Almost snatched me off the ground!"

"Ohoooooo!" Viola screamed.

"Yeah! That's *right*! I had to hold on to a tree! That sure was a powerful kite! An' pur — d-a-y! That sure was one pretty kite. If you think I'm lyin' I'll take you up on it! I'll show you! I'll make you one an' you kin fly it yourself!"

"Take 'im up on it, Amerigo," cried Viola mockingly.

"Yeah!" Rutherford declared, "but you have to wait a while. You too li'l to fly a kite *that* big! Shucks, it'd blow that li'l cat up to the moon!"

I been there before! he thought, and grinned with secret satisfaction.

"I hear they givin' you a brand-new schoolhouse, all to your self!" said Mrs. Derby with a broad smile, just as he reached the top step of the front porch the following evening after school.

"Yes'm."

"Won't be long before you big enough to whip your daddy! You smart as he is already!"

"No'm." Wondering: This year? as he ascended the dark corridor stair.

He entered the house. The late-afternoon sun fired the cracks in the grass-green window shade. Looks just like a leaf. He looked at the clock, an electric clock with the face set in a polished wooden frame. It blazed like silver. He could hear it ticking. It was four o'clock:

"When you turn the long hand till it gits to twelve — an' the short hand till it gits to four — then it's four o'clock. — Understand?"

"Yessir."

★

"Come on, 'Mer'go!" Tommy yelled back at him. He stood on the corner of Independence Avenue and Troost, staring dumbly at the cracks in the pavement. His eyes followed them along the sweeping decline from the hump of Troost Hill down the burnished maple-leafed grape-studded way to Garrison Square.

"He passed at four A.M.," said the stranger — just as a bunch of noisy children straggled past him in an array of noisy colors that mingled with the colors of the leaves falling from the still trees. The pleasant and yet nauseating odor of old wine-soaked barrels stung his nostrils.

Bra Mo's old truck wheezed by on its way to the coal yard.

"Hi, 'Mer'go!" he yelled, but *his* mind was filled with the frenzy of color that fell down through the gold-misty rays of sunlight, swelling the great Troost Hill into a mountain of leaves!

"Com on, 'Mer'go!" Tommy was yelling from the opposite corner.

He stepped irritably from the curb and approached the vast frontier of the new way to school, a way untrodden by the feet of his father and mother, his uncles Ruben and Sexton, his aunts Edna, Ruth, Pearl, Nadine, and Fanny, his grandmothers Veronica and Sarah, or his grandfathers Rex and Will — a way that the reverend and Mr. T. Wellington Harps would never go.

"Look out!" Tommy cried. A loud jagged sound whizzed past his face and bathed him a backwash of cold air that caused his eyes to fill with water and the loose ends of his unbuttoned jacket to burst away from his immobile body.

"You gonna git *killed!*" Tommy exclaimed, holding the lapel of his jacket in his clenched fist. "Didn't you see that truck? You better learn to look where you goin'!"

He walked blindly across the street. A few yards from the corner he came to an empty store whose dirty plate-glass window made his forefinger dirty. Another step and a host of distinctive fruit smells greeted his nostrils.

He stared at the pyramid of coconuts, at their little round eyes. *"People's like that,"* he heard Mr. Derby say. "Looka there!" he cried, but Tommy was way up ahead. He moved on, a little anxious now, because of the sound of the streetcar rolling down the avenue, noticing, however, the huge bunches of grapes. *The biggest grapes in the w-h-o-l-e w-o-r-l-d!* feeling the cool round ripples of bright green laughter bubble up in his throat, just as the sack slipped from his fingers an instant before the loose grapes sprang over the kitchen floor in all directions: "*Dumb*bell!" Viola exclaimed laughingly. "*Frog eyes!* Frog eyes!" A sharp pain at the back of his head, his cap flew into the air: *"Whoopie!"*

The voice was well ahead of him now, breaking the virgin trail for a cluster of grape-colored voices, yelling: "WHOOPIE!"

"Leroy," he thought, suddenly remembering that he was on his way to school, and that Leroy, Etta, and Sammy would be there, too.

Now a streetcar rolled ominously *up* the avenue, its square windows void of faces.

At the corner of Independence and Forest he paused in front of a candy store window. He gazed at the thick pulpy Indian Chief tablets with the big Indian head crowned with feathers of black and gold against a background of red. *"Pontiac!"* he heard Rutherford say, eyeing the penny pencils and the long yellow ones for a nickel. They lay next to the orderly bunches of pen-point holders — black, blue, red, yellow, and green. Fat round A's, B's, and C's spread out over the ruled spaces of his mind and aligned themselves in marching formation along the edges of the deep black crevices between the floorboards of St. John's and advanced through the breach at Independence and Troost and overtook him at Forest Avenue where they were joined by legions of wineballs upon which grains of sugar glistened like stars!

"You gonna be late, man!" Tommy shouted from the middle of the next block. He and the others cut up through the ravine of a rather steep hill.

"Come on up this way!" Turner yelled over his shoulder, but he followed his father's voice down the avenue to the corner.

"An' there it is!" he exclaimed. "I *told* you!" pointing to a big rambling junkyard at Independence and Pacific.

Suddenly he heard a bell ringing like that of a g-r-e-a-t b-i-g alarm clock coming from far away! He looked anxiously down the street. There was no one in sight. One solitary cloud stood motionless in the sky.

"Boom!" — A leaf fell from the big cottonwood tree in the churchyard. There's the church! His mouth felt acrid and dry and a wave of cool air wafted his face as a bunch of frame houses jostled by. Tired, panting for air, he paused to catch his breath. His heart pounded in his ears. There was no sign of the schoolhouse. Maybe it's *next* year! An overwhelming joy suffused his mind. But then he spied the upper stories of a strange and yet familiar redbrick building with many windows, standing earnestly in the morning sunlight. He looked at the sky, as though he would question the cloud, but it was gone.

Finally he reached the stone wall bordering the playground. He beheld the Stars and Stripes waving listlessly in the breeze.

Boom! the big front door banged against the back wall. He stepped inside: *Boom!* the door closed heavily behind him: *Boom! Boom! Boom!* the sound echoing down through the corridors. The steps whined noisily as he climbed the broad wooden stairs. He stepped onto the clean planks that ran side by side the full length of the hall.

"Boy — your momma was late every day!" Rutherford exclaimed above the din of voices that poured through the transoms above the doors ranged along the hall: *"An' lie? Oooo-whee! She could really tel l'um!"*

"Well, you've managed to be late the *first* day!" said a voice.

He looked up into the narrow mustard-brown face of a middle-aged man with short-cropped iron-gray hair and small brown eyes that blinked nervously, causing his thin, slightly hooked nose to wrinkle in the indentation just above the bridge.

"Well — you've managed to be late the *first* day! Tisct-tisct," sucking the air through the narrow gap between his front teeth in two quick bursts of menacing sound.

"I-I —"

"Come with me!"

He followed him down the long hall. Pictures hung upon the cream-colored walls, mostly of bearded old men with bushy mustaches and fiery expressions in their eyes, as if they were really mad about something! Some of the men in the pictures were white and some were black, and in the very center of the wall there was a picture of George Washington. *"The father of the country!"* Tommy had declared.

How does he know?

They came to a door.

"Wait here."

You have to stay after school, he thought, and maybe get a whipping!

"If you hit that boy one more time — I'll . . ."

"You may go in and find your seat," the man was saying, while he looked up into his splotched purple face with awe.

He stepped into the room and a flood of warm autumnal sunshine filled his face. He saw the silhouette of a woman sitting erect at a desk, hands clasped, in the far corner of the room beside one of four large windows. He timidly advanced, and was suddenly surprised by a wave of sniggering voices that rose upon the air. Half blinded by sunlight, he gazed upon an orderly crowd of black, brown, and beige faces, all of which were about as big as his own, sitting wide-eyed behind orange lacquered desks arranged in rows that extended the full length and breadth of the room.

His glance took in the clean blackboard, which was bordered by a thin chalk line upon which the A-B-Cs were written in large fat letters and small fat letters.

ABCDEFGHIJKLMNOPQRSTUVWXYZ — gimme! He imaginatively stretched out his hand and collected Unc's nickel.

"What is your name?" the woman was asking.

"She was tall and thin lookin'," he replied to Rutherford's inquiry that evening as to how Miss Moore was looking these days: "with a lot a powder on. Her face looked purple. Like Miss McMahon's when . . . But 'er eyes wasn't Irish."

"What you mean, Irish?"

"Blue."

"Where'd you git the idea that all Irish people got blue eyes, boy?"

"They was real dark brown — almost black! . . . 'Cause they is!"

"*Are!*" Viola corrected.

"Are — what?" Rutherford asked.

"Irish eyes. An' they was black almost, like Aunt Tish's, an' she looked kinda like 'er, too, only 'er hair's long like Gran'ma's, but black instead of silver —"

"You think Momma's hair is silver?"

"Ain' it? Gran'ma's got *good* hair, prettiest hair in the w-h-o-l-e w-o-r-l-d!"

"Will you listen to this joker, Babe?" Rutherford grinned with apparent satisfaction.

"Him an' the *whole world!*" said Viola. "*My* momma had pretty hair, too! Even if it was nappy, but when it was just washed, it usta shine like nobody's business!"

"She ain' lyin', Amerigo!"

"Miss Moore's was wound 'round the top a 'er head with a big pretty comb — an' b-i-g hairpins!"

"What is your name?" the woman was asking.

"Amerigo," looking self-consciously at the faces of the children. Their eyes shone like dog- and cat-eyes in the bright rays of sunlight.

"Amerigo — what?"

The faces grinned, lips curved into peach-, prune-, and plum-colored crescents filled with big white milk teeth. Sniggers burst involuntarily through their noses.

"*Jones!*" he blurted out, unconsciously drawing himself erect. The words resounded with a booming resonance that frightened him.

The woman stood up, her figure tall and gaunt under her soft tower of hair:

Who in the hell are you *to be accused!*

"*Amerigo Jones!*"

"Take your seat here," the woman was saying.

His eyes followed the direction indicated by her hand, the third seat in the front row. The polished nail of her forefinger glistened in the sun.

"Like a magic wand. Like a queen! White as a white woman's, but she's a Negro just the same!"

"Sit down, son," said the woman gently.

"You have to bow to the queen," like the prince on the radio every Saturday. He bowed to the Queen!

A burst of laughter exploded within the hot blaze of sunlight that flooded the room, like a sudden shower of spring rain, splaying stars in a dusty yard beside a low redbrick house, running under the gate and down the alley, whirring in a glistening stream around the sewer grate and into the dark depths of a rushing sound that was as wide as the sound of the sea. . . .

Meanwhile the purple coloring upon the queen's cheeks grew perceptibly deeper.

I'll love her always! Next to mom and dad and Aunt Rose and-and Miss Chapman. *Her no more than him.*

"Sit down, Amerigo," said Miss Moore hoarsely, but he could not hear her because of the wide sound of the sea. . . .

"Luuuuuuve! oh, love, Oh careless love! You go to my head like wine! You cost me the love of a many a poor girl — an' you nearly broke this heart of mine! Ohooooo —"

"You better wash them dishes, little niggah! Ha ha!" Rutherford laughed.

He looked confusedly into the darkness of the middle room and saw his father's silhouette bending over the ashtray on the table beside the bed, fishing for a cigarette butt.

"What?" asked Viola abstractedly.

"Your son's singin' about *careless love!* Ain' that somethin?"

"Naw! If that don't beat all!" She laughed from the front room.

"Yeah!" Rutherford turned toward him with a broad mischievous grin: "What do *you* know about careless love?"

He held the washed cup in midair with his right hand while his left groped futilely for the dishcloth hanging on the nail beside the sink. Soapy water dripped from the rim of the cup. He beheld his father's bowing figure in bold relief against the light that filled the front room where Viola sat in the comfortable chair wrapping a long thin band of olive-green tissue paper around the wire of an artificial American Beauty rose that she held between her fingers.

He's doing it just the same! It looked like his father's figure was actually bowing to his mother. He wondered how it could be possible, since he's in one room and she's in the other! Then he remembered what Tommy said about rain falling on one side of the street while the sun shone on the other.

Tears stood in his eyes, and the thick aching sensation in his throat prevented the unsung words of the song from issuing from his mouth.

That night, just after Viola and Miss Vera whose hair Viola was straightening had said good night, he knelt beside his bed and said his prayers, concluding: "God bless Miss Moore — I mean, *Mom an' Dad*! . . . Dad an' Mom . . . an' Aunt Rose . . . Miss Chapman — an' *then* Miss Moore!" Then he crawled in bed and settled himself under the covers. Bits of conversation filtered in from the kitchen,

"Honey, we sure made a killin' on that fish fry last Sad'dy night!" Viola was saying.

"Guuuuuurl — wasn' that a killer?" Miss Vera replied. He could see her broad ugly-pretty smile and her small headful of reddish brown hair all greasy and shining in Viola's black hands. "Sold all the tickets I had — an' coulda sold a lot more!"

"Well" said Viola, "they sure partied 'um down to the bricks, all right. We'll have to have another'n soon, so we kin have a New Year's formal that's a wingding!"

"Yeeeees, yeeees!" Miss Vera exclaimed: "Snap! Snap!" He saw her bosom quiver when she snapped her fingers, he saw her hips moving when she walked. He wriggled restlessly into the deeper regions of the red room. . . .

Yeeees! Yeeees! The sound creeped through his closed eyelids, kneaded itself into two heaving mounds of flesh, which suddenly burst through the open lapels of Viola's bathrobe as she bent over the washtub on Toodle-lum's back porch.

"Why you — you — li'l black rascal!" she shouted, *"you lookin' down my bosom!"*

He turned his eyes away, only to look up, past another obtruding breast, into Miss Moore's accusing face:

"Shame on you — still suckin' your momma's titty!"

He grew smaller and smaller, until he disappeared into the depths of the black room. It was shot through with brilliant bursts of light, *like the stars on the silver screen. Only brighter!*

"All right! Let's hit 'um!" Rutherford shouted. And he floated to the surface of the black room and emerged into the cold washed air of the morning, engulfed in a vague, dumb, shivering sensation of movement and sound smells of morning, fired by flashes of intense wet color.

And suddenly he was astonished to find himself walking up the avenue toward the schoolhouse, over a way that was now known to *him,* in a time that had expanded *and* contracted into definite sequences of events that had made a vague and yet profound impression on his mind — as he moved along the narrow path, no wider than the width of his body, heel over toe,

in a playful humor now, along the black crevice that separated the curbstone from the side walk.

"Unh!" said Rutherford wearily as he entered the kitchen at five-thirty
on a Monday evening. "The I-talians done moved out an' the apartment on
the first floor's empty!"

Just then Viola's face appeared in the frame of the kitchen window.
Rutherford stepped to the door, saying, "Git your daddy his house shoes.
My corns is *cryin' — you hear me?*"

"Yessir."

"Hi," Rutherford said to Viola as she entered the door.

"Hi," said Viola, grunting under her heavy load. Rutherford took the sack
from her arms and she sank into the chair near the sink, rubbing her wrists.

"Hi, Mom," he said, handing Rutherford his house shoes. Then he took
off his mother's shoes and fetched Rutherford's old pair of house shoes for
her. She nodded thanks. Her face was ashen from the cold, thawing now in
the warm damp air of the kitchen, the tip of her nose a deep purple color.
That's Indian blood, he thought.

"The whiskey's gone! Did you notice?" Rutherford asked, stretching out
his hands before the oven.

"I noticed it when I was comin' up," said Viola. "My *arms!*" still rubbing them.

"Luggin' 'em groc'ries is a mess, all right!" said Rutherford sympathetically.

"They feel like they gonna break off! It's a low-down dirty shame!"

"What's that?" asked Rutherford, reaching for his paper.

"That you have to buy groc'ries *all the way out there* where the rich
white people live — *millionaires!* — an' *lug 'um* all the way through town
on a crowded streetcar just to save a few lousy pennies on a can a this or
a pound a that! An' do you think any a those white men would git up! An'
let a — let you sit down? Honey, they watch you loaded down to the bricks
an' don't even bat a eye!"

"Yeah, it's tough, all right," said Rutherford. "What's this?" noticing
now a clean white envelope on the kitchen table. Amerigo looked nervously out the window.

"What is it?" Viola asked. She looked worredly at him and handed the
note that she withdrew from the envelope to Rutherford.

"What?" he exclaimed, "late for school *agin?* Me an' your momma
workin' an'-an' damned near freezin' to death to feed you an' all you gotta
do is go to a nice warm schoolhouse an' be on time — an' you can't even
do that! What's the matter? Huh? Huh?" Amerigo looked at the floor. "*I*
know what's the matter: daydreamin'! You worse'n your momma was. You

gotta *go* some to be late more'n your momma was! Got your head in the clouds *all the time!* You don' see nothin'! Don' hear nothin'! What do you *think* about *all* the time? Huh? Why — you damned near late *every day!* An' come bringin' home a M on your grade card last time! An' you so smart an' all that . . . an' in arithmetic! I was one a the best li'l niggahs in arithmetic in the w-h-o-l-e school! Whasn't I, Babe?"

"You was good, all right. I wasn't so bad, myself!"

"Yeah," said Rutherford, "an'-an' you wanna go to *college!* Ain' that a *killer!*" His face grew serious. "Amerigo?"

"Yessir."

"*Look at me* when I talk to you!"

Startled by the violent tone of his father's voice, he snapped his head erect and looked into his face.

"Yessir." His lips trembled visibly, tears ran from the corners of his eyes, and a lump rose in his throat.

"I-don't-want-to-have-to-tell-you-'bout-bein'-late-for-school-no-more! You hear? Do you hear me? No more!"

"Yessir," he whispered. "Yessir, yessir, yessir."

"Yessir," he had replied to Mr. Grey's angry command that morning, a little while after the last bell had rung:

"Come with me, young man!" his face twitching nervously.

"Mr. Grey," Miss Moore had protested, laying her arm protectively upon his shoulder, "don't you think it would be better to let —"

"That will be all, Miss Moore!" said Mr. Grey.

"But, Mr. Grey, I — "

"Young man, come with me!" He grabbed him roughly by the arm. Miss Moore's face turned purple. "Mr. Johnson! Somebody get Mr. Johnson!"

"Yes, sir!" replied Mr. Johnson, who suddenly emerged from the little crowd of teachers who had gathered in the hall. He carried a long push-broom in his hand.

"Yessir?" smiling slyly.

"We'll have to teach this young man a lesson!" said Mr. Grey. "What would you do about a young man who is *always* late for school?" He spoke over his shoulder, as he raced down the hall, dragging Amerigo along with him.

"Let me see, now," said Mr. Johnson, rushing to keep pace with Mr. Grey. "I don't rightly know just what I'd do at the moment!" He smiled and rubbed the smooth jet-black surface of his pomaded hair with the tips of his fingers.

"Is the fire hot?" asked Mr. Grey.

"What fire, Mr. Grey?"

Mr. Grey turned on him with a look of extreme agitation.

"I reckon so," said Mr. Johnson, "I — "

"Come-come!" said Mr. Grey to Amerigo, who had tried to slow down in order to catch his breath. "Late thirteen times in the past five weeks. We'll have to show *this* young turtle. Ey, Mr. Johnson?"

An acute pain smote him in the pit of his stomach, causing him to grip the muscles of his bowels, while a sweetish-sour spittle rose to his throat. His eyesight grew hazy and his temples throbbed. He followed Mr. Grey down the hall, past George Washington, down into the dark gray cement-floored basement where they played when the weather was bad. Empty now; their footfalls echoed throughout the vacant rooms that shot off from the main passageway through another passageway that led them past the gym where the odor of sweat rose, causing him to suddenly jerk his head aside. Just then Mr. Grey sucked the spittle through his teeth, causing Amerigo to stumble and Mr. Johnson to scuff the sole of his shoe against the floor. They were walking past the shower room where they bathed every Thursday. He could hear the hilarious screaming of naked children no bigger than he, he saw their bodies glistening in the falling water. And then the sound ceased abruptly: Boom! Mr. Grey had opened a huge iron door, motioned for him and Mr. Johnson to go in, and had closed the door securely behind him: Boom!

They stood at the top of a cement staircase, looking down into the great furnace room. The huge furnace loomed up from the smooth concrete floor, a black iron house from which a quiet howling came. Like the wind in the empty house! he thought. He looked toward the upper reaches of the room. Hoary shafts of light streamed through three small windows near the ceiling. He followed the light down to the huge coal bins standing against the south wall opposite the furnace, which occupied more than half the area of a room almost as large as the gym. The bins were filled with great pyramids of coal.

"Come-come-come! Tisct-tisct!" Mr. Grey grabbed him by the arm. He started to cry and pull back. He looked to Mr. Johnson for help, but he had already descended the staircase and now stood looking up at them with an expression of agitated expectancy upon his face. He was a tall slender man, but now he looked very short, very small beside the huge furnace, and his dusky skin seemed to be made of the same tough iron of which the furnace was made.

Amerigo helplessly allowed himself to be dragged to the foot of the staircase. He stood trembling and whimpering in front of the furnace. Mr. Grey held him firmly by the shoulders.

"Do you know what this is?" Mr. Grey demanded. "This is a *furnace!* This is where we put bad little boys who come to school *late!*"

Amerigo's body shook convulsively. He looked up into the face of the furnace, the upper half of which was full of deep cylindrical holes.

They looked like eyes. A cold blast of air washed over his body: "Naw! Naw!" he cried. "Let me go! P-l-e-a-s-e let me go! I won't do it no more! M-O-M!" writhing in Mr. Grey's grasp: "MAAAma!"

Meanwhile the eyes stared at him, the conscienceless yellow eyes.

"*Open 'er up,* Mr. Johnson!" Mr. Grey laughed.

Amerigo tried to break away. He fought with all his might, but Mr. Grey caught him by the leg and held him fast. A warm stinging sensation oozed between his legs and wet the seat of his pants.

"I said OPEN THE FURNACE DOOR, Mr. Johnson!"

Mr. Johnson opened the door. A brilliant yellow light cut a thick wedge into the gray atmosphere of the room and illuminated their faces, firing the pupils of Mr. Grey's greenish brown eyes.

"Put more coal on! Tisct! Tisct!" Mr. Grey had him now; he couldn't get away. "Thirteen times tardy! We'll have to teach this one a lesson that he'll *never* forget! Be *still!*"

Mr. Johnson stared at Mr. Grey for a moment, gritting his teeth so hard that the strained muscles of his jaw made a deep crease in his cheek.

"All right, Mr. Johnson!"

Mr. Johnson grabbed one of the huge widemouthed shovels that leaned against a square cement pillar, stepped over to the pile of fine rusty-looking coal, and scooped up a shovel full. The shovel made a ringing sound as it scraped against the floor. He raised his arched body, lifting the shovel to the length of his arms, took two long sweeping strides toward the furnace, swinging the shovel back in an elliptical plane, its mouth aimed at the mouth of the furnace, and with one quick agile lunge swished it in: Woomb! It landed evenly upon the bed of coals, emitting a cloud of smoke permeated by a spray of yellow flames that shot up through the bed of fire like long yellow blades of grass.

Beads of sweat stood out on Mr. Johnson's face. The command obeyed, he stood rigidly, his shovel by his side, growling angrily at Mr. Grey.

"NOW!" Mr. Grey cried. Amerigo felt himself swinging into the air, his head advancing near to the flames — and back. He tried to scream. His mouth stretched wide open and the veins of his neck and throat swelled out in tight blue chords against his black skin. BUT NO SOUND CAME!

"You going to be late again?" asked Mr. Grey, laughing nervously within the vacuum of imprisoned sound. He tried to answer:

"NAWSIR! NAWSIR!"

But no sound would rise above the terror that stretched his jaws and strained his lungs. At the same time a wild uncontrollable laughter: Ha! — hahaha haaaaaaa! — filled his mind and terrified him even more.

"Are you going to be on time from now on? SPEAK!"

"Open up your mouth, boy, an' tell us what you see!" cried a shrill voice. NO SOUND CAME.

His head grew nearer the flames.

"SPEAK!"

He shook his head weakly from side to side, again and again, his face now bathed in a shower of sweat, the stench oozing uncontrollably from between his legs and down into his stockings. Mr. Grey released him. He crumbled to the floor, sobbing dumbly, shaking his head.

"I think he's learned his lesson, Mr. Johnson," Mr. Grey was saying. "Haven't you?" suddenly turning his eyes upon him again.

"No more . . . no more . . . no more . . ." he muttered with great effort: ". . . No . . . more . . ."

"No more, you hear? No more!" Rutherford was saying.

"Yessir," he whispered hoarsely. He clutched Viola around the waist, burying his face in the pit of her stomach and crying. His body shook convulsively.

"What's the matter, baby?"

He merely howled and shook his head.

Then he felt strong hands on his shoulder.

"NAW-NAW! NAW, sir! —" he screamed, and fell to the floor, kicking and screaming.

"AMERIGO!" Rutherford cried.

"Naw! naw! naw!"

"WHAP!" A flat crashing pain resounded against the side of his head, and he felt himself swinging into the air. He pressed his head against his mother's bosom. He felt her warm tears upon his face. A joyous confusion spread over him.

"Unh! Babe," Rutherford exclaimed in a frightened voice, "I ain' *never* seen 'im like *this!*"

"He's a little feverish," said Viola softly. "Here, baby," carrying him into the front room where she took his clothes off and laid him down upon the sofa. Noticing that his underwear was stained with excrement, she signaled for him to be quiet, rolled them into a neat little bundle, and went casually into the kitchen. Rutherford looked up from his paper.

"How is he?"

"Aw, he'll be all right. I'll wash his face. He'll be better soon as he gits somethin' in his stomach."

"Sometimes it seems like I don' know that boy at all," Rutherford sighed, shaking his head in bewilderment.

Viola's wounded glance fell to the floor.

From the front room Amerigo watched her put the kettle on and take the wash pan from the nail beside the sink and put the soap in it. On her way to the front room she stopped and took off her coat and hung it up in the closet.

"You stand there by the fire, babe, the water'll be hot in a minute." She smiled tenderly at him.

Him no more than her. He watched her move silently, sadly into the kitchen and draw the hot water from the kettle. Again she advanced toward him, her image growing darker as it filled the middle room door. She was kneeling before him.

"Now," she said. He threw his arms around her neck and pressed his trembling naked body against her.

They ate supper in silence: lima beans, oxtails, and corn bread. The kitchen was warm and damp because the walls, windows, and curtains were sweating. The cold blue evening air outside looked like water.

"It raaaained forty days! An' it rained forty nights!" the reverend declared. *"Didn't it rain? Didn't you hear it? Listen! L-i-s-t-e-n! Have mersey, Je-sus!"*

The next time it'll be by fire! he thought.

"Sister Bill's movin' out south," Viola was saying. "An' Allie's *done* gone! They got a house with a yard an' grass an' ever'thin'."

"On Park, ain' it?" Rutherford asked, biting into a fresh slice of corn bread.

"Yeah, Sixteenth Street. I sure don't blame 'um none — for gittin' out a this *alley!* With all these drunken low-lifers an' — " She lowered her voice and shot a glance at the toilet door, "dopers an' hustlers an' ever'thin' else you kin take the time to name. Looks like we gonna be the last ones to leave away from down here."

"You gotta have money to live out south," Rutherford replied. "Them nig-gahs movin' out south! Payin' all they sal'ry out in rent an' can't even eat! I see 'um. *Big shots!* Drivin' around in Cad'llacs an' gotta sleep in 'um at night. Unh-huh! We all right here. Ninety percent a them jokers is on relief. What's that? Owe the man for every stick a furniture they own. Lot of 'um don' even own the clothes on they back. At least we got enough to eat. An' we ain' on no relief. An' the stuff that we have got that we gittin' on time is almost paid for — that is if you ain' already gone downtown an' bought somethin' else."

"Ol' lady Crippa's talkin' 'bout raisin' the rent."

"Raisin' *what* rent!"

"*This* rent! I told 'er 'bout 'er promisin' to paper these walls. Ain' been papered in three years, I said. Look!" throwing a wide-eyed glance at the walls, causing Rutherford and him to do likewise. "Just look! It's all yellow an' stained from sweatin' so much. It's a wonder we all ain' got pneumonia in this damp gas heat!"

"That ol' woman don't never fix nothin'," added Rutherford irritably. "That old porch about to fall down. An' all she kin do is to figure out ways to squeeze more money out a somebody. For cryin' out loud! Well — we ain' *payin' nothin'*! Not a cryin' dime more! An'-an'- if she don' paper this dump, we'll clear out a this rat trap! You tell 'er that!"

"Why don't *you* tell 'er! Always tellin' *me* to tell somebody somethin'. *I* done *told* 'er already. She just laughs. She don' believe it. We been fools for so long now, she can't git it in 'er head that we'd just up an' move! I think that old woman'd drop dead if we ever left here!"

"She'll just have to go to hell then, 'cause I'll tell 'er! Tell 'er in a minute! Just wait till the next time she starts some a that raisin'-the-rent-money crap! I'll tell 'er to her teeth!"

The telephone rang.

"Go an' answer the phone, son," said Rutherford.

"The Jones residence . . . hello? . . . hello? . . ."

"Who was it?" Rutherford asked, as he entered the kitchen.

"They hung up."

Rutherford shot a cutting glance at Viola. She looked into her plate. There followed a long tense silence that lasted for two minutes.

The telephone rang.

"I'll git it!" Rutherford declared, almost knocking his chair down, springing from the table.

"Hello? Aw — hi, Allie Mae. Eh . . . uh . . . I don' know."

He stole glance at Viola. She smiled a barely perceptible smile — with her eyes only.

"I don' know," Rutherford was saying. "Here — I'll let you talk to Viola. S'long. All right. Yeah. Yeah — Unh-huh. Okay o-o-o-kay . . . well . . . Yeah? Well, take it easy. I'll give 'er to you. . . ."

Viola went to the phone. Rutherford took his seat at the table and stared fixedly into Amerigo's eyes. He studied his empty plate.

Him no more than her. He shot a glance at the dirty clothes hamper and clamped his lips tight. . . .

★

"Well, take it easy," Rutherford was saying. Dressed and ready to go, he stood before the kitchen door. Viola was taking her straightening combs out of the cabinet drawer. Amerigo was drying the dishes.

He's going to the barbershop, he thought. To old man Moore's . . . Bra Mo . . . Queen Moore — some more — anymore . . . down on Twelfth Street.

"An' that old man kin go!" he heard Rutherford exclaim. "When he wants to. Catch 'im when he ain' all juiced up an' he'll cut you a head a hair that won't don't. Scissors an' comb. None a that sugar-bowl jive with clippers. Beveled down, Jackson!"

"I have to git mine all cut off," Amerigo thought with not a little resentment. "An' down on the avenue instead a out on Twelfth Street."

"Well, girl, I'm gonna leave it with you," Rutherford was saying. "After I git my hair cut, I think I'll drift down on Eighteenth Street an' try to see if I kin run into ol' T. C. or Willard an' some a the boys. I ain' got but about a foot an' a half, so I'll be home early — unless one a the cats opens up a keg a nails!"

"Okay," said Viola blandly. "Don' do nothin' I wouldn' do!"

"Bye, son," said Rutherford.

"Bye."

He watched him leave with admiration, and thought: He's the best-looking man in the w-h-o-l-e w-o-r-l-d! Embarrassed, he let his glance fall into the soapy water. Brilliant clusters of rainbow-colored soap bubbles floated upon its surface like little jeweled islands that broke up and disappeared — or multiplied! — when he wiggled his fingers.

Suddenly he was singing: "I'd work for you," as Rutherford's footfall faded upon the stair: "slave for you . . . I'd be a beggar or a maaaaaid for you! If that ain' love . . . it'll have to do . . . until the real thing comes along!" He closed his eyes. "I'd gladly move . . . the earth for you, to prove my love, dear, an' it's wo-orth for you —"

"If that ain' love!" cried Viola, joining him.

He opened his eyes. She stood in front of the gas stove fastening her apron, her head thrown back: "It'll have to do. Now gimme some harmony, there. You take the tenor an' I'll take the alto." He smiled at his mother, and they did the thing together:

"Until — the — r-e-a-l thing — comesa — looooooong!"

They grinned at each other with satisfaction.

"Wait! Wait a minute!" she cried, suddenly raising her hand as a sign for him to pay attention. Her eyes flashed, her lips expanded and her teeth sparkled.

Like pearls. Ain' *nobody* in the *whole world* got no teeth no prettier'n hers!

"Wait a minute!" she was saying, and he waited within the aura of excitement that was now poised upon the fingertips of her extended right hand.

"Snap!" went the finger. "I got it! Some think . . . the world was made for fun an' folly — an' so do I! Eh . . . let me see . . . how does the rest of it go? Boy — you shoulda heard your daddy an' me sing that! We was in the seventh grade. In Miss Phoenix's class. He was first tenor an' I was alto. I led the whole section!"

"I hope they'll still be singin' it when *I* git in the seventh grade." he exclaimed, but Viola didn't hear, she was still searching for the lost words to the song.

"Aw — it'll come back," she said, "I kin just hear it so plain! Ain' that funny?" Her expression gradually grew calm and thoughtful. "Then there was 'The Sweetheart of Sigma Chi.' Your daddy usta love that, too."

"How did it go?"

Viola lifted her head toward the ceiling and began:

"The girl-of-my-dreams-is-the-sweetest-girl-of-all — the girls I know. Eeeeech co-eeeed — like a rain-bow trail, lost — in the afterglow. The blue of 'er eyes — an' the gold of 'er hair — like a haze in the western s-k-y! An' the moonlight beeeeams! . . . on the girl of my dreams, the sweetheart — of — Sig-ma — Chi!"

He gazed wondrously upon his mother's face, through the darkened windowpane of the moving streetcar, at the red-lipped woman with snow glistening in her hair, but no more after the conductor cried out, "Union Station!"

"I kin sing 'um down to the bricks when I want to. . . ." Viola was saying. Then she looked curiously at the straightening comb in her left hand and exclaimed: "That gal's late agin!"

"Who?"

He perceived a cool fluid sensation on the backs of his hands. The water's cold.

"Allie Mae! That gal don' know what time means! You just watch, she'll come traipsin' in here all out a breath: Aaaaaw, girl, you know, I just couldn' git away! Momma this an' momma that — an' Doris the other!" Laughter followed this speech, accentuated by the immaculate sparkle of a solitary gold tooth.

"That's the style," he thought.

There was a knock at the door.

"Sssssh!" she whispered, "here she comes! Watch what I tell you!" She moved swiftly to the front room, paused in front of the door, and assumed a casual air, while he watched from the kitchen with a broad smile of anticipation upon his face.

Viola opened the door.

"Allie? Is that you!"

"Aw, girl, I just *couldn'* git *away*! Oh! — I'm winded!"

"Tee! hee! hee!" he shrieked from the kitchen door.

"Come on, girl!" said Viola laughingly, shooting a glance at him, "I thought you wasn' *never* comin'!"

"At the last minute Momma come draggin' in half dead an' I had to cook supper, a course. An' then Doris! That gal's gonna be the death a me yet!"

The two women advanced slowly through the middle room, gradually picking up the glow of the kitchen light, Viola taller and more imposing. Miss Allie Mae was real little and cute, just like a little girl! But she isn't prettier than Mom . . . even if she is lighter.

A wave of uneasiness disturbed the smile upon his face as the two figures emerged from the depths of the middle room. They were right upon him, and suddenly Miss Allie Mae's bright pretty smile had caused him to knock the saucepan off the drainboard: Boom!

"Oh!" Miss Allie Mae exclaimed, looking anxiously after the sound. "G-i-r-l!" turning to Viola, "I'm a nervous wreck! Hi, babe!"

"Hi." He dropped his eyes.

"That Doris," said Miss Allie Mae, "honey — come home with a face as long as Eighteenth Street!"

"What was the matter?" Viola asked, taking her hat and coat in the middle room, returning with Rutherford's house shoes. "Here, put these on an' take a load off your feet."

"Thanks, girl. Oooooo-whee! Rutherford's shoes are c-o-l-d! But they sure feel good!"

"What's the beef with Doris, honey?"

"Yeah, girl — that little miss got to have a ballet dress! Kin you beat that! Here I am, slavin' like a dog, takin' all this crap off the white folks *an'* these no-good men, tryin' to feed 'er an' keep 'er clean an' decent — an' she gotta have a ballet dress! Where-am-I-gonna-git-the-money? I asked 'er. An' she started cryin' the blues. Mary Ann an' Cosima an' them's gittin' ballet dresses an' shoes an' things! An' then I told 'er: But you can't have ever'thin' just 'cause ever'body else's gittin' 'um."

"Ain' that the truth!"

"Your momma ain' rich! I told 'er. Your daddy's good lookin' enough, but he ain' givin' you a cryin' dime! I'm all by myself — an' gotta help Momma, too! Mary Ann ain' got no daddy, neither, she said. Smart as a little devil when she wants somethin', girl! An' that's the truth, too!"

"Who's Mary Ann?" Viola asked, placing a little powder box full of shiny black hairpins on the table.

"Ain' I give you the low-down yet?"

"Naw, girl, what's the low-down?" Viola arranged her straightening combs on the shelf of the stove. Then she started removing the pins from Miss Allie Mae's hair. Meanwhile Amerigo waited for the low-down on Mary Ann.

"Clean that dishpan good, Amerigo," said Viola, shoving the chair in front of the kitchen table. Miss Allie Mae sat down and wriggled her body into a comfortable position. Viola immediately set to work.

"Now — what's the low-down, girl?"

"Aw! I almost forgot. Well — Mary Ann is my neighbor's daughter. Big shots, child! 'Course, they ain' rich or nothin'. Prob'ly ain' got no more'n me. But they sa-ci-ety folks, honey. You know, always havin' teas an' piana recitals an' things. Last year I think she was the president of the committee takin' up funds for the N.A.A.C.P."

"Unh-huh."

"Well — anyway, girl, 'er name — it's the momma I been talkin' 'bout, now — 'er name is Agnes Martin. Divorced, girl! Three boys an' a girl. Mary Ann's the youngest. I think she must be 'bout Amerigo's age. An' strict! She don' take no stuff off 'um little darkies. Watches Mary Ann like a hawk an' makes the boys — big as they are! — walk the chalk line, I'm tellin' you!"

"Where's 'er ol' man?"

"I don' know. They been divorced a long time, it seems like. Ain' that just like a man! — to walk off an leave a woman with four children! But he seems to take pretty good care of 'um, though. They got a nice house. It ain' no castle in Spain! But the roof don' leak, an' it's painted nice, an' it's got a nice little yard in front with a lot a pretty flowers an' bushes an' ever'thin'. Anyway, like I was sayin' — she makes 'um walk the chalk line, honey. All of 'um's nice an' mannerly an' clean as a pin! One of 'um's fixin' to graduate from high school. Hear he's goin' to college to study bein' a 'lectrical engineer — or somethin' like that, girl. I don' know how you say all that, but you know what I mean."

"Naw!"

"Yeah, girl. High-class folks! Kinda stuck up, though, honey."

"Yeah?"

"An' when we moved out there, an' Doris started at the new school, they started dancin' classes. An' you know Doris, she takes after her daddy, she just loves to dance! If she didn' dance so much she could maybe git somethin' in her head. I'm gonna have a time with her in a few years. Wild, honey — *already!* Got a boy-friend!"

"Ain' that somethin'!"

"Yeah, girl! Well, anyway, she had to have ever'thin' the rest of 'um had. An' you *know* they took the cutest ones first an' picked over the rest. *A course,* the white-lookin' ones, an' them that had good hair didn' have no trouble. Doris's hair might be a little nappy, but she ain' black! An' she's got good legs, too! Took that after 'er momma. Besides, Mary Ann's darker 'n Doris."

"Color ain' ever'thin'!" Viola said with a bitter smile. "An' dancin's dancin' — whether you're light or dark. As for legs, all you need is two! That's all Clara Bow's got."

"You tellin' me, girl! Well — anyway, they didn't wanna take 'er in at first."

"Ain' that a shame!"

"An' now they havin' that recital that the Gammy Bamma saror'ty's sponsorin' an' they so biggidy they can't see straight! But I went up an' told 'um: Doris kin dance as good as *any* of 'um — even better! Even if she *has* got nappy hair!"

"What did they say?"

"They couldn' say nothin'. When she gits fixed up, I told 'um, she looks just as good as the rest of 'um. They let 'er in, too!"

"You did just right!" said Viola, sweeping the big white comb upward from the nape of Miss Allie Mae's neck. "But who is this Cosima?"

"Ho! ho!" he laughed. "I ain' never heard a no name like that!"

"Looks like you ain' never heard a the sayin' that children should be seen an' not heard when grown-ups are talkin', neither!"

"Aw, Mom."

"She's the daughter of J. J. Thornton. You know, the one with the photography shop on Eighteenth Street. Tall, thin, with real good hair. Looks like a whitie. The photography shop is on the second floor an' the momma — she looks white, too — 's got a fun'ral parlor on the ground floor. Ain't you seen that fun'ral parlor there with all them ferns an' things in the windows?"

"Aw yeah! Now I know where you mean. Don' never see nobody in there, though. Does she ever git any business?"

"I don' know. I don' think she does the embalmin' herself. I think she gits G. G. Hopkins or A. J. Akers to do it for 'er. Anyway, Cosima's 'er daughter."

Cosima. He stared at the flowered pattern on the wallpaper that had turned yellow because of the gas heat. C O S I M A. This time the word echoed within the warm volumes of familiar feeling and assumed animate form in his mind, along with the name of Grandma Sarah whom he could not remember. He tried to ferret her image from the faded flowers, but was distracted by the silent question: how can you see somebody that you've never seen? Like Grandpa Will and Grandma Sarah? — faces flooded his mind — and Old Lady and . . .

"You gittin' through, there, boy?" Viola asked. He was staring at Miss Allie Mae with his mouth open. "You in a trance or somethin'?"

"Yes'm." He finished drying the dishpan and started to hang it on the nail beside the sink.

"Just leave it *there,* boy! I told you I'm gonna use that dishpan in a minute!"

"Aw, I forgot."

"She's a cute little thing. . . ." Miss Allie Mae was saying.

"Who?" Viola asked.

"Cosima."

"Aw yeah. I was so busy keepin' a eye on this dreamer here, I almost forgot what we was talkin' 'bout. She is, is she?"

"An' smart as a whip to boot. Kin play the piana like nobody's business — *already,* child! Read music better'n most grown-ups. Pretty brown hair, reachin' down 'er back. Oh, she's their little pride an' joy!"

"Kin she dance, too?"

"I don' know. I think she's gonna play for 'um. Well, girl, you kin just imagine how *glad* I was to come home — after workin' hard all day — an' hear all *this* mess!"

"Unnnnnh-huh!"

Viola began to Miss Allie Mae's scalp and knead it with her fingers.

Meanwhile he took a seat opposite them and watched Miss Allie Mae's little bosom heave slightly as her head swayed under the persuasion of Viola's fingers.

"What's bal-lay?" he asked.

"Dancin' on your toes like they do in the movies," said Viola. "I could do it real good, if I wanted to. Don't you remember, Allie, when I got them ballet shoes an' started dancin' like them white gals do in the movies?"

"Who you tellin'! You was a dancin' fool! You oughtta seen your momma, baby — "

"He was too little," said Viola cautiously.

"Aw, yeah . . . Yeah, that's right."

He pricked up his ears.

"I could go to the show," said Viola, "see 'um doin' it — once! honey — an' then come home — an' do it down to the bricks!"

"An' she could, too, Amerigo!"

"I could do the splits standin' up against the wall,"

"L-i-m-b-e-r!"

"just as good as on the floor. An' I mean layin' my head against my thigh! Ruben might a been the *tappin'est* fool in town, but *I* was the best on toe!"

"Rutherford made you stop, didn' 'e?"

"Yeah, girl. He said it kept me too thin. I guess it did, at that. But it didn't make no bit a difference to me, 'cause I loved dancin' better 'n eatin'."

"That sure ain' no lie," said Miss Allie Mae. "We usta go to the dance, Amerigo, an'-an' Rutherford, he'd be wore out. But your momma, she'd be just as fresh as a daisy. Hey-hey!" She threw her head back with a hearty laugh, and glanced meaningfully up at Viola, who also burst into laughter.

"Sure is funny! Tee! hee!" he exclaimed. Viola gave him a silencing look, while Miss Allie Mae withdrew into the secret recesses of an indulgent smile.

A jet of steam issued from the spout of the teakettle:

"We gonna be the last ones to move away from down here. . . ." he heard Viola saying, and was amazed that her lips were still as she draped a big white dish towel around Miss Allie Mae's shoulders and fastened it with one of the safety pins she had stuck into the shoulder of her apron.

Aunt Lily's moving up on Campbell, he thought. An unexpected sadness stole upon him as he traced the way from the alley to Eighth and Campbell Streets along the seam of the embroidered tablecloth.

"Looks like ever'body's movin' out a the alley all at once!" said Miss Allie Mae, bending over the sink. "I swear, I don't see how you an' Rutherford kin stand it. Ouch!"

"Aw — is it too hot, honey?" Viola exclaimed, shooting a quick laughing glance over her shoulder at him, releasing next a forceful stream of cold water from the spigot.

"Oooooooow!" cried Miss Allie Mae, while Viola innocently mixed the waters with the tips of her fingers.

"There now, is that better?"

"Aaaaah!"

"Yeah," said Viola. "A lot of 'um's movin', but we sure ain' in no hurry! Ever'body an' his brother's on relief, payin' ever'thin' out for rent — an' ain' even got enough to eat. An' we ain' never been on nobody's relief! But it ain' none a Rutherford's fault. Honey, if I didn' do hair, an' sew, an' work every day, girl, I don' know *what* we'd do! Dependin' on ol' man Mac! He just loves ol' man Mac! An' ol' man Mac don' do *nothin'* but work 'im like a dog an' make fine speeches. Eatin' at the table with the white folks! What's that if they ain' puttin' no money in your pocket!"

"Is he still fallin' for that same old three-six-nine, honey! Rutherford oughtta quit when things git better — if they ever gonna git better. You know them folks across the water's talkin' about w-a-r! An' the smoke from the last one ain' even cleared away yet! But like I was sayin', as good lookin' as he is — an' smart to boot! — why he could go places, gurl, with a little luck!"

"He's a good man, all right," said Viola. "He's steady, he's good to his family, an' he brings his pay home every week! That is when ol' man Mac pays 'im. That's more'n you kin say for most of 'um. An' what he don' know ain' worth knowin'! He kin figure ever'thin' out, if he put his mind to it. Reads all the time. An' it ain' nothin — *nothin'* — you kin ask 'im about what's happenin' in the world that he don' know at least *somethin'* about it. But he ain' got no — no git-up-an'-go! You know what I mean? As long as there's enough to eat in the house an' ain' nobody sick or nothin', he's *satisfied!* If I didn' go out an' buy a rug or a stick a furniture once an' a while, you think he'd buy it? I have to tell 'im to git a haircut, to buy a pair a shoes or a new suit. He don' even know what size shirt he wears!"

"*We was poor, Amerigo,*" he heard his father say, his voice trembling within the aura of a sad sound that swelled in his throat. "*I kin remember when we usta have to git in bed in the daytime just to keep warm. Waitin' for Momma to come home with somethin' to eat. An' when she did come home, late in the evenin', she'd be e-v-i-l! An' as long as there was some-thin' to eat an' a fire in the winter ever'thin' was all right. Momma was quiet an' peaceful-like, an' we usta have a lot a fun.*"

"You kin straighten up now, Allie," Viola was saying as she wrapped a bath towel around Miss Allie Mae's head. "How 'bout a bottle a brew?"

"Yeah, child, I thought somethin' was missin'!"

Viola shot a glance at him and he immediately got two bottles of beer from the icebox, opened them, and poured their contents into two glasses that Viola handed him from the cupboard.

"Amerigo's sure growin', girl!" said Miss Allie Mae, eyeing him with a pretty smile as she sipped her beer. "That's you all over agin, an' gittin' more like you every day! Big pretty eyes. I wish *I* had them lips! He's sure your boy, all right. How you like your new first-grade teacher, Amerigo?"

"All right."

"*All right!*" Viola laughed. "She's the apple of his eye, girl! He even writes 'er letters in 'er vacation! Yellah woman with long pretty hair."

"Aw Mom!"

Miss Allie Mae laughed and threw her head back in a sudden provoca-tive gesture that caused her beer-moistened lips to part and her eyes to flash with reckless mirth.

"What's 'er name, Vi?"

"You remember ol' lady Moore?"

"Aw naw! Ol' lady *Moore?* She still kickin'? Why she musta taught my momma!"

"It's about time for her to retire, I guess," said Viola, "at least that's what I heard. Maybe next year."

"Unh-unh! . . . Ol' lady Moore," said Miss Allie Mae thoughtfully. "There'll never be another'n like her!"

"Sure won't, honey."

"*Next year?*"

"Yeah, next year!" said Viola, taking a sip of her beer.

"I wonder who'll be takin 'er place?" Miss Allie Mae asked.

"One a them young 'uns, I guess," said Viola. "The ol'-timers all seem to be retirin' — or dyin' out."

Sssssh! whispered a voice.

"But-but! . . ." he struggled to protest, but his voice made no sound above the roar of the cold burnished leaves and crystalline drops of rain and then snow that fell and fell, filled the hollow eyes that stared up into the hoary sky.

"Who's the new principal now that ol' man Bowles is dead?" Miss Allie Mae was saying. "He sure was a fine man!"

"He sure was!" said Viola. "I loved 'im like he was my own father. An' all the white folks respected 'im, too! He sure wasn' no grinnin' Uncle Tom! Not him!"

"Who they got now?"

"Ol' man Grey."

"Is that so! He's a mean 'un, honey. An' the way he kin look at you. Ugh! Usta be over to Yates when I was there. We usta call 'im Ol' Grey Mule! Hey! hey!"

"He's a stubborn man, all right," said Viola.

"An'-an' rabbit! 'Cause he usta wrinkle his nose all the time," said Miss Allie Mae, "an' suckin' his front teeth! Does he still wrinkle his nose, Amerigo?"

"Yes'm."

"He's got a boy oughtta be finishin' high school about now. Ain' worth a *dime,* girl. *Always* into somethin'!"

"That's *always* the way, girl, big shots! All educated an' high society an' they kids turn out worse'n any a ours!"

"Got a daughter, too. Cute little thing. I think she's in high school, too. I forget what year. Wild as the March wind!"

"He always looked like he was half sick to me," said Viola.

"Yeah, girl, I guess that's why he's so mean."

"I bet he sure makes you all walk the chalk line — huh, Amerigo?"

He wriggled uneasily in his chair.

"I guess you'll be gittin' your grade cards pretty soon. All full a E's an' S's!"

He stared fixedly into the shadows under the table:

"Mrs. Jones," he heard Miss Moore say in a grave voice: "I'm glad you could come down to see me. It's about our young man —"

"He, uh, he ain' — isn't getting into no — any trouble, I hope. What-what's the trouble, Miss Moore?"

"Dreaming. Amerigo Jones is so busy dreaming that he doesn't seem to be with us half the time. It isn't that he isn't intelligent and *can't* do the work, he simply doesn't pay any attention to anything except what's going on inside that busy head of his. *And,* the gentleman's l-a-z-y!"

"That spells lazy," he thought.

"I'll git-get his father to talk — to speak to him. *Then* he'll straighten up an' fly right! I mean . . ." grinning with embarrassment, "or he won't know the reason why!"

"Does he get to bed early enough?"

"Why, yes, ma'am! He has to be in bed by eight when he has to go to school, but he kin stay up till nine or so on Sad-Saturday."

"Well, he's often very late. I keep him after school, but it doesn't seem to help." She blushed and flashed a wink at Viola. "And he's not with the other children. He must wander off by himself on the way to school."

"I don't know what he could be up to!" said Viola, "But-but you kin-can rest assured that-that I'll find out! No tellin' *what* his daddy'll do when *he* finds out!"

"I'm afraid that if he doesn't make a great improvement, he may not be able to pass next year."

"Aw naw!" Viola burst out uncontrollably: "Don't you worry about a *thing,* Miss Moore! When his daddy gits through with *him* he'll be the smartest thing in the whole school!"

"Well, I hope so, Mrs. Jones. Things will be different for those of his generation *who are prepared.* I wouldn't be a bit surprised if he didn't have something to say to us. It is up to us to help him say it."

"All full a E's an' S's," Miss Allie Mae was saying. And then her voice blended into Rutherford's voice:

"I waited 'specially till Wednsd'y night to tell you, Amerigo, so it wouldn' be no women here. Don' be scaired, I ain' gonna whip you." He saw his father sitting in the comfortable chair, himself at his feet, staring ashamedly at the bright flowered pattern in the rug:

"Your momma tells me that you ain' doin' so hot in school. Always got your head up in the clouds, thinkin' 'bout somethin' else. What you thinkin' 'bout? Huh?"

His eyes filled with tears.

He looked up at his father, and his blurred gaze drifted past his face and came to rest at the feet of the Spanish lady who stood upon the silver balcony under the silver stars. He chose one.

Huh?

He looked at the strange man who stared at him as though he expected him to say something. He lowered his eyes once more to the pattern in the rug.

"You're smart! You know that? You one a the smartest children I ever seen. Barrin' none. That means white ones an' all! An' deep, too! You ain' got no business *flunkin' out* in school! Ain' another child in the whole North End that's more thought of than you. Your momma an' me's tryin' to help you all we kin. You got a nice clean home. Your folks is decent folks. Ain' no lot a gittin' drunk an' cussin' fightin' all the time — like with half these niggahs down here. What they gonna say when *you* come flunkin' out in school an' can't go to high school? Huh? Got to go to high school before you git to college. How you gonna amount to somethin' when you can't even git out a the first grade! You kin be smart as Solomon! But if you ain' got a piece a paper in your hand to prove it, your name is mud. You end up like me, workin' in a hotel. I coulda been a-a lawyer, or a doctor or somethin' if-if I-I'd a had the chance to git a education. Now I want to see your homework — every day — from now on! You hear me?"

"Yessir."

"An' if you come up with some more bad marks on your grade card, I'm gonna get somethin' from you. You understand what *that* means, don't you?"

"Yeah," Viola was saying with a heavy sigh, "it won' be long now! Half the North End's waitin' on that grade card. An' I *know* he ain' gonna let 'um down!"

"Ain' that sweet!" said Miss Allie Mae.

"Yeah, girl, Unc done promised 'im a dime for ever' S an' a quarter for ever' E!"

"Naw!"

"No kiddin', honey! An' Mister Harrison's givin' 'im a quarter for ever'thin' over a M. Why, he *should* make a killin': ol' lady McMahon, Aunt Nancy, Bra Mo, an' Mrs. Derby — an' you *know* Miss Sadie's gonna give 'er *baby* somethin'! Sure is nice, the way *ever'body* just *loves* him!"

"Yeah," said Miss Allie Mae, "that's right, all right. You an' Rutherford's doin' a good job on that boy. Makin' a gen'leman out a 'im. Tippin' his hat an' sayin' 'scuse me to the grown-ups an' all. Why I noticed it often — he's got better manners'n most men, even the educated ones!"

"That's what ever'body says," said Viola. "'Course, I ain' sayin' he's nothin' special, mind you, he ain' no better'n nobody else's kids, but that's sure what the people a-l-l say, honey, the black *an'* the white! Them white gals down at the laundry usta be just crazy about 'im, an' the reveren' an' all the sisters an' brothers at Saint John's —"

"He said his piece so nice!" said Miss Allie Mae, "on the First Sunday program — in front a the whole church, girl."

"I didn' hear it, but I heard all about it. I was too nervous, girl. I git to thinkin' 'bout what if he makes a mistake or somethin'!"

"He spoke like a li'l man!"

He stirred uneasily in the warmth of the women's praise.

"Yeah, girl," said Miss Allie Mae, following her own train of thought, "I try to see that that young 'un a mine toes the line, too. Little devil! Takes after 'er daddy. Gittin' more like 'im every day. Say, speakin' a men, when's the last time you seen ol' T. C.? I ain' seen that boy in a coon's age. He still workin' at the station?"

"Supposed to be," said Viola, "but you can't never tell about T. C., though. Day after pay day you got to go lookin' for 'im. An' when you *do* find 'im, he's broke. He'd give his head away if it wasn' sewed on tight!"

"Is he still with Mabel? Now there's a sweet girl —"

"She's crazy about T. C. but he just won' do right to save his life. An' she ain' the first one to fall for 'im like a ton a bricks. You git 'im all fixed up — an' he's a good-lookin' man!"

"You tellin' me!"

"It's a dirty shame!"

"How's his momma? There's a saint of a woman if there ever was one. So kindhearted. No matter what he does he kin always go home. It's a good thing she's got that house an' a few roomers."

"I guess she's all right, the last time I heard. T. said he was comin' by this week. That means we might not see 'im till this time next year!"

Next year sometime, he thought, startled by the loudness of his thought, which suddenly emerged from the teeming din of voices that tumbled into his path.

He tried to place his feet squarely in the middle of the long crevice separating the sidewalk from the curbstone — through the endless street that was This Year, faltering now and then, fighting the golden air in order to balance himself with his arms, looking warily both ways at the dangerous intersections: Independence and Forest, Christmas Day and New Year's Day, which in order to pass he had to show his report card: An E, three S's, and an M! He heaved a deep sigh as he tipped his Sunday hat and smiled along the perilous paths of the North End like the good little boy everyone knew and expected him to be.

"Look out, 'Mer'go! —" Tommy cried.

"What?" He looked around curiously, when suddenly he saw a knot of strange little curly black heads advancing toward them just as they were crossing Troost Avenue. He stumbled dreamily on the fringe of the crowd next to Tommy and William, Carl and Turner, Sammy, Etta, and Mildred, a short stoutly built black girl who had started late to school. She moved well out in front of the others.

"Let's git them muthafuggahs!" she cried, her fists doubling into knots that appeared to be as hard as the muscles in the calves of her short stubby legs.

"Aaaaaaaaw!" His mouth flew open with astonishment.

"Come on, you niggahs!" she cried.

He found himself amid a profusion of flying fists and arms as the two little knots of black and white children fused into one seething mass of arms and legs. A ringed fist grazed his face and caused him to bite his tongue.

He was through it. He trembled all over. His sheep-lined coat was torn. He touched his right cheek. Blood! He started to cry.

He was running.

"*A nigger done it!*" cried a familiar voice: a throbbing pain shot through his big toe, and then a searing pain from the bruise on his knee. The pavement grew hot under his feet. . . .

The siren screamed louder! His chest heaved up and down and he breathed with great effort. His legs moved with leaden sluggishness up the ravine of the hill at the corner of Independence and Pacific Street, and down the other side, down past the church and the bunch of frame houses, until a bell like the bell of a huge alarm clock rang:

"Look!" Tommy cried.

They stopped in front of the wall bordering the playground. A little girl was writhing on the ground. She wore a pretty pink dress, white stockings, and shiny patent-leather shoes. Her eyes stared wildly into the sky. Flecks of foam spouted from her mouth, and she gasped for air. ". . . Like soap suds . . ." He watched her smooth orange skin grow purple, and then blue. Suddenly she clamped her mouth shut and her eyes walled around in her head.

"'Lectra's havin' a fit!" Leroy cried.

"Gimme that stick!" Tommy cried.

"What stick?" he asked.

"Aw, man — *that* stick!" pushing him aside and picking up a small twig near his right foot. She fought and kicked and uttered grunting sounds. "Grab 'er hands!" Tommy shouted.

He grabbed the arm nearest him, Leroy grabbed the other, while Tommy forced the twig between her teeth and pried her mouth open, grabbing her tongue with his fingers.

"It's purple!" Amerigo said.

"Here!" said Tommy nervously, "that's what the teacher said to do when she gits a fit to keep 'er from swallowin' 'er tongue."

"Aw, can't nobody swallow they tongue! You crazy!" he exclaimed.

"Aw, yeah, they kin, too!" said Tommy, "That's what Big Rabbit said, an' the nurse, too. They *sure* oughtta know!"

"I don't care. . . ."

The air seeped into her lungs, her body grew quiet, and a peaceful expression came into her face. Her black eyes shone with a burning brightness. Her hair was long, silky, and black, done up in two big pretty braids with blue ribbons tied at the ends.

Electra was smiling at him.

Her teeth are almost as white as Mom's. . . .

She extended her hand to him. He took it and helped her to her feet. Then he, his companions, and the golden Electra walked on down the street. The last bell rang just as they stepped onto the playground.

"'Mer'go loves 'Lectra! 'Mer'go loves 'Lectra!" Etta shouted first, then Leroy, Sammy, and the others took up the cry. Tommy grinned at him. He dropped Electra's hand, but they cried even louder now. He pushed her away from him — too hard, for she fell to the ground and cut her hand on a stone. He started to help her to her feet, when a powerful impulse drew his attention to the classroom window above:

Boom! Miss Moore stood looking down upon him, a faint sad smile curling the corners of her thin purple lips.

And suddenly the sniggers of children filled his ears. Sunlight filled his eyes. She was pointing her finger to a seat on the front row: *You have to bow to the Queen!*

"Bal-dy! Bal-dy! . . ."

"That's Frog-eyes, man!"

"Them's eyes of the world! Tee! hee! hee!"

"Just *loves* 'Lectra!"

"Who?"

"Eeeeeelec-tra! The crazy girl!"

He stalked into the building, took his seat, and did not lift his eyes from the deep black crevices between the floorboards that ran to the wall, and beyond.

"FORGIVE ME! PLEASE FORGIVE ME!" he sang to himself as he walked through a maze of quiet afternoons that enveloped him in an aura of volatile blue pain he could not evade, no matter how hard he tried:

"FORGIVE ME!" he sang to the dumb crowd of images that danced before his eyes with the bright frightening clarity of thoughts reflected in a pool of water.

"I DIDN'T MEAN TO MAKE YOU CRY!"

As the wind rose and howled through the branches of the frozen trees, and broke into myriad telltale articulations that now and then drowned out his voice, obscuring the time and the place. . . .

"I LOVE YOU! AN' I NEED YOU. . . . DO ANYTHING, BUT DOOON'T SAY GOOD-BYE! LET BY — GONES . . . JUST BE BY-GONES."

That ol' lady must a taught my *momma!*

"She'll be retirin' next year, I guess."

"Who they gonna git in 'er place?"

"One a them young 'uns, prob'ly."

"I wouldn' be surprised if ol' man Grey didn' go, too, honey. They don' stay long on the North End."

"FOR WE ALL MAKE —"

"What you gonna git on your grade card this time, 'Mer'go?"

"MISTAKES — NOW AN' THEN!"

"What you gonna ask Sanie Claus to bring you?"

"Aw — it ain' no."

"FORGIVE ME — PLEASE FORGIVE ME, MY DEAR."

"Haw! haw! haw! haw!"

"AN' LET'S BEEEEE — SWEETHEARTS — AAAAA-GIN!"

The sound of a needle cracking in the empty groove of a spinning phonograph record followed, and then a flashing particolored silence exploding within the aura of the red room, gradually giving way to the deep rich tremulous blackness as his nervous hands sought refuge between his restless thighs.

"I'M SO — REEEEE!"

Sunlight trails blazed through blue skies turning rose, turning gray, casting a silvery sheen upon the burnt red cobblestones that lined the alley, upon the parallel rails of iron that divided the avenue into three strips of asphalt littered with the droppings of men, animals, and machines.

"Tee hee hee hee!"

Shimmering inkwells in orange lacquered desks. Big letters and small sprawled stiffly between thin blue parallel lines and gradually gathered into words and phrases like the words and phrases that filled the spaces between the invisible lines of the *Shadow* the *Voice* and the *Star:*

An exceptionally enjoyable dance recital was held on Monday evening, Aug. 9th, by Miss Judith Williams' young people's dancing group in the

main auditorium of North High School. The program was sponsered by
the ladies of the Bamma Gamma Sorority whose president is popular Miss
Marjorie Flowers, active socialite of this city. The music was provided by
Miss Cosima Thornton, daughter of Mr. and Mrs. Elijah Thornton, and the
members of the ensemble included . . .

Wriggling into patterns of numbers that harassed afternoon with tedious
demands for the right answer to the question that crashed to the frozen
ground with a Boom!

"Now?"

Up Pacific Street and through a rubbish-strewn alley to Forest, across
Forest to Belvedere Hollow, past Gloomy Gus's old shack to Troost, which
his eye followed involuntarily, inevitably all the way down to Garrison
Square, and then to the old schoolhouse — torn down now.

"I'M SO — REEEEE!"

Turning up Troost, past Cousin Rachel's house where a little tobacco-
brown girl with nappy hair, big drooping eyes, and a sagging wet bottom
lip smiled at him from the porch, bewildered by the anger in his eyes.

"Hi, 'Mer'go."

"Hi."

Ruben fell in about twelve.

I'M SO — REEEEE.

He turned down the avenue until he came to the litter-strewn entrance of
an empty building with two big double doors. The green paint was peeling
from their panels. He stared at the dirty window of the glass cage that stood
between them, at the round hole at the top and the rectangular one at the
bottom. That's to put the ticket through. It was empty now. He ran his
finger along the edge of the dirty signboard leaning against the wall. In vain
he sought the shiny photographs of Ruth Etting singing to the American soldiers wounded in France, and Buck Jones and Silver; Tom Mix and Tony,
and old Rin-tin-tin! Hoot Gibson and Tim Tyler and Ken Maynard and
Douglas Fairbanks Junior and *The Count of Monte Cristo* by Alexander
Dumas, Charlie Chaplin. Idle, empty stood the billboard, marred with the
perforations of useless thumbtacks that now held in place merely the
unpainted squares where the Stars of the Silver Screen used to be.

He kicked a can as he stumbled across Aunt Edna's alley. A man lay on
the ground, his head but a few feet from an uncovered garbage can. Flies
swarmed around the rotting food in the can and around his head, in his
eyes, and in the corners of his gaping mouth, which was stained with a
thick crust of dried blood.

He crossed the avenue at Campbell Street. Three old Italian men sat on
wire chairs in front of the pool hall. They were short, stout, and gray, with

thick mustaches that were stained yellowish brown where their thin black cigars stuck out of their mouths. They wore white caps and white shirts with their collars open, and their faces were red from the sun. They stared vacantly to the north, toward a little crop of green hills beyond which lay the great river. The breeze came from there. It rippled through the big cotton-wood tree beside the path that led to the alley. He unconsciously searched the path for signs of the dead gambler's body. Nor could he discover any blood from the gunshot wound.

The hole was too little. It was a little cooler on this side of Campbell Street because it was shaded by the trees that stood in the yards that stretched to the top of the hill in little grassy terraces. In his imagination he ascended them, up to where the great Admiral Boulevard lay sprawled out in the sun.

He wondered how long it would be until five o'clock. He tried to gauge the redness of the sun, and decided that it would not be long. Then he came to the inevitable halt at the backyard gate.

"I did it!" exclaimed a voice, and he was titillated by a feeling of unsup-pressable joy that rose with a bittersweet sourness to his throat. In order to distract it, he looked at the ruin of brick and plaster that was once the empty house. Weeds shot up through the bricks and from the mound of ashes where Old Jake found the star. He touched it to see if it was there. Now he gazed with a vague feeling of awe at the lot in back that used to be the yard. It was almost obscured by a tangle of long burned grass in the midst of which towering sunflowers seemed to have sprung up at random. Fat indo-lent grasshoppers crawled along their stems and slept upon the broad fuzzy leaves, while bees swarmed around the dark sticky centers of their blossoms. Flies flitted in and out of the sun's rays, playing follow the leader.

"Look at ol' Amerigo go!" he heard Tommy exclaim, as he cleared Carl's shoulders in a game of follow the leader. As the brilliance faded from his eyes, he discovered in the far corner of the lot, near the fence, a young peach tree, standing in the shade of the great elm trees alongside Miss Ada's apart-ment. He looked up on her porch. She doesn't live there anymore. . . . Mr. Jim an' Miss Gert lives there. . . .

He thought of Aunt Rose who lived out south now with a profound feeling of regret, for he saw the big red house at the juncture where Fifth Street crossed the trafficway.

"Looks like we gonna be the last ones to move away from down here," said Viola sadly.

He ascended the steps to the back porch:

"Heeeeere kittykittykittykittykitty!"

He looked down on Aunt Lily's porch. Flies swarmed around the puddle surrounding the drain, which gave off a sour stench. An old woman was bending over a saucer into which she poured some milk from a can. Her head was covered with a white bonnet bordered with fine ruffles like Miss Barnum's, and her stiff white hair was tucked up under the edges. Her tawny arms and neck were long and skinny, but sturdy, and streaked with big blue veins. There was a string around her neck to which was attached a ball of asafetida.

She straightened up spryly and shaded her eyes from the sun with her hand: "Hi, boy! You home from school already?" He studied the big black mole over the right side of her heavily defined upper lip.

"Yes'm!" thinking, "She isn't as old as Old Lady." He gazed upon her large bony face with its raw cheekbones, big plain thin-lipped mouth, and square chin. A matchstick was clamped between her teeth and her bottom lip bulged with snuff. He watched the cat lapping the milk from the saucer. It was very small, white, dirty looking. She's from Georgia, he thought, but said:

"How's Miss Fanny?" A soft round pale yellow woman who always sat in the rocking chair in the middle room where the bed used to be when Aunt Lily lived there, she always had a painful look on her face, with her pink lips curled up so that her four gold teeth showed. Georgia peach.

"She's in the Lord's hands, son," the old mother said with a sigh as she moved heavily into the house.

"She looks like a white woman, almost," he said to Viola and Rutherford at the supper table that evening.

"Prob'ly is," said Rutherford, "that is, more white'n colored. They all mixed up down there."

"Who?"

"The white an' the colored."

"Where?"

"Down South."

"They come from Georgia!"

"An' you know what I heard?" said Viola.

"Naw, what?" said Rutherford.

"That old woman's seventy-nine years old! She sure don't look it. *Seventy-nine!* An' she washes an' irons — "

"Unh!" Rutherford exclaimed.

"Yeah!" said Viola, "I'm tellin' you! An' she walks — walks! — all the way to the river almost, down under the via-duct! Does a full day's work, walks back home late in the evenin', an' then *cooks!* An' looks after 'er daughter!"

She's in God's hands, he thought.

"That's what I call a real woman!" Rutherford exclaimed. "But them days is gone. They don' make 'um like that no more. Been workin' like that all 'er life, I guess. Out in the open, eatin' plain food. Gittin' plenty a rest. In 'em days they'd work up to the time the baby was due. I ain' kiddin'! I heard Momma tell how in her day they'd have the baby — an' then go back an' finish a week's washin'! Huh!"

"What's the matter with the daughter?" Viola asked.

"Kidney trouble!" Amerigo replied.

"How do you know?" Rutherford asked.

"I asked 'er!"

"Ain' that a *killer!* The people ain' been in the house two minutes — an' this little niggah knows all about 'um! Been callin' on *ever'body!* Like he was the mayor or somethin'! Ha! ha! Beggin' for all the milk bottles an' aluminum an' things to go junkin'! But I usta be worst then he is, though. Only I'd steal 'um!"

"Don't be puttin' them kinda ideas in his head!" said Viola.

"Aw Babe, you know I'm just kiddin'. But let me tell you somethin', son. It's all right to be nice to people. You a friendly person. You got a talent for that. Why, take me. I could live in this alley *twenty years* an' I wouldn' know half as many people as you. You just like your momma. But there's one thing I wanna tell you. It ain' polite to ask women what's the matter with 'um when they sick."

"How come?"

"Well — it kin be embarrassin'! I mean they have all kinds a fe-male trouble an' things. *You* know what I mean!"

"Aw . . ."

"Hi there, shorty!"

He peered through the screen door opposite his and beheld the pock-marked face of Miss Sadie standing in the door in her negligee. He was just coming home from school.

"Hi there, shorty!" the woman was saying, but now he discovered that the voice was younger than Miss Sadie's; fresher, it sparkled with a cutting humor, causing the sad sound to shimmer like broken glass in sunlight.

Miss Lucille, he thought, marveling at the fact that he had at first thought that she was Miss Sadie who had long since moved away. He peered at the new image behind the screen. She was always laughing. He remembered that she had pretty light brown skin, lighter than his mother's but not as light as Miss Fanny's from Georgia, and a flat, slightly turned-up nose. Her eyes were dark brown and full of mischief, and her lips were soft and pink, and there was a tiny mole over her upper lip near the corner of her mouth on the right side.

"Hi," he said huskily.

Aslantwise he looked at her fresh flowered dress; at her shapely bare legs, which terminated in a pair of house shoes trimmed in fur through which a plump clean big toe protruded. His mind was suddenly filled with the memory of her dress, wriggling slowly, sensuously, down where her hips swelled out into T. C.'s big hands, to the rhythms of a funky blues, on a soft evening after Viola had straightened her hair and Rutherford had gone to the barbershop, when the darkness was charged with night light and cricket-song, and cigarette tips flashed red from the porches of neighboring houses, and Mr. Morgan, her husband, had gone to work as a waiter at the Southern Mansion downtown.

He's her husband, reveling within the crepuscular light of a secret that had cast alluring shadows upon the walls of the red room and filled his mind with the soulful plaint of an unheard voice:

"In the evenin' . . . *In the evenin'* — *Momma, when the sun goes down. In the eeeeeevenin'!* — *Momma, when the sun goes down! Ain' it lonesome* . . . *ain' it lonesome* . . . *when your lover's not around.* . . . *When the sun goes dow* — *own."*

Flat Nose! he heard Rutherford yell, and he smiled at the woman behind the screen with uncontrollable affection.

"What you grinnin' at, you little big-eyed mutt?"

"Last night I lay a-sleepin'," sang the blue voice. *"I was thinkin' to myself. . . ."*

"Nuthin'," he replied.

"Last night I lay a-sleepin'. . . . I was thinkin' to myself. Ain' it lonesome . . . *ain' it lonesome* . . . *when she's out with someone else* . . . *when the sun goes dow* — *own."*

He entered the kitchen in a mild state of agitation.

"Boom!" banged the kitchen door, and he was stung by the painful regret that Miss Sadie had moved without ever taking him to the circus. She lived way over on the west side.

"Bra Mo! Aw, Bra Mo!"

"Eeeeyo!"

"Fifty pounds!"

"Yo!"

He went down on the front porch and stared into the alley.

"Corina, Co-rin-aaaa! Where'd you stay last night?" A man's voice accompanied by a guitar. *"Co-rina, Co-rina — where'd you stay last night!"* The music came from Mrs. Shields's house across the alley. He tried to peer through the screen door. *"Your hair's all messed up,"* sang the man as Bra Mo lumbered up the path that used to lie between the empty house and Aunt Nancy's house with a cake of ice on his shoulder. "An' your dress ain' fittin' you right!"

Fifty pounds. . . . Twentythirtyfortyfiftysixtyseventyeightyninety a hundred!

"Corina, Co-rina!"

Miss Pearl stepped out onto the porch in her bathrobe. Her hair was parted in the middle and plaited into two long thick braids that hung down over her shoulders. She eyed him sensuously, contemptuously, and then glanced expectantly up and down the alley. Then she winked at him, laughed, and swished back into the house.

"She thinks she's so hot!" he heard Viola saying. "Goin' with a trashman. Hear they gonna git married an' live down on the city dump!"

"Well, you know, it's like they say," replied Aunt Rose. "All that glitters ain' gold! I know it ain' new — but it's true!"

"Where'd you stay last night!" the singer was still singing, his voice suddenly drowned out by a truck rumbling down the alley. He happened to catch sight of Old Lady who, startled awake by the truck, cocked her good eye down the alley, swatted at a fly with her flyswatter, and dozed off again.

"Where'd you stay last night?"

Jew Mary's moved down on the Avenue, next to The Blue Moon. That's where Katie works.

"Your hair's all messed up."

A big black woman slowly advanced up the alley.

"An' your dress ain' fittin' you right!"

"Hi, Miss Minnie!"

"Hi, baby!" Her big perfect face smiled up at him.

"Your dress sure is pretty!"

"Well, Lawdy! If you don' take the cake! Hee hee! B-o-y — where'd you learn to sweet-talk a woman like that! If that don' beat all!"

"Mom says that a woman likes for you to tell 'um when they lookin' nice an' things."

"Well," she stopped at the foot of the steps to catch her breath. Her voluptuous bosom heaved up and down. "You — you listen to what your momma tells you, heah? Whew! 'Cause she sure is raisin' you right. Mercy!

This alley's about to *kill* me! When you . . . when you comin' over? I got somethin' good for you!"

"What you got!"

"Aw — but you don' like none a that —"

"None a what?"

"Nothin' but a li'l ol' lemon meringue pie."

"Uhmmmmmm!"

"When you comin'?"

"When kin I?"

"Right now, if you want to. Just as soon as I git home an' git my shoes off. My dogs is barkin' loud enough to hear 'um down on the avenue!"

"Aw I forgot somethin'."

"What's that?"

"My momma told me not to eat at nobody's house."

"An' that's right, too!" grinning broadly. "I don't want you not to mind your momma!"

"Maybe I could just come over an' look at it."

"Sure is pretty all right. Well . . . I got to git up there an' git that man's somethin'-to-eat on the table. . . . Your momma home yet?"

"No'm."

"Well, you ask 'er if you kin have a little piece — just to look at."

"Yes'm. I got six milk bottles!"

"That's fine. You gonna have a lot a money Sad'dy. Come to think of it, I got a bottle or two you kin have. You goin' junkin'?" She looked back over her shoulder as she turned up the new path freshly worn through the ruin of the empty house.

"Yes'm."

He watched the slow heavy fluid movement of her hips and suddenly found himself staring at her straddled legs swelling from under her dress, which wrinkled around her thighs as she writhed with pain on a cold winter's day. Last year. More than last year.

"I don't think it's broke, Miss Minnie," he heard himself saying, just before he had run down the slippery alley and climbed the steps leading to Old Lady's porch. "Old Lady! Old Lady!" Cary, Old Lady's third great-grand-daughter, opened the door and he burst into the warm room, which reeked with the smells of gravy and biscuits and fired meat and asafetida and burned hair and baby-pee: "Old Lady! Miss Minnie's done sprung 'er leg 'cause she fell on the ice but it didn' come from that 'cause Mister Roy beat 'er up. We heard 'um fightin' an' he blacked both 'er eyes an' swole up 'er jaw — an' — an' he done gone away an' left 'er — an' she's all by 'erself an' I'm takin' care of 'er. She said if I told you you'd know what to tell me to do."

"Eh?" Old Lady scooted her rocking chair a little closer to the big fat-bellied coal stove that squatted on its stout bulldog legs in the far corner of the room.

"She said if I told you, that you'd know what to tell me to do!"

She cupped her right palm behind her ear and focused her good eye upon him. He stepped back in awe of her wizened face. After half a minute she took a swig from her gin bottle and wiped her mouth with her gnarled hand. The knuckles were large and round and the nails looked hard and tough.

She saw A-bra-ham Lincoln! He saw the tall tall man with the bushy beard and deep sad eyes standing over her, while she looked up at him, hand cupped behind her ear, her good eye spelling out the words that fell from his lips.

"Go 'cross the alley, boy, an' look around on the . . . on the hill, there . . . till you come across some weeds with stickers stickin' out a they round heads stickin' up out a the snow. Pull up a mess of 'um an' bile 'um. Wrap 'um up in a clean rag an' put it where the swellin' is. As hot as she kin stand it! An' keep on doin' it. Did you make a fiah in the stove? D'you make a fiah — eh?"

"Yes'm!"

"Go on, then . . . an' do what I told you!"

"It's gonna be all right, Miss Minnie. Old Lady told me what to do an' I done it. You just lay right there an' keep warm an' I'll be back in a minute."

Last year, he thought, lifting her big strong leg. He slid the hot towel under it and let it down slowly.

"Oh Lawd!" she sighed. "Oh Lawd!"

"I know it hurts, but Old Lady said I gotta do it — an' keep on doin' it till it gits better."

He wrapped the towel around her swollen knee and the lower part of her thigh and tried not to see the dark junction which was covered with a tuft of soft black hair. He fastened the towel with a safety pin he had found in the drawer of the sewing machine. Singer . . . Singing machine! Then he rushed to the kitchen and found the wash pan and the washrag and dipped it into the cold water he had drawn from the tap. He wrung it gently and folded it in half and laid it on her forehead.

"Uhmmmmmm. God bless you, baby! He give you a good steady hand. I won' never forget this."

"Ssssssh."

He quietly rushed upstairs and brought back a bowl of soup that Viola had made for her.

"Uhmmmmmmm!"

"Sssssssh!"

He settled her back on the pillows and arranged her dress properly and covered her with a blanket. A good proud feeling came over him.

"*Don't never turn a stranger from your door,*" said Aunt Rose, and then her voice blended with that of the reverend, and with the voice of an unknown man accompanied by a guitar: "*It may be your best friend — you don't know!*"

"Sssssssh." He tiptoed quietly out of the room so as not to disturb the slumbers of the stranger.

"How is she?" Viola asked at supper.

"She's a whole lot better, I think. I went down to Old Lady's like she said an' she told me what to do. Git some weeds like Granpa Will an' Jesus woulda done an' wrap 'um —"

"Granpa Will an' *Jesus!*" Rutherford exclaimed. "You hear that little niggah, Babe?"

"An' I wrapped it 'round 'er leg r-e-a-l — r-e-a-l hot! Like she said. An' it h-u-r-t! But it's —"

"You raised up the woman's dress, boy?" Rutherford asked with a mischievous smile.

"Yeah! An' . . . an' . . . an' then — I fastened the towel together with a safety pin an' things."

"You done good," Viola said, looking at Rutherford sternly. "You always did have a way with the sick. Remember the time he massaged Miss Betty's back, Rutherford? She let him do it. An' it got better, too!"

"Maybe we got a doctor in the fam'ly!" said Rutherford. "Think you better start a hospital, son. Goin' around peepin' up women's dresses!"

Boom!

"Naw, I didn' neither!" His cheeks swelled up under his eyes, which were on the verge of tears, while his lips pouted with guilt as his body contracted into a ball of flesh that grew smaller and smaller, gathering around a hard little core of feeling that had caused him to scoot his chair farther up under the table.

"Well —" Miss Minnie was saying over her shoulder. "Come over when you kin, you heah? Primm's gonna be home in a little while."

"Unh!" said Viola's voice, "a long time after last year."

"Unh! I see Miss Minnie's got herself a new man! Seems real nice, too!"

"Well," said Rutherford, "that other niggah she had didn' do nothin' but beat up on 'er all the time."

"She done got smart!" Viola said.

"How do you mean?"

"She don' have to worry about him beatin' up on 'er. She's big enough to be his momma!"

"He don' seem no fool, though. I think that joker's educated. He's got a trade. If she stick with that joker she'll have somethin' one a these days."

"She's a hustler, too," said Viola. "Works hard as a man! You know how southern folks are. They work an' save. Live on bread an' water — like the Jews — just to save up a few pennies. An' then they open up a little business. An' the first thing you know they on big time. Half the joints on Eighteenth Street an' Twelfth Street that Negroes have is owned by southern Negroes."

"Amerigo . . . son . . ." Mr. Primm's boyish tenor voice. He beheld his meager face, his dark reddish brown hair that extended far down the sides of his face in long sideburns. A shimmering drop of spittle clung to the bowl of the eternal pipe clutched between his teeth. His eyes twinkled merrily, while his hands busied themselves with a little spatula that he used to apply the sticky black printer's ink to the flat iron disk of his printing press.

"Amerigo, son . . . let me tell you somethin'. You know people ask me, Primm, why did you marry that big black woman? Well, I say, I like big black women. She looks *good* ta me! But that's not the only thing, she's loyal."

"What's loyal?"

"That's when somebody'll stick by you through thick an' thin. Like your momma."

"Aw."

"An' she ain' too proud to work. Don' have to have a whole lot a clothes an' things like that. Times are hard now, but they won' be hard always. She's workin' at the rag factory an' I'm workin' at the market. But do you think I'm gonna be doin' that all my life? Why, hell no! I'm gonna work an' save these pennies, an' then one day we gonna move away from here. Listen to what I tell you! Gonna build a home! Start with the basement first, if we have to. Live in it. A year. Two! You think one a those pretty high-yellah gals'd do that for a man! Some men just look for beauty, but I know better! Beauty's deeper than skin color. Hot damn! I've had more knots on my head than you kin count foolin' with these so-called pretty women! You see what I'm talkin' about? *You'll* find out when you get a little bigger!"

He focused his eyes on the little trail that cut up through the ruin of the empty house. The sun tinted the crumbling plaster orange. The bricks, which had been stacked into pillars two feet square and five feet high, seemed to support the early-evening sky that settled down between the houses. He could hear the water shooting from Mrs. Crippa's water hose. She's watering the garden. One day, some day *I'm* going to have a b-i-g b-i-g house with a b-i-g b-i-g yard! He saw quite suddenly the quiet majestic building standing in the snow in the heart of the Plaza. "Full a grass, an' flowers, an'-an'-I'm gonna water it a-l-l the time!"

He stepped out on the back porch. He looked down upon Mr. Derby, who was cleaning a big mess of fish with a large hunting knife. He could hear Mrs. Derby humming in her kitchen. He frowned with revulsion as a swarm of flies and Miss Jenny's dirty-white cat gnawed on the entrails he had dropped on a piece of newspaper. The entrails glistened in the sun, leaving bright red stains on the paper, while the blue-green wings of the flies flickered. The fish's dead eyes were shining.

"You kin have 'um —" said Mr. Derby, stretching out his hand without looking up.

"How does he know!" running down to accept the proffered bladders. Just as he got back to the porch, Rutherford stepped out of the kitchen door.

"What you say, there, sonny!"

He looked into his father's face, and then stared at the bladders in his hand.

"What you say, there, sonny!"

"Yessir," he muttered, confounded by a sensation that made him exclaim to himself: This has happened before!

"Stay out there, you two, till I call you!" Viola yelled from within the house. They hadn't heard her enter.

"Aw-aw!" said Rutherford with a bitter grin, looking imploringly at him and then into the kitchen, unconsciously twisting the evening papers in his hands like the man at the poultry store when he wrings the neck of a chicken. He saw the big turkey, headless, with his horny feet hanging down. . . .

"She's gonna kill me like that one a these days!" Rutherford was saying.

"Like what?"

"That gal's gonna go an' buy somethin' on credit — an' I'm gonna go stark ravin' mad — an' kill her, you, *an'* myself!"

Amerigo peered anxiously through the kitchen screen.

"Reeeeady!" Viola yelled.

"Yeah!" Rutherford replied, "How much did it cost?"

"Well, come on — if you comin'!"

They rushed into the front room. Amerigo arrived first. Viola was nowhere in sight.

"She must be hidin'!"

"Come on out an' let us have a look at you, girl!" said Rutherford. They

stood facing the front door. Presently the middle room door behind them
squeaked on its hinges. They turned around.

"Hot dog!"

"Unh!" said Rutherford, speechless.

Viola stood in the frame of the middle room door, with the light from the
windows flooding her face. She was freshly powdered, her lips were
painted, and her eyes flashed with excitement. She unclasped the long silver
fox fur that was draped across her shoulder by pressing a sheath under its
throat, which caused its mouth to fly open and the tip of its tail to be
released. She caught it before it could fall to the floor and deftly slung it
over her arm and assumed a careless air of tempting nonchalance.

"Like the white women in the advertisements in the *Star.*"

"Ain' that a killer-diller, Rutherford?" smiling ecstatically. She whirled
on her toes. "Just too too divine! It's the latest thing! An' look how smooth
an' silky the fur is!" She extended the pelt for him to inspect. "You kin just
see that it's the *real thing!* An' I got it at a *bar*gain! Why just think in a year
it'll be *all paid for!* I got three new heads to do reg'ler, an'-an' Susie wants
me to make 'er a hat like mine, an'-an'-Eeeeee! I'm just tickled *pink!* You
just wait till I come steppin' out in *this!* Won' them gals turn green! Old
Patsy's been stickin' 'er nose up in the air about that imitation fur she got
from R. C. But you just wait!" She popped her fingers, and her eyes blazed
with a new fire:

"An' — aw yeah! I almost forgot! Just guess what we gonna have for
supper tanight!"

"What?" Amerigo exclaimed.

"Some good ol' buffalo fish! Some good ol' gol-den bantum corn on the
cob! An' corn bread, an' buttermilk with Spanish onions an' tamadas an'-
an'- Whee! Rutherford, I'm so *ha*-ppy!" She threw her arms around his
neck. Amerigo squeezed himself in between them, grasped them both
around the waist, and laughed with a fearful agitation.

"This woman's done gone an' put us in debt for another *twenty* years!"
freeing himself from her embrace. "Ol' lady Mac ain' even got furs like that
— an' ol' man Mac's got *seven* hotels!" He smiled ironically, scratching his
head. He stared at the fur while Viola strolled up and down the room,
posing in various attitudes on the sofa, on the chair, handling the fur with
first one hand and then the other. Presently he leveled his gaze upon her.
His expression was grave. She returned his gaze with a smile poised haz-
ardously upon her face.

"How much did it cost?" he heard Rutherford ask, and his heart leaped
into his throat. "Did you take the money?"

Is he gonna kill 'er now?

"Amerigo," said Viola coolly, "you go down an' git the fish Mr. Derby promised. An' don' go lollygaggin' 'cause you have to go to the store an' git a pound a lard when you git back."

"Yes'm." He moved nervously toward the kitchen, not daring to look back. As he stepped out onto the back porch he heard the too cool, too calm, insistent aftertone of his father's voice:

"How much did it cost?"

The pleasant smell of buffalo fish filled the air. Steam rose from the boiled potatoes, from the golden bantam corn, and from the corn bread that Viola cut into slices. Like a cake, he thought, avoiding the intensely thoughtful faces that silently presided over the evening meal.

"Hi there Joneses!" cried Miss Lucille, peeping through the screen door.

"Unh!" Rutherford exclaimed in mock indignation, "gittin' so's a man can't even eat his supper no more without people stickin' they nose in his plate!"

"Hi!" said Viola with a strained smile.

"Mom bought a new —" Ouch! he grabbed his shin. Viola cut him with a killing glance, and he clamped his mouth shut and stared into his plate.

"Tee! hee! hee!" Miss Lucille squealed. "Big mouth! Comin' out?"

"Yeah, girl," said Viola, "we'll be out in a little while."

"Honey!" said Miss Lucille to Viola: "somebody sure gave you a rough deal: a polly parrot for a son an' a Frankenstein for a husband!"

"You better *slide* on down them steps, woman," said Rutherford with a malicious grin, "'cause I sure don' see how you gonna *walk* down — not on them flat feet a yourn!"

"You just be glad you don' have to carry me, muckle-head!"

"Muckle-head! You hear that, Babe? That woman didn' git out a the kinnygarden till she was forty-five! An' she come callin' *me* muckle-head!"

"You got me mixed up with your momma, boy!"

"Aw-aw!" said Rutherford.

"Eat your supper, there, boy!" said Viola. He was giggling hard. "By the time these two git through wisecrackin' your food'll be cold!"

"Cracker Jack baby!" he muttered to himself.

"What did you say, little niggah?" said Miss Lucille, sticking her nose against the screen.

"Nothin'!"

"Look out, there, girl!" said Rutherford. "I know you ain' gonna punch no hole in my screen with that flat nose a yourn, but you might dent it just the same!"

"I'll be waitin' for you down on the porch, hot stuff! That is, if you don' *choke* to death stuffin' your gut on that fish!"

Miss Lucille's voice trailed away and blended with the mellow sounds of suppertime that issued from all the doors and windows and flowed into the yards, into the shoots and paths between the houses and out into the alley.

"Mom?"

"Boy, if you don' stop crammin' that food in your mouth! You'll swallow one a them fish bones an' choke to death!"

Boom!

That gal's gonna kill me like that one a these days! He smiled self-consciously at Viola, carefully avoiding Rutherford's glance. He took a sip of buttermilk.

"Mom? Kin I go over to Miss Minnie's an' git a piece of lemon marangue pie? Just to look at?"

"You bring me a piece — just to look at, too!" said Rutherford. "If you don' git out a here, I'll *brain* you!"

He made a dash for the door.

"But come right back!" Viola called after him: "'Cause you got dishes to wash!"

"Aw Mom!"

"SKIN — M-A-N!" cried a loud melodious voice from the alley just as he was getting back from Miss Minnie's.

"The skin man!" Rutherford said.

Amerigo looked over the porch banister into the alley. No one in sight.

"He's a little early, ain' he?" Viola asked.

He made a run for the front door.

"Amerigo Jones! You come back here! Or do I have to ask your daddy to tell you?"

"Aw Mom!"

"You hurry up an' finish them dishes an' *then* you kin go out. While you 'aw-Mom'in' you could be through!"

"Ain't you got no homework to do?" Rutherford asked.

"Just somethin' to read an' somethin' to spell. . . . But I done it 'cause I thought we was gonna have it tamarra instead a taday."

"He's always got a excuse!" said Rutherford, "but I don' wanna hear that bull too often, you hear? Don' make me have to check up on you."

"HEAH'S YO SK-IN M-A-N! YOU GIT-F-I-V-E FAH A NICKEL! AN' TEN FAH A DIME! I'D GIVE 'UM A-L-L TO YOU — BUT THEY AIN' NUNNA MINE! — SKIN MAAAAAAN!"

A siren shrieked down the avenue.

"Skin man! Aw-skin man!"

"EEEOH!"

"Ovah heah!"

"Well I sure ain' bashful, lady!"

"Tee! hee! hee!"

"If you got the dime, I sure got the time!"

"Skin man!"

"I'm comin', mistah — can't you see how hard I'm breathin'?"

He stood in the kitchen alone, his hands immersed in the gray soapy water, his fingers caressing the smooth round surface of a glass, the wave of voices rising and falling in the alley, washing upon the shores of his mind, which was filled with the image of all the black people, the brown and the beige ones, sitting on their porches in relaxed evening attitudes, their faces alive with animate flashes of humor that sparkled in their eyes, as their heads were flung back by the recoil of raucous laughter. He identi-fied each of the multitimbered voices that blended in jovial conversation and spattered against the cobblestones like summer rain bubbling down the alley. Then it emptied into the avenue, where it picked up the noisy reflec-tions of the neon lights that shone from the store windows and from the chrome-rimmed headlights of passing automobiles and from the streetcar that rolled past filled with still more faces emitting bursts of transient sound. He *felt* the streetlights come on! And blazen sharp trails of light along the dangerous edges of broken glass strewn among the cobblestones.

Meanwhile, from the top of the alley came the steady din of dangerous traffic speeding east and west along the great Admiral Boulevard — more quietly now that five o'clock had come and gone and the sun had left only a faint trace of crimson, blending into a mauve rind of sky that lay just above the treetops to the west.

He could hear and see it all, as he stared vacantly at the faded flowered patterns on the wall before him.

Days getting longer, he thought. Days getting hotter and then it will be summer and then — God damn! Aaaaaw! Hot dog! God damn! He laughed to himself, thrilling to a vague feeling of wickedness as his mind was enveloped by the sad-sweet-long-lazy-lost-impatient feeling that was summer, when school was out and the playground stood empty and the bell was silent. In the scorching sun and in the shade, dripping ice and lemonade. Ice cream and soda-pop, and rubber-gun fights in the wet shade of porches and basements. Amid the pricky bushes on the hill at the top of the alley and in the gray-dusty lot next to old man Whitney's house, the sanctified church often pitched a tent at night and sang and shouted and beat tambourines and rolled on the ground to the beat of clapping hands, stamping feet, and the rolling bass of an old out-of-tune stand-up piano. The white people drove up in cars from the great Admiral Boulevard and gave them money once, twice, three and four times, until they couldn't get any more when they took up the collection.

He thought of the quiet hot afternoons when he had to take a nap on the pallet in the front room darkened by the drawn window shades through which brilliant points of light appeared. On Sundays Viola and Rutherford went swimming at the bathhouse on Eighteenth Street, or over in Kansas with Miss Ada and Mr. Willard and Harrison, his brother who looked just like him: Twins! Their daddy was a b-i-g fat man who could lie on the water without swimming and read a book. Mr. Chainey, and T. C., who used to be a lifeguard. Rutherford was teaching Viola how to swim and Amerigo couldn't go with them because he was too little.

A sad feeling swelled his cheeks into a pouting attitude. I don't care, I'm going to Aunt Nadine's where Grandma is!

The quiet flowery street opened up before him and his eyes took in the soft landscape bulging with tufted blue grass spangled with golden dandelions and clover. He gathered a bouquet of the soft fuzzy purple flowers and ran home to Grandma Veronica, who sat on the front porch, staring blindly out at the sun from the shade cast by the big cottonwood tree.

"Look Gran'ma! They're purple! I got 'um for you!"

He smiled at the thought of the smile upon her face.

Then suddenly he heard a scream, followed by a heavy thud, and the crash of pans and dishes to the floor. "Gran'ma! Gran'ma!" He rushed into the kitchen and found her lying on the floor, holding her back. She grunted with pain when he tried to roll her over. There was a deep gash in her back. Blood! She groped futilely in an effort to gain her feet. He tried to help her but she was too heavy. "Call somebody!" she had cried, and he had dashed out into the street and found a man, the mailman, who helped her to her feet.

"Just half an inch more," the doctor had said, "and her spine would have been seriously injured."

"Don't you *never leave 'er agin!*" Viola said.

"I *didn'* leave 'er!" tears blurring his vision. "I won' *never* leave 'er agin!"

"An' he never did!" said Grandma Veronica. "He never got too busy to think about his gran'ma, if she wanted somethin' or not. The rest of 'um, maybe, but not him!"

Summer undulated before his eyes in waves of heat, like the waves of heat that came from the oven in wintertime. It settled upon his skin and trembled

in beads of sweat upon his face and soaked the collar of his white shirt at
church, and did not go away, not even at night, no matter how hard he tried
to wipe it away.

"Boy, you're b-l-a-c-k!" he heard Viola say, as he looked at his arms and
noticed the degree to which the sun had burned his skin.

"Dark," said his voice, looking with astonishment at his sunburned arms,
and exploring his face with his fingers to see if he could feel the blackness,
and grasp the tremulous emotion provoked by the word *black*.

"The blacker the berry the sweeter the juice!"

"You have to taste it to find out, Momma!"

"Heh heh heh."

"If he was a white man!"

Followed by a profound silence, trembling within the hot wet blackness
that was summer.

"Boy! Ain't you through yet?"

"No'm."

"Listen," lowering her voice cautiously, "I got somethin' to tell you:
When somethin' happens in this house — no matter what it is — you keep
it to yourself, you hear? Fixin' to tell Lucille about them furs! What me or
your daddy does ain' nobody's business. The first thing you know she'll go
down an' buy a cheap imitation pair just like 'um! Like she did that red
dress a mine. She looked it over good, saw just how it was made, an' then
went downtown an' bought one *just like* it. Not a little like it — *just like
it!* Nothin' makes me saltier than a copycat! Now you mind what I tell you,
you keep your mouth shut, you hear?"

"Yes'm."

"If you don' hurry up, it's gonna be time for you to go to bed pretty soon."

"Yes'm."

She went to the toilet. He heard the discreet sound of paper tearing, followed by the flushing of the flush-box, the gentle creaking of bones, then the
door swung open and she stepped into the kitchen straightening her dress.

She had to pee, he thought. He tried to suppress the thought when their
glances met the instant before she stepped toward the sink and made a sign
for him to move the dishpan so she could wash her hands. He wondered
why she had to wash her hands when he couldn't see any dirt. *Why you
have to wash your hands an' face just to go to bed! . . . an' on Sunday
mornin' when you just had a bath on Sad'dy night!*

A sudden loud whistle burst in upon his thoughts. It came from the yard.

"T. C.!" he cried excitedly.

"T. C." Viola exclaimed, as though she had not heard him say it, looking
toward the screen door with a broad smile.

Then another whistle just like the first one: One long, two short, three long. It came from the alley: Dad! He thought enviously, sadly reflecting that he could not whistle like that no matter how hard he tried.

"That usta be our emergency signal!" he heard Rutherford saying. "We'd git to fightin' an' the rocks'd start to flyin'. Things'd git a little tough an' I couldn' see no way out a that mess an' then I'd whistle — or he'd whistle — an' one or the other'd come a-runnin'!"

"One time, 'Mer'go," T. C.'s voice was saying, "me and old Rutherford was swimmin' in the river, ha — ha!"

"Hot damn! I *knowed it!*" Rutherford exclaimed. "That niggah's been razzin' me 'bout that for *twenty years!*"

"Aw-haw! haw! haw!" T. C. laughed. "We was swimmin' in the river, 'Mer'go. Me an' your poppa. He was a swimmer! Haw! haw! That little joker caught a cramp! M-a-n , you ought to a seen him strugglin' an' scufflin'! That cat tried to whistle! Every time he'd work up his mouth he'd spout water like a whale! Had his lips all screwed up an' wasn' no sound comin' out! I was swimin' behind him, laughin'. He went down three times, too! That Missouri River was dangerous, Jack. You ever git caught in one a them whirlpools *right* — that's the *end!*"

"That's the truth, Amerigo!" said Rutherford. "It's a wonder we didn' git drowned in that river at least a dozen times!"

"Anyway," T. C. continued, "ol' Rutherford was just a spoutin'! Hold on! I yelled, I'm a-comin'!"

"Hold on to what, niggah?" said Rutherford. "He come tellin' me to h-o-l-d o-n — an' me about to drink that river dry! I had the worse cramp I ever had in my life, you hear me? I thought I was a goner!"

"I grabbed that joker," said T. C., "an' he started to fightin'. An' that li'l joker was *strong!* He was li'l, but he could whip anything his size, 'Mer'go, an' them big cats wouldn' fool with 'im neither. Huh! git that little niggah man an' he'd *bite* you to death! An' scratch? Scratch like a cat! Well, he like to got us *both* drowned. I got away from that cat. Started to treadin' the water, Jack. Prancin'-like. An' then I squared off on that joker. Haw! haw! I hit 'im with a c-l-e-a-n right cross. Right on the button! An' that cat saw stars!"

"Battlin' T. C. B.!" Rutherford grinned.

"Aaaaaaaw! An' then, 'Mer'go, an' then I dragged 'im in. An' when I done pumped half the river out a that cat, he rolled his bloodshot eyes an' said — you know what he said?"

"Naw!" said Viola.

"What?" Amerigo asked.

"Niggah — what you come hittin' me for? Ah-ha! ha! Ain' that a killer?"

"Hi, T.!" he yelled from the kitchen door, watching the big man approach. His smooth healthy black skin stood out against his fresh white shirt. The collar was open and the sleeves were rolled up to the elbow and he wore a light brown straw hat that appeared almost white in the light that streamed from the kitchen door.

"What you say, there, big shot?" said T. C., stepping into the kitchen. He grabbed him by the armpits and swung him up toward the ceiling, and then down between his straddled legs, and up again, while the laughter bubbled uncontrollably from his throat until he almost choked.

"Whew!" T. C. exclaimed. "Vi, what you feedin' this joker? He's h-e-a-v-y! Let me feel your muscle!" He stood Amerigo on his feet, and he raised his right arm and strained to raise his biceps as high as possible.

"Feel that little joker's arm, Vi! Got a build like a prizefighter!" He rained blows on T. C.'s stomach and tried to jump up and catch him by the neck.

"Hi, T.," said Viola. "Amerigo! Cool down an' let T. C. catch his breath. Don' be so bothersome!"

"Aw Mom, I was just —"

"He don' hurt me none, Vi. Let 'im play. Put-up-yo'-dukes, Jack Johnson!"

He fell into a fighting stance, but Viola gave him a look that made him drop his guard.

"You oughtta try that bad left hook on some a them little boys that run you home every day!"

"What?" said T. C. with surprise. "You mean they runnin' my boy home?"

"Yeah! —" said Viola, "— they knockin' knots on his head an' tearin' his clothes half off a him. *Somebody* better show him how to take care of hisself."

"Unh!" said T. C. "We got to put a stop to *this!* B-o-y — me an' your daddy was the battlin'est little niggahs on the whole North End! By the way, where is that joker?"

"He's down on the front porch shootin' the bull with Lucille. They at each other's throats like cats an' dogs! That woman couldn' resist a crack if she was dyin'! Come on down. Had your supper?"

"Aw, I ain' hungry!"

"Boy," Viola grinned, "I ain' never seen you in my whole life when you *wasn'* hungry! It's a dirty shame the way this man kin eat, Amerigo! Here, pull up a chair, T., an' I'll see what I kin find."

Viola took the remains of the corn bread from the oven and a bowl of boiled cabbage from the icebox. She emptied the cabbage into a pan and put it on the stove and lit the gas. Presently the strong pleasant smell of cabbage filled the kitchen. Meanwhile she put the remaining piece of fish

in the skillet, warmed it, and when the cabbage was hot, loaded his plate
and set it before him.

"Look at what old Vi's puttin' down!" he exclaimed, laying to the food
as though it were his first meal in years.

Viola peeled an onion, washed it, diced it, and scattered it over his cabbage.

"You knowed it, didn't you!" he exclaimed, looking up at her with
childish affection while she admiringly watched him devour the food.

Viola set the bottle of beer before him and started for the glass.

"Ummmm-umh!" he grunted, waving her back. He raised the sweaty
bottle to his lips, and the foamy contents disappeared into his massive
throat to the rhythmic shuttling of his gurgle-pipe.

After a while a soft mound swelled the white belly of his shirt, he heaved
a contented sigh, belched, wiped his mouth with the back of his huge hand,
and scooted his chair away from the table.

"That'll git it every time!" he said.

"WHAT!"

Rutherford stood in the kitchen door. "I *thought* somethin' was wrong!
Me settin' down on the porch — all innocent an' ever'thin' — an' this
joker's up here eatin' me out a house an' home!"

"Too late now, Jackson!" said T. C. with a beautiful grin: "You shoulda
locked the barn door be*fore* the mule got away! Ah-ha! ha! What you say
there, man!"

"What *you* say! I thought the law must a had you or somethin', ain' seen
you in so long!"

"Aaaaaw, you know how it is, Rutherford."

"Yeah, *I* know, you been runnin' around with those low-lifers on Twelfth
Street. Lettin' 'um drink you up an —"

Viola shot a significant glance at Rutherford, who immediately ceased to
speak, and they both watched Amerigo staring at T. C. with such absorbed
attention that he failed to notice that they were looking at him.

"Ain't you through yet?" said Rutherford.

He continued to stare at T. C., absentmindedly drying the dishpan with
the dishrag.

"Ain't you through yet?" he repeated.

"That little joker's out a this world!" said T. C.

"Amerigo!"

He looked at Rutherford dumbly, as though he did not recognize him:
"Yessir."

"Naw — he ain' finished yet," said Viola: "Looka here!" pointing to two
pans filled with water on the back burners of the gas range.

"Them's soakin'!" he exclaimed.

"That cat's *always soakin'* somethin'!" said Rutherford.

"An' what about these?" said Viola, pointing to the dishes T. C. had used.

"Aw Mom! That ain' no fair! Them don' count till tamarra!"

"Git me a bottle a brew, boy!" said Rutherford, "before I lose my temper an' kill you!"

Boom!

"An' I *know* you ain' gonna forget your Uncle T.!" said T. C.

"Git me one, too, babe," said Viola.

"Come on. Ever'body, let's go down on the porch," said Rutherford.

"Wait a minute!" said Viola, suddenly dashing into the middle room. They all looked expectantly after her.

"She's gonna kill me like that one a these days," said Rutherford's voice. Why's she doing it? he wondered.

WHAP! Rutherford's palm glanced off Viola's shoulder. Amerigo leaped out of bed and rushed toward his father with his fists doubled up:

"Don't you hit my momma!"

"Git back in that bed!"

Why's she doing it?

"Hey! hey!" T. C. shouted. His handsome face broke into a smile. Viola was whirling about the kitchen in her silver fox furs.

"Ain' that somethin', T.?" she said.

"G-i-r-l — them's a killer! You sharp as two tacks! You kin ba-*lieve* me!" The frown upon Rutherford's face deepened.

"You know, Rutherford," said T. C., "you're a lucky joker to have a wife like Viola. A woman that'll stick by you, Jack! An' be a good mother an' all that. An' on top a that, she's proud. Yeah! Always *did* want to be somebody. That gal's one a the dressin'est women on the whole North End. Yessir! An' she don' only know what to wear, but how an' when to wear it! Class, Jackson. That's what I like! Boy," he turned to Amerigo, "you got a good-lookin' momma!"

"Yeah," said Rutherford, "that's true, all right." His frown had faded now, and a slightly confused, slightly embarrassed smile worked its way into his expression. "Ol' Vi sure likes fine togs, all right. You know one thing? She got more clothes then ol' man Mac's wife. No kiddin'! I'm scaired to open up the closet half a time — afraid a new pair a shoes'll fall out an' bust my brains out! No crap! An' me a porter in a cheap hotel! An' in the deppression to boot!"

"Turn around there, Vi," said T. C., "an' let's have another look at you!"

She walked and whirled and turned and smiled, and charmed the smiles deeper into their faces, until a bright tension shimmered in the air and created an atmosphere that was like the Fourth of July. A great lump of affectionate feeling for his mother rose to this throat, and he thought: She's the prettiest woman in the w-h-o-l-e w-o-r-l-d!

"Let's go down on the porch," Rutherford was saying. He, Viola, and T. C. moved toward the front room. "Douse that glim," said Rutherford to him over his shoulder, and he, glancing at the dishes that T. C. had used and the pots soaking on the stove, thrilled to a dizzying sense of escape, which caused him to knock his knee against the chair as he rushed for the light switch too eagerly. A sharp pain shot through his body, and tears rushed into his eyes. He gasped in an effort to suppress the pain, as he stumbled through the house in the dark and down the dark stairs to the front porch where a little group of barely visible people sat huddled around the lamp-ringed tranquility of the evening.

The air was alive with cricket-song! Moths and gnats flitted in and out of the lamplight and crashed against its shade with a faint tinny din. Fireflies darted in and out of magic globules of phosphorescent light, against the massive darkness of the big cottonwood tree that towered above Sammy Sales's house, which stood opposite Toodle-lum's house on the Charlotte Street side, west.

Like a Christmas tree, he thought, fascinated by the light, oblivious to the voices that droned about his ears. But Christmas won't come for a long time. After summer goes away . . . and all the leaves on the trees fall off and school starts, and geography and history and l-o-n-g di-vision!

"You got to be smart to calculate numbers!" said a voice.

"Loooooooooooooooooong de-vision!"

"That boy's got a head like a preacher!"

"Loooooooooooooooooong de-vision!"

"Open up your mouth, boy, an' tell us what you see!"

He gazed at the ruin of the empty house, now a vaguely red promontory strewn with shattered pieces of sparkling glass. He sought out the spot where Mr. Everett had pointed, fixed his attention upon two pieces of splintered glass — which suddenly appeared as eyes shining up out of the ground!

"I wouldn' be surprised if they wouldn' be at it agin!" a voice was saying.

"It's a pity he had to die like that, hungry an' alone," said Aunt Lily's voice.

"Naw, I wouldn' either," said another voice. "All you kin read in the papers these days is pictures of generals an' armies! An' those Germans is *smart!* They know all about war. Makin' all 'em high-powered machines an' things: submarines, poison gas! A — they got more ways a warrin' than I got blues!"

Someone sighed within the shadows of the porch.

"People's starvin' over there. Things ain' gonna go on like that much longer."

"Things seem to be breakin' a little better over here, though. Maybe that'll help. An' I'll tell you one thing, you watch this new joker, a Democrat they gonna git to run for governor of New York, maybe. Maybe not next year, but you just wait. Roosevelt! Franklin Delanor Roosevelt. Aristocrat, Jack! Tough man! He's comin' up. Goin' places. You wait an' see if I'm lyin'. If anybody kin keep us out a war, he kin."

T. C., he thought.

"Well, maybe he kin," said Rutherford, "but I don' believe that no one man kin keep nobody out a nothin'! It's capital that rules the world! Them big shots on Wall Street. The ones that make the guns an' airplanes an' submarines an' all that jive! Us scufflin' for a livin' — ain' got nothin' — got to do what the man says. An' I mean the paddies just the same as you an' me. War ain' nothin' but a business."

"We missed the last 'un," said T. C. thoughtfully, "but I think they'll git us *all* if we have to go agin!"

"Where?" Amerigo asked.

"To the war," said Rutherford.

Amerigo looked into the corrugated shadows that cut the houses into segments of light and dark up and down the alley. He looked at the sky and tried to penetrate the mystery of war. He looked at the trees that glistened with the light of the fireflies. A heavy oppressive feeling filled his heart.

"How kin you stop it?" he asked the company aloud.

"What?" asked Rutherford.

"War!"

Cricket-song filled the silence, which gradually receded into a vague sea-sound accented by occasional bursts of laughter issuing from the shadows of neighboring porches. The streetcar rumbled down the alley and slowly faded out of hearing into the sea-sound charged with cricket-song, which suddenly ceased, overwhelming his mind with a terrific silence echoing the loud boom of war!

"Pray," said a voice. Miss Jenny. He could see her silhouette against the streetlight.

Now I lay me down to sleep, I pray the Lord my soul to . . .

"He's got the whole world in his hands! . . ." sang a great booming voice.

"How you like your new principal?" T. C. was asking. He listened with detachment to the woman's voice that answered:

"He don' come till next year."

Mom. Next year?

"Ol' man Grey's leavin'. That's what you said it said in the *Voice,* didn' it, Rutherford?"

"Yeah, that's right, Pr'fessor John D. Powell from Atlanta Georgia! Hey! hey! A real distinguished-lookin' cat! Looks like a whitie. There was a picture of 'im in the papers. An' a young 'un, too!"

"It's about time some of them old diehards got out a the way," said Miss Lucille, "an' let some a the young 'uns have a chance!"

"He must be a hell of a educator," said Rutherford, "with all them degrees he got behind his name!"

"An' old Amerigo's in the fifth grade!" T. C. exclaimed. "M-a-n, don' seem like *no* time since that little joker was born. I usta throw 'im up in the air like a rubber ball! First thing we know we'll look up an' he'll be comin' out a one a these high-powered colleges! A big shot! An' gittin' married to one a them pretty little society gals!"

"Yeah!" said Rutherford.

"Won' even speak to us no more!" T. C. grinned.

"We'll have to come around to the side door then!" said Rutherford.

"Don' start that stuff!" said Viola.

"Old Vi'd be s-a-l-t-a-y!" said Miss Lucille.

"Hey! hey!" T. C.exclaimed. "He's got the makin's of a great man, too! *He* got a *head* on *his* shoulders! Rutherford, he don' think like you an' me, man!" He slapped Rutherford on the back. "He don' think like none a these jokers 'round here. He wants what the white man wants — already! You know? Ain' *no*body in the whole North End that don' know that little joker! An' I mean, respect him, too! Momma said she heard him teachin' Sund'y school last Sund'y. He didn' know she was listenin' an' he was bringin' that jive *home* to them little jokers! An' when the gen'ral assembly time came, he stood up an' spoke before the whole Sund'y shool! Had old rev. grinnin' an' scratchin' his head! Yes sir! Momma goes to church e-v-e-r-y Sund'y an' *she* said she ain' never heard nothin' like that!"

"Unh!" Viola exclaimed, "he didn' tell me nothin' 'bout that!"

"If you'd go to church sometimes yourself," Rutherford grinned, "you'd see what your son's doin'! Ha!"

"Now don' start that stuff, Rutherford Jones! I believe in the church as much as anybody!"

"Why don't you join up, then?"

"Ain' no sense in joinin' the church till you ready to do right, an' know you ready, an' kin live like the Good Book says! Just joinin' the church to be joinin' don' cut no ice."

"You ain' fixin' to start givin' up dancin' an' beer an' havin' fun, are you, Vi?" said Miss Lucille. "You know you don' have to lie to me!"

"Naw, girl!"

"That woman," said Rutherford, "kin drink more beer — unh-unh! — more beer'n the breweries in Milwaukee kin brew!"

"Oooooooo," Viola cried, her laughter infecting the others.

"You ain' exactly no amateur yourself there, brother!" said T. C.

"Don' do as *I* do, do as I *say* do!" said Rutherford. "That's what Momma usta tell us!"

"Well," said Viola, "when the time comes to join the church, an —"

"When she gits old an' fat an' evil!" said Miss Lucille. "Tee! hee! An' then she'll sit around an' give the young 'uns hell, like all them old sancty sisters up at Saint Johns!"

"At least I try to see that Amerigo goes an' learns what's right!"

"Yeah," said Rutherford, "when old Vi gits old, see, with one foot in the grave and the other'n on a banana peel an' can't party down to the bricks no more an' done spent all my money on clothes — "

"What you got, Vi?" said Miss Lucille, but Viola pretended not to hear.

"She's gonna git eeeee-vil!"

"Aw, Rutherford!" said T. C.

"An' righteous, Jack!"

"What *you* talkin' about, Rutherford Jones," said Viola, "I don' see you breakin' your neck to join no church!"

"Don' need to, I'm good enough already."

"Ain' that a killer!" Viola said.

"Rutherford Jones!" said Miss Lucille, "if they didn' already have a president in hell, I'd sure vote for you!"

When he threw his head back to laugh, he caught sight of Miss Jenny's silhouette, rocking quietly, calmly, to and fro.

"She's in the Lord's hands." The laughter died in his throat.

"Naw, but seriously!" Rutherford was saying: "I try to treat *ever'*body right! Like I like to be treated. I believe in the *sense* of the Bible . . . in the meanin' underneath. An' I don' need *nobody* to read it for me!"

"Look out, there, Jack!" said T. C.

"That's right!" Rutherford insisted, "an' goin' to church ever' Sund'y — givin' all my money that I done slaved for all week to some jackleg preacher to ride around in a Cadillac an' wearin' twenty-dollar 'dos an' di'mond rings an' all that crap! That ain' gonna make me git to heaven — if it is a heaven — no faster! An' you, neither!"

Mrs. Derby shook her head with a serious air and said:

"I agree, Mister Jones, they's a powerful lot a sinnin' goin' on in the world. Always have been. But the way I heard it is that the people ain' the church!"

"Tell 'im, Mrs. Derby!" said Viola.

"Tell 'im *what!*" Rutherford exclaimed.

"Let 'er talk!" said Miss Lucille. Mrs. Derby cleared her throat:

"If all the peoples was good they wouldn'a had to build no church. Our Lord an' Savior, Jesus Christ, wouldn'a had to die on no cross. They is —"

"But — " Rutherford tried to interrupt, but the others shushed him down.

"They is sinners! The world was *born* in sin. Some a the biggest sinners is sittin' right up there in the church. But that's — that's why we *need* a church!"

"A-men!" said Miss Jenny.

"That's all well an' good, Mrs. Derby," said Rutherford, "I ain' disputin' that. An' I believe that every man — e-v-e-r-y man — got the right to worship like he believes. But let me ask you somethin': What do you think was happenin' before there ever was a church?"

"You gittin' deep now, Jack!" said T. C.

"That's dangerous talk, Rutherford," said Viola seriously.

"Life *is* dangerous! An' the truth is dangerous! That's why ever'body's sayin' one thing an' doin' somethin' else!"

"How does he know?"

"But they is a church!" Mrs. Derby was saying: "Man is born in darkness, an' the Good Book brought the light!"

"There was people before there was a Bible!"

"But there wasn' *nobody* before the Lord!" said Miss Jenny.

"Goddamn! She got you there, Rutherford!" T. C. shouted. "Aw . . . excuse me, Miss Jenny."

"Got who?" Rutherford retaliated: "What about all them Cath'lics an'-an' Jews! People in Africa — an' China an' them. They goin' to hell just 'cause they ain' Baptists? Now, I don' care what other people think. The church is a good thing — if a man believe in it — an' try hard to do the right thing. But I don' believe that no man kin be saved by just goin' to church! An'-an' if God *is* God, He gotta be God for ever'body! E-v-e-r'-b-o-d-y! An' to tell you the honest truth, I don' know — don' nobody actually know — what really happened before man came to the earth. You know they got people — scientists an'stuff like that — that don' do nothin' but dig up old bones an' rocks an' things tryin' to find out what happened. An' they say that man comes from a monkey!"

"I knowed you wasn' nothin' but a monkey all the time, Jonsie!" said Miss Lucille. "An' I know what you gonna do when the deal goes down.

Just like ever'body else! You gonna fall down on your black knees an' ask
that jackleg preacher to pray for your black soul!"

"I'll go to hell first!"

"Don' talk like that, Rutherford!" said Viola in a frightened voice.

"You gittin' too deep now, man!" said T. C.

"If I don' mean it," Rutherford declared, *"I'll take a bloody oath on my
momma!"*

"Rutherford!" Viola cried.

Sea-song poured into the gulf of silence.

"Fourth!" Amerigo said absentmindedly.

"What *you* talkin' about, li'l niggah?" said Rutherford.

"T. C. said I'll be in the fifth grade next year. I'll be in the fourth!"

"What's that got to do with the price of tamadas!"

The fourth grade, he thought, embarrassed by the upsurgence of a wave
of pride in and love for his father.

"I took ever'thin' apart . . ." he heard him say, *"an' I remembered where
it went. An' then I cleaned what was dirty, an' replaced what was worn
out. An' then I put it all back together agin. An' I polished it till it looked
like new!"*

The words faded away, and he gradually became absorbed in a large and
transient mood filled with images of falling stars and generals with big
mustaches and armies in the brown part of the Sunday paper — of Franklin
Delano Roosevelt who might one day be able to stop the fireflies from flitting in and out of the massive shadows of the cottonwood tree. If anybody
could keep the globules of corrugated light from cutting the houses into
segments of light and shadow that trembled when the streetcar rumbled
down the avenue upon the soft fuzzy surface of Viola's new fox furs that
were dead. . . .

He managed to catch a glimpse of Old Jake's horny feet and long dangling neck, just before . . .

"AW-LAWD!"

A horrific scream burst from the dark bosom of the tree towering above
Sammy's house.

"What's that?" cried Miss Lucille, "It ain' Sad'dy night *yet!*"

The all looked into the bosom of the tree.

"Sounds like —" Miss Derby began.

"AW-LAWD!"

"That's Mrs. Sales!" said Viola. "At least it sure *sounds* like it!"

Sammy's grandma, he thought, recalling the image of the tall yellow worried-looking woman shuffling up and down the porch stairs, talking to herself in a high-pitched whining voice.

"What the hell's goin' on?" shouted Mr. Dan, the foot of his pegleg emerging from the shadows of Mrs. Shields's porch.

Meanwhile all the windows and porches were suddenly filled with curious whispering people who gradually, cautiously stole into the alley and peered through Mrs. Shields's gate at the disheveled figure that stood in the door on the upper story of the house.

"MAH BABY! MAH BABY!" she screamed, hugging her large bosom and rubbing her stomach.

Like she has to go to the toilet, Amerigo thought.

"AW LAWD! LAWD, HAVE MERCY!"

"She's just drunk!" cried Mr. Mun from downstairs.

"Naw, she ain'," said Miss Anna in a grave quiet voice. She moved toward Mrs. Shields's gate and the crowd burst into the yard. Amerigo made a dash for the alley.

"Git back up here!" Rutherford commanded.

"SOMEBODY CALL A DOCTOR!" yelled Miss Pearl, who at this minute stepped out onto the Sales's porch.

"What's the matter?" asked Miss Emma.

"This child's done gone an' killed 'erself!"

"My Gawd!" Mr. Everett exclaimed.

"How, Pearl?" asked Mrs. Shields.

"She took poison, Momma, a whole half a can!"

"She took poison!" whispered the spectators.

"Poison?"

"What kind a old poison?"

"Lye, honey!"

"Aw-aw!" said Rutherford.

"Doctor ain' gonna do'er no good!" said Miss Jenny.

Pray, Amerigo thought.

"Ain' that a cryin' shame!" said Viola.

"Lawd a mercy!" sighed Mrs. Derby.

"That lye's tough!" said T. C. "that's what we use down at the station to clean out them big drains when they git all stopped up! An' I mean, it eats up e-v-e-r-y-thing!"

The sound of a siren turning down Charlotte Street stirred a new wave of excitement. He imagined the big ambulance stopping in front of the house, and the two black men who took the stretcher from the back and rushed up the stairs, and came slowly back down, staggering under the

weight of their burden covered with a blanket. He managed to catch sight
of the big scarf tied around its head, and the eyes staring up toward the sky,
and the feet wrapped in gunnysacks, cold, hungry, alone, just before they
slid it in.

The ambulance drove away. He stared at the crowd of heads bobbling in
the light streaming from the door of the dead woman's room.

Fireflies! he thought.

Another siren pierced the noisy din.

"A nigger done it!"

"Git back! Git back!" A white man's voice, immediately followed by the
sound of the rumble of feet stamping down the stairs.

And suddenly there was a host of shadowy figures clothed in a motley
array of colorful costumes: bathrobes, underskirts, shirtless, barefoot,
some completely dressed from head to foot. They streamed out of the yard
into the alley, under the corrugated light that cut them into fragments of
light and shadow, causing them to exclaim in awed tones:

"I wonder what could have made 'er do a thing like that?"

"Maybe 'cause 'er old man left 'er!"

"Wasn' no good, no how! I wouldn' kill *myself* over *no* man!"

"You don' know what you'd do if your love come down!"

"Men — is just like streetcars, honey: There's one comin' e-v-e-r-y minute
or so! Hey! hey!"

"It wasn' that," said Miss Anna.

"What was it then?" asked Mr. Mun.

"I don' exactly know. She been sick for a long time. Can't find no work.
Couldn' work if she did. Times is hard! Poor baby. She had the blues, I
guess."

"Well, maybe you right, I ain' disputin' that. But they gonna have to *kill
me* before *I* die! I ain' gonna give up till my corns stop achin'!"

"You gonna live as long as Ma-thus-a-la! Hee! hee!"

"Me, too!"

"You sure said *that* right!"

"When the Lord call you, you got to come," said a quiet voice from the
shadows of the porch.

"But He don' tell you what train to catch, Momma."

Behind Miss Jenny's silhouette stood the thick wavering form of Miss
Fanny, barely visible against the faint light from the coal oil lamp that
glowed softly behind her.

"How you feel, baby?" Miss Jenny asked.

"Evenin'," said Mrs. Derby.

"Evenin'," said Rutherford, Viola, Miss Lucille.

"How you doin'?" T. C. asked in a husky voice.

"How you feel, baby?"

"I feel the same, Momma. Just the same."

"You better lie back down before you catch your death."

"Was Pliney here?" asked the sick woman.

"Naw," said Miss Jenny, "not chet. But he'll come. He'll come."

Miss Jenny rose and entered the house. She closed the screen door softly. From within they heard soft, patient, motherly sounds. Finally the light faded from the lamp and gave way to a silence still charged with the rumors of war:

"*Boom! Boom! Boom! Boom!*" popping and flashing in bursts of fire that flew from the dark-bosomed tree where the fireflies flickered.

Her name was Jessy, he thought.

"It's about your bedtime, ain' it?" said Viola.

He looked into the strange woman's face. "You have to git up early in the mornin'. Tamarra's your big day!"

"What's happenin'?" T. C. asked.

"He's goin' to the art gallery to git some art appreciation!" Rutherford said mockingly.

"Art what?" said Miss Lucille. He could see her grinning in the dark.

"They didn' have jive like that when *we* was in school," said T. C. "Ain' that somethin'! Well, I know my boy here's gonna learn it, if they's somethin' to learn. Walk away with a-l-l that high-powered stuff! Mingle among the best of 'um, Jack! Show the whities who we are. What we kin do if we have half a chance!"

"Better teach that little darkie to earn a loaf a bread!" said Miss Lucille tartly. "Fill his head up with all that kind a stuff an' then send him back down here to this slum to hustle pennies on street corners!"

An unspeakable rage filled his consciousness while familiar voices now filled the channels of his ears:

"I'm gonna be a doctor when *I* git big!" said Carl. "They make a lot a money, man!"

"Aahahahahah'm gonna be a be a . . ."

"What you gonna be, niggah?" cried William mockingly.

"I know what I'm gonna be, too! be, too!"

"*I'm* gonna be a big-shot politician!" said Turner. "Tell you niggahs what to do! Take in all the money, Jack!"

"Aw-man," Tommy declared, "*you* can't be no politician! Who's gonna vote for a colored man?"

"Don' *need* no votes if you work with the mob! Did you see *Scar Face*? You see how *that* cat got started? Eh-eh-eh-eh-eh-eh-eh! Machine gun, Jack!"

"You crazy!" Tommy said.

"I'm gonna be a tailor," said William.

"You know what I'm gonna be?" Tommy asked.

"What?" they answered in chorus.

"A artist." He withdrew a piece of paper from his pocket, unfolded it and showed it to the others.

"Looka there —" Lem cried, grabbing it and holding it up to the street-light. "That's Momma! Looks just like 'er, too!"

She's dead, he thought.

"I bet you can't draw *me!*" he challenged Tommy.

"Bet you I *kin!*"

Tommy turned the paper over, placed it on a piece of cardboard that he found in the alley, and began to draw furiously. After a few minutes he handed the paper to him:

"Look at *that,* man!"

"Looks just like that cat!" Turner said.

"Aw naw, it don'!" he cried, scowling at the big-eyed face on the paper.

"Aw *yeah* it *does!*" said William. "Who's that, man?" he asked Willie Joe, who'd just came up the hill.

"'Mer'go . . ."

"What you gonna be?" Tommy asked, "You're so smart!"

A prince! he thought, A king! The smartest man in the w-h-o-l-e world! The president of the United States of America. A preacher, teacher. He looked at the sky, and then at the trees: "I'm gonna be a symphony leader! With a hundred — two hundred — with a million trumpets an' things! — with *me* doin' the leadin'."

"Aw man — you crazy!" Turner exclaimed.

"Haw! haw! haw!" Lem laughed so hard he almost fell off the porch banister.

"I'm gonna do it, too!"

"Yeah —" Tommy said, "in the municipal auditorium! Downtown, Jack!"

"Aw naw! I'm gonna go in France an' places like that, like Ira Eldridge an' —"

"Who's that?" Tommy asked.

"Don't you know who that is, man? You don' know nothin'!"

"Who was he, smarty!" Tommy asked.

"He was a Negro! A actor! An' he never was no slave, neither! An' he went all over the world actin' on the stage — an' ate with kings an' queens an' princes an' things like that!"

"When was that?" Turner asked.

"In slavery time."

"How could he be doin' it in *slavery time* — an' not be no *slave hisself,* niggah! Ho! ho! I got you! You kin sure tell 'um! A spook — actin' — in *slavery* time — gittin' booty from queens!"

"Tee-hee-hee-hee-hee-hee-hee-!" Willie Joe squealed.

"Yeah, he did, too! Niggah! It was Ne-groes that was free when all the other Ne-groes in the South was slaves! An'-an' he was like that. An' *I'm* gonna be one, *too!* Like old Paul Robeson, man! Only *I'm* gonna be the biggest! I'm gonna stand up there on that stage in a real tux, like Duke Ellington, with that little old white stick in my hand directin 'um *down!* Man, Let my hair grow reeeeeeal long! So it kin fall in my face, like it does old Chikoffski in the show!"

"How your nappy hair gonna fall in your face, niggah?" Turner shouted. "You better slick that moss down with some Murray's!"

"I don' care. An'-an' the people — big shots! — all over the whole world! — millions of 'um'll be clappin' an' clappin'!"

"Let's give 'im the claps, men!" cried Turner:

"Clap! clap! clap! clap! clap! clap!" They laughed and yelled, while he bowed deeply, again and again, his hair falling into his face, like Chikoffski in the show.

Gradually the uproar subsided. In the thoughtful pause that followed a small voice said:

"*I* wanna be a *shoeshine* boy!"

They all stared into the face of Willie Joe.

". . . hustlin' pennies on street corners!" Miss Lucille was saying.

"You ain' *my* momma!" he cried, surprised by the tears that filled his eyes.

"That's right, 'Mer'go!" cried T. C. "Look out, Lucille! This boy's your even change! He's got more brains than you, me, an' his momma an' poppa put together! Don' let 'um hold you back, Amerigo. You go on out there an' look at them pictures like the rest of 'um. That's where the white man's gittin' his. Yes, sir! Mister Charlie don' like to see you readin', or sittin' quiet-like, thinkin' about somethin'. He likes to see you laughin' an' full a booze! 'Fraid you might learn somethin' *he* don' know! Them high-society niggahs know it! They sendin' they kids to learn all that stuff . . . all that high-powered music. Like — what's 'er name? What's the name a that *tough* little girl — s-m-a-r-t! always givin' 'em piana recitals all the time. . . . Ain' no older'n Amerigo. . . ."

C-O-S-I-M-A, he thought. Funny name.

"You mean Cosima Thornton," said Viola.

"I guess that's her. Her old man's got that photography shop over on

Eighteenth Street. Looks like a whitie. The momma t —"

"Cosima Thornton," said Viola. "Allie knows 'um. Doris has been dancin' with 'um a long time."

"How *is* old Allie?" T. C. asked. "I ain' seen that gal in a coon's age! She's a cute li'l sleepy-eyed gal!"

"Her brains is 'sleep, too!" chuckled Miss Lucille.

"She's all right," said Viola. "Just the same as ever. Worryin' 'erself over Doris . . ."

"Yeah, well . . ." said T. C., picking up his thought: "All them. An' them big-shot doctors and lawyers out south. You got to have *class* these days! Even the preachers is gittin' hip. Ain' no more a that bein' *called* crap — an' openin' up a storefront with a few hus'lers in the choir! Naw naw! Them days is goin'. Am I right, Rutherford?"

"Right as rain!"

"Yes sir! Now you got to be educated! Got to put-that-jive-on-the-line! Without all that jumpin' an' shoutin'. These new little niggahs like 'Mer'go want talkin' — lecturin' — to!"

"Lawd! You young 'uns sure got problems, ain't you!" Mrs. Derby exclaimed in a quietly mocking tone, shooting an invisible stream of snuff juice into a can filled with water that stood beside her chair.

"Amerigo's gonna be the president!" said Rutherford with a sly grin. "What's that got to do with art? That little niggah'd better be studyin' how to keep his poppa out a war!"

Boom! Boom! Boom! Boom! echoed the volleys of war throughout the porous red room . . .

"Well, so long, Jackson!" T. C. was saying.

"So long, man. Take it easy!" Rutherford replied.

"I got to do it, man!"

"Wait a minute there, Thomas C.," said Miss Lucille. "I'll walk you a piece."

"Take it easy, there," said Viola.

"So long, Vi!" said T. C. "We'll have to open up a keg a nails agin soon!"

"Unh! — will you listen to that joker!" Rutherford exclaimed. "We prob'ly won' see this cat no more till doomsday!"

"Bye!"

"Bye . . ."

"S'long . . ."

In the darkness of the middle room Rutherford was saying:

"Like I was saying . . . I want you to look —"

"Sssssh!" whispered Viola, "he'll hear you."

"I want you to look —"

"AW — LAWD!" shrieked a woman's disheveled voice.

"passed away at four A.M."

"Sssssh!"

"I want you to —"

Pray.

"— look nice just as much as *you* do. But here we are scufflin' an' scrapin' to barely git by, to have somethin' to eat an' a roof over our head. People barely kin work agin an' *you,* buyin' furs! Shit! You scare me to death! No kiddin'! For me to do somethin', I have to think about it a long time. An' then I'm half scaired somethin'll go wrong! But *you!* You do the impossible just like it was the most natural thing in the world!" Silence. Then: "Nobody, nobody in his right mind'd buy fox furs on what we make. E-v-e-r since I kin remember I been payin' for livin' I done already done! Or borrowin' for the livin' I'm doin'! Just as soon as we git one bill paid — I'll be damned if you don' go an' put the man's hand in our pocket *agin!*"

"I'll be payin' most of it myself!" Viola whispered. "I *know* you can't afford to buy all the nice things that other women have on the sal'ry you make. That's why I work! So that you an' me an' the baby — all of us — kin have some a the things we couldn' have otherwise. If we waited till we *could* afford somethin' we never would buy somethin' new! At least we kin have ever'thing the rest of 'um have — an' — an' git a little fun out a life!"

"What I care what the rest of 'um have!"

"Sssssssh!"

"*Be damned* what the rest of 'um have! It'd be different if we was borrowin' money to pay for somethin' to eat. But for *furs!*"

Pray.

Now I lay me down to *Boom!* . . . I pray the Lord my soul to *Boom!* . . . If I should die before I *Boom!* . . . I pray the Lord my soul to *Boom!*

He stifled the booming cannon throbbing between his legs with his fist, and disappeared shamefully into the total obscurity of the black room.

"Mister President?"

He stirred sluggishly.

"President Jones! Let's git up an' git with it! It's time to git ready to go to the art gallery an' learn all about how to run the country. Now listen! You awake!"

"Yessir."

"All right. Now I heated some water for you, an' laid out your clothes. I want you to git up an' wash your face an' hands good. An' don' forgit your neck! An' put on your clean underwear an' your white shirt, your Sund'y shoes. I done already shined 'um for you. Here's the quarter for the bus an' four bits to keep in your pocket — in case you have to buy somethin'.

"I know you gonna act like a gen'leman an' listen good to all they tellin' you, so I don' have to tell you that. Ah got to go now, so have a nice time an' take it easy, you heah?"

"Yessir," he nodded from the side of the bed, watching his father go through the door. He leaned out the window and watched him start up the alley, taking long strides through the deep snow. He tried to discover his tracks, but the burnished cobblestones yielded not a sign.

He tiptoed into the middle room and crawled into bed beside his mother.

"Uhm," she grunted irritably, opened her eyes, and looked at him.

He turned restlessly on his back.

"I'm gonna make you git up in a minute!" said Viola.

He looked at the Indian maiden upside down, at the disciples sitting around Jesus in the picture over the bed. Their figures were elongated, and their heads rested on the bottom of the picture frame, while their outstretched hands seemed to push the table against the ceiling.

He turned on his side in order to have a look sideways. The weight of his shoulder pressed against Viola's arm.

"Git up now!" she commanded. "Shoot! You too big for this jive. You ain' no baby no more!"

He lay very still.

"Boy?"

The word echoed throughout his consciousness:

"I'm a *boy!*" He carefully stretched himself out to his full length until his toes touched his mother's toes!

"What time is it?" asked Viola, suddenly sitting up in bed. The shoulder strap of her nightgown fell off her shoulder and exposed her left breast. "You better git out a this bed. You got things to do!" She adjusted her shoulder strap.

He stood in the kitchen door, facing the brilliant bar of oblique sunlight alone. The streetcar ground hotly up the avenue. She's at work now, he thought, and tried to discover within the shady depths of the elm trees in Miss Minnie's yard the big rich apartment building with the big red neon sign burning the word B-I-A-R-R-I-T-Z into a night sky filled with falling snow.

The art gallery! A sudden spark of happiness flickered in his mind. The great building loomed up out of the darkness. The brittle snow crunched beneath his feet, as he spread the thick lather of soap upon his face and neck.

That's the prettiest house in the whole world! He put on his fresh white shirt, and then the iron-pressed trousers of his Sunday suit.

"An' don' forgit to grease your legs!" he heard Viola say just before she dashed out the door. "You don' want your legs lookin' all rusty!"

He rubbed Vaseline on his legs, and then put on his shoes and socks. He combed and brushed his hair three times, slicked it down with Murray's, and put Rutherford's stocking cap on and made a knot in the back and rolled it up till it fit his head real tight, the way Rutherford did. After he had finished his Post Toasties, he took the skullcap off and admired the tiny wavelets of hair that rippled over his skull in the front room mirror. Then he carefully put on his cap, cocked it on the side the way Rutherford had showed him, the way it was in the photograph in the album where at age three he stood beside Rutherford dressed in a light tweed double-breasted overcoat and cap just like his father's. He stared his face out of focus in an effort to measure the time since he was three. It resounded deftly within the vast dark gray regions of memory in a volley of colorful explosions, in bursts of black and white interspersed with big red numbers: Nine! Eight! Seven! Six! Five! Four! Three! *Boooooom! BOOMmmmmmmm! BOOOOOOOOOMMMMMM!*

"Boy!" Viola had exclaimed.

He stepped out the door into the sunlight that flooded the front porch, over the clean spot where . . . He unconsciously looked at it, even though it was gone. Under the spell of a strange elated feeling he descended the stair and made his way through the cellarlike coolness of the shoot. . . .

He swaggered proudly up the avenue, carefully avoiding the rocks and bottles and tin cans. Tommy and the others were half a block ahead of him. They called out to him, but he pretended not to hear. He walked alone.

"Look at that s-h-a-r-p little niggah!" said Mr. Hicks who used to sell popcorn at the show, just as he passed the big frame house where Aunt Pearl. . . . He walked straighter and held his head higher, unconsciously obeying Viola's admonition to: "Hold your head up an' walk like a man!"

"Hi, Tony!" said Miss Mamie.

She goes with dago-Sam at The Blue Moon.

"Mornin', Miss Mamie!" He tipped his cap.

"Ain' that nice! A *real* gen'leman!" she exclaimed to a passerby, a tall tawny red-eyed man with greasy overalls looking about him as though he had lost something. He looked distractedly at Amerigo for an instant, scratching his uncombed head with a huge dirty hand, and then continued his search — somewhere down between the cracks in the dirty asphalt street.

Just as he reached Troost Avenue a boy about his own age and dressed up as he walked awkwardly down the hill, as though he felt a little uncomfortable in his Sunday suit on a Friday morning.

That's the new boy.

"H-h-h-hi!" he smiled a broad smile, bearing a set of white rabbit teeth, which exaggerated the size of his mouth, so that his round peanut head seemed too small and his skinny neck too long.

Listen to that little niggah stutter! he exclaimed to himself, barely able to suppress the impulse to laugh. He eyed the big black mole over his upper lip. His name was Isaac. Amerigo was warmed by his sincere, anxious, and somewhat fearful smile. Something about Isaac reminded him of Toodle-lum, and yet he was different. He studied his impression, as Isaac drew nearer, remembering the first time he had seen him, last First Sunday when he had joined the church with his mother. Her name's Mona . . . moan.

"A be-u-ti-ful black woman, I wanna tell you!" he heard Rutherford exclaim. "Like a African queen! An' dig-na-fied, Jack!"

"Come on," Amerigo said.

"O-o-o-o-kay," said Isaac greatfully.

They marched together up the avenue until they came to the corner of Independence Avenue and Pacific Street, where they joined the unavoidable stream of children bound for school. . . .

"Mom?" Viola was just stepping into the kitchen that evening.

"Hi, baby!"

"Mom? Kin-I-go-to-the-show? Tommyan'Turneran'them's goin' . . ."

"Ain't you forgot somethin'?"

"No'm."

"Seems to me you have."

"What?"

"You done got to be such a big shot that you can't say good evenin' to somebody when they speak to you? I see the art gallery ain' improved your manners a bit!"

"No'm." He fidgeted uneasily on the orange crate.

"No'm — what!"

"Evenin'."

"That's better."

"Kin I go?"

"I don' know 'bout you goin' all the way down on Twelfth Street at night. Better wait till your daddy comes home an' ask him."

"But Mom!"

"You heard what I said! I don' want to have to tell you agin. What's come over you this evenin'? Well, how did it go!"

"What?"

"What! Boy!"

Boy.

"Boy! *I* believe you losin' your black mind! The *art* gallery! You went, didn't you?"

"Yes'm."

"Better take off them clothes before you git 'um dirty."

He moved dreamily through the kitchen, apparently oblivious to the woman who stood at the drainboard taking groceries out of a brown paper sack.

"An' hurry up! Your daddy'll be home in a minute. An' straighten up that front room. It looks a mess! I don' know what's got into you taday. . . . the house all dirty . . . an' look at these dishes! Standin' all over the table!"

He made his way into the middle room where the sun lay aslant the bed. He absentmindedly took off his clothes and hung them up and put on his everyday pants and shoes and shirt, and then proceeded to straighten up the front room, and then the middle room. He was just putting the dust mop away when the front door banged.

"Boom!"

"All-*right,* Viola Jones!" Rutherford exclaimed as he strode into the house. "Them white folks like to *killed* me ta*day,* you hear me! How's the president!" Amerigo smiled at him, and he looked at his father with the eyes of a stranger as he stepped into the kitchen.

"I don' know *how* he is!" said Viola. "Must be excited, I guess. I haven' been able to git a word out of 'im. Come home an' the house's all dirty — that ain' like him at *all!* If *that's* what art's gonna do to 'im, he better stay home from now on!"

"Unh!" Rutherford exclaimed: "What happened, Pres?" He rolled up his sleeves in order to wash his hands.

"Nothin'."

"*Nothin'!* You go way out to the art gallery — such a high-class joint — minglin' with all the whities an' all you kin say is nothin'? Did you have a good time?"

"Yessir."

Rutherford dried his hands. Viola poured the hash into the bowl and set the steaming biscuits on the table.

"Take the tea out a the icebox, babe," she said to Rutherford, and when he had placed it on the table they sat down.

"Well, how many of you went?" Rutherford asked.

"Just our class an' Miss Fortman, on a big bus all to ourself. An' we didn' go the way the streetcar goes, we went another way till we got to the station, an' then we kept straight on out till we got to the end of the Troose line an' then turned in a street for a while an' then up a path till we come to the art gallery. An', Dad, kin I go to the show? Tommyan'Turneran'em's goin'. Mom said I kin if it's all right with you?"

"What that got to do with *art?*"

"Aw Dad, kin I?"

"I said it's up to you —" said Viola to Rutherford, "but I ain' too hot on him goin' all the way down on Twelfth Street all by hisself with a bunch a little ragamuffins."

"Aw, Viola, that ain' no place to go! When *I* was that little joker's age I could go to the end of the *world* by myself!"

He ate halfheartedly, picking at the strange food on the plate with the faded blue flowers. He stared at the chip on the edge where he had banged it against the sink, and suddenly the fork felt strange in his hand. He sipped his iced tea. His head back, his eyes wide open, he stared past the vague oval form that was his father's head through the screen door beyond which lay the amber evening. It made the red bricks of the houses look velvet, and the whiteness of Mrs. Crippa's porch look silver where the huge angular shadow from Miss Minnie's house cut a deep wedge into the upper story, while the creamy-white globe of light shining through her kitchen curtain took on the appearance of a little ". . . moon! When it's reeeeeal big and a real thin cloud goes over it. Like angel hair on the Chris'mas tree when . . ."

He squinted at his mother. She ate quietly, thoughtfully. . . . Painted! . . . A sudden unconscious curiosity caused him to scoop up a fork full of hash to see if it were real. He smiled with some secret satisfaction — secret even to himself — as the hot lavalike mass slid down his throat. He washed it down with a swig of tea-colored paint wondering if it made the inside of his stomach brown. Suddenly he realized that the sausage-shaped excrement that plumeted into the water in the toilet stool was . . . brown! . . . and reveled in the observation that the excrements of dogs and cats and horses were brown, even when they ate yellowan'redan'white . . . an' greenan'blue! He sucked the air into his mouth to see if he could taste the blue color! The red of the setting sun, the greenredan'purple of the vegetables in Mrs. Crippa's garden. He chewed the particolored flowers spangling Viola's dress!

"What in the *world* are you doin', boy!" Viola asked.

He tried to taste the orange, sun-hot, brown-edged, ripe-peach color of her voice.

"Boy!" Rutherford shouted.

Gold! he thought, a split instant before he caught his breath and stared wildly at the hairy-faced man who fixed him with an imperative stare. He sank into an obscure cool-blue silence.

"I sure don' see why you need to go to no movies, no way —" said Viola, "the way you dream all the time!"

Red! The thick color filled his eyes and coursed hotly down his cheeks.

"What's the matter, baby?" said Viola.

A storm of color flashed through his mind. He began to tremble.

"Maybe he's sick!" said Rutherford.

The soft fudge-brown pressure of Viola's palm upon his forehead.

"He ain' got no fever. How you feel, honey?"

Yellow and . . . Nothin' — he whispered hoarsely.

"Ever see somethin' like that?" Rutherford asked. "Just *look* at that li'l niggah an' he breaks out in a flood a tears! Babe, you better let that cat go to the show before he washes us all away an' I can't read my paper — an' I'll be maaaaad!" He scooted his chair away from the table. "What they showin', Pres?"

"*The Revenge of Zorro!*"

"*The Revenge of Zorro!* That cat's been re-vengin' for forty years! No kiddin'! Amerigo, I remember that joker when I was just a li'l bitty boy!"

I'm a boy! Blue . . . blow your . . .

"That was a good 'un, Vi . . ." Rutherford was saying. "You must a put your finger in the hash tonight."

Viola smiled distractedly at Rutherford, and then cast a worried glance at him.

"Maybe you'd better stay home, hon, an' go to the show tamarra night."

"Aaaaaaw — Mom!"

"Let him go!" said Rutherford. "It ain' gonna hurt 'im. Besides," he said from the middle room, "I don' wanna git flooded out a my house!"

Next time it'll be by fire! he thought.

"Got somethin' to show you niggahs!" said Turner as they headed out Eleventh Street. His eyes twinkled mischievously as he sucked on the matchstick that dangled recklessly from the corner of his mouth.

"What?" asked Willie Joe.

"It ain' nothin' for you, little niggah!" said Turner. "You too little!"

"I ain' too little!" cried Lem.

"Huh! You ain' nothin' but six years old!" said Tommy to his little brother.

"Aaaaah'm eight! Eight!" said Toodle-lum.

"I'm the oldest!" said Tommy.

"Me an' you an' Carl!" said Turner. "The rest a them niggahs's too little. To go where *I'm* talkin' 'bout you got to run fast — make a quick git-away!"

"Me, too, me, too," said Toodle-lum.

"Aw, niggah, you can't run!" William declared.

"*I'm* the fastest!" said Amerigo.

"Think we oughtta let that li'l niggah come, man?" said Turner to Tommy.

"Where?" asked Willie Joe.

"*I'm comin', too,*" cried William. "You ain' gonna leave *me* behind! I'll tell *Tom!*"

His eyes filled with tears and the corners of his mouth turned down just as they reached the corner of Eleventh and Forest Avenue. They waited for the light to change, and then they headed toward Tracy. Just as they neared the corner Turner whispered something in Tommy's ear, which they giggled at secretly.

"I'm gonna *tell!*" William screamed. "You just wait an' *see* if I don'!" Tears washed down his face, which contorted into a mass of reddish brown clay while a stream of blue-green-grayish snot oozed from his left nostril and blunt sucked peppermint-white teeth protruded from tomato-red gums framed by fleshy lips the color of wet inner tubes.

"I'm gonna tell — you just wait an' see if I don'!" he was saying, while the others grinned at him. Willie Joe walked nearest.

"W-H-A-P!" William slapped him upside the head.

"Don't you laugh at *me, niggah!*"

"WAAAAAAAAH!" screamed Willie Joe, his fudge-brown face breaking up into a mass of bulldog wrinkles, his eyes glistening wet starlike through squinting eyelids.

"Heh heh heh!" Turner laughed.

"You hit 'im agin an' I'll beat *your* head!" said Tommy. "I don' care if you *are* my brother! Pickin' on that little boy!"

"He ain' got no business *meddlin'* then! An' if *you* go somewhere, *I'm goin', too* — or else *I'm gonna tell Tom!*"

Meanwhile Amerigo searched the four corners of the converging streets for the bank, mentally reviewing the way they had come.

"Aw, it ain' no bank around here!" he said skeptically, looking ahead eastward.

Tommy and Turner laughed. Willie Joe wiped the tears from his eyes, while the two older boys gazed at the two-story apartment building on the northeast corner of the street opposite them: a dirty, dark, wine-red building. Three smooth stone steps led to a little porch that gave onto the entrance. Through the thick glass door he could see the inner hall and two of the three apartment doors. Discovering no signs of life he inspected the neighboring house, a one-story unpainted frame house where Negroes lived, with a little grassy yard swelling up in a soft mound that gave onto the porch on which there was a swing. It was empty, and the rusty-black door behind the rusty screen was shut.

After that came a weedy lot that swept up toward Tenth Street. He took it in with a glance — and then the boulevard.

Prettier than the boulevard at the top of the alley, he thought, but the boulevard at the top of the alley is bigger!

The after-supper traffic was heavy. Cars sped both north and south along the double lanes surrounding the bush-lined park, which extended from the great Admiral Boulevard down to Twelfth Street, where it was interrupted by the Twelfth Street car tracks, and continued on out south, as far as he could remember.

They ran through the park, playing cowboy and Indian, lingering here and there in order to steal a glance at the scantily dressed sleepers who lay huddled near the bushes in order to escape the summer heat, in groups, in pairs, or alone; on blankets or newspapers; surrounded by the random conversation, sighs, and giggles that burst intermittantly through the din of traffic.

Now they stood upon the great stone porch and looked down at the dazzling light that flitted noisily up and down Twelfth Street, swirving dizzily around the North End of the park opposite the porch. The porch had ornaments with geometric patterns of blooming flowers in a gaudy assortment of reds and whites, fragile yellows and blues, soft velvety purples and burnished browns.

Meanwhile the obsolete cannons in the park pointed their muzzles dangerously to the north. Volleys of flickering light exploded against the resisting darkness above and between the buildings and ricocheted against apartment windows and bombarded the proud stone porch itself.

Amerigo squinted his eyes, and the whirling globules of light from the street below swelled like raindrops on his eyelids. They dropped into the troubled darkness of the front room. The green light changed to red, and the tip of Rutherford's cigarette pulsed in angry worried flashes that converted his face into a mask silhouetted against the middle room window full of stars:

"Boy?" said Viola's voice:

"Boy? Boy? Boy?"

From every direction it came, converging upon his consciousness until he dissolved into the luminous exploding sound issuing from the still cannon.

"Boy?"

He stretched himself out to his full length and strained his ears and eyes in order to feel the unknown reaches beyond the luminous tenor of his mother's voice. He breathed in the hot smells of the summer night: sweat, dust, fried fish, chicken, barbecue, beer, gin, and whiskey exuded from cafés, bars, and restaurants and from the pores of the motley crowd of black, brown, and beige people who milled up and down the street adorned in the colors of flowers, of birds, of winter snows. Talking, laughing, singing — crying sunlight! — uttering crystal and rainbow, sea-blue and Christmas candy, bile-green and conscienceless-yellow, to the insistent beat of myriad feet and clapping hands.

He looked at the blazing marquee of the theater. A streetcar clanged down the street behind him, just as the strong seductive smell of popcorn filled his nostrils and his feet sank deep into the soft rug after he had pushed his money through the bottom — rectangular — hole of the glass cage where the pretty red-lipped woman sat, hair glistening with snow until shortly after the station when she disappeared into the darkness saturated with the articulate smells of starch, sweat, peppermint candy, Murray's hair pomade, freshly pressed trousers, talcum powder, chewing gum, shoe polish, and the exploding apparition of big red and black numbers flashing upon the Silver Screen.

BOOM!

"The comedy!" cried Turner. "Men, we're just in time!"

"Hot dog!" Amerigo cried, tearing the flap off his popcorn and stuffing his mouth full of the hot salty crisp butter-greasy starlike flakes.

"Gimme some," said a wet soggy little voice just beside him.

Black-and-white figures on the silver screen, reflecting on the foreheads, cheeks, chins, pupils of attentive eyes, and gold and silver crowns of bared teeth.

An African scene: bushes and grass and trees and vines.

An angry lion appeared.

"Gimme some,"

He looked into the starry eyes of Willie Joe and thought: This has happened before. His breath quickened to a sudden excitement that was so intense he had to divert his eyes to the screen.

Negroes in the bushes. Bones in their hair. Rings in their noses. Big white thick lips. Enormous white eyes. Enormous teeth: grinning grinning grinning grinning grinning grinn ingrinninginninginningin . . .

Drums beating: *Boom! Boom! Boom! Boom!*

"Gimme some . . ."

He stuffed another handful into his mouth.

"Look! The lion's comin'! The lion's comin'!" cried Toodle-lum with great excitement.

"We know it, man!" said Turner.

Boom! Boom! Boom! Boom!

Negroes in hair-raised white-frightened flight. White soles of big black flat feet flapping in the breeze.

An Englishman appears carrying a long rifle and wearing a monocle, helmet, and khaki pants, then shoots the lion in the behind. The lion gets angry:

"Grrrrrrrr!"

"Aw-aw!" Amerigo cries.

All the fright-white Negroes run into a grass hut.

The lion chases the Englishman, who runs after the Negroes, who tremble behind the door of the hut. The hut trembles.

The Englishman knocks on hut door: *Boom! Boom! Boom! Boom!*

The lion is getting closer.

"Aye say, eold man, ah you theah?" The Englishman inquires of the trembling Negroes in the hut, while the lion comes closer and closer until he is eating-close:

"GRRRRRRRRRR!"

He pounces upon the Englishman, pushes him through the door of the hut behind which the trembling Negroes cower. Now that the angry lion is in the hut, they are running and running — all of them — until they get smaller and smaller, the lion, too: smaller and smaller and smaller until they all disappear.

"Gimme some . . ."

Laughter in animate crystal flashes. Silhouetted heads bobble to and fro, from side to side, until a torch-bearing woman appears upon the screen with an American flag draped around her body real pretty-like. Like a statue at the art gallery! The interior of the great building fills his mind so completely that he forgets to spell out the big white letters that you can't rub off with your fingers that flash across the screen. The music swells around the pop and crack of a long black whip and Zorro, dressed in black with a mask, on a big white horse like Buck Jones's horse, Silver, rears up on his hind legs and leaps over a deep crevasse between two mountains and dashes toward the burning farmhouse where the pretty girl and her crippled old father are holding off an attack of rustlers aided by a horde of renegade Indians with a *Boom! Boom! Boom!* of rifle fire amid the swish and crack of gutting flames excited by the pounding of horse's hooves and arrow-hiss, blood-gush, bone-crush, knife plunge and tomahawk-thud!

And now the flaming wall is falling upon the pretty girl and her crippled old father. But fear not: Zorro, the Avenger —

"Aw-aw now!" cried William.

— is on the way!

"Will he arrive at the ill-fated scene in time to save Will Slokum and his pretty daughter, Mary, from the devouring flames?" cried a booming voice: "Chapter Four will reveal the exciting destiny of the friends of — ZORRO — THE AVENGER!"

"Hot dog!" Amerigo cried.

"I'm comin'!" said Carl.

"Me, too!" said William.

"Gimme some."

"Ain' no more, man!" he said irritably, thrusting the nearly empty box at Willie Joe as they filed out of the movie. They passed through the lobby ringed with bright light that for a moment hurt his eyes and obscured the edges of the shapes of things and people. After that his mind was overwhelmed by the strange clarity of the scene, the sounds and smells that mingled with the remembered image of Zorro dashing to the rescue of Will Slokum and his pretty daughter, Mary, cringing beneath the falling flaming wall.

A taxi swerved around the corner and sped up the boulevard toward Eleventh Street. A brown-skinned woman sat in the backseat. He had caught a glimpse of her thigh, and had discreetly diverted his glance, but then looked again, and had been too late. He followed the pulsating taillight to the top of the hill.

A profound excitement came over of him as they approached Eleventh Street. The night was quiet. They moved thoughtfully through the shadows of silent trees. As they were nearing the middle of the block, a car glided quietly by and hesitated, catlike, at the corner of Tracy Avenue, in front of the redbrick apartment house with the glass door. It slowly turned the corner and moved up toward Tenth Street. Then suddenly its headlights flung their shadows into the middle of Tracy Avenue just as they reached the apartment house. He went around the block, he thought, noticing that the car had stopped. The headlights went out, at which their elongated shadows disappeared from the street. The car door closed cautiously, and a white man with slick hair paused under the lamppost and lit a cigarette, looking carefully up and down the street as he did so, and then dashed into the building.

"All right, men, follow me!" said Turner in an excited whisper.

"Where?" asked Willie Joe.

"Sssssh! niggah!" cried Turner, poking him in the ribs with his elbow.

"That *hurts!*" said Willie Joe.

"I *told you* them li'l niggahs too little!" Turner cried in exasperation.

"For *what!*" William demanded. "*I* ain' too little for *nothin'!* An' if *you* goin', *I'm* goin', too!"

"Well, hush up then," said Turner. "Follow me an' do what I tell you."

They turned cautiously up Tracy Avenue and walked past the apartment house. The shades of all the windows facing the street were drawn, but pinpoints of rosy light appeared through the cracks. They stole up to Tenth Street.

"Wait a minute!" Turner whispered, watching a suspicious car roll down the street. Then he faced Eleventh Street and studied the windows and doors of the houses on both sides of the street.

"On your toes, men!" he whispered, "an' be ready to make a fast git-away!"

They came upon a parked car in the driveway that gave onto the back-yard of the apartment house.

"Cover that car!" Turner commanded softly. Willie Joe and Toodle-lum looked in the window.

"E-e-e-e-empty . . . empty," Toodle-lum whispered.

"Forward, men!" whispered Turner.

They stole into the yard. It was covered with cinders that cracked and squashed under their feet.

"Ssssssh!" said Turner.

Suddenly the back door of the apartment on the ground floor opened, flinging a bright yellow slant of light across the yard. They crouched breathlessly under the porch. Amerigo's heart pounded wildly, his eyes fixed upon the ominous shadow that emerged from the frame of yellow light. It had a long pointed head and a hooked nose. It looked out. Listened . . .

Sweat ran down Amerigo's face and tickled his nose. He started to scratch but stopped because the sound of his bitten-off fingernail against his sweating nose made too much noise.

The head disappeared and the light scudded back over the cinders into the house.

Total darkness.

Cricket-song!

"Sssssssss!" Turner whispered, nervously poking Tommy with his elbow.

"It ain' me, man!" said Tommy.

"What?" said Willie Joe.

"Sssssss!" Turner whispered, "you gonna git us *all* killed! Now come on an' be quiet!"

They crept into a little shoot four feet wide between the apartment and the house next door. Amerigo could see the parked car through the widely spaced boards of the narrow fence at the end of the shoot. He tried to remember if its owner had had a long head and a hooked nose. He stumbled over a can.

"God *damnit!*" Turner whined. "Be *careful*, you niggahs!"

"Wasn' none a me!" Lem whispered.

"Me neither!" said William

"Mmmmmme-me-me neither," Toodle-lum mumbled.

"Sssssst!" Turner touched Tommy's shoulder and Tommy stayed the others. They stood dead still. Faint rays of moonlight filtered over the roof of the neighboring house and filled the shoot with a subtle silvery blue light.

Turner signaled for them to move deeper into the shoot, to hug the wall of the apartment house in order to avoid the moonlight.

"Ssssssssh!" he hissed quietly, and came to a halt. He pointed to the two windows overhead. They looked into the bedrooms of the apartment. Their shades were drawn but there was a little space about an inch wide at the bottom of the one on the left and a little less at the bottom of the other one. They were both filled with rosy light.

Turner and Tommy who were the tallest merely stood on their toes, gripped the sill with their fingers, and stared excitedly through the crack. He tried to squeeze in between them but he was too short. Lem, Willie Joe, and Toodle-lum who were even shorter tried to scramble up the backs of Turner and Tommy who poked them irritably with their elbows and continued to fix their attention upon the rosy slit at the bottom of the window.

Meanwhile he discovered three half bricks on the ground, which he stacked one on top of the other, and then stood up on them, on the tips of his toes, so that, straining every muscle, as it were, he was barely able to see, over the tip of his nose, through the tiny aperture. His eyes widened and all his senses took in the rosy room filled with the huge bed covered with a white sheet. A soft, round, pink-skinned young woman with brown hair lay upon the bed with her legs spread apart, the right one drawn toward her chest. She supported herself with her elbow. She was looking up at the naked slick-haired man who stood looking down at her. Trembling. Sweating. Looking. She was smiling and her lips were moving. He could not hear what she was saying, but it sounded as though she were saying: "Now?"

The unheard word echoed within the chambers of his pounding heart. His body ached all over. *He* began to tremble. His sweating fingers were slipping from the sill. The bricks were slipping under his toes. Desperately he tried to secure his grasp. The woman began to squirm teasingly in the bed. Her smile deepened. Her lips parted and her tongue darted between her teeth. She drew her leg higher and repeated the unheard word.

He fell to the ground with a loud crash.

"Gaaaaaaaad daaam!" Turner cried, followed by the frightened scramble of a blind herd of stampeding feet crashing through the darkness, while he lay dazed at the foot of the window. With a dreamy detachment he watched the rosy border at the bottom of the window being pushed upward by a pink hand until it approximated the size of the window frame. A naked face and bosom, half submerged in shadow, stuck out of the window and looked toward the yard end of the shoot where the noise was coming from. Like the Africans in the show! he thought, but was suddenly horrified as her eyes swept down the shoot and looked right at him. Now he caught sight of the big gun she held in her right hand.

"Little black sons of bitches!" she cried angrily. She pulled the shade down until it reached the bottom of the window frame. He was plunged in silvery blue darkness.

She didn't see me! he thought, crouching on his hands and knees. He started to crawl toward the back of the house. Like the Indians. But now the back door opened and light sprawled across the entrance to the shoot. The figure of a man whose upper body was cut off by shadow shot a bright beam of light over his head and pinned him to the ground. He lay as though he were dead. The light flicked out. The door banged to, was bolted. Silence.

His face was wet with something that stank. Slowly, cautiously, he crawled through the filthy shoot, carefully avoiding the tin cans and broken bottles, hugging the shadows until he gained the street. Then he ran all the way home.

The violent yellow moon stared at him through the window of the front room. He closed his eyes and sank heavily into the black room.

Now?

He lay upon the big white bed with his legs drawn against his chest. A naked woman stood over him. She had a long whip in her hand.

"Touch the bottom rungs of the chair!" she commanded. *"Now!"*

He tried to scream when the whip bit into his flesh, but the sound stuck in his throat.

"Now!"

The whip descended again — and again. Welts rose upon his naked body. He tried to cry out, but his voice failed him. The pain found him no matter where he tried to hide, and veined his body, like a leaf pierced by a fiery constellation of stars.

"STOP!"

A purple-splotched face appeared.
"If you hit that boy *one more time, I'll . . ."*
He slipped into the warm ooze of an obscurely intense feeling of shame.

Saturday morning was a raw-yellow, noisy-blue morning. The sun stared knowingly through the window. He opened his eyes. Then he closed them and moved his head into the shade. He listened to the familiar noises that came from the kitchen and from the middle room where Viola lay, breathing three times more deeply than he.

"Hi Sonny!"

Rutherford stood over him. He pretended not to hear. Rutherford stepped out the door. He lay still and waited for Viola to wake up.

She woke up, sat on the side of the bed, and yawned. She looked at him. He clamped his eyes tight. She tiptoed barefoot to the toilet. She brushed her teeth and washed her face and combed her hair. Then she broke the beam of sunlight that stretched out toward him from the middle room window as she stepped behind the door in order to slip out of her gown and into her underwear, stockings, and finally her dress.

"S'long, babe," she said, as she slipped down the steps.

His eyelids quivered guiltily. He stirred, as though the sound of her voice had awakened him.

"Uhn . . . S'long."

Her footfall faded. He leaped out of bed and rushed to the toilet, and poured the remains of the hot water into the wash pan and scrubbed his face, arms, and legs. He stared curiously, guiltily, at the chalky white stuff that stained his thighs, which he could not rub away with his fingers.

It's in the bed, too! he said to himself as he covered the stain with the sheet. He straightened up the front room, the middle room, and the kitchen. Then he gulped down the oatmeal and milk his father had left him. He hurredly rinsed the breakfast dishes and stacked them on the drainboard. Seconds later he was dashing down the front steps.

He sprang up the alley and turned into the path behind Mr. Harris's old house. It stood next to Aunt Nancy's house, almost at the top of the alley.

"There's that cat!" Turner cried. "What happened, man?"

"Oooooo wow!" laughed Willie Joe, louder than all the others. "What happened to you maaan?"

"You niggahs run off an' left me, that's what!"

"I waited for you at the corner," said Tommy.

"Me, too!" said Carl.

"That's what *you* say!" he said.

"Didn' I, man?" said Tommy to Turner.

"Yeah, m-a-n," Turner replied. "But we couldn' wait all night. We was hot!"

"They catch you?" asked Willie Joe.

"You see I'm *here,* don't you! But m-a-n, that sure was close! Just as I fell I heard old Turner cuss, man —"

"Just as that cat was about to git that pussy!" said Turner.

"Yeah! An' then I heard you guys beatin' it through the shoot —"

"I was first!" said Tommy.

"But I was right on you, Jack!" said Turner.

"I was third," said William.

"Me, too!" said Willie Joe.

"What *you* mean, *me, too,* man?" said Turner. "Can't be but *one* third."

"I was really comin', though!" said Willie Joe.

"What was you doin' back there, 'Mer'go?" Tommy asked.

"Them old bricks fell down under me, an' the woman that was naked on the bed — man! She sure was pretty. All naked with *real* big titties — she stuck 'er head out the window an'pointed a g-r-e-a-t b-i-g f-o-r-t-y — f-i-v-e six shooter! at you niggahs. She was m-a-d! Man! Oooooooo-whee!"

"But we was hittin' 'um!" cried Turner.

"An' I was lyin' real real still in the shadows, man."

"Man, I bet you was s-c-a-i-r-d! Hee! hee!" Willie Joe laughed.

"Naw, I wasn' either!"

"Aw man, you *know* you was scaired, man!" said Turner.

"Shucks! You'd be scaired, too. That gun was b-i-g! She cocked it an' took aim, but you cats was *gone!*"

"Done cut out!" said Willie Joe with a grin.

"An' man! When she went to shut the window it looked like she was lookin' right *at* me. But I didn' move!"

"That little niggah *couldn'* move!" cried Turner. "He was scaired shitless!"

"An' when she shut that window an' pulled the shade down, man, I was just fixin' to run when the back door opened up. A big m-e-a-n-lookin' cat stuck his head in the shoot with a b-i-g flashlight in his hand. I couldn' see *what* he had in his other hand. An' he flashed it up and down."

"What did you do?" Tommy asked.

"He dug a tunnel in the ground!" Turner laughed, joined by Willie Joe and the others.

"I hugged the ground like a Indian, Jack!"

"Old Toodle-lum was last!" cried Willie Joe.

"Aw naw I wasn', neither! You wasn' in front a me, neither . . . neither . . ."

★

"Let's go, you guys!" said Tommy. They made their way up the hill to the rubbish pile behind Mr. Mose's yard where they immediately set to work examining empty cans for Libby labels.

"How many you got?" Carl asked Toodle-lum. Toodle-lum withdrew a bundle of labels from his pocket and they compared their bulk.

"I got the most!" cried Tommy, triumphantly showing his.

"I'm gonna git me a bike!" Amerigo said.

"Aw man, you can't git no bike with what you got," Tommy said, "you'd have to have a million of 'um!"

"Yes I *am!*"

"Aw man, you crazy!"

"I don' care."

"I'm gonna git me a BB gun," said Turner: "Eh-eh-eh-eh-eh-eh-eh-eh-!"

"Aw man, they don' have no BB machine guns!" said Tommy.

"Aw man, I know it. I'm just playin'."

"I want a huntin' knife!" said Tommy.

"That's sharp!" Carl exclaimed. "Me, too!"

"Me, too!" said Willie Joe.

"Looka there!" cried Lem, "I got one!" pouncing on a can with a rusty label with a picture of a cow on it. He carefully removed the label and added it to his roll.

Tommy found an electric bulb, which he burst, extracted the brass fitting, and dropped it into his gunnysack in order to sell it later at the junkyard.

They cut through Mr. Mose's shoot and descended upon Campbell Street, skirting the hill where they had a few skirmishes with the renegade Indians, and finally filtered down behind the row of apartments where the Italians lived, and onto Harrison Street. Through the raw-bright land that was Saturday morning, they searched for treasure: bottles for grasshoppers, june bugs, and ladybugs, fancy cigar boxes, oddly shaped cans, copper wire and brass, aluminum pots and pans, lead plumbing fixtures, milk bottles, wine jugs, anything they could sell to the junkman. They drifted down below Fourth Street, past the Field House and the ruins of the old Garrison school-house whose remains sprawled out under the towering Clairmount Hill. They gleaned all that was to be found in the lots on Third Street, and finally entered the wild entangled jungle that spread down around the railroad tracks. Beyond the tracks lay huge industrial barns and storage sheds and big dingy factories with huge dirty windows divided into little square panes,

some of which were broken, their big pipes spewing rusty water into the
great river.

Through the weed-encumbered paths they went, exploring the marshy
hollows for frogs, beating the bushes for snakes, cutting long dried stalks
of weeds to be used as weapons against inevitable danger.

Finally they climbed up to Cliff Drive, with its sweeping expanse of park
bedecked with tall fir trees. Like at Swope Park and the art gallery, he
thought, seeing the splendid array of trees and bushes that surrounded the
noble building.

"Look!" Tommy cried.

They all stared at the dead snake stretched out on the hot asphalt drive,
regretting that the speeding automobile had prevented them from taking it
alive!

They came to a clump of red-haw trees. They stuffed the miniature
apples into their pockets until they bulged. They bit into the sour-sweet
pulp of the tiny fruit and flung the cores at each other. They played marbles with them. They played war with them.

"*Boom!*" cried Turner, bouncing a red-haw on Willie Joe's head.

"*Boom!*" cried Willie Joe, discharging a barrage at Toodle-lum who
ducked agilely behind a blackberry bush. Amerigo plucked one but it tasted
sour.

"*The blacker the berry the sweeter the juice!*" said a voice.

"Look out for snakes, men!" Turner cried.

"What ol' snakes!" Lem cried, jumping back suspiciously.

"Black snakes! — that's what!" Tommy cried.

"I don' see no snakes!" Amerigo said, bravely raking the bushes with the
end of his spear.

"You will if one of 'um bite you!" said Tommy.

"I don' care."

They stood in front of the reservoir, staring at the cool clean water from
behind the thick wire screen attached to iron posts embedded in the surrounding low cement. From the center of the reservoir a fine spray of water
shot up into the sunny air.

"That's to clean the water!" said Tommy.

"*Man* — I'm sure hungry!" said Turner.

"Me, too!" said Willie Joe.

"Bet you I could eat all the pork chops in the world!" said Lem.

"Listen to that joker!" said Turner.

"I'll take the chicken, Jack!" said Tommy.

"I'll take the turkey!" Amerigo said.

"*Huh! I* want some a that chicken, too!" said William reproachfully.

"How you gonna have some if *I'm* gonna have it *a-l-l,* man," Tommy exclaimed.

"I'll tell Tom!" The corners of William's mouth dropped, his eyes filled with water.

"To the junkyard, men!" said Turner, staying William's tears.

"Let's go thataway!" said Tommy, "it's closer!"

"Aw — thisaway is closer, men!" Turner protested.

"You kin go thataway if you wanna," Tommy declared, "but *I'm* goin' thisaway!"

So Turner and his brother, Carl, and Willie Joe went thataway, while Tommy, his brothers William and Lem, Toodle-lum, and he went thisaway: through the strange yet familiar North End where Rutherford and Viola, T. C., Uncle Ruben — *Boom!* — Aunts Edna and Fanny and Ruth and Pearl and Nadine and Uncle Sexton and Grandpa Rex and Will and Grandma Sara and Veronica had gone before him:

"Man — we usta be death on cats!" said Rutherford's voice. He looked anxiously at the sky. He beheld the great hill in the distance. Its grassy summit jutted out into the burnished yellow light of the afternoon like a mountain.

"Clairmount Hill!" Tommy cried.

"Hey! hey!" Amerigo shouted.

"I *told'um* it was thisaway!" Tommy cried.

They walked on through dirt streets lined with weatherworn frame houses until they finally came to a sort of broad dirt square that gave onto the city dump, a great mound of rubbish and tin cans glistening in the sun. They scampered up the mountain of rubbish and finally reached the top, which gave onto the asphalt playground of the new Garrison School.

The playground was empty. They climbed over the rail and ran this way and that, screaming with a sudden burst of expansive joy, as though trying to occupy the whole playground all at once, as though they would fill it with the motley-colored sound of a throng of playing children.

Amerigo made a dash for the cement staircase that lead to the upper playground, casting a wary glance at the furnace room as he ascended, experiencing a dizzying sensation of relief as T. C.'s voice boomed out:

"How you like your new principal, 'Mer'go?"

Next year.

Sadly he scanned the empty window of the first-grade room for the melancholy purple-lipped smile of the "queen."

He looked at the windows of the fourth-grade room. That's Miss Fortman's room. He saw her large, handsome brown-skinned face smiling at him, her full bosom heaving with an exuberance that reminded him of Viola.

"Whee!" he cried, as he pushed the swing into the air, leaped in, tightened his grip on the heavy chains, and watched the asphalt swoop under his feet! The bright blue, endlessly blue sky filled his face, higher and deeper! — higher! and deeper! — until his feet swung up above his head and a sudden nervous jerk on the chains caused him to fall backward, grazing his shoulder against the iron stancheon that supported the swing.

"Whee!" He trembled with fear. "Whee!" relieved now that the swing was slowing down and the others were not looking.

"Come on, Amerigo!" cried Tommy, but he held on tight until the swinging stopped, until the ground stood still, and he rested safe in Old Jake's arms.

"Boom! Boom! Boom!" resounded the scurrying feet upon the asphalt pavement, heads bobbling behind the wall, moving up Pacific Street, his wobbly legs pursuing them.

"Come on, 'Mer'go!" cried William.

He caught up with them just as they reached the bakery side of the avenue.

They were staring through the window at the trays of jelly rolls, cinnamon rolls, sugar buns, cream puffs, fruit cakes, nut rolls, and butter rolls ranged along the shelves.

"Ohmmmmmmmm!" Willie Joe licked his lips and rubbed his belly.

"Come on, you guys!" Tommy urged, and they turned into the junkyard and spread the booty before the scrutinizing eye of the merchant.

"Forty-seven cents," said the man, digging into a leather purse with dirt-encrusted fingers. He was a tall skinny fairly young white man with friendly brown eyes. Amerigo stared at his long nose.

"Hot dog!" Tommy exclaimed.

Willie Joe got a nickel. Toodle-lum got a dime. William got thirteen cents, Lem four, Turner thirty-eight, and he thirty-six.

"I got the most!" cried Tommy proudly.

"That ain' nothin'!" said Amerigo.

"Come on!" said Willie Joe. They went to a nearby grocery store and each got a quart of cold milk. Then they went over to the bakery and bought a box of assorted two-day-old cakes. Then they crossed the street, climbed the little ravine of the hill until they reached the top, where they sat upon the yellow clay and enjoyed the spoils of conquest. The cold milk sloshed down their hot dry throats and spilled down their chins, as their wide vacant eyes stared into the blue heavens. They bit into the firm sugar-crusted cakes that made their hands and mouths sticky with icing and with jelly. . . .

Meanwhile life hummed quietly, indifferently in the street below.

I hope it never changes! he thought, remembering the milk bottles that Miss Minnie had promised him, the nickel that he would collect from Miss

Lucille for going to the store, the sixty cents he had earned delivering relief groceries in the Western Flyer.

As he was hoping that it would never change, he perceived a faint amber tinge in the rays of sunlight that diffused throughout the afternoon, as they slowly walked home through the avenue that stirred with a subtle nervous agitation at the prospect of another week coming to its end.

The sun rang out like a great golden bell! Like a Heavenly Bell, shimmering upon the blue-golden air, upon the green-golden trees, upon the red-golden houses with the gray-green-golden porches, which he knew were there, though he could not see them, as he lay in the Sunday beams that shone through the window.

The way to church, and church, rang out with golden song. The reverend warned the faithful congregation against the consuming fires of hell, while the emerald-green, gold-edged wings of the flies flitted in and out of the open transoms through which summer sounds floated, animating his words and intensifying the eternal pain and suffering that was to be the fate of sinners.

"Save me, Je-suus!" cried a voice.

"He'p me, Lawd!" said another.

Boom! his hip crashed against the ground in the darkness of the shoot an instant before the naked woman . . . like a statue at the art gallery . . . stuck her head out the window and glared angrily toward the mouth of the shoot.

"We all a-l-l sinners!" shouted the reverend.

"Yeah!" someone shouted, followed by a piercing soprano note that broke up into particles of light that froze in a golden sheen upon his forehead. He wriggled in his seat, and finally dashed madly, gladly out into the free air and followed the golden clouds home. . . .

"Don' forgit to tell Aunt Rose that I kin do 'er hair whenever she wants me to, you hear?" said Viola. He shook his head affirmatively as he rose from the dinner table. "An' don' stay in the show all night. School ain' out yet!"

"Yes'm."

"You got your clean handkerchief?"

"Yes'm."

"Where's your money?"

"In my pocket."

"Straighten your tie."

"Git out a heah, boy!" said Rutherford.

He stepped greatfully out through the door and headed up the alley, south. He walked out Eleventh Street, east, cautiously past the redbrick house on the corner of Eleventh and Tracy. It was quiet. Strange in the Sunday sunlight. Must have a hundred rooms . . . fifty anyway! He saw a woman lying upon a big white bed in every room and a naked slick-headed man standing over her, sweating and trembling.

He looked at all the windows of the apartment and at those of the neighboring house. A stiff, unsuppressable agitation caused the pants of his Sunday suit to bulge just below his belt buckle. He looked at the sky, and then at the trees, eased his hand into his pocket, and covertly sought the shaded spots of the sidewalk, near the houses, out of general sight, as he proceeded down Tracy to Twelfth, Fifteenth, and Eighteenth Streets, past the mission house, the liquor store, the ice cream parlor, and up past R. T. Bowles Junior High School where he would have to go before he could go to North High, and then college and then — hot dog!

"Aaaaaw shit!" shouted a woman from the apartment opposite the school. He looked up on the porch at a brown-skinned woman of twenty-five dressed in an underskirt, the left shoulder strap of which hung down over her shoulder. She wobbled unsteadily and glared angrily down into the street.

He stared at the patch of hair between her legs against the sunlight.

"What you lookin' at, you little big-eyed bastard?" she shrieked.

He tipped his hat respectfully, smiled a weak apologetic smile, and hastened up the street.

A little past Nineteenth Street he came to a bridge. He looked down at the shining rails that sped east and west through the city.

Gradually the tension in his pocket relaxed. He left the bridge and continued up Tracy Avenue until he came to a group of apartment houses with wooden porches and dirty yards cluttered with wild grasses and weeds and sunflowers, but in the yard in front of the last house on the corner the grass was cut. It was soft and prickly wet, like the fresh-cut fur of an enormous green kitten, nestling around a two-story redbrick house with a clean cement porch with a neat little swing painted green. Flower boxes full of bright red flowers stood on the banister and flower beds teeming with an assortment of blooming flowers grew along the front and side of the house.

His eyes took in the sweeping hill opposite. Through the bushes he could see the buildings of Western College. That's where Ardella went, he thought . . . but *I'm* gonna go to Harvard and Yale where all the big shots go, Jack! I'm gonna know all about *every*thing in the w-h-o-l-e world! He saw Viola's face breaking up in a smile of approval, amid a din of teeming voices splashing against the shores of his consciousness like summer rain . . . splaying stars in the gray dust that flowed under the gate and clattered down the alley.

"Open your mouth, boy, an' tell us what you see!"

"That boy's got a head like a preacher!"

"Whose little boy is that?"

"Why — that's Rutherford an' Viola's little boy!"

"Don' he look nice!"

"Smart! An' *manners,* too!"

"A reg'ler little gen'leman!"

"— look at them eyes!"

"Look at that walk!"

"Just like a little white boy!"

He opened the gate and entered the path. All the soft grasses rared up in approval as he passed. A sparrow dipped its wings in salutory tribute!

"Give 'im the claps, men!"

Clap! clap! clap! clap! clap! clap! clap! clap!

He bowed from the stage of a great hall filled with millions of clapping hands, ". . . *In England an' France! . . . Like old Paul Robeson, only bigger! . . . Bigger than . . . bigger'n Ira Eldridge! . . . Bigger'n Stokowski at the show!*"

Clap! clap! clap! clap! clap! clap!

"From all the waves in the sea . . ."

Clap! clap! clap! clap! clap!

"From all the stars in the sky!"

"You ain' got no money, honey, but you sure got a whole lot a nerve!" cried a husky male voice that came from the spinning phonograph record in the room behind the screen. The shade was drawn, but a blazing right angle of sunlight fired its side and bottom edge, diffusing a pregnant green light throughout the room.

"Naw! — you ain' got no money, honey, but you sure got a lot a nerve!" The guitar whined plaintively. He rang the bell.

A tall shadow in a sky-blue dress filled the screen and partially obscured his view of the large round table around which three men sat.

"Jus' 'cause you know that I love you —"

"Good afternoon, Mister Jones!" said Ardella tartly.

"Hi," stepping self-consciously into the cool sweet smell of whiskey, beer, gin, the blues, and the animate expressions in glazed eyes sweltering in the nurtured shade of a hot Sunday afternoon.

"Hi Aunt Rose!"

"Why, hello, baby!" She smiled from the doorway of the little hall that connected the kitchen and the bedroom to the parlor. Now she moved heavily into the parlor and joined the men at the table.

"Been to church?"

"Yes'm," moving deeper into the room.

"More'n anything in this world!" cried the man who was still singing the

blues. *"If you had a dollah —"* One of the men signaled Ardella to pour another drink. *"If you had a dollah — for eeevery lie you told!"*

"You'd be rich, wouldn' you, Dan?" said Aunt Rose to the man sitting next to her. He downed his whiskey in one gulp, a tall, lean smooth-skinned black man in a clean lumber jacket over a white shirt that was open at the throat.

"I don' know as I'd be ex-*actly* rich, but I reckon I'd need a small train just to carry my change in!"

"You'd a been rich as Rockerfelloooo 'fo you was ten years old!"

"Have a seat, Mister Jones," said Ardella, "an' pour yourself a drink. That is, if we humble folks are good enough for you."

"You cut out that foolishness, Ardella," said Aunt Rose, "you know that boy don' drink. Come around here, boy, an' let your auntie have a look at you. I ain' seen you in a long time. This is Mister Williams, Amerigo," indicating the tall man on her right: "Mister Williams, Mister Jones."

"Say, I know this little darkie!" exclaimed Mr. Williams. "He looks just like Viola, don' 'e?"

"Spittin' image of 'er!" said Aunt Rose.

"Why, I knowed your momma, boy, when she wasn' no bigger'n you!"

He put his arm around his waist and drew him to him. The strong smell of whiskey perfumed the air when he spoke, and droplets of spittle flickered out in rays of diffused sunlight.

"You turned out to be a f-i-n-e lookin' young man!" continued Mr. Williams. "Well, sir, if *I* could just go back an' start all over agin!"

"How many times have you *an'* I wished that!" Aunt Rose sighed.

"If! if! if!" Ardella said, rubbing her flat stomach. "*If* one of you gen'lemen would offer a lady a drink." She smiled bitterly and moved toward the Victrola.

RCA, Victor! he thought.

She put on a record.

"Drink up, girl, I'm buyin'," said the second man, a yellow-skinned freckle-faced man who motioned sleepily at the bottle on the table. Aunt Rose looked at Amerigo with a private knowing smile:

That's my daughter, it said. That's my pride an' joy! Take a good look at 'er an' at the rest a these niggahs, Amerigo, an' see how it is to be dead before your time! An' please try not to judge your auntie too hard. She's had a hard time. But she loves *you!* You hear me, she loves you!

He felt Ardella's oblique glance, darting between her mother's eyes and his eyes, just after the record began to spin, the needle to crack, the piano to play — then a mellow commenting trombone backed by an ingratiating fiddle and a signifying drum:

"If I ever git on my feet agin!"

He diverted his gaze to the floor while Ardella poured herself three fingers of whiskey, threw her head back, and gulped it down with a frown, her head recoiling to its former position as she set the glass on the table just in time to catching him stealing a glance at her:

You think you're smart, don't you? he felt her eyes saying. You and that big-eyed momma of yours. All dressed up in your Sunday suit! Been to church, heard every word the reverend said. Smart, too. Real smart! Gonna be somebody someday. Then Momma's gonna point to me and say: 'Now why couldn't you have been like him? Why couldn't you have tried!' You little shrimp! You aren't any better than *I* am! You're no smarter than I am! You're luckier than I am, though. . . .

"*If I ever git on my feet agin!*" the woman sang.

I don't hate you! No, I don't! I hate Momma! But she's all I got. She's *all I am!* And she loves you. I don't hate you. I just wish you were somewhere else — miles away! I wish you and your big bright eyes had never been born! Maybe, maybe it would have been better if *I* had never been born, if I were dead.

"Yeah," Mr. Williams was saying, "if things was *then* the way they is *now* —"

"It ain' never too late," said Aunt Rose, shooting a glance at Ardella.

"It's too late for *me!*" said Mr. Williams.

The third man, a little blue-black man dressed in a gray suit, with huge gnarled hands with enormous pink fingernails that he drummed nervously on the table, looked up from his drumming.

He's got hands like Bra Mo, Amerigo thought.

"It's too late for me," Mr. Williams was saying. "Momma's dead, Poppa. I got a sister — but she's so good a Christian that she turns 'er head the other way when she sees me comin' down the street. Hell! I been in too many crap games, too many sportin' houses. Never could keep still long enough to git married. *I* got a few kids . . . here an' there. Yeah! but they don't even know my name! Ain' got no schoolin'. Been out workin' ever since I was ten. An' I got more gray hairs then I got black 'uns. Heh! — an' you *'spect* me to go where this boy's goin'?"

"What you got to say to that, Josh?" Aunt Rose looked at the little man in the gray suit who looked like Bra Mo.

"Well, the way I look at it is this: that a man ain' no more then he thinks he is. You kin be born high an' you kin be born low, but here's one thing that I do know: Ain' *nobody* comin' till he gits called! Maybe He call you when you young, like Jesus, or when you old, like Job. But whether you git called or not ever' man — ever' livin' ass — got the price to pay! 'Scuse me, son, but I got to call it like I see it."

"Your momma tells me that you been to the art gallery," said Aunt Rose.
Clap! clap! clap! clap! clap! clap!
"Yes'm! Last Frid'y. We went in a bus for nobody else but us! Went that-away! Out a big boulevard lined with r-e-a-l pretty trees. After we passed the station an' Memorial Hill, then we turned into a driveway an' stopped in front of a g-r-e-a-t big buildin'! With a park around it full a real real pretty trees — an' pur-d-a-y! — with a lot a leaves an' things that ain' like none a the ones around here!

"We went between the tall black shiny posts, bigger'n a telephone post — with real funny things on top where it held the roof up that looked like baskets of fruit cut out a stone. The roof rested on that. An'-an' on the front a the roof shaped like a triangle was a picture cut in the wall. They call that skulpcher —"

"Go ahead, boy!" Mr. Williams exclaimed.

Aunt Rose smiled with approval.

"S-c-u-l-p-t-u-r-e —" said Ardella, "I know a little bit about that, myself."

"That's what I said!"

"Go on, honey!" said Aunt Rose:
Clap!clap!clap!clap!clap!clap!

His voice became lost within the voluble swell of voices that reverberated throughout the great hall. "Just after the entrance where you give your coat an' hat an' a tall gray-headed white man in a blue-lookin' uniform with writin' on the pocket pushed the gate open — almost like on the streetcar — after the conductor turns the handle an' the money falls.

"There was a g-r-e-a-t big pretty room! With big big big rugs on the walls with pictures on 'um of knights of the Round Table, an' big horses all covered with iron so they couldn' git stuck with spears an' cut with them big long swords —"

"S-o-r-d-s!" said Ardella.

"Yeah, an'-an' standin' up side the wall was a-was a r-e-a-l horse made out a stone like in a picture, with a man on top of 'im, all dressed up in a iron suit with a long spear an' a shiel' an' — "

"D!"

"Shiel*d!* — an' axes an' big balls with a lot a stickers stickin' out of 'um connected to a chain — to fight with."

"That sure is somethin', all right!" said the freckle-faced man, who had aroused from his slumbers. "An' then what?"
Clap! clap! clap! clap!clap!clap!clap!

The armor and mail clashed and clanged in hot combat, the legions of brave warriors gushed with blood induced from their bodies by spear, lance, pickax, mace-and-chain. Horses hooves wildly churned the turf into a slimy mass stained red by the thick coils of blood that oozed from the wounds in the necks of the walleyed dead men. . . .

"There was some steps made out a real marble on that side of the room an' on the other. They went windin' up an' around — a little bit like the steps on Twelf' Street in front a the show."

"*Th!*" said Ardella.

"*An'*-an' on the wall that the steps wind up aginst — on that side — was a real big picture. Pur-d-a-y! With a pretty blue sky an' pretty green trees, an' under the trees some men was standin' with long white beards all dressed up in sheets an' sandals, lookin' at another man who was talkin' to 'um. He had his arms all stretched out like he was sayin' somethin' important. An' the wall over the other steps had a blue sky, too, with real tall good-lookin' men with straight noses an' big eyes an' pretty legs — just like a woman! — ridin' naked on pretty horses, like Indians racin'!"

Cloppidycloppidycloppidycloppidycloppidycloppidyclop . . .

"But we didn' stop there —"

"Where?" asked Aunt Rose.

"Downstairs in the basement. Only it wasn' like no basement around here. It was a basement like a front room, only it didn' have no rug on it an' stuff like that, with a real shiny floor that you couldn' see no dirt nowhere. It had a lot of glass closets with a lot a pretty rocks that the Indians usta use for bows an' arrows an' hatchets an' tomahawks for huntin' an' a g-r-e-a-t big hat with a lot a feathers for the chief. Pontiac, Jack!"

He stared at the right angle of blazing light that fired a fringe of shiny hair on Aunt Rose's head.

"*You woulda been a wonderful woman, if you hadn' a . . .*"

"*She dyes it. . . . Sssssssh.*"

"An' dresses an' a lot a pretty beads an' bracelets . . ." his voice was saying.

"Did they let you go through the whole buildin' by yourself?" asked Aunt Rose.

He gazed into the cool clear skies of her eyes. He watched her tapering brows take flight like a pair of birds in the velvet picture on the front room wall:

"Did they let you go through the whole building by yourself?"

"The gentleman's dreaming," said Ardella, "he must be in love!" Her prune-colored lips spread out in a sensuous smile, and her eyes narrowed into slits, so that the whites were barely visible through the feathery sheen of her eyelashes. He shivered, a funny feeling crept between his legs, and he dropped his glance to the polished floor.

"What was she like, son?" Aunt Rose smiled tenderly. Her eyes articulated the assurance that she understood, that she *really* understood, that she *knew*.

"Who?" in a flood of embarrassment.

"The guide," said Ardella. "You had a guide, didn't you?"

He looked puzzled.

"The young lady who took you around an' explained ever'thin'," said Aunt Rose.

Ardella was still smiling sensuously.

He stood a-tremble before the young lady with the soft red hair and large green eyes spaced far apart. The sun glistened upon her moist red lips, as she signaled for the class to sit down upon the floor in front of the long wooden box with the carved figures. The class obediently crumbled to the floor in a mass of heads, eyes, arms, and legs akimbo, while he remained standing, his foot caught in the shadow of the iron bars of the Spanish window.

She smiled at him and motioned for him to sit down.

He writhed in a fury of embarrassment, but remained standing. Giggles spilled from his classmates' mouths onto the floor.

This is my Sund'y suit! he thought.

An instant later *her* hand touched his shoulder, like a magic wand. His will flowed out of his body and he sank to the floor.

Her lips were red, he thought, staring through the window of the speeding streetcar, marveling at the crest of snow that spangled her hair and at the sunlight that fired her lips so brilliantly that the sight of them hurt his eyes.

He studied the movement of her throat as she spoke. It was framed in the blazing white collar of her blouse.

I bet it never gets dirty, he thought.

She unconsciously touched her neck with her fingertip and shifted her attention to the box with the carved figures, explaining that it was used by the rich Spanish noblemen to store their treasures of: . . . balls an' grasshoppers, june bugs an' rubber-guns, Libby labels an' glass stars in . . .

And presently the group had sprung to its feet and was moving through a series of beautiful rooms. He walked at her side, sipping the sweet wisdom from her . . . licked-wineball-colored . . . lips!

"The young lady who took you around an' explained ever'thin'," Aunt Rose was saying.

"An' there was a —"

"*Were!*"

"Yeah. A whole lot a pictures, too, with real people in 'um — in every room! — pictures of watermelons an' or'nges an' grapes that looked like you could eat 'um off the wall, but they was painted. An' they was a lot a cows an' sheep an' old brown houses in the middle of big yellow fields with men an' women workin' in 'um, plowin' an' tyin' up hay into bundles . . . an' sittin' an' talkin' an' laughin' an' dancin' — real funny-like, with they legs all stuck up in the air, all funny-like. But they wasn' movin', an' you couldn' hear what they was sayin', but they *was* movin' — an'-an' you knowed — knew they was sayin' *somethin'*! Ain' that funny?"

"What?" asked Aunt Rose.

"That you kin see somethin' movin' that ain' even movin'? An' that you kin hear somethin' that you can't even hear! *You* know what I mean! There was a cat playin' a violin in one picture, an' I could hear it just as p-l-a-i-n —"

"You lucky, son," said Aunt Rose, "there's a lot a folks can't even hear it when they hearin' it!"

"An' then — in a-nother picture there was a little boy in a blue suit that was *laughin'*! An' he looked just like it, too! Sort a dancin'-like, but he wasn' movin'. I looked away an' then looked back agin — real quick! — an' he wasn' gone nowhere, but he was still dancin' just the same, Jack!

"An' there was another picture — the prettiest picture in the w-h-o-l-e w-o-r-l-d!"

"What was *that?*" asked Ardella.

"The picture of a man with a iron hat on his head made out a gold. His head was kinda in the shaddow-like, so you couldn' hardly see what he looked like, but you could see 'im just the same. But you could see his hat best. It was gold an' shiny. A man from olden times. He's called *The Man with the Golden Helmet,* Jack! — an' —"

"B-o-y!" cried Aunt Rose, "was there anything you *didn'* see?"

"No'm. An' *listen!* There was a b-i-g b-i-g room — from China! *All the way from China!* With a lot a shiny horses an' things made out a glass, an' dishes an' vases, an' on a wall — real tall — was a statue of a b-i-g man with pretty ears! The biggest ears in the w-h-o-l-e — w-o-r-l-d! An' long eyes that looked like he was half asleep. He was sittin' down with his legs crossed — Indian-fashion — an'-an' his hands an' his fingers looked like a woman's. But he wasn' sleepin'. If he was sleepin' he'd be lyin' down. He was thinkin' about somethin' that he knowed."

"Knew."

"Unh-huh. Kinda dreamin'-like."

"What was he supposed to be?" Mr. Williams asked.

"He was God. Not exactly God 'cause *he* was dead. Like God — only *they* call 'im Booda. Funny name!"

"You must be hungry after —" Aunt Rose began.

"But how kin He be God when GOD'S *GOD?*"

"Ain' no use in me lyin'," said Aunt Rose with a sigh, "I really don' know, but I reckon those people over there that believe in 'im's gonna git to heaven just as quick as any a the rest of 'um. Your cousin Ardella went to college, ask her."

"I don't know, Momma," said Ardella.

"Come on back in the kitchen," said Aunt Rose. He followed her into the kitchen. It was smaller than the kitchen of the old red house on the hill. It was on the ground floor and looked out onto a porch walled in with narrow slats running crisscross.

He sat down at the little table in front of the narrow north window that looked onto a neighboring house. While Aunt Rose busied herself about the stove, a brown-and-white collie dog poked its long thin muzzle against the screen and whined in a friendly way.

"Go 'way, Queenie, I done fed you once taday," said Aunt Rose without looking up from the pot she was stirring.

Ace is dead. He suddenly realized that Queenie was there instead of Ace.

He observed unconsciously that Aunt Rose's feet and legs were swollen, that she moved with greater difficulty, a faint groan or grunt accompanying each radical shift of position. And that almost always now her tightened lips betrayed the laughter in her eyes.

She's getting old. He felt sad, as he ate the chicken she offered him, even though he wasn't really hungry. But then after a while it made him hungry because it was so good.

"Why's that?"

"Why's what?"

"That you kin git hungry even when you ain' — aren't?"

"I hope you don' never have to be hungry when you hungry," she said, caressing him and pressing a coin in his hand. "Buy yourself somethin' good for the show."

"Thank you, ma'am."

"What show you goin' to?"

"The Lincoln an' the Gem."

He told her what Viola had told him to tell her, said good-bye to her and to the men sitting around the table. The Victrola was playing again: *I'm a big fat momma — with meat shakin' on my bones!*

"Bye, Ardella."

Every time it shakes, some skinny woman lose 'er home!

"Bye, baby," said Ardella in a tone so warm that it made him turn around in the middle of the path, amid the cheering crowd of blooming flowers, and wave with a self-conscious flurry of emotion.

*

He closed the gate. The eyes of the world were upon him. He walked Sunday-suit straight, swaggering a little, as he stepped upon the toe of the gentle unpaved hill, his glance taking in the neat cluster of apartment houses on the northeast corner. A Negro owns them. One day when I get big I'm going to get me one! And Dad can run it. He can have it because I'll give it to him and Mom! *Him no more than her.*

He looked up at the clouds floating in the sky, and at the leaves pearling on the trees whose branches were permeated with burning flashes of sunlight. Like long shiny needles of fire sticking in your eyes! . . . through your face . . . through your nose . . . through your clothes: throughyaclothesthroughya nostthroughyaclothesthroughyanosethroughaclothes! . . .

Like real real real sharp icicles — stickin' through the summer!

He quickened his step in order to get to the show before summer came because when summer came he would have to go to Aunt Nadine's. He had to hurry before summer was over because when summer was over he would have to go to school where the new principal was, in Miss Hunt's class . . . With pretty brown hair on her head and around her eyes and on her legs. Like a white woman's!

Georgia peach!

The heat dripped in beads of sweat down his neck, rolled down the pits of his arms, shone like diamonds on the backs of his hands. He slowed his pace as he ascended the hill to keep from sweating out his white Sunday shirt. He sought out the shady patches of summer, pausing only for an instant upon the brink of autumn when school would start.

Now it was behind him, to the rear and to the left of his left shoulder. He was approaching the boulevard. It stretched all the way from the great Admiral Boulevard to where he was now, and beyond: All the way to . . . to . . . to — past the art gallery!

He stopped at Nineteenth Street and looked both ways, gazing absentmindedly at the four big letters painted on the redbrick wall of the building on the opposite corner: Y-W-C-A. That's where Mom's club has their teas. American Beauty Art.

Clap!clap!clap!clap!clap!clap!

As he entered the reception room in his Easter Sunday suit, new last Easter . . . Lookin' sharp as a tack, Jack! . . . the Christ-redeeming sun firing the long white curtains and animating the smiles on the ladies' faces, which were crowned with festoons of spring flowers while the tips of their glistening eyelashes dipped into subtle profusions of powder and rouge that blushed upon the mounds of their elated cheeks. The whole spectrum of red-colored lips admired the sparkle and glitter of a host of chattering teeth sprinkled with silver and gold. Manicured fingers flew in pursuit of subtly intoned innuendos as they discreetly adjusted the delinquent folds of lace, taffeta, chiffon, muslin, or silk, resurrected from the pain and sweat of the infernal kitchens, laundries, and apartment houses of the white districts of the great city.

Like real pretty flowers! They were stirred by a dignified ripple of social excitement, consecrated with a cup of tea locked between thumb, fore-, and middle fingers, tilted into the gulf of pursed lips while eyes wandered critically examining the corsages of roses that were crucified, bound with tassels of gold and silver ribbon to the hostesses' shoulders:

"Viola Jones, president!"

Clap!clap!clap!clap!clap!clap!

"Hi, baby! Ooooooooow! Don' he look nice!"

"Hi, Miss Susie!"

"Hi, there, boy!"

"Hi, Miss Vera!"

"Come here, let me kiss you!"

"Hi, Miss Patsy!" He burned hot under the deep-bosomed scent of powder and perfume and the scorching tip of burned cork, straightened hair, and clean sweat, observing with awe the bush of down emerging from the deep fold between her breasts.

"Hi, there, Babe!"

"Hi."

Viola stood behind the long table with the lace tablecloth laden with cookies and candies and nuts. She's the prettiest! He admired the way she turned the spigot of the polished silver urn and released the sparkling tea into the brittle white cup that he would have to hold carefully. "An' don' forget to drink slowly an' *munch* on that cookie! 'Stead a *devourin'* it with one gulp!"

Meanwhile the handsome dark lady in pink with big sad eyes sat before the baby grand and sang, to the acompaniament of her rippling fingers:

"I theeenk! . . . that Iee shall nevah seeee . . . A po-em — lovely as a tree," tilting her head upward in order to gaze upon the tree through her closed eyelids: "A tree whose hungry mouth is pre-essed . . . a-gainst the earth's sweet flowing brea-est —"

"Aaaaaaaaaaw!" The napkin slipped from his knees and glided across the floor.

"A tree that looks — at God all day-ee. . . . And lifts her lea-fy arms to pray — ee. . . ."

He stared ito the brilliant light flowing through the window. He watched the lamppost tree lifting its leafless arms to pray, until the handsome lady in pink finally confessed:

"Poems are maaaaaeeeed —" neck and eyes straining, lips stretching to produce the soaring note. "— maaaaaeeeed! — by fools — like me . . ."

She made it!

"But only Goooooooood — can make — aaaaaaaaa trrreeeeeeeee!"

Joyce Kilmer. "Mom?"

"Sssssssssh!"

Clap!clap!clap!clap!clap!clap!clap!

"Mom?"

"What?"

"Kin I have some to put in my pocket?"

"All right — here." She gave him some of the nuts from the table. "It's about your time, ain' it?"

"Yes'm — Bye."

"Bye, baby."

He swaggered through the festive room teeming with sweet-smelling delicate-petaled good-byes from members and friends of the American Beauty Art Club who, according to the *Voice:*

". . . enjoyed a gala turnout at their annual Easter tea at the YWCA, Sunday, April 12th. The salon was decorated with American Beauty roses, which were also used for the charming buffet centerpiece. The musical entertainment was provided by that popular sweetheart of song, Miss Mary Williams, and a good time was had by all. The members, seated left to right are: Mrs. Viola Jones, president, Miss. . . ."

There were no speeding cars, so he crossed Nineteenth Street and was freshly stimulated by the recollection that it was Sunday, and that he was going to the Gem Theater to see Warner Oland in *The Adventures of Charlie Chan.*

He passed the cool entrance of the YMCA building with its glass doors and polished brass handles. . . . His ears were suddenly beset by a din of phrases and initials spread themselves across the off-white pages of the *Voice* in fuzzy black letters. Annual YMCA Membership Drive Gits Underway. Mr. L. P. G. Chan, B.A., M.A., Ph.D., DET, NATIONAL Secretary of the Urban League, speaks out against race prejudice . . . aginst social injustice . . . aginst . . . for Warner Oland's Credit Union . . . Station . . . League of Nations . . . I pledge allegiance to the A.E.I.O.U. fifty cents you went away . . . The PTA Ca — mitte's meetin' at the YWCA, WPA, NRA, NEW DEAL, YO' DEAL, NO DICE? DAR? KKK? FEPC . . . of the National Ass — so — she — aaaaa — shun for the Ad-vance-ment of Painted People . . .On! On! Metokas an' Galeders!

The black, white, and grayish personages who filled the squares and rectangles on the pages of the *Voice* came to the forefront of his mind in a procession of colors: smiling ladies and gentlemen bursting with crimson distinction, deep tragic purples and criminal greens, mellow beauty-queen browns, snooty beiges and off-whites, serious fudge-browns, scholastic gray-blacks, and everywhere the gold-rimmed black-blackness of the One and Only Living God.

Eighteenth Street spread out before him like a huge page of the *Voice*. All the buildings appeared as photographs and the flickering signs as headlines. He stood on the corner and watched the motley-colored procession of figures walking up and down the street, talking, laughing. He breathed in and out the picturesque smells of barbershop and pool hall, drugstore and tavern, the Sunday-afternoon heat, the slightly wilted after-church freshness of Sunday suits and dresses reflected upon the polished surfaces of parked and moving automobiles, agitated by nervous lights upon the marquees of theaters, the honking horns of taxis and the voluable mellifluence of friendly greetings:

"Hey Joe!" cried one tall dark man to another tall dark man on the opposite side of the street. Just then the streetcar rushed between them, casting the greeter's reflection on its windows like a chain of photographs whisked through the air.

"Hi, man!"

"You lookin' mighty sharp, there!"

"Aw it ain' my world, I'm just livin' in it!"

"Now who you shuckin'!"

"Yeah! Ha! ha! Say —"

"What?"

"You don' look so bad, yourself!"

"Don' give me 'way, daddy!"

"Take it easy, man!"

"Got to do it!"

"I'd work for you — slave for you . . ." sang a long-legged passerby, "I'd be a begger — "

"Or a ma — aid *for* you!" Amerigo answered in the style of Pha Terrell. The singer threw a broad smile over his shoulder and waved.

"If that ain' love, it'll have to do — until the real thing comes along!"

He followed him up the street with his eyes. But then his attention was suddenly distracted by a loud roar coming from the direction of the ballpark just below Eighteenth Street.

He struggled with temptation to run down and watch. Satchel Paige's the greatest! And old Babe Ruth . . . candy bars . . . Jack Johnson! T. C. . . .

Wilcox . . . Jesse Owens, the world's fastest human! — an' — an' JOE
LOUIS, the BROWN BOMBER! — hot dog!

He turned up Eighteenth Street and crossed over on the . . . sunny side of
the . . . so that he could see The Blue Moon where Viola and Rutherford
went out, where he would go out when he got big enough. He walked past
Streets Hotel and Elnora's Café, where the food's real good and expensive
and only big-shot spooks can go in. He stared in the pool hall and barbershop where Rutherford and Williard and Harrison — twins — and Mr.
Zoo shot pool and sat outside in Harrison's car and drank whiskey — Old
Crow, Old Taylor, Vat 69, Four Roses, and Sneaky-Pete'nHooche-coocher!
Booze! Joy-juice . . . firewater . . . liquor . . . a fifth a pint a half of a . . .

He stopped at the corner of Eighteenth and Vine:

"I shook hands with Pi-ny Brown" he sang, "an' could hard-lay keep
from cryin'. . . ."

Joe Turner and Pete Johnson, Jack! He gazed at the picture of Cab
Calloway in white tails and tie on the poster in the drugstore window

"Once there was a gal named Minnie the Moocher!" he sang out uncontrollably, "I'm gonna . . ." He was oblivious now to Joe Turner and Pete
Johnson and stepped blindly into the street just as a cab swerved around
the corner and wriggled in between two parked cars like a snake.

"Better watch out where you goin', there, little niggah!" cried the driver,
grinning broadly from under his driver's cap, "I'm *crazy!* I done killed *four*
cats taday, an' it's *Sund'y!*"

"I'm like a ship without a sail —" boomed a voice from the loudspeaker
over the record shop across the street, "I don't know where to turn. I've
learned a lot of things that I've tried hard not to learn. Won't someone help
me find the girl that once was mine, so I'll be happy again!"

Dan Grison! he mumbled excitedly to himself, with Jimmie Lunceford,
with the greatest reed section in the w-ho-l-e w-o-r-l-d! Willie Smith on
alto, man! And old Trummy Young on the trombone! "Ain' what you do
— hit's the way that you do it, Jack!" Hawkins, Evans, Chu Berry, Lester
. . . I'm the Hawk!

"I'm Chu Berry!" cried Turner's voice.

"I'm Lester!" cried Tommy. "Man — that cat kin blow up a *breeze!*"

"I don' care, I'm the Hawk!" He saw himself up on the stage, taking a
swinging solo with a golden saxophone, his jaws full of air like Mr. Zoo's,
blowing fast an' fancy an' high an' low — all at once! The piece came to an
end, the band fell in behind him, and the drummer went crazy on the drums.
Old Chick Webb, the fastest drummer in the w-h-o-l-e — w-o-r-l-d!
Humpback. He bowed for the Hawk and for Chick Webb and for the band.

Clap!clap!clap!clap!clap!clap!clap!clap!

Looking in the window of the clothing store on the corner opposite the record shop, he examined the gambol-striped pants and the white, gray, and beige beaver hats, the shoes — Florsheim — Stacy Adams' and Edmond Clapps! Like the reverend's. He tried to mesure the time until he could wear shoes like that, and long pants instead of knickers, and a pimp-chain. *Uncle Sexton was a . . . Sssssssh! . . . Solid, Jack!*

He continued up the street past Lincoln Hall where Benny Moton used to play.

He entered the confectionary store next to the Gem, burning with resentment against the time until *then . . .*

"May I have a milk shake, please?"

"Milk shake, comin' up!" yelled the pretty young girl with freckles behind the counter, giving him a wink that drove his embarrassed gaze through the smooth concrete floor.

She set the tall frothing glass before him. He sucked on the straw and stared unconsciously at her protruding hip as she bent over the refrigerator in order to scoop up a dipper full of ice cream. The scooping done, he listened to the whir of the electric fans hanging from the dirty-green ceiling. He listened to the sounds of the street, Eighteenth Street, a long dirty colorful street. Finally the sound of air bubbles at the bottom of his glass and the abrupt end of the sweet pleasant coolness flowing into his mouth caused him to lick his lips regretfully and climb down from the stool and step out into the four o'clock sun.

"One please," he said to the middle-aged woman who pushed the ticket through the hole at the bottom, and entered the dark light-spangled room and seated himself among colors and smells that he knew by heart.

Before the main feature came on, and the Preview of Coming Attractions and the two comedies . . . Fat 'n Skinny and the Three Stooges . . . and the newsreel, there was a Musical Revue featuring the Nicholas Brothers, two brown-skinned little boys in gray knickerbocker suits, white caps, socks, shoes, and handsome smiles that tickled his funny bone. They had rhythm in their feet that made the floor smoke just like it was really burning, just before the sign said THE END.

They are the dancin'est cats in the w-h-o-l-e — w-o-r-l-d! Beside Bill Bojangles Robinson an' Uncle Ruben. I can do it, I bet! I could do it if I wanted to. I'm *gonna* do it, I'm gonna grow up and be a dancer like that, and have my picture in the *Voice,* Jack!

And then the comedies, and then:

The Adventures of Charlie Chan, starring Warner Oland.

Hot diggedy! He's Chineese. Confucius say, Man who cook carrots an' pees in the same pot, he verry dirty! Aaaaaaw!

When Charlie Chan's adventures were over he stayed to see the Nicholas Brothers again, and then he stepped out into the street regretting that he could not dance like them, right now! He wondered how it was that they could and he couldn't.

He walked down Eighteenth Street, west. Seven o'clock amber filled the sky and mellowed the summer laughter that filled the street.

"They had to have somethin' new, a dance to do, up there in Harlem, so —" He stood under the laughing voice that burst from the loudspeaker.

Old Fats Waller, man! He smiled with delight because he was alive and all dressed up and had been to the Gem Theater where he had seen the Nicholas Brothers, and was now on his way to the Lincoln Theater to see Basil Rathbone, a Englishman! Aye sae, eold maan, ahr you theah! The overgrown pussycat snapping at the seat of his pants while the bone-haired Africans fled, white-soled feet flapping in the . . .

"Someone started truckin'!"

"One please." He took the ticket from the pretty lady's manicured finger and gave it to the dark well-groomed man who tore it in two and dropped it into the tall box with glass like the box on the streetcar and released the smooth trapdoor until they fell through the hollow eyes at the foot of the trees. . . .

The music came on seriously, settling down with the fog around the big pretty . . . spooky . . . house in England, with the wind howling like people and the dog howling like somebody was going to die, and the shadowy patterns of the leaves from the great trees that stood in the yard veined its gloomy facade. The shutters banged against the only window with a light where a pretty lady dressed in a white gown combed her long pretty hair sadly — until she saw the tall good-looking man . . . Basil Rathbone, Jack! . . . standing behind her. He started talking to her as though she were crazy. Real educated! I'm going to talk like that. "Realleh, mah deah, we simpleh caun't geo on like thisssss — eneh longah!"

"Please, John, or aye shall geo m-a-a-d!"

Hot ziggedy! He settled into the melancholy mood saturated with evil and intrigue, admiring the clothes and manners of the actors, the way the bad man sipped the soup which she suspected was poison. . . . Poison's green. . . . Watching him extract the long black pipe from the pocket of his perfectly fitting tweed jacket and load it as though it were a pistol, shooting, after a fearful flame-flare, lethal volleys of smoke into the air — *Boom! Boom! Boom!* — while the sad pretty lady trembled amid its shattering reverberations.

Boom!

The lights of Eighteenth Street hit his eyes and blinded them with their brilliance. Gradually he saw the long line of dressed-up adults waiting to enter the show. He scanned their impatient faces and was secretly pleased that he had already seen the picture. Then the thought of their just beginning to experience the pleasure that was all over for him caused his spirits to droop.

Sad that he had already seen the Nicholas Brothers — twice — he moped up Eighteenth Street. He stared through the windows of the ice cream parlor, tasted with phantom tongue the crawdads spread out upon the cart in front of the pool hall. He envied the men and women who could stay up late and who now chatted and laughed and drank in the taverns and did not have to go home. He cast one last longing look up toward Vine Street, stretched his imagination past the Gem where the *Voice* was, and then turned down Paseo Boulevard and headed toward Fifteenth Street.

The stars were bright. He looked at the trees, the bushes and flowers in the park. He heard the invisible crowd cheering the ball players, the roar of children splashing in the pool in the bathhouse behind the wooden enclosure. The chlorine stung his nose and burned his eyes, which had turned as red as fire after he had climbed out of the water and Bubbles, the life guard, had said:

"Say Abe, look at this little joker! Look at them legs an' shoulders. He's built like a boxer!"

"Damned if he ain'!"

He increased the length of his stride, stuck out his chest, and suddenly shot his deadly left into his invisible opponent's vulnerable chin, legs engaged in a steady shuffle, eyes fixing him with murderous intent: "Like Joe Louis!" Jim Donovan yelled from the center of the ring in Madison Square Garden, "in New York City, the biggest city in the w-h-o-l-e — w-o-r-l-d! Above the roar of the crowd, louder then the roar of a million — of a hundred million lions . . . the winnah! — and still heavyweight champ-e-ion — of the w-o-r-l-d . . . J-O-E — Lllllouis!"

"eeeeeEEEEEEEEEE — Y-A-Y!"

Eyes filled with happy tears, he looked up just in time to see the red shimmering traffic light at Fifteenth Street. There was a hamburger stand on the opposite corner and a big signboard above and behind it with a pretty redheaded woman smiling down upon a brand-new shining Ford car.

"Ford's got the fastest pickup," he heard Rutherford say, "but the Chevy's better for distance."

He saw Rutherford sitting in the comfortable chair, the bird-of-paradise lamp shining down upon him, as he bent over the imaginary steering wheel, heels dug into the flowered pattern of the rug, the ball of one foot for the brake and the other for the clutch, using the long green-stemmed ashtray

for the gearshift, explaining that he should feed the gas gradually, ". . . an'
release the clutch smooth at the same time till the motor goes
aaaaaaaaaaehmm! An' then shift to first, into your knee, an' then gas it
agin, mash down on the clutch an' shift to second, straight out an' slightly
at a angle a little past neutral, an' then do it agin, an' then back to third —
an' then b-r-e-e-z-e, Jack!"

The light changed. He mashed down on the gas, released the clutch, sang
the gears across the busy street and shifted into first just as he reached the
other side, and then he did it again, and then he b-r-e-e-z-e-d on down to
Twelfth Street.

"Hi-de-hi-i — de hi! He de-hee-de he! OOOOOOOOOO — you push
the first valve down an' the music goes round an' a-round — o-o-o-o —
o-o, an' it comes out here!" His tails flapped in the breeze and his hair fell
into his face and he fell into a trucking shuffle like Cab.

He stood at the corner of Thirteenth Street and looked at the pretty little
house with the neatly trimmed lawn that looked like napp green hair to see
if he could see a light — That's where Miss Fortman lives — glowing in the
presence of the handsome buxom, brown-skinned fourth-grade teacher
who had smiled seductively when she had greeted him at the door. . . .

"Here's the flower boxes you wanted. Policeman Jackson let me use his
saw. . . ."

"Thanks, baby! They look just wonderful! Now you come right in and
I'll see if I can find a cookie and a glass of milk in the kitchen."

He waded through the thick soft rug and took the chair that she had
offered him in front of the polished dining table. He admired the beautiful
buffet, which was of the same wood as the table, against the opposite wall
with two glistening silver candlesticks at each end.

She entered the room with a slice — a real hunk! — of three-layer chocolate cake and a big glass of cold milk!

He looked at her quivering bosom, and bit into the soft creamy cake,
casting moon-eyed looks of eternal gratitude. Just as he was finishing the
cake he noticed a sharp odor coming from the kitchen.

Smells like doodoo! he thought, but then he guiltily rejected this conjecture,
struggling all the while to avoid her gaze. But before he could stop the rush of
air that burst from his lungs, he heard his voice asking: "What you cookin'?"

"Good old cabbage and salt pork — and corn bread!"

Cabbage! That's what *we* eat!

"Unh!" he had exclaimed to Viola upon arriving at home, "She was
cookin' *cabbage!*"

"Schoolteachers eat cabbage like ever'body else! What did you think she
ate — orchid petals?"

"Green!"

He shifted into third for the breezy stretch to Twelfth Street.

Where he came upon a row of brick and frame houses. He studied the neat little signs beside the doors and scanned the facades for the one that might belong to him.

Guggenheim. That's a funny name. He tried to remember his face when he was four and Rutherford was twenty and almost had to die from double pneumonia and called the doctor and Dr. Guggenheim had come with a little black bag and a beard.

"Distinguished, Jack!" cried Rutherford, "an' none a that how-much-money-you-make crap! An'-an' when kin you pay? Naw, sir! He's the kind a doctor who examines you first! German Jew. From the *old* country! Old man Mac sent 'im."

"Yeah, he really was somethin', all right," said Viola. "An' I mean, anytime we called 'im — day *or* night — he was *there*! Fresh as a daisy! An' c-h-e-e-r — ful! I had to set up with your daddy all night, an' when I wasn' there old Allie'd set up with 'im."

"Delirious for nine days, Jack. They didn' know if my number was up or not!"

"You don' remember that, do you babe?" Viola asked, "that time I left you with your daddy to go to the store? An' Rutherford decided to take you for a ride in Johny Crippa's car!"

He tried to remember this father getting out of bed:

"Come here, sonny, your daddy's gonna take you for a walk — a ride maybe." Taking him by the hand and stepping barefoot onto the porch in his pajamas, sweating profusely. Lifting him into his arms at the head of the steps and almost falling down. Aunt Lily heard him.

"Rutherford — c-h-i-l-d — what you doin' out a bed!"

"Gonna take my son for a walk."

"You want to *kill* yourself! . . ."

"Stand back, woman!" pushing Aunt Lily aside, stumbling down the steps and across the yard and through the shoot. The long sharp hairs of his beard scratched against Amerigo's cheek and his breath smelled . . . green.

He studied the window decorations of the drugstore on the corner of Twelfth and Paseo:

"An' he almost did it, too!" Viola exclaimed, "but Aunt Lily was on 'im like white on rice! She held on to 'im. Finally Jenks heard all the commotion, looked out an' saw what was happenin', an' took him back. Aunt Lily said Jenks tried to take you out a your daddy's arms, but he wouldn' let you go. He just wouldn' let you git away. Aunt Lily said you was just

a-laughin' to beat the band! An' when I got home I found you two — 'sleep!
— Yeah! Sleepin' in the bed side by side, just like nothin' ever happened!"

"Old Guggenheim brought me out a that mess!" Rutherford exclaimed,
"you hear me! After that I started gittin' *strong!* An' hong-r-a-y! Didn' I,
Babe? They had me on a diet. Sssssssheeed! Couldn' eat nothin'! Viola kept
bringin' me that old hog-hoof tea — "

"That's what the doctor *told* me to give you — an' that's what I gave
you!"

"I got so sick a that damned tea I'd git *mad* when I'd see 'er comin' with
it. One day I saw 'er comin' with that cup an' I yelled out: Aaaaaaa naw
you don'! You bring me a T-bone steak smothered in red gravy an' onions
an' some fried patatas. N-O-W! An' she brought that steak. An that was
a-l-l, Jack!"

He examined the boxes of patent medicines in the store window and
studied the hot-water bottles with the mysterious long rubber tubes screwed
into their necks. Embarrassed as to the enigma of their purpose, he stared at
the bearded faces of the Smith Brothers on the cough-drop boxes.

I'll be a doctor, he thought. With a beard and a black coat, and make
everybody well, operations and stuff.

The mellow summer night beguiled him with its song, subsumed by the
clapping of myriad approving hands. The glittering marquee of the theater
dazzled his eyes, while the undulating forms of countless women stirred the
impatient blood in his veins. The applause gradually died away and in its
stead an unsuppressable sense of dread. He beheld the dingy apartment
buildings. He peered through every window and saw what was happening
in every room — between the carelessly drawn shades.

He approached *the* apartment. The parked cars stood out in front. From
the dark interior of the car nearest the corner the crimson tip of a cigarette
illuminated the pale fingers of a hand and revealed a gray face with small
beady eyes that stared at him knowingly.

He crossed the street and sped up the hill, feeling the eyes on his back,
peering through his clothes. He shifted into second and then sang into first
at the summit.

At Tenth and Harrison the Troost streetcar overtook him. He watched its
big red taillight whir out, down past Campbell Street, near the house where
he was born, next to the Silver Laundry, in the basement. Where the sidewalk shines like diamonds.

"Sometimes I wonder why . . . I spend the lonely nights! . . . dreamin' of
a song," he sang thoughtfully: "The mel-o-dy . . . haunts m-y rev-er-ie —
an' I am once-agin-with you . . . When our love was new."

He turned down Harrison Street. St. John's loomed into view, its huge windows filled with light. The roar of the great organ absorbed the melody of his song, cooled the fires in his blood, and caused the lids of his eyes to fall heavily under the weight of his lashes, like the branches of great trees. He saw them, great fir branches, swooping down from the rims of his eyes.

He stood before the door of the church and listened:

Deeee — eee — ep ri-vah, my home is ooovah Jur-dun. . . . Deeee — eee — ep ri-vah, Lawd. . . .

A quartet. The Mills Brothers — Brothahs! Four brothers and a guitar! He plays like a real trumpet with nothin' but his hands. The father plays the bass with his mouth since the son died, John . . . Doom doom doom doom — dum-doom-ma-doom-doom! The Ink Spots, Jack! I'm gonna be a quartet with a guitar. A crooner — Russ Colombo! Naw — Clarence Rand! Bbbbing Crosby: *When the baluuu . . . of the night . . . meets the gold . . . of the day . . . someone . . . waits f-o-r — me!*

He walked down Campbell Street to Eighth Street. Aunt Lily's light was on. I'll go and see 'er next Sunday. Next year. He greeted the men, women, and children who sat out on the porches and steps and played in the street: "Hi, Turner an' Carl an' Guinny an' Josephine an' May an' Helen an' Betty an' Dorothy an' Mable an' Frank an' Ersaline an' Cornelia an' Mary-Louise an' William an' Jail!"

"Looks like we gonna be the last ones to move way from down here," said Viola's voice.

He paused thoughtfully at the great Admiral Boulevard.

Go! said the green light.

Tomorrow's Monday. . . . He tried to peep through the window of Mrs. Crippa's front room as he entered the shoot. Too high.

He looked vacantly at the sprawling lot next to his house just before he unhooked the gate, whistling in order to overcome a subtle fear that rippled through his mind. His foot on the bottom step of the stair, he peered for an instant into the pitch-black reaches of Miss Jenny's porch. Then he noticed that the light in the kitchen was out. They're gone.

He entered the dark kitchen and immediately turned on the light. It shone too brightly, and threw a heavy wedge of light into the darkness of the middle room.

A creaking sound! As from the step of an unfriendly foot. From the middle room! He held his breath. No sound but the sound of voices coming from the alley, of a truck running down the avenue, a radio, now laughter, crickets! Suddenly a teeming din of sound!

He turned on the lamp in the middle room. He caught a glance, from the corner of his eye, of a strange face! He stood unconsciously before the mirror and stared at his face. It stared back at him.

A step on the front stair!

Not Mom or Dad! Not Miss Lucille. Mr. Morgan! Amerigo recognized the jingle of his keys. He saw the round, well-dressed figure of the man who worked as a waiter at the Southern Mansion, downtown.

"That's a sharp cat!" said Rutherford's voice. "Old Morgan usta be on big time in the old days. Hustlin' was good, an' that joker laid right in there. I remember seein' when I was just a little boy!"

"Married me when I wasn' nothin' but a baby!" said Miss Lucille. "Sixteen! I didn' know no better. Filled my head with a lot a air. Good-time Charlie! Hot damn! He was out havin' his black fun an' I had to look out after myself!"

How did he know? he wondered, hearing Miss Lucille cry out one evening, in the kitchen through the toilet door: *Why what do you mean!* just before his fist resounded against her face: WHAP! followed by tears and half-swallowed recriminations that seeped through the cracks in the toilet door while he, Viola, and Rutherford ate their evening meal in silence.

"That cat sure knows what to do, don' he!" Rutherford whispered maliciously. "Why — what-do-you-mean? Huh! Startin' out all bad an' ever'thin', like he wouldn' find out about her an' T. C. WHAP! He went — an' that wrapped *that* up!"

He and his mother had maintained a noncommital silence in which the telephone vibrated insistently. Rutherford looked into their faces to see if they had heard. They looked into their plates.

He listened to the quiet breathing of the night.

He's gone to bed. He heard Mr. Morgan's shoes drop to the floor.

The large seashell-sound rose from the alley, the avenue, and the great Admiral Boulevard. He turned on the light in the front room. Are Mom and Dad out together? Where? Mentally he scanned all the streets passed through. He looked in all the windows.

He walked back through the empty rooms strewn with discarded clothing and entered the kitchen where he found a leg and a breast of chicken, bit into a cold biscuit, and drank a glass of milk.

When he had finished eating he took off his Sunday suit and hung it up in the closet. He looked at his naked body in the mirror. Like a boxer . . . a Greek jockey . . . strap. He turned out the light in the kitchen and in the middle room and entered the front room and made his bed. Just before he turned out the light and slid between the covers of the red room, he cast a glance at the Sunday *Star* and the *Voice* whose pages lay sprawled upon the comfortable chair. . . . In the dark with no moon. Tears coursed down his cheeks and fell upon the sheet.

He walked through the noisy Monday morning enchanted by its colorful sound: toe over heel, heel over toe. He heard — just as he passed the cottonwood tree at the bottom of Campbell Hill — the quick step of summer at his heels. He quickened his pace, in case it should overtake him, realizing, however, that by the time he reached the old empty building where the show used to be, it was no use, that summer had come and gone! That he had felt within the brilliance of a hot summer day the freezing blast of winter, whose light had transformed itself into huge flakes of snow that had filled the naked arms of the trees!

Now, in the languishing autumn of spring, whose new leaves were heralding summer, he heard whispers rumoring the blood-golden course he had taken. His body waxed hot, and was cooled in a wash of sweat that stormed his mind like summer rain, as his muscles strained in order to stay his fleeting pace. Up and down country hills, in and out of Aunt Nadine's garden and up and down the excrement-splattered ladder of the pigeon coop. Green fields strewn with purple flowers rushed prickly into his face, filling his hands with their softness, which he revealed to Grandma Veronica's blind eyes.

Backward the forward rush! Like from the back of the streetcar! Nights and days receded into "Next year," which was *already* this year! Stars *fell up* into the early reaches of daylight and vanished, and the moon metamorphosed into the sun before his very eyes! Before he could cross Harrison Street "Next year" had insinuated itself — in a whirl of color — into the falling leaves that transformed the big white bed at the foot of *Zorro's Friday Night Revenge* into a great mound of snow through which he strained to look up into the inarticulate mouth of the trembling slick-haired winter in order to hear the answer to the unheard question. It sounded like, "Was it, Now?"

September! Next year *already!* He was astounded. In the fifth grade in Miss Hunt's class with the new principal comin' — already there. Waitin' — *ing*. Beyond the hill at the corner of Pacific Street and Independence Avenue, opposite Uncle Charlie's junkyard and the church and the bunch of . . .

Boom!

The shock of sound and color rising from the playground.

"That niggah sure thinks he's cute!"

"Thinks!"

"Talkin' like a sissy!"

"Walkin' on his toes like a punk!"

"Yeah! In them short pants. Tee! hee!"

"Frog-eyed devil!"

"Black-as-the-Ace-a-Spades!"

"HIS MAMMY DON' WEAR NO DRAWERS!"

Earl Lee's voice filled the cinder-dusty lot next to Mr. Whitney's house at
the top of the alley, just after he had come back from Aunt Nadine's:

"HIS MAMMY DON' WEAR NO DRAWERS!"

"Aw-aw!" Turner cried, "I'm gonna *see* this! I *know* A-mer'go ain'
gonna let *no* niggah talk about Miss *Viola's* drawers — an' let 'im git away
with it!"

"I don't play that stuff, Earl Lee!" his voice said in a distant artificial
tone. Just like Socrates was saying it. He saw the big picture of the fierce-
eyed Socrates painted on the art gallery wall, gesticulating to the other
Greeks under a blue sky.

"I don't play that stuff, Earl Lee!"

"I know that your *mammy* plays!"

"Aw-aw!" cried another sheeted figure. And a blinding rage rose to his
throat and tears filled his eyes amid war cries of the advancing horde of
Indians and the sound of pinto pony hooves mingled with the rattle of
armor and mail as the barbed mace crashed against the enemy's face and
the thrust lance flew home, knocking him from his horse, at which they
rolled down the side of the mountain and came to a death-locked stop on
the edge of the deep ravine at the bottom of which, many fathoms below,
lay the Chinese temple in which the great Buddha sat, legs crossed, arms
reposed, dreaming the conquest that caused Tommy to yell:

"Git that niggah, 'Mer'go! Use your right! Uppercut 'im!"

"Swish!" went the telling sword blade, splitting the dragon's mouth. Up
swung the tomahawk, severing the bleeding scalp.

"That's right, man!" Turner yelled, "run that niggah home! Show 'im he
can't talk about your mammy's drawers!"

"Hot dog! Look at ol' Amer'go!" cried Willie Joe.

"*DON'T,*" cried Rutherford, "*never back no man up in no corner! If you
win the fight, ask him if he's got enough, an' if he's got enough, quit! Shake
hands an' forgit it!*"

"You got enough, niggah?" cried Socrates.

The enemy lay whimpering in silence.

"All right, then."

He led the triumphal march through the sun-splayed alley. The cool
sweaty sheen of victory prickled his face, dripped from his armpits, trembled

between his taut thighs. With exhilarated gratitude he accepted the homage
of the crowd.

"What happened to you?" Viola had asked when he entered the kitchen.
"Your face is all dirty an' your nose bleedin'. Did you fall down?"

"No'm."

"What happened to you, then?" asked Rutherford.

"I had to fight."

"Unh!" Rutherford exclaimed. "Must a been somethin' pretty bad to
make *you* fight!"

"Who'd you fight?" asked Viola, spreading one of Rutherford's shirts
out on the ironing board.

"Old Earl Lee!"

"What'd he do?" Rutherford asked.

"Nothin'."

"Nothin'! You beat a man half to death for nothin'? An' I *know* you
must a *won*, comin' home all bruised up, with your shirt all torn. Look at
that, Babe!"

Viola examined the shirt.

"That don' look like no tear to me. That looks like a *cut!*"

"Damned if it don'!" Rutherford cried. "Unh! That little niggah sure was
cuttin' at you! Cut your shirt off your back! An' it must a been with a razor,
too, 'cause ain' no knife gonna cut so clean an' even like that!"

"What'd he *do?*" Viola asked.

He began to tremble with agitation.

"Nothin'."

"He must a done somethin'," said Rutherford, "or said somethin'. What'd
he say?"

"My momma don' wear no drawers." he muttered.

"Your momma don' *what!*" Rutherford asked, suppressing laughter.

". . . My momma don' wear no drawers!"

"Your momma don' wear no *drawers!*" Rutherford grinned broadly.
"Well, why didn't you show the little niggah?" He mischievously grabbed
the hem of Viola's dress, revealing the pink underskirt.

His glance, burdened with rage and embarrassment for his father,
dropped to the floor where it lay shattered in a seething heap of sharp
blinding rainbow-colored impatience that now checked his gait and caused
him to swagger with assumed nonchalance onto the playground. He cast a
wary eye at the tall imposing figure of the red-headed man surveying the
upper and lower playgrounds from his post at the head of the concrete
stairs, field whistle dangling by a chain from his neck, like a general surveying his camp.

His "Englishman's" sun helmet shaded his eyes, and the sleeves of his white shirt were rolled up to the elbows, one of which rested upon the rail, his doubled fist supporting his red-headed chin, while the tufted hairs of his neatly trimmed mustaches roofed his fleshy upper lip, which was now quivering in anticipation of the command for Chester Owlsley to stop beating his sister, Emma's, head against the asphalt.

Minutes later they were marching through the sniggering crowd into the office where there was a can in the closet, filled with water, in which a coiled leather strap lay like a malignant rattler's tail, thirty-two inches long and an inch and a half wide.

The tears were gone, but their eyes were still red when they entered the classroom a little while after the bell had rung. Miss Hunt suppressed the smile in her eyes and told them to take a seat in a voice that was a little too stern, as she smoothed her blouse over her pretty bosom with a discreet tapering off-white hand, allowing her sweeping lashes to fan the hot embers glowing within the pupils of her eyes, causing the new principal's face to approximate the color of his hair.

Amerigo looked enviously from one to the other, and finally allowed his gaze to rest upon Miss Hunt's face. As the door clicked subtly to, he insinuated into his glance an expression of intimate confidential adult deprecation of the childish behavior of the punished criminals who stared sheepishly at the blackboard upon which the multiplication tables were written in a pregnant feminine hand.

"Aye say, eold man, ahr you theah!" he whispered, at which the class laughed hilariously. Miss Hunt relieved the heat in her bosom with a smile, while he admired the soft wisp of hair that fell into her face, just before she cleared her throat and took up the inevitable textbook.

Silence.

And then her gentle tongue kissed away the tedious drudgery of reading, writing, and arithmetic. In a passion of ambition to learn, to excel, question after question burst from his lips in Rathbonian articulations. His words kissed her words. His thoughts pursued her thoughts — through the soft, the dangerous, the daring waters of the world. Together they tracked the virgin snows of endless mountains, caroused upon exotic islands in all latitudes, and fed upon the fruits of the earth's bountiful gardens.

"Sailing, sailing, swiftly sailing, com-rades sing!" she sang in tremelous voice.

"Sssssh! Ssssssh!" she whispered to still the enthusiasm of he who would sing the loudest and best, only for her . . . only for her.

Oh how he envied the blackboard from which she rubbed the multiplication tables, the piece of chalk with which she wrote the spelling list, oscillating between his jealousy of the chair upon which she sat and the skirt that she adjusted at the knee when she folded her legs, unconsciously wriggling her ankles, as her questions caused anxious fingers to pop like whip-ends in the air.

Then the hated bell rang.

Patterns of noisy light burst from all the rooms and cascaded through the hall beneath the stern glances of William Lloyd Garrison, Frederick Douglass, Booker T. Washington, Abraham Lincoln, and the father of America. I pledge al-legiance to the flag of the U-nited States of A-mer'ca an' to the Republic for which it stands, one nation, indivisible, with liberty an' justice — for all!

"All of me! Why not take all of me?" he sang quietly: "Can't you see . . . I'm no good without you."

"Sssssssh! Ssssssh!" rippled through the wriggling chairs of the auditorium. The new principal, Mr. Powell, rose to his feet and signaled to the student body to be silent.

"We will now sing the Negro National Anthem!"

He looks a little like Dad, he thought, admiring the handsome figure in the white shirt and dark brown suit. A little golden key at the end of a golden chain swung from the third button into his vest pockets like curtain cords. Like the reverend's. "And he's got good hair, too! It swept back from his domed forehead . . . like Aunt Rose's . . . like it was made out a stone like at the art gallery. In-*tella-gent!*"

". . . The Negro National Anthem!" he was saying, and there followed a rumble of chairs and the gentle cracking of supple bones stretching the host of bodies into respectful attitudes. The introduction wriggled from Miss Tucker's, the seventh-grade teacher's, fingers and excited the air into their lungs where it strained to be released by the downfalling hand of Principal Powell:

"Now!" declared the hand.

"Lift every voice and sing! Till Earth and Hea-ven ring, ring with the har-m-o-ny of li — ber — ty! Let our rejoycing r-i-s-e! High as the listening skies! Let it resound loud as the roooooling sea!"

Heads up, shoulders pushed back, eyes peering into the bright sunny vistas of the rolling sea. . . .

Land!

"Let us march on! till Vic — to — ree — is won!"

"Up from the human wilderness of slavery!" declared Principal Powell, "and into the bright air of freedom, eating of the fruits of knowledge and culture, facing the responsibilities of enlightened citizenship in a better America, in a better world — that is our reason for living!"

. . . Like Thomas Hayes and Marian Anderson and Paul Robeson and Ira Eldridge — and *me!* — he thought.

"We must learn to read not only with our eyes, but with our minds, with our spirits! We must learn to write not just words, but those deep human feelings — which all men possess — that communicate man's desire to live in freedom and harmony with himself as well as his fellow man. We must learn how our government is run so that we can vote for our rights, and for *the Right,* even though it be against our personal interest. That is what it means to be an American! The one great duty of life is to serve others, to live for others!

"The time to start is now, the place, right here. It is my desire to see you become organized into classes with each class representing a unit with collective as well as individual voting power. We're going to establish good government at Garrison School, and we're not going to put our personal interests above Garrison's interests. The president, to be chosen from the seventh-grade class, will be responsible to the whole student body and to the faculty for the intelligent, efficient governing of our school. I can think of not greater ambition for a young man or woman than to aspire to this lofty position —"

Hot dog! I'm gonna be the president! — I'm gonna . . .

"We must learn to govern ourselves so that when we reach the age of citizenship we shall be able to fulfill our rolls as citizens of the city and state, of the great nation in which we live. The future belongs to the educated, to the heard and honest worker, to the dreamer with a vision. Let us all strive to be better human beings, to be smarter human beings, to be the makers of our destinies!"

Clap! clap! clap! clap! clap! clap!

"Let us sing, in closing, 'My Country 'tis of Thee.'"

"My country, 'tis of thee, sweet land of li-ber-ty, of thee I sing! — Land where my faaather died! . . ."

Crispus Attucks, the first man to die for his country . . . in a boat with George Washington, the father of the country, crossing the Pa-to-mick . . . and Harriet Tubman and the Underground Railroad with John Brown's body lies buried in the . . . and President Lincoln, the sixteenth president of the United States, who walked five miles just to give somebody back a nickel that somebody forgot that came into his store because he was a poor man and liked to help poor people, so when the South wanted to keep the Negroes a slave, he said, We're going to free the slaves because slaves are people just like everybody else and because slavery is bad like it says in the Bi-ble and so he wrote the Emancipation Proclamation that said that there couldn't be slavery . . .

"— Land of the pil-grim's pride! —"

In the cold snow and freezing wind at Plymouth Rock . . . Ford's got the fastest pickup . . . where the Indians should then know to plant corn that they ate at Thanksgiving with the Indians eating at the same table because they were so good to them, giving them New York that used to be New Amsterdam when they gave it to the Dutch where Franklin D. Roosevelt comes from like the windmills and pretty houses with a lot a rooms that you kin see one through the other at the art gallery above the Indian room in the basement beside . . .

"From ev-ev-re — ee moun — tain-side . . . let free — dom — ring!"

With liberty an' justice for all . . . Like in England an' France where they sure kin . . . can . . . an' Scotlan . . . *d!*

He let the noisy mob rush past him when the recess bell rang. He bowed graciously and allowed Miss Hunt to pass, casting a respectful glance at the gracefully turned calf that swelled up from her delicately wrought ankle. In the hall he stopped before the portrait of Frederick Douglass and studied the intense expression upon his patriarchial face, surrounded by white wiry hair that partially obscured the collar of his shirt. His brilliant eyes peered out from under fierce bushing brows, while his mouth clamped down upon the last definitive unalterable inexorable word: *FREEDOM!*

Freedom! He pronounced the word, screwing determination into his face: Freedom!

Next he stood before the quiet, gentle clean-shaven boyish face of Booker T. Washington:

"Cast down they bucket where thou art . . ." said the great man.

"That's from the Bi-ble. The reverend said that, that's what Jesus tol — *d* the disciples who were fishermen first."

He moved dreamily down the hall and stopped before the portrait of George Washington. He compared his face to Rutherford's face:

He wasn't the father of the country 'cause he wanted to be. — He had to . . . to be . . . . Wasn't nobody else! A wave of pity for the poor father of the country came over him, cold, ailing, alone, facing the invincible armies of the redcoats, caps, carryin' all them bags at the Union Station.

He stared into the brilliant sunlight streaming through the great hall window, head high, chest out, arm resting majestically upon the banister, oblivious to the cries of the children playing outside. He was so intent on his meditations that he remained undisturbed by the vague fragmentary

VINCENT O. CARTER

image of Miss Hunt and Mr. Powell, who observed him from the shadowy corner at the opposite end of the corridor.

The bell rang. He saw the in-rush of his tattered ragamuffin army with aristocratic disgust!

Again the bell rang. He strode behind the lines, high-leather-booted, cape swaying, evaluating the stamina of his bond slaves, coarse hunters and trappers who straggled along the avenue with the eyes of a worried general on the eve of the decisive battle.

Boom! Boom! Boom! Volleys of late-afternoon sunlight setting fire to the trees!

"Lift every voice and sing!" he cried encouragingly, thinking sadly: We caunt possebleh beat the eneme with *thisss* armeh! To General Handcock. . . . Cock is a bad word . . . pussy! Poon-tang! Twoit! . . . We caunt possebleh beat the enemeh with *thisss* twoit! To a worn-out soldier who suddenly appeared in the person of Miss Mona he said:

"How's Isaac?"

"He's dead, son."

"He was a good man. Arrange the funeral for nine A.M. tomorrow. Carry on!"

Attucks dead — from a single shot. We'll see that he gi-gets a medal. A gunshot wound in the heart. The first man to die for his country!

Down past the barrel shop. Sun, shining upon a sea of varied green, colorless, and brown bottles and jugs, metamorphosing between squinting eyelids into a great array of flowers saturating the great auditorium of St. John's with sweet-smelling scents arranged around the thin powdered face of the sleeping Isaac, who was dressed in his Sunday suit with a white shirt and black tie, his frozen hands folded naturally on his stomach.

Sobs of the bereaved family filtered through the strains of,

"Steal a-way, steal a-way, steal a-way to Jeeeee — sus! Steal a-way, steal a-way hoooome. I ain' got loooong to staaay here. . . ."

"My Lord!" cried Minnie Simms in a strong tremelous voice. "He calls me! He calls me by the thun-dah! . . ."

Boom!

"The trumpet sounds"

Gold.

"with-in-a-my soooul. . . ."

Boommm!

"I ain' got loooong — to staaay here."

"Green trees a bindin'!" whispered the flowers through the snow, like a great silver coffin filled with the hoary voices of the dead, dead shadows filling the thumbtacked squares: Gone. Wondering at the absence of the billboards in front of the show that had long since been hacked into fire-wood by the freezing population: "Burned to — to ashes . . . dus-*t* to dust . . . to clay . . . brown — like it was painted."

"I ain' got looong to stay here. . . ."

The reverend, tall, dressed in black — the shad-ow — of death, I shall fear no evil — emerged from the sea of flowers.

"Let us pray."

Prayer rose in a seething spray of articulate whispers that swelled into crystalline droplets of tears that rained down upon the sleeping Isaac and reverberated within the golden swell of the great organ. Someone was singing:

"Go-in' hooome, goin' home, I'm a gooooin' home, Qui-et-like . . . some still day, I'm a-goin' home."

"Where it's *really real!*" suddenly opening his eyes and looking *enviously* at Isaac, wondering: Does he know?

"It's not far. . . ."

He stretched out his body to its full length in order touch the bright star with his toe:

"— just close by, through an o-pen door. Work's all done! — care laid ba, go-na roam no more. . . ."

"Toe over heel, heel over toe."

The reverend raised his head. His hands gave the sign for silence:

"Here lies Isaac who is dead. . . ."

". . . *passed away at four* A.M. . . . *Sssssh!*"

"an innocent lamb of the Master's flock."

"Here lies Crispus Attucks who is dead, the first to fall from the back porch banister: Boom! Nine times. First he fell, then half lay, half fell, blood spurting from the hole in his neck — *Boom! Boom! Boom!* — that wouldn't heal 'cause the hole was too little. *Twenty-caliber. Rachel did it!*"

"Freedom!" Frederick Douglass declared.

"Cast down thy bucket where thou art!" replied Booker T. Washington.

"Here's your nickel back," said Honest Abe.

"We gonna give 'im a medal," said the general, "an' name the Attucks school after 'im — "

"An' Lincoln university after *me!*" said Mr. Lincoln.

"An' *somethin'* after *me, too,* or *I'll tell Tom!*" declared Frederick Douglass.

"Cast down thy bucket where thou art," replied Booker T. Washington.

"I'm the father! Ain' nobody else!" said the general with resignation.

"And now Amerigo Jones," the reverend was saying, "one of Isaac's best friends, would like to say a few words."

He climbed the back porch stair, looking down upon the clean spot where the sleeping Isaac lay.

"What you *dreamin'* 'bout, child!"

He looked dumbly into Mrs. Derby's face. She stood on the porch with a dishpan in her hand, smiling curiously. Her conscienceless yellow eyes glistened from the cool blue depths of shade.

"Nothin'." He continued up the long long stair, his progress somewhat impeded by the weight of the heavy autumn sunlight, which charged the air with a winterlike severity.

The seasons flooded his mind in a spectrum of hot and cold colors that inspired cries of anguish and joy up and down the alley. Pages of number-less books sprouted from the branches of the trees — and fell. Words rained down and filled garrulous throats, arousing in him the impatient desire to stretch out to his interminable length and be free, like Frederick Douglass.

Cast down your

"Bra Mo! Aw Bra Mo!"

It was Maxine. She was ten, a little brown-skinned girl with a hooked nose who had recently moved to 618 where they still used to be on the first floor. He glanced excitedly into the shoot in order to catch a glimpse of her face, making mental note of the fact that her hair was nappy, that her hips were broad, and that her legs were bow.

"Bra Mo! Aw Bra Mo!" her coarse young voice echoing myriad con-scious moments of that infinitely timbred cry, which caused the tides of change in his alley to ebb and flow, filling the windows and doors of every house, setting in motion that humble figure who strained cheerfully under the burden of fire in winter and wet dripping cold in summer.

"Bra Mo! Aw, Bra Mo!" An unheard voice, high and thin, laughing like brass bubbles bouncing over the cobblestones.

"Well," said Viola's voice, "Miss Minnie's gone. You'll have to go a long way to visit 'er now."

"You take the Quindera bus —" said Miss Minnie, "Tenth an' Main, an' ride to the end of the line an' walk straight on till you come to a big white house on the corner, then you turn left a little piece an' then you ask somebody. You'll find it, all right. Mind you, it ain' much yet, just a little gopher hole in a heap a dirt. We got a few chickens, some geese an' ducks, an' two sows an' a shoat. We gonna live in the basement till we kin scrape up enough money to build the first floor — Like I say, it ain' much, but it's our'n, an' we ain' payin' no rent to no white man, either! We workin' for ourselves, an' it ain' nobody's cockeyed business *how* long it takes!"

"That's my woman!" exclaimed Mr. Primm's voice, which suddenly condensed around the stem of his pipe and swelled into a shimmering droplet of spittle that finally fell — *Boom!* — into the three empty rooms on the second floor of 618 where Mr. and Mrs. Derby *used* to live.

Miss Betty lives there now. A youngish-looking gray-haired woman with large sleepy eyes, tawny unhealthy skin, and a feathery black mustache fringing her upper lip. Her shoulders drooped, and the former refulgence of her breasts seemed to have sunk down into her little round belly, causing it to swell, as though she had swallowed a little watermelon-sized balloon.

"She sure kin cook, though!" Viola exclaimed.

"Yeah," said Rutherford, "she puts down some a the best light rolls I ever *did* eat!"

Amerigo saw her, sickly, sleepily, miserably dabbing into a soft airy mound of dough with her arthritic hands by coal oil lamplight, her wavering shadow hovering over the stove that flowed dangerously with the heat of the fire he had scavenged from the condemned houses of the surrounding neighborhood at ten cents a basket, but which he had given to her, because she was old and sick.

"How's your buddy doin'?" Rutherford's voice was asking.

"She ain' doin' so good. Have to hold 'er up so she kin cook to keep 'er from sleepin' on 'er feet an' fallin' into the stove."

"That's too bad. A old woman like that, too sick to work, with nobody to look after 'er. She couldn' git along, I don' believe, without you."

"Ain' nobody else."

"Saaam-my! Saaam-my!" Mrs. Sales called from the bosom of the cottonwood tree behind Toodle-lum's yard.

"Aw — I hear you!" Sammy cried from the first floor of 618. A feeling of regret and confusion took possession of him, as he relived the scene:

Sammy kissing Maxine under the steps, mashing his belly and grinding his hips against hers and squeezing the cheeks of her behind with his fingers.

His mother killed herself, he thought, watching Maxine's wiggling hips. That's his girl. He's twelve.

"Saaam-my!"

"I'm comin'!" breaking from Maxine's grasp with a show of irritation. "You wait right here till I come back, you hear!" he commanded, and dashed off.

Just then William Young came up the alley. He was tall for thirteen and wore long pants and smelled like sweat and tobacco. He looked rough, tough, and dirty, but he was good looking, with long slicked-down hair. His perfectly shaped teeth were of a greenish yellow color.

Maxine shot a smile at William. William leaped onto the porch and grabbed her around the waist.

"Quit now!" she grinned, while he, Willie Joe, Annie, Geraldine (Turkey-legs), and Toodle-lum looked on.

"Quit!" William exclaimed, addressing his audience, "ain' that some shit!" — at which he grabbed her more firmly and screwed his belly against hers so fiercely that she frowned as though she were in pain, uttered a delirious grunt, threw her arms around his neck, and buried her lips in his mouth.

"Aaaaaaaw!" he had cried: "I'm gonna t-e-l-l! I'm gonna *tell* Sammy!"

Amerigo had dashed through Toodle-lum's yard and come to a breathless halt at the kitchen door of Sammy's house. Sammy sat alone at the table, stuffing a piece of corn bread into his mouth.

"Sammy!"

"What, man?"

"She's *kissin'* 'im, I *saw* 'er!"

"Who?"

"Maxine's kissin' old William!"

"Naw!"

"Yeah! Honest!"

"Come on, man!"

"Aw-aw, now!" he had cried, racing with Sammy to the scene of the crime.

William stood on the step facing them with his hand in his pocket.

"He's got a knife!" he whispered to Sammy.

"I don' care!" Sammy exclaimed, "he kin *have* 'er! Now git this, see?" He waved his finger in Maxine's face. "We're through, see! Finished! Washed up! Git it?"

With that he dashed back home to finish his beans and corn bread, leaving him to fidget nervously under Maxine's reproachful gaze.

"What'd you have to go an' tell for?" she said. "Wasn' none a your business."

"Stool pigeon!" cried William with a vicious sneer. "A dirty double-crosser. I oughtta beat your big head!"

"Let 'im alone," said Maxine, a subtle smile insinuating itself into her face. With deliberate slowness she drew William into her arms and kissed him, darting her tongue between his lips and wriggling her behind in Amerigo's face.

"I hate a meddler worse 'n a liar!" exclaimed Rutherford.

Supper was over, the dishes washed, and the homework checked. He stood on the porch and listened to the playful voices of his companions in the alley.

"Why ain't you out playin' with the rest of 'um?" Viola asked from within the kitchen.

He pretended not to hear.

"You hear your momma talkin' to you, boy!" said Rutherford.

"Nothin'," he muttered, perplexed by the mystery of Right and Wrong. Of silhouetted shadows wriggling sensuously in the frames of screen doors in the cool summer evenings, while strange voices whispered through the long copper wires that stretched from the lamppost to his house and deafened his ears with their silent reverberations, causing Rutherford's lips to tighten and Viola's face to lose its expression, except for the eyes, which uttered a subtle plea for silence, just before his glance fell into his plate.

His eyes followed the wires from his house back to the lamppost, and from that lamppost to the next, looping noisily up the alley, humming, popping, cracking! The din of forbidden words wriggled themselves into kissing lips. Lip-locked mouths grunted painfully, while hips and bellies writhed within the voluminous redness of nine o'clock. He pulled the covers over his head, but the voices found him just the same.

"What'd you go and tell for?" Viola exclaimed from the big white bed, while Amerigo stood above her trembling, staring into the vortex of a shattered sense of Justice. And then the sky turned dirty. The trees appeared ominous. Stench rose up from the drains in front of Miss Jenny's porch and from behind Maxine's house. Rusty water standing in dirt-encrusted cans in the trash box turned bile-green. In vain he struggled to avoid the vile odors. Finally a warm sticky feeling oozed between his legs and formed a cool pool upon the sheet, the meaning of which, in the light of day, he was at a loss to explain.

"Willie Joe? Is that *you?*" cried Viola from the back porch the following evening. He was just entering the yard.

"Yes'm!" His face was dirty, but his mouth stretched itself into a clean milk-white grin framed in elliptical folds of prune-colored flesh, with deep wells at either corner to indicate where the dimples were.

"Boy! You're growin' like a *weed!* I almost didn' *recog*nize you!"

"Yes'm!"

"What grade you in now?"

"Secon'."

"Well, that's fine!"

"How you doin'?"

"All right."

"Well, I'm gonna see. I'm comin' down to the school tamarra night, an' I'm gonna be checkin' up on you!"

"Yes'm. Kin 'Mer'go come out an' play?"

"If he wants to."

"Aw Mom! I don't wanna play with that little boy!" he exclaimed, thinking: *We simpleh caunt goe on like thisssss!*

"Amerigo?"

"Ma'am?"

"You could make me very happy if you would do me just one little favor."

"What?"

"Call me 'Mother.' *All* the little white boys out at the Biarritz call *their* mothers 'Mother' an' it sounds *so* nice!"

"Aw *Mom!*"

"Go out an' play with Willie Joe."

"Aw *Mom!*"

"You heard me! He's comin', Willie Joe."

"Come on, *niggah!*" stalking down the steps.

"I thought you weren't supposed to use that word," said Viola.

Freedom! cried Frederick Douglass.

"Cast down thy bucket where thou art," replied Booker T. Washington.

"Come on, Willie Joe."

"Well, well, Mrs. Jones, it's a pleasure to see you!" Principal Powell said with a warm smile the following evening at PTA meeting. Viola warmed herself in the educated glow of the light overhead, eyes sparkling, teeth sparkling, gold crown shimmering like the timber of Rutherford's voice. "It's a pity that *Mister* Jones couldn't come out tonight."

"Oh, eh, well, he was . . . wasn't feeling very well, but I'm *sure* he'll come next time!"

Aaaaaaaw! Amerigo said to himself, hearing Rutherford exclaim:

"What in the *heck* — am I gonna be doin' down there with a whole bunch a women? Listenin' to them little jokers answerin' a lot a questions they done memorized already — just to make 'um look good for one night! *You* go — an' represent me. I'm gonna lie up here an' read my Shadah!"

"Who knows what evil lurks in the hearts of men!" said the Shadow. "The *weed* of crime bears bitter fruit. Crime does not pay!"

How does he *know!*

"Well," Principal Powell was saying, "I surely hope he'll be able to come to the Beau Brummel's Ball we're giving next month. I have you on my guest list!"

"Oooooo!" Viola exclaimed, "that'll be, I mean . . ."

The bell rang, titillating the night air with an enthusiasm that encouraged the multiplication tables to arrange themselves in proper order, the hemispheres to apportion themselves upon the globe as Mother Nature and the geographers intended, while the mountains, rivers, and lakes ranged themselves within the longitudes and latitudes that hummed very discreetly in order not to give the lie to the satisfied expression upon Miss Hunt's face as she eyed Mrs. Powell, her fingertips sweeping away the anxiety from her smooth cheeks, which were *lighter,* caressing the waves of her soft brown hair, which was *better,* while her shoulders alluded with a sudden backward thrust that *her* belly was not full with child.

Sssssssssh! warned the wires under the cover of his Sunday suit.

Then the telephone rang. And all the nice little boys and their nice little mothers and occasional fathers ran into the hall to answer it.

"Oh! why hel-*low,* there, Mrs. Jones!" cried Miss Fortman. "I suppose you've met Miss Hunt already?"

"Eh, yes — " said Viola, "I've been visiting Amerigo's class, and I've — oh! — I'm just — so *impressed!* The children spoke so nice an' — and . . . and all, and . . . I sure hope Miss Hunt isn' having too much trouble with him. Eh . . ."

"Oh noooo!" Miss Hunt exclaimed. Affecting a whisper. "Amerigo's one of my brightest pupils!"

"Oooooo!" Viola exclaimed.

"That's *my* boy!" said Miss Fortman.

Cabbage! he thought, and suddenly flushed hot in the tropical heat of the bosoms and hips and powdered smiles that ricocheted between their animated faces — so quickly that he grew dizzy from the loudness of the discreet thought that forced its way into the expression on Booker T. Washington's face:

My momma is the prettiest woman in the w-h-o-l-e w-o-r-l-d!

He looked at the night sky through the great hall window and caught a glimpse, by reflection, of Frederick Douglass's angry face.

"Can I drop you off?" Miss Fortman was saying.

"Oh! Eh, no! No-no, don't bother!" said Viola nervously. "It's not far. *Really,* it's —"

"Eh, in Cosy Lane."

"Where's that?" They flowed out of the building.

"It's —" Viola began.

"Oh, here's the car —" said Miss Fortman. "Please —"

The taxi driver jumped out and opened the door and they got in. Huge bars of yellow light shot through the windows of the schoolhouse and slanted into the asphalt floor of the playground as the building disappeared in the darkness.

When they reached Uncle Charlie's junkyard, they turned into the avenue. Its funky darkness was agitated by a humid heat charged with the scintillating stench of whiskey, wine, gin, and beer-wet lips locked in tongue-hushing embraces and taut thighs grinding out the rhythms of the shameless dance for which God, in His anger, would punish them, in the end.

Viola wriggled nervously and now and then looked at Miss Fortman with a strained smile:

Ssssssssh!

"Oh!" said Miss Hunt, "I'd certainly be afraid to walk down this street — even in the daytime!"

"It's rough, all right!" said Miss Fortman, looking at Viola for confirmation. Viola looked at her hands.

Just as they reached the alley, the car slowed down. A man in a lumber jacket was kicking another man who lay doubled up on the ground in the stomach.

"You cocksucker! I'll kill you!" yelled the kicker, and kicked his prone victim again. Blood spouted from the corners of his mouth and stained the front of his shirt. He motioned feebly for someone in the crowd to help him. The man kicked him again, in the mouth.

"Drive around them, can't you?" said Miss Fortman fearfully.

"We live up there!" Amerigo said.

Viola poked him sharply in the ribs.

The fighting man pulled out a razor. A siren approached from the downtown end of the avenue.

The taxi driver backed agilely through the dispersing crowd, swirved around in front of the advancing streetcar, and shot up Campbell Hill.

"We kin go up to the boulevard, an' then go down the alley from the other way!" he said, catching sight, at the turn, of the tears in his mother's eyes.

"Where *is* it!" asked Miss Fortman impatiently. "I hope we don't get a flat tire," looking suspiciously at the broken glass that glittered between the crevices of the cobblestones.

Like stars!

He imagined that they were driving through the Milky Way. At the avenue end lay a smoldering heap of red glowing fallen stars. In their midst a man was cutting another man to death.

The squad car had already arrived. Its siren was still shrieking, even though the policemen had already gotten out of the car and were swinging their clubs furiously. But gradually the siren ceased, and the silence was filled by excited exclamations up and down the alley. Doors slammed to, eyes peeped from behind still curtains, the questions: Who? What? Where at? How? swallowed up by the sound of another siren approaching, just a few seconds before the long white ambulance pulled into the mouth of the alley.

"You kin back up into Mister Jackson's yard," he said, "an' then turn up the alley, an' git out thataway!"

"Thanks *awfully* much for bringin' us home!" said Viola, "I sure hope —"

"You're welcome," said Miss Fortman. "Well, we'll be seeing you."

"Good night, Mrs. Jones," said Miss Hunt. "Good night, Amerigo."

"G'night!"

They entered the front room. Rutherford stirred in his chair where he had been dozing.

"Unh! I must a dozed off a minute, there. How was it?"

Viola did not look at him. She went into the middle room and took off her shoes.

"Well?"

"It was very nice," Her voice trembled. "The school was decorated, and all the classes were in session — just like every day in school. The children had drawings on the walls. An' — and some of them were real — very good! They had their lessons and the parents could ask them questions." She sat on the stool in front of the vanity dresser and stared at the mirror in the dark. "And Amerigo," she paused to blow her nose and wipe the corners of her eyes. Then she rose and entered the front room where he stood by his father's chair. "And Amerigo, I'm not just saying it because he's our son, was one of the smartest. They all said so! Miss Fortman an' Miss Hunt. She's the new one, a little yellah gal with wavy hair. An' cute! She even thinks her shadow's white! She kept rolling her eyes at Professor Powell, and he wasn't taking any notice of her whatsoever what with that nice-looking wife he's got. She's pregnant. And he ignored her, too. And what I mean to tell you, they're simple people, and not putting on all that big-shot stuff. . . . I mean, putting on airs. And guess what? He's in the Beau Brummells! And we're on his guest list for their formal at the Mi-ni-ci-pal Auditorium! Isn't that just too too divine? Only big shots belong to that club, and *we're* invited!"

"Unh!" said Rutherford, "we gonna be mixin' with high sa-ci-aty. Hey-hey!"

"Be serious, Rutherford. You *know* I ain' — that I'm not stuck up! And all those so-called big shots don't impress me at all. But it *is* nice to be accepted by nice *ed*-u-cated people who're really *doing* things and — and then to wrap it all up, Miss Fortman just *had* to bring us home! That avenue was bad enough, but when we got —"

"What you talkin' all fancy for?" said Rutherford.

"What!"

"Talkin' like your son. Huh! First my son an' then my wife turnin' into Englishmen on me!"

Viola's eyes flashed with anger.

"An' he's *right,* too! He oughtta learn to talk better. That's what he's goin' to school, tryin' to git — get an education for. *We* know better . . . but we don't do noth — anything — about it. I've scarcely seen a man smarter than you, as far as brains go — when it comes to figuring things out and reading and knowing what's going on and all that. . . . *But what good does it do* — if — if you don't do something with it? I was so *ashamed!* We had to drive through this *slum* with all those low-lifers, crazy winos — killing each other — right on our very doorstep! They were scaired, afraid to come up this alley. Sometimes I'm afraid, too. And then the law — the police came — and the ambulance. They had to *back out* from in front of *our* house. We try to be respectable people, *but they don' know that!*" She wept freely now. "An' — an' they never will, because they'll be scaired to come down here, an' we'll be ashamed to invite 'um —"

"*Ashamed a what!*" Rutherford shouted. "*I ain'* ashamed a *nothin'!* We honest hardworkin' people. We pay our debts an' don' bother *n*obody! An'-an' don' nobody bother us!"

"You know why? Huh? 'Cause you don' go down on the avenue when *you* go out. You hang out on Eighteenth Street. You come home and tell me what a nice time you had at Harrison's — an' what a nice apartment *they* got out on Twenty-Fourth Street, an' what a tough wagon *he's* drivin'. You dream of bein' able to go out on the lake on Sund'y mornin's to go fishin' with Woodie an' them, but you can't, 'cause you ain' got no car an' they spend too much money for you. You ain' no more satisfied than me, but you too scaired to do somethin' 'bout it! When Amerigo does to high school — he'll be graduatin' *year after next!* — where's he gonna invite his high school friends?"

"Why, *hell* — heck —" Rutherford stammered, "*here!* If they — if they —"

"*You think they're gonna come down here!*" Viola screamed. "An' git *cut up!* Or *killed,* maybe — on the North End! An' after that he's got to go to *college!* An' he'll be *ashamed* of us!"

"Aw Mom!"

"Naw! I don' *blame* you, I'd be ashamed, *too!* To have to bring your nice girlfriend *down* here — to *Cosy Lane!* Ain' that a *killer!*"

"Boy," Rutherford said, "your momma's *mad,* you hear me?"

"Miss Fortman is the secretary of the Bon-tons. I sent 'er a invitation to our cocktail sip. I wouldn' even be surprised if she didn' even come now."

"Well," said Rutherford with a show of embarrassed joviality, "that wrapped it up, you done made me mad, Viola. I'm goin' to bed!" Grinning childishly he rose from the chair, stretched himself, and yawned in an exaggerated manner.

You're supposed to cover your mouth when you yawn, he thought, comparing him to Principal Powell, Frederick Douglass, Booker T. Washington, and the general.

Sssssssh!

"I'll have to have a new dress," said Viola in the dark. "Can't wear the same one I wore last year."

"Sssssheeeed! You make me salty with that same old jive!" Rutherford whispered. "Where in the hell — heck you think we gonna git the money?"

Amerigo stretched himself out in the bed until his legs trembled with the taut strength of the great rebellious slave who snatched the whip from his master's hand and fled to the northern side of Freedom. He, the great Frederick Douglass incarnate, stood upon the stage of Garrison School and accepted the diploma for graduation with honor, he stood upon the stage of R. T. Bowles Junior High School and received the diploma with honor, and upon the stage of Northern High, and finally he opened the great doors of Harvard and Yale, and strode across the pages of the *Voice* in multicolored splendor!:

Now a great conductor:

Clapclapclapclapclapclapclapclap!

A Preacher!

Clap clap clapclapclap!

A Principal!

Clapclapcl . . .

A bearded doctor in a black suit!

Clapcapclap.

A Greek Jockey!

Clapclapclapclapclapclap!

A tap dancer like Uncle Ruben, the Nicholas Brothers, an' Buck an' Bubbles an' Bill Bo-jangles Robinson!

C-a-a-a-a-alapclapclapclapclapclapclapc . . . l . . . a . . . pp . . .

An actor like Basil Rathbone an' Ronald Colman an' George Sanders an' Laurence Olivier an' Douglas Fairbanks Junior an' Senior. "We realleh caunt geo on like . . ."

Claaaaaaaap-clapclap — Claaaaap-clapclap!

A big-shot lawyer!

An' now we'll have a few words from the Chairman of the Board of Trustees, Lawyer Jones!

AAAAAAAAAAAAAA-Men!

An' now we'll have a few words from Undertaker Jones, Chairman of the Finance Committee!

"He'p'im Lawd!"

An Educator!

"Cast down thy bucket where thou art!"

Freedom!

"Not 'cause I wanna — 'cause I have to!"

A barrage of shattering explosions revealed a big white bed. The naked woman smiled up at the trembling white-haired grizzly-bearded man:

Freedom?

He sank into the . . .

Ssssssh!

He writhed within the pitch-black alluvia of a suffocating impatience that even the warm breath of the light-giving sun could not penetrate:

"Boy!"

"Sssssssheeeed!"

"Boy!"

"Yessir."

The sun shone with hurting brightness on the dirty way to Freedom. With a profound feeling of revulsion he walked amid the hovels of the enslaved, sprawled along the northern district of his Consciousness, along the glistening streetcar tracks that conducted the noisy streetcar up and down the avenue, past the house where they "found Aunt Pearl dead with —"

Ssssssh!

"an' had to be buried in —"

Sssssssh!

Past Cousin Rachel's. She made Uncle Ruben git kil —"

Sssssssh!

"Have an accident 'cause the hole from the twenty-two-cal —"

Sssssssh!

"wasn' big enough by the time Doc Bradbury came . . ."

At Pacific Street he had to turn north, past the junkyard where —

Sssssssh!

"works."

But quickly! And past the church, the bunch of . . .

On he rushed, the boy, through his shedding skin, imprisoned within the fleeing bone, in hot pursuit of a pair of wings that "Awl a God's chil'un" did not have yet!

That evening at the supper table:

"Boy!" said Rutherford sharply, "don' eat so fast — an' stop pilin' all that food on your plate! Leave some for somebody else. Now-put-one-a-them-pork-chops-back!"

He put the pork chop back on the serving platter, his body shaking with uncontrollable rage, tears running down his face. He stared stubbornly at his plate with his mouth ajar until the half-chewed meat grew cold.

"You know what I mean," said Rutherford, "stuffin' your mouth so full. Both jaws! Almost like he wasn' even tastin' it. An' two pork chops at once. You kin have *three*, if you want 'um, but one at a time. Now go ahead an' eat, an' stop bein' hurt over nothin'."

"I ain' hungry."

"Well — you finish what's on your plate, we don' waste no food in this house."

He indignantly stuffed the food into his mouth.

"*WHAM!*" Rutherford's open palm flickered across the table and burned the right side of his head. A burst of starry light spilled through his eyes and nose as he fell backward, arcing through the sky and finally crashed against the floor.

He trembled where he lay. Viola's face rushed toward his, her arms scooped him up into her bosom, their bodies swinging upward in a little flurry of flickering light, blue from the gas flame under the teakettle, bright yellow from the bulb hanging from the ceiling.

"Leave 'im alone!" Rutherford commanded. "He's almost as big as you. He kin git up by hisself. I'll either make a man out of 'im — or kill 'im!"

He whimpered in his chair and thought:

I'm gonna git me a *job* . . . an' make my *own* money!

He speculated upon the places where he might seek work as the tears dried on his face. The whole shopping district of the great city opened up like a bright shining vista wherein lay wealth, fame — the world!

Clapclapclapclapclapclapclapclapclapclap!

He stumbled through a great black dangerous forest teeming with hideous faces, with arms and clawlike hands that lashed out at him. He sank into deep holes, quagmires and pools of quicksand, barely escaping, only to be confronted by huge huge uprooted trees and great massive stones that ensnared his limbs and tore his flesh.

Finally, more dead than alive, he stumbled into the light of day, trembling in the early-morning coolness, frightened by the excited twitter of the birds. He stared dumbly at the torn sheet, and then at the front room filled with blue light pierced by yellow rays of sun.

Night ain' nothin' but a great big shadow, he thought. He knew it!

He listened to his mother and father breathing in the middle room, back to back.

The alarm clock went off. Rutherford's hand flickered out: WHAM! and silenced it. His head fell back upon the pillow for several minutes, and then he sprang up, as if jerked by an invisible hand. Red-eyed, awry-haired, he stretched himself from the side of the bed, the big toes of both feet curving up like thumbs.

Rutherford glanced at him. He turned his back, but nevertheless felt his father's gaze and heard the jingle of the keys in his hip pocket and the up-swish of his trouserlegs and the dull metallic rattle of his belt buckle, fol-lowed by the thud of his shoes. They strode sluggishly, resignedly into the kitchen and stopped in front of the sink and waited until the water ceased to flow into the teakettle, and then moved back to the stove, and again to the sink — through the eternal machinations of morning.

"Bye hon," said Viola softly, as she left for work.

He pretended not to hear.

Alone, he stared through the empty rooms of the apartment. Then sud-denly he jerked himself out of bed, as Rutherford had done, and dressed himself.

Now? whispered the unheard voice. . . .

He headed southward, up the alley, avoiding Rutherford's track through the invisible autumn snows. He cut through the shoot between the second from the last of the little row of buff-colored, one-story stucco houses where Mr. Jason and Mrs. Pritchett lived. A little stiff-legged yellow woman who walked that way because Mr. Jason hit her with a hatchet. Hatchet-leg!

He crossed the boulevard in a hatchet-legged gait, cutting the southwest corner of the park into a triangle, and then took a hatchet-legged hop, skip, and a jump over the asphalt to Charlotte Street past the house where Howard Robbins lived with his mother, Stella, who had killed her husband.

"Shot 'im four times!" said Rutherford, "an' got *away* with it!"

"To bad for the baby, though," said Viola, "he ain' no older'n Amerigo. Think a how it must feel, to go through life knowin' that your momma killed your poppa! An' then in school an' all. You know how kids are."

"Who killed Cock-Robin?"

I did! cried the Sparrow, with my little six-shooter! *Boom! Boom! Boom! Boom!* Four times!

Straight out Charlotte Street to Eighth, Ninth, and Tenth Streets. Here he halted and looked cautiously toward Locust Street where Rutherford's hotel was. The coast clear, he sped across Tenth Street and down the hill to Eleventh Street until he came to the grade school where white kids went.

His sense of adventure increased as he grew nearer town.

He regarded City Hall with awe and respect.

So tall — and b-i-g! New and clean — with all those rooms full of desks and pencils and with big thick brown linoleum floors and big warm radiators in the winter and air-conditioning in the summer, and electric fountains that give cold water when you mash down on the clutch!

He frowned with displeasure at the bums carousing on the steps and sleeping on the lawn. Realleh!

Then, as he moved toward the corner, he suddenly thrilled to the memory of March, when the wind swept down this broad street and swirled in eddying currents around the buildings, sucking the hapless pedestrians down into whirlpools of air, causing faces to flush with pink surprise, and tear-blind eyes to blink, and rebellious wisps of hair, furling scarves, ties, and coattails made a hot dash for freedom. Whee! as the ell of an inflated skirt swooped up around a pair of naked thighs! And a bedeviled hat whipped miraculously into the air! Whoop — ee! amid the crowd of outstretched arms and hands grasping futilely at the turbulent emptiness that scattered the contents of parcels hither and thither and sent frisky dogs barking through the streets!

Whoop — ee!

The light changed and he flowed with the crowd across the street and stopped in front of the telephone building and looked through the huge windows with letters that you could not rub off even if you could reach them: B-E-L-L T-E-L-E-P-H-O-N-E C-O-M-P-A-N-Y! He observed the women who sat at the little barred cages. . . . Like at the show . . . gazing at the long line of people waiting to pay their bills. At the same time he enjoyed the bizarre reflection of the stream of pretty cars and taxis, of rich-looking white people with expensive dogs and well-dressed children, flowing up and down the street behind him.

Wraaansch! went the blast of the bronze-brass horns of the big buses, interspersed with hisses: *Pschht!* of their air brakes, as they slowed down in the driveways of the bus depot on the corner and came to a stop. Their big doors swung open; the redcaps rushed up to carry the bags of the passengers who streamed into the station.

He turned down Walnut Street and entered the big drugstore on the corner. Standing before a white-jacketed young man with sandy hair and a bland pimply face he said:

"Do you need somebody to sell watches, razors, an' soap an' pencils . . . or candy? . . . What you sellin'?"

"No," said the young man.

He stopped resignedly but undauntedly into the street and made his way up the hill to Main Street. He rejected the flower shop, seeing that they already had a woman to sell flowers and a pleasant-looking white boy of sixteen to deliver them. He looked enviously at the young man, and then stuck his head in the door of the luxurious men's clothing store on the corner, but decided not to apply for work when his intruding head was confronted by the cold stare of a pudgy-faced bald-headed man in an immaculate dark brown single-breasted summer suit and brown-and-white shoes that were new. . . .

A long black limousine came to a halt in front of the Muehlebach Hotel. A beautiful bouquet of orchids stood in the window of the flower shop, in a crystal vase resting upon a velvet cloth that was artfully draped across an ebony table. A mirror framed in silver hung behind it. "I'll try there."

Seconds later he was back on the street.

"Besides, you'd need a decent suit of clothes!" the lady had said not too unkindly, smiling at his shabby corduroy pants, rusty-toed shoes, and torn leather jacket. He caught a glance of himself in the mirror on the way out and was ashamed.

I don't care, he thought standing before the entrance of the great hotel, trying to decide whether or not to go in.

Freedom! cried the immutable voice, and in the next instant he was confounded by the triple image of himself reflected in the long glass panes of the swinging doors. He floated, flushing with prickly excitement, into the rich leather-upholstered atmosphere of the lobby, reverberating with subtle sniggers and discreetly amused noses and the distracted glances of eyes resting upon the fine sawtoothed edges of the *Star*. He stood before the registration desk.

The clerk had dark brown hair, brown eyes, a straight nose, and pouting lips. His shirt was very white and his pretty suit had M-U-E-H-L-E-B-A-C-H written on it. He was sorting the mail.

Amerigo waited.

The clerk did not look up.

"Eh, 'scuse me."

The man sorted his mail.

"Eow, aye beg yoahr pahdon, sah!"

The man did not look at him.

"Eh," he had just begun, when a well-dressed gentleman with a pleasant smile stepped up to the desk.

"Oh! Good morning, sir!" said the clerk, and handed him a letter.

"Thank you," said the gentleman, and stepped into a nearby elevator.

"Eh."

The clerk sorted his mail.

He turned and tried to confront the other faces in the lobby.

No one looked at him.

Cast down thy bucket where thou art.

He stepped, crestfallen, into the street. Fixing his attention upon the tarnished beauty in the antiques shops, he moved down toward the power and light building. Auntish shops! That means old. . . . I don't care!

He stood on the corner. He was staring at the tops of an orderly mass of used cars in the lot across the street. Beyond the lot rose a redbrick building upon the wall of which a big picture was painted: black men in white coats, with toothy smiles and gray heads, carrying silver trays laden with beautiful things to eat to elegant smiling white ladies in furs and richly dressed white gentleman in tuxedos with shiny lapels. Above the picture, painted in big white letters, the sign:

S-O-U-T-H-E-R-N M-A-N-S-I-O-N.

"Hot ziggedy dog!" he shouted.

He had followed the sunlight into the darkened room. A long silver mirror extended the full length of the upper half of the north wall and reflected the crystalline shimmer of a galaxy of beautiful glasses of all sizes and shapes arranged on glass shelves. As his eyes became accustomed to the darkness, vague details of the room's interior came into view: the soft red rug upon which he stood, extended beyond the stream of light that threw his shadow into the barely perceptible frame of the rear door. It had no handle and was painted a dull black color, so that except for the thin, intensely black crevice that outlined it, it looked like a part of the wall.

He yawned, a strange and yet familiar heaviness surprising his eyelids. I've been here before, he thought, sinking deeper into the rich warm dreamy darkness, which suddenly became alive with shadowy planes of fiery light that illuminated the edges of the tabletops, the backs and edges of seats, legs and rounds of chairs. A pile of neatly folded table linen blazed from a far corner and burned its reflection in the flying wing of a baby grand piano. Subtle shimmerings of light reflected from the surfaces of brass instruments, of a bass fiddle leaning against the wall, of the drums! Throbbing silently under their covers, filling the room with soft pulsing rhythm, while the silver trays, ashtrays, cream pitchers, and salt-and-pepper shakers on a table near the linen table shone like highly polished jewels.

His eyes followed the silver sheen along the edge of a round pillar up to the ceiling where a chandelier, like a great glowing ember, filled the room with sparkling particles of powdered light, like fine snow suspended in a twilight air.

While the music played softly, the hushed whispers of the smiling brightly jeweled porcelain-faced ladies and gentlemen bade the white-coated, head-less, handless, legless waiters with sparkling teeth and eyes to bear the glis-tening silver trays laden with beautiful things to eat: crystal flasks filled with ruby and emerald liquids, bunches of crystalline grapes, halved lemons the juice of which clung like tears to the rinds. Like at the art gallery, he thought, Flemish!

"What kin I do for you, sonny?" said a voice.

He looked at the chandelier, and then at the burning points of light that gathered upon the surface of a chromium ball of a post three feet high through which a thick red cord looped, separating the tables from the bar. In this burning ball of light — quite suddenly — a pale, round, middle-aged face appeared, surrounded by a tangle of false-looking reddish brown hair, with a long nose and tired sagging purple cheeks that were only prevented from falling upon her several chins by the pursed purple lips of her wide mouth. She stood behind the bar. The cigarette dangling from the corner of her mouth supported a thin column of smoke that spiraled up into the great beam of sunlight that flooded through the front door and threw its undu-lating shadow upon the black back wall.

"What kin I do for you, sonny?" the woman was saying.

"I'm lookin' for a job."

"What you wanna do a thing like *that* for?"

"So I kin make some money."

"Well, what kin you do?"

"I-I kin — can — do *anything*!"

"E-R-N-EEE!" the woman shouted, the tip of her cigarette burning a crimson hole in the foggy sunlight while the timbre of her voice jarred loose a spark of fire that shot into the profusion of smoke that streamed from her nostrils and obscured her face like a tangled curtain of wrinkled gauze.

"EEEEEOW!" answered a loud voice from beyond the black wall.

"Back there," she said.

Boom!-Boom . . . Boom-Boom . . . Boom-Boom. The handleless door swung gently to and fro and finally came to rest within the confines of the thin black rectangular crevice that interrupted the whiteness of the kitchen's front wall.

"What does the gen'leman want, Mister Hopkins?" said a penetrating bass voice, just as he caught sight of a pair of beautiful black pink-nailed hands extending from the sleeves of a white cook's jacket that wielded a long French knife with a swift casual precision. The movement produced a pleasant sharp-gray swishing sound pregnant with the light reflected by the whitewashed walls and the bright array of aluminum pots and pans that hung from racks built onto the back of the long table that hid his face.

He made his way through the jungle of pots and pans until he discovered the long black face with a long sharp nose and almond eyes that belonged to the knife-sharpening hands and penetrating voice. He wore a tall starched cook's cap and a white hand towel around his neck. The naked bulb hanging from the ceiling not far from his hand created an aura of brightness that made the big range behind him look like a great furnace. Its upper shelf was lined with heavy black cauldrons, kettles, and pots of various sizes. The giant spoons, dippers, sifters, colanders, and the biggest egg beater he had ever seen in his life aroused subtle fears in him. And then there was the rack of sharp knifes beside the table, and the big meat grinder at the far end of the table, which was stained with blood. He watched the man's movements with awed fascination, unconsciously breathing to the compelling rhythms of the sharp swishing sound.

Then he gradually became aware of a second sound, like that of an electric motor of, say, a streetcar, accompanied by intermittant chopping sounds, like a hard stick beating out a solid rhythm on a wooden drum.

"What does the gen'leman want?" said a second voice, but this time it was a softer fuzzy-timbred voice. He followed the subtly amused glance of the tall-hatted man and discovered the chopper against the adjacent wall near an open window with bars looking onto the alley where he could see the rear end of a blue truck with a sign written in fancy white letters on it:

R-I-T-Z C-R — the unfinished word crashing into the face of a brown-skinned man wearing a white cap that was not as tall as that of the swisher. His lips were fleshy, his nose blunt, and his white jacket stained with dirt and blood. Amerigo moved closer and waited for him to look up from the pile of parsley he was chopping. He started to speak but the chopper turned around and opened the door of a big white refrigerator that stood directly behind him.

That's where it comes from. Amerigo was pleased to have located the motor.

The chopper — Mr. Hopkins! — took a cylindrical can from the refrigerator and set it on the table. Then he shot an unexpected glance at him that took his breath away:

"Ah-Ah —"

"When you Ah-in' —" said Mr. Hopkins, "you lyin', an' when you uh-in' — you don' know!"

"I'm lookin' for a-a-a —"

"Watch out, now. Take your time!"

"for a job!"

"He's lookin' for a job, Mister Peady," said Mr. Hopkins, smiling at Mr. Peady, who was ripping the belly of a big fish with swift casual precision.

"Doin' what, Mister Hopkins?"

"Mister Peady said, 'Doin' what?'" said Mr. Hopkins.

"Waitin' on tables!"

"Waitin' on tables," said Mr. Hopkins to Mr. Peady.

"How much experience he had?" asked Mr. Peady.

"How much —" Mr. Hopkins began.

"None! I mean . . ."

"He means *none*," said Mr. Hopkins, scooping up a handful of chopped parsley and dropping it into the can.

"I don' think he kin wait," said Mr. Peady.

"Aaaaaw — *yes* I kin! Just gimme a chance. *I'll* show you!"

"How come?" asked Mr. Hopkins, looking at Mr. Peady, who flipped the severed half of the fish onto the table, revealing the fine white ribbing of bones that wove the pink flesh into a kind of a leaf.

"How come?" Mr. Hopkins was asking.

"He can't even wait till he gits big enough to hold a tray —" said Mr. Peady, "let alone wait on the customers! Tell 'im, Mister Hopkins, that they got waiters *waitin'* in line that been waitin' *forty years!* Tell 'im that the one thing wrong with the world taday is that they got too damned many waiters! They the lyin'est! cheatin'est! stealin'est! no-goodes'! Snakes in the *world!* An' don' *never* leave one by hisself with your old lady!"

Mr. Hopkins grinned, revealing a mouth full of tobacco-stained teeth. "You heard Mister Peady. He's the *Chef.* Been Cheffin' a *hundred* an' forty years! Mister Peady usta burn in heaven till the Lawd give 'im a job down here 'cause all them cute little angels started gittin' fat! Now He didn' mind it so much as long as them black angels got fat, but when them little blond, blue-eyed angels started gittin' fat, *too!* Good Gawd-a-mighty! It looked like they just couldn' git enough of Mister Peady's good home cookin' . . ."

"What kin you do, Mister — uh — I don' believe I caught the name, sir?"

"A-merigo!"

"Uh — what-was-that?" asked Mr. Hopkins, cupping his palm behind his right ear.

"Amerigo Jones!"

"Aaaaaah! You one a the *Jones* boys! He says his name is Jones, Mister

Peady, but he didn' say what else he kin do. It's a cinch he ain' no waiter, like you say."

"I kin cook!" He turned to Mr. Peady: "Just as good as you!"

"He kin *what,* Mister Hopkins?" Mr. Peady exclaimed.

"Mister Jones," said Mr. Hopkins, "didn' I tell you that Mister Peady usta *burn in heaven?*"

"Ain' his momma's cookin' good enough for 'im?" asked Mr. Peady. "I bet he's got a *good*-lookin' momma! An' a rich old man. Why — Mister Jones's settin' pretty! Cookin' ain' nothin' but a lot a hard-assed work! Have to work like a dog all day an' half the night — an' the snakes gittin' all the credit! I maybe could help 'im," he said to Mr. Hopkins, "but I'd just have 'im on my conscience. I wouldn' even condemn no waiter to be no cook!"

"*You* doin' it!" he retorted.

"Yeah! But just take a good look at me! Old. Broken down before my time. An' ain' got a cryin' dime to show for it! You take my advice, son, you git yourself a education. Finish high school. Go to college — if your old man'll send you, an' if he won', work your way through. Learn to be one a them big-shot doctors! Yeah! Or a lawyer, so you won' have to work so hard. Then you kin stay home nights an' make your old lady happy."

"I think Mister Peady done spoke his mind, Mister Jones," said Mr. Hopkins with a kind thoughtful smile. "No bones, Mister Jones. What did you say your first name was?"

"Amerigo."

"With a name like *that* you oughtta run for *pres-a-dent* — or at least a congressman!"

The naked glare of the bright bulb, the shimmering reflection of the aluminum pots and pans, the throbbing rhythm of the refrigerator motor, and the intermittent chopping sound of Mr. Hopkins's knife whirred in a sickening constellation of dread, rage, and humiliation that growled from the pit of his stomach as the silent white door boomed softly to and fro. He followed the sun-blazed path through the darkened room of the Southern Mansion to the door.

Trembling as he half walked, half stumbled down the street, he grew dizzy, and the air that rushed into his hot lungs burst into a spray of icy coldness that permeated his whole body and chilled him to the bone. A cramping pain shot through his stomach and shocked him into a sense of urgency that propelled him down one dull street after another, heedless of the tarnished clouds that lowered blandly overhead while the indolent traffic droned indifferently through the dead hour of the morning.

Presently he had turned into a broad street that looked familiar, and his thoughts quickened to a growing excitement caused by a subtle sense of recognition. Minutes later he was standing on a bridge looking down upon a great network of rails that glistened like a great silver cobweb. And then his eyes, in excited anticipation of his thought, beheld the great Union Station!

His face brightened with a vision of new possibilities: To be a waiter-or-a-porter-or-a-cook on the railroad!

He gazed up at the high ceiling where the great chandelier hung and realized at that instant that the station reminded him of a church, not like St. John's, but like the ones in the books at the library with a huge lobby and great wings on either side giving onto a long center hall filled with strong rays of sunlight that streamed down through the great windows upon the little people below — moving around like ants, Ant Rose, Ant Tish, Ant Jamima — *aunt!* — and standing in long lines in front of the cages where the ticket sellers sold tickets to places written in chalk that you could rub off with your fingers — if they wasn't — *weren't* — so high up — on the black-boards, numbered: One-Two-Three-Four-Five-Six-Seven-Eight-Nine-Ten. *I'm* ten. He looked up to see what route the tenth pair of rails had indicated.

Meanwhile people sat nervously or resignedly on the long wooden benches, surrounded by bags and packages, smoking cigarettes, eating fruit and candy, while redcaps pushed heavy luggage carts or followed passengers dressed up in their Sunday clothes to and from the tracks. People of all sizes, ages, and colors, he noted unconsciously, selecting one, a policeman:

"'Scuse me, could you tell me where to go to be a porter-or-a-waiter-or-a-cook — to ask somebody, I mean?"

"Why, you'd have to go to one of the commissaries down on the track, sonny," he said. "Now, you go —" pointing to a staircase.

"Thanks!" he gasped over his shoulder, rushing toward the staircase, which he descended until he reached a landing covered by a roof. His eyes swept along the rails and there, on the first pair, right in front of his eyes stood a big beautiful streamlined train!

"Hot dog!" he cried out. "The Silver Streak!"

At that instant he saw its long graceful coaches speeding through the pages of the *Star* and through the red-and-black-lettered months of last year and this year and next year's calender hanging on the walls of barbershops and pool halls.

Quietly, patiently it lay couched under the roof, eyes dim, windows dark, like a looooooooong pretty snake! A big overgrown pussycat — Grrrrrr! — waiting for the numbered blackboard upstairs to make up its signifying mind which way to go. *Go fly to the eas . . . t, go fly to the west, go fly to the one you love the best! . . . Realleh!*

"*Peeeeeeeeeep — peeeeeeeeeep!*" tooted a piercing horn accompanied by the whine of a motor and the rumble of a chain of baggage wagons, causing him to jump behind a pole in order to avoid being run over.

"*Uuuuuuga! Uuuuuuuga!*" Another noisy caterpillar sped by, pinning him to the pole just as he tried to escape. And in its wake a loud swishing sound subsumed by a low rumble, rushing down through the shed, setting its steel housing a-tremble! It grew louder . . . like a big hot wind! — and shot out into the sun, its tail wagging under the bridge, and under the water — to France and England! Like a fish! Like a whale! Silver!

"Watch me, sonny!" A voice crashed through the worn wooden panels of a swinging door giving onto the platform. A graying brown-skinned man was pushing a tall metal rack containing many trays laden with all sorts of pies and cakes: brown and red-pink-white-egg-whitewithcherry titties . . . aaaaaaw!

He pushed through the swinging doors and looked into a big steamy room full of dirty pots, baking pans, and tall metal racks like the one that had just rolled out the door and yelled at him. A young round-faced Negro with green eyes, reddish nappy hair, and pouting lips, dressed in a wet smudged-white . . . was white . . . jacket, a pair of dirty brown pants, and run-over shoes was scrubbing a big fat dirty pot.

" 'Scuse me . . ."

The young man kept on scrubbing without looking up.

"Eh. Aye beg yohar pahdon, could-you-tell-me wheah theh hiah cooks, waitahs, or portahs?"

"NAW!"

He stepped quietly back through the door and onto the platform. He walked on until he came to an office. A white man sat behind the window in a summer hat that was shoved back on his small gray head. He wore metal-rimmed glasses with bifocal lenses. A long yellow pencil stuck out from behind a big red ear. He looked out over the upper lenses of his glasses and pursed his lips at him.

"Do you need a cook-or-a-waiter-or-a-porter?"

"Nope."

"Or somebody to do somethin' else?"

"Nope."

"Are you the one that does the hirin'?"

"Yep."

"Maybe next week?"

"Nope."

"Next year!"

"Uhmn."

★

He stood on the sidewalk with his back to the station and contemplated Memorial Hill. He walked through the parking lot, crossed the busy boulevard, and ascended the steps that led to the path up the hill to the terrace where the fountains were. He beheld the monumental figures on the great wall who stood in warlike attitudes. *Boom! Boom! Boom!* resounded the fierce cannon. Bayonetted, muddy-booted men with bandaged legs peered through the hollow eyes of gas masks as they clambered over the top.

He climbed the staircase on the right and peeped into the windows of the adjacent rooms where he saw plaster-of-paris no-man's-lands hovering between barbed-wire defense positions of battles the names of which he had heard, but which he had already forgotten.

Finally the general reached the top of the stairs and stood upon the battlement in front of the towering torch of Freedom and looked down over his city. The streets south to north swept straight through to the river and were cut into neat little squares by the streets running east to west; crystal-like clusters of redbrick and gray stone buildings stood in the squares bordered by slate-gray strips of asphalt and cement.

His weary eye wandered over the skyline. It was broken by the power and light building with its tower and ball of light turning lollipop-red, then off-white, like the grate of the gas stove in the front room, and then Christmas-green — but not in the daytime. A little to the west of the center of town, the telephone building, City Hall, and the courthouse huddled close together, as if they were in cahoots.

"Vote!" cried Rutherford, *"for what?"*

He cupped his palms and shaded his eyes like the vigilant Indian Scout atop his pinto pony to the rear and to the left of him and scanned the windows of all the buildings, row on row, square on square, east to west and north to south, in an attempt to divine the room that reverberated with the monumental question:

Now?

He looked at the sky. A subtle tinge of red stained the clouds. A sense of five o'clock urgency rose in a sudden swell of dinning sound that rippled through the trees and echoed within the chambers of his heart with a terrible violence:

Boom! BBBBOOOOM! BBBBBOOOOOOMMMM! BBBOOOMM-MMMMMMMM!

His eyes swept along the banks of the river. He tried to discover his coming-out place. He tried to measure the distance up through ten years of garrulous pulsating sounds, smells, shapes, and colors, which had fired the leaflike shades of many rented rooms floored with parallel planks between which the fathomless crevices had run side by side — beyond the walls of St. John's and the schoolroom and the art gallery and the Union Station — into the large voluminous room that was the future, where the reverend and Mr. T. Wellington Harps and Rutherford would never go — to the ticking of clocks!

Four . . . four a — o'clock, he thought.

And now he saw his own towering bearded figure striding up out of the river: Amerigo Frederick Douglass Booker T. George Washington Jones! He stepped majestically, whip in hand, from square to square! Leaping over City Hall, the courthouse, *and* the telephone building in one bound!

He stood at the foot of Memorial Hill. At his back the swarm of cars crawled around the station. The clouds were streaked with blood and the sun-shattered trees torn into shreds of quivering light. Just as he reached the battlement the windshield of an unseen automobile, swerving into a curve somewhere on a distant hill to the east, deflected a volley of golden fire that blew a hole through his chest:

Boom!

"If he'd a been a white man!" said Rutherford.

General Douglass half stumbled, half fell down Memorial Hill.

Boom!

Growing smaller as the blood from the hole that was too little congealed, as the —

Boom!

— grew louder:

If I'd been a white boy they'd a — would have given me a job!

Cast down thy bucket where thou art.

Gallery.

The weight of a heavy blackness pressed him down through the busy streets, squeezing him within the minimal bounds of some arbitrary modicum of undignified space reverberating with a terrifying boom!

At last he stood in front of the courthouse. He walked up the steps and entered the building. It was full of offices. He entered the first one he came to. A thirty-five-year-old white man with his hat on and a burning cigarette dangling from his lips sat back in a chair with his brown-shoed feet propped up on a desk, reading a newspaper.

A detective! Amerigo studied the dark round spot on the sole of his right shoe and then his blue half-length socks with their fine diagonal stripes. A crust of ash fell from his cigarette. He looked at him as he brushed it away, and returned to his newspaper.

Amerigo pushed open the swivel gate behind which the detective sat and walked through the open door of the rear office. He studied the disorderly desk, the books in the bookshelves, the typewriter, the telephone. He searched for guns, blackjacks, rubber hoses, seeing the mangled face of a young man whose name he could not remember on the front page of the *Voice*.

"Ain' that a shame!" Rutherford had said.

A sudden sense of fear whisked him out of the office into the hall.

He mashed down on the clutch and took a sip of water from the electric water cooler, and then made his way to the upper floor where he discovered a Negro woman dusting the panels of a big double door.

She looked at him and kept on dusting. A white cloth was tied around her head. He observed that she had Chinese eyes and bad feet. He hesitated before the door and cleared his throat. She continued to work.

"Eh . . . 'scuse me. Kin I go in?"

"You a citizen ain't you?"

"Aw — I meant —"

"What?" She stretched her ailing fifty-two-year-old body to its full imposing height and fixed her gaze upon him.

"Nothin' . . . ing."

He pushed the door open and entered the beautiful courtroom. It was furnished with dark brown highly polished wood, solid, sturdy, and new looking as though it had never been used, and yet was old, unmovable, as though it had been there forever.

He studied the imposing throne where the judge sat, the gavel he held in his hand, the *Boom! Boom! Boom!* of which seemed to be validated by the flag of the United States of America hanging from the pole behind the bench.

Boom! Boom! Boom! went the gavel — through the loudspeaker of the little table-model radio in the front room of 618:

"I see you're back again, Sam," the judge was saying.

"Well, ya honah, sah, I —"

"Just wait a minute now, I'll ask the questions and you just give the answers. You're charged with disturbing the peace again, and beating up your wife, Sarah. You broke her nose and knocked out four of her teeth. Now, what have you got to say for yourself?"

"I'm jus' sorry 'bout the whole thing. I . . . I — "

"I what?" asked the judge.

"I was jus' drunk, I guess. An' if you jus' let me off this time I promise I won' do that no mo'! Naw, sah! I mean that! I take a dirty oath on my —"

"Just a minute!" the judge broke in. "You're on the air, you know . . ."

"Yessah."

"Sarah, you got anything to say? It was your nose he broke."

"An' he blacked both a . . . both of my eyes, too, Judge! Eeeeevah Saaaaad'y night he come home all drunked up an' eeeevul! Done spen' all his money an' then he start beatin' up on somebody! An' I told 'im last time, if he do it agin, I was gonna call the law an' have 'im locked up! An' — "

"Is that what you want us to do, lock him up?" asked the judge.

"Well," said Sarah, "he ain' no bad man, Judge. He's a good man when he's sober. An' . . . eh . . ."

"Well now, you called the officers and had him brought in. What do you want us to do?"

"Like I say —" said Sarah, "he's a *good* man when he's sober an' all that."

"All what?"

"When he straighten up an' fly right. You *know* what I mean, Judge. An' if he promus . . . promus to act right — I'm willin' to give 'im anothah chance."

"You gonna straighten up an' fly right, Sam?" asked the judge.

"Yessah," Sam muttered.

"What's that? Speak up so all the listeners can hear you!"

"YES, SAH!"

"Yes, *sah* what?"

"Yes, sah I sho' is gonna straighten up an' fly right!"

"All right," said the judge, "I'm going to let you off light this time. The fine will be twenty-five dollars. You take Sarah home and get her teeth fixed, and don't let me see you before this bench again!"

"Naw, sah!" said Sam.

Amerigo stepped out into the corridor, descended the stairs, and entered the street. His body writhed uncomfortably in his tight black skin. It pressed in upon him, as though it were a suit of rubber many sizes too small. His thoughts, trying to expand, strained against the contracting wall of skin.

He turned eastward down Twelfth Street. The buildings loomed ominously around him at dizzying heights, plunging him into the cool depths of late-afternoon shade. He stepped into the driveway near the corner and was wafted back onto the sidewalk by a buffeting breeze set in turbulent motion by a black van that swerved into the drive. Black Mariah! he thought, as fear caused the skin to draw still tighter around the struggling tension within him.

He *had* to follow the van into the basement of the courthouse — with his eyes only, at first, thrilling to an exciting temptation that made him hesitate in the middle of the drive. There's where they give them the third degree!

Without realizing it, he had entered the basement. He was standing before an office next to which was a big room closed off with real bars. He peeped in.

"WHAT THE HELL ARE YOU DOIN' THERE!" exclaimed an angry voice.

From the corner of his eye he saw the towering figure of a white policeman with a gun and bullets around his belt, just in time to duck under a big red palm swinging toward his head.

"If I catch your little black ass in here agin, I'll kick the *shit* out a you!" the officer declared.

Trembling from head to foot, teeth chattering, he strained his will in order to hold his buoyant flesh back to a walk.

"I said, GIT!" shouted the voice somewhere behind him.

W A L K! cried Frederick Douglass.

Rattle! Rattle! rattle! His stick grating against the iron bars.

W A L K!

Sunlight from the street bathed his face. A feeling of relief accompanied by a seizure of violent trembling confused his diminishing feet as he stumbled over the deep crevices between the great blocks of cement paving down the long long street. With much difficulty his shriveling legs strained to span the endless inches of the way back through the ravaged no-man's-land of the Ten Year Siege.

Meanwhile the sun mercilessly bombarded the helpless clouds. Blood rained down upon the poverty-infested hovels of the North End and upon the fallen flesh of the dying trees, while the cool airs of evening sucked their bared nerves, which were jarred by the rumble of iron wheels and the whining of automobile motors, clotting the evening's gaping mouth with dust.

He cautiously made his way down the sheer wall of the curbstone until he finally reached the cobblestone bed of the street. He climbed down into the deep trenches between the stones in order to avoid the dangerous traffic overhead. The way was encumbered by slimy pools of spittle, the droppings of dogs, burned-out matchsticks as big as tree trunks, and huge smoldering cigarette butts that gave off stifling vapors of strangling smoke. A terrific pain burned his chest when he breathed, and his eyes filled with water.

Now an uncanny sound slowly dawned upon his consciousness; it was like that of a great fingernail, scratching a metal surface. He crouched close to the side of the trench and wiped the tears from his eyes and tried to peer down the passageway. A huge beast was coming straight toward him! Its long feelers fingered the air threateningly, and he gradually perceived that the blood-chilling sound was being made by the horny shell of its reddish brown body, scraping against the stones of the trench, as it crawled upon its grotesque legs. He turned to flee in the opposite direction, but at that instant a series of loud explosions burst upon the air above him. Then there was a great rumble, as of thunder! — A hot steamy dung-colored mass flowed down into the trench and blocked his path. He looked behind him and saw that the beast was getting closer. Gathering all his strength, he clawed his way up the stinking excremental mound, slipping backward as often as he advanced, strangling on the vile fumes, until he finally reached the summit. But no sooner had he gained the street than a great wheel crashed into the pile of manure and sent him plummeting back down into the trench. Then flashes of darkness and light, followed by the thunderous grating of giant feet and the Boom! Boom! Boom! of the spiking heels of women's shoes! He pressed himself flat against the floor of the trench. Gradually he perceived a rank bile-green odor that was even more suffocating than the others. He could actually feel the poison creeping into his lungs, into his eyes, into his very skin. He vomited and fell into a fit of coughing that so exhausted him that he had to lie for an indeterminable period of time with his nose stuck in a little crack in the trench wall through which a little jet of fresh air blew. As his strength slowly returned, he discovered that he lay in a warm slimy ooze. He struggled to one knee and stared into a great beady eye — and froze with terror. The eye did not move. There was no sound except the sound of the distant traffic overhead. He waded through the ooze and managed to crawl around the mangled body of the cockroach, and made his way toward the distant curbstone at the other end of the cobblestone street.

By grasping the crags of the rough cement that jutted out into the gap between the sewer grating and a segment of the curbstone he managed to climb very slowly up the sheer dangerous incline to the sidewalk. When he reached the top his hands and feet were bleeding and there was a throbbing gash in his knee.

A car raced toward him! He half stumbled, half fell into the hole of the sewer cover and clung to the rough inner edges while his feet dangled high above the raging sewer waters below. Straining to hold his grip, he stared dumbly into the pitiless eyes of the cat, and felt its hot panting breath upon his face. Tiring, he tried to support himself by resting his foot on one of the jutting twigs growing out of a crack in the curbstone, but he could not reach it. The strength in his hands slowly gave out. He longed for death. . . .

"HEEEEEEEER — KITTYKITTYKITTYKITTYKITTY!" A woman's voice!

It's too late, he thought.

"F R E E D O M!" cried another insistent voice, and with a terrific effort he managed to crawl out of the sewer. He fell down, exhausted, at the base of the fireplug. . . . When he regained consciousness he could not walk immediately, but had to crawl along the cracks at the base of the buildings.

Time out of mind waxed and waned upon the rugged shores of his barren consciousness. In some age, some season, he found himself entering a great canyon bordered by high shelves of stone that supported towering redbrick walls. He was engulfed by a cold dank smell that was vaguely familiar. Having regained the use of his legs, he walked on and on, surmounting the hazards of crag and crevasse, surviving a near-fatal encounter with a huge brown bird.

I've been here before! he thought continually, gradually taking heart in the pleasant feeling the thought gave him.

After a long while he stood before a great wooden gate. He easily walked under it and was immediately upon a broad cement shelf full of cracks and craters, as though it had been bombarded by another planet. It was closed off by a huge fence on one side and a forest enclosed within a latticed fence on the other side. Two huge buildings whose back porches faced each other sealed off the other two sides. Suddenly he was stricken with fear:

The cat!

He scanned the porch at the bottom of the three cement steps.

"M-O-M!"

His voice was so small that it merely reverberated within the frustrating frenzy of fear that squeezed all the potency out of his lungs.

"MAAAAAAAHM!"

He fell upon his hands and knees and cautiously approached the steps from the far side of the yard, along the edge of the forest: Mrs. Crippa's garden!

BOOM!

There was a great explosion. He looked up on the big porch behind him because the noise had come from there. A giant gray-haired women dressed in black stood shaking out an enormous white sheet that billowed out over the yard like a great sail. He jumped into a crack and covered his head with his arms in order to avoid the clods of bread that plummeted about him. When she had finished she folded the sheet and laid it on the banister, and then took up a very large package from the porch.

"HEEEEEEER KEEDYKEEDYKEEDYKEEDY!"

"MRS. CRIIIIIIPA!"

"HEEEEEEERE KEEDYKEEDYKEEDYKEEDYKEEDY!"

She mumbled something to herself, as she stepped into the yard and placed the package on the lid of the garbage can and returned to her porch.

BOOM! went the screen door as she entered the kitchen. Meanwhile he crawled toward the foot of the steps, seeking shelter along the base of the garbage cans.

BOOM!

Miss Betty stepped out onto the porch and poured a bucket of dirty water down the drain, disturbing the horde of blue-green horseflies dozing along its edge. Now they beat the air above the sewer with their monstrous wings, and swept up into the yard, and circled around the garbage can while he huddled in the damp misty crack between the last can and the foot of the stair. Finally they swooped down upon the paper package, filling the air with the din of their buzzing.

"Miss Beeeeeetty"

She looked directly at him.

"Miss Betty, IT'S MEEEEEEE!"

She turned absentmindedly and entered her kitchen.

BOOM

BOOM!

Rutherford stepped out onto the porch. He looked over the banister down into the alley, glanced at the mouth of the shoot, and finally settled down upon the orange crate and unfolded the pages of the *Star.*

"DAAAAAAD"

Miss Jenny appeared on her porch with a bowl of milk in her hand.

"KIDDYKIDDYKIDDYKIDDYKIDDY!"

"DAAAAAAAAAAAAAAAD!"

Boom! she entered the house.

Slowly now, tediously, he inched his way up the hazardous stair, which was stained with the coagulating blood of the six o'clock sun! . . .

"WHERE'N THE HELL HAVE YOU BEEN?" Rutherford shouted. He was looking at him!

He *sees* me!

He gasped for air and felt his lungs expand. He flexed the trembling muscles of his body and felt his black skin give way to his awareness of his father's recognition of him.

"Come here!" he commanded.

Amerigo approached him cautiously, coming to a halt a few feet from where he sat, well out of range of his long powerful arms. He stood upon the clean spot that was no longer clean, looking down upon his faint shadow, which impressed itself upon the blueness of the evening. His head had slid off the edge of the porch.

"You hear me talkin' to you?" Rutherford was saying.

Dumbly he studied the floorboards of the porch.

"Baby?" A woman's voice.

She sees me, too!

"Leave 'im alone!" said Rutherford, "I want to know where he's been —
till six o'clock! Who in the *hell* does he think he is? This ain' no restaurant
— no ho-tel or nothin' — where he kin just come an' go as he pleases. I
come home an' found the front door *an'* the back door all open. Didn' even
make up his bed. I'm gittin' sick a this crap. The bigger he gits the less he
tries to help us. Us out workin', tryin' to take care of 'im, an' he don' even
appreciate *nothin'*! So busy playin' — *all day!* — that he can't even come
home an' make up his bed. Ain' even got time enough to eat his supper. You
better git 'im out a my sight, before I beat all the black off that little
niggah!"

Viola eyed him significantly, and he moved covertly, under the protective
complicity of her gaze, into the house.

"Wash your hands an' face," she said.

He washed his face and hands. Then he sat down to the table and faced
the bowl of lukewarm fried cabbage alone. He crammed his mouth with
corn bread, onions, and salt pork so that he would not taste the cabbage.
He swilled down his buttermilk. All the while he felt Rutherford's gaze,
through the *Star,* through the screen, intensifying the glare of the naked
light overhead. As he was finishing, the screen door opened and Rutherford
stood over him.

"An' when you git through, I want you to wash up the dishes. Look!"
He opened the oven door, "all *them!* Pots an' pans you been *soakin'*! An'
clean all that crap from behind the sink."

"Yessir."

Rutherford stalked into the middle room where Viola was making up the
bed.

"What you doin'?" Amerigo heard him ask. "Let *him* do it! He been out
playin' all day. Let him earn his keep! I better go down on the porch 'fore
I kill both a you."

He heard Rutherford going down the stairs, and Viola's footfall as she
approached him.

"Babe!" Rutherford called from the corridor, "you come on down here
with me, an' leave that little niggah by hisself!"

She smiled sadly at him and turned to join Rutherford.

"A *one*-two-three-fo'! A-*one*-two-three-fo'!" shouted a husky voice from
the alley, accompanied by the sound of tramping feet:

"Column right — ho!"

Laughing commentary up and down the alley.

Mr. Man o' War, playin' army, he thought, seeing Maxine, Sammy, Willie Joe, Annie, and the rest marching single file.

"Column lef' — harch!"

"Hee! hee!"

"Aaaaaw — do it, then!"

"When war do come, we sure gonna be ready!"

"Mark tiiime — hark!"

Tramp! tramp! tramp! tramp! gradually accompanied by a low growl coming from the distance, growing louder, drowning the tramp-tramp-tramp-tramp of the time-marking feet, which now slowly rose to the foreground of sound, as the growl moved farther up the avenue. Tramp! tramp! tramp! tramp! between the noisy rattle of Bra Mo's truck and the bang of a neighboring screen door: Boom!

"Momma, where's Toodle-lum?"

"I don' know, Pearl, ain' he with you?"

"No'm."

"Toodle-lum! Aw-Toodle-lum!"

The streetcar! he thought suddenly, recalling the growling sound that had drowned the tramp-tramp-tramp of the marching feet. He looked warily into the dark middle room, and cast a suspicious glance into the invisible darkness behind the screen door. That wasn' nothin' but the streetcar! he reassured himself, crawling around the mangled remains of the cockroach.

Then he gathered the dishes together and stacked them on the drainboard. He poured the hot water into the dishpan, watched the soap flakes fall from the corner of the box like snow, turned on the cold water, and watched it foam like beer. He slid the dishes in, plate after plate, in a long chain of plates, of cups and saucers, a glistening chain of knives, forks, and spoons.

Gradually all the sounds from the alley, the boulevard and the avenue, and from the neighboring houses faded into the background of his consciousness. His mind forgot what his hands were doing, and his hands worked independently of his eyes, which had closed him into the voluminous feeling of blackness, from the depths of which an unheard voice echoed from a long way off:

"Deeee-ee — eep ri-ver! My home is oooooo-ver Jordan. Deeeeee-ee — eep ri-ver, Lord, I want to crooooooss o-ver intoooooo — campground!"

His blind fingers lifted the dish towel from the nail and rubbed it over the surfaces of the plates.

"Oh — don't you wa-an-na go-ow — "

Plate after plate.

"to that go-ah-spel pee-eace! To that praaaah-ah-mised la-and where aw-awl is peee-eace? Deeee-ee — eep ri-ver, L-o-r-d! I want to crooooss o-ver intoooo — campground!"

He scrubbed the pots and pans and cleaned the tray under the burners of the gas range. He scrubbed the kitchen table clean, let down the wings, and spread a fresh tablecloth on it, to the accompaniment of the unheard voice singing the quiet melody that was enclosed within the dark chamber behind his eyes. Tremulously his lips repeated the words:

"Deeee-ee — eep ri-ver."

He cleaned the trash from behind the sink and scrubbed the shelves of the cupboard and rinsed the dishrag out and poured the dirty water into the sink, wiping the greasy ring from the dishpan and hanging it up on the nail between the sink and the cupboard. Then he sprinkled the scouring powder into the sink and scrubbed it until it sparkled. That done, he rinsed out the dishrag again and hung it on the nail beside the dishpan, and hung the dish towel beside the dishrag. Then he swept the floor.

And suddenly he was finished. The melody had fled in the face of his self-consciousness, and the words of the song were crowded out of mind by thoughts that were animated by the clean shining objects in the orderly kitchen. Like Booker T. Washington's, he thought for an instant, and then the thought suddenly disappeared as quickly as it had come, into the blue darkness of the middle room and became lost within the depths of a pleasant melancholy feeling. He turned on the rose-shaded lamp and began putting the room in order.

"You ain' been blue," he sang, hanging Rutherford's pajamas on a hook in the closet, putting Viola's stockings in the middle drawer of the chest of drawers: "Nooooo-no-no . . . ! Yooooou ain' been bluuuuuuue —" arranging the shoes in a neat row in the little space between the bed and the chest of drawers, dusted the bedposts and the vanity dresser and the back, runners, and rounds of the wicker-bottomed rocking chair. "Till you've had that — mooood indigo. That feelin' . . . comes stealin' —" His eyes closed before the mirror of the vanity dresser. "down to my —"

"Now git to bed!" said an imperative voice.

Boom!

He opened his eyes and stared into the mirrored image of Rutherford's face. The skin tightened around his diminishing body and the floor rushed up to meet his downcast gaze.

"Yessir."

He sank heavily into bed. He heard Viola ascend the stairs and enter the room. He closed his eyes when she arranged the covers.

"Good night," she whispered. He did not answer. She went into the kitchen where Rutherford was. Low mumblings filled the front room. Now there were other voices, four. Then laughter, and movement, the icebox door opened and shut, beer bottles hissed open, and finally there was the smell of frying hair.

"Sund'y," said one of the voices.

Sund'y! He felt the word whirl around in the darkness under his tight skin like a sun, deeper and deeper into the blackness flowing like a river, flowing like a deep black river, fluid black flesh flowing like a deep black river: *I want to c-r-o-s-s . . . o-ver into. . . .*

A bell!

A bell ringing.

A bell ringing from a tower in the town.

Birds twittering amid the sound, golden sound, sunny sound, ringing in a rosy blue wash, sunny-golden, filling the front window, while a long beam of fluid gold sunlight slowly advanced through the kitchen door. He listened to its advance, egged on by the ringing bell. The bell ringing from the tower of the Catholic church down from the spaghetti factory, down on Cherry.

"Cherries are ripe! Cherries are ripe!" twittered the sparrows, the robins sang "Again, again!" while the Sunday-morning air rushed in and out of Viola's and Rutherford's lungs, Amerigo's the fastest, then Rutherford's and then —

Boom! The Sunday *Star* landed on the porch with a gentle thud. A tingling coolness tickled his feet, as he ran down the corridor stair and onto the porch, just in time to catch the streetlights dozing faintly yellow in the face of the rising sun, just before they dropped off to sleep. Out!

By the time Rutherford got up to go to work he had read and neatly folded the funny paper and lay opossum-fashion, waiting for him to leave.

Now that he had gone, he waited for the sun to steal into the middle room and fire the hem of the sheet of Viola's bed. He waited for her to feel the heat of the burning sheet, and stir, and stare, pink-eyed, into the mirror of the vanity dresser, and wonder, and then suddenly know, and look at the clock and yell:

"Boy? You awake? It's time for you to git up an' go to Sund'y school!"

Clean, dressed up in his Sunday suit, he stepped out into the redeeming light of Sunday morning. Head high, shoulders back, he walked under the burning wires and was not afraid. The Lord smiled down out of heaven: Surely goodness and mercy shall fa-ah-low me — ee all the days of my life, and I shall dwell in the house of the Lord — for ever!

He sat attentively in his Sunday school class and listened while Sister Mayfield spoke of how angry it made Jesus when he found the money changers in the temple, and how He got mad for the first time in His precious life, and drove them out!

The bell rang. He handed the collection money to Sister Mayfield, collected the books, took his seat, and waited for Sunday school to close. Meanwhile the reverend eased in quietly and took a seat near Sister James. She rose to her feet with a tired grunt and asked for the secretary's report and sat down again. The secretary made her report. Then Sister James rose again and smiled a greeting to the reverend, thanking him for his presence. "The members of Saint John's are truly blessed —" she said, "in havin' a faithful leader who never forgits to look after the tiniest members of his flock!"

"A-men!" said Aunt Nancy.

The reverend smiled upon his flock, and his flock beamed under his loving gaze.

"I'm — I'm especially glad that the reverend's here this mornin'," said Sister James, "'cause the Lord's work has been called to my attention. An'-an' I felt that it's my duty to speak out, to root out the truth from its hidin' place!"

"A-men!" said the reverend approvingly amid a chorus of a-mens resounding throughout the room.

"I believe that!" Sister James continued, "I believe that if your house ain' in order, you oughtta clean it up! When you hear the Lord come knockin' on your door it's too late then!"

"Speak to 'er, Je-sus!" cried Brother Jones. Smiles animated the faces of the congregation.

"I — I was checkin' the rolls down through the years," said Sister James, "tryin' to keep track a our young 'uns. I know most of 'um by heart. Know they mommas an' poppas. But every now an' agin a face drops out a sight, a name escapes your mind — an' you wonder what happened!"

"A-men!"

"Now, we're startin' our membership drive pretty soon, an' I kinda wanted to account for ever'body. Well sir! The Lord sure works in mysterious ways! I got to — got to lookin', an' a-lookin', an' not findin', till I come to the conclusion that some a our most reg'ler members are still sinners!"

"AAAAAAW!"

The reverend scrutinized the children, as though he would ferret out the money changer.

"They names," Sister James was saying, "don' appear on the rolls — *nowhere!* One in partic'lar happens to be one a our most outstandin' members! A-mer'go, honey, do you know you still walkin' in sin?"

"NAAAAAW!"

"That you ain' been baptized in the name of the Redeemer, Jesus Christ!"
Suddenly the room was full of huge accusing eyes looking at him.

"That you ain' been *born* agin? Help me, Jesus! Help me touch this child's heart!"

"AAAAAAA — MEN!"

"An' there are others, too!" continued Sister James. "Reveren', I think we oughtta just *be* late closin' the Sunday school this mornin' an' extend the invitation to these children to join the Lord's flock!"

"AAAAA-MEN!"

The reverend rose, a tall handsome shadow trimmed in gold.

"Yeah!" he sighed, "I think we a-l-l oughtta say, A-men!"

"AAAAA-MEN!"

"We oughtta utter — from the depths of our hearts — a word of thanks to this good sister, who is never — never! — too tired to work for Jesus. A-men!"

"A-MEN!"

"I don' know — the Lord knows! — how it sometimes happens that our children just get pushed out into this sinful world like counterfeit money an' we expect 'um to pay the price of salvation with it!"

"Yes, Lawd!"

"Tee! hee!"

"Talk to 'im!"

"An' then," said the reverend, "then one day there comes a vigilant, God-fearin' soul who hears the word: Go separate the brass from the gold! An'-an' declare what is false to be false! God bless Sister James! Now, Amer'go an' the rest a you young folks, we gonna bow our heads in silent prayer for *you!* With all our love, with all our hope, with all our will, we gonna pray that the Vision of our Lord an' Savior, Jesus Christ, fills your hearts an' eyes, that you'll be able to *see* God's-only-begotten-Son — *alone!* — with the cross on his back. *Alone!* wearin' a crown of thorns upon His precious head, climbin' up Calv'ry Hill!"

"Oh Lawd! Lawd! Lawd! Lawd!" sang a mournful voice.

"A-*looooone!* Among the taunts! an' the jeers of the Roman soldiers! Under a thunderin' sky with stained bloody clouds! I-IIII-I want you to feeeeel! FEEEEEL! feel the nails tearin' holes in the palms of His gentle hands an' feet. Fee-eeee-eeel! Aaaaaaw-feel! Help me, Jesus! if You please!"

"Uhmmmmmmm!" moaned an anonymous voice.

"FEEEEL the sharp steel! piercin' His side. Look! See the look in His eyes when He raises up His head toward heaven, an' mumbles in His weakness: My God oh my God! why — oh why — hast Thou forsaken me?"

A low primeval moan rose from the back of the church, a black alluvial moan.

"See His head fal-fall-faaaal upon His chest! An' now watch death steal into His immortal eyes. See how His lips tremble upon the words His bleedin' heart *commands* them to say? *Forgive them, Lord, for they know not what they do!*"

"Yeah!"

"Forgive the sinners, the liars an' the backbiters an' the backsliders! Forgive the innocently born for they know not what they do!"

"A-MEN!"

"That was a day, children!" declared the reverend. "Children! Christians of tamarra, the hope of the God-fearin' future! Are we gonna let Jesus die in *vain!* Are we gonna waste the precious blood of Christ upon the barren rocks of sin? Have pity! Have mercy upon Him, the only Son of our Great an' Lovin' God who first had pity on *you*. Who gave His-only-begotten-Son that *you* might live!"

The moan grew into a deep mysterious chant that had no words, and which only the old folks knew. It trembled upon the air like a living thing. It throbbed like a heartbeat. It swelled and broke upon the shores of the mind like waves of sea. It churned itself into a seething foam of passion that slowly receded into the secret depths of a primordal stillness: still . . .

"Rise! and prepare to face your God!" the reverend commanded.

Amerigo, paralyzed within his black foul flesh, watched the sinners rise from the midst of the throng of eyes.

"Don' hesitate! Come *now!* Come down an' accept the hand of fellowship in Christ. Tamorra may be too late! For if you deny Me here on earth, so will I deny you before My Father who is in heaven!"

"Praise Je-sus!" cried Brother Dixon.

Meanwhile the false coins moved tremulously down the aisle to the table where Sister James stood with her eyes closed and her lips bent upon a silent prayer, while the reverend greeted them with the welcome hand of forgiveness.

Amerigo felt the great man's eyes upon him where he sat. He gazed into the Old Testament skies trimmed in bright halos of gold.

"Won't you come?" whispered the reverend. "Come to Je-sus just now!"

He could not move.

"Now?" whispered the reverend. He began to sing tenderly: "Come to Jee-sus, come to Jee-sus, come to Jeee-sus just now! Just now. Come to Je-sus just now. He will help you, He will help you, He will help you, just now, just now, He will help you — just now."

"Now?"

"A-He will *save* you, He will save you, He will save you, just now . . . just now, He will save you, just now!"

"Oh yes, He will!" cried Sister Mayfield, placing her warm velvet hand upon his trembling shoulder.

"He will saaaave you — just now."

The congregation hummed the melody softly. He remained in his seat. Presently all the eyes turned toward the reverend. He said:

"We thank the Lord for all those who have come under His protection this mornin'!"

"A-MEN!"

He shook the hands of the downcomers and asked them if it was their wish to join St. John's Baptist Church, to be accepted in Christian fellowship and abide by the rules of the church, according to the ordinances of the Holy Bible and the authority invested in him by God?

"Yes," they all said: "Yes."

"Yes."

"Yes."

The congregation rose. The reverend raised his hands and bowed his head in an attitude of silent prayer. Then suddenly the heads raised and the eyes broke up into patterns of shuttering lashes. Sound issued from moving lips and shuffling feet. The congregation hastened to answer the call of the great organ that could now be heard from the main auditorium.

The choir was already marching to the choir stand, singing the opening hymn. Meanwhile Amerigo darted out the side entrance and followed the path to the street. He crossed over to the unaccustomed side, where white people lived, and walked in the shade of a strange tree, east for a while until he came to a broad boulevard running north and south and turned north until it turned west where it became the great Admiral Boulevard, running parallel to the avenue. Now he crossed the boulevard, north, and followed a pleasantly shaded street until he came to the crest of a hill from which he looked down toward the great river. He gazed at the broad vista for some minutes, and then wandered unconsciously down an alley, through a shoot, south, up an empty street, and then turned west, into the boulevard again.

The dull Sunday-morning traffic sped past him. Now and then he came to a fruit stand perched on the sidewalk. He passed the bakery. He came to the white church just in time to see the people streaming quietly onto the side walk.

Finally he stood on the corner of Admiral Boulevard and Troost. He looked down the hill toward the avenue and tried to discover the house behind the trees where Isaac used to live. Unable to find it, he gave up the search, crossed Troost, and walked down the gentle slope past the candy factory, a few apartment houses where white people lived, and on to Campbell Street. As he turned down the hill he smelled Sunday dinners cooking, biscuits and fried chicken, mashed potatoes, peas, corn, stewed tomatoes, raisin and apple pie, mingling with the redeeming light of Sunday morning, but he did not hasten his step.

Nor was he excited, as he usually was, when he, Viola, and Rutherford sat down to Sunday dinner and Viola gave him the leg of the chicken.

"Ain't you hungry?" she asked.

"No'm."

"Unh!" Rutherford cried.

He wriggled nervously in his chair. After that there was a knock upon the front door.

"Oooo-oo!" cried a feminine voice. It was already advancing through the middle room. "Brother!" said Aunt Nadine, stepping into the kitchen.

"Hi, sister!" said Rutherford.

"You go right on eatin'," said Aunt Nadine, "don' let me disturb you. I just thought I'd drop in on you. Don' never see you at church!" She sat, gasping for breath, upon the proffered chair, the staves of her corset straining against the fabric of her dress like thick veins.

"Get a plate, Amerigo," said Viola.

"You shouldn' draw that straitjacket so tight, there, girl!" said Rutherford with a sly grin.

He set the plate on the table before Aunt Nadine.

"Amerigo's growin' like a weed!" she said, "Gonna be a man before you know it!" She smiled a fine yellow-toothed smile, while her cheeks swelled up under her large and rather pretty eyes like two dark brown apples.

That's Dad's sister, he thought, observing that her nose and hair were like Rutherford's, and reflected that his wasn't, and wondered: How come?

"He's wearin' my drawers already!" Rutherford was saying. "Yeah! An' my socks, too. Viola sneaks an' gives 'im all my ties. I can't hardly find a decent rag to wear no more. I'm sure glad that little joker can't wear my shirts yet!"

"Aw, but *you* ain' got but *one,* brother!" Aunt Nadine declared, biting into a breast of chicken. "What if you had *three!* Eeeeev'ry time you look around it's a nickel for this an' a dime for that an' a dollar for the other! It really adds up! An' *then* — after you done made all that sacrifice to feed 'um an' bring 'um up — they go off an' leave you!"

"Yeah," said Rutherford, "that's part of life, I guess."

"Church must a run overtime, Nadine," said Viola, "you're a little late taday."

"Scandal, honey."

"What happened?" Viola asked.

"The reverend had to straighten that fidgety Lucy Mae out! Switchin' around — showin' all 'er belongin's!"

"What'd she do?" Rutherford asked.

"Sung a solo this mornin', you know — she finally wormed 'er way into the senior choir — an' she got up there an' closed 'er eyes, honey, an' got to swingin' 'er head an' ever'thin' else! Well, sir! She was singin' like she forgot where she was!"

"What you mean?" Viola asked.

"Well, the reveren' let 'er finish, an' then he called 'er down in front a the whole church! This ain' no nightclub! he said. Gittin' so you can't tell the Lord's music from the devil's. An'-an'-then he told 'er, when you sing in *this* church, sing from your heart an' not from your hips!"

"Naw!" Viola exclaimed.

"An' he's right, too!" Aunt Nadine declared. "All these cake eaters an' jitterbugs an' blues signers singin' spirituals ever' whichaway! I think it's a c-r-y-i-n' shame!"

"Unh!" said Rutherford. "I bet she sure felt like crawling under a rock!"

"She started cryin'," said Aunt Nadine. "He told 'er it wasn' no use cryin', she'd better be prayin' to the Lord to purify 'er soul!"

"Ain' that a killer!" Rutherford exclaimed, "embarrassin' somebody like that — in front a the *whole* church!"

"He's right, too!" Aunt Nadine declared heatedly. "A leader ain' no leader unless he kin speak out the truth before *ever'body!* An' she wasn' the only cobweb in the attic this mornin'." She looked at Amerigo significantly.

"What else happened?" Viola asked.

"They kept the w-h-o-l-e Sund'y school overtime just on account a your son."

"What did he do?" Rutherford asked gravely. He and Viola looked at Amerigo, who looked into his plate.

"The *star* member of the Sund'y school," said Aunt Nadine, "ain' even been baptized, ain' a *real* member of the church, ain' no Christian!"

A dead silence descended upon the room. He looked at his mother and at his father and at his aunt, all of whose gazes settled upon the lower levels of the room, as though they were searching for the answer to the mystery there.

"Mine ain' no better'n yourn," Aunt Nadine was saying to herself. "Lord knows I try to git 'um to go to church but they just won' go. An' Charley, he won' help me none."

"That boy's been goin' to that church — ever since he's been big enough to walk!" Rutherford said angrily.

"But he ain' never been *christened!*" said Aunt Nadine, "never been *baptized*. An' if you ain' been *christened* an' you ain' been *baptized* you ain' been born, you ain' *nothin'* or *nobody!* You walkin' in *sin!* An' then, when they *did* extend the invitation to join, this young man *refused!*"

"He's *right!*" Rutherford exclaimed with trembling lips. "He don' *have to* join nobody's church till he gits *damned good an' ready!* An' I don' care if he *never* joins the da-gum church! You supposed to join the church *of your own free will,* not 'cause they *embarrass* you to death! Pointin' at you, an' makin' you stand up in front a ever'body, like a damned fool! Make you think all the sin in the whole world is your fault. If *I* was Jesus Christ —"

"Watch out there, now, brother!" cried Aunt Nadine.

"Naw! if I was *God* I wouldn' *want* nobody to follow me just 'cause I had to browbeat 'um!"

"I know, brother!" said Aunt Nadine.

"You know what, Nadine? You think just 'cause you *live* up there in that damned church you goin' to heaven?"

"I know — you a hard one," said Aunt Nadine, "but the Lord's gonna punish you one a these days, you just mark my word."

"I'm punished *already!* What *more* kin the Lord do to me! I'm a black man in a white man's world. I could just as well be dead, an' you givin' me all that jive 'bout the *Lord* ain' gonna make no difference —"

"There's freedom in the Lord, Rutherford," said Aunt Nadine.

"There's freedom for *you* in the Lord," said Rutherford. "The only freedom *I'm* ever gonna know is what I find in *myself,* in thinkin', an' under*standin'* things an' —"

"You'll pay for those words one a these days, Rutherford Jones," said Aunt Nadine, "Amerigo's gonna grow up an' break your heart an' it's all gonna be your *own* fault! Why — already he's switchin' an' struttin' like a man! A smooth talker! Got a word for ever'body. I see 'im, all right. Hat all cocked on the side of his head, walkin' down the street like a proud cock!"

"Ain' no child in that church that's better thought a than Amerigo!" said Viola with deep emotion. "He goes to church every Sund'y! An' he ain' no liar an' he ain' never been in no trouble."

"Kin I go now, Mom?"

"Goin' to the show — on *Sund'y!*" exclaimed Aunt Nadine.

"I'm goin' to the *art* gallery!"

"He goes *every* Sund'y," said Viola with a triumphant twinkle in her eyes.

"Yeah," said Rutherford, "he's *the only one* — the only spade in the whole joint. An' he's *accepted,* too! Holds his head up an' don' take no crap from *no*body! 'Cause he's got *class!* I ain' like that. You an' none a us was like that, but he's got it!"

"So that's what the rage is now!" said Aunt Nadine, "Yeah, well, we'll see what happens. A reg'ler young man!"

"Go on, son," said Rutherford tenderly, and he fled.

Autumn advanced imperceptibly upon winter, which had already anticipated a spring, shimmering in the reflections of summer's light, burned the infectuous impatience out of his lungs, and he burst into a fit of coughing that sent the malignant seasons flooding through the pores of his skin and through his nostrils. He sneezed his spittle-spangled way to school, and blew his nose — between bursts of feverish words drawled out in English accent — until the skin burned like a Bermuda onion. In knee pants and knickerbockers General Douglass strode through the galleried halls and in and out of the sixth-grade classroom catching the graceful long-legged words that leaped from Miss Griffet's, the sixth-grade teacher's, lips into his waiting arms. Around and around they whirled, her questions and his answers, his questions and her answers, until a bell catapulted him into a world of exile that was home, and the phlegmatic weeks culminated into dreaded Sundays through which he fled to the sanctuary that was the art gallery.

And the rims of his eyes burned as he moved through paths illuminated by searing flashes of white and rainbow riddled with bright filaments of gold.

"— That's the chief of the Mo-hawk Indians!" he exclaimed, thinking: Crow.

"I know it, man!" Tommy said. They studied the phophorescent red feather-headed face that hung in the frame on the clubhouse wall.

"Man o' War!" he heard Rutherford exclaim. "Where'd that niggah ever think up a name like that! Sounds like a hoss!"

"He's a soldier!" he had exclaimed. "He was in France — Frahn-ce — in the World War, and he got decorated for savin' two army nurses from the Rind River!"

"The Rhine!" said Viola. "Here you are fixin' to graduate next year an' can't even talk yet. Take your elbows off the table."

He took his elbows off the table.

"Yeah, the Rhine," suddenly caught up in the excitement created by Mr. Man o' War's ejaculatory utterance: *Ooooo-whee!* on the previous evening, as they all sat around the clubhouse table that stood under the portrait of the Indian chief. He had inched closer to Maxine, and trembled nervously when she let her arm dangle idly between his legs: *Ooooo-whee!*

The capricious toothy smile of Mr. Man o' War filled his mind, his strongly ridged lips stretching across his dusky face, his large nostrils expanding, his wide eyes flashing brilliantly. Gray hairs issued from his long tapering ears, as he scratched his small round closely shorn salt-and-pepper-colored head with his small black dirty-fingernailed hand. Mr. Man o' War was gazing at the Indian chief, as though he expected him to confirm the reason for his exclamatory utterance:

"Oooooo — whee! That was the *coldest* water I ever did see! Old Jerry was a comin' like a bat out a hell! An' it wasn' nothin' in front a us but that cold cold water. An' on top a that it was night an' it wasn' no moon. An' I was wounded, too! Well, sir! When that hospital blowed up I thought I was a goner! An' them nurses, they was pur-d-a-y! Man! Well, I told the little redhead to stay on this side till I come back for 'er, an' took the blonde first. She was from Chi — never will forgit! Well, I started across with 'er an' that current was s-w-i-f-f! I thought I never *would* git to the other side! But I made it, all right. But I was *tired!* An' then, an' then, I had to go back for the redhead. Man-oh-man! I hit that water a-*gin!* Whew! When I got over there she was just a-waitin' an' a-tremblin'. S-c-a-i-r-d! Jerry was *close!* An' when I say close, I mean *close!* Well, I caught my breath for a minute, an' then I took hold of 'er. Good-Gawd-a-mighty! That was the softest woman God ever made! But I didn' have no time to think 'bout nothin' like that, I had to fight that water! Almost didn' make it this time, too! But I finally made it. When we got to shore I dragged 'er up in the woods. An' then I passed out. The next thing I knowed was that I woke up in a hospital. A purdy little French nurse was smilin' down at me. "Sa va?" she said. That means, You feel all right, you know. An' I said, Wee wee! That means, Yeah! Man, I was in France!

"An' now," he was saying, "he's just waitin' till he gits-gets his pension that the gov'ment's gonna give 'im an' he's gonna be real — verreh — rich! An' he's gonna build us a bran . . . *d*-new clubhouse — an' . . . *d* everythin' . . . g!"

"That cat must be shellshocked!" Rutherford exclaimed.

"Shellshocked or not," said Viola, "he don' do nobody no harm. Matter a fact he does a whole lot a good. Got 'um learnin' how to tie knots, an' how to save people that's been wounded, like in the Red Cross, bandagin' an' stuff. Learnin' army rules an' regulations. You see how he had 'um drillin' all summer! Keeps 'um out a trouble. Now he's got 'um organized into the Mohawk Indians."

"We got that old room behind Policeman Jackson's house," Amerigo said, "that's the clubhouse for meetin's an' parties an' things. We cook things, too, real — verreh — good."

"I hear old Basil Rathbone's got a sweetie!" said Rutherford.

"Who?" Amerigo declared. "Aaaaaaaaw!"

"Look at that little joker blush, Babe! Hey! hey! A lady's man!"

"*'Mer'go loves Max — ee — een! 'Mer'go loves Max — ee — een!*" cried Willie Joe's voice.

"Aw-naw I don'!"

"Aw yeah, you do!" cried Lem. "I saw you in the show Frid'y night! Just a kissin' on 'er an' squeezin' 'er titties!"

"Aaaaaaaaw, you sure kin tell 'um!"

"*You* sure kin tell 'um!" Turner cried. "She had 'er hand in that cat's pocket!"

"Hot dog!" William cried. "Look at ol' 'Mergo! Got him a sweet patooty!"

"I ain' studyin' you, man!"

"Well, it won' be long now," Rutherford was saying, "look up one a these days an' he'll have one a these little gals in a fam'ly way an' you'll be a grandma, Vi. Ha! ha! An' sal-t-a-y!"

"Aaaaaw, naw he won'!" Viola exclaimed. "That boy's gonna finish high school an' go to college an' amount to somethin'."

"I ain' never never never gonna git married!" he exclaimed. "I'm gonna go to college an' git-get to be some 'un b-i-g — a real big shot an' make a whole lot a money! An'-and then I'm going to buy you an-*d* Dad a pretty house with grass in the front *and* in the back, and a —"

"A private room!" said Viola, "for each one where he kin put his own things —"

"Yeah," said Rutherford, "with a din, with tools an' things to make things. An' maybe a little boat to go fishin'."

"An' a Ford to pull it!" he exclaimed. "They have the fastest pickup!"

"How do *you* know?" Rutherford exclaimed. "You can't even drive."

"*I* know!"

"That sure would be nice, all right. . . ." Rutherford said.

"You could have a six-family flat — a hotel even!" Amerigo continued. "I could run it for you. We could git old, an' lie up an' git f-a-t! Hey! hey!"

"Not me!" Viola exclaimed. "None a that gittin'-fat jive for *me!*"

"I'm gonna be in Miss Tucker's class next year!" he said.

"I see in the *Voice* where she's supposed to be retirin'," said Rutherford. "A new teacher's comin', a little yellah gal named Sparks."

"Aw naw she ain'!"

"I read it, muckle-head!"

"I don' care!" he muttered under his breath. A feeling of rage made his lips tremble.

"Tommy's done left you," Viola said. "Goin' to R. T. Bowles already."

"Ain' that somethin'," said Rutherford. "I was down on the avenue the other evenin' — an' didn' see *nobody* I knowed! Like somethin' swallowed ever'body up. An' the avenue's just half a block away! I bet you I ain' been down there more'n, more'n three times in the past year!"

"All a *our* friends are out south," said Viola. "If, if it wasn' for Amerigo, we wouldn' even know the neighbors. Ever'where you look there's nothin' but winos and hus'lers. Mister Harrison's out on Twenty-Ninth Street now. Got his *own* house. Allie said she saw Mrs. Harrison at church Sund'y an' she sure looked nice."

"Did you find some pretty wallpaper for the paperin'?" Rutherford asked.

"You know old lady Crippa! She found the cheapest paper she could find — an' *then* had the nerve to talk about *us* payin' for half of it!"

"Ain' that a shame!"

"Well, we been here for so long. We wasn' nothin' but babies ourselves when we came. This boy's already eleven, an' we're twenty-six . . . seven!" Her glance fell upon the table. "Yeah! She figures she kin do whatever she wants. Can't blame 'er, though, she's been gittin'-getting away with it for so long! She'll be asking for more rent next."

"*I'll* be dang!" Rutherford exclaimed.

"Yeah! She's already complainin' about prices goin' up. Times are gittin' a little better, but they still tight."

"We oughtta stop lettin' that woman run over us. We oughtta move, that's what we oughtta do!"

"You been sayin' that for almost twelve years!" Viola exclaimed with laughing eyes.

"Has it been that long?"

"Will be next year. Take a look at your son."

Rutherford looked at Amerigo, and he looked at his father. An angry voice rose from the depths of an angry silence:

Who do you think you are to be accused!

Amerigo Jones!

"Will you look at this cat?" Rutherford exclaimed. "Big as me! Graduatin'! Unh! That new principal's sure puttin' 'um through. Hot damn! He's even got old Amerigo gittin' to school on time! An' I ain' had to look at that joker's homework since he came!"

"An' Amerigo — an' all of 'um's crazy about 'im, too! But he don' take no jive!"

He's like Dad, Amerigo thought, only he's a little lighter — and he's got a good education. But he isn't any smarter! Crow.

"Very soon now, you're going to be graduating from Garrison School," he heard Principal Powell saying. He stood before the class on a thoughtful afternoon when the mellow glow from the lamp overhead warmed the cloudy light that filtered in through the windows. He could see its reflection in the rimless glasses that he removed from his eyes as he rubbed the pink depression in the bridge of his nose with his thumb and forefinger.

"I'm gonna git-get me some glasses like that! In — *tel* — a — gent!"

"Very soon now, you're going to be graduating from Garrison School. Most of you can read and write a little, and you're supposed to be able to do a little arithmetic."

He shifted his glance to the gray window.

"But that's only the beginning. You don't really *know* anything yet. Why — that's hardly even a beginning! There's geometry and algebra and calculus, beyond which begins the poetry and drama of numbers, the abstract symbols of space, time, and movement! And then there's history — the history of the whole human race! Behind *and* ahead of you. White or black, you're a part of the human family. You're a part of everything that lives, and everything that lives is a part of you."

"How does he *know?*"

"Many sincere and brilliant men have written the record of their lives, their thoughts, their discoveries, down on paper. Their writings comprise the literatures of the world. Literature is just another way of talking, of discussing, in order to find out what is good, what is true, what is beautiful. These are the questions in life that should come to mean the most to you in the end, no matter what you aspire to be, no matter what you study. A good education is just a tool that helps you to design and build your thoughts in a clear, orderly, and beautiful way. If you expect to do beautiful work, you have to keep your tools sharp, and you have to master the use of them. The more you know, the more you see, and the more you can see the greater your possibilities of understanding perhaps the one thing that is the most important, *yourself,* and your relationship to the world in which you live.

"I sincerely hope that your preparation for life doesn't stop here. I'd like to see every one of you here go on to high school, and finish! And then go to college, and finish!"

Harvard and Yale!

"I've been to two colleges."

"Man!" Harry Bell exclaimed.

"No — three!" Principal Powell smiled and scratched his head and then fit his glasses to his eyes and peered into the grayness beyond the window, as though to check his calculation. "As a matter of fact" — he turned his bright expression upon the class — "all in all I've been to four colleges!"

"Hot dog!" Amerigo cried.

"And I have the feeling every day that I've hardly scratched the surface. And not — not of what there *is* to be known, for who can know all there is to be known? But of what *I* am *capable,* with all my limitations, of knowing! Do you understand what I mean? Can you follow me? I — I *still* don't know the simplest things — like what time it is."

Four o'clock! ticked the Big Ben clock, as Amerigo sat upon the clean white floorboard staring into the brilliant sunlight flooding the screen door and against the window shade, causing it to look like a veined leaf spangled with . . .

"What time it is," Principal Powell was saying, "like — what is *really real* and what is *not* really real? What is *really true? and what is false?* what is the meaning of life, and why — why was I born? Where do we go from here? when we die?"

To heaven where the streets are paved with gold! Amerigo started to raise his hand and tell the principal, but hesitated for some deep mysterious reason that was intimately connected with the word *star.*

"Do you know how many stars are in the sky?" he was asking.

Amerigo stretched himself to his full length, as if to count them with his toes. Like Dad said, it's warmer . . .

"More than there are grains of sugar in the sugar bowl!" Principal Powell exclaimed with a childish grin. "More than there are grains of sand in the deserts of the world!"

Aw!

"Yes! Plus all the grains of sand on the bottoms of all the oceans! And each little star is a world, and each little world is much bigger than the one in which we live. Just think of that! The Milky Way is just one little constellation of whirring worlds. But there are numberless constellations of whirring worlds! Myriad constellations of whirring worlds!"

A million of them!

"More than we can ever hope to see. And somehow we are all a part of that. Isn't that beautiful?"

"Sure is!" said Chester with a satirical smile.

Tee! hee! hee!

"Doesn't that make life interesting? Worth living to the full? Every instant, every day, eternally new! A new world eternally new! A new sky eternally illuminated by a new light! Moving! Changing! *All the time!*"

A subtle fear tinged with anticipation thrilled through his consciousness.

"This is the world," Principal Powell continued, "of which you are a part, like a drop of water in the sea, like a little cloud floating in a b-i-g sky. Live! and . . ."

"Aaaaw, I almost forgot!" Viola exclaimed.

"Live! — and . . ."

"What?" Rutherford asked.

"The reverend's dead."

"Naw! Unh! When?"

"This afternoon. Allie called an' told me!"

"What did he have?"

"A heart attack. He just up an' died. Just like that!"

Amerigo closed his eyes and watched the constellations of stars whirring in the sky. More than is in the sugar bowl or the Sahara Desert . . . falling through the gold-rimmed glasses at the foot of the tree. . . . Like Isaac an' Crispus Attucks. . . .

"Why did he die?"

"Who?" Rutherford asked.

"The reveren'?"

"The reveren'! What you mean — why did he die? *Ever*'body dies!"

"How come?"

"How *come?* 'Cause they do, that's all!"

"But there are some people who are dead that haven' died."

"What's this little joker talkin' about, Babe?"

"That's your son!"

An' there's some that are alive that are dead like Frederick Douglass and Booker T. Washington . . . Him no more than him! and Jesus. . . . An' some that's alive but asleep . . . like Boodah . . . Sorta dreamin'-like, but not really dreamin' . . .

Amerigo gazed into the depths of his father's troubled eyes. The soft blue light of evening mellowed the yellow light that filled the kitchen. The alley hummed like a seashell.

"I think the funeral's gonna be next week. . . ." Viola said.

The shadow of death as the tall figure of the reverend rose up from behind the array of flowers that surrounded the sleeping Isaac. . . .

"He preached last Sund'y as hard as ever, Allie said. He was even makin' plans to go to the Baptist Convention. They gonna have a big shin-dig in Chicago this year."

"Well, he's gonna miss this 'un," said Rutherford.

"I guess so," said Viola.

Amerigo saw his horny feet dangling just before they shoved him in the ambulance and drove up the alley.

"He shouldn' a had to die like that," said Aunt Lily.

Come to Je-sus, come to Je-sus, come to Jeee-sus, just now! He felt the reverend's eye upon him as his body contracted within his shrinking skin. He will save you He will save you. He will save you, just now. . .

"I did it!" his voice whispered. "I did it!"

He gazed vacantly up at the ring of downlooking faces. Tears fell through the hollows of his eyes under the earth at the foot of the trees.

"He died for *you!*" cried the reverend: "*Alone!* Amid the jeers of the Roman soldiers. *Alone!* On the cross that *you* might live!"

"How kin somebody die for somebody?" he asked suddenly.

"Can't *nobody* die for *nobody!*" Rutherford exclaimed.

"Jesus did."

"He's got you there, Rutherford!" said Viola.

"That's somethin' different."

"Kin-Can somebody be born for somebody?"

"Eat, boy!" said Viola. "Your food's gittin' cold!"

That night the alley shone like a cold dusty river teeming with dusty stars swirling dangerously in its swift currents. More than is in the desert . . . in the sugar shaker . . . the salt bowl . . . haircut on the floor of the barber-shop . . . that's all . . . that's all.

He grabbed the blonde first and dived into the red room. He swam and swam through the cold swift water. Finally he reached the other side. He dragged her up on the bank. She pulled him down toward her parted lips.

"I can't now —" he said, "I gotta go back for Mom. Naw! I mean Aunt Rose. . . . Aunt Rose! Cosima. She's got red hair and a soft fuzzy name!"

He leaped once more into the cold purple water and started back, and got very tired before he got to the other side, but he finally made it. Miss Hunt was waiting, trembling, scaired. He crawled ashore, to the place where she lay. His lungs ached as he gasped for breath. His arms and legs were as heavy as trees. His eyes came to rest within the depths of her eyes. Irish.

Now?

He sank into the cold black swirling waters of the Rhine. . . .

"Unh!" cried Rutherford the following morning, "looks like old Man o' War an' all them veterans gonna git straight — sure enough!"

"What?" Viola asked sleepily. He looked into the middle room where Rutherford stood gazing into the paper, blocking his view of the Indian maiden, his nose almost touching Jesus' nose.

"What?" Viola was asking.

"I see here that they gonna git they pensions!"

"Naw!"

"Yeah! I know things gonna be jumpin' now! Unh! unh!"

"Kinda makes you sorry you missed it, don' it?"

"Who me? What's them few pennies mean to you — if you got a bullet runnin' around inside you like ol' what's-his-name? You know who I mean, or a silver plate in your head! One arm, lose a leg, or somethin'!"

"Man o' War ain' got no plate in his head."

"I ain' neither!"

"But you ain' gittin' no pension!"

"Naw, I guess you right, but I *am* goin' to work, an' you better git out a that bed if you don' wanna be late agin!" He looked into the front room at Amerigo. He pretended to be asleep. "An' you better hit 'um, too, sonny!" he said, dropping the paper in the comfortable chair on his way out. "So long," he said, as he shut the screen.

"So long," said Viola.

"Bye," he said.

He lay still and waited for Viola to leave. When she had gone he jumped out of bed and gobbled up his breakfast and rushed out into the alley filled with warlike excitement.

"Wh-wh-wh-when's — when's he gonna git it . . . git it?" Toodle-lum asked excitedly.

"Taday!" Lem shouted.

"Aw man," Chester said, "they can't git it taday when it was just in the paper taday!"

"What *you* care, niggah?" William exclaimed. "*You* ain' gonna git none a what *we* git — *you* ain' in the club!"

"I bet you I know who's gonna git some!" said Chester with a malicious grin.

"What you mean, man! I don' play that stuff!"

"Don' have to," said Turner, "you was born, wasn' you? A chicken ain' nothin' but a bird! An' a bird ain' nothin' but a turd with wings! Ha! ha!"

"They gonna git it real . . . verreh soon, I bet!" he said. "Hot dog! An' then we gonna git a new clubhouse an' —"

"Man oh man!" Willie Joe exclaimed.

"Tee! hee! hee!" giggled Annie and Geraldine a few yards behind the men.

Meanwhile, the bells reverberated throughout the hours, which culminated into days that trembled within the redeeming light of Sunday morning.

Come to Je-sus whispered the reverend, surrounded with billows of flowers, peering up through closed eyelids into the long procession of eyes looking down into his hollow eyes at the foot of the blossoming trees.

Come to Je-sus, just now.

Three days and three nights of singing and preaching, animated by the ringing bells in the towers in the town and along the long black wires swooping from pole to pole along all the known ways in the land of Eleven Years, and beyond:

"He looked so *natural!*"

"Yeah — just like he was asleep."

"How much did the funeral cost, honey? You heard?"

"Naw, but it must a cost a fortune!"

"Did you hear what *I* heard?"

"Naw, what did you hear?"

"Well, I ain' supposed to tell nobody, but if you promise not to tell — "

"You know you kin count on me to keep my mouth shut!"

"Well, it wasn' told to me directly, mind you, but I got it from somebody who got it from somebody else who was *there* when his wife *told it!*"

"Naw!"

"Yeah, girl!"

"What was it all about?"

"About Sister B. P. I ain' mentionin' no names — an' Deacon J. J. H."

"I *knowed* it! I *figured* one a these days she'd git to switchin' an' git caught with 'er pants down."

"Well, that's just what happened, honey. His wife caught 'um *at it.*"

"You mean doin' the *thing,* honey?"

"I mean they love was comin' *down!*"

"These big shots, honey, they the biggest devils in the church! An' did you see the way they was carryin' on at the funeral! All that cryin' an' carryin' on ain' natural, honey!"

"But it was kinda sad, though," said Viola. "That candidate spoke *so* nice, an' the music an' the flowers an' all were *so* lovely. I tried to hold myself back, but girl, I got to cryin' an' blowin' my nose! I thought I never *would* stop!"

"Did you git some a the flowers?" Miss Allie Mae asked.

"Unh-huh. Pressed 'um in the Bible — where the text was."

"Well, that was one a the biggest doin's *this* town's ever seen!" said Miss Allie Mae. "Shoulda seen the white folks lookin' when we rode through town in them long black limousines, honey! All togged down to the bricks!"

"You tellin' me! I wasn' lookin' so bad, myself! I had old Amerigo sparklin' to beat the band!"

"He spoke so n-i-c-e!" said Miss Allie Mae. "I was as proud as I could be!"

"G-i-r-l — I was *scaried!* He was up there in front a *all them people* — an' my knees was shakin' all the time he was recitin'."

"Ain' that a shame!" Rutherford's voice broke in. "Ol' Viola don' never go to church unless somebody kicks the bucket! Ha! ha!"

"RUTHERFORD JONES!"

"Yeah! gits all togged *down* — an' c-r-i-e-s — up a breeze!"

"Don't you believe 'im, Amerigo!"

"He knows! Boy, when's the last time your momma been to church? Not since Sue's mother died. An' she didn' even *know* 'er!"

Tears accompanied by embarrassed laughter rolled down Viola's cheeks.

"I don' know," she said in a confused voice. "I can't explain it but all that beautiful music an' the beautiful flowers an' all. An' the reveren' spoke so nice. An' then the daughter started cryin' — an' the family an' all. *You* understand what I mean, don't you? How you kin feel sorry for people that's died that you don' even know? It seems like to me . . . It seems like *ever*'body oughtta have *some*body to *stand up* for 'um when they die. It — it oughtta be somethin' *beautiful*. Aw — I don' know. It ain' somethin' that you kin just explain just like that. But it don' even have to be no funeral, sometimes I just cry 'cause I feel sad about somethin'. An' even if you don' know what it *is* — it makes you feel better."

"They GOT IT!" Chester cried on a bright Saturday morning. "The first of 'um's gittin' it taday!"

"How do *you* know?" he asked.

"Some of 'um's got it already. Mr. Dan's got his. An' old Frog, an' Mr. Slim, 'cause he was wounded."

Suddenly a crowd of children had gathered in the alley.

"You look thisaway an' I'll look thataway!" cried Willie Joe.

"Aw niggah!" William shouted, "you don' come tellin' *me* what way to look!"

"Toodle-lum!" Mrs. Shields called down into the alley.

"Yes'm . . . yes'm . . ." Toodle-lum whined.

"You come up here on this porch!"

"Aaaaaaw, bigamaw!" he cried, his face twisting into a painful grimace. Water filled his eyes, and he beat his thighs with his skinny little fists and gnashed his teeth. "Man o' War's comin'! comin'!"

"I don' care *who's* comin'! You better git your li'l behind up here before I come down there an' git you myself!"

"Aw let the boy alone!" shouted Mr. Everett from downstairs. "That crazy niggah ain' comin', no way, but they ain' doin' no harm!"

"Well," said Mrs. Shields, "you stay where I kin see you!"

"Yes'm . . . yes'm."

The sun advanced toward eleven-thirty. The traffic in the alley increased.

Music from the houses spilled out into the street. People leaned on porch banisters and looked up and down the alley for signs of lucky veterans.

"Aw he ain' comin'!" Miss Myrt shouted from her post in the second-story window of Tommy's house. "That niggah done found a yellah woman an' left town!"

"*Aw* naw, he ain'!" William cried.

"He *said* he was comin'!" Amerigo shouted, "an' he is, too!"

"*Said!*" Tommy exclaimed. "His mouth ain' no prayer book!"

"That niggah oughtta be hoss-whipped!" declared Miss Betty, "promisin' these kids, an' then don' show up!"

The twelve o'clock whistle blew.

BrrrrrRRRRRUUUUUUUMM! There was a loud roar at the foot of the alley.

"LOOK!" Amerigo shouted. "It's HIM!"

A big red shiny chromium-plated motorcycle shot up the alley. In the saddle sat Mr. Man o' War dressed in black riding pants and boots, a black leather jacket, and a white aviator's cap with goggles.

Halfway up the alley he gunned the motor: *ZOOM!*

Boom-Boom! went the exhaust.

"HOO-R-A-Y!" the children shouted.

"It's *MEEEE!*" he shouted, coming to a stop. Laughter from every house splashed over the banisters and down the steps where it glistened in the twelve o'clock sun.

"I *told you!*" Amerigo cried to Rutherford who was just then coming down the alley.

"WHEE WHEE!" shouted Mr. Man o' War. "It's gonna be *ice cream an' s-o-d-a — p-o-p!* for *eeeeevah*-body!"

"EEEEYAAAAY!"

The children swarmed around him, examining his boots and jacket and his shiny new motorcycle.

"Indian Chief, Jack!" Tommy cried.

"Yeah! Now git!" cried Mr. Man o' War.

And suddenly all the children were scrambling up the steps to the porches and half stumbling, half falling down again with cups and glasses and plates and spoons, which, within a matter of minutes, flushed prickly-red, green, and root beer. Soft mounds of vanilla, chocolate, strawberry, lemon, and pistachio-nut ice cream spotted their noses and dripped from their chins. Willie Joe was enviously eyeing the bowl that Sammy, Policeman Jackson's dog, had to himself, when suddenly ZOOOOM! ZOOOOOOOOMM! the Indian Chief burst upon the air. Mr. Man o' War waved to the crowd.

"Fare thee well!" he cried, pulled his goggles down over his eyes, and he was gone!

"Ready for action, Jack!" Turner cried.

"So long, Man o' War!" resounded throughout the alley.

"That's a crazy niggah as sure as I'm born!" cried Mr. Everett with a smile that was more affectionate than anyone could ever remember seeing on his face.

"Where'd he come from?" Mr. Mun asked.

"Aw, I don' know," Mr. Everett said. "Just looked up one day an' there he was with all them kids around 'im, tellin 'um stories. He sure could tell a story. Had 'um laughin' an' cryin' sometimes, too. Yes sir, next thing you knowed, he had 'um marchin' up an' down ever' whichaway!"

"An' now he's gone heaven knows where!" said Miss Anna thoughtfully, with a faintly wondrous smile on her face.

"So l-o-n-g, Mister M-a-n o' W-a-r!" Amerigo shouted.

"You'll never see the likes a him agin, son," said Mr. Dan. He cocked his pegleg in the air and whisked the tip of his Diamond-head match along his hip, its flaring yellow flame burned the tip of the Bull Durham butt that dangled from his pursed lips, and suddenly the burned-out match lay smoking between the crevice of two cobblestones at his feet.

"You'll never see the likes of him agin, son," Mr. Dan's voice was saying.

And then the alley grew quiet with the sounds of thoughtful eating. Suddenly the twelve-thirty whistle blew. Big Tom's truck zoomed down the alley, paused for an instant when it reached the avenue, and then turned west and headed toward town.

Sunday morning blasted out like a clarion:

"Boy!" Viola cried, "what you doin' home from church so early. You been fightin'? Somebody after you? Hold on there, an' catch your breath. Now, what happened?"

"N-n-no'm!"

"What's the matter?"

"The church burned down!"

"WHAT!"

"Yes'm! I saw it burned up. I saw it. An' it was on the radio, too, an' don' nobody know how come!"

"Unh!" Viola exclaimed.

I did it, he thought, as the reverend stared up at him from the coffin:
He died for you!

Sunday was suddenly illuminated by a great flame that had sent St. John's crashing to the ground. On his way to the Gem and the Lincoln he stopped and stared at its charred remains. He looked at the space where the

Sunday school room used to be, where Sister James used to sit, in front of what used to be the wall beyond which the parallel crevices between the floorboards ran. He peered into the basement filled with smoldering ashes. Like bones! he couldn't help thinking, surprising himself, while his thoughts ran on against his will: Like white bones with no meat on them . . . flesh . . . He stared dumbly at the great tangle of charred beams that sprawled grotesquely on the floor of the great auditorium. A rush of free air issued from his lungs. A subtle joy filled his heart: *I did it!*

Who among you here — in God's house taday! said the voice, and he fled, terrified, through the redeeming light of Sunday afternoon. . . .

Upon his return at dusk he stared at the monstrous shadow. He listened to the gentle breezes whispering through the summer night. Staring into the black cavernous foundation, he unconsciously tried to ferret out the hollow eyes that flashed conscienceless-yellow from the cool shady depths of Aunt Lily's . . . Miss Jenny's . . . Miss Betty's . . . porch, after Old Jake had poked his staff in and found the star. He fingered the dark room that was his pocket. Gone! A profound, barely perceptible fear rippled through his mind: Gone?

. . . Searching the skies of the red room for the missing star. . . .

Do you know how many stars are in the sky?

He sank into the desert sands of the black room.

The sun that shone Monday morning shone like a great fire. A star searching the skies. He questioned the tolling bells.

Sparkling pieces of ice frosted his iced-tea glass at supper. He sucked a piece into his mouth. It burned his tongue. He bit into the burning flame. It chilled his teeth to the bone.

Water isn't any thing but fire! He laughed aloud.

"What you laughin' at?" Rutherford asked.

"Nothin'."

"I wonder what they gonna do now?" Rutherford asked Viola.

"I was just thinkin' 'bout that, myself. I was just talkin' to Aunt Nancy this evenin'. She was sayin' what a shame it is for the new preacher. Here it is his first week a bein' elected to pastor an —"

"They choose one yet? I thought this one was just temparary."

"No, he's the pastor, all right, but now he's gotta build a new church to pastor in. Allie said they talkin' about rentin' the municipal auditorium — the little theater — till they git it built."

"Unh!"

"Yeah!"

"Won' that be a killer!"

"Right smack dab in the middle of town!"

"That joker's got class, you hear me!"

"An' educated, too!" Viola said. "You know, they had preachers from all over the country tryin'. They preached an' shouted an' jumped up an' down till the times got better, but he won out. An' that's somethin'! They say he's good lookin', tall an' dark, with a deep mellow voice an' a quiet way."

"What's his name?"

"The Reveren' Doctor John Phillip King."

"Hey! hey!"

"An' sing!" Viola continued. "Allie said, he got to singin', Oh when I come to the end of my journey, an' almost had *her* shoutin'!"

"I'd sure like to see that!" Rutherford exclaimed, shoving a forkful of salad into his mouth. "Old Allie shoutin'!"

Throughout the summer Sunday mornings he made his way to the heart of the great city on his way to the municipal auditorium. He sat within the plush interior of the little theater and saw the great stage when the reverend looked down upon his proud congregation.

"It pleases me!" he said in a well-modulated voice that flowed through the loudspeakers overhead, "to look down into tha faces of my people an' see 'um sittin' in the *front* row of the municipal auditorium!"

"A-MEN!" shouted the congregation.

"AN' on the *third* row, in the middle, an' in the balcony — *ever'where!*"

"Tee! hee!"

"Speak, Je-suuus!"

"Truly, truly" said the reverend, "the Lord works in mysterious ways! He burned down His own house an' built His temple in the devil's stronghold! He made it His temple! Where ever'body's welcome! Where ever'body kin walk right in the front door! Follow me, now, I don' want no misunderstandin', but it . . . it seems to me that things, maybe things, help me, Jesus, that things haven' turned out so bad, after all . . . when you try to look at it through God's eyes. In order that somethin' kin be *born agin — somethin's got to burn!*"

"A-MEN!"

"Yeah! you don' git somethin' for nothin' in this world! You gotta go through the fires of *hell!* to git to heaven! Moses beheld the burnin' bush and was amazed that though it burned, it was not consumed! Saint John's Baptist Church is more alive right now than it ever was!"

"A-MEN!"

"But we won' stay in the devil's house. We don' need it! The Lord done proved His point. Where His spirit dwelleth there dwelleth He also!"

"A-Men!"

"Now, we're gonna pray to God for courage, an'-an' strength-an' faith-aaaan' *money.* We're sure gonna need a lot of it —"

"A-Men!"

"— an' build the Lord a *new* temple — a new Saint John's Baptist Church!"

"Help'im, Je-sus!"

"A place of worship that we kin *all* be proud of!"

Like the art gallery, Amerigo thought, as he followed the stream of black, brown, and beige faces, flowing west until the white faces gradually faded away and a gray, reddish, sweaty, pungent, rhythmic, dusty, blood-spattered, gold-spangled, laughter-ridden, pain-ridden, teary-eyed humor filled the sky: heel over toe, toe over heel: east to west, west to east, and then south, along the shining rails come Sunday, animated by a burning sense of pride, because the municipal auditorium's not far from the Muehlebach Hotel and the Southern Mansion and it's on the way to the art gallery, where everything's so pretty — an' clean! Different from the North End, from the slums!

"I see where Saint John's gonna buy the old Fifteenth Street dance hall," said Rutherford at the end of a day when the wind had blown warmer, and he had spread out the pages of the *Voice* and waited for Viola to finish frying the fish.

"Unh — unh!" she exclaimed, "what a time we usta have there!"

"In a couple a months," said Rutherford.

"In a couple a months it'll be spring!" Viola said.

"Yeah, an' old Amerigo'll be graduatin'!"

Amerigo watched the bar of sunlight advance toward the foot of the table.

"He's gonna need a new suit," said Viola, emptying the boiled potatoes into a bowl.

"With long pants!" said Amerigo.

"I don' know about that."

"Vi-ola, you can't have that boy graduatin' in no short pants! He's almost as big as you!"

"Ever'body's *supposed* to have long pants!" Amerigo declared, "— and a navy-blue suit with a white shirt, and a tie, blue or black, an' . . . d white shoes. Hot dog!"

"That'll be my black ruin!" Rutherford exclaimed.

"What?" Viola asked, lifting the fish carefully onto the platter.

Buffalo, Amerigo thought, anticipating the hot salty crisp taste of the first mouthful. She set the plate of corn bread on the table.

"Well," Rutherford said, "he's wearin' my socks, my ties, my drawers *an'* shirts. Now he kin almost wear my *pants!*"

"That's what you git for havin' me!" Amerigo said, and burst into a fit of laughter that infected Viola and Rutherford, who shot swift subtle glances at each other.

Suddenly the fish had disappeared, all but the bones.

Like a leaf, he thought, looking at the skeleton that he had carefully spread out along the edge of his plate. He stuck his fork into the blind eye.

I did it! He sipped his buttermilk.

"An' then next year," Rutherford was saying, "next year he'll have to git up early to go all the way out on Nineteenth Street to school."

"I know!" Amerigo declared. "It's like on the way to Aunt Rose's."

"An' you gonna have to work hard!" said Rutherford. "None a that foolin' around, 'cause if you don' make it there, you can't go to high school, an' *then* college is *out!*"

"Your daddy's sure tellin' you right!" said Viola. "Just think, you'll be graduatin' in *June!* An' here it is April already! Ever'body's comin', Aunt Rose, Ardella, your daddy an' me, an' Aunt Lily an' Unc, Flat Nose. An' even old T.'s gonna git all dressed up, just to see you graduate!"

One day, during the busy-bee lull of a lazy afternoon in the beginning of June when the heat of the sun melted his eyelids and his chin sagged upon his chest, a penetrating voice shocked him into a state of fearful awareness:

"Amerigo Jones!" It was Principal Powell.

"Yessir."

"Would you come up here, please?"

He half walked, half stumbled up to the great man's desk.

"Sit down."

He sat on the chair beside the desk and inadvertantly crashed his knee into the wastepaper basket.

"'Scuse me."

"Now," said the principal, "I should like to know how you would like to have your name signed — *should* you happen to graduate."

"Hot dog!"

"Surely you don't mean that!"

"Aw, Oeh, neo sah."

"What *do* you mean?"

"I mean I'd like it."

"It?"

"To be signed: Amerigo Frederick Douglass Booker T. Washington Jones."

"But that's not your name, is it? It's not the name your mother and father gave you."

"No sir, but that's what I want!"

"Well, let's compromise: Amerigo F. D. Jones."

Franklin Delano.

"Jones," he was saying.

"Yessir," replied the Father of the Country.

Boom!

A great clap of thunder shook the dark sky, followed by a bolt of lightning:

"Oh!" rippled through the surprised crowd whose attention had been fixed upon Principal Powell.

"Amerigo did it!" Chester whispered.

"What!" Amerigo asked.

"Made it rain, niggah!"

The graduating class, ranging in rows behind Principal Powell, burst into snickers that caused him to turn around and give them a silencing look.

"Too bad it rained," said Viola in the taxi after the ceremony. "But it was nice. All the kids looked *so* nice. An' that little girl that spoke — spoke so *nice* an' clear! She was so tiny for twelve."

"She's ten!" Amerigo exclaimed, "an' they had to hold 'er back to keep from graduatin' too young."

"Well, she sure spoke like a little lady all right!"

"Yeah, it was real nice, all right," said Rutherford.

"They said I did it," Amerigo said.

"What?" Rutherford asked.

"Made it rain."

"How come?" Viola asked.

"'Cause I come in long pants. I was lookin' s-h-a-r-p! Hot dang!"

"Be careful, there," Viola warned, "you almost said somethin'."

"Walkin' all cute!" Rutherford exclaimed. "An' like to fall down. Haw! haw! haw! An' didn' win *nothin'!* Not even a booby prize! They kept callin' the names a the ones on the honor list an' I kept waitin' to hear my son's name — an' I ain' heard it *yet!* But that little Chester — what was his name?"

"You know it, Amerigo," said Viola.

"Chester Owlsley."

"Now *he* must be a tough little joker! Had the highest marks in the whole school."

"He kin do long division without writin' it down in his head. But his sister, Erma, is better in English, an' his other sister, Emma — they're twins — is better'n both of 'um, but she's sick all the time an' has to stay home."

"Well, you ain' missed a day!" said Rutherford. "What happened to *you?* You supposed to be so smart an' all."

"That don' matter!" said Viola. "You got through, didn't you, babe? It won' be long now!"

The taxi swerved into the alley.

Amerigo sat on the porch and ate his crawdads and drank his beer.

"He kin have a glass a beer. He's a man now — or he soon will be," Rutherford had said.

"Aaaaaaw naw he ain'!" Viola had exclaimed. "That boy ain' nothin' but twelve years old. Why, he's just a *baby!*"

"Do you remember how old we was when we got married?" Rutherford asked.

"That don' make no bitter difference!" she replied.

"Drink your beer, boy," Rutherford said.

"Yessir."

"But one glass is all you git!" Viola declared.

He sat on the porch and drank his beer and ate his crawdads, and watched the stars fill the sky. The moon flushed red and then orange against the lamplight up and down the alley. Meanwhile he indulgently accepted the congratulations of the neighbors and answered all the question and suffered with those to whom fate had denied the opportunity that he had been privileged to enjoy.

The nine o'clock whistle blew and stirred the fireflies around Sammy Sales's tree.

I can stay up tonight, he thought, laughing to himself with secret pleasure, titillating uneasily upon the verge of an enthusiasm the limits of which he has at a loss to discover.

"Aw, swing them hips!" cried a man's voice from the alley. They all looked down and saw Fay, a tall, pretty, muddy-yellow woman of twenty-four, switching up the alley.

"She's really puttin' it on, there!" Rutherford exclaimed.

"Yeah," said Viola, "she's gonna break 'er backbone, if she ain' careful!"

"Tee! hee! hee!" Amerigo exclaimed. "Look at that broad walk!"

Rutherford and Viola looked at him. The grin froze on his face.

"What did you say!" Rutherford asked.

"Nothin'."

"Well, you better not say it agin! Look at that broad walk! You must think you a *man* or somethin'!"

"It's about your bedtime, anyway, ain' it?" Viola asked.

"Aw, Mom!"

"Well, you straighten up an' fly right, then."

He trembled within the happy stillness of ten o'clock, soothed by cricket-song, singing the tale of the hero who graduated from elementary school and who was going to junior high school for a year, after which the great doors of North High would open, and the secrets of its many rooms would satisfy his thirst and his hunger to know. Once wise, he would win the prizes of the world. Mom and Dad, and Aunt Rose, and Aunt Lily — the whole North End — would be so proud.

Be a race man!

Fight for the rights of our people!

Things is gonna be a lot better for you than it was for us — if we don' git tangled up in another one a Europe's wars!

"Ain' that the *truth!* We oughtta stay over here an' attend to our *own* business — an' let them Frenchmens an' Germans kill they*self* up if'n they got a mind to!"

"We all in the same boat!" Rutherford exclaimed.

"What you mean, we *all* in the same boat?" T. C. exclaimed. "We got two big oceans between us an' them. We kin just lay over here, Jack! Cool as a cucumber, an' when they start cryin', Come over an' help us, tell 'um, Unh-unh!"

"We're a half a block from the avenue, T. C.," Rutherford said, "but if *one* house starts burnin', *all* the rest is goin', too. A plane kin fly everywhere a bird kin fly, an' birds fly everywhere, you hear me?"

"Well, *I* sure don' want nothin' to do with no war!" T. C. exclaimed. "I didn' *start it* an' I ain' *gittin' nothin' out a it!* Let these white folks fight they *own* wars."

"Mrs. Jones," Miss Jenny whispered, slipping quietly out onto the porch. "Did you hear what I heard?"

"Naw, what? Good evenin', Miss Jenny."

"'Evenin'. Mrs. Crippa's tryin' to raise the rent!"

"Naw!" Viola turned to Rutherford. "You see, I just knew it was comin'!"

"I got it from the folks downstairs," Miss Jenny said.

"How much?" Rutherford asked.

"What*ever* it is is too much!" Viola said. "She's done gone too far this time!"

"Yeah!" Rutherford said, "we oughtta *move!*"

"We oughtta start lookin' for a place right now!" Viola said.

"But someplace close to the hotel," Rutherford said, "so I won' have to pay no carfare."

"Maybe you could study up for one a those civil service jobs," Viola said. "They pay good an' you don' have to work too hard."

"Yeah," said Rutherford, "but, Babe, you know I ain' got enough education. You gotta have at least a high school diploma."

"With all that readin' you do! You could do it like — *that!*" snapping her fingers.

Rutherford grinned with embarrassment. "But old Amerigo's goin' to high school next year. He'll be out a high school — *an'* college — in no time. He'll git him one a them high-powered jobs, Jack! An' we'll have it made! Hey! hey! Won' that be somethin'?"

Viola looked down into the alley. The shades of the streetlights cut hard eleven o'clock holes in the cobblestones. A sad sound seeped down through the crevices between the cobblestones, filled the holes and rose until it filled the crevice that was the alley, and rose until it flooded the sky and made the stars shimmer as though Amerigo were seeing them underwater. Tears rolled down his face, as he gulped down a breath of air.

"You're sleepy, boy," Viola said. "You better go to bed now. You been up late enough for one night."

He said good night and ascended the stairs. Minutes later he turned out the light, slipped into bed, and reached for the star with his toe.

"We oughtta start lookin' for a place right now!" Viola whispered from the middle room, and he turned over over on his side and gazed at the sky.

I hope it never changes. The way to Garrison School stretched out before him. He bolted upright in a seizure of fear.

Next year, said a voice, which catapulted him into the deep mysterious regions of the black room. Stars rained down and covered the way to Garrison School, buried all the houses and all the trees.

It ain' no Sanie Claus!

Aw — yes it is!

Aw — naw it ain'!

I don' . . .

The stars rained down and rained down and filled the black room: Four! . . . Three! . . . Two! . . . One! — *Boom!* . . .

"Rutherford!" Viola exclaimed, just as he was stepping in the door the following evening.

"What you say, there, Vi?"

"Guess what?"

"What?"

"I was talkin' to Sister Bill an' she said that she heard from Mister Williams that they were plannin' to move next month — an' she thinks it might be somethin' for us."

"Where is it?" He took off his coat and hat and handed them to his son, who put them away and brought his house shoes. "Thanks, son."

"It's up on Tenth Street. It's got four rooms an' a bathroom. An' it's about the same distance from the hotel. But I don' know if we kin git it 'cause they don' want no kids."

"What you think we oughtta do?"

"I think we oughtta take a look at it," said Viola. "Ain' no use waitin'. It wouldn' cost but a little more'n we payin' here when the old lady raises the rent. Ever'body we *know* — practically — 's *gone*. Amerigo's graduated. Ain' a *thing* to keep us down here."

"Maybe we could talk to 'er," Rutherford said.

"I done *tried* that! She come givin' me that old who-struck-John about prices goin' up an' all that jive — *you* know how she is. An'-an' I said in that case, we'd have to *move*."

"You done *told 'er?*"

"Yeah! Wasn' nothin' else to *do!*"

"Unh!" He rolled up his sleeves and started washing his hands and face while she sliced the potatoes for the hash. "What did she say?"

"She sure made me hot! Come laughin' an' said 'Oh you won' move, Viola, you been here too long,' throwin' up 'er hands ever' whichaway — you know how she talks."

"Yeah. An' what did *you* say?"

"I said we done already found a place — an' . . . that we'll be movin' next month!"

"Ain' that *somethin'!* Boy, your momma done gone an' talked us out a house an' home! Hot damn! Here it is — almost winter! — an' we gotta move — an' ain' got no house! Now you kin see what I had to put up with all these years!"

"Yeah, I told 'er —" said Viola.

"Well — if you told 'er, I guess that's *that*. Now lay that hash on me, all this talkin' about movin' done gone an' made me hungry!"

"Won' *she* be surprised!" said Viola with a triumphant grin. "She don' really think we'll do it, *yet* — we been takin' all that jive for so long. An' just think, it'll be close to the car line an' we'll have a bathroom! Won' have to be ashamed to tell people where we live. Livin' on a *street* for a change an' not in no alley!"

"Hey! hey!" Rutherford exclaimed.

Evening settled down around the kitchen. A strange blue-black light filtered through the curtained windows and mingled with the yellow electric light, giving off a cold color that made the kitchen feel uncomfortable. The new cheap wallpaper spangled with strawberries was beginning to sweat. The smell of the paste that the paper hanger had used to stick it on was still in the air. It made the hash taste funny. He tried to peer beneath the paper and see the faded purple flowers on the old yellow paper, but remembered with a pang of regret that it had been scraped away, that he had helped to scrape it away. He looked about him. The table, the cupboard, the chairs, the plates, even the gas stove, appeared strange, temporary, in the sweating brightness of the room. And now mysterious sounds rose from the alley and filled him with impatient alarm:

Boom!

A nigger did it!

Ruben fell in about.

One-two-three-four! — Hup-ho!

Boom!

I did it!

A clap of terrific thunder, a great flash of yellow light that caused Principal Powell's voice to falter, during which pause Chester had exclaimed:

Amerigo did it!

What?

The rain dropped through the hollow eyes and washed the bleached bones clean until they shone as bright as the star that Old Jake had held up to the sun.

"Looks like it's gonna be all right," said Viola to Rutherford the following evening. "Mister Williams talked to 'um an' told 'um that we was decent folks an' that Amerigo wasn' no baby — that he's in high school an' goes to church an' has good manners an' all an' that you an' me's workin' steady. I went an' met 'im. His name is Mr. Christian. Him-*he* and his wife have been there for twenty years. He looks after the place like nobody's business! An' old lady Crippa's fit to be tied!"

"I bet!" Rutherford replied.

"An' Amerigo," said Viola, "I know we don' have to tell you this, but just the same, we *do* have to be a little careful 'cause they're so funny about kids. It ain't you I'm worried about, it's about a lot a kids runnin' in an' out a the house when we ain' home. An' you gonna have to stop singin' so loud an' trompin' up an' down the stairs like a hoss! It won' hurt you to walk for a change."

"Yes'm."

The following evening Rutherford appeared on the back porch with two large suitcases.

Is he goin' away? he wondered, his thought accompanied by a sudden terrific pounding of the heart.

"Hi, son," said Rutherford.

"Hi."

Viola came home soon after with the groceries. She smiled and talked as usual. She cooked a good supper, fried apples and short-cut steaks, which were not disturbed by the telephone ringing. After supper familiar voices came from the radio, provoking laughter and dramatic suspense. These gradually became lost within the procession of songs that issued from Amerigo's lungs as he washed the dishes. He was in no particular hurry now, because there was no school tomorrow, no fear of the possibility of not being graduated from Garrison School.

Each evening more and more suitcases appeared, and wooden and cardboard boxes and piles of cord string and rope and little cans with nails. Suddenly a bizarre disorder pervaded the rooms. The front room rug lay rolled up in a corner and the windows stood stripped of their curtains. All the perfume bottles on the vanity dresser had disappeared. He wound his way through a labyrinth of jagged piles of kitchen utensils and upset furniture, old bottles, cans, shoes, a host of useless things that frustrated his memory. He noticed that his mother was having the same experience, for now she was saying:

"Unh! *Here's* that old hat! The first one I ever made. You remember that hat, Rutherford?"

"You got so many hats I can't keep track," he replied, trying to place the hat.

"Look at this!" Amerigo exclaimed, holding up a tiny bottle containing a tooth.

"I sure remember *that!*" Rutherford declared, "a perfectly good tooth! G-i-r-l, you oughtta be hoss-whipped!"

Viola grinned, and her gold tooth sparkled in triumph.

"*The Last Supper* by Leonardo da Vinci!" Amerigo proudly exclaimed as Rutherford took the picture down from over the bed and wrapped it carefully in newspaper. Then he took down the calendar with the picture of the Indian maid and rolled it up and put a rubber band around it and stuck it in a corner of one of the packing boxes.

"I don' see what you takin' that ol' out-a-date calendar for," said Viola.

"Aw, Mom, can't I have it?" Rutherford looked at Viola in confusion.

Like at the show . . . he gazed at the two clean spaces on the wall where the picture and the calender had been.

"What?" she asked absentmindedly.

"Nothin'," he said sadly, as the familiar order of the rooms of 618 Cosy Lane continued to change.

Day after day.

In the red room filled with packing cases he tried to visualize the new house, the new way to school. At times he saw the charred remains of St. John's, reexperienced subtle feelings of relief and guilt. He tried to measure the distance from the new house to the municipal auditorium, to the art gallery, the Fifteenth Street dance hall that was not becoming the new St. John's, to R. T. Bowles Junior High.

Then one day he watched two big men grab the chest of drawers and carry it down into the alley and put it into the huge moving truck. He took the bird-of-paradise lamp down himself and handed it to the third man who stayed in the truck and told everybody where to put things.

When everything was in the truck the third man swung up the huge tailgate and rattled the chain through the iron rings, and made it fast. It was twilight when the truck moved up the alley.

"Bye, baby!" said Miss Jenny softly.

"Bye."

"Be good now!"

"Yes'm."

"*I hate to see . . .*" sang a deep-throated voice from the interior of the Shields's house. Toodle-lum sat on the porch looking down at him. He waved, almost shyly. Toodle-lum waved back.

"Come on, Amerigo," Rutherford said, "we'll walk. It ain' far."

. . . the evenin' sun go down.

They walked slowly up the alley through the twilight.

I hate to see . . .

"So long Mister Jones, Amerigo!" It was Aunt Nancy, just stepping out onto her porch.

"So long Miss Nancy," Rutherford said, tipping his cap. Amerigo simply smiled.

. . . the evenin' sun go down! . . .

The cobblestones were of a gray-reddish color. *'Cause my baby, she done lef' this town. . . .*

They nodded to all the people on all the porches.

If I'm feelin' to-morrow . . .

The lights came on just as they reached the top of the alley.

just like I feel today

He turned and looked down the alley lined with porches cut up into faint circles of corrugated light.

just like I feel today . . . the man was singing. And a great whirring sound filled his ears. It was like the sound in a seashell.

I'm gonna pack my bags — an' make my get-a-way! . . .

"Come on, son," Rutherford said tenderly. He took his hand and they started across the great Admiral Boulevard.

I don' live down there no more, he thought.

"If it wasn't for the powder —" he continued the song to himself, unaware that the voice of the singing man was well out of range.

The new street was paved with bricks, and there was a little yard in front of the new apartment that was crowded with sunflowers that almost reached the second story, their huge heads bowing down toward the wild grass and flowers that grew below. A little walk led to the cement porch of the ground floor. Mr. Christian, the janitor and rent collector, lived on the south side.

"This our mailbox, here," said Rutherford.

He glanced at the mailbox his father pointed to and read: RUTHERFORD JONES, VIOLA JONES, AMERIGO JONES on a little card that fitted into the space just below the top flap with the slit in it where you put the letters in. There were six mailboxes, but before he could read all the names Rutherford was already ascending the stairs. The porch was painted gray, and the apartment on the south side appeared to be empty, but the screen door of the apartment on the north side was open. A stout black woman and a little black girl eight years old with bowlegs and short nappy hair stood looking at them.

"'Evenin'," Rutherford said.

"'Evenin'," said Amerigo.

"'Evenin'," said the woman in a juicy friendly voice, her face and the face of the little girl who looked just like her breaking up into a smile.

They ascended the second flight of stairs.

"Hot dog!" he exclaimed, as he looked out at the great city that sprawled far to the south.

"An' there's the ballpark!" said Rutherford, pointing to the southeast.

They took in the view, which was interrupted only by one or two apartment houses to the south and southwest. A private hospital and nurse's home stood on the corner at Eleventh Street and next to that, north and opposite 1015, a big frame house and a couple of smaller houses stretched up to Tenth Street where there stood a big empty building with large dirty, plate-glass windows.

The tall buildings of the downtown district towered above the houses opposite his house.

"There's City Hall!" Amerigo exclaimed. "An'-an' the telephone buildin' . . .g! An'-and the power and light!" Suddenly he visualized the new way to town.

To the north, across Tenth Street, beyond the vacant lot that filled the corner, stood the ruins of the old St. John's.

"Come on, son," said Rutherford, "we better git in here an' help your momma, 'cause if we don' she's gonna be sal-t-a-y!"

They entered the house.

"Hi, you two!" said Viola. "The movers just left. It's gonna look real nice when we git it all fixed up. Get the floors lacquered an'-and the woodwork washed an' the windows, an' the curtains up an' ever'thin'. That's what you can do, Amerigo, while your daddy helps me movin' all these heavy things. I had 'um put the couch over there and the comfortable chair over there, an' we kin put the gas stove over there in the corner, an' the mirror goes on the wall, there an' the bricabrac shelf in that corner, there —"

"Wait-a-minute, woman!" Rutherford exclaimed. "Damn! Let's git one thing done at a time! Boy, your momma shoulda been a general or some-thin', the way she kin give orders an' don' do nothin' herself!"

"Well," said Viola, "we'll see who's gonna git the most work done. Let's git at it! We got galores a chores to do before that grub goes on the table!"

All the while Amerigo had been arranging the room in his mind, according to his mother's description. A smile burst upon his face.

"What you grinnin' about, you little sharp-mouthed thing!" Viola said.

"It's gonna be just like it was at home!"

"This is home!" Rutherford declared.

"Aw, yeah." He grinned self-consciously, comforted by the fact that there was a window in the south wall of the front room and one in the west wall where the door was. The sofa faced the window. When I go to sleep I can look out . . . He gazed at the south window. The roof of the neighboring house was very close. I could leap it, I bet! He peered very far down into the shoot in order to calculate the risk, and having calculated it, put the thought of jumping onto the neighboring roof out of his mind.

When supper was over they worked far into the night. They spoke very little, each bent seriously upon his task. The "middle" room gradually began to look familiar: the vanity dresser on the left, the rocking chair in the left corner, the tie rack with the color chart on the wall to the right of the vanity dresser with the straight-backed wicker-bottomed chair. Opposite the dresser stood the bed, and in this wall there was a window. At the foot of the bed was the chest of drawers, underneath which Rutherford's house shoes had magically appeared. The telephone stood silently upon the end table Amerigo had made in the carpenter's shop at school, and above the telephone hung the Indian maiden and over the bed the picture of the Last Supper.

He listened unconsciously for the streetcar to rumble up the avenue, but instead it hissed out Tenth Street, a new modern streamlined streetcar with two big pedals, one for the brake and one for the clutch, and a lot of switches and fancy light — and *f-a-s-t!*

It stopped at the corner of Tenth and Troost to take on passengers, and then leaped — lunged — down Eleventh Street, and paused resiliently, stayed by the red light and the swift current of whizzing cars and buses that went all the way to Independence. The bell rang, a soft, pleasantly penetrating catlike bell, and it sprang down to Twelfth Street. If he ran through the house to the back porch, he could catch the flicker of its taillight just as it glided past the A&P, like the Silver Streak! Like a whale! Over the bridge and over the bridge and over the sea to France and England!

He entered the new dining room; it had a window facing south. The trunk stood in a corner, and in the middle of the room stood a bright new dining room table. Almost like Miss Fortman's! Rosewood . . .

"Is that rosewood?" he asked Viola.

"Naw, it's walnut."

"Aw," thinking: Walnut Street. English! Realleh! Wall-nuts — aaaaaaaaw!

"M-a-n!" he exclaimed, as he beheld the new coolerator that had suddenly replaced the old icebox.

"Oooooo-whee!" Bra Mo exclaimed, sweat dripping from his smiling face, "sho gotta have it to git it up there with this one!"

"Seventy-five pounds!" he said proudly, noticing the feather edge of gray that ringed Bra Mo's head, reflecting that his face seemed to wrinkle more than it used to when he smiled, and that one of his strong white teeth was missing. He shoved the ice into the box as though he were glad to be rid of his burden.

"Look!" Amerigo exclaimed proudly, "I'm almost as big as you!"

"Yeah, I see you catchin' up with the old man!"

"Mom said she'll pay ya Sad . . . you Saturday."

"Aw . . . eh . . . that's okay. Yeah, that's all right."

He took out his dirty little flap-eared book, which also appeared to have grown old, and wrote down his account with the ancient blunt-edged pencil. . . .

The little corridor between the middle room and the dining room was just large enough to fit the new cedar chest where Viola kept the sheets. Rutherford had screwed hooks into a panel along the wall above where you could hang your hat and coat, and there was enough space between the end of the chest and the wall for umbrellas and things like that. This little corridor gave onto the bathroom, which contained a south window over a bathtub, and between the tub and the door were the washbasin and the toilet. To get hot water you had to heat the long cylindrical boiler in the kitchen next to the gas stove. Rutherford had made a shelf in the corner over the bathtub for the toilet articles, and Viola had hung the hot-water bottle with the long tube with the plastic nozzle with the holes in the end of it on a hook screwed in the back of the door, which, along with all the wood-work, was painted apple-green and the floor was lacquered mahogany and there was a soft yellow rug in front of the toilet stool, you put your feet on when barefoot. Another larger one draped over the side of the tub.

"Nice! nice! Nice!" he heard Miss Parks — the seventh-grade teacher, instead of Miss Tucker who had retired before he had had a chance to sing: *Some think the world was made for fun and fol-ly — and so do I!* — say: "There are *many* words in the English language besides the word *nice — interesting, charming, pleasant, agreeable — anything* but *nice!*"

It's realleh cha'ming! he thought, stepping over the freshly lacquered border of the floor into the corridor and went into the kitchen. It was just like the kitchen of 618, only there was no toilet door in the northwest corner of the wall near the window.

Viola had painted the cupboard white and the chairs white with green leaves on the side panels and on the backs of the chairs, like the green leaf on the big red apple that the Spanish lady had been holding in her hand longer than he could remember.

He walked down Troost, the new way to Aunt Rose's, the new way out south, cutting across the busy juncture at Twelfth Street and down past the ice cream factory. He waited for the light to change at Fifteenth Street and dropped down to Seventh Street, past apartment buildings gray in the sun with grass yards, stores closed on Sunday. Just as he reached the corner he gazed up at the porch of a weatherworn house that was bathed in the shade of a large tree. Suddenly a blast of brilliant sunlight blinded his eyes and his heart pounded violently in his ears. Children's giggling voices filled his ears. On the porch, in the swing, within the cool aura of shade sat an old lady with a wizened purple face and thin faded purple lips. She sat very still with her arms folded in her lap, with her shoulders straight and her head erect, as though the slightest movement would cause the tower of long coiled iron-gray hair, held in place, he knew, by a huge white comb, topple down.

The Queen!

He stood in the path leading to the porch, whispering softly to the still waxed figure: "Miss Moore?"

"Eh? Oh, what is it? What did you say, young man?"

Her voice was very old and thin, but precise and clear. Not like Old Lady's, like a witch, but like a queen, like an old dead queen that's been put under a spell and has to wait a long time on the porch and not say a word . . . until the prince comes . . . and kisses her on the cheek and she wakes up, a new and beautiful queen! With tears of joy running down her face. Oh my beloved! she has to say, and then he says, Oh, my beloved! I've found you at last! And then they return to her father's kingdom where the wedding bells ring out, and they live happy ever after.

"Miss Moore?" his voice was saying, "don't you remember me? My name is Amerigo Jones from the first grade."

She looked dreamily at him. A vague distant smile wove a web of wrinkles in her face, and she touched her hair with the thin pale fingers of a tremulous hand.

"Amerigo Jones!"

"Yes'm! My mother's name is Viola Jones and my father's name is Rutherford Jones, and they used to be in your class, too!"

"Oh, yes," she whispered, as if in a dream. "My! Eh, Won't you sit down? Yes, sit, do sit down. Eh . . . How old are you now?"

"I'm twelve and next year I'm going to R. T. Bowles Junior High."

"Hum? Ah, yes, that's . . . that's fine!" She lapsed into an absentminded silence that lasted for some minutes. Suddenly a car whizzed noisily by and startled her. "Uh! What's that? Ah, yes, I see. That's nice."

"She's dead. Asleep."

He wanted to kiss her on the cheek, but he only gazed at her in silence. From somewhere within the house a clock was ticking. Gradually he grew impatient within the pale aura of her dream.

"I have to go now."

"Yes yes, that's fine."

"Aunt Rose is waitin'-waiting."

"You must come to see me again sometime, young man. Eh, what did you say your name was? Ah yes — eh —"

"Amerigo. Amerigo Jones."

He bowed to the Queen.

"Ah yes. Yes."

The giggles swirled through the channels of his ears and washed him down into the street and up the hill. After a while he turned into a pleasant little yard and stood before the screen door. From the shaded interior of the room he heard the clock ticking, and he was amazed that time had followed him, had *overtaken* him.

He rang the bell, and a tired but familiar voice bade him to enter.

She's getting old. *Now I lay me down to sleep. . . .*

"How you like your new home?" Aunt Rose was asking.

"All right." He sat in the rocking chair near the bed — it took up almost half the space in the little room — a brass bed with shiny bedposts the tops of which you could screw off and hide things in. The mattress was very thick and soft and the sheets were very white and the blankets were very fluffy and light and clean. She lay with her head propped up on a huge white pillow, very brown and wise and clean and quiet. She gritted her teeth now and then because of the pain in her heart. He pretended not to notice. He looked at the three long windows with the green shades that diffused a soft green light throughout the room, and stared as long as he could at the pinpoints of light that broke through the shades behind the embroidered curtains. Like a church . . . a very small church. He noticed that the light was further diffused by the narrow mirror in the vanity dresser with wings on either side, so that you could close the panels toward the middle and cover up the larger mirror, if you wanted to. Like the pictures of Jesus and the Virgin Mary in the middle and the angels and things on the sides. Triptych. Tri means three, like in triangle.

"All right," his voice was saying. "We got a new icebox, a coolerator, and a new dining room set made out of walnut on credit. I have to go down to the furniture store on Twelfth and Main and pay the bill every month."

"Well . . . that's nice," in a weak, breathy voice.

"Is there anything I can do for you, Aunt Rose?"

"Naw, honey, ain' nothin' nobody kin do — 'cept the Lord."

Pray, he heard Miss Jenny say, wondering how it would be if Aunt Rose died, how the world would look, what would happen to the house and the grass and the flowers and Queenie and Viola and Rutherford . . . and *me?* If she wasn't there when they needed something or somebody, not just to give you something, but to talk to and be around and look at. He bent down and kissed her.

"Boy! You better *git* away from here — with your foolishness!" she muttered in a breathless spasm of painful embarrassment and joy. "You gonna come up to see me when you start to high school? I know your old auntie ain' much, I ain' got no education an' all —"

"Aaaaaaw! I'm comin'. It's just right down the hill. I kin come almost every day!"

"You got a sweetheart?"

"Aaaaaaaaaw shucks!"

"Well, you gittin' to that age. Your momma an' daddy wasn' much older'n you when you was born. Little big-eyed devil! You bring your girlfriends around when you wanna an' let your auntie see what kind a company you keepin'. I'll be up an' out a this bed one a these days, the Lord willin'."

"Yes'm."

If I should die before I wake, I pray the Lord my soul to . . .

"Next thing you know, you'll be goin' to North High," she was saying, "an' then we'll have to think about you goin' to college."

"Yes'm."

And suddenly he was looking around the corner to see if he could see September coming, just before he crossed over to Twenty-Second Street. Gradually he became lost in a usual late-summer Sunday, except that it was a little sad, its heart was weak, diffused with a mellow somber heat agitated by subtle airs that issued from winter's thin purple lips.

As night fell he walked the familiar way home, until he got to Eleventh Street, then he cut west to Harrison and turned up the hill and into the little yard where the sunflowers stood almost a story high, bowing their heads toward the wild grass that Mr. Christian had freshly cut. The scent filled his nostrils as he climbed the stair. He stood on the porch and looked at the city by night. Scattered clusters of light shone from the tall buildings, and the lights from the shops and lampposts shone from the streets.

The front looked the same as the old one, almost the same. He tried to discover what was different and decided that it only looked cleaner and fresher, newer. Everything was in its old place, but in a new way. Like in the middle room that isn't really — realleh — the middle room because of the other room that's got the new ice — coolerateh — and walnut dining room table and flowers in the window with the trunk in the corner. Eh! . . . with the big medical book behind it with pictures of men and women all cut up in little pieces, just to show how babies are born, and how men and women look on the inside naked. They put it theah on purpose!

He thumbed the pages and inspected the bodies, the round red chamber where the baby lay with its head down and his feet up, like he was doing a somersault!, spinning through cool blue worlds of light that emptied into the deep alluvial regions of the black room, and then the red room:

"Them's the facts of life, men!" Turner was saying.

"What?"

"You ain' a man till you git the claps!"

"What's that?" Willie Joe asked.

"Gonorrhea," Tommy said.

"Aw."

"Kids!" Turner exclaimed.

"Well," Tommy said, "I don' want *nobody's* claps!"

"It ain' what you want that makes you fat, it's what you git!" Turner exclaimed with a knowing grin.

"Man — you crazy!" Tommy said.

"*I* sure don' want 'um!" William exclaimed.

"M-m-m-me n-n-n-neither . . . me neither!" Toodle-lum said.

"How you gonna git the claps when you ain' even had no pussy!" Carl said. "Toodle-lum! Aw haw! haw! haw!"

"M-m-m-m my n-n-n-name is Charles! My name is Charles. I ain' studyin' you, now . . . ain' studyin' you."

"I bet *you* ain' had none! Ha! ha!" William said to Carl.

"What you wanta bet?"

"I'd like to git ol' Etta!" Turner said. "I bet she got some good booty!"

"Old Etta! M-a-n! I bet she kin really do it!" Willie Joe said.

"Listen to that little niggah!" Turner exclaimed, thumping Willie Joe on the head.

"Ouch!"

"That little cat can't even git a pee hard-on! Ha! ha!"

"Tee! hee! hee!" Lem squealed.

"Ha! ha! ha!" Amerigo laughed.

"What *you* laughin' at?" Turner said. "You ain' had none. Old Maxine wants to give it to you, but you too chicken to take it —"

"That's somethin' bad!"

"How you think you got here?"

"What you mean, niggah?"

"I mean your old man had to pull down them pants!" Turner said. "Ask Tommy, if you don' believe me!"

"You niggahs sure are nasty!"

"Come on an' git it!" Viola cried at suppertime the next evening.

"Mom?"

"Well, it's about time, you hear me!" Rutherford exclaimed, stepping up to the sink to wash his hands. He looked at his father with great emotion. He watched the huge muscles in his arms ripple as he rubbed the soap between his hands. He suddenly saw his father naked that time when they went to the bathhouse and dressed in the same locker. He trembled with embarrassment and rage.

"Wash your hands, too!" Viola was saying. He beheld her naked, her breast protruding between his upturned eye and a bearded face with a booming bass voice that made him sink tremulously into his chair and bite into his hot dog sandwich with exaggerated gusto.

"Did you hear your momma tell you to wash your hands?" Rutherford asked.

Boom!

He rose from the table and guiltily moved toward the sink. The gummy bread stuck to the roof of his mouth and almost choked him when he tried to swallow. Finished, he sat back down.

"An' don' fill your mouth so full," Viola said, "that food ain' gonna run away. Take your elbows off the table. Somebody's think you never learned no table manners at all!"

A sudden naked impulse caused the telephone to ring.

Now?

The shrill reverberation filled the darkness of the black room and pictures flashed through his mind like the pictures on the silver screen: a woman, prostrate, naked, upon a big white bed. The man stood over her, naked, trembling.

Now?

"Dad?" he cried from the moon-dark shoot outside, but his voice made no sound.

The telephone rang. Viola picked up the receiver, smiling as she spoke, and drew her leg toward her chest, while Rutherford trembled. A face with eyes peering in the window, *his father's face* looking in, and it was *he* who stood over the bed. Trembling.

"Dad?"

No sound save the sound of a flash in the dark accompanied by the thud of his body falling heavily upon the newly lacquered floor, shocking him awake. The silhouette of a huge black form between him and the window.

"D-A-D!" he screamed. The form bent down and enveloped him in an aura of soft warm flesh.

"It's all right, babe," Viola whispered softly, "you just had a bad dream."

The bedroom light flashed on, revealing the inquisitive lines of Rutherford's strong dark face.

"Has he got a fever?"

"Naw, I don' think so," said Viola, rubbing his forehead.

"Well, put 'im in the bed an' come to bed yourself — it's late."

The light flashed out. Darkness filled his eyes. His body sank once again between the troubled sheets. She covered him with the blanket. Just before the smell of her went away he felt the soft moist pressure of her lips upon his cheek. Then her silhouette was suddenly absorbed by the massive darkness between the windows. The sound of her movements faded — until the cloudy gray morning came and bedeviled his mind and eyes with a teeming, seething jumble of pictures that beat upon the waves of his consciousness so fiercely that he was only aware of a great spray of hurting excitement that filled the air and now and again shimmered rainbow, like powdered crystal caught in a ray of sunlight.

Occasionally the seething particles of light and movement congealed into recognizable forms and he found himself walking down a dusty street with his eyes fixed upon an undulating hip beneath a pale pink dress from which a pair of shapely black velvety legs extended, toe over heel, heel over toe, forcing him to hide the heat that burned between his legs with a pocketed hand, grateful that the grinding wheels of the streetcar distracted his attention long enough for him to realize that he must cross the street and turn south along the new way to school.

Nervously he burned through the cool shades of September, gathering around the light of the passionate leaves that fell and piled up like mounds of glowing cinders at the feet of the half-naked trees.

As he approached the R. T. Bowles Junior High School, the scampering leaves swelled into sensuous volumes of movement and sound that made his heart pound with wild excitement. The big brick-red building, sort of like Garrison School but a whole lot bigger . . . different, with halls with lockers along the walls with locks that you opened by turning a little knob to the numbers to the left and to the right until it opened; halls animated by the sounds of boys and girls, laughing and talking, darting in and out of rooms according to the directions of men and women teachers who pointed this way and that.

"Hey! hey!"
"Look at that hinkty little chick!"
"Yeah — Mae West!"
"Aaaaaaa mess!"
"Haaaaa-ha!"
"I wanna see my ba-bay! See my ba-bay ba-ad!"
"Yeah!"
"Goin' to the dance?"
"What dance?"
"Count's comin', honey!"
"Gotta be there!"
"Me, too!"
"Who you goin' with?"
"With my ever-lovin' mellah man!"
"She's the sweetes' wo-man that I've ever had!"

"With Jimmie Rushing, honey. He's fat, but he's cute!"

"What you say — man!"

"Gimme some skin!"

"There — you got it!"

"Hey, baby! You sure lookin' fine. Damn!"

"What you mean?"

"I mean, do you love me, honey. Do you love me true? Do you love me as much as I love you? An' you sapposed to say: 'Course I do! An' then I say, Well jump back, honey, jump back!"

"Who wrote that. I *know* you didn' make that up all by yourself!"

"You smart ain't you!"

"He! hee! hee!"

"If I-ee didddden'tt care . . . more than words ca-an say!"

"Honey I kin truck down to the bricks!"

"Aw, that's old. They peckin' now, doin' the Susie Q an' the Big Apple. An' I hear they doin' a new step they call the Shag in Chi. Johnny Twine kin do 'um *all,* honey, an' b-a-l-l — room!"

"He's cute, girl, with them broad shoulders an' mellah hips!"

"The rest of 'im ain' bad, neither."

"Now that you sayin'!"

"Confucius say —"

"What he say?"

"Aw nothin'."

"Confucius was a square!"

"Yeah, he wasn' nowhere!"

"Yeah he was, he was from Delaware!"

"Where's Delaware?"

"I don' care!"

"Ha! he! ha!"

"Say, baby — you gonna give me some a that booty?"

"Aw — you sure are baaaad!"

"Come here."

"What for?"

"*You* know *what for!* You wanna meet your daddy after school?"

"Not if I kin help it. Where?"

"Aaaaah-ha! ha! ha!"

"A tiskit a taskit, a brown an' yellow bas-kit! I —"

"Ole Ella, man!"

"Mella as a chella!"

Slang! Amerigo's contemptuous voice exclaimed: "We simpleh caaunt geo on like thisss!"

"Listen to that *cute* cat! Where'd you come from, niggah?"

"Why — whaat dew yew *mean?*"

"Ain' that a *bitch!*"

"Aaaaaaaaaaw!"

His mouth flew open just as the last bell echoed throughout the busy halls, and he found himself sitting in a room at a desk with initials scratched into its lacquered surface that were not Rutherford's or Viola's, staring at a woman who was the homeroom teacher, who held in her hand a stack of cards that she passed down the aisles. Name here, address there, this there, that there:

"When you've finished," said the woman, "pass them to the front. No, the address goes *here,* not *there!* Can't you read? Pass them up! Pass them up!"

Talk talk talk talk.

"Quiet please!"

Giggle giggle giggle!

A bell ringing.

Tramp tramp tramp — out into the hall and down the hall and into another room with another teacher with cards to fill out quietly-quickly-talk-talk-talkgiggle-giggle-giggle: myriad-colored, multitimbred, soft-throated, curly-headed, lemon-breasted, grapefruit and honeydew. Rose-lipped Shirley, taut-thighed Othella — and June, vivacious June with the wild lips burning! If I ever had a chance to . . . if . . . if, he thought, smothering the speculation with his pocketed hand:

Bell in and bell out.

And then the tortuous way home through the jabbering streets, the autumn-leafed tramp tramp tramp thinning out along their separate ways home. In time a sort of hysterical calmness induced by fatigue that resulted from walking ground his body down to a neutral thing, which permitted him to fly in pursuit of his harassed thoughts up the avenue and finally through a shoot behind two squat redbrick two-story houses and across a cinder-strewn yard into the alley past the filthy cluster of mean crumbling redbrick houses littered with a bunch of grimy little children who stopped crying and fighting long enough to stare at him, and into his own backyard.

"Good evening, Mister Christian." He was just coming up out of the cellar.

"Good evenin', son," he said, smiling.

Yellow teeth! He looks mean! Beady eyes like a crawdad. Black! I mean, *dark!*

"How was it, babe?" Viola asked.

"All right. Ever'body's got his own locker to put his hat an' coat an' books an' things in, an' goes to a new room every time the bell rings to learn somethin' else. I like English best."

"How do you *know*," said Rutherford, "this is just the first day!"

"Who's your teacher?" Viola asked, casually looking up from her plate.

"Eh . . . eh . . ." He dropped his fork on the floor.

"Aw-aw," Rutherford exclaimed, "it's one a them high-yellah gals, I *bet!*"

"Naw-it-ain'-neither! She's brown-skinned! 'Er name's Miss Jennings." Amerigo stared at the ceiling, hardly breathing, oblivious to the glances that flickered between Rutherford and Viola. "A *real real* pretty brown! A pretty copper Indian-brown!"

His voice echoed within the pregnant savory silence of the kitchen at suppertime. It was almost like the old kitchen. He could almost feel the presence of the old alley. The song of evening filled his mind. *I hope it never changes!* he thought with a suddenly emerging feeling of joy. He gazed past Rutherford's head. The sun shone copper-amber upon the red bricks of the tall four-story apartment building across the alley. A copper-colored girl stepped out onto the porch. Her silken hair fell in natural curls around her rather plain yet attractive Indian-looking face. She was built rather low to the ground and her legs were sort of bow. She sat down on the top step and her flowered dress slid up over her knees. . . .

"You in a trance?" Viola was asking.

"You in a trance?" asked a strange faraway voice. He waited for someone to answer.

"You in a trance?" the voice was saying.

"Naw — he's in love!" said Rutherford's voice.

"Who?" he wondered, gazing at the fulsome bosom of the girl on the porch.

"Haw — he's in love!"

"Aaaaaaw!" suddenly conscious of his mother and father again, looked guiltily into Viola's smiling face and lowered his gaze. "She's from Denver."

"How do you know?"

"I asked 'er! She said we could. We all told things about each other, an' I asked her where she was from an' she said, Denver, Colorado, an' I asked her if she knew where Daniel an' Fisher's was —"

"Unh!" Rutherford exclaimed.

"— an' she said, Yes. An' then I asked 'er if she knew Miss Jerusha Summers who worked there makin' chocklits —"

"Boy, are you crazy?"

"How come?"

"Denver is a big city, that's how come . . . with thousands of people. How do you think she's gonna know Jerusha — just 'cause we do?"

"It's a dirty shame!" Viola said, "she writes us long lovely letters all the time. An' she never forgits a birthday. She sent us that be-u-ti-ful box of candy last Christmas — an' we didn' even write her a card an' thank 'er!"

"Je — rusha!" he said, pronouncing the word as though he liked the sound of it.

"You always were crazy about Jerusha," said Viola, smiling and remembering, staring into her teacup as though she were seeing her face. "I bet old Elmer'll be sick a hisself for-the-rest-of-his-black-life! For goin' off an' leavin' a girl like that — *stranded!* — in a strange city with nowhere to *go!*"

"She was just a girl," said Rutherford, "but she had *cha*racter, Jack!"

"She slept with me, an' you an' your daddy slept tagether. An' when she got back to Denver she never forgot us. We oughtta write her — "

"Why don't you write, then?" said Rutherford, pouring himself a second cup of tea.

"Why don't *you?*" Viola said. "Your fingers ain' broke!"

"We'll git our son to write," Rutherford said, "he's in high school, gittin' all *edu*cated an' ever'thin'!"

"I'm going to Denver when I git big!" — the thought of Miss Jerusha filling his mind with ancient yearning, seeing the small delicate light-brown-skinned woman, almost as little as Miss Allie Mae, lying beside Viola with the soft light of the bed lamp shining down upon her face, weeping softly, as she told how Mr. Elmer went off and left her and how grateful she was that she could stay with them. He wondered how Mr. Elmer could do a thing like that to such a pretty woman. Anger and resentment against Mr. Elmer welled up within him. He bitterly regretted that he was so small, that he could not avenge her. If a thing like that *ever* happened to me! I'd . . . I'd . . .

His mouth ajar, his mind overwhelmed by the thought of Beauty in Distress, he gazed out into the expanse beyond his father's head. The sun shone upon the copper skin of the girl sitting on the porch. It glistened upon her hair. A distant, abstract rage filled his chest, his throat:

"If — if —"

"If what?" Viola asked.

"Nothin'."

Nothing. The speculation for which there were no words catapulted him once again into the burning atmosphere germinating with particles of sound and color and movement, and caused him to lose all awareness of himself, of his beginning or of his end. What had once been his ears were now volumes filled with sound, what had been his eyes were orbits filled with light, what had been his body a configuration of driven snow, finally coming to rest, a burning droplet upon a wrinkled sheet, exposed to the light of day.

★

"All right — let's hit 'um!'"

He opened his eyes and looked once more into Rutherford's face.

"It was early one Mond'y mornin'!" It was big Joe Turner's voice that he heard, books under his arm: "an' I was on my way to school. Yeah!"

A cold amber sun, and the gray streets stretched out before him.

"It was early one Mond'y mornin' — an' I was on my way to school!"

Through the falling leaves: *Boom! Boom! Boom!*

"That was the mornin' that I broke my mother's rule!"

Rustling through the big doors on the Tracy Avenue side of R. T. Bowles Junior High, up the wax-exhaling stairs and down the busy corridor, darting in and out of the busy traffic, hurried by the warning bell, seeking and finding the room that corresponded to the subject written on the card and sliding into his seat at the sound of the last bell, the first of a series, the first of the third before English, which he liked best.

She was twenty-five as she spoke. Her hair was soft and black and it gathered around the oval contours of her face. Her eyes were dark brown and clear, like a new baby's eyes that only looked at clean things. Her skin was flawless and her mouth perfect and her teeth were so even and white that they looked like they had never been used!

"*I was in love with you, baby —*" the Blues Singer was singing.

She was tall, but not too tall, taller'n me-than I! too tall.

"*— way before I learned to call your name!*"

Pretty titt . . . breast . . . bosom — chest! Chest!

"*I was in love with you, babeh!*"

Her arms tapered gently from her shoulders and her hands were fine and clean and her nails were nicely polished, natural like Mom's like they don't ever . . . get dirty.

"*way before I learned to call your name!*"

Her hips swelled amply, modestly below her waist, around which a thin belt held her pleated skirt in place. Navy-blue. She had a little belly, but his eyes scanned it quickly.

"*An' now you in love with someone else. I know you gonna drive me in — sa — ane!*"

Someone else?

Boom!

"This is Langston Hughes," she was saying, alluding to the autographed photograph on her desk, "a very fine poet." She knew him *personally.* They were *friends.* He was very *intelligent.*

A poet writes poems, he thought. Like Omar Khayyám. . . . A tree . . . I-ee thinkk thattt I-ee shall nevah see. . . . a bough, a jug of wine and. . . . Someone else?

"'A Negro Speaks of Rivers,'" she was saying. "Eh, Amerigo, Amerigo Jones," looking about for the face to correspond with the name on the list. "Will you please read the poem?"

"I've known rivers."

As his voice droned out meter and rhyme, he searched the banks of the great river for his coming-out place. He saw himself striding forth, stepping over the crystal squares of the great city, leaping over the power and light and the telephone buildings in a bound! *Boom!* resounded the volley or ricocheting sunlight, and the wounded general half stumbled, half fell down Memorial Hill. Through the hazardous silence of the Twelve Year Siege he crawled and finally pulled himself up the steep incline of the closing line:

"My soul has grown deep, like the rivers. . . ."

"Why — you read that beautifully!" declared Miss Jennings.

Giggles resounded throughout the sunlit room. A very young voice whispered:

You have to bow to the . . .

"Lillie . . . Bryant! . . ." she was saying. "I'd like you to tell the class what you think the poem means in your own words."

A pretty little light-brown-skinned girl with thick black hair, heavy eyebrows, and strongly accented cheekbones began to speak:

"I've known rivers, Eh, I think that he's tracing the history of the Negro and . . ."

He was gazing at Miss Jennings's beautiful brown neck. Ann Jennings . . . Ann Jones. When I'm twenty-five she'll be . . . too tall.

There was a mole on the right side of her neck, almost under her chin, near her, Eve's apple! He stared at it, while Lillie explained the meaning, and then Ruth Brashears, a tall skinny girl with a longish oval face, large greenish brown eyes, and a pleasant friendly smile. After she had explained, Carrol Tolbert, a round-headed, fat-cheeked, dark-brown-skinned boy with sensuous lips and a full set of big strong white teeth and sparkling mischievous eyes, raised his hand:

"— all he means is that a river ain' nothin' but a hair of the ocean's nappy head — that needs combin'!"

General laughter. Miss Jennings smiled.

"See Carrol T. before you pee!" he muttered under his breath.

More laughter. Miss Jennings looked confusedly at the class while he continued to stare at her neck.

Miss Jennings unconsciously rubbed the spot on her neck, glancing at him with a subtle expression of curious agitation. She played with the gold chain she wore, pinched the hem of the neck of her dress together, and finally folded her arms upon her bosom and allowed her head to sink a little forward.

The bell rang. He rose and marched triumphantly into the hall, his eyes and all the outlets and inlets of his sensibility filled with the sound and the fury of Miss Jennings' beautiful neck!

"Our love . . . if a dream, but in my re-va-rie. . . ." he sang at the top of his voice along the way home. "I can see that this love was meant — for me. . . ." He became his voice. He became the song. He floated along the glistening streetcar tracks, was run over by a southbound streetcar. ". . . My dreams . . . are as worthless as tin to me!"

"*Zoom!*" the northbound streetcar stirred the breeze that wafted his face.

"Without you — life would never begin to beeee! — Soooooo — love me! — as I love you in my re-va-rie. . . . Make my dreams a real-i-tee. . . . Let's dispense with for-mal-i-tee. . . . Come to me! . . . In my rev-a — reeeeee!"

"Sing it boy!" shouted an old man just as he was reaching the corner of Eleventh and Troost.

He looked vacantly at the man, and then past him, at the little church on the other side of the street, near the garage on the northeast corner. She goes there . . . Episcopalian.

He peeped through the crack of the double door and gazed at the empty seats and at the altar, which was different from the pulpit at St. John's. Sort of like a Catholic church, but not as fancy.

Suddenly the seats filled with quiet serious-looking dignified people. Big shots. Sunlight filled the altar. The choir stand flushed with singers dressed in white half-length robes. He could hear *her* voice singing, funny, but real dignified, without a whole lot a shouting and stuff. And then the music filtering through the crack in the door died down, and the preacher talked, lectured, like in a class room. Real educated!

I'm gonna be a Episcopalian and sing in the choir. I'm gonna . . . But when I'm . . . she'll be . . .

He eased away from the door and stepped quietly into the street where the noise of his fears were absorbed by the sound of traffic.

"Hi, Amerigo!"

William, a pretty little black boy with wavy black hair, stood on his front porch, smiling at him.

"Hi."

Sort of like Toodle-lum, but his hair's curly in a different way. More wavy-like, like an Italian's! Toodle-lum's was — Was?

He thought about the alley and all the old faces that had lived down there, and the new.

I oughtta go down and see Aunt Lily. I oughtta go down next week. Next week.

Suppertime came and went. Crickets sang in the grass. The city lights sparkled like diamonds.

In bed in the dark the stars gave off a sad blue burning light. When I'm twenty-five she'll be too tall. Realleh! Mr. Dillahd will have her. He wants her. He closed his eyes upon the sunny red classroom. The door opened and Mr. Dillard entered, a tallish, slightly round, clean-cut young man of thirty with glistening pomaded hair. He strode across the room, his face contorted into a self-conscious smile, as he tried to ignore the whispered remarks of the students:

"Oh!" sighed all the girls.

"Ain' he ka-ute?" exclaimed Ruth Regal.

"Look at that mellah moss!" Clista whispered, "tee! hee!" with a little squeal that made everyone laugh.

Her name is Jones, too. Amerigo laughed at her funny turned-up nose and the dimples on either side of her mouth that gave her face a doll-like expression.

Meanwhile a faint smile played around the corners of Miss Jennings's eyes and mouth as she accepted the soft-spoken information that Mr. Dillard's nervous lips imparted. He tried to catch the word as it fell:

Now?

Now? echoed throughout the red room, causing sharp pangs of regret to force him deeper into the red room, bloodred, turning black, shimmering in the moonlight. Tirelessly he swam through the freezing waters, until he finally reached the island, where he dragged Miss Jennings safely to shore. He lay her head upon a soft volume of poems by Langston Hughes. She opened her eyes and stretched out her arms in gratitude. Now? she whispered.

Boom!

The next afternoon at school La Verne, who was tall and oval-faced with big pretty eyes spaced far apart, said:

"Mister Walker's the cutest!"

"That ain' no lie!" said Ruth Regal.

"Ol' Ruth is black," Carrol whispered to Tracy who sat beside him, "but she's tacked. I'll take 'er — an' won' give 'er back! Ha! ha! ha!"

"I'll take 'er, too!" Tracy said, a wheezing laughter shaking his skinny frame.

"With that fine curly hair," La Verne continued. "An' he knows how tog, too!"

Mr. Walker, the English teacher, walked down the hall in a soft white linen summer suit like he knew what time it was.

"You'll never be a movie star," he sadly heard Viola say, "but you got a good heart and a good head — develop those. Anyway — beauty is as beauty does."

When the last bell rang Mr. Walker stood before the main entrance of the building, immaculate in the three o'clock sun. His dark glasses gave an air of mystery to his dark handsome face, while his heavy but neatly trimmed mustache proved that he was a man. It was red. On top of that, he was tall, and his legs were long and straight, creases sharp. His lips parted suddenly and his face broke into a healthy smile. Miss Jennings rushed out of the building dressed for tennis. He opened the door of his dark blue convertible, she got in, and he entered from the other side. He said something to her:

Now!

She said something to him:

Now?

And they were off!

His heart sank with grief as he watched the car's fluid motion down the street to the corner — and away! — though the hateful street, under the hateful sun. The two-faced sky was fair for *them,* the flowers bloomed for *them.* The sudden breeze that chilled him wafted *their* faces, *kissed their lips!*

Amerigo stared at her neck.

She said something to him. He said something to her.

Amerigo stared at her neck.

As she threw her head back to laugh, eyes flashing, teeth sparkling, breast heaving — somewhere along the fair hot way — she touched her neck. He *knew* it, because suddenly the air rushed quietly from his lungs and the beat of his heart faded from his ears. He heard the old folks singing at church in a deep mysterious way a wordless song that had no melody, but yet a melody, though you couldn't just learn it, you simply opened your mouth that wasn't *your* mouth anymore, and sang the song that you couldn't even hear, *because you had become the ear,* that wasn't an ear anymore, but the song. He simply became the song. . . .

That evening after supper he stood motionless before the kitchen sink staring vacantly into the dishpan.

"What's the matter with you, boy?" Viola asked.

From the corner of his eye he perceived another figure approaching from the depths of the middle room. Closer, closer still, until it stopped beside the first figure that stood in the door. They were staring at him.

"Your son's blowin' his top!" said the taller figure. A heavy bearded voice.

Tears trickled down his face.

"You sick?" Viola asked.

He shook his head.

"Somebody do somethin' to you?"

Silence.

"Well — what's the *matter*, then?"

"Nothin'."

"Come on, Babe," said Rutherford, "leave 'im alone."

The two figures receded into the darkness.

His lips trembled, his tears fell into the dishpan.

They don't care! They don't know. Don' nobody know. He stared at the rainbow bubble. He picked up the glass. The bubble burst.

Somewhere in the darkness beyond the kitchen window another passionate leaf fell to the foot of a tree: *Boom!* It jarred his consciousness. Another! And another! An instant later, a month later, until the earth lay covered with the raucous sound from which he tried to separate his awareness of himself, as he climbed the steps of the R. T. Bowles Junior High School and entered the busy hall:

"You heard the latest?" asked a voice.

"Naw — what, honey?" asked the second voice: girls.

"They say that Principal Thompkins is beatin' old Mister Dillard's and Mister Walker's time with Miss Jennings, and that he's just waitin' till he gets his divorce so he kin marry 'er!"

"Ain' that a *killer!*"

Someone else?

He shuddered within the cool recesses of an early Monday morning when he was on his way to school.

The bell rang. He stepped blindly into the room.

"Sssssssh!" whispered Carrol T., pointing to a little tortoise that he had placed upon Miss Jennings's desk. The class settled down in secretive silence and waited for her to enter the room.

She entered.

Giggles.

"Ssssssssh!" Carrol hissed.

Her eyes swept curiously over the class. She subtly straightened her dress and touched her hair. She stood before the desk. She looked down, and then up, and then a smile lit up her face. Her eyes shone. Her teeth sparkled. The class burst into a gale of laughter. The tortoise drew its head into its shell. She tried to coax it out but it wouldn't come.

"Come on!" she whispered seductively. Crooking her right forefinger and pursing her lips, she beckoned to him. A sensuous smile inflamed her eyes and worked itself around the contours of her mouth. When she winked at the tortoise her lips quivered.

It's *true!* he thought.

Suddenly the room was filled with the blinding whiteness of the huge white bed. Miss Jennings lay upon it with her leg drawn toward her chest. She smiled up at Mr. Thompkins who stood above her. Trembling:

Now? she whispered, temptingly beckoning to him with her crooked forefinger and winking at him: Now?

"I sure wish *I* was that turtle!" said Carrol T. out loud, "I bet you *I'd* come out!"

He sat choking in the sun-filled room amid the sound of laughter that, shimmering upon the rims of her eyes, was about to fall, when suddenly, head thrown back, teeth bared, her eyes met his, and the laughter froze upon her face, congealed in her throat, as her fingers groped nervously behind her ears and along the quivering flesh of her neck in search of her lost composure.

It's true! her glance admitted, in a helpless, barely perceptible shade of apologetic brilliance.

Boom!

Someone else!

"He's a fine man!" he heard Viola say. "At least that's what ever'body says. They say his wife sure gave him a hard time. An' I hear he's got a little girl, too."

She should have a principal, he thought. Not just a teacher. And he'll be good to her too. She'll be a big shot in society — a prominent social figure and all. He's a terribleh luckeh chap! Man.

He entered the office the following afternoon just after the last bell had rung. "May I speak to Mister Thompkins, please?"

"A student to see you, sir," said the secretary, a brown-skinned young lady with rimless glasses.

He stepped into the office. It was like Principal Powell's, only bigger. He looks like Principal Powell, too! Edu-cated!

"What can I do for you?" Mr. Thompkins was asking with a friendly smile. Amerigo studied his handsome dark brown suit.

With a vest, Jack!

He admired the little golden key that dangled from the third button, and the YMCA membership pen in the buttonhole of his coat. There was a pencil in his manicured hand, which he tapped gently against the ink blotter on his desk, where papers were neatly arranged. Moving toward the desk, he observed that Mr. Thompkins' skin was about the same shade of brown as that of Miss Jennings and that his hair, though not as good as Mr. Walker's, was neatly cut. He was a tall man, and there was a humorous twinkle in his eye, though his general expression was one of thoughtful sadness.

His wife gave him a hard time.

"What can I do for you?" he was saying. "Won't you sit down?"

Amerigo sat down.

"Eh — I-I've been thinking about what I want to be when I, about what profession I would like to take up, when I get to be a — when I finish high school. I just wondered if you had a minute . . . minute . . . to spare . . . ta . . . to . . . kind a tell me what you think about it."

Mr. Thompkins leveled his gaze upon him.

"If you catch a joker starin' at you," he heard Rutherford say, "stare back at him, an' hold it!"

He stared back at him — and held it. Mr. Thompkins reared back in his swivel chair, took a deep breath, and looked at the ceiling, as though he were searching his past, a thoughtful, sad past, for the right word, for the right beginning, as though he were reaccessing the way through his own Forty-Three Year Siege.

"Well, son, I don't really know if there *is* a right way to know — so — so early. I've wanted to be so many things since I've been old enough to think about it."

He's the one for her, he thought, scrutinizing his man carefully, hardly conscious of the warm serious words that now fell in the background of his mind. *He* should have her. He can give her more than I can, but if she ever needs me I'll love her forever. I'll love him, too. When I get to be a man. When I finish college I'm going to be a poet like Langston Hughes, and she'll read my poems and . . . and be sorry, and I'll forgive her. She'll see. They'll *all* see.

"Well," Mr. Thompkins was saying, "that's about all I know to say, son."

He thanked him and left the office.

"After you've gone . . . and left me cryin'!" he sang to the burnished leaves that fell around his feet: "After you've gone — there's no denyin'. You'll feel blue!"

She'll see!

"You'll feel sad. You'll miss the sweetest-lovin' daddy that you ever had!"
Too tall.

The wind swept the dead leaves over the earth. The last flowers flushed hotly with the feverish pangs of death, bowing their heads under the weight of the early-morning frost:

There'll come a time — now don't forget it. . . .
But I'll forgive her.
There'll come a time . . . when you'll regret it.
I'll show her!
S-o-m-e d-a-y — when you grow lonely —
The wind moaned through the empty branches of the trees. . . .
Your heart will break like mine — an' you'll w-a-n-t me oooooon-ly —
Too tall.
After you've g-o-n-e — after you've gone aaaaaaaa — way!

The wind blew the helpless seasons into the endless space that was Next Year. Snow fell. Rain fell. Rain. Hail. Snow fell. Sparrows picked at the frozen earth. Santa Claus came:

"Merry Christmas!"
"Merry Christmas and a Happy —"
Boom! Boom! Boom! Boom! Boom!
Is it Next Year?
"Naw, it's this year!"
"I don' care."

"W-e-l-l, it won' be long now, babe!" Viola exclaimed, "just a little while longer an' you got it made!"

He looked up at her from the depths of his despair. Her bright warm smile bore down upon him with the cruelty of the hot summer sun. *She* had been away then, Miss Jennings had been away, in Denver, for three whole months! His letters had stretched out under the bridge and under the bridge and under the bridge to:

Dear Miss Jennings . . . Dear Miss Jennings . . . Dear Miss Jennings . . . Dear Miss Jen . . .

"What?" Viola had exclaimed, "you writin' that woman *agin!* She ain' had time to answer the *last* one *yet!* Did you tell 'er about all the books you been readin'?"

"Yes'm."

"What did you git from the library this time?"

"I got the poems of Omar Khayyám an' . . . and —"

"Who's he?"

"He's an old poet. And *The Big Sea* by Langston Hughes. He's colored! A Ne-gro! and the *Republic* of Plato and —"

"Who's that?"

"There's a picture, a mural of him on the wall at the art gallery."

"That's deep stuff, there, boy! You gonna read your letter to me when it's finished?"

"Yes'm."

Viola's laughing voice scratched the grooves along the surface of his mind like a phonograph needle scratching the empty grooves of a record. Nobody understands! His black skin tightened around his awareness of himself until his eyes bulged grotesquely and his ears protruded into the hostile air about him like antennae registering the intensity of the cruel laughter directed at him.

If I'd have been tall! he thought bitterly, and old, light, half white with curly hair! If — if I had lived out south in a house with bushes and a lawn and trees, and Santa Claus wasn't Santa Claus only because he *had* to be. If spring would only wait *till I get ready!* How long?

I'll love her always, he thought with a heavy feeling of futility that was agitated by a feverish anticipation of raw green grasses springing up through the snow, of buds swelling on the branches of the trees, along the perilous way from Aunt Rose's up to Twenty-Third Street. He passed the white house on the corner, *her* house with the fresh white curtains and the polished windows, with the bright green lawn shaded by the pretty trees — under fair skies and foul — just before he dashed around the corner and down the hill and up to Troost to catch the streetcar, south, to the art gallery, where they *have* to take you in, even if you're *ugly* and *black* . . . and weren't baptized until the new reverend had stood up in church and said:

"Well, sir! — Ain' this a glorious day!"

"A-MEN!"

"Eh, now! eh . . . Ah . . . eh . . ."

"Help 'im, Je-sus!"

"Aaaaaaw-nooow! Praise the Lord! I feel at h-o-m-e! In God's house! You know. when you been saved — after a long hard struggle with the devil — with yourself!"

"Tee! hee! hee!"

"You jumpy as a child at Christmastime! You look up into the starry sky an' you see *God!*"

"YEAH!"

"Aaaaan' you look at the *trees* an' you see *God*! You look into your neighbor's face an' you see *God's holy work!*"

"YEAH!"

"Eeeeeevrywhere — eeeeeeevery whicha way you look — you see Gloray! Gloray! Gloray! — An'-an' —"

"Talk to 'im, Jesus!"

"An' it makes you wanna go out into the street an' stop ever'body you meet and ask: Do you see what I see? In the brilliant face of this glorious day, do you see the shining presence of our Lord and Savior, Jesus Christ?

"You wanna — *speak out!* Somethin' within you won' *let you be still!* You have to tell the *world* that you found Jeeee-suuus! Now I wanna ask *you* somethin': Have *you* found 'Im? *You!* — who have come to worship in God's new shinin' temple. Have you found Him? If you have — stand up! Stand up an' be counted!"

The great mass of black, brown, beige faces rose around him like a great swelling wave, undulating in the alluvial heat of a great tension that agitated two thousand hearts into beating as one:

Boom! Boom! Boom!

The tension swelled into a deep dark fomenting mass of sound that rose like a dense mist above churning waters, and the song without words swept upon the shores of his consciousness, like a river, like a sea — all seas. One Sea! — and slowly receded into the stillness from which it came.

"Look around you!" the reverend commanded, "an' see if you see a soul flounderin' in a storm of doubt! Trapped in the whirlpools of sin! An unborn thing strugglin' for eternal life: point-him-out!"

Myriad black pink-nailed fingers pointed at him:

Boom!

"Who made you?" cried the reverend: "*God!* Who blew the breath of life into your body that you might become a livin' soul? *God! Who!* aaaaaw *who* sent His only begotten Son upon the earth that *you* might know the bliss of life everlastin'? *God!* Don't you love 'Im? Huh! Now I'm gonna utter the most beautiful words that the ears of man is ever likely to hear. For you! David — David wrote 'um, but I like to think of 'um as my own — your — ever'man's — love song to God:

"Our Father, who art in heaven, Hallowed be Thy name. . . ."

Two thousand voices spoke as one voice. The deep alluvial waters rose and flooded his heart and swam in the orbits of his eyes. He stood up and groped his black sinful way down the aisle like one gone blind and came to a halt when he could walk no more.

"A-MEN!" rang throughout the great assembly.

The reverend took him by the hand. And suddenly a great pain smote him in the heart, for while the reverend was extending the invitation to join St. John's in Christian fellowship, his mind was filled with thoughts of *her!* His breast heaved with exhilaration in the thought: *She'll be proud of me! Now I'm like everybody else. She'll see.*

A week later when the reverend declared: I now baptize you in the name of the Father, the Son, and the Holy Ghost, and the chilly waters swirled over his head and he emerged clean in the redeeming light of Sunday morning amid the jubilant chorus of hallelujahs and a-mens, he saw only her face reflected in the face of Viola who sat trembling in the pulpit, her eyes stained red with tears.

When he was dry and saved he wondered: Will *she* love me now?

Too tall, said the *Voice* after Rutherford had unfolded its pages the following Friday evening and read:

Mr. and Mrs. Theodore Jennings of Denver, Colorado, wish to announce the engagement of their daughter, Ann, to. . . .

"Boy!"

He opened his eyes, though he had not been asleep, and looked at his father.

Now, the time that ain' long is now!

He watched Rutherford step out the door. Then Viola, minutes later.

"Bye, hon. You git up now, you don' wanna be late on your first day." She slipped a dollar into his hand. "Don' tell your daddy," she whispered with a confidential smile, and slipped out the door.

Heel over toe, toe over heel, along the new way, the new way that his straining toes had rehearsed time out of mind.

He came to a pause at the corner of Eighteenth and Woodland and looked up at the two-story house with the photographer's shop on the ground floor, with the sign in white enamel letters that you couldn't rub off, that read: J. B. THORNTON, PHOTOGRAPHER. There's where *she* lives. He heard Miss Allie Mae describe the funeral parlor . . . *with all them ferns an' things in the windows* . . . He looked for signs of *her*. Funny name. Cosima. He crossed the street.

There was an old building on the opposite corner. The sign on the plate-glass window said, THE VOICE, and he unconsciously turned its pages down through the years, and heard Mr. Jordan say: "I'll bet you want to be a schoolteacher when you grow up?"

"No sir."

"What then?"

Now, all of a sudden, he felt himself caught up in a stream of faces mostly new, moving up the hill. He gazed shyly, excitedly around him, questioning the shimmer of a flashing eye, a dazzling smile, the quick movement of a nervous hip that knew it was being looked at: creamy beiges and dusky browns, a choice of copper-reds, balancing dangerously upon the high heels of new shoes, startling the crowds of fresh curls adorning their heads. Wondering if *she* were one of them, he walked straighter, with his head high and his shoulders back.

He came to Nineteenth Street where the Methodist church stood on the northeast corner and the Attucks School opposite it. Crispus . . . the first man to . . . gunshot wound . . . single. . . . It looks like Garrison, William Lloyd.

Freedom!

Meanwhile the crowd grew thicker, the voices louder.

He stopped at the bridge a little past Nineteenth Street and looked down at the shining rails that led to Denver, Colorado, west, and New York, east — and over the sea and over the sea to France and England.

Presently he came to a stone wall about four feet high, at the edge of a gentle green lawn that swelled into a large hill to the southeast, leading his eye to the great redbrick building that sprawled out upon its summit: stately, immutable, immaculate, efficient, *i*'s dotted and *t*'s crossed, replete with the resolution to every *if*.

He stopped and stared at the long rows of polished windows three stories high, seeing within every room a desk, a blackboard, and rows of seats flushing with noisy pupils toeing the parallel crevices between the floorboards running side by side at the sound of a bell:

Rrrrrrrrring!

And he followed the crowd into the large auditorium, very much like the one at the art gallery — only bigger, much bigger, but the floor's just the same. Several men sat on the stage, modest, intelligent-looking men with unslicked-down hair, serious attitudes, and golden keys dangling from the buttonholes of their vests. Like the men on the pulpit at St. John's, only different, not as expensively creased nor as shiny. Edmond Clapps! Give 'um the . . .

The middle man stood up and moved to the front of the stage.

"Mr. Bowles?"

"Sssssssh!"

He gave a sign like the reverend for the student body to rise.

Like Mr. Powell.

"Let us sing the Negro National Anthem!" he said, and his face suddenly sprouted a grizzly beard and his eyes grew fierce. He raised his master's whip into the air and brought it down with a crash against his knee: *Boom!*

"Lift every voice and sing! . . . till earth and heaven ring"
Rrrrrrrring!
"loud as the rooooooooolling sea!"
The aftertones of the song burning in the air, the assembly sat down. The little man in the middle with the thick mustache and yellow skin, the gray suit that was half a size too large and a little wrinkled smiled like a shy boy and prepared to speak.

Mr. Cook . . . H. O. . . . In-*tel*-la-gent!

"We, the members of the administration and faculty of North High, welcome you! To those of you who are new among us, we hope that an important phase of your life will begin here. There will be many things to learn —"

The history of the whole human family.

"— and many feelings to explore. And for those of you who pass successfully through these doors, the knowledge afforded by an even greater institution of learning lies before you, that of the university!"

Harvard and Yale and — God damned! Aaaaaaaw! Tee! hee!

"Opportunities for Negroes in America are slowly but steadily increasing. With *hard work, patience,* and *perserverence* — we are entering the mainstream of American life."

"Places that you and I will never see! . . ." cried the reverend.

Dead!

"The continuation of that advance is up to you! The future belongs to those who are *prepared.* Don't let your color hold you back, don't let it cramp your imagination, cripple your initiative!"

Open your mouth an' tell us what you see!

Dead!

"We do not know what the next few years will bring. There is hunger and poverty and political unrest in the world —"

. . . but fatback an' beans is good!

"The possibility of war is not unseemly —"

. . . 'cause Jerry don' know that fat meat's greasy!

"though we still have time to hope and pray —"

Pray.

"— that reason and love can influence the hearts of men."

What can *I* do?

"And that is all the more reason why we must make these moments here at North High count —"

. . . of *Monte Cristo* by Alexander Dumas — Basie!

"We must live them to the full. We must learn all we can. There is no substitute for a good education —"

Tools.

"There is no substitute for *love, compassion,* and *human* understanding."

How many stars are in the . . .

More!

"But life is not all work. It means playing, too. Here at North High we hope that you will avail yourselves of every opportunity to partake of as many extracurricular activities as common sense will allow in order that you may round out your personalities and . . ."

Clapclapclapclapclapclapclapclapclapclapclap!

Rrrrrrrrring!

The assembly broke up into patterns of light and movement through which he ran, frantic with the fear that he could not fully embrace the total volume of the moment whose approach he could hear resounding from the chamber of the little red drum, as he raised his bottom just high enough to let it fall upon its resonant surface with a boom! that made the water rush into his eyes and laughter to bubble up from the depths of his throat and trickle down the folds of his several chins. . . .

"Amerigo Jones?" A little old lady with off-white purple skin, good gray hair coiled into a little tower held in place with combs, looked at him expectantly as he entered the office. He stood before the desk in front of the sun-filled window.

Like the Queen! in her old-fashioned navy-blue dress with lace trimming around the neck and sleeves, and the long golden chain hanging from her neck and a brooch at her throat. Younger . . . but not as old as Aunt Rose or . . . Aunt Tish!

"I hear Aunt Tish's dead!" said Viola's voice.

"Naw!" said Miss Allie Mae. "Poor Gloomy Gus! I wonder what he'll do now — without her to take care of?"

"Die, too, I guess. They been tagether so long they'd even started lookin' alike. Now they say he's lyin' up in the hospital with somethin' they don' know what it is — an' ain' even tryin' to live!"

"Sssssh."

"Amerigo Jones?" the lady was asking. She drew her leg toward her chest and smiled at him.

"Yes'm . . .Yes."

"Won't you sit down?"

He sat down.

"I'm Miss Birdie, the student counselor. It's my job to decide what courses you should take. Do you intend to go to college?"

"Eh — yes'm. I'd-I would like to go. Yes."

"Do you think your parents will be able to send you?"

"Eh."

"What is your father's profession?" She took up her pen and prepared to write upon the white card in front of her.

"He's —"

The Father of the Country. But not because . . .

"A maintainance man — at a hotel."

"Does your mother work?"

"Yes'm. She works — is employed — at — at a hotel — an apartment hotel, as a head maid."

"I see. . . ." She tapped the point of her pen gently against the edge of the large green ink blotter that partially covered her desk. "Amerigo, don't you think it would perhaps be wiser to learn a trade? And prepare yourself for some practical profession, in case you might not be able to go to college?"

Cast down thy Booker T. began, but before he could get it out the angry voice of Frederick Douglass had overpowered his senses with the word *Freedom!* and he blurted out:

"No'm! I'm gonna go to-to *college!*"

"In that case, are you interested in the sciences or the humanities?"

"Eh."

"I mean, would you like to become a doctor, or a chemist, a mathematician, or would you like to teach, or perhaps be a lawyer or a social worker or something like that?"

He dropped his eyes and studied the floor for a moment, trying to take in the myriad possibilities that flashed and popped in his mind like the movie reel on the silver screen just before it got dark and the pictures filled his eyes: Ten! Eleven! Twelve! Thirteen! *Boom!*

"or something like that?" her voice was saying.

"I don't know yet. . . ."

"You have time, son."

She's saying something else.

"I suggest the general college preparatory course for now — and then we'll see how you do."

Rrrrrrrring!

The red room divided itself into long rows of rooms. Within each room a woman, lying upon a white bed at the foot of which he stood, trembling:

Rrrrrrrring!

They drew their legs toward their chests and articulated the question —
which resounded upon the air like the myriad-timbred voice of a Great
Host:

What do you want to be when you get to be a man?

The word *MAN* boomed in his ears with a deafening sound. It overwhelmed his senses and set his body to trembling so violently that he could
hardly contain himself. And he ran, desperately, frantically, from room to
room, confronting the upturned faces whose smiling lips intoned the pregnant question:

English?

— A soft dark-eyed woman with a deep autumnal smile who spoke of
the beauty of the literary idiom ". . . over the sea and over the sea and over
the sea to France and England."

Dramatics?

Ruth Regal and Lillie Bryant and he among unknown heads bent toward
the black soft-spoken iron-gray-headed little man with the face of a lovable
bulldog: Mr. Larson, founder of the Larson Players who gave plays at
Lincoln Hall where Principal Powell played in *The Emperor Jones* by
Eugene O'Neill. Like Ira Eldridge! Like I'm gonna-going to be . . . do-when
. . . if I wanna-wish to. After the first two years, we'll see.

Algebra?

Pretty little Miss Dark-brown Thin-lipped Big-eyed Forty-year-old
Algebra, taxing the star-crossed imagination with the enigma of the
infernal X.

That means Hell, son.

General Science?

Tall, thin-lipped, off-white, smiling and laughing and joking, pumping
the little hand generator that made the lightbulb light up like the lightbulbs
in the alley. . . . His son's a freshman, too. Smart. Off-white. Plays tennis.
Him and-*He* and Cosima!-in-the-paper.

Reserve Officer's Training Corps?

"T-a-l-l and s-t-r-a-i-g-h-t!" A nut-brown, strong-lipped, plain-nosed,
sharp-eyed, straight-talking, curly-headed man. The general! Sergeant
Shores of the regular army: "Tramp! tramp! tramp!" I pledge allegiance to
the flag of the United States of America, and to the Republic for which it
stands, one Nation, Indivisible, with Liberty and Justice — *for all!"*

Physiology?

Miss! — Tall, dark, healthy and robust, but fine, dignified, well poised
upon the square heels of low-quartered shoes, enveloped by an aura of perceptible sadness that intensified her forty-three-year-old explanations of the
circulation of the blood and the functions and interactions of the eye, the

ear and the heart: Preachers! She's been waitin' on that cat to marry'er for *forty* years — an' ain' nothin' happened yet!

Rrrrrrring!

Rrrrrrring!

"Let's hit 'um!" Rutherford cried the following morning, and he ran and ran, until he came to a room at the end of a hall where he stopped and listened in front of the glass door. From within a sudden burst of beautiful seashell-sound, a chord that grew into a phrase that swelled like a great wave and remained suspended in the air, and then:

"NO! No-no-no-no — *no! Idiots!* You *dumb!* s-t-u-p — i-d sons of — All right! All right! Now! Let's begin — againe! Wait!"

Suddenly the door swung open.

"Whatttt do *you* want?"

He stood gaping at a little man not much taller than he, who looked more like a boy than a man, with a clean hairless face and closely cut hair and a slightly humpbacked nose. His lips were fleshy and there was a nervous twitch in his right eye. A trace of mischievousness in his smile gave the lie to the aggressive attitude suggested by his tenacious grip on the door handle.

He looks sort a like a chipmunk . . . or a rabbit!

"Whatttt do *you* want?" he was saying.

"I-I-I want to join the choir. They tol'-*d* teold me at the office to come, but I-I couldn't find it."

"Caun't you *read!* What's your name?"

"Jones."

"*What* Jones!"

"Amerigo Jones!"

He began to laugh in an exaggerated manner, his large boyish teeth flashing, his nervous but sturdy little frame trembling beneath his egg-white shirt, which was too large.

He's Mr. Rogan, he thought admiringly. He got a scholarship to the university. The youngest teacher on the faculty.

"A — *merigo* Jones!" Mr. Rogan cried, tugging comically at his oversized pants. The belt had been drawn to the last notch, but they still gathered around his flea-sized waist like a sack, sagging in front, while the cuffs stacked in several folds over the insteps of his oversized shoes.

"Ladies and gentlemen!" he exclaimed to the members of the class. "This fine-looking young man — *who has interrupted our rehersal by snooping* outside the door! — is *Mister A-merigo* Jones! And I *know* he sings! Because with a name like *thattt* — *and* being late, *too,* he'd *better* sing! SING!"

Boom!

— In a flash Mr. Rogan had sprung to the piano, a loud chord resounded from the keyboard.

". . . Sing! . . ."

The pupils only smiled at first, but now their smiles deepened, laughter bubbled from every throat. Amerigo's mouth was standing wide open, but no sound escaped. His ears filled to overflowing with the peals of laughter that animated all the faces with the bared teeth and sparkling eyes, faces that were mostly new.

"That's a c-chord, *Mis*ter Jones!" Mr. Rogan screeched. "Sing: ah"

"Ah . . ."

"Ah — ah — ah — ah — ah — ah — ah — ah — aaaaaaaaah!"

"Ah — ah — ah — ah — ah — ah — ah — ah — aaaaaaaaah!"

"Sit — ohav theah," said Mr. Rogan, looking down his nose at him, "with the tenors."

He took his seat with the tenors.

With the second tenors, he reflected with a pang of regret, consoling himself, however, with the thought that Paul Robeson sang baritone. But tenor's the highest.

He looked around at the new faces except for Carrol T., who was sitting back with the baritones and Ruth Brashears and Lillie Bryant who sat with the altos and little Clista Jones with the sopranos, the tenors and basses were brand new. . . .

He watched Mr. Rogan, his rimless glasses mirroring fragments of the windows and the globular light overhead, now banging away at the piano, now waving his arms frantically, as they, the choir, he too, strained to produce the high notes and the quick that rippled from the tips of his fingers and flickered from the pupils of his eyes and quivered upon his lips, which made him smile or frown, or fold a phrase gently within the palms of his fine hands and cuddle it, as though it were a bird, and suddenly release it, send it flying, soaring through the air, beyond the southern windows!

"Ohhhhh — my good Lo-ord!" shouted the first tenors, and his mouth flew open with wondrous admiration.

That's Roscoe Howard! he thought, remembering the enthusiastic sighs of the girls the first time he had heard the choir sing.

A tall, smooth black young man from Texas, like the reverend, with wavy hair and feathery eyelashes, like Dad's, his lips quivering beneath his thin mustache and regular nose, trembling with the vibrations of the sad sound suspended above the sustaining hum of the choir, which now replied:

"Show me the waaaaaay! to entah the charriot — an travel along!"

"Gonna serve my Lord while I have breath!" the sopranos declared.

Earline! A name he had come to know with a nervous sensation of pleasure and regret, adoring the shy quivering dimpled voice that made her bosom heave and her eyes shine and her fingers fidget with the note she was trying to pass to Roscoe.

"Wait!" Mr. Rogan shouted. "Miss Whisonant! Is this a choir rehersal or a *crap game?*"

"I don't know, Mr. Rogan," she answered in a mincing voice.

"It is *nottt* a crap game, Miss Whisonant! NOR is it an English composition class — Now *pass* that damned note to Roscoe — or put it in your pocket, but in GOD'S NAME STOP TWISTING IT!"

Earline blushed amid the gale of laughter that immediately swept through the room.

She loves Roscoe, Amerigo thought, sorry, infinitely sorry, that he could not sing first tenor.

"Now take it from where we left off!" Mr. Rogan was saying.

"Ohhhh — my good Lo-rd!"

"Show me the waaaaaay!" This time the basses answered.

Cecil Jefferson. His regular black face with the playful mischievous eyes made him think of Turner's eyes when he said: "Give 'um the claps, men!"

"Show me the waaaaaay!" the basses were singing, and as they held the note, Cecil's bottom jaw extended, dropped, like the jaw of a great steam shovel, as though the low note were rolling out of his mouth, up from the bottom of the great river.

He loves Edna. Alto. The word *love* detached itself from the words around it, separating into sonorous notes that tripped up and down the scales of the song — now inflaming the tenors, now the sopranos, now descending to the deep shades where the solemn basses pined for the altos.

"Gonna serve my Lord while I have brea-eth!" the baritones declared, and he observed that Sidney was a baritone and that they sit behind the altos. He's gonna get a scholarship and be a great singer! He loves Willa, second soprano.

"So I can see my Je-sus aaaaa-fter de — ath!" Virgil. He had long eyelashes like his sister, Ruth. First tenor real-verreh high! But not like Roscoe. Loves Margret Raves who isn't in the choir. Off-white, pretty bosom, and a gap between her front teeth like the Wife of Bath. But she doesn't love him.

The notes arranged themselves into a minor chord, as his affections vascillated between Edna who was Jeff's and Earline who was Roscoe's and Willa who was Sidney's and Margret who wasn't Virgil's. They were all older than he and would graduate next year and go to college. A familiar feeling of dread gathered around the thought of next year when they would go away, when the singers of the song would go away, when the notes would receive their diplomas and go off to college.

I hope it never changes! said a voice from the shadowy reaches of the past, as he sang his way through the days and weeks, searching for the four little notes through the medium of which his energetic second tenor might send the sad sound soaring through the air to engulf the burning question.

"Boy!" Viola declared, noticing the urgency with which he stuffed a biscuit into his mouth. "You gonna *kill* yourself if you keep on goin' like you goin'!"

"Gotta go to the choir rehearsal!"

"Rutherford, talk to your son!"

"Stop crammin' that food in your mouth like your momma tell you!"

"He's runnin' from mornin' till night!" Viola declared. "Don' *never* stay home no more. Singin' in that choir, an' runnin' out to Roscoe's an' Earline's an' 'em's all the time! I don' see how he has time to *study!* Comes home every evenin' *loaded down* with books an' don' *neeeeever* open 'um!"

"That little joker sure likes to carry them books!" Rutherford said: "Hey! hey! A intel*lec*tual! Well, sonny, before you git out a here *tanight,* I want to see your homework!"

"Aw Dad! I did it! Eny-anyway, all I had to do was mostly readin' — a reading assignment."

"Zaaaaaaaawlways got a excuse! Well, we'll see what you been doin' when your grade card comes. Singing' *all* the time! Better be tryin' to git somethin' in your head. It's a cinch you can't sing you way through college, that is, if you git in at all!"

Boom!

IF?

"Anyway," Rutherford was saying, "what you doin' out to Edna's house *all* the time! *I* thought *she* was supposed to be *Jeff's* girl!"

"She *is!* We're just friends, that's all."

"Unh! You *is* a fool! Wastin' all your time talkin' to somebody *else's* girl an' ain' gittin' nothin' out a it. Better git yourself a girl a your own. What do you talk about — till twelve o'clock at night?"

"Life!"

"Unh!" he grinned, "what do *you* know about *life,* little niggah, ain' never missed a meal since you was born! Git me that paper, boy!"

He fetched the paper for his father and resumed his meal in a frustrated silence, hovering on the periphery of his chosen circle of friends who were all held together by the song. An irrepressible sigh stuck in his throat and prevented his biscuit from sliding down.

Better got you a girl of your own! said Rutherford's voice, and he made a mental review of the faces his own age, the faces from R. T. Bowles. He ran toward this one and that one, but no sooner than he arrived than they divided themselves into pairs that whispered and giggled intimately, noses touching, lips touching, arms locked in hip-grinding embraces within the aura of tiny red lights — rose and blue — burning weakly in smoke-filled rooms, to the pulsating rhythm of the slow sad song, inflaming his sensibility with a desire and shame that dissolved in the hot rushing waters of disgust.

Better git you a girl of your own!

All of a sudden it sounded like Tommy's voice.

I don' care answered another voice, and he heard the needle pop and crack in the whirring groove of the phonograph, and a tall melodious articulate voice declare:

"If I — ee diddidn't care-eh . . . more than words ca-an say — ee. . . ."

I don't care! Anyway, the kind of girl I want . . . I want a girl who . . . who . . .

The overwhelming import of this speculation forced the soggy biscuit down his throat, and he looked up in time to hear his father exclaim: "Unh!" behind the pages of the *Star*.

"What?" Viola asked.

"Looks like things gittin' tough! Every day now, you don' see nothin' but headlines 'bout military conferences an' stuff. Germany's makin' pacts an' treaties. Looks like Europe's choosin' sides before the big bang!"

"Well," said Viola, "I sure hope *we* don' git mixed up in that mess!"

"We all goin' when the wagon comes," said Rutherford gravely. "I'll tell you one thing: If England goes, we goin', too! Ain' never been a war in history when we didn' help England!"

"The Revolutionary War!" Amerigo said with a facetious twinkle in his eyes.

"Aw, li'l niggah — you know what I mean!"

"Ne-gro!"

"Listen, li'l niggah, you don' go correctin' your poppa, you heah?"

"He's *right!*" Viola exclaimed with an amused grin. "That's what he's git-getting an education for! Aw say, I almost forgot to ask you, how's ol' T. C. doin'?"

"That's a cryin' shame!" said Rutherford, shaking his head. "That joker throwin' away that good job at the station. He didn' say nothin' 'bout that. An' then he went to workin' on the *road* gang, layin' track! He thinks he's

so strong! 'Em ties like to *killed* 'im! An' now he's half sick — an' won' go
to the doctor. Teet' all fallin' out."

"He's got such beautiful teeth!" Viola said sadly.

"Yeah . . . I spoke to ol' man Mac for 'im an' he kin start to work with
me Mond'y. We're shorthanded as it is. It's hard to keep somebody with
that measly sal'ry the ol' man's payin'."

"Did you ask 'im 'bout that raise?"

"I ain' had a chance yet, the ol' man bought a new hotel an' it's keepin'
'im busy. An' you know ol' lady Studhoss ain' gittin' up off a *nothin'* unless
the ol' man says so."

Amerigo rose from the table.

"Eh . . . I'm goin' now, Mom."

"Put on your coat, it's cold outside."

"Aw Mom!"

"Put on your coat!" Rutherford said.

"Yessir."

He put on his coat and dashed out into the street. . . .

Oh Skylark! have you anything to say to me? he sang, his ears filled with
the dulcet intonations of Billy Eckstein: Won't you tell me where my love
can be? Is there a meadow in the mist, where someone's waiting to be
kissed? He scanned the meadows spreading out under the misty autumn
evening and the splinters of light that escaped from the shaded windows of
the houses he passed. Skylark! Have you seen a valley green with spring,
where my heart can go a-jour-ney-ing?

Through the whirl of eventful days crowded with painful movements,
which fell to the feet of Friday night:

Hey! hey! no more classes till Mond'y!

"Goin' to the pajama party?"

"Where?"

"At Baby Miller's down on Fourteenth Street."

"You goin'?"

"You *know* I'm goin'! All them fine mellah chicks?"

"Can anybody go?"

"Aw man, you too nice. A pajama party ain' nothin' for *squares!*"

That evening after supper:

"Mom?"

"What?"

"Can I go to a party over on Fourteenth Street at Baby Miller's house?"

"You invited?"

"*Anybody* can go!"

"I guess so, but be home by eleven o'clock!"

"Aw, Viola!" Rutherford exclaimed, "to be home at eleven o'clock he's gotta leave at *ten* — an' *you* know a party ain' even *warm* till it's almost over. You be in here by twelve o'clock, boy — but I mean twelve, you heah!"

"Yessir. Mom?"

"Now what?"

"You got any change? Just in case I have to buy somethin', or break my leg and have to get a taxi?"

"Boy, you gittin' expensive! You better get yourself a little job so you kin earn your own spendin' money. Here." She gave him fifty cents.

"That ain' no lie, Amerigo," Rutherford said. "You ain' no baby no more, you gittin' to be a *man.*"

His senses quickened to the word *man.*

"You *always* goin' to the show, an' to dances an' parties — football games an' stuff. It ain' gonna hurt you to earn a little money to treat your girlfriends —"

"I haven't got a girlfriend — and I'm not *going* to have one, till I find the right one. One that's intelligent, with good manners, and I'm realleh in love with her. And then I'm going to marry her — after I finish college and get to be somebody and have enough money for a home with nice furniture and everything. A real lady who plays the piano, maybe," and has red hair he thought, with snow shining in it, in a blue uniform with a white blouse and a real verreh white collar and pretty teeth and soft brown skin with a gold chain around her neck, copper in the evening sunlight, and tall and straight with polished fingernails like a queen! His heart throbbed with emotion as the images of all the women he had known fused into one over-poweringly beautiful apparition that shone with celestial splendor.

"You gonna have a hard time finding the kind a woman you want. . . ." Viola said thoughtfully.

"You better git out a here, if you goin'," Rutherford said.

Sharp as a tack in his Sunday suit, he shifted into first with a swagger, and then into second on the wing of a song and then — breezed on down to Fourteenth Street.

Someday she'll come along, the girl I love! And she'll be big and strong, the girl I love, And when she comes my way —

Rrrrrrring!

The door opened. He stepped into a warm corridor softly illuminated by a rose light that almost obscured the coats, hats, pants, shirts, blouses that hung on hooks around the walls. A tall slender large-eyed woman looked down at him. "Come on in, son, and take off your clothes," she said, and disappeared into the adjoining room. Before she closed the door he caught a glimpse of several girls whom he did not quite recognize swimming in the soft seductive light, two lounging on the rug with cushions under their elbows and one standing against a wall. They wore semitransparent pajamas through which he could see the purple patches on their bosoms. A pajamaed couple were dancing: close, slowly, hardly moving, arms locked, lost in the intimacy afforded by their closed eyelids.

The woman reappeared.

"Ain't you undressed yet?" handing him a pair of pajamas.

"No'm."

"Well, git at it or go home. This ain' no sideshow!"

She entered the kitchen through the door on the right, through which he caught a glimpse of Baby Miller with her arms around a boy whom he did not know. She was kissing him on the lips and rubbing him all over with her hands. Another boy whom he did not know but whom he had seen at school stood near the refrigerator sucking on a cigarette in a strange way. His eyes were glassy like the eyes of the men and women after they used to come out of Miss Sadie's apartment, and he smiled as though he were dreaming. The kitchen was full of smoke.

A feeling of desire, like nausea, rolled up from the pit of his stomach into his throat. His back pressed against the door he had entered, his hands blindly, instinctively grappled for the knob.

Saturday morning he made his bed quickly in order to hide the stain on the sheet, which was all that was left of the warm ooze into the depths of which he had slipped through what had been left of Friday night into the black room. He cleaned the apartment, polished it, shined his father's shoes and his own and pressed their trousers, and waited for five o'clock and supper.

"Did you have a good time at the party?" Rutherford asked once they were seated at table.

"Yessir."

He bit into the juicy hot dog sandwich and licked the mayonnaise from his lips. Viola poured the beer. He drank, freeing the gummy bread that clung to the roof of his mouth,

and waited for the evening filled with the smell of popcorn, frying hair, and more beer, and the gossipy voices of Viola and Miss Ada to float into the front room and lull him to sleep. . . . He turned toward the window and stared at the night light, which grew brighter, though his eyes were closed, and his thoughts wandered through the red corridors of North High, peeping into the forbidden rooms filled with the objects of all his desires. He tugged at the covers and wriggled this way and that to divert the distracting airs that delayed his descent into the deep dark blackness where the song lay, still, waiting for the redeeming light of Sunday morning.

He opened his eyes in time to catch Rutherford's flickering hand silencing the alarm clock, and he marveled at the familiarity of the scene: his father sitting on the side of the bed, yawning and stretching, young and strong and dependable, like the rhythm that was always beating — so that you don't even hear it most of the time — a continual sound that had become a part of his own conception of sound, a rhythmic sound that he had heard all his life. Now he saw life as one long day. One morning when Rutherford stopped the alarm clock and dressed and made his breakfast and called out to him to get up, when Viola dashed up and out minutes later, her voice kissing his ears with some word of affection or admonition. One evening around the supper table held together by one stream of conversation in which Rutherford was the Oracle of World Events, speaking of the machinations of men beyond the intimate walls of home, the alley, Tenth Street, the North End, the downtown of the great city, that vast throbbing pain that was the United States of America, over seas and deserts, steppes and fjords, from the summits of great mountains into the valleys of foreign cities and houses of justice — along the frontiers of angry nations feverishly preparing for war!

Boom!

Time reverberated within his consciousness and he tried to measure its length: Five feet, two! Fourteen and a half years old. Mom and Dad are twenty-nine. He's six feet! She's five feet, four, but she breathes the longest, then Dad, then me. He tried to calculate the length of time: Loooooooooong division!

"Boy!" cried Viola in her usual startled voice, as though somewhere deep down inside of her body was a bell that rang and shocked her from the world of sleep into the world of eternal morning.

"Boy —"

He looked at his mother with a smile.

Him no more than her. I mean He no more than her!

"— look what time it is!" she was saying. He noted that her articulation was perfect, and he wondered why people spoke good English at certain times and bad English at other times. Viola sat upright in the bed, her eyes pink, her fine skin veined with wrinkles from the pillow, adjusting the wanton shoulder strap. "You'd better *git* out a here an' go to Sund'y school!"

There! She's changed her speech again! He tried to listen to his mother's and father's words down through the years to see if it were always so.

"Aw Mom!" he heard himself saying, "that's kid stuff. Sunday school! It's enough to have to go to church, but Sunday school isn't church! Listenin'-g to all that shouting and carrying on!"

"All right, if you don' go to church, you don' go to no show! I *mean that*! Now you git-up-and-git-out-a-here!"

He sat among the familiar smells and sounds and colors of St. John's, listening to the usual offering of the men's chorus — they sang "Precious Memories" *again* — and the junior and senior choirs. More or less the same general announcements were made, followed by a song to warm up the congregation. Mass psychology! And then the reverend rose, cleaned his eternally dirty glasses with the biggest, whitest handkerchief in the world — beside Louis Armstrong's! — as he always did, and geared his mind to the exposure of the holocaust of sin that lurked in the hearts of men, in a world that, but for the Grace of Gawd, would be doomed to Eternal Damnation.

He'll start with the text first and then make his point.

And suddenly the church seemed to expand in all directions. The reverend grew tall, and the sound of his voice echoed throughout the long, sometimes sad, sometimes jubilant, day that was Sunday. But in the undulation of light and shade upon his consciousness a feeling of dread came over Amerigo. Baptized, saved, he sat full-statured amid the righteous, the reverend's words droned in his ears like the beating wings of an incorrigible fly, agitating his sense of awareness like the drop of sweat that rolled from the ends of his pomaded hair down his neck and moistened his — Rutherford's — shorts, which tightened around his crotch, enmeshing him in the irksome throes of doubt, as he tried but failed to reconcile the reverend's words to the disquieting *Boom!* that echoed from overseas and to the hiss and crack of the telephone wires that looped from pole to pole, inflaming the tip of Rutherford's cigarette down through the dark part of one long day.

"A-men!" shouted a sister, and he involuntarily frowned, enraged by the earthen gruffness of her voice.

"He's the Lil-laaaaay!" the reverend was shrieking in his old-time religion voice: "of the va-laaaaaay!"

"A-MEN!"

" — he's the bright and mor-ning star!" The congregation began to sing. And he listened disdainfully to the laboring voices, which sounded amaturish and pathetic against the polished phrases of the North High Choir, as the noble strains of: Jaaaaaaaa-su, pri-i-ce-less trea-ea-sure! wafted in his memory. That's Bach! A secret uncontrollable pleasure caused him to glance discreetly from left to right, and then at the trees through the crack in the transom, and at the sky. He felt *his* body growing in stature, while the church and the reverend grew smaller, until, finally, he sat a giant among a throng of dwarfs. Realleh!

With a great feeling of relief he stepped out into the frosty afternoon decked with autumn-tinged clouds and finally into the dinner-scented atmosphere that was home.

One meal . . . one Sunday dinner, after which Rutherford dozed among the pages of the *Star* and the *Voice* and Viola busied herself around the house and Amerigo made his way through the town to the art gallery.

As he passed through its columns he noted with pride that they were Corinthian columns because they looked like baskets of fruit, different from Doric and Ionian. The marble had been imported from Italy, the home of Michelangelo, the Renaissance, and Mrs. Crippa. He entered the hall with a feeling of easy familiarity, glancing only casually at the medieval implements of war, the tapestries, and even the mural upon which Socrates spoke to his companions under the eternally fair skies of ancient Greece.

He followed the stream of quiet, discreet, well- but simply dressed people into the auditorium and listened to the sons and daughters of the society folks of the city stumble through Mozart, Bach, and the pas de deux. Ahem!

Then he boarded the streetcar and stayed on until all the pleasant prosperous colors and forms ran out of sight, and the streetcar gradually took on a dusky hue that was animated by sonorous gusty voices that caused him to think of the alley and streets like the alley that he could only escape via the redeeming light of Sunday afternoon.

He got off at Nineteenth Street. It was cluttered with dirt and poverty. He listened to its noisy jocular fatalism. He glanced in the windows of the beer halls with disdain, and tried to reconcile Bach and Mozart, English Literature and the broadly articulated *a* to the impulse that forced him up towards the Gem Theater.

You a mean an' evil woman — an' you don' mean no one man no good! screamed an earthy voice through a loudspeaker, and his heart involuntarily beat faster, while his eyes ravished, against his will, the shapely bowlegs and broad swaying hips of a cocoa-brown young woman who walked proudly beside a tall willow-limbed young man dressed in a zoot suit — fifteen bottoms, thirty-two in the knee, triple a's shining like the reverend's, snow-white big-apple hat spreading like a gable . . . Clark . . . over a big fine house.

But I don't blame you, baaa — bay — I'd be the same way — if I could!
A sadness — a mixture of envy, loneliness and proud defiance — welled

up inside him. It caused him to walk straight, too straight, as he passed the cluster of boys and girls whom he recognized from North High. They were from the south side. They talked and laughed familiarly, arm in arm, waist in arm. I don't care! he thought as their voices faded out of hearing. He walked straighter, straining not to allow the haunting music to filter through the channels of his ears, his bones! Dem bones, dem bones, dem dry bones . . . Malleus, Inkus, Stapes! And still the impatient rhythms pounded in his blood and in the hard tight secret bound by a thousand snares within the wrinkled folds of Rutherford's shorts.

After the show he walked up Eighteenth Street past *her* house. As he drew near he shot a guarded glance from the opposite side of the street. A tall, lean white-looking man sat in the doorway of the funeral parlor and a short slightly rotund white-looking woman sat opposite him. Mrs. Thornton. And *she* sat between them, though he did not really see her because he dared not look at her, as he blindly nodded a greeting and tipped his hat, noticing that she was hemmed in the vortex of the triangle formed by her parents' knees. Nor could he tell if they had returned his greeting, because he was afraid to look back, but he felt that they hadn't returned it, he couldn't remember having imagined that they had, nor could his breath quicken to the conjured up afterimage of a possible smile.

He half walked, half marched up the street and turned the corner south to Nineteenth Street until he came to the boulevard and down the boulevard to Eighteenth Street again where he stood and stared at the frightening procession of apparently happy people who were making the best of the early hours of the evening. He spoke to a few North High students as he made his second round up Eighteenth Street and entered the ice cream parlor almost a block west of where he had encountered the Thornton family. He drank a milk shake without tasting it.

Somebody clicked a nickel in the music box and he tried not to hear the insistent tenor sing: *If I-ee diddidn't care . . . more than words ca-an say-ee, If I — ee diddidn't care, would I — ee feel thissss way — ee. If thissss isn'tttt love, then why — ee do I — ee thrillll?*

"Take it easy," he said to the waiter, a senior at North High. Rollins. "He's little but he's tough!" he heard Roscoe say. "He's the toughest cat on the whole football team! The only way you gonna stop him — is *kill* 'im!"

As he stepped into the street the singer was asking:
And what makes my head go 'round and 'round — while my heart stands still?

He worked his way through the jostling crowd that gathered around the entrance to Lincoln Hall and climbed the stair and paid for his ticket at the door and strode with great dignity into the funky bluesy atmosphere simmering with the heat of the sensuously swaying bodies. He cautiously scanned the faces he encountered with a barely perceptible smile, which projected — offered up for sacrifice — a timid question that quivered upon his lips. He moved toward the orchestra at the far end of the hall, past the crowded chairs that lined the wall. He unobtrusively approached a girl who sat alone. Her eyes, the set prim line of her lip, said, No. He pretended not to have noticed her and greeted with exaggerated cordiality her companion, Stacy, who had just returned with a bottle of Coca-Cola. He swaggered on, flinging a greeting here, one there, eyeing the dancers with an air of critical approval or disapproval, interested now only in the more anthropological aspects of the dance, until he reached the bandstand and became so absorbed in the music that he didn't care to look for a partner when the music stopped playing. He greeted Alphonso, the drummer.

"Hi, Al!"

"Hi, man!"

Boom boom boom boom. An invisible foot tapped out the beat and the music started. He inched his way toward a girl who stood near the window in the opposite wall. He cleared his throat and studied the phrase: I beg your pardon, but may I have this dance? No, he decided, that's not . . . Eh . . . would you give me the pleasure of. He drew closer. The trumpet player stood up to take the solo. He was on top of the girl now.

"I beg your pardon!" he blurted out.

"What?" looking at him with an expression of disdain.

"Eh."

"Come here, bitch!" A young man in draped pants appeared from nowhere and whisked her away. She grinned and fell into his arms and into the pulsing rhythm of the song. He stood gaping at them, and at the same time an excruciating pain smote him in the bowels. He trembled with humiliation and rage as he watched them glide smoothly over the floor, hips coordinating like the gears of a powerful machine, with grace, improvising, now that the trumpet solo was over, to the double beat of the bass.

I would have treated her like a lady, he thought, and then he sadly found himself wondering why the sky was blue and why birds sang. Why was blood red? And then all the faces in the hall blended into one face, the movement became one movement, and he was swept involuntarily into the dance that he had inherited from his Uncle Ruben.

He bought a Coca-Cola he didn't want and took a seat and became a spectator. Suddenly Roscoe and Earline appeared smiling and, without knowing why he did it, he turned his back on them with a confused mocking gesture, and quickly turned around again, but they were gone. "Wait!" his voice trailing sadly into the thought: I was just . . . just playing. But they were gone, swallowed up in the crowd. He fretted impatiently in his chair, crossed his legs and studied the hall, the ugly naked lights over the bar, the dark musty recesses of the cloakroom into which couples now and then disappeared and reappeared rearranging their clothes. He studied all the shoes with their pointed toes and Cuban heels, all the sharp creases and high-waisted pants, pimp chains swinging, all the glistening sheens of pomaded hair and sweating foreheads bent with religious concentration upon the dance.

The orchestra was playing the last piece. He looked around with desperation. "Would you like to dance?" he asked a skinny-looking girl who sat two seats from him. She nodded. He took her by the hand and trembled onto the dance floor. He took a breath and shifted to his right hip, and then to his left, the way Viola and Rutherford had said, the way Uncle Ruben would have done.

"Git the beat," he heard Rutherford saying, "an' then shuffle to the right an' to the left, or slightly forward, or back, an' then turn — s-m-o-o-t-h! — without bendin' your knees too much."

He tried it, but he was trembling so violently that he stumbled. He started again — and stumbled again. The girl sighed impatiently. He was afraid to look at her, but he grinned self-consciously and tried again. Gradually he lost consciousness of himself and of the girl. He was moving within the warm swirl of the music. The girl settled her belly within the smooth rhythmic space of two swift backward strides, and his shorts, damp with sweat, tightened about his groin, and in the pause, just before the turn, he pushed her away, smitten with shame, and fled through the crowd and down into the street, his ears full of the mocking laughter that did not stop until he finally fell into the deep velvet reaches of the black room.

"Keep yo' han' — on-a the plow — h-o-l-d on!" the choir sang to the congregation of the Methodist church on Nineteenth Street. Mr. Rogan stood before them in his Sunday suit — too big! — his eyes closed, arms outstretched, holding on:

"Hold oooooonnn! Hold ooooonnnnn!"

He searched the faces of the congregation. Mr. and Mrs. Thornton sat in front, with Cosima between them. She plays for the choir. Methodis . . . *t!* He stole a glance at her, perusing her face, the simple appropriate dress she wore. Suddenly he became aware of Mr. Rogan's cutting glance and heard him screaming, though no audible sound escaped his angry lips — Look at *me,* damnit! — as Rutherford's strap fell across his naked legs.

"Kee — ee — eep yo' han's oooon the plow — hooooold on!" followed by approving a-mens throughout the church, and when the service was over he lagged behind in order to catch a glimpse of *her,* but missed her in the confusion, and stalked down toward Nineteenth Street alone.

"Hi, Amerigo!" A soft brown girl with neatly arranged coarse black hair and a pretty face was smiling at him.

"Hi, Mary Ann." He was somewhat cheered because *she* was Cosima's best friend! He searched for something to say to her as they made their way to the corner. Then suddenly he thought: Maybe *she* might see us! He glanced up at her house on the corner and wondered which window she might be looking through, the bedroom? the kitchen? He grinned nervously at Mary Ann and tried to imagine Cosima eating.

Cabbage! said a malicious voice, but he forced the thought out of his mind by uttering a hasty good-bye to Mary Ann and rushing down the street, hurrying he knew not where or why. Gradually a depressed feeling took hold of him and he became absorbed by the thought of the grueling machinations of still another Sunday night in the year that was swiftly approaching next year.

Thanksgiving dinner was good and exciting — and exhausting!

And after that the wind howled through the streets as though it were in pain, freezing the branches of the trees, and the puddles of water that lay in the streets, froze the rain, and then snow, which the wheels of the automobiles churned into a dirty pudding that was finally heaped in piles beside the sewers and drains all along the way to North High:

"Glo-o-o-ri-ous! is Thy Name, Al-might-ty Lord!" rang throughout the approaching Christmas season, which was illuminated by a frozen hoar-gray light mellowed by a warm rose-tinted familiarity that engulfed his awareness of himself in some organic way, and a long string of Christmases stretched out to a length of fourteen and a half years.

"Glorious is Thy Name!" he sang with gusto, drowning the peals of roaring laughter that spilled from the mouth of the mechanical Santa Claus as the snows, one Snow, one continous falling, blocked up the chimney hole and covered the faces at the foot of the trees.

The bells rang from the towers in the town!:

"Merry Christmas!"

"Haaaaa-lay-lu-jah!"

"Merry Christmas!"

"Haaaaaa-lay-lu-jah!"

"What did Santa Claus bring you, baby?"

"Aaaaaaw — there isn't any."

"Haaaaa-la-lu-jah!"

Throughout the volumes of the gray room at four o'clock when the little columns of fire in the gas stove cast crisscross patterns upon the . . .

"One pattern!" Then:

"Aaaaaaah-ha!" Rutherford exclaimed, stepping into the crowded front room reverberating with lusty exclamations of:

"HAPPY NEW YEAR!"

It's Next Year just the same! he thought, his glance falling upon the flowered pattern of the rug, agitated by a sweet, slightly nauseous smell. He licked the eggnog from his lips and smiled at Viola and Rutherford and at the host of friends in the room: One Year! he thought triumphantly, feeling last year emerging into his awareness of this year. Trying to recall the year before that, which was gone, dissolved, like the year before that and the year before that and Ten . . . Nine . . . Eight . . . Seven . . . Six . . . . . . Five . . . . Four . . Three . . TwoONE YEAR!

"Next Year!" he exclaimed, laughing uncontrollably.

"What's the matter with you, boy?" Rutherford asked Viola with flashing eyes, "That little glass of eggnog's done gone to that little joker's head!"

At which he shrank from the sight of the protruding breast into the diminutive reaches of the silent question that struck his ears with such a force that sleep did not come easily, and he had to wander through the endless volumes of the red room, which divided now into myriad rooms washed by the waves of scorching yellow laughter. . . .

Frantically he swam, her long red sweeping hair a blazing flame. Finally they reached the hot red sand of the burning beach where he lay her gently down, and bent down to cool her parched lips with a kiss, and was plunged into the cold black silhouette against the frost-covered front room window.

A muffled sigh from the middle room! Bedsprings whining!

"Don't you hit my momma!" he screamed, but there was no sound. I *hate her!* pulling the covers over his head. Him, too! Emboldened by rage, he steeled himself for the Fifteen Year Siege.

"Now is the month of May-ing, when Merry lady are playing —"

"NO!" Mr. Rogan shouted. "This is Palestrina, not W. C. Handy! Stop jiving the damned rhythm. It goes like this: Tum *tum* tum *tum* tum *tum* tum, tum *tum* . . . . tadum tum tum tum. Tada *dum* tum *tum* tum-*taa*! — Tada *dum* tum *tum* tada! It's spring! Nature's pregnant —"

"Hot dog!" Jeff exclaimed.

"Cecil, shut up!" said Mr. Rogan. "Listen! It's spring. The flowers are blooming, and — and new leaves are budding on the trees. Look! Look out that window!"

Beyond the window spring was ablaze with timid colors fidgeting in the sun. Silver clouds were trying to impose a capricious gloom upon the afternoon, but neither the flowers nor the new leaves, nor the birds nor the slender grasses shooting up from the lawn were taking them seriously. . . .

"You're in a wood," Mr. Rogan was saying, "In a beautiful forest! Perhaps just walking because you're young, or — or on a picnic. You hear the sound of laughter behind that bush over there! A girl — a beautiful girl — and a boy —"

He likes boys, he thought, his imagination overwhelmed by a sense of mystery.

"More laughter!" he was saying, "playful and gay — in another direction, maybe, burning with the same fever that radiates from the sun. You run here! there! hesitate, trembling, listening, like a bird, like a squirrel, tail high, listening, like a deer, like a faun! You chase the sound, but it's no longer there. It's over there! Just beneath that knoll! You run and run, and your whole being sings with a joy that-that would *kill* you if it continued any longer. Listen! Now-is-the-month-of-May-ing! When mer-ry lady *are* play-ing. Tra la-la la la la *laaaa!* Trala la la laaa lala! Now *sing!*"

"Now-is-the-month-of-May-ing —"

"That's it!" he cried with a passionate smile, his fingers flitting through the air, the voices gladdening to the heat, to the burning, to the painful emergence of that wet shining thing that was spring.

Rrrrrrrring!

They dashed out into the hall, he leaping faunlike up the four steps leading to the upper hall. Just as he turned the corner Lydia screamed. He looked back and saw her standing on the stair, holding her belly with her arms, her face ashy, trembling violently while the blood trickled down her legs and lay in a lump at her feet. A crowd gathered around her and gazed at the lump of blood.

"It's a baby!" cried Carrol T.

"Stand back!" Mr. Haines, the janitor, stepped into the crowd. "Take her to the nursery!" he commanded and Ruth and Earline who stood nearest gathered the crumbling Lydia into their arms and took her away.

"Now get movin'!" Mr. Haines shouted. "*All* of you!"

He was a short dark-brown-skinned man with gray hair who wore glasses over his serious bluish brown eyes. He took off his jacket and covered the dead baby. Then he went away and returned with a bucket of sawdust, which he strew over the blood until it was all absorbed and then scooped it up with his shovel, the way Mr. Johnson at Garrison School had scooped up the coal in the furnace room, and threw it in the big trash can that he carried downstairs. . . .

The corridor grew still, as though in all the rooms nobody spoke, as though they were listening to the consuming flames of spring.

Rrrrrrring!

(((((((((((((. . . ing . . .)))))))))))))

Next year I'll be a junior, he thought as he walked home, not quite able to realize that the summer vacation had started, suspecting every moment that he had made a mistake, mistrusting the sense of freedom that stole upon him, the sense of loneliness because of something finished, and of something about to happen at the end of that hot expanse of time that stretched out before him.

One summer.

He stared at the sun until his eyes ached, then looked away and blindly walked into a tree. Someone laughed. As his vision returned he could just make out the retreating forms of a knot of girls ahead of him, one with long reddish brown hair. Cosima! overwhelmed by a welter of confusion, rubbing the lump on his forehead. He picked up his cap and stumbled on his way feeling like a fool.

Summer grew hot and wet with sweat. At night when he could not sleep he would quietly pull on his clothes and walk all the way out to the art gallery and sit in the grassy porch and if the moon shone stare into the shadows of the luxurious trees. It was his secret place, where all was peace, where he was beside himself with a painful joy too deep for thought. At some point, when his spirit was exhausted, he would return home. Fatigue would overtake him on the way and he would be grateful for the kindness of sleep into whose embrace he would sink and remain until the envious sun and the twittering birds confronted him with a new and painful reality.

"Amerigo!"

He got up and ate his breakfast and started out for Mr. O'Casey's barbershop where he worked shining shoes, but where he was not destined to work long because he did not smile at the customers and "hustle," as Mr. O'Casey said.

Mr. O'Casey was a kind gray-headed man of fifty-four with gallstones and brown eyes, but Irish just the same.

"Now porter —" he began no sooner than he had arrived, continuing yesterday's conversation, Friday, because today was Saturday, the big day in a barbershop. "Now porter, I know you're a fine young colored boy, gittin' an education an' all, but you gotta *smile* an' say *sir* to the customers when they come in. The minute they hit the door you gotta be on your feet! Standin' there, greetin' 'um with a smile. 'Wanna shine, sir,' you gotta say, or: Good evenin', Mister So-an'so! How about a shine, there! Or somethin' with a spark to it! An' *then* you'll make money, an' I will, too! But when you set over there in that corner, there, readin' books — an' don' pay 'um no mind, porter, waitin' for 'um to ask *you* — you never *will* git nowhere!"

"I caun't dew it!" he exclaimed to Rutherford that evening at supper.

"You caun't dew what!" Rutherford asked, slipping into his house shoes, while Viola fried the hamburgers.

"I caun't say all that, play no Uncle Tom for no white man, an' I ain' — I'm nottt — going to, eithah. I went there, theah . . . and sat in a cornah and waited. I didn't mind asking the customer if he wanted a shine. Would you like a shine, sir? I asked them, and if they said yes, I *gave* them a shine, the best shine I could. Then I went back and read my book. There was nothing else to do."

"Unh! Did you talk to 'um with a English accent? Hot damn!" he laughed. "No wonder you done lost your job, talkin' to the white folks like you better'n *they* are. You gotta learn to hustle, boy. Use psychology. You gittin' to be a *man!* It ain' no shame to shine shoes. It's honest work. It won' kill you to smile an' be nice to people. One a these days you'll have to. I mean — do it when you don' feel like it! You think I like to run the elevator, humorin' drunks an' crackers that think that just because they tip you a lousy quarter you got to kiss they behind? You know what a white woman said to me the other day? She said, Rutherford, you know one thing, if you was a white man, I'd marry you. She thought she was payin' me a compliment! I had to just smile an' say nothin'. Some things you got to just take an' go ahead on an' keep your dignity. Ain' nobody in that hotel is more respected than me! From ol' man Mac on down!"

"Well, I ain' gonna play no happy niggah for nobody!"

"You didn' understand what your daddy said," said Viola. "Wash your hands."

"You're young yet," said Rutherford, sitting down to the table. "You'll learn, or end up dead before your time. It's fine to git a education an' all that — talkin' all fancy — but you gotta git along with people, 'cause as long as you need the money they payin' you to live on — they don' have to understand you!"

"Supper's gittin' cold," said Viola.

"I'm Amerigo Jones!" he muttered under his breath, "an' I kin be anything I wanna be . . . to be — and I don' care!"

He sat down to the table with a feeling of dread, fear, and anxiety because of the facts of life that lurked outside the kitchen walls, beyond the walls of North High, and the invisible walls of Next Year, rising higher with the heat.

"Well, sir," said Aunt Rose as he entered the house on a sultry Sunday afternoon near the end of August. "Well, sir! I see you didn' forgit your auntie after all!"

"Aw Aunt Reose!" he grinned guiltily.

"I know how it is. You ain' got no time for a old broken-down woman like me. But I don' blame you none. Only I would like to hear from you once an' a while — just to know how you doin' an' what you learnin' at school." Her eyes twinkled mischievously, and he observed that her health had improved, though she still moved heavily and with that economy of effort typical of the aging.

Older still, he thought, but at least she isn't sick — ill — anymore. He stared at her, marveling at her strength, remembering how worn out and used up she had seemed when he last saw her. Like — as though — she were going to die. He suppressed the sad feeling as she sat down on the stairs with a heavy grunt and drew him to her. Like an old, old lady. He wondered if she, too, had seen Abraham Lincoln.

"What you starin' at, boy?"

"Nothin'."

"Yeah," she sighed, "I know, your auntie's gittin' old. Every time I look at you I think about your mamma an' poppa an' 'em, when you wasn' no bigger'n a pup. Me an' your gran'ma. Seems like yestiddy. But it wasn' yestiddy — it was a long time ago." She straightened his tie. "You glad to be goin' back to school next month?"

"Yes'm. I'm going to be a junior. They know but they don't know they know."

"What?"

"It's a sayin' . . . g. A freshman don' — doesn't — know and he *knows* he doesn't know, a sophomore doesn't know, but he *thinks* he knows, a junior knows but doesn't *know* he knows, and a senior knows and he *knows* he knows!"

"Ha! Well, sir! It looks like *I* been a freshman all my life! 'Cause the older *I* git the less I seem to know! The best *I* kin do is *try* not to *make the same mistakes over agin* an' put my trust in the Lord! Been to church lately? Your momma's been tellin' me that she can't hardly make you go no more."

"Aw . . ."

"What's the matter, you gittin' too educated to go to church?"

"No'm, but all they do is a whole lot a hollerin' . . . g and shouting and saying the same thing over and over again . . . and calling that preaching! The reverend *says* he's got an education, but that he likes to talk *plain* because he's *got that old-time religion that was good enough for his dear old mother!* But we're living in *this* time! Splitting infinitives over all that stuff about Eve coming from Adam's rib and all . . . all that, like he's never *heard* of physiology and Darwin's Theory of Evolution — or the *Republic* of Plato and . . . and Shakespeare and all of them."

"Well, your auntie ain' got much education, neither, but I know one thing, there ain' *no* fool like a *educated* fool! An' that there's more to the Bible than's on the printed page, an' that if you talkin' to folks that a lot of 'um ain' got much education, just plain simple workin' folks, you gotta talk so's they kin understand you — that is, if you know what you talkin' about, yourself —"

"Yeah!" he interrupted, "but if they keep on talking *down* to the people all the time, how are they ever going to learn something? If I were a preacher I'd go to Harvard or Yale or something and try to talk as well as I could and teach the people in an educated way. The Bible's *plain,* but I never did see so many big words I couldn't understand!"

"That's right, son, you all right!" throwing up her hands in a gesture of surrender. "Your auntie's got to do it *her* way an' you got to do it *yourn*. I reckon that if it's the *truth* we're after, an' we look hard enough, we gonna end up in the same place, God willin'." She flashed a wink at him, and he felt a little silly, like a child, when he was six or seven years old.

"Had your dinner?"

"Yes'm . . . Yes."

"Come on."

They proceeded to the kitchen where she served him up a piece of apple pie and a glass of milk. He raised the glass to his lips.

"How many girls you got?"

He choked and almost spattered the whole table with milk.

"None!"

"Now you kin tell your auntie! You kin tell me. I bet you a little devil!"

"Honest! I haven't got a girl. I wouldn't have *any* of them . . . eneh! You oughtta . . . to see the way they act — carry themselves — doing it in the halls behind the lockers by the gym and —"

"Doin' what?"

"And letting them feel all over them and everything. That's not the kind of girl *I* want! *I* want a *lady!* Somebody . . . somebody that you kin re*spect* and take her flowers an' . . . and kiss her hand. Treat her nice —"

"Don't you know no girls like that?"

"No'm. They all stuck up! No'm . . ."

A feeling of wonder and humility came over him, as he thought of a certain two-story house. Too tall.

"Eh . . . your momma tells me that you're mighty keen on that little Thornton girl —"

WHO — meeeeeeee! How does she *know?* He was unbearably surprised to hear it uttered as a fact for the first time, stamped upon his consciousness by the certainty of Aunt Rose's voice, retelling a known fact in a disinterested tone, as of some happening in yesterday's newspaper, as though she had possibly said: It looks like the Germans really mean business, placing her hopes, however, on the strength of the Maginot Line and the diplomatic skill of the British statesman with the umbrella, thankful that we, America, were safely insulated by the two oceans and the Monroe Doctrine and a group of screechy politicians called the Isolationists. *Your momma tells me that you're mighty keen on that little Thornton girl.*

WHO — meeeeeee! rang in his ears like the happy bells of Let's Pretend and shook him with their titillating vibrations, forcing his mouth ajar, his eyes to shine, the piece of apple pie on his plate to remain uneaten.

Meanwhile Aunt Rose merely grinned at him. Finally she said:

"Well, you picked a good one, son." A serious, even grave expression passed over her face, causing him to search for a deeper meaning in her words when she added. "You show them society niggahs who you are."

She's thinking of Ardella, he thought.

"You gotta aim high if you want to amount to somethin'."

He wondered if *she* knew!

She's *got* to know!

The full impact of Aunt Rose's knowing, of Viola's knowing, dawned upon him as he stepped into the redeeming light of Sunday afternoon and headed for the art gallery. He looked into the face of the knowing sky, listened to the whispering trees. He trembled with excitement, with the embarrassment, the joy, of one who was being talked about.

Clapclapclapclapclapclap . . .

He wandered through the polished halls of the art gallery, among the living pictures, the living statues, through the living atmosphere of historic times that he knew by heart, but which he now beheld as if — not for *the* first time, but for *a* first time — for the first time in the glorious age of her knowing. Lost within its pleasant aura, he was suddenly confronted by Old Jake with his golden helmet.

"She's got to know!" he said.

And as he passed quickly out of the gallery, he decided not to look at the fiery Greek's face, but upon gaining the door, he felt compelled to put his feeling to a final test. He looked back.

"Eh — your momma tells me that you're kinda keen on that little Thornton girl," said the great man, and Amerigo burst blindly through the door and buried his sensibility in the soft breast of evening, which lay waiting, burning with all the virulent colors of autumn, tingeing his delirium with a fearful apprehension of sadness. The thought: "It's too good to be true" would have articulated itself into words had he not done his utmost to suppress it.

Speeding northward on the streetcar, the gradual shabbiness of the streets had a sobering effect upon him. He became aware of where *he* lived, and where *she* lived. And that she had *already* won a scholarship, according to the *Voice* and that *he* would probably have to stay at home and attend junior college, *and* work as well, and *then, if* things went well, *if* he won a scholarship, he *might* hope to attend whatever university it designated, because, although Rutherford had finally gotten a raise, which was *not* very much, he could *never* afford to send him to Harvard or Yale.

His shoulders sank deeper under the weight of impending reality. Gradually the noisy rumor about him and Cosima seemed a mockery. The thought of her knowing struck fear in his heart and caused him to walk straighter than ever after he had stepped down from the streetcar at Eighteenth Street. I must not let them see! he thought.

After the movie he strolled indifferently past *her* house, but she and her parents were not sitting out front, so with a casual air he glanced up at the windows. They were dark. Disappointed that he could not show his indifference he turned down the avenue, and then thought: Maybe she's at church! He turned back toward Nineteenth Street, and when he arrived at the church he eased the door open and peeped in. There was no sign of her.

Feeling foolish, guiltily, even ridiculous, he turned down Nineteenth Street and interested himself in the men and woman he met, and in the unique way in which the shadow from the lamppost fell across the broken bricks in the sidewalk. Then he observed that the YWCA was dark, and then watched with an air of superiority a couple talking on the corner. The boy held the girl by the waist and spoke softly to her and the girl smiled at the boy as though he were the only boy in the world. He began to sing softly as he approached them, but they did not notice him, so he resentfully left them to their folleh and grew more intensely involved in his song, a song with no words, with meaningless words he made up himself, sad autumnal articulations of pain, filling a melody that he had never heard before, but was familiar just the same. At Eighteenth Street he gazed left and right at the banal procession, turned right and followed the persistent sound of the *Boom! Boom! Boom!* that came from Lincoln Hall. Now he was getting the hang of it, could ask the right girl in the right tone of voice at the right time and move in any direction at will to the beat — and s-m-o-o-t-h — of the rhythm and grind of the axising hip and release from quivering lip a flow of nervous images gleaned from the better movies and Palgrave's Golden Treasury and smile with discreet sarcasm upon the primitive machinations of the mob: an aristocrat in a class of his own, proudly, defiantly alone.

There was no one at home when he got there. In bed, in the red room, he tossed impatiently, waiting for the plodding events (the sound of separate keys in the lock, the peaceful or complaining settling down to sleep of Viola and Rutherford, their quiet measured breaths which he must compare to his own, the envelopment by darkness and the sound of swift, dangerous waters, the ignoble release and finally the total abandonment into a state of oblivion) to pass, and the sound, the inevitable sound of Rutherford's voice:

"All right — let's hit 'um!"

The eyes of the world were upon him as he marched to school, a junior who *knew* with a desperate pounding of the heart, but *knew not* that he knew, a lieutenant in the ROTC, a member of the North High Choir, Quartet, Special Singers, and Glee Club, nervously contemplating the hazards of Chemistry! History! Geometry! French! And gladdened by the prospect of English Literature and Sociology: Tramp tramp tramp tramp, through the foggy morning.

Looks like smoke. That's corny! He became aware somewhere in the half-sleeping part of his mind of the clouds of smoke that followed in the wake of the Great War that boomed overseas, that had shaken the Maginot Line, obscured the boundaries of half a dozen little countries, and caused a whirl of speculation as to whether England would get into it, and Russia, and what would happen if they did, now that Italy, Il Duce, had made a pact with Hitler. The wind moaned through the trees and broke up into a din of articulate whisperings that mingled with the rumble of the streetcar that sped across Fifteenth Street. Uncle Billy's face flashed before his mind and his voice separated itself from the other faces and declared: *One a these days you'll look up an'* . . .

The oppressive feeling that was chemistry and geometry, and the thought of her knowing fused with, dissolved into, a vague ubiquitous fear inspired by Uncle Billy's prophecy, which, though it did not, could not, penetrate the deeper levels of his consciousness, filled his mind with a profusion of movement and sound that gathered around the word *Cosima*. Not daring to think that it could really be true, he hoped rather that some beneficent fate, some undertone of faith subsuming the dread inspired by the words *next year,* might relieve the tension that filled the silence in which the aftertones of the word *Now?* rang like a bell in the tower of a town.

"What you say, Dad?"

He looked into the raw-boned handsome face of Roy Earle. Earle looked down at him with a smile that revealed a broken front tooth, and struggled beside him with the lazy movements of a natural athlete.

"Oh! . . . eh hello theah!" thinking: "He's in the Golden Gloves, and on the football and basketball teams. Goes with Betty Love. Betty Love with long black curly hair with sideburns and slightly bow legs." His resentment of Roy's intrusion upon his thoughts deepened, as he struggled to suppress the image.

They turned into Eighteenth Street. A knot of girls passed them just in front of Street's Hotel.

"Hi Roy!"

"Hi Roy!"

"Hi Roy!"

"Hi Roy!"

They looked back with seductive smiles.

"What you say, baby!" grabbing the nearest one by the waist. Loraine Turner, freshman. Her bosom bounced when she walked, short little peach-colored girl with lipstick and high-heeled shoes. "Look at that f-i-n-e bitch!" Earle exclaimed with a grin. "Ha — ha! . . . How'd you like to have a piece a that, dad?"

His mouth flew open.

"Aaaaaaaw! Roy Earle!" Loraine giggled.

She *likes* it! Amerigo observed with bewildered amazement as she struggled loose from him and he patted her on the behind. When she caught up
with the others she whispered something to them and they burst into shrills
of laughter, and looked back at him and giggled and switched their hips, at
which Amerigo's face grew hot with rage, disgust, and envy.

They were stepping off the curb at Eighteenth and Vine. Roy asked:

"How you makin' out with Cosima?"

"Why — what — what-do-you-*mean!*"

"Aw-haw haw haw! Man. I know you stuck on that hinkty chick!
Eeeeevery time I see 'er in the cafeteria or in the hall I see you, standin' or
sittin' not too far away! Just gazin' at 'er — like she was Lena Horne!"

"Aaaaaaaaw, maaaannn!"

"She's a fine chick!" Roy said. "Goddamned *virgin!* Has to stay home a-l-l
the time. Her ol' man got the key to that pussy belt hisself! Ain' nobody gittin'
none a that cock! Gotta have dough. Be a doctor's son or one a them big-shot
niggahs!"

He wants me to hit him, he thought. He'd like that, him being in the
Golden Gloves and all.

"Ha!" Roy laughed to himself.

"What are you *laughing at!*"

"Old Chubby Collins tried to take 'er to the dance last year. He's a cock-
hound!"

"His old man's a lawyer," he said, "why didn't her old man let her go?"
He tried to control the tremor in his voice.

"He was afraid he'd try to git in them drawers! Ever'body knows Chubby!
An' his ol' man's worse than him! Comin' to school in that bad Oldsmobile
— all shaaaaarp! — like he was a movie star or somethin'!" They walked
on quietly a few yards. "But that don' cut no ice with me!" Roy continued,
as if to himself.

"Whaat?"

"Foolin' around with these virgin queens. I ain' tryin' to win no home, I
just wanna lie up between a cool pair of thighs an' git my *rocks* off!" He
grinned with apparent satisfaction at the agitated expression on his face.

Everybody knows! he thought with a heavy heart, just as they were
turning up Woodland Avenue. He was glad that he remembered not to look
at the house. But now they heard voices from behind, girls' voices, *her*
voice among them, laughing and talking gaily. He and Roy shifted to one
side to let them pass, a little beyond the bridge. The sudden thought of Miss
Jennings threw him into confusion.

"There's your ol' lady, man!" Roy yelled, and for an instant Amerigo
contemplated dashing his brains out on the rails below. Instead he fled to

the other side of the street and half stumbled, half walked up the hill, alone, his eyes fixed upon the ground, and tried to pretend that he had not heard the derisive "Huh!" that had issued from the lips of one of the girls.

Was it Cosima? he wondered. That she had to hear it from that bastard! Like *that! Her!*

His diminished black body moved laboriously toward the summit of the great hill. Over the hazardous terrain of the age of her knowing.

Finally, after a tremendous effort, he entered the music room and took his seat a little before the bell rang. The hated room bubbled with the telling of the events of the last summer. Things had changed. There were several new men in the choir. Roscoe, Edna, Earline, Cecil, Virgil, and Sidney were gone. Dave was going with Susie now, and Betty was "sweet" on John, Willie and Pauline had had a "falling out," Odell had been a playground instructor, Lydia had dropped out of school and had a job. Cosima entered the room and took a seat just in front of *him.*

Rrrrrrring!

As the sound died away, Mr. Rogan entered in a flutter of nervous effeminate movement, in a perfectly tailored new blue serge suit, an off-white silk shirt, a soft blue tie, and a new pair of tan shoes.

"Look at that cat!" Carrol T. exclaimed, at which the others also exclaimed and whistled.

"All right!" cried Mr. Rogan, feigning anger, but the uproar continued.

"I said *all right!* Shut up! or get the *hell* out of here!" Silence. Then after two minutes, posing now behind the desk, his nose stuck up in the air, as though the room were filled with a bad smell, he began in an artificial tone: "I'm — eh — verreh pa-leased to see that seo meneh of you — eh — ledes and *gent*lemen have managed to return to us." He spoke of the schedule of concerts the choir was to give in the coming year, and concluded by announcing that the choir was to have an accompanist. "To those of you who don't know her," shooting a facetious look at Amerigo, "I'd like to introduce Miss Cosima Thornton, who has been studying music at the conservatory and is one of our most promising young pianists. Miss Thornton, would you be seo kind as to take a seat at the piaaaano!" She rose and seated herself at the piano. "All right," he resumed, "we're going to run down the old repertoire so that Miss Thornton can get acquainted with some of our standard arrangements." He raised his arms, held them suspended for a second, and then down! — at which the word, "OOOOOOOOOOOOOOOOOOO!" issued from sixty-five mouths. "My good LO — ORD — show me the WAAAAAAY!"

He studied her face in profile, as her fingers flitted excitedly, nervously over the keys, as her lips trembled and her eyes darted over the notes on the page.

She looks kinda like Mom. He studied her large brown eyes and the strong ridge that outlined her lips. But her eyebrows were different, rather heavy and almost meeting over the bridge of her nose, while a soft, barely perceptible fuzz grew on the side of her face. Her hair was different, too, a thick mass of reddish brown curls, which made her head seem to large for her thin neck and sloping shoulders. She's sort of ugly! he thought with astonishment, suddenly smiling as a burst of warm affection flooded his senses. She reminded him of Toodle-lum! His smile deepened, a smile of remembering. How ridiculous it was, and yet how accurate the comparison seemed! But then, there was in her nature a nervous explosive quality that Toodle-lum did not have, not merely thinness, fragility, but the flighty fragility of a butterfly! And she always wore flowing things with a close neckline and skirts just a little too long. Now she made him think of Aunt Rose! Something about the lively expression in her eyes, they seemed to talk, to give expression to nuances of feeling that rendered words unnecessary. He stared at her neck.

Gradually he became aware of a dead silence that seemed to engulf him and interrupt the flow of his reverie like an intrusive sound. It woke him up. He looked about him, at Mr. Rogan, at *her*, sitting at the piano with her hands folded in her lap. She looked at the piano keys, but the rest of the class looked at him with expectant smiles on their faces.

"Mister Jones!" said Mr. Rogan in a cold incisive tone, "please forgive me for dis*turb*ing you, but would you be so kind as to tell me who — in your opinion — is directing this choir?"

"You."

"Oh? I thought by the way you have been staring at Miss *Thornton* instead of looking at *me* that *she* was directing it!"

General laughter, gales of laughter, splashing against the cobblestones up and down the alley like summer rain, and swirling through the holes in the sewer lid where it whirred like the sound of the sea.

"Now let's try it — a-gaine!" said Mr. Rogan. "And let us pray that the *lunk-head* second tenors come in on time!"

"Oooooooh — my good Lo-ord — show me the waaaay!"

Rrrrrrrrring!

He allowed himself to be washed through the door and down the hall into the French class where *she* sat in the first row, he in the third next to Mary Nixon who sat next to Mary Ann who smiled sympathetically at him, while the pretty-legged French teacher lectured and then asked questions. He stumbled through a translation and got his lip hung up on the *eu,* and was more than grateful when the bell rang. He fled toward the stinking odor of sulfuric acid that was chemistry under Mr. North, the shy, boy-faced chemistry professor whom he imagined to have been born in a test tube. He sat on the front row two seats from *her,* lucky Melvin Humphreys on the other side, whispering and smiling about something. By straining a little he could see, without attracting Mr. North's attention, the tip of her nose and the fine pattern of the hairs on her legs.

Geometry was a desert, a wasteland dominated by a frightful tyrant, a neat brown-skinned man of small stature with wavy slicked-down hair and a mustache and polished fingernails and a mellow voice like Ronald Colman's. There was a rumor afloat that he was mad as a result of shellshock during the World War and was subject to fits of violence when one could not ascertain the third side of a triangle. Besides, *she* was not there. And he was hungry, and tired, he could *never* sit still. The effort of avoiding geometry wearied him. The bell rang and he fled to the cafeteria, where he managed to find an inconspicuous place two tables away, facing *her.* Once, or was it his fancy only? It seemed that she smiled faintly — ever so faintly! — at him!

After lunch, English. Miss Southern, over forty-five, well preserved, with a worldly, slightly wicked sense of humor, and wise. Like a queen, but not *the* queen, more like Queen Elizabeth I, but darker, of course. She had a skin like tan satin, with a smudge of pink on her cheeks under her dark burning rimless spectacled eyes. Her speech was perfect and she never washed her face with soap. Creams.

He and Cosima sat *side by side!* in a heavenly atmosphere that reeked with the scent of sonnets.

"And don't be afraid when you read Shakespeare!" Miss Southern was saying. "He wasn't anything but a man. Made out of flesh and blood, just like any other man. They're all alike, anyway. This one just happens to have been a genius. His language is personal. His sonnets are kind of like — like the blues. Just imagine Bessie Smith or Billie Holliday singing about trouble, about being tired and worried, about being in love with some no-good man. You're old enough to know love. Think about the one *you* love, the fair skies and muddy waters *you've* seen — and then *read* the man! Now who wants to read?"

Fingers popped in the air like whip-ends, while he stared dumbfounded at the page of verse and struggled to discover his voice, to set his tongue, to squeeze an upsurging feeling into audible shape. He squirmed in his seat in order to get his body into the right position, and when the impulse was ready he raised his hand and popped his fingers desperately. But he was too late.

"All right, Miss Appleton — you try," Miss Southern was saying. She began to read.

NO! That's not it! That's not the way to say it! he thought, unable to sit still. Before she could finish he was wriggling in his seat so excitedly that

Miss Southern had to give him a silencing glance, which she, with benevo-
lent humanity, tempered with a smile. When Miss Appleton had finished
she nodded to him and said: "All right, Amerigo, say the thing."

He took the book tenderly in his hands and fixed his eyes upon the
opening line, struggling all the while to control the emotion that so overpowered his voice that it was only with the greatest effort that he could
utter the first word. It half stumbled, half fell from his lips in a hoarse
groan, followed by a fit of stuttering and desperate attempts to pick up the
line. Then he fell into the throes of an impotent rage, and then the burning
heat of a crushing humiliation, followed by a feeling of dread, and then
silence. A terrible infinite silence, ringing with the aftertones of remembered words that intimidated him by the suddenness of the impact with
which they bombarded his consciousness:

Now?

The other students had begun waving their hands. He cleared his throat
and struggled to speak.

"Ruth," said Miss Southern.

NO! he thought, It's coming! It's coming!

His lips quivered.

"Ruth — you try. . . ."

Ruth read, and when she had finished, Miss Southern and all the members of the class agreed that she had read the sonnet very well. He could
only shake his head in protest. That was not it. She had not said it. The
anguish one felt due to the indifference of his beloved was not like that at
all. He searched for the right words with which to explain to the class and
to *her* what he meant. But the spiteful bell rang before he had a chance to
gather his murdered feeling into his arms and breathe the breath of life into
it. He was the last to leave the room. As he passed through the door, his
eyes met those of Miss Southern who regarded him with the faint trace of
a sympathetic smile.

She knows, he thought, and proceeded wearily to the next class, and to
the next, and ever and ever to the next, filled with the reverberations of the
questions that he burned to answer, but failed to answer, again and again,
because the magnitude of his feeling damned up the stops of his sensibility,
rang in his eyes and ears, filled his mouth, his nostrils, like the pealing of a
great bell, filled the channels of his being with a great roaring wind that
broke up into a flux of incoherent intonation, as though of a world being
consumed by flames. Through season after season of still another year.

★

"You sick?" Viola asked. They were having supper.

"No."

"You look kinda peaked to me. Stick out your tongue."

He stuck out his tongue. Rutherford looked up from his paper and looked at him searchingly.

"What's the matter, son?"

"Nothin'."

"That all you gonna eat?" Viola asked, noticing that he had eaten only one pork chop.

"I'm not hungry."

Rutherford returned to his paper, to the big headlines spread out across the front page of the *Star* telling about the war that was raging in Europe. It said that England was in it, alone now, and that France had fallen and that the president was urging all-out aid to the Allies and that an increase in the national budget was requested. There were maps with the countries of Europe drawn on them with scales and numbers at the bottom to indicate the distances and arrows to show where the German armies were, where the submarines were, and where the Allies were retreating to and from.

Over the sea and over the sea and over the sea to . . . he thought, relieved to be able to articulate a thought, any thought, as he slipped into the bloodred room, regretting and yet strangely welcoming the loud *Boom* of war. It made him smile, then snigger, and then slobber, and choke, and momentarily awaken to the thought: I did it! He laughed, as he sank deeper into the depths of the room that was as red as blood, through the bottom of the redness that was blacker than he.

Boom! Boom! Boom! Boom! Boom! Boom! exploded from the porch six times.

"Let me have a crack at it!" T. C. cried. He stepped beside Rutherford and leveled the big forty-five upon a nearby star.

AWHOOM! AWHOOM! AWHOOMAWHOOM! AWHOOM! AWHOOM!

"Hot damn!" Rutherford exclaimed:

AWHOOM! the forty-five replied, amid the ringing of bells and other bursting, exploding sounds that echoed throughout the city. Like a big chain reaction, he thought, from over the sea and over the sea. . . . And from a strange part of the South Pacific, hearing the tramp tramp tramp of marching feet and the banners of war interspersed with stars heralding the coming of Our Lord and Savior, Jesus Christ, the King of Peace.

"F-o-r — unto us a child is bor-orn!" he could hear the choir singing, "unto us, a Son is given! Unto us —"

AWHOOM! AWHOOM! AWHOOM! hallelujahed the smoking forty-five.

SkeeeeeeeWHOOM! enjoined the screaming shell, ripping its way through the crying waters. And a gutted ship sank to the bottom of the sea.

This year! said Uncle Billy.

He looked at his mother and father and the host who gathered in the front room, their faces flushed with optimism, animated by a frenzied relief due to the fact that at last something was happening.

"God is on *our* side!" exclaimed the bells and Joe Louis.

"Pray," Miss Jenny whispered.

God bless A — merica! Kate Smith sang out, just after the moon had gone over the mountain.

"This our country, too!" Rutherford's voice exclaimed. "If they let us fight. And then — when it's all over — they'll see how loyal we were. They gotta give us our rights then!"

Next Year? He saw his question explode into a great flame and fall around the charred ruins of Harvard and Yale.

He, the battalion adjutant of the North High ROTC, strode through the yellowish blue light of an early Monday morning on his way to school, Sam Brown belt, brass buttons, and shoes shining, glistening saber clanking at his side, a senior who *knew* and *knew* that he knew. A worried fretful impatience stole upon him as he proceeded up Eighteenth Street. As he drew near *her* house his breath quickened. Her door opened and she stepped out and crossed the street, little jets of steam escaping from her mouth. He behind her, but not too close. From the bridge they heard the first bell ring. She quickened her pace. He behind her at a discreet distance. There was no one else on the street. He could hear her tiny feet crunching through the frozen snow.

In a kind of sweet miserable delirium he persued her, his eyes and nose running from the January cold, but not too close. Her hair bobbled up and down, and by the way she carried her head he knew that she knew that it was he who followed her, though at a respectable distance.

He stared at her neck, and she began to walk faster, as though fired by a sense of urgency. He, too, accelerated his pace, his saber clanking against his leg. Once, when he almost tripped over it, she looked back, and their glances met for a fleeting instant, just as they gained the walk over which they sped in anticipation of the last bell:

Rrrrrrring!

She flung the door open and held it for him, lowering her gaze, while their burning faces were bathed in the wash of hot air from the giant radiators that sent them scuttling down the fall to their lockers. They arrived at the door of the music room at the same time. He smiled confusedly, stupidly, made a slight bow, as to a queen, and allowed her to pass through the door. Then he came after, but not too close.

The snows fell hard throughout January all over the world, according to the *Star* and the *Voice*. Headlines came more often now, more maps and arrows and pictures of troops in frozen attitudes, as though the men and machines had suddenly been caught unawares by the hypnotizing winds that had turned them into grimacing statues. The great ubiquitous BOOM! resounded on land and below the freezing waters, and the names of the dead were spewed out upon the pages of the *Voice* every Friday. . . .

With the advance of spring, the snows melted and the rains came, laying bare the fallen fruit of the cold season. Blinded by the searing brightness of *her* eyes, smarting from wounds inflicted by *her* cutting glances, or supercilious smiles flung at him like hand grenades, he rallied all his strength in order to meet the onslaught of an army of trees writhing in the agony of giving birth to a new generation of leaves. Flowers boomed! And freshets of rain and malicious winds lashed at the exposed love-infected nerve.

"Now-is-the-month-of-May-ing!" they sang, and he wondered how long he would be able to stand it.

"Hi, Amerigo." Mary Ann greeted him with a tender smile that seemed an expression of patient sadness. They had a secret. Only to her had he confessed his love for Cosima, her best friend. It was almost like having confessed to Cosima herself.

"She likes you," Mary Ann had said one March day when the wind had howled like a hungry dog.

"How do you *know?*"

"Because she *said* so, that is, not *exactly* . . . in so many *words,* but she talks about you all the time."

"I tried to call her, but her father always says she's busy or not in, or something like that."

"He doesn't think *anybody's* good enough for her!" said Mary Ann. "Are you going to make the honor roll?"

"I don't know."

"They're going to select the speakers for the commencement exercises from the honor students. If you could just get your name on that list. Maybe that would help."

"Do you think so, Mary Ann! And I'm *already* in the choir and the Glee Club and the Special Singers. I'm gonna be the battalion adjutant in the ROTC, and when I have to go to the army I'll probably make second lieutenant right off. Old Carrol has already been elected editor of the yearbook, but I can make business manager, I think. The one that sells the most ads gets it. And that'll mean that my picture will be in the book at least ten times! And I'm the chairman of the entertainment committee, too. I proposed at the last meeting that we have dances for the senior class every Friday evening from three-thirty until six-thirty. If Mr. Thornton won't let her come out at night, maybe he'll let her stay a little after school. He wouldn't have to *know* it. She could tell him she was staying for something else."

"We could try," Mary Ann answered sadly.

He took her hand and led her around behind the library where they sat on the steps and faced a pleasant little lawn with a green pelt of grass. She looked at him with tenderness as he continued to disclose the plans through which he hoped to win Cosima.

"Wouldn't it be *wonderful* if I could take her to the senior prom!" he exclaimed. "Who's taking you?"

"I don't know."

The hopelessness in her tone aroused a feeling of pity in him. She's like me, he thought, wondering exactly what he meant, looking at her now, really looking at her, for perhaps the first time. And then he suddenly realized that they were alone, but then took satisfaction in the fact that no one could see them, no one would talk. And if they did, what could they *say?* Everyone *knew* that Mary Ann was Cosima's closest friend. In fact, it now occurred to him that she and Cosima were strikingly alike, only Cosima was bright and clear and sharp, like a photograph, and Mary Ann was dark and subdued, sort of like a negative. Thrilled by a sense of discovery, he continued to compare them. Mary Ann played the piano, too! Not as well as Cosima, of course, but well, very well, indeed, and she was a member of the same society, accepted by the same circle of friends. She was on the honor roll the same as Cosima, but Cosima would be valedictorian. This proximity to Cosima seemed to enshroud Mary Ann in a veil of mist. That is to say, he became acutely aware of her dark brown color, as though it were some sort of encumbrance, through which she must struggle before she could shine like Cosima, as though it had clogged her sensibility, dulled her reflexes just a hair, causing her to appear but a parody of Cosima. How pretty her face is! He didn't dare say *beautiful* out of deference to Cosima. If it were not for — what? He contemplated the effect of touching her up, speculating as to just what alteration would transform her into that electrifying, magical, queenlike being who flitted over the horizon of his fondest dreams.

When they parted he gave her a note for Cosima. It contained the sonnet that he had not been able to read in class. On his way home he imagined her reading it in secret, feeling the passion with which he would have read it had his heart not overwhelmed his voice. She would place it under her pillow and listen to his words in the dark.

Even as he uttered them now, in the dark, from the depths of the red room. He turned on his side and discovered that the stars shone brightly. It seemed a good omen.

He was already awake when Rutherford called, and all along the way to school he plotted his campaign. He would concentrate on the yearbook, making a mental list of the districts he would canvass for ads. He would try to get the dances organized as soon as possible, so that he might get a chance to dance with *her,* to talk to *her* all the sooner. He suddenly realized that he had never talked to her, never had a real conversation with her. In fact, he had hardly heard her voice at all, except in class, only to answer a question, which answer was usually brief and *always* right. Reserved and shy, he reflected admiringly. A real lady! Yes, he must get the dances organized as soon as possible. To dance with *her!* Hey! hey! But dignified! None a that grindin' and stuff. On the toes, Jack! In a graceful whirl on the toes! Round and round! The dance, that was it. And the honor roll? At this point the incorrigible doubt assailed him: a loooooooooong chemistry equation deployed and encircled him, while history threatened his rear. "We realleh ccaun't geo on like thissss!" he exclaimed aloud in an effort to cheer himself up, but anxiety made him cast a quick glance at the trees, at the sky in which the sun glared threateningly. He reflected that if he could only pluck it out of the sky and put it in the icebox, keep it cool, he might check the advance of spring, and he would have the chance to do all the things he wanted to do, all the things he hadn't done in sixteen years, but which he must now attempt to do in three — not quite three — months!

By the end of March time had become a heavy weight that had insinuated itself into his blood, turning it into iron; his head was a heavy iron ball and his clothes were of mail, everything he touched seemed so heavy that he could not take hold.

The first dance had finally been arranged for the second week in April. He had wanted one every week, but the administration had objected because of the expenses. So the second week in April came and the dance was on. The orchestra played smooth and easy, like John Kirby said. Like Basie and Lunceford. The senior class turned out full force, but *she* didn't come. He danced with Ruth, Helen, and Mary Ann. He did the boogie with pretty little June Williams. But not one dance with Cosima Thornton. *She* was not there.

"What happened, Mary Ann?"

"I don't know." She touched his arm consolingly.

"Did you give her the poem . . . eh . . . the note?"

"Yes."

"What did she *say?* Did she read it?"

"I don't know. I guess so. She probably did." Her eyes darkened.

"Wanna dance?"

"If you want to."

They danced. He kept his eyes fixed on the door. She really was not there. He looked at the side of Mary Ann's face, at her mouth which was very close to his, taking secret pleasure in the thought that he might kiss her if he wanted to, if he *dared,* and enjoyed the virtuous feeling that resulted from rejecting this temptation out of deference to his Queen.

It was a nice dance, a pretty dance, but *she* had not come. A light shone in the upper windows when he passed her house on the way home that evening, but he couldn't see anyone behind the curtain. Up and down Eighteenth Street people stood in groups talking about the war over in Europe, but he didn't stop to listen. Something has happened, he thought, but just what it was he could not say. He walked distractedly home trying to figure out why she hadn't come.

All through supper he stared blankly at the big black letters sprawled across the pages of Rutherford's paper.

"Man-man!" said Rutherford, more to himself than to anyone in particular.

"What?" Viola asked.

He looked at his mother with deep affection, as though he were just returning after a long absence and was rediscovering her. She's getting a little fat. He let his gaze rest upon her full face. She looked buoyant, as though she were slightly filled with air. Her hair was evenly streaked with gray. But she's still nice looking, though. . . .

"What?" she was asking, and he observed his father. His hair was black, though they were the same age. But he's getting a little fat, too.

"Boy — looka there!" he heard Viola teasing him. "You gittin' faaaaaaat! Got a bay window like nobody's business!"

"Aaaaah-ha!" he had exclaimed with some embarrassment, drawing in his stomach and sitting a little straighter in his chair.

He doesn't have to go to war, Amerigo thought. Too old. He measured the time, counted the suns and moons, the raindrops and snowflakes, measured the volume of the wind: I'm sixteen . . . and he's . . . they're thirty-one . . . -two . . . because . . .

"Man-man! . . ." Rutherford was saying.

"What?"

"I see here where ever'body that ain' called yet's gonna either have to go or work in a defense plant. You *know* where *I'm* goin'!"

"It's takin' a war to *blast* you out a that hotel!" Viola exclaimed. "You might as well be makin' some of that good money, too."

"Things gittin' tight," Rutherford continued. "Ol' Uncle Joe's been bidin' his time so far, but now the Russians an' ever'body else's gotta pee or git off the pot if we gonna git out a this mess, 'cause them Germans are terrible — you heah me?"

I'll have to get up early in the morning, he thought. Rutherford's words had merely reminded him that tomorrow was Saturday and that if he were not careful Jerry Evans would beat him out of the business manager's post. Then, too, there was the commencement speech to write, just in case he was accepted by the honors committee. Miss Southern was the chairman, so the speech would have to be good. And if that was not enough to occupy his mind, final examinations were coming up soon. Loooooooong division! a voice whispered, and he heard the poisonous hiss of chemistry, watched the steel-helmeted dates and isms that were history, climbing over the top. He should get the next dance arranged. So many people to call and all. And the choir was singing next Thursday at the synagogue. . . .

He slipped into bed feeling that Saturday had already come and gone, that something had happened. He *knew*, and he *knew* that he knew, but he didn't have time to stop and figure it out. It was what the little groups of people standing throughout the red room were talking about. A black man hanging from a tree with his eyes popping out kept exclaiming, *I did it!* And he laughed and laughed, and somebody was sitting on the big red drum that went Boom! Boom! Boom! — which made him laugh louder and louder, until he almost choked with laughter, until it swirled in swift currents around him and he sank deeper into its waters, struggling now to get his breath. His chest burned. His heart pounded in his ears. Futilely he fought the current. Just before he died he thrust his head into the silhouette that suddenly appeared against the window filled with light.

The pillow! He threw it on the floor, and lay back down, alongside death, and closed his eyes. Tomorrow's Saturday. He wondered what time it was now, how long it would be before Saturday came and went and the something that had happened happened and he would be free! . . .

"I made it," he exclaimed to Mary Ann the following afternoon at four o'clock.

"But the grades aren't even out yet!" she exclaimed.

"Aw, I don't mean that, I mean I sold the most ads for the yearbook. I'm the business manager."

"That's *wonderful!*" she cried, a bit too joyously, he thought. Her eyes shone as though they were wet under the long fringes of her eyelashes. He couldn't avoid looking at them, and she, perceiving this, blushed deeply, which caused the dimples on either side of her mouth to make her face look pretty, even beautiful! he hazarded to think.

"Come on," he said, taking her affectionately by the hand.

"Where?" she asked.

"I'll show you."

"Here," he said at last. They stood before the gate of Aunt Rose's yard. April had washed it clean. All the grasses and new flowers were shining, immaculate even behind the ears.

Clapclapclapclapclapclapclap! thundered the myriad invisible hands as they entered the yard.

Aunt Rose stood behind the screen, her body forming a huge bulky silhouette that filled the door.

"Why come on in —" she exclaimed before he had a chance to ring the bell, "come in!"

He opened the door and stepped back so that Mary Ann could enter first. And presently they were sitting at the big round table all decked out in Aunt Rose's finest linen, with beautiful cups and saucers that he had only seen in the china cabinet, and bright polished spoons of real silver.

"One lump or two, miss?" said Aunt Rose.

"Please call me Mary Ann."

"All right, Mary Ann."

"Two, please."

"Lemon or cream?"

"Lemon, thank you."

"How about you, Amerigo?"

"Huh? Eh — two. I mean three! Please."

"Lemon? Cream?"

"Eh, no'm — neither . . . ne*i*theh one, thanks."

They sipped their tea and he felt like a sissy, drinking from that thin little cup that was so light that he could hardly feel the weight of it in his hand. Two gulps and the tea was gone. He stared at the biscuit in his other hand. He had intended to eat it as he drank the tea. Frustrated, he looked at Aunt Rose with a confused smile. She smiled back and they laughed, Mary Ann, too, they all laughed heartily. The ice was broken.

"So you're goin' to teacher's college —" Aunt Rose was saying to Mary Ann. "That's fine. I wish you all the success in the world. I knew my boy could pick 'um, all right —"

He looked anxiously at Mary Ann. He tried to interrupt Aunt Rose, but she was drifting through the mellow haze of a pleasant speculation. "Amerigo's a lot different from the others, Mary Ann, he's a dreamer . . . got his head in the clouds. Always did. Like his momma. Aaaaaalways did wanna be somebody. It does my heart good just to look at the two of you. How many kids you plannin' on havin'?"

He blushed to the roots of his teeth while Mary Ann laughed as though his embarrassment were tickling her to death.

"She's very nice," said Mary Ann, as they left the house. She locked her arm in his and pressed her cheek against his shoulder as they walked, while he strained to control the uneasy feeling that her nearness gave him. He consoled himself that it wasn't *his* fault, that *he* hadn't done it. Done what? He stopped abruptly and looked at her as though she were a stranger.

"What's the matter?" she asked him in a tone that betrayed the fact that she knew, releasing the grip on his arm with an expression that once again obscured the beauty of her face and metamorphosed her into a negative of Cosima. He looked at her now as though he were trying to discover Cosima in her face. It's no use, is it? her expression seemed to say. And once again he had the feeling that something had happened, and he knew that he knew.

"You got a date for the dance yet?" he asked her.

"No!" She turned away from him.

"I mean —"

"I *know* what you mean!"

"Has anybody asked *her* yet?"

"No! Nobody dares."

"Will, will you ask her for me?"

"Why don't you ask her yourself!"

"I never get a chance to see her alone. Always in class. And you *know* how everybody talks! Old lady Southern saw us coming in class together the other day and she called her and said something to her. I couldn't hear it, but you *know* what she said, and I do, too! They don't think I'm good enough for her. I —"

"I've asked her already," said Mary Ann in a quiet even voice that was a little frightening.

"WHAAT?"

"I *know* you're blind as a bat, Amerigo Jones, but are you deaf, too?" she shouted.

But he didn't hear her, the bells of the world pealed in his ears, and he struggled to scream above the roar:

"W-h-a-t — d-i-d — s-h-e — s-a-y?"

"She said she'd see. Mrs. Thornton wouldn't care so much, but it's *Mister* Thornton — he's the one you've got to —"

"All I want to *do* is take her to a *dance!*" he uttered painfully. "I'm not going to *eat* her!"

"Amerigo," said Mary Ann, "that dance is two months away! There's still time! Besides, the world won't come to an end if —"

The pained expression on his face made her stop, as though she, too, heard the loud pealing of the bells, all the bells in the world.

"Amerigo! I made it! I made it!" Mary Ann shouted as she rushed up to him the following evening.

"Congratulations," he said, forcing a bitter smile.

"Oh," said Mary Ann, "I'm sorry. I didn't mean to —"

"That's all right. That's . . . that's all right."

"But you can *still* read your speech!" she said consolingly. "You don't *have* to be on the honor roll. The announcement came out today, the speeches are going to be judged on the basis of quality alone — and on how well you say it. You've still got a chance. Is it ready?"

"Ready? Oh — what's the use!"

"What's the *use!* A-merigo Jones!"

"What do you want me to *do?*" he screeched. "You *know* that if I'm not on that list, and everybody *else* who's making a speech *is* — I don't have a chance!"

"You can try!"

"You think I *could?*"

Again her eyes shone as though they were wet, as though they would extinguish the ravaging fires that consumed the world.

"I *know* you can!" she declared.

Her gaze was steady, her smile full of hope. Their faces grew close.

"Maybe I could," he whispered. "Aaaaaaaaaw —"

"Now what?" she asked impatiently.

"I've hardly even started it. And it has to be ready day after tomorrow. And there's the *dance! That's* not even *half* ready!"

"Oh!" cried Mary Ann, "I almost forgot. . . ."

"What?"

"She's coming. She asked Mrs. Thornton and she said yes before her father had time to object, only she has to be home by six o'clock."

All the next day he struggled under a mountain of cares, while his classmates flitted in and out of sunny rooms, sporting their blue and gold ribbons that furled in the freshets of spring air bursting from bellowing lungs, from windows thrown open, from slamming doors, as though March was still pursuing April who was stuck on May!

All day long the torturous bliss inspired by the knowledge that *she* would come was rendered less bearable by the insinuating bells:

Rrrrrrrring!

A veil of light fell from the sky and caught the twelve o'clock sun blushing in its nakedness. And then May shivered sensuously into the afternoon.

Rrrrrrrring!

He took a quick peep into the gym to see if the stand for the orchestra was set up. The janitor hadn't started yet. On his way to find him he remembered his speech and ducked into the auditorium to have a look at it. As he unfolded the crumpled sheet of paper a feeling of futility came over him. He stared dumbly at the hasty lines scrawled on the paper, and suddenly felt the woman's gaze upon him while he stood at the foot of the bed, trembling with indignation:

Now?

Rrrrrrring!

He dashed into the choir room filled with *her.*

"It's our last farewell, dear No — or — th High. . . ." they sang. The principal's son had written it. He was lying in a sanatorium, dying of tuberculosis. Ssssssh!

"and how proud we are to say good-bye. What the future holds, has not yet been told, but you've shaped us in a way to make us b-o-l-d! To say we'll w-i-n. . . . our battles ever, and. . . ."

She's coming! he thought, feeling the shock anew, as though Mary Ann had just said it.

"W-h-a-t — d-i-d — s-h-e — s-a-y!"

Rrrrrrring!

Gentle airs wafted through May's hair and the sun blushed with impotent rage and, though it was only four o'clock, the moon was already making a faint trace in the sky. The Allies were on the offensive as the orchestra tuned up. One could hear the fragments of sound up and down the halls, dashing in and out of empty rooms, as though they were in search of a chord and a sequence and a rhythm that would convert them into a song.

Everybody was there, but he didn't see *her* at first, though he knew she was there. The fury of the sound screaming in his ears told him that she was there. He raced futilely about, attending to this and that nothing-in-particular. And once, from the corner of his eye, he *saw* her just as plain as day, sitting there with Mary Ann, just like anybody else. But he didn't know it. Even when the music started. They were playing "Stairway to the Stars." Ella's tune, he observed curiously, realizing all the while that he had seen her and didn't know it.

Now? a voice whispered, cutting the threads of his sensibility like a razor, and suddenly he became conscious of her. . . . She's right behind me! . . . In his confusion he began looking into all the places where she was not — on the ceiling in the sheen of light reflected by the metal rim of the bass drum, *in* the drum, between the skins! The music stopped. He crossed the hall and waited for the music to start. It started. He turned and stared at the musicians. In the Mood, it was "In the Mood" that they were playing. He turned around to stare at the dancers, but saw only *her* face, *her* eyes, not looking at him, but skirting the periphery of his gaze. Another face, dark, wet, sadly smiling, near *her* face. Somebody said something but he didn't know who it was, there was so much noise. Why are they making so much N O I S E! . . . I . . . I . . . can't *hear!* He stumbled forward for some reason, some utterance had escaped his lips. His arm was sliding lightly around her waist, not too tightly, lest he break her, or get her pretty yellow dress dirty. He thought he held her hand, but it was hard to tell, it was so small, so light, like Aunt Rose's teacups. I must not touch her! he kept thinking. G-r-a-c-e-f-u-l! Swing into the turn — now! From the corner of his eye he caught a glimpse of her face. Her nose was close to his. So *close!* Under the nose the lips. The lips!

Somehow her thin little chest lay close to his, but gently, and the piece was almost over. Will she let me gain? He wanted to ask her for the next dance. He cleared his throat in order to ask her for the next dance, and her ear, in anticipation of his utterance, informed her eye, and her nose, which followed suit, touched his!

After that, sometime after that a bell rang, and all that he knew, could remember, was that somewhere in the world, at sometime in the world, there had been a dance, and that *she* had come!

"Son?"

He looked up from his speech into Viola's face. She knows, he thought, and then he dwelt upon the novelty of hearing her call him *son*. She very rarely did that. Rutherford did more often. It was his way of being affectionate, of expressing some difficult side of love that he could express no other way. He always said it at some unexpected time, when he felt he least deserved it, but it never surprised him. It warmed him and made him want to cry. Viola usually accomplished this with a kiss or a bowl of soup. For this reason the word *son* now assumed the gravity of that excess of love and passion reserved only for very serious situations.

"Son?" The word stood suspended, frozen, in the air like a fatal sentence: "Son? Do you know that time it is? It's almost three o'clock. Even if you do finish that speech by tomorrow morning, you'll be too sleepy to say it right, let alone say it by heart."

He looked at the hysterical scribblings on the page. So banal, so inadequate, not what he wanted at all, not what he really felt. But I've got to try! he exclaimed to himself. She's afraid I'll mess it up! Resentment against his mother subsumed his feeling of self-pity. She always was afraid! Afraid that if I sang in the amateur contest people would laugh. Afraid that I'd forget the poem in church. Always afraid of what people might say. I don't care! He bent his eyes upon his speech and gradually became oblivious to her presence; nor had he seen the sandwich and the glass of milk she had placed beside him an hour ago.

The red room echoed with the reverberations of his speech. He tried to catch them with his hands and hold on to them, but they evaded his grasp, they hid in the cool dark channels of his ears and along the banks of the swirling waters of the Western Front of his consciousness:

Amerigo, honey, do you know that you ain' been born agin? That you still walkin' in sin? Sister James asked. And he grew smaller under the glare of the multitude of staring eyes.

As he emerged from the baptismal waters, he beheld the tear-stained face of Miss Southern. A feeling of guilt smote him.

"She's coming," she said sadly.

"W-h-a-t — d-i-d — s-h-e — s-a-a-a-a-a-y?" the sound of his voice swallowed up by the roaring din of fragmentary words.

"Boy!" Rutherford shouted, "if I have to call you agin —"

He stirred sluggishly, feeling cold and old, like after New Year's when everything has happened. He lumbered heavily to school through the snow-laden streets of May, dreading the fact that he would have to relive it, to say it again, that which had already been said. His head ached. He ached all over, and inside where you couldn't see it. In his pocket, the speech, like a piece of counterfeit money. Maybe it's good! he tried to reassure himself. Maybe there won't be enough time to hear everyone today and I can try tomorrow! His step quickened to this thought, his hopes revived. As his finger touched a sharply folded corner of the speech in his pocket, he experienced a familiar sensation that he tried desperately to remember, but only meaningless fragmentary images came to mind: of the alley in the rain, of Bra Mo sliding a cake of ice onto his shoulder and how it glistened in the sun and dripped like ice dripping from the wires and shades of the lamp-post in the spring, he thought of Next Year when . . . Yeah! — *then* I'd have a *chance!* He hurried now, practically ran, to receive his stay of execution.

Meanwhile three Allied submarines had been blown out of the sea, everybody was talking about a place called Dunkirk, and Mr. Churchill's voice sounded grave as compared to Mr. Roosevelt's, which did not, however, stop the bells from ringing.

Stepping into the English class, it occurred to him that it was all the fault of the bells. If they forgot — *once!* — Stopped! Just didn't ring — all the bells and clocks — in the world — *there would be time!*

Rrrrrrring!

Miss Southern, looking like Fate, sat stoically before the class. He sat next to *her.* She was calm, as though *her* place in heaven were assured! Mary Ann sat at her side, resigned, to be sure, but confident. Miss Southern cleared her throat and announced in impeccable English, the kind of English that makes you feel a moron, how the speeches were to be judged. She wished everybody good luck, and then she called on the first candidate:

"Amerigo Jones!"

"Come to Je-sus . . . Come to Jeeee — sus . . . Come to Je-sus, just now . . . just now . . . just now . . . just now . . . just now."

How long had he been sitting on the steps behind the library, amid the roses smelling all over the place, while the birds crapped on the walk? An ant crawled near his foot and he crushed it with a vengance.

"Well," he said bitterly as Mary Ann came around and sat down beside him, "don't tell me! Cosima made it. And you made it. And there'll be four or five of you who are the other white lights!"

She remained silent.

"Don't pity me, damnit!" he shouted.

"You made battalion adjutant," she said in a monotone.

"But I didn't make major, did I! NO!"

She pretended not to have caught the irony of this remark.

"Has anybody asked you to go to the prom yet?"

She lowered her eyes.

"Why not?" he shouted. "You read your damned speech as good — as well — as *she* did, didn't you? You play the piano! And *no*body could *doubt* your virtue! Why not? The sun's yellow! How-how is it that everything it touches turns black? How's that? What are you going to *do?*"

"What are *you* going to do?" Mary Ann retorted.

"She said no?"

"*She* didn't say it, her *father* said it," said Mary Ann, shrugging her shoulders. "He's going to take her himself."

"W-H-A-T? You mean he's going to humiliate her like that! He'll be the only father in the whole school! Well, my momma isn't coming with me. I'm a man!"

Boom!

Mary Ann heard it and looked at him. He looked at her, surprised that she had heard it.

Dunkirk.

"What are you going to do?" she asked again.

Confronted by the all-out boldness of her gaze, he retreated across the choppy canal of a humiliating silence.

"I'll go with you, if you want me to," said Mary Ann. Her voice was still, like a depth charge: down . . . down . . . down.

Boom!

"Let's go!" he heard himself saying, in a voice that was younger. The words were enshrouded in an aura of release subsumed by a feeling of dread. The alley flashed through his mind, vaguely, painfully, hot and cold sensations shot through his body. He involuntarily rubbed his knee and wiggled his toe.

"Do you mean it!" Mary Ann was saying.

He looked into her smiling face without really seeing her, his eyes filled with blood, his ears filled with the sound of sirens screaming, the pavement burning under his feet, like the world was on fire, unaware now that they, he and Mary Ann, were racing homeward, hand in hand, as though they were being pursued by some common enemy who could follow them anywhere.

That evening at the table bright with tomato salad and iced tea, Viola, noticing the nervous light in his eyes, asked:

"Who you takin' to the prom?"

"Mary Ann said she'd go," he said sullenly.

"Oh! That's nice!" Viola exclaimed.

"I thought you was takin' that little Thornton girl!" said Rutherford with a sly grin.

"Aaaaaaw!" he muttered, avoiding his father's gaze in an effort to conceal his confusion, a mixture of shame and hatred.

"All that callin' up you been doin', an' love-letter writin'. What's the matter — she turn you down?"

Viola looked into her plate as she spoke:

"Mary Ann's one a the nicest girls in town — an' one a the most respected. She's pretty, too! I'd be *proud* to take her, if I were Amerigo."

"Who's takin' *your* gal?" Rutherford asked with a seriousness in his tone that betrayed the smile on his face.

"Her *father!*" he answered contemptuously.

"Her *father!* Ain' that a killer!"

"She wanted to go! I *asked* her. But her father wouldn't let her."

"It must be terrible for her," said Viola.

"I think I kin git the old man's car. . . ." said Rutherford quietly.

"Naw!" said Viola.

"Yeah! He come up to me taday an' said, Well, Rutherford, I see they gonna take you away from me. Looks like it, I said. He bit down on that stogie an' then he said, I hear that boy a yours is graduatin'? Yes, sir, I said. An' then he asked me if he could drive, an' I said no, an' then he said, 'Why don't you take the limousine an' drive 'um to the ball?' An' I said, that'd be a killer. An' he'll need flowers for the young lady, he said, an' a little change to put in his pocket — an' then he handed me this twenty-dollar bill!"

"Wasn' that nice!" Viola said.

They all smiled now, each from within his own private world of remembering, up from the depths of cherished hopes and disappointments and speculations that had stretched out through the days, the years, as the sun rose, and the moons, and the clocks keeping time with the falling snows and with the rains falling.

"I have to start at the defense plant Mond'y," Rutherford was saying.

Boom!

He's too old. Amerigo studied his father's forehead for traces of his receding hairline, for a gray hair or two, and, finding none, marveled that he was older just the same. He's heavier, he thought, remembering the first time he had really noticed it. Then, too, his voice and his movements were more solid now, something in him seemed set, finished, irrevocably fixed.

"You'll need a new suit!" Viola was saying, in much the same tone as she used to say, "I'll need a new formal," caressing the words embodied in the reflection that she had never gone to the circus after Uncle Ruben had died. Still fondling the green velvet suit that Miss Sadie had given him, remembering suddenly that she had not taken him to the circus, either. The star! he exclaimed to himself, as though he were answering a question that he could no longer remember having asked.

As the evening light grew softer the ghostly voices blended into the song that rose from the alley.

I hope it never changes!

The thought boomed noisily within the vast voluminous vacuum that was next year when he could go to college, if. . . .

"A new suit!" Rutherford protested. "Unh! — a tux!" then: "Maybe we could rent one and have it altered. An' he kin wear my studs, an' those golden cufflinks Sexton gave me before he died."

Rutherford rose thoughtfully from the table and took the old battered World War cup from the hook over the sink and turned on the spigot until the cold water bubbled in it.

One cup! he thought, as his father brought the cup to his lips.

After that they went out onto the porch and gazed into the evening filled with stars that fell down into the buildings and shone behind the windows and in the headlights of the cars throughout the great city.

One morning the following week when he met her on the way to school Cosima did not speak to him.

She knows!

He slipped her a note in the music room, but she dropped it into the wastebasket. She turned her back on him in the English class, and acted as though he did not exist. The week dragged on in this desultory way toward Friday night, the night of the senior prom. Only Mary Ann seemed happy over the event, though even *her* eyes avoided his when she and Cosima were together. When they were alone, discussing the prom, her eyes were excited and triumphant and bitter by turns. He began to be aware of a certain brashness in her laugh that he had never noticed before. Once when they were walking down the hill, he staring moodily at the pavement, she squeezed his arm affectionately, and when he looked at her in that tolerant way of his, she laughed at him in a cruel way that shocked him and threw him into a fit of confusion. He looked at the sky and at the trees, helpless amid the volleys of laughter.

Even when Friday night came and his mother and father fussed excitedly about him, arranging him and telling him how to act and continually asking him if he had forgotten anything — his keys, his handkerchief, his money — he felt ridiculous. His lips quivered with remembered, anticipated pain, which became even more intense as she stood on Mary Ann's porch, ringing the bell.

Rrrrrring!

A serious, handsome, well-poised woman of perhaps forty-six appeared at the door. In her expression, her bearing, the critical way she scrutinized him as she welcomed him in, with a distant, subtly skeptical cordiality with which she reacted to all men, a divorced woman.

"Won't you come in?" indicating the way into the parlor with a gesture of courteous resignation. It was a woman's parlor, homey, shining, with a piano and a big coal stove with polished chrome fenders, pictures of the family in well-dusted frames on the cobwebless walls, a big old-fashioned sofa with lace doilies on the arms and back where you pressed your head, if you dared taking the liberty of relaxing to that degree, because the lady's manner was *serious*.

They sat facing each other, he with the box of flowers in his hand, looking expectantly for Mary Ann. "She'll be down in a minute," the lady said.

During their casual conversation about school he wondered if she knew about him and Cosima. He thought he perceived a half-condescending, half-resentful twinkle in her eyes. She knows! He fidgeted on his seat. He looked at his hands. His nails were dirty! He tried to hide them. The doilies on the chairs were so white! The ashtrays sparkled as though they hadn't been used since her husband left — twenty years ago. Within his clinched palms he could *feel* the dirt under his nails. And his stiff white collar was cutting his neck, and a light film of persperation was causing it to burn a little, and Rutherford's shorts were beginning to tighten around his thighs because the sofa was covered with velvet material that prevented his pants from sliding evenly when he moved. But now, to his infinite relief, he heard a noise at the top of the stair.

"Ah!" the lady exclaimed, no doubt as much relieved as he, and a little theatrically, he thought, a pleasant smile beguiling her face, no longer a resenter of men, simply a mother, enjoying the happiness of her only daughter at one of the most important moments of her life. Mary Ann stood at the top of the stair in a blazing white dress.

"Ah!" he exclaimed, carried away by her unexpected beauty.

She smilingly descended the stair with a studied ladylike dignity, her rich black hair falling around her nut-brown skin, eyes shining, the whites with a silvery shimmer broken by those long shadowy lashes that swept downward like the boughs of trees! over rushing waters reflecting moonlight.

When she reached the bottom of the stairs he presented his elegant flower box. It was tied with a luxurious silver ribbon fixed with a long pearl-headed pin. MUEHLEBACH FLOWER SHOP was written across one corner in elegant script. She beamed ecstatically as she fumbled with the ribbon and finally opened the box. Within it a lining of white silk paper upon which lay a corsage of three cold pale gardenias.

Boom!

A deep dark despair descended upon him.

Like a grave! Suddenly he was thinking of Cosima — as something, someone, dead!

"Aren't you going to pin them on?" her mother was saying, smiling sweetly at his stupefaction as he fumbled futilely with the corpse of his beloved Cosima, pearl-headed pin in hand, jabbing at the delicate shoulder of Mary Ann's dress.

"Here, let me!" said the mother, overcome by his confusion, pleased that her daughter had provoked such powerful emotion in the young man, pinning the flower on her own shoulder, pretty much as Viola had relieved his anxiety during the past few months and up to the very last when she had pinned the flower in his lapel, forcing Rutherford to exclaim:

"Aw, let the man go, for Christ sake!" pressing the twenty-dollar bill in his hand — plus five! he had discovered, as he had stepped out the door, as they, he and Mary Ann, were now doing, waving good-bye to the lone figure silhouetted behind the screen.

She's crying, he thought.

When Mary Ann saw the limousine she could only exclaim: "Ah!" in a short breathless gasp that seemed to complete her feeling of happiness. Rutherford opened the door with the courteous impersonality of a real chauffeur. In the backseat they held hands, but they did not look at each other. He could not look at Cosima, cold, pale, austere, unforgiving, impaled upon Mary Ann's shoulder.

When they arrived the ball had already started. Soft music drifted down the corridors in distorted bursts of sound permeated by excited bursts of conversation and laughter. Just before they entered the hall he gave the toe of his new black shoe a quick swipe against the leg of his pants and wondered if his hair pomade was making his forehead greasy. There was nothing he could do about his nails at the moment. Mary Ann looked good enough to eat.

They entered the hall. A bevy of faces rushed up to meet them, all of Cosima's and Mary Ann's friends, in long pale organdies and taffetas and crepes, smiling, sparkling, with exclamations of congratulations and dramatic undertones of surprise, while he stood amid them covered with confusion subsumed by a feeling of blasphemy, of sacrilege, that such merriment should take place in the presence of the martyred dead. He looked stealthily around to see if *she* were there, but before he could complete his survey, he felt himself being swept away and flung into the midst of another group. Mary Ann showed her corsage to all her friends and flaunted her triumph he thought suddenly. He felt sick in the stomach. He felt dizzy. He made an attempt to escape.

"Come on, Mary Ann," he said, "let's dan —" but before he could utter the words, she let out a delighted squeal and ran toward the corner where *she* stood, alone: in a wine-colored organdy dress with a hooped skirt and a long stole of the same color draped over her shoulders. She looked as though she might have stepped out of another century, a lovely century peopled with beautiful, sad ladies who had suffered with dignity in the hands of misfortune, some queen whose king had abandoned her through some unavoidable importunity of fate, one to whom "something had happened." Moved by the impact of his thought, a sense of fatality stole upon him and forced him to try to measure up to the tragic import of the moment.

"Oh, Cosima! I'm so *happy!*" Mary Ann was saying, throwing her arms around her. "Look!" thrusting forward the austere corsage on her shoulder. The gardenias looked so white, as though they had been compressed of the purest snow, the flesh of snow, at the feet of the ice-laden trees. Cosima kissed Mary Ann on the cheek without smiling, at which instant her gaze met his. It was as cold as death!

He and Mary Ann were moving away. While they were dancing he noticed that Cosima's father had reappeared. No one asked her to dance. She danced with her father, a tall, lean, thin-boned man with sensuous pink lips, who looked at the world through the slits of spectacled eyes, as they turned about, she like a moth imprisoned by the flame, the bright globes burning in the ceiling reflecting in the polished rims of his glasses.

They went home early. He caught a glimpse of her — behind Mary Ann's ear — just as her stole whisked through the door.

After that Mary Ann's ebullience became oppressive, the dance grew tiresome, the gardenias on her shoulder began to wither in the heat, to be crushed in the jostle of the dance. Finally the last piece had been played and the senior class had filed out of the hall in pairs. The "hip cats" were going to a nightclub and have a "ball," and the "squares" were going home. Mary Ann leaned heavily on his shoulder, smiling a dreamy smile. As he slipped her wrap over her shoulders, she fell back into his arms and turned her face to his — under the staircase near the main entrance, they were alone.

Now? her eyes seemed to whisper.

He beheld her with an expression of hatred that he struggled to disguise by planting a feeble kiss upon her lips. Then he grabbed her by the arm and fled to the safety of the waiting limousine, she laughing all the while as though she were drunk, or a little mad.

He often saw them together during the few remaining days of the semester, but now they both avoided him. *Something had happened,* he knew, but why isn't she mad at Mary Ann, *too!* And then: *Boom!* COSIMA KNEW IT ALL THE TIME!

In his despair he tried to console himself with the thought that actually she did love him, but had sacrificed him to the will of her father, the will of the white niggers! he added bitterly. Gradually a subtle hope fired his imagination and shone like a little sun upon the horizon of his consciousness in the form of the thought: This can't be the end! . . . Somewhere . . . somehow.

Next Year! thundered a voice.

BOOM! retorted the shattering explosion from over the sea and over the sea and over the . . .

When Next Year came Cosima went off to the university. Amerigo stayed home and waited for the command of the booming voice, the smoking breath of which obscured her face, but not the thought of her. It moved like a specter behind the cold blue haze that filled the early-summer mornings, and the hoar-white mornings of winter, one winter, filtering through a little square mud-spattered window, while a bell rang from a tower in the town. . . .

A rosy glow permeated the porous blue-black darkness charged with the aura of a hard yellow Sunday summer light. The howling wind outside suddenly died down. Stillness.

Cosima's face was clearly visible. The smile on her lips intoned more clearly the question that pierced the air more easily now that all was still, save the occasional *Boom!* of the falling things of the forest. In the still pause between midnight and dawn, he heard it:

Now?

"Yes!" he whispered, and half lay, half fell at his beloved's feet: "Yes!" *Boom!Boom!Boom!*

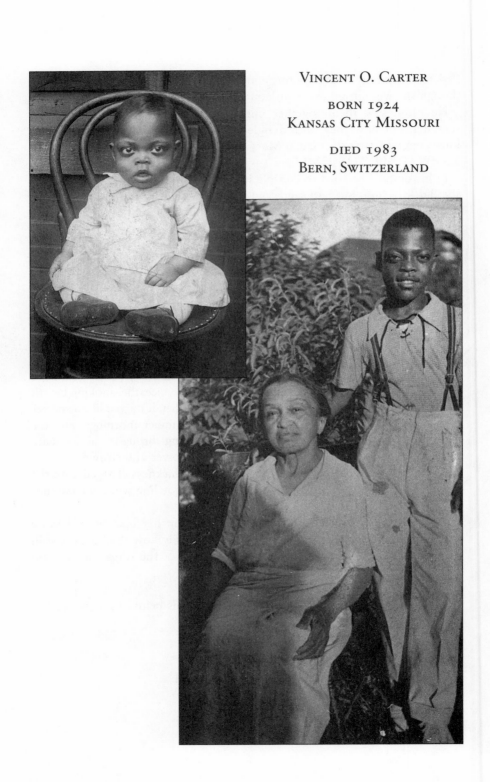

VINCENT O. CARTER

BORN 1924
KANSAS CITY MISSOURI

DIED 1983
BERN, SWITZERLAND

PUBLISHER'S NOTE

The one substantive change that we have made to this work, with the support of those who knew Vincent Carter, is to impose a new title. The author had intended to call his book *The Primary Colors*. The title we chose instead, *Such Sweet Thunder,* was also used by Duke Ellington and Billy Strayhorn for their 1957 tribute suite to Shakespeare. It comes from *A Midsummer Night's Dream,* in which Hippolyta says,

> The skies, the fountains, every region near
> Seem'd all one mutual cry. I never heard
> So musical a discord, such sweet thunder.